BERING STRAIT
by FX Holden

Independently Published
Typeset in 12pt Garamond

fxholden@yandex.com

From a working draft titled 'Under the Hammer'

With special thanks to the following weapons and military tactics technical advisers without whom this book might have been a fantasy, rather than hardcore future fiction!

Gary Carillo, Austin, Texas, USA
Richard Campan, Villeneuve Loubet, France
'SSnake', SBPro, Hannover, Germany
And the crew of SIMHQ AAR

RUSSIA

Lavrentiya

The Diomedes

Anadyr

Saint Lawrence

Nome

USA

Eielson AFB

The Bering Strait

250 km
150 mi

N

○→□ Mercator

CONTENTS

IF A TREE FALLS

Bering Strait, August 2032

The iceberg had calved off the Arctic ice pack two years earlier. After wallowing for a while in the ocean off the coast it had been picked up by the transpolar current and then flung into the Beaufort Gyre, a swirling maelstrom of hurdy-gurdy waters that circulated between the East Siberian Sea and the Beaufort Sea off Alaska. Like a small child thrown off a playground carousel that was spinning too fast, it was dumped into the mouth of the Bering Strait, slowing but moving inexorably south at a stately two to three knots.

The violence of its birth and the impact of wind and tides had seen its original tabular shape worn away until just a thin sliver of a dome remained above the water. Below the water, 200 tons of ice and trapped rock served as both ballast and rudder, driving the berg forward. At 800 feet long, it was at least twice the size of the iceberg that sank the Titanic.

And it was headed straight toward the Russian super-freighter *Ozempic Tsar*!

The bridge of the *Ozempic Tsar* was silent. Under a panel of windows with a 360-degree view of the sparkling sea around it, a bank of screens and instruments flashed and blinked. Two doors, one to port and one to starboard, let out to an over-bridge watch station in which sat Ozempic Line Maritime Apprentice Fyodor Leonov. He was taking the approach of the huge iceberg very calmly.

The *Tsar* was outfitted with the latest in subsea sonar and high-frequency radar for detecting both shipping and subsurface objects, and as it bore down on the iceberg at a combined closing speed of 18 knots, the sonar was the first to react. A collision warning alarm began to sound throughout the ship, but there was no panicked shouting, no thud of feet running on steel decks.

The AI controlling the ship's radar directed a beam toward the suspected location of the iceberg, but saw nothing. Indecision might have paralyzed a human captain, but the *Ozempic Tsar* had no such problems. Confirming that the sea lane to starboard was clear of other traffic, the massive super-freighter feathered its starboard screw, punched in portside bow impellers, dialed its speed back to 10 knots and began a grindingly slow, skidding turn to starboard. It was helped by the fact it was carrying a bulky but lightweight cargo for this journey, but without perfect information about the speed and bearing of the iceberg, its computers calculated a 10% chance that the ship would not clear the object ahead of it in time.

A new alarm began to sound throughout the ship, warning the six-person crew of mostly security personnel to get to emergency stations and brace for impact. Leonov stayed seated, and no one else responded. There was no sign of panic either above or below decks.

Slowly, the bows of the super-freighter swung around and the ship's radar was able to pick up a return from the dome of ice that was riding above sea level. Now the AI could use two inputs, the radar and sonar, to calculate the position, speed and bearing of the iceberg and it revised its estimate of the likelihood of collision to zero. Immediately it began replotting a track to get itself back on course once the iceberg was passed. As the iceberg slid along the *Tsar*'s port side, a comfortable two miles away, the ship sent a warning message about the berg to both the Russian and US Coast Guard channels, giving its position, speed and likely heading given prevailing currents. And then it canceled the blare of klaxons ringing out over its empty decks.

Pimple-faced and ruddy cheeked, Apprentice Fyodor Leonov was from a long line of merchant sailors and distantly descended from Captain Viktor Nikolaevich Leonov, a two-time Hero of the Soviet Union. Steely nerves were hard coded into his salty DNA, even though at nineteen he was the youngest among the small crew. Entering the Maritime Academy, he had been desperate to prove himself to his fisherman father and hadn't been able to believe his luck when he was told his first seagoing assignment was going to be aboard the most advanced freighter in the entire world! He had spent most of the first day of the voyage just thinking about the look of pride in his father's eyes as he'd waved goodbye to Fyodor and his ship in Anadyr.

The *Ozempic Tsar* was proof that the future of merchant shipping was autonomous. The fourth of its kind in the Ozempic Imperial Line, it was first to make the polar voyage from Archangelsk in Russia to Hokkaido in Japan completely unmanned. As its name implied, the *Tsar* was very much a king of the seas.

It had a capacity of 400,000 deadweight tons and had sailed with a consignment of powdered lithium from a dialysis plant in Anadyr. It was 1,300 feet long, with a draught of 75 feet, steered not by a shore-based human helmsman like its remotely piloted sister ships, but by a Norwegian-designed AI core that managed both navigation and systems overwatch

The crew aboard the *Ozempic Tsar* were mostly there to deter hijackers, but there was no way to pilot the ship or alter its course if the ship was boarded at sea, and the engine room, cargo and fuel supply were completely sealed against intruders. Young Leonov had been given basic training in how to repel pirates using the ship's anti-boarding defenses and, in the unlikely event pirates made it aboard, how to secure himself deep in the bowels of the ship inside its invulnerable panic room. Not that pirates were a big problem in the Arctic seas yet, but a fully laden super-freighter with absolutely no crew to guard it would have been a tempting prize if precautions hadn't been taken.

The *Ozempic Tsar* was a 250-million-dollar miracle of progress in the field of self-piloted freighters and proof that the Russian oil oligarchs who built her had shown amazing foresight in realizing that global warming could be an upside business opportunity if it meant a permanent polar freight route could be opened as the Arctic ice cap melted. They had a dream that they could take Anadyr from a small local container port to

7

the biggest port in the Russian Far East in coming years, shipping the riches of the Chukotka gold, copper and lithium mining region to markets on the East Coast of America and beyond, whose demand for the raw materials for batteries to supplement their renewable energy obsession was insatiable.

The *Tsar* also held the world record for the Anadyr–New York transit, completing the 3,000km trip in sixteen days, requiring as it did little time in port for crew rest or replenishment, and taking its fuel from the sea as it sailed, using solar and wind-powered catalytic converters to turn the seawater into hydrogen for its engines. Taking the northern sea route also shaved nearly two weeks off the trip from the container terminal at Anadyr, which otherwise would have had to go via the Panama Canal.

Up in his watch station, his head turned toward the iceberg now sliding past the *Ozempic Tsar*'s port bow, Apprentice Fyodor Leonov could have been forgiven a moment of pride. Feeling his ship slice through the slight swell of a brisk, sunlit summer in the Strait, thinking nothing in the world could stop it!

Unfortunately, Apprentice Leonov wasn't really capable of thinking at all, because like the other five members of his crew, he was dead, and didn't really care anymore about what a magnificent ship the *Ozempic Tsar* was.

And he cared just as little when two PIKE anti-ship missiles appeared on the horizon, tails streaming liquid fire, and then buried themselves deep in the *Tsar*'s guts before they detonated their 1,000lb blast-fragmentation warheads.

After which the still unimpressed Apprentice Leonov set his own world record, for the fastest trip to the bottom of the Bering Strait on an autonomous pilotless freighter.

TUNDRA TCON

The AI controlling the *Ozempic Tsar* managed to get several longwave, satellite telephone and high-frequency radio burst transmissions away before it was silenced by the cold, dark waters of the Strait. It also managed to fire a tethered distress buoy from its bow section that bobbed up to the surface of the sea even as the carcass of its host ship settled on the seabed 15 fathoms below. Fixed to the ship by a gossamer-thin carbonite string with the strength of tensile steel, it sent the position of the now doomed *Tsar* to its owners, its insurers, and to the nearest naval air and sea rescue service – which happened to be the Arkhangelsk headquarters for the Coast Guard of the Russian Federal Security Service.

The comms operator who received the mayday immediately and instinctively hit the alert button, which sounded a klaxon across the base at the hangar where the Sikorsky Skywarrior naval rescue quadrotor and its crew were stationed. The next thing he did was call up the international ship register to identify the ship that was in distress so that he could send imagery to both the Sikorsky crew and any other nearby shipping that might be directed to help.

The next thing he did after that was to sigh, reach over and click a checkmark next to the ship on his screen to advise the rescue crew what type of distress call they were responding to.

Bloody robot ship.

He was from three generations of fishermen and sailors, and had a grandfather who had served on the cold war flagship the *Kuznetsov*, striking terror into the hearts of the weak NATO fleets every time it sallied out of the Black Sea past Gibraltar and into the Atlantic. A ship crewed by heroes of the Soviet Union, back when Russia had heroes. Men braving radiation leaks and the constant threat of annihilation in nuclear fire to keep Mother Russia safe from a Western alliance bent on its destruction.

Now half the fleet were Unmanned Combat Warships, and the rest were slated for either conversion or retirement. 'Sailors' didn't stand watch on the decks of ships, in the freezing air of Baltic seas, watching for torpedo wakes or missile contrails; they didn't even sit deep in the Command, Control, Communications and Intelligence centers of their warships, watching glowing green screens for radar returns or listening for the acoustic signatures of submarines. They sat in reverse-cycle air-conditioned trailers on a shoreside base and watched the world through the sensors on their drone ships, only taking control when they needed to tap in new navigation orders or use their linked sensor arrays to explore and identify unknown contacts. And even the humans were redundant, because the drones were programmed with failsafe routines that would kick in if contact to Archangel was lost, or an enemy attack rendered comms unavailable.

The comms operator looked again at the image of the *Ozempic Tsar* on his screen and paged away from it in disgust. Four hundred thousand tons of cargo, steel and silicon sitting and breaking apart on the floor of the Bering Strait. It might not even have had a crew aboard.

Apart from environmentalists, the owners and their insurance company, who gave a damn?

In the Situation Room of the Russian 3rd Air and Air Defense Forces Command, Captain Andrei Udicz gave a damn. He was watching the same cry for help from the *Ozempic Tsar* scroll across his screen and he turned his face from the screen to look at the five other officers in the room.

"The ship in question has been confirmed as the *Ozempic Tsar*, Comrade General," he reported. The ship was famous even among Russian naval officers. "It has deployed a distress buoy, which indicates that at least part of the hull is lying on the sea floor."

General Yuri Lukin, leader of the 3rd Command, sat with his fingers on his expansive belly and looked up at the ceiling.

"How long until we have visual confirmation?" He was flanked by several intelligence officers and aides.

Udicz looked down at the tablet in front of him. "I can have a pair of Okhotnik drones over the site of the incident within … eight minutes," he said. "And I have two rotary-wing drones on standby if we need more eyes."

"Incident? You mean attack, do you not, Comrade Captain?" the General asked, arching his eyebrows. "Our satellites picked up the bloom of a violent explosion. The *Ozempic Tsar* was carrying no explosive cargo. Inert cargo ships do not just explode in the middle of the Bering Strait."

"Yes, Comrade General," Udicz replied carefully. "Perhaps it hit another ship, or an iceberg?"

"A high-explosive iceberg?" the General asked.

"There is a commercial fishing vessel within ten clicks of the site of the attack, Comrade General," Udicz said, ignoring the jibe. "They will be the first people on the scene. The Navy has directed them to search for wreckage."

Lukin fixed his gaze on Udicz. "Let us assume the *Ozempic Tsar* was not destroyed by a collision with a highly explosive iceberg. Let us speculate, Captain, about other causes," Lukin invited. "*Military* causes."

Udicz moved from one foot to the other, like he was being invited to step into a trap of some sort, but couldn't see what kind, yet. "If I should speculate about a military cause, Comrade General, I would speculate that such a catastrophic loss could only be caused by one or more long-range anti-ship missiles such as the US fields on any one of their several destroyers currently deployed in the Strait."

Udicz was probably the only officer in the meeting who had actually seen one of the deadly PIKE missiles up close and in action. Two years ago he'd been part of an official Russian delegation observing a NATO fleet combat exercise. Not as a friendly gesture from the Americans, of course, but because for any such exercise involving three or more nations bordering the Russian Federation it was a treaty obligation. He still remembered the chill he felt, standing on the bridge of the

American stealth missile cruiser the USS *Zumwalt*, watching as a US submersible fast-attack drone reared up out of the sea beside them, popped its hatches and loosed a volley of four of the deadly anti-ship missiles in less than a minute before sliding beneath the waves again. Forget the missiles, though. It wasn't the sight of the small gray-green stealth catamaran appearing from nowhere and firing missiles over the horizon that had made him shiver, either; it had been the thought that the machine could be launched below the waterline of the very cruiser he was standing on, and then pilot itself under the surface through the Kattegat Strait, down the Gulf of Finland, and park itself invisibly on the mud riverbed alongside the Cruise Ship terminal in St. Petersburg, ready at any time to detonate a nuclear warhead in the heart of the city.

Of course they had deployed detection systems in the river now, and for the Americans to even attempt to do so as a test or exercise would be regarded as an act of war, but Udicz had to wonder if they had got their countermeasures in place in time. What was to say there wasn't already an American submersible drone snuggled under a pier in the old imperial capital, covered in silt and just waiting to unleash Armageddon on command.

"Difficult to confirm though, I imagine," the General mused. "Such an isolated body of water, and not even a crew member as a witness."

"The American PIKE is a surface-to-surface stealth missile. Our satellites, even infrared, would not have picked up the launch. But the Navy may be able to recover sensor data from the ship's black box, assuming it is still reporting via the buoy," Udicz said. "That might provide visual or even audio evidence of a missile strike. The staggered-pulse engines of the US PIKE missile have a very distinctive acoustic signature."

"Not very definitive evidence, though," the General grumbled. "Readily deniable. Video and audio files are so easily doctored."

"I agree," Udicz said. "But why? Why would the Americans do something so stupid? Unless it was an accident."

12

"Accident?" Lukin said. "It strikes me, Udicz, that you would have to be very determined to *accidentally* sink a ship the size of a small island."

Carl Williams had only been an environmental science attaché at the Moscow Embassy for three weeks. With 700 full-time staff in the Russian Federation, 200 of whom were based in Moscow, Carl was only one of several new staff who had moved into the Embassy compound on Bolshoi Deviatinsky within the last month, and he still had that newbie halo hanging over him.

He had met neither the Ambassador nor his nominal manager at the Embassy yet, and really hadn't got much further than his orientation paperwork and some training in Embassy security protocols.

As a National Security Agency analyst he would normally have an office in the Controlled Access Area or 'Tophat' of the Secure Chancery Facility, but Carl was an 'undeclared' officer attached to the Embassy's Economic Affairs section and so, instead of working in the Chancery, he was still learning how to get from his accommodations to the commissary for breakfast and then down through the labyrinthine New Annex basement tunnels to his desk monitoring Russian Federation Far East Military Command traffic.

The traffic was of course encrypted and couldn't be broken in real time, even by the adaptive neural network natural language AIs he had at his disposal as an NSA analyst. No, his job instead was to look for patterns in the volume, origin and target of Russian Eastern Military District comms and try to tie them to complementary intel from either signals intel or human intelligence sources and see if they could confirm suspected meetings, military exercises, military equipment tests or even civil emergencies.

He had grown up as a kid on stories and films about the great cryptologists of history, like the men and women who broke the German Enigma codes using the world's first electronic computers at Bletchley Park in the UK. Or the NSA cryptographers who helped avert World War Three by decrypting the Russian fleet signals during the Cuban Missile Crisis and were able to tell the Kennedy brothers that the Russian destroyers had orders to sail only as far as the line of blockade, and no further.

They had worked in rooms of buzzing, clacking equipment, discs of tape whirling, coding machines spitting cards into a fug of cigarette smoke as they desperately fought to break enemy codes ahead of invasions, revolutions or Scud missile launches. Even the generation of code breakers he had been born into had grown up needing to be able to read computer code, looking for potential exploits in a soup of alphanumeric gibberish.

As Carl walked past the other attachés into his cubicle-sized office in the LED-lit basement corridor under Novy Arbat that had been converted into a listening station, he threw his sandwich on his desk, put his paper cup of coffee down next to it and glared almost resentfully at the tools of his trade. Instead of whirling reels of tape, he had a telephone headset. Instead of card readers spitting out index cards, he had a small laptop PC full of apps, including one which he could use to stream the latest TV shows. And instead of having to read and write code, he had HOLMES, the NSA AI system that was his own personal analytical assistant.

HOLMES was the name Carl had given the system – it was an acronym for Heuristic Ordinary Language Machine Exploratory System. Which sounded better than NLLS 1.5 or Natural Language Learning System 1.5. He had toyed with calling the system NESSIE, but that had an association with the Loch Ness monster he didn't think was appropriate because, unlike the monster, HOLMES was not a mythological creature.

Carl sank onto his seat, pulled on his headset and logged in using his voice recognition code.

"Good morning, Carl," HOLMES said in his ears. "Did you sleep well?" In addition to a cool name, he had also given the AI a plummy British male voice to match.

14

Carl's hair wasn't brushed and if anyone had paid attention, they'd see he was wearing the same t-shirt today that he had worn yesterday. In fact, they might even question whether he'd taken it off when he went to sleep.

"Cut the chat routine," Carl said grumpily. "Sitrep, anomalous traffic, Sector 42, all incidents since I logged off last night."

There had been a bump in traffic in that sector before he went off duty last night but he wasn't expecting anything. HOLMES was supposed to send a text and email alert to him and the watch officer if it detected a major incident worthy of deeper analysis. It hadn't, so anything that it had logged could only qualify as routine.

"The most noteworthy event last night was the apparent loss of a Russian flagged commercial freighter in the northern approaches to the Bering Strait at 0215 Pacific Standard Time."

Carl's immediate reaction was 'so what'. Sure, terrible for the crew and everything, but civilian shipping disasters weren't exactly his priority. "Loss? What do you mean, loss?" Carl asked. "Contextualize."

"The *Ozempic Tsar* was a 400,000-ton fully autonomous cargo ship sailing from Archangelsk in Russia to Hokkaido in Japan via the polar route when it issued a mayday on open maritime emergency frequencies to say it was taking water rapidly following an explosion in its engine room and cargo bays and was sinking. It then deployed an emergency locator beacon."

Carl looked up at the ceiling, hands behind his neck. "Cargo?"

"The registers at Lloyd's show that the primary cargo was 162,000 tons of processed lithium."

"Value of the cargo?"

"Landed value one point nine six three billion US dollars."

Carl put his coffee down so quickly it splashed out of the cup and over his empty desk. "Billion? Did you say nearly two billion?"

"Yes, Carl. Do you want me to source more intel on this incident?"

"Access all available intel, compile and report," Carl replied. Two billion dollars? Someone had just lost real money. Either the owners, the buyers or the insurers. He picked up his coffee and sipped. How did it get so cold so fast? He should really get one of those absorb and release gel-lined mugs. Those things could keep soup warm all day, they should be able to solve his cold coffee problem.

"Do you want a full or brief report?" HOLMES asked, coming back to him within about three minutes.

"Brief," Carl said. "Very brief."

"Open source and US Coast Guard intel indicates the *Ozempic Tsar* issued its first mayday call at 0210, issued two more between 0210 and 0214, and ceased mayday transmissions at 0215. A distress beacon was released and started transmitting the ship's location at 0216, at which time the US Coast Guard logged it as a probable sinking, cause unknown."

"Boring. Location?"

"The distress beacon transmitted the *Ozempic Tsar*'s location as latitude 65.74 longitude 169.69, which is five miles inside the Russian Federation Exclusive Economic Zone west of Big Diomede Island."

"Their problem, then," Carl said. "Not even international waters. Any salvage operation initiated yet?"

"Satellite intel indicates there are a number of civilian and two Russian naval vessels at the scene."

Carl perked up slightly. The Russian Pacific fleet base at Vladivostok could be expected to direct maybe one vessel to check out an incident involving an autonomous ship with no human life at risk; to investigate the area, recover the distress buoy and download the black box data. But two showed a higher than normal level of interest.

"Associated military communications activity," he said. "Three degrees of separation." He was asking in shorthand for HOLMES to look at intelligence reports from around the time of the incident, including first-hand, second-hand and even

16

third-hand source reporting. It was about as broad a search as he could ask for, a total fishing exercise.

"Signals intel analysis indicates a spike in Russian Pacific Fleet Command traffic 33 minutes before the incident and then for two hours following the incident, after which traffic returned to near normal levels except for comms to and from vessels in the area of the incident," HOLMES replied. "Do you wish to deep dive or continue?"

Carl had been trained to follow his instincts. With AIs like HOLMES to do the actual analysis, instinct was the only competitive edge humans had over neural systems now. AIs were the masters of cold hard logic, but they sucked at Wild-Assed Guessing.

"Continue. Related air or land-based military traffic analysis," Carl replied.

"Satellite and signals intel indicates two Russian Federation Okhotnik Hunter drones were sent to the scene of the incident, arriving over the wreck at 0225 and returning to their base in Vladivostok at 0245. Their flight track is indicative of a dedicated reconnaissance mission rather than a standing combat air patrol."

OK, this was starting to get interesting. Not a lot interesting, but a little. Ten minutes after the Russian freighter sinks, and two Russian drones are already on station right over the top of it, transmitting images? Pretty convenient they just happened to be available. Carl didn't believe in coincidences like that.

"Wait, you said there was an uptick in Far East HQ comms traffic 33 minutes *before* the incident?"

"Yes."

"Origin and target?"

"The origin of the transmission was Russian Pacific Fleet Command. The target is unknown."

Carl sighed. "Deep dive. Other non-routine Russian military traffic in the area of Bering Strait between the uptick in comms traffic at incident minus 33 minutes and incident time zero."

"There was a non-routine code burst on a Russian Federation military channel six minutes and twenty-eight seconds before the incident. The origin of the code burst was 100 miles north of Saint Lawrence Island. No other non-routine traffic reported."

Damn, damn, damn. He got up from his desk, leaned up against one of the walls in his broom cupboard-sized office and began bouncing on his heels. A ship explodes. Six minutes earlier, a burst of Russian military traffic from the middle of the Bering Strait. Thirty-three minutes before that, an uptick in Russian Eastern Military District traffic. *Wait.*

"HOLMES, assume the transmission six minutes before the sinking was from a Russian Federation naval vessel. Do we have any data on Russian naval vessels within missile range of the freighter at that time?" It was a long shot, but maybe a Russian missile test had gone haywire.

"Checking Satellite, Signals, Human Intelligence ... no Russian naval vessel within range within the communications window," HOLMES said. "Do you wish me to expand the search to vessels of other navies?"

"What? Repeat, contextualize."

"I have a 98.4% match on both a possible launch vessel and missile type," HOLMES said. Carl could swear it sounded pleased with itself. "The time to target projected from the location of the comms burst at six minutes to the time of first mayday call from the *Ozempic Tsar* matches the profile of a US PIKE long-range stealth anti-ship missile launched from the Finnish *Scorpène*-class submarine FNS *Vesikko*."

Carl snapped forward in his chair. "Say again? Expand!"

"Signals intel indicates the FNS *Vesikko* sent a message to Finnish Fleet Command at Heikkila, Finland, one hour before the incident, reporting its position, bearing and speed. The FNS *Vesikko* is a refurbished French *Scorpène*-class submarine equipped with the US PIKE long-range stealth anti-ship missile. My analysis shows that if the *Vesikko* had maintained its stated bearing and speed, its estimated position would correlate with the location of the anomalous comms transmission 100 miles

18

north of Saint Lawrence Island. A PIKE missile fired by the FNS *Vesikko* at this position would have taken six minutes and eighteen seconds to reach the *Ozempic Tsar*, which correlates with the timing of the anomalous radio transmission. The triangulation of these three data points gives a 98.4% certainty that if the *Ozempic Tsar* was destroyed by a naval vessel, it was a PIKE missile fired by the FNS *Vesikko*."

Carl was starting to sweat. He wasn't a small man – in fact he was carrying about fifty pounds more than he probably should be, but it would usually take a lot more than just sitting in his chair in the cold corridor under the Embassy compound to make him break out in a sweat. This sweat wasn't exertion, it was fear.

"Would a what-you-call-it missile ..."

"PIKE."

"Yeah. Would one of them be enough to sink a 400,000-ton freighter inside ten minutes?"

"If it successfully struck the ship's hydrogen storage or fuel cells, one such missile would be sufficient. Standard military doctrine would dictate two are fired to secure catastrophic target destruction."

Carl whistled. "A double tap. Just to be sure."

"Please repeat. Was that a question or comment?"

"Neither. Please tell me there were no US naval vessels capable of firing a PIKE missile inside that kill zone at the time of the incident."

There was a slight pause, then HOLMES responded. "The nearest long-range cruise missile-capable US vessel was the subsea drone USS *Venice Beach*, which was on station 290 miles south-southeast at the time."

"Inside missile range?"

"Three hundred nautical miles," HOLMES said. "The USS *Venice Beach* could also have engaged the *Ozempic Tsar* with its missiles at that range but it would have had to fire 30 minutes earlier. I am unable to locate any US Pacific Fleet Command traffic to or from the USS *Venice Beach* at that time."

"But that *is* around the time of the Russian Pacific Fleet comms burst. They might have been reporting on a suspected US missile launch. Dammit, this is ugly. HOLMES, deep dive Navy command and control logs and check whether the *Venice Beach* fired a PIKE missile in the last 24 hours. Check whether any US Navy vessel in the Northern Pacific has fired any sort of weapon at all. Check for any intel indicating that Russia has the capability to hack a US naval vessel and order it to fire one of its missiles. I want you to run three scenarios: one, the Finnish submarine sank the Russian freighter. Two, the USS *Venice Beach* sank the freighter. Three, an unknown Russian vessel, aircraft or land-based missile battery sank it. Summarize potential supporting data and assign probabilities, then send the report to my laptop with a copy to the Senior Defense Attaché and NSA Russia Desk."

"Will do, Carl. What should I title the report?"

Carl thought about it. "Heading: Battle of Bering Strait. Subhead: Who killed the *Ozempic Tsar?*"

"Yes, Carl. Compiling."

Carl drew a dot on a page and wrote *OzTsar* next to it, then a ring and FNS *Vesikko* at 6 minutes 18 seconds. Further out at 30 minutes, USS *Venice Beach*. It was the time correlation between the position of the Finnish sub, the flight time of a PIKE missile, and the timing of that comms burst from the middle of the Bering Strait that bugged him the most.

"HOLMES, do you believe in coincidence?"

"I do not indulge in beliefs, Carl."

"Point taken. HOLMES, book me some serious bandwidth. Something stinks here."

HOLES IN THE CHEESE

The US Ambassador to Moscow, Devlin McCarthy, had several firsts to her name but the one she liked best was that she was the first black Irish American to be named Ambassador to a top tier post like Moscow. In fact, Devlin was pretty sure she was the first black Irish American in the State Department, let alone in Moscow. She wasn't the first ever black Irish American, that she knew for a fact, because that honor went to her father, his father, and his father's father. Further back than that, she hadn't checked. She loved her grandfather's explanation, though – he insisted his ancestors were Viking slaves, captured Moors bought in the slave markets of Hedeby and shipped to Ireland to serve in Viking families during the reign of Harald Bluetooth.

It was a great story, and she told it to anyone brave enough to ask her about her family history, which most of the Embassy staffers were too timid to do. She wouldn't mind if they did – it would give her a chance to break down the Ice Queen reputation she seemed to have brought here with her. Small talk wasn't something people seemed comfortable trying on her, so luckily she was comfortable with their small awkward silences. She really didn't think she deserved the rep she had. Sure, she was fifty-ish and twice divorced – she never had much of an interest in lifelong attachments – and she spent most of her waking life at work, but she did take two weeks' holiday every year to be with her now-adult daughter, always taking her somewhere outdoorsy for at least a week, followed by a week somewhere nice like a beach resort or theme park. When Cindy had hit her adult years she'd been expecting her to find something better to do in the summer than hang with her absentee State Department mother, but Cindy hadn't missed a holiday yet and these days there was a third guest with them, Cindy's new daughter Angela. Devlin figured the fact they'd stayed close said something nice about them both.

Apart from her annual family get-together, then, most of her daily life was polite society and diplomatic doublespeak. So she relished days like today when she was summoned to meet with the Russian Foreign Minister Roman Kelnikov at his State offices inside the Kremlin walls. His Ministry was on the ring road that circled Moscow, but the fact he was meeting her here indicated to her she was in for a bit of diplomatic theater where frank views might actually be exchanged.

She sat in the back of her two-ton armored limo with two bodyguards up front, one facing forward, one backward, and her personal aide beside her. In the days when cars needed a driver, they'd needed a detail of three – one to drive, two to guard. But driverless vehicles had freed up the third spot either for additional protection, guests or, in this case, legroom. As they approached the River Gates that led directly into the Russian Foreign Ministry underground car park there was the usual ceremony with credentials and Kremlin guards running a sweep of the car and its occupants. They all had to demount and go through biometric scanners before they were allowed back into their car and inside the Kremlin walls.

As their car found its assigned parking bay, Devlin patted the small printed folio on her lap. She never took a tablet or telephone into Russian Government offices because, since passive data retrieval had become a thing, it was the work of seconds for a concealed scanner to strip an electronic device of all its data. The great privacy backlash of about twenty years ago when people got sick of their data being stolen, their identities cloned and their secrets sold to the highest bidder had seen a revival in the use of good old-fashioned paper that had to be physically stolen, held and read before it gave up its secrets. All truly sensitive information these days was only held on paper.

And the information in the folio on her lap was about as sensitive as it came.

"Tea?" Kelnikov asked, motioning to the samovar on a silver table next to his desk. His office was big enough to hold a large oak desk which legend said had been gifted to the Russian Foreign Minister Molotov by Minister of the Reich Ribbentrop. There were also two long sofas, both facing in towards a less formal teak coffee table decorated with fresh flowers and fruit.

Devlin had been told her security detail and her aide were welcome to wait in the anteroom today. The meeting she was invited to attend with Kelnikov was to take place under four eyes only. When she'd walked in, he'd been sitting at his desk talking with a secretary and he'd risen to shake Devlin's hand, then sat back down again at his desk. No fruit for her today, then.

"Yes please," Devlin said to the offer of tea, and the secretary fussed arranging tea and a plate of small dry cakes for them both, then hurried out of the office.

"You look well," Kelnikov smiled, his bald head glistening in the light of the overhead lamps. He was about sixty, overweight, known to have an occasionally recurring barbiturate habit and a predilection for preying on ballerinas from the Bolshoi, where he had a private box. Devlin found him completely and totally without charm. "I think you have even got a little early summer tan, is that possible?"

Oh, so that's how you want to start? Devlin thought, immediately shifting herself into cold, minimalist mode. She ignored the poorly disguised barb about her color.

"Why was I summoned here, Mr. Secretary?" she asked.

"Invited," Kelnikov smiled, thin lips parting over yellow teeth. "As you know, if you had been summoned, there would have been a public press pronouncement to that effect. We are not there yet."

"Where are we, then?" she asked. Fortunately her people had done their work and knew exactly what it was that she had been 'invited' to talk about. She had been both forewarned and forearmed.

Kelnikov reached into his desk and pulled out a small folder tied with a string, which he took his time untying. He pulled out a large photograph and slid it across the table to her.

"The *Ozempic Tsar*," he said, pointing at it. "The most advanced autonomous pilotless freight vessel in the world, and valued at more than 250 million of your American dollars. On its most recent voyage, it was carrying a cargo of 1.9 billion US dollars' worth of processed lithium."

"Then I sincerely hope it was insured," she said, immediately playing the ball back at him. "Because my information is that it is now lying at the bottom of the Bering Strait."

His hands were folded and resting on the desk in front of him, but he fanned them wide now. "Oh please, do tell me what information you have on the demise of this pride of the Russian merchant fleet?"

She had been planning to save her ammunition, but his racist remark, his obsequious manner, his slimy smile, all conspired to make her want to have this audience over and done with as quickly as possible. From her own folio she pulled Carl Williams' intel report and placed it so that the cameras which she assumed were in Kelnikov's office could take a nice clear shot of it. She was about to tell him what was in it anyway.

"We are happy to share the intelligence we have on this tragedy. I'll give you the short version," she said. "Thirty minutes before that ship was sunk, a Russian naval communications center at Anadyr sent a message to a Finnish submarine, the FNS *Vesikko*, sailing 20 miles southwest of the *Ozempic Tsar*. Six minutes before the *Tsar* sent out its first mayday, that same vessel reported it had fired its missiles." She watched with satisfaction as Kelnikov's eyes narrowed and he pursed his mouth. "Six minutes later, at least two subsonic submarine-launched surface-to-surface missiles hit the *Ozempic Tsar* and detonated its hydrogen fuel stores. The explosion was so catastrophic it was registered on one of our thermal imaging satellites as a possible ICBM missile launch bloom, but luckily for you, our AI detected that it had the wrong heat signature and our military alert level was not raised."

Kelnikov spoke in a tight voice, verging on anger. "You accuse us of collusion in this crime? What proof do you have?"

"You know that there would be no conclusive satellite imaging available for the undersea launch of stealth cruise missiles."

"Then you have nothing," he said, suddenly happy, reaching into his folder again. "Whereas we have this." He took out another photograph and almost threw it at her.

It was a satellite photograph of a ship, with latitude, longitude and date stamp clearly visible. She could guess what ship it was, but Kelnikov spoke before she could say anything. "That is a US Navy vessel, the USS *Venice Beach*. An unmanned guided missile cruiser, armed with anti-ship missiles." He took out another photo and flipped it at her so hard it spun on the table in front of her.

She stopped it spinning and held it down with a single finger as she looked at it. It showed a large metal plate on the deck of what looked like a fishing vessel, with the word *TSAR* stenciled across it. If she had to guess, she'd guess it would turn out to be a close match for the name a certain Russian freighter had stenciled across its stern. Next to the wreckage lay a crushed tubular shape about two yards long and what looked like a mangled engine of some sort.

"Does your report tell you what that is?" Kelnikov asked gleefully.

"Actually it does," she said. "I'm guessing that tube next to that clearly faked stern plate is the housing of a US PIKE anti-ship missile."

"Salvaged, not faked, and yes it is!" Kelnikov said, building up a head of steam now. "You don't deny it? The missile that destroyed a Russian freighter while it was moving through Russian territorial waters was American!"

"Your tone is accusatory," Devlin said. "But I have seen no evidence to justify your anger being directed at the USA."

Kelnikov leaned over and jabbed his finger angrily down on the photo. "Your missile, fired by one of your ships!"

She laughed, realizing as she did so that she was ignoring ten years of training and practice in protocol. Kelnikov's face clouded. No, it boiled.

"Just *what* about this act of naked aggression do you regard as funny?" he demanded. "Tell me!"

"How about you tell me something?" she asked, speaking in firm controlled tones. "PIKE missiles have been exported to thirteen countries, two of which have unfortunately recently moved out of our sphere of influence and into yours. One of those is Finland. I don't deny the missile in that photograph may be a PIKE, but I strongly deny that it was fired by one of our ships. Our information indicates it was fired by a Finnish submarine which was in communication with Russian Far East Military Command."

"You accuse Russia of sinking a Russian merchant vessel? What nonsense."

"The *Venice Beach* did not fire those missiles. Finland, however, recently signed a defense cooperation treaty with Russia. One of Finland's refurbished French *Scorpène*-class hydrogen-electric submarines was in the area and would have been more than capable of this attack."

"Again, I ask you what proof you have for this baseless accusation?"

"The same as you have for yours," she said coolly. "None." She closed her folder. "Was this the only matter you wanted to discuss today?" she asked.

Kelnikov slapped the table, but if he expected Devlin to flinch or jump, he was disappointed. She'd seen him in this state many times and had been waiting for it. She did little more than blink at him. "You have 24 hours," he said, "to admit responsibility for this heinous act, issue an apology and offer suitable reparations to the owners of the *Ozempic Tsar*."

"Or..."

Kelnikov glared at her. "Or, as you Americans are so fond of saying, 'All options are on the table'."

Back in her limo, Devlin fished out the intel report again and looked at it carefully. She handed it to her aide. "I see that the origin of this report is NSA Moscow. Find out which

26

analyst wrote it, will you? By the look on Kelnikov's face, I knew more about this *Ozempic Tsar* incident than he did, and that was a damn nice place to be. I want to write a note to say thank you."

ANOTHER DAY IN PARADISE

If there was a shittier rock on the whole planet than Little Diomede Island, Lieutenant Commander Alicia Rodriguez wanted to know where. Because she'd be on the first plane there and she'd wallow in its complete shittiness and then be able to return to Little Diomede happy that she wasn't actually living on the shittiest damn rock on the whole damn planet.

Or in fact, not even *on* the shittiest rock, but *under* it. At least if you were living on top of the rock, you'd get 360-degree sea views. Sure, you'd be looking through fog, out over windblown white caps, not seeing much apart from shitty seabirds and ice floes, but you could at least look east and tell yourself that right over there, just over the horizon, that was Alaska in the good old US of A. And if you looked west, you could tell yourself you were looking at the Evil Empire reborn and get a bit of a thrill telling yourself you were manning the closest US military base to Russia and they didn't even know you were there.

But no, she wasn't living on top of the rock. She and her personnel were living in the cave that millennia of beating waves had carved under the pockmarked, moss-covered basalt of Little Diomede. Who had discovered the cave? If she ever met them, she would beat ten kinds of crap out of them as a thank you. But it probably wasn't even a person. It was probably a drone, which was kind of ironic.

Rodriguez wasn't sure exactly how many years the facility on Little Diomede had been under construction, but she knew why it had been built. A Pentagon position paper had warned that with the opening of polar shipping routes, an increasing amount of vital commerce was now moving through the Bering Strait, giving it the potential to be as strategically important as the Strait of Hormuz between Iran and the Emirates was in the last century. When Russia expanded its naval base at Lavrentiya in the early 2020s, as part of its 'Pivot to the Pacific', diplomatic tensions had risen, and the US had looked for responses. It could have recommissioned the old Marks Army Airfield at Nome but strategists pointed out that since the advent of hypersonic cruise missile technology, large fixed infrastructure such as an air base was near impossible to defend, and while it had political and economic value, its true value in a conflict would be very limited.

The idea for a secret base *under* the rock cap of Little Diomede had been born.

There had been nothing there but a tiny fishing village twenty years ago. The Navy had bought out the two dozen or so villagers, turned their houses into barracks and then moved in construction crews. They'd created a plausible cover story by building a naval radar dome on the crown of the island, and the first thing they did was throw up a hulking great storage shed next to the dome and fill it full of mining gear to sink a shaft straight down through the middle of the island to the cave below. Then they began hollowing it out. The Russians showed a lot of interest while the radar was being built, and sent a flight over to scan and photograph it every time it got an upgrade, but as long as they couldn't see the US putting anti-missile systems there or building airstrips on Little Diomede, they generally ignored it, apart from the occasional electronic countermeasure attack trying to jam it when one of their naval battle groups was moving through the Strait.

At first it was conceived as a missile launch platform with ground-to-air ordnance concealed under the large radome and an autonomous anti-shipping missile system hidden in the cavern, covering the eastern approaches to the Strait. Navy solved the question of how the island would be covertly supplied by dredging the floor of the sea cave, widening it, and putting in a submarine dock.

But it was with the widespread adoption of unmanned aircraft that Little Diomede came into its own. Plans were soon laid to base thirty aircraft under the Rock, a mixture of reconnaissance Unmanned Aerial Vehicles and Unmanned *Combat* Aerial Vehicles, commonly known as drones. Little

Diomede wasn't intended to be a manned military base. It was to be a 'second strike' facility. In the case of full-scale nuclear war, or even a major regional conventional war, it would wait out the first strike or first wave of attacks and then strike back, its thirty fully autonomous attack aircraft in range of all major Russian military and civilian targets in the Russian Far East and, unlike ICBM silos, able to carry out multiple strikes thanks to automated landing, recycling and relaunch capabilities. The only personnel who would remain on the base when it was operational would be a handful of service technicians, staying topside in the radar facility during peacetime and deploying under the Rock in time of war.

Except the whole automated landing, recycling and relaunch concept was still just that, a concept.

The challenge the Navy threw at the planners for Little Diomede was seen as impossible at first. New aircraft variants had to be developed and systems just didn't exist that would allow drones to be landed, refueled, rearmed and relaunched without human assistance. The first phase of the project, before they did a full build-out of the base, was to prove that it was even viable to stage drones out of the Rock. And that meant that during the pilot phase, they needed humans to launch, land and recover the machines. Navy had done as much as it could ashore in Defense Advanced Research Projects Agency, or DARPA, test facilities to automate the loading of fuel and ordnance and transport of the drones from hangars to launch ramps, but the litmus test was whether those systems would function at all in extreme environments like the Bering Strait.

The Rock was essentially supposed to operate as a concealed aircraft carrier, but where an aircraft carrier had hundreds of personnel dedicated to aircraft operations, the cavern under Little Diomede could take no more than fifty. It wasn't that the enlarged cavern wasn't huge, but once you took out the existing dock infrastructure, added hangar space for thirty drones, storage for parts and fuel, and the machinery needed for getting the aircraft airborne and recovering them after a water landing, there wasn't much left over for all the humanity needed to service the robots. Everything that could be automated was. They could draw a lot on the systems that had been developed for the latest generation of supercarriers, but tailor-made kludges were needed for multiple systems.

So where on an aircraft carrier you had separate teams for aviation fuel, plane handling, aircraft maintenance and ordnance, just to name a few, under the Rock all those functions had been boiled down to Air Boss Alicia Rodriguez and her small team. They were no ordinary assemblage of personnel. She'd had to put together a tailor-made team of launch/recovery specialists, air traffic controllers, machinist and electrician mates, plane captains for aircraft maintenance, aerographers for weather forecasting and ordnancemen to fit the weapons into the auto-load magazines. They'd pulled Rodriguez off the USS *GW Bush*, where at twenty-six she'd been one of the Navy's youngest ever 'mini-bosses' or Assistant Air Commanders, and told her she could have her pick of personnel from any vessel she named. She'd drawn up a shortlist of personnel who had served in at least two functions aboard a carrier, preferably three. They'd given her twenty bodies, and she'd argued for thirty, ending with twenty-four. She split them into two shifts, and all of them had to understudy a different function so they could back each other up. She didn't have enough people for redundancies.

The drones that Rodriguez and her crew were put on the island to service had been designed for carrier ops and didn't need a long runway; they were built to be launched from a catapult and needed significant modifications so that they could fly right into the mouth of the cave and drop down onto the water to be retrieved with a crane and sling. Rodriguez had heard it had taken Northrop Grumman Boeing two years to work out how to fit retractable skis to their machines instead of wheels, and another two years to work out how to avoid them sucking seawater into their air intakes every time they splashed down.

Fuel for the drones wasn't an issue, because a purification and catalyzation unit was installed that could supply 200 liters of liquid hydrogen and 400 liters of potable water an hour. A repurposed S8G nuclear power plant from a decommissioned *Ohio*-class submarine provided power to the entire base.

Being as it didn't officially exist, the drone wing under Little Diomede didn't have a typical Navy designation; in organization charts it was buried deep under Naval Network Warfare Command and was simply known as 'Auxiliary Unit 4' or A4, but to the aircrew and officers based there, Little Diomede Air Base was just 'the Rock'.

Rodriguez had been an aviator, most recently a 'shooter' or launch catapult officer, before she'd been promoted to Mini-Boss, but in the role of Air Boss under Little Diomede, she doubled as squadron CO. Normally she would have had to 'fleet up' through a squadron department head role, then Executive Officer or XO, before being assigned a squadron command, but things under the Rock were far from normal.

Besides which, there was only one pilot on Little Diomede right now and none of the aircraft had yet been certified for operations. So her only pilot was going stir crazy waiting to get one of the machines onto the Cat and into the air so she could fly it back in through that cave mouth and try her skill at 'threading the needle' as she called it. A drone pilot could theoretically fly their aircraft from anywhere in the world with a fast satellite link, but with A4 they were trying new tactics with line of sight comms and that meant a pilot co-located with her fighters, at least in the test and certification phase.

The lone pilot's name was Lieutenant Karen 'Bunny' O'Hare and Rodriguez had not had a part in choosing her. For a start, the woman wasn't even American. She was Australian, and had come across from the DARPA Joint Unmanned Combat Aerial Vehicle program where she had been the lead pilot testing and perfecting the water landing capabilities of the next-generation Fantom fighter. On paper, it made perfect sense that the pilot who had led the testing of the seaplane version of the Fantom would also lead the establishment of the unit for which they were designed, but Rodriguez soon learned there was more to Bunny O'Hare than appeared on paper.

She had cut her teeth on F-35s in the Royal Australian Air Force before an 'attitude problem' earned her a 40 day detention and suspended discharge. But she'd acquitted herself so well as a combat pilot flying missions in tandem with drones that she came to the attention of recruiters at DARPA and was headhunted into their dedicated next-generation attack drone program, which had delivered a new weapons platform to specification, but now needed a new breed of pilot to fly it. DARPA was looking for pilots whose flying and social skills were less important than a talent for continuous partial attention and an ability to contribute to AI coding and development. For the first time in her life, Bunny's attention deficit disorder was actually an asset.

The aircraft that had emerged from the revitalized attack drone program, the Fantom, was a real killer. Twenty-six feet long, with a wingspan of 33 feet, it was powered by two hydrogen-fueled Reaction Engine Scimitar powerplants giving it the ability to hit a maximum airspeed of Mach 1.8 or 1,300 mph and carry a payload of 10,000lb – ranging from recon pods and GPS-guided precision air-to-ground munitions to the latest Cuda air-to-air, hit-to-kill missiles.

Unlike Rodriguez, and despite her frustrations, Bunny liked Little Diomede. She had grown up in the Australian outback, and she liked it being *cold*. She also liked the idea of being the only pilot on an island with two dozen aircraft to fly. Did she miss bossing her F-35 around the sky in the real? Hell yeah, but unlike a lot of other aviators, Bunny already lived in the future and the future was remote-piloted, semi-autonomous, and she would never go back. In her F-35 Bunny only ever felt in control of her own machine, even flying as flight leader. Hell, half the time whatever fool she had on her wing didn't do as they were ordered, or screwed it up. Chewing out one too many fellow pilots for shitty results in training exercises was one of the things that got her transferred to drones, but she couldn't help calling human error for what it was – dumb ass error. And you couldn't afford a wide margin of error in modern combat where the distance between dead and alive was measured in milliseconds.

At the stick of a Fantom, though, she commanded not one machine, but six. Not one wingman, but five. She flew the queen bee in the formation, and the other five machines were slaved to hers, executing her orders exactly as she issued them, right or wrong. If she screwed up, lost a machine, missed a target, there was no one to blame but herself.

She didn't often screw up, but when she did, Rodriguez was glad they had a few hundred feet of solid rock over their heads, because she was sure the Russians could have heard Bunny swearing down in Vladivostok. And right now Bunny was only getting flight time on simulators, so Rodriguez could only imagine what she'd be like if she was in a fight for real. Like a lot of combat pilots Rodriguez had met, Bunny seemed to start every day looking for a target to hit.

And today, that target was Air Boss Alicia Rodriguez's catapult officer.

"With respect, you said 'tomorrow' three days ago, Lieutenant," Bunny was saying, staring at the ops-ready Fantom waiting to be loaded onto the electromagnetic aircraft launch system, or catapult, down on the flight deck. She was facing down Rodriguez's shooter, Lieutenant KC Severin, and several of Rodriguez's flight operations personnel were sitting on their asses on a rock shelf behind her, enjoying the show.

"And that aircraft has been ready for two days, as promised, Lieutenant," Severin said. He was a small man, but he was all muscle and had been Rodriguez's assistant on the *GW Bush*. "It's the Cat that's the problem. No matter what we dial into the catapult, it's delivering 196,000 pounds of thrust and by our reckoning, that will send your little paper planes into the lip above the egress chute like bugs into a windscreen."

"So I'll punch in a little elevator trim," Bunny said. "Stick the drone to the rails."

"Good idea, Lieutenant," Severin said, irony in his voice. "Tell you what, why don't we tie your butt to the shuttle, send you through that chute with 196,000 pounds of thrust, you hold your arms out and flap, see if *you* can stick to those rails."

They'd had to come up with their own terminology for the world under the rock. The drones were launched through a 50 by 50-foot smooth bored tunnel straight through the rock that emerged from a cliff face 500 feet above sea level. It was called 'the chute'. The drones landed by flying under the overhanging rock and into the mouth of the cave at sea level, which was called 'the Slot'. The artificial harbor inside the cave consisted of a simple rectangular submarine dock beside which the drones launched, and the seawater filling the cavern was known as 'the Pond'.

The chute exited the Rock directly east, toward Alaska, masking the egress of the drones from anything but a luckily placed satellite or high-altitude recon overflight. To further confuse any imaging, a mooring had been created outside the egress port, and several old fishing boats were tied up there, the remnants of the fishing fleet that had once sailed out of Little Diomede. Demasted, they were small enough that there was no risk to the drones taking off and landing, but numerous enough that any overhead image would just see a cluster of ships, with a launching drone, if it was unlucky enough to be caught entering and leaving, just a blurred dot.

"This base is supposed to go to Phase II in six months, you know that, Lieutenant," Bunny sighed, and turned to appeal to Rodriguez. "Between now and then I have to do the forms on 30 drones, ma'am. There's going to be a submarine full of Secretaries of this and Admirals of that, docking in the Pond in about 20 something weeks, and after six hours underwater in some stinking tin can, followed by a shower, some strong coffee and crappy food, they are going to stand right here..." she pointed at the platform they were standing on next to the flight deck, "... expecting to see me fly a Hex of Fantoms out that chute, dodge a few lurking F-35s, blow the hell out of some barge in the Eastern Strait, and then watch as I gracefully and professionally glide them back through the Slot to a perfect water landing and recovery."

No matter how annoying, arrogant and disagreeable she could be, Bunny O'Hare was seldom wrong, and although she was bitching she did it with a smile and a rolling Australian brogue. Rodriguez turned to her catapult officer. "How much longer, Lieutenant?"

Severin bought himself some time to answer, looking down at a tablet screen. "We're reconfiguring the catapult software, ma'am. Four hours. Then we have to test and recalibrate. Six hours total. If we can, we'll get it done by 2300, midnight latest. Next shift can do the fueling and pre-flight for the Fantom, 2 hours. If all goes well, we'll be good to launch at 0300."

To anyone else but Bunny O'Hare, laying down a flight time of 0300 would have gotten Rodriguez at least a groan. The Australian just smiled. "Permission to get some beauty sleep, ma'am," she said, before saluting and turning on her heel.

Rodriguez watched her go, then returned to Severin and his smirking team. "If that Cat hasn't been reconfigured, test fired and made ready by 0200 it's *your* asses I'll be launching off that catapult, gentlemen."

OPERATION LOSOS

Headquarters of the Russian Federation 3rd Air and Air Defense Forces Command, Khabarovsk, Russian Eastern Military District.

Colonel Yevgeny Bondarev, Commanding Officer of the Russian 6983rd Air Brigade or Snow Leopards, stared at his unshaven, gray-skinned reflection in a mirror, stuck in the act of trying to decide whether to shave or throw up.

A lot of things made Bondarev feel like throwing up, but this time it was the thirteen glasses of brandy he'd put down yesterday afternoon and evening with his Brigade staff, and as a man who didn't drink heavily, he was hurting badly. It had started innocently enough, a group of his officers inviting him to dinner to mark the anniversary of the death of his grandfather, Hero of the Russian Federation, Victor Nikolaevich Bondarev. After a nice three-course meal with wine, however, the night had descended into speeches, each accompanied by a toast to his famous grandfather, but when the speeches ran out, there was still brandy left, so there were more toasts – to absent wives, newly born children, newly married daughters or sons, recently departed fathers or mothers and, of course, to the apparently immutable President Navalny, now in his second year at the helm of a resurgent Russia.

There was something else too. He was trying to remember, had he proposed a toast to his own daughter? It had crossed his drunken mind, but had he said it out loud? Damn – he couldn't remember! He'd kept his daughter a secret until now because the mother was a foreigner with whom he'd only had a casual fling before she had moved back home. But if it became known he'd had a relationship with a foreigner without declaring it – worse, had a child with the woman – that kind of 'oversight' could bite you on the ass. He grabbed his razor in one hand and his shaving cream in the other, then dropped them both as the bile rose in his gut and he spun around to face the toilet.

Wiping his mouth with a towel, he rested his forehead against the cool tiles. He'd know soon enough if he'd been indiscreet.

Usually Bondarev would doze through a staff meeting like today's, his brain numbed by the reading of minutes, follow-up on administrative actions, edicts about the misuse of supplies and a long list of transfers. He was a combat commander, not a bureaucrat, one of the few at the table who had actually led in war and personally downed three enemy pilots over Turkey, though it had given him no satisfaction.

Today, however, despite the rising acid in his gut and the pounding in his head, he was focused on the figure at the end of the long mahogany meeting table, General Lukin, one of the few in the Air Army hierarchy who had Bondarev's respect, because Lukin was known to be fiercely loyal to his pilots and ground crews, and not afraid to stand up to Kremlin stupidity. What got Bondarev's attention right now was that Lukin appeared to be more interested in reading the room than the papers in front of him. Bondarev got the sense that whatever he was about to announce, it was well rehearsed. The man was no longer in his physical prime, was carrying a few pounds more than was probably healthy for him, but he was still a fairly fit fifty years old. He was sweating. And he looked like he'd aged five years since Bondarev had seen him on video link two days earlier when the *Ozempic Tsar* had been lost.

"Gentlemen, you are all aware that two days ago the United States, without provocation, attacked and sank a merchant ship of the Russian Federation in the Bering Strait, well inside the Russian Exclusive Economic Zone," he said, and paused. "An ultimatum was given to the United States to acknowledge its responsibility, apologize and offer reparations to the owners of this advanced and very expensive vessel." He looked around the room. "The ultimatum has expired, and as

38

expected the United States has not accepted responsibility for the destruction of the *Ozempic Tsar.*"

As the General finished, he looked up and nodded to an aide at the back of the room who had been standing there holding a stack of lightweight tablet PCs. The man began walking around and distributing them, and Bondarev put his thumb on the DNA lock that woke the screen. He saw a dozen folders on the home screen, all of which started with 'LOSOS', the Russian word for salmon.

"Operation LOSOS," Lukin said, guessing their thoughts. "What you are holding are your personal orders for the upcoming operation to secure the Bering Strait from future acts of piracy by the US or any other nation and guarantee free passage for international shipping traffic." The large OLED screen behind the General came to life and an intelligence officer that Bondarev recognized as a young Lieutenant from his own Brigade staff stepped forward. He remembered she had been seconded to the 3rd Command staff for a special project – now he knew what it was. Whatever was going down, it had not been triggered just two days ago, it must have been in preparation for months. He got a sudden feeling he was about to be a part of a major chapter in the history of his nation, but on the right or wrong side? That was yet to be seen.

Lieutenant Ksenia Butyrskaya drew a big breath and straightened her back. Bondarev noticed she kept her hands firmly clasped behind her back, probably so that their trembling didn't give her away. "Our intelligence indicates that the attack on the *Ozempic Tsar* was most likely conducted by an unmanned US warship which fired two PIKE anti-ship missiles. Operation LOSOS..." she began. She swiped a hand quickly across the touchscreen to show an aerial reconnaissance photograph of a small airfield. Bondarev noted the presence of a light aircraft, helicopters that were probably air-sea rescue machines, and what might have been a military transport aircraft. He saw nothing of real significance. Butyrskaya continued, "... has a single objective. In an internationally sanctioned peacekeeping action we will take and hold the US island of Saint Lawrence, specifically the airfield and radar installation at Savoonga, capture any US military personnel on the island and leverage control of the island to ensure the safe passage of international air and maritime traffic through the Bering Strait." Butyrskaya paused, expecting the room to immediately explode with questions.

In fact, there was a stunned silence.

Bondarev spoke first. "Are we declaring *war* on the USA?"

Butyrskaya looked to Lukin. He shook his head slowly. "There will be no formal declaration of war. And our objective is to take Saint Lawrence with minimal use of deadly force. The US keeps only a small military police force at its radar base, there are no ground troops garrisoned there. The forces allocated will be more than adequate to contain them. Operation LOSOS will involve more shouting than shooting."

Bondarev looked across the table at an old friend, Lieutenant Colonel Tomas Arsharvin. One of those he'd been drinking with last night, they'd served together in Syria during the border conflict with Turkey and saved each other's asses more than once. Bondarev guessed he would be the one who knew what was really going on, but he couldn't ask him here. He'd have to save that until after this charade of a briefing. Arsharvin caught his look and tried to read his mind. "We are acting under the authority of the Barents Euro-Arctic Council to preserve the rights of all international shipping to traverse the northern polar seas without interference." Arsharvin's voice sounded hollow, letting Bondarev know what he thought of that flimsy diplomatic cover.

Bondarev couldn't help himself. "*Sweden* supports us taking military action against the US?" he asked disbelievingly. The Barents Council was a subset of Arctic nations comprising Norway, Sweden, Finland and Russia that had come together to lobby for fishing rights in the Arctic waters that were opening up as the icecap receded. Norway had dropped out after a dispute several years ago but the other three nations continued to make treaties with each other under the name of the Barents

40

Council – even if, until now, no other country had paid them any mind.

"Sweden abstained," Arsharvin said, his voice betraying nothing of what Bondarev knew he must be thinking. "The vote was carried on a majority."

And what the hell have we promised Finland? Bondarev was going to ask, but kept that question to himself. "The United States will not let Russia occupy its territory in the name of a tinpot fishing coalition. It will react with violence such as we have never before seen," Bondarev commented, looking around the room. No one was meeting his gaze.

"Perhaps they should have thought of the consequences before they sank the *Ozempic Tsar*, Comrade Colonel," Butyrskaya said, clearly wanting to say more.

General Lukin held up his hand. "Thank you, Lieutenant," he said. He brushed at an invisible hair on his lapel and then spoke to the officers at the table, not to Bondarev in particular. "The United States is riven with internal division. It has shown a reluctance to engage in international affairs of any consequence and our activities in Africa, the Pacific and the Baltics have brought only bluster from their President and State Secretary and whining in the United Nations. In every situation where we have moved our agenda forward, the United States has conceded and returned to its own political bickering."

Another silence followed, into which Butyrskaya unwittingly stepped. "If they were strong, they would have challenged our Navy with theirs. Instead, they resort to an ambush on unarmed civilian shipping."

Finally Bondarev heard a voice other than his own. Colonel Artem Kokorin, commander of the 573rd Army Air Force Base, the Lynxes, slapped a hand down on the table. "We are not fools here. I do not believe we are risking all-out war with the USA for the sake of a freighter owned by a rich fool and piloted by a robot!"

Lukin fixed him with an ice-cold glare. "Russia does not want war, comrade. The Bering Strait is a strategically important waterway and the USA has seen fit to challenge the freedom of our ships to traverse that waterway. This peacekeeping action will assert the rights of all shipping to move through the Strait and we will withdraw as soon as the USA acknowledges its perfidy and gives assurances it will pay reparations and guarantee freedom of navigation."

Kokorin nodded, then leaned toward Bondarev and whispered under his breath, "Bullshit." Lukin waved at Butyrskaya to continue her briefing. She pointed at the tablets in front of them. "Your unit-level orders are being sent to you as we speak and your officers recalled for detailed briefings. Operation LOSOS will be initiated at 0100 hours on August 24th." She saw faces tighten and nodded. "Yes, that is six days from now. As soon as special forces have secured the airfield and radar station garrison at Savoonga on Saint Lawrence, Colonel Bondarev's Snow Leopards will provide air-to-air and air-to-ground cover for ground operations, then will stay on station to protect the airlift of ground-air defense units and garrison troops by Kokorin's transport units. We expect to have full control of both air and sea in the operations area within 24 hours of the arrival of special forces troops in the target area and full control of the territory of Saint Lawrence within 36 hours."

"If my Sukhois and Migs are running a combat air patrol over a US territory at the same time as their radar and airfield there goes dark, there will be a reaction. I predict a maximum of 10 minutes before the first US F-35s arrive to order us to leave their airspace. What are we to tell them, if they bother to ask before they shoot?" Bondarev asked.

Butyrskaya smiled. "That has been anticipated. Immediately before special forces land, we will declare a submarine emergency in international waters off the coast of Saint Lawrence," she said. "One of our boats will send a mayday and declare a nuclear containment breach. Arctic Fleet assets in the area will be directed to respond and will start moving at speed to the area and provide ship-based anti-air cover. All international shipping and aircraft will be asked to divert to allow our rescue efforts unhindered freedom of action.

42

The US might send reconnaissance aircraft, but the cover story should be enough to prevent a full-scale air defense response until we are in control."

"And if they don't buy this cover story?" Bondarev persisted. "I have the resources to rotate a combat air patrol of one squadron over Saint Lawrence for that period, but if we sustain any losses, I assume I will be able to call for reserves from 2nd Command?"

Butyrskaya looked at Lukin and opened her mouth to speak, but Lukin spoke first. "We will not be mobilizing any more units than absolutely necessary, so as not to forewarn US intelligence. This operation will be run entirely with the resources of 3rd Command. Central Military District will not be drawn in."

"We should pre-position reserves," Bondarev continued. "We cannot…"

"Reserves will *not* be needed," Lukin said, in a tone clearly intended to end the discussion. "Does anyone else want to raise strategic concerns?"

"Rules of engagement," Kokorin said. "The smokescreen about the submarine might enable us to get assets in place, but it won't hold if the US gets satellite or air recon confirmation that we are moving troops onto Saint Lawrence." He looked at Bondarev. "If my aircraft are tasked with transport and low-level air-defense suppression, I want to know Bondarev's fighters will be able to protect us without having their hands tied."

"We will not tolerate US interference in our peacekeeping operation," Lukin said. "You will be free to fire on any land, sea or air threat in the operations area." At last, something Bondarev liked. His leaders might be throwing him into an uncertain battle on a flimsy pretext, but at least they were not restricting his freedom of action.

Lukin waited for other questions and when there were none, he picked up his tablet and nodded to his staff. "Gentlemen, I will not keep you any longer. You have a vital peacekeeping mission to plan and the clock is ticking."

As the others stood, Arsharvin made his way to Bondarev's side. "My office, as soon as you are done with your staff meetings," he said.

Bondarev grabbed Arsharvin's arm as he was about to walk away. "This isn't about the *Ozempic Tsar*, is it? It isn't even about that stupid island."

Arsharvin looked up at the ceiling to where small dome cameras sat capturing every audible word and gesture. "My office," he whispered. "And bring a bottle of your best stuff. What I have to tell you is worth it."

NO REST FOR THE WICKED

When Rodriguez's shooter declared the electromagnetic catapult operational, word spread through the Rock like Severin had put a post on Twitter. There were currently thirty-seven other people serving underground in the base and it seemed all thirty-seven of them had some reason to be working in the docks or on the deck somewhere where they had a good view of the chute. Rodriguez couldn't blame them – it was the Rock's first operational launch in weeks. Until now, they had only had simulations, and then three test flights, before the Cat was taken offline. Tonight they would be putting one drone in the air and seeing how fast they could do it. The eventual goal was one machine every three minutes, or a full 'hex' of six machines inside 20 minutes. She sighed. If they were to be certified combat capable, that's what it would take, but it would strain both her people and the cantankerous Cat.

She looked around the launch bay. When she was down on the 'flight deck' or in her command trailer up behind the dock for a launch, she wore a yellow Air Boss shirt over her green flight suit with its simple squadron commander gold oak leaf on the shoulder. The deck was awash with multicolored shirts.

Half of her twelve-man crew was finalizing pre-flight checks on the drone; the other half was operating the Cat and its feeder system. It was supposed to be an almost fully automated system, but something always glitched. Unlike on a carrier, the Fantoms under Little Diomede were originally designed for 'cartridge launch' – made to be launched off the back of a truck like an old ICBM, fitted into launch canisters and fired into flight by a rocket-propelled launch arm like a bullet out of a gun. Here under the Rock, they'd modded the canister system and put the canisters on a conveyor belt so that a whole hex could be loaded onto the Cat and launched one after the other in quick succession. Supposedly, once they were pre-flighted and loaded into the canisters, it only took one plane handler to lock the drone into the catapult shuttle and a single shooter to operate the launch system. As the base development moved into Phase III, even those two roles would be automated. That was the theory anyway.

"You miss being up in Pri-Fly, Boss?" a voice said from behind her. "The grand ballet of colored shirts, the smell of jet fuel and Red Bull ..." She recognized the voice of Commander Justin Halifax and turned. He was the senior officer on Little Diomede, CO of the Naval Computer and Telecommunications Area Master Station which hosted her unit, therefore her senior officer. He commanded the communications station and dock operations but he wasn't an aviator, so he left day to day flight operations largely to her.

He had an office and quarters in the radar installation which was the Navy's cover on Little Diomede, and only took the elevator down to the cavern every few days to check on progress or investigate the frequent hiccups. Nonetheless the lure of a launch had pulled even him down from topside. He stood looking skeptically up at the roof as though it was about to drop on his head. Rodriguez's private theory was that he was claustrophobic, but that was OK, because that meant with nearly half of all personnel under the Rock under her command, she had a pretty free hand down here.

"Miss my shooter's position more to be honest, Sir," she said with a smile. "Less ballet, more rock and roll."

Halifax looked around the cavern. "Everything still on track for launch?" he asked.

"Yes, sir," Rodriguez said. "We've got the Cat pulling like it should now. We're good to go."

"Good," he nodded. "We have to start ramping up the test flights, Lieutenant Commander. We're two weeks behind," he pointed out. "And I'm not planning to be the one telling Naval Air Forces Command in Coronado we can't hit Phase II transition."

"No, sir." Rodriguez looked over to the trailer parked at the top of the submarine dock, where she knew Bunny O'Hare would be sat at her bank of screens, going through her own

46

pre-flight routine. "But we're still short a pilot, sir, and the one I have is an Australian-born DARPA test pilot. I'm supposed to have moved Navy aviators into that trailer by now."

Halifax looked annoyed at being reminded. "I know. We're not exactly top priority down here, with all the shit going down in Korea. I heard they deployed two more squadrons of Fantoms there this week."

"Any word on my request for blast doors to seal off the Pond, sir?" Rodriguez asked. "We might be under 500 feet of rock, but that won't help if Ivan drops a nuke right outside. Right now, even a minor cyclone could push so much water and ice into the Pond we'd be out of commission."

He sighed. "I tried again. It's still no. They're not investing in any more infrastructure before proof of concept."

From down by the flight deck she saw men in green jackets who had been crouched around the locking bar on the drone stand up, and her yellow-jacketed catapult officer spun around and gave her a thumbs up.

"Roger, Cat 1. Moving to the Island," Rodriguez said into her mike. The Island was the nickname they gave to the drone command trailer, which here served a similar function to primary flight control inside the command island on a carrier. "If you'll excuse me, sir?" Halifax had told her he wanted to be topside for the launch, standing over the lip of the chute to see how visible the drone was exiting the cave at night. Baffles should mask the exhaust from the naked eye, and Navy had an infrared satellite parked overhead for this test flight, trying to pick up a signature, but he had wanted to see for himself.

"Actually I'm coming with you, I need to talk to O'Hare," he said. He hunched his shoulders, ducked his head and followed after her.

Rodriguez frowned, but led the way across the dock to the trailer and thumbed the lock on the door to let herself and the CO in. The trailer was parked broadside to the flight deck and had been modified from a standard drone control center, being lengthened by about 10 feet with the addition of a stool, extra comms gear and windows to allow Rodriguez to look out on the catapult and recovery dock. Otherwise it was a standard drone trailer, with a bank of screens and controls for two pilots. The second chair was empty, as Rodriguez had pointed out.

"CO on deck," Rodriguez said as she pulled open the door.

"As you were," Halifax said before O'Hare could react. She was busy punching data into touch screens in front of her.

"On track for launch 0230 hours, ladies and gents," Bunny said without taking her eyes off her screens. "Fantom is singing like a bird." She pointed to data from the drone, streaming across a screen. Rodriguez had no idea what it meant, but Bunny sounded satisfied.

"Good, I have a change of target for you. Requires a new mission profile," Halifax said. He had a tablet under his arm and held it up, then tapped away at it. "Sending to you now."

He finished sending and handed the tablet to Rodriguez. Now she understood why Halifax had sounded a little mysterious. The original Operations Order was for a full-scale launch and recovery test. The flight plan had called for Bunny's Fantom to exit the Rock and head east over the Alaskan coast to the Yukon Delta, test its cameras with some night vision shots of a fishing camp near Dall Lake and get safely home again, hugging the terrain and wave tops to try to stay off the radar. North American Aerospace Defense Command – NORAD – had been tasked to try to identify and track the flight to see if the Rock could be identified on radar or satellite as the point of origin. But now she could see they were being given a different sort of test, perhaps to see how Rodriguez and her team performed under pressure. Change the target at the last minute, change the mission profile, stand back and watch the chaos unfold. Well, if Halifax wanted to see her fail, he'd be disappointed, she'd make damn sure of that.

Bunny opened a dark screen and pulled up the data Halifax had sent her. Now she turned around, a puzzled look on her face. "The target is USAF Eielson Air Base?" she said.

"Correct, Lieutenant," Halifax smiled. "Someone in the Pentagon thought it would be a good test of Air Force air defense systems to see how close you can get one of your drones to Eielson field before they threaten to shoot it down. You have mode 7 crypto IFF on your machines, correct?"

"Yes, sir," Bunny replied, still sounding dubious. The Identify Friend or Foe system was something that by default she would engage, to ensure she wouldn't be shot down by mistake.

"Then monitor Air Force comms and keep the IFF off until we pick up an imminent shoot down order," Halifax said. "The exercise will conclude either when you have simulated a missile launch on Eielson, or when you are forced to light up your IFF."

Bunny bent to her screens and started punching in the new data.

"If we even get close, this will not do wonders for Navy–Air Force relations, sir," Rodriguez said, smiling and handing back his tablet.

Halifax looked across at her, tucking the tablet under his arm. "Stop grinning, Air Boss. The new mission profile calls for a Fantom in ground-attack configuration, not recon." He glanced down at his watch. "Your people have 23 minutes to pull that Fantom off the deck and either dial up a new bird in ground-attack config or reload it with air-ground ordnance."

SCOTTISH VODKA

It was 0220 by the time Bondarev was finished with his staff meetings and felt comfortable that preparations were in hand. The first task had been convincing his officers that this was not just an exercise – they were about to conduct the first sanctioned Russian attack on US territory in history. The fact Saint Lawrence Island was only 60 miles from the Russian Chukchi Peninsula was irrelevant. Bondarev and his men knew it might as well be Washington, DC, the way the USA would react to Russian troops on US soil.

Bondarev was third-generation Russian Federation military. He didn't question the orders of his political masters, not in front of his subordinates anyway. But if he was to be part of starting a world war, he wanted to know why, and he knew it wasn't because some shipping magnate had lost one of his shiny new toys.

Arsharvin's office was actually two rooms joined by a door. Bondarev walked in on a scene that looked like the one he had just left; tired men poring over maps and screens. It also looked like he had walked in on an argument, but they jumped to attention when they saw him.

"At ease," Bondarev sighed and pointed at the door to the inner office. "The boss in there?" He didn't wait for an answer, but walked over and tapped on the door with the neck of the Scotch bottle he was carrying.

"Come in!" Arsharvin boomed, and Bondarev pushed the door open to find his friend leaning back in his chair, boots up on his desk, staring at the ceiling with a telephone to his ear. He grimaced at Bondarev and pointed at a chair, then a tray with empty glasses, holding up a finger to show his call was nearly finished.

Bondarev unscrewed the cap of the bottle and poured a generous measure into each glass as Arsharvin put his phone down. He got up, closed the door and then took the bottle Bondarev was holding, nodding appreciatively. "Macallan 25?"

"Might as well enjoy it while we can still get it," Bondarev said.

"It will be worth twice as much on the black market a week from now," Arsharvin pointed out to him. "After the US slaps on sanctions."

"Yeah, but what good is a full bottle of whiskey to a dead man?" Bondarev said, slumping into a chair. "I have a bad feeling about this."

Arsharvin parked his backside on his desk. He was tall, still annoyingly fit, with broad shoulders and a square jaw; he even had a dueling scar on his left cheek below the eye from his days as an elite fencer. "I won't lie," he said. "You could be on the front line of World War Three in a week's time and we could all be dead in two."

"Cheers, then," Bondarev said dryly, throwing down his Scotch and letting the taste dwell in his mouth before he poured another. "What the hell, Tomas?" Bondarev asked. "The polar shipping route is so important we're willing to risk nuclear annihilation for it?"

Arsharvin leaned in so that he couldn't be heard in the office outside. "This isn't just about Saint Lawrence Island, Yevgeny."

"I knew it."

"We are going to annex the Bering land bridge."

"The what?" Bondarev frowned.

"Western Alaska. The whole of the Alaskan peninsula from Koyuk and Buckland west to Nome. Two hundred square kilometers with Saint Lawrence Island in the south, giving us control of the entire Bering Strait."

"Why in the name of ..."

"It's the new Panama Canal, Yevgeny!" Arsharvin said. "Do you know how many ships took the polar route through the Bering Strait ten years ago? Five hundred. This year so far, that number is five *thousand*."

"And so? We are already building up Anadyr, Lavrentiya. We have the biggest ports in the whole North Pacific. What more do we win by militarizing the seaway?"

Arsharvin drew two lines in whiskey on the table, then a single line across the middle like he was cutting a throat. "If we controlled the entire Strait and charged a toll at the same rate as they do down in Panama, the tolls alone would be worth a billion dollars a year."

"That is pennies," Bondarev scoffed. "It would cost us that much to keep it free of ice, blockade and police it."

"Pennies now." Arsharvin tapped his nose. "With five thousand ships moving through. But when it is fifteen thousand, twenty thousand ships? Would you scoff at three billion dollars? Five billion? Control the Strait and you control the polar route. It's not just the money, it's trading leverage, geopolitical leverage..."

"World war..." Bondarev added. "Nuclear Armageddon. Have we learned nothing from our misadventure in Syria?"

"What happened in Syria was between Iran and Israel. Besides, the Middle East is all in the past. The Russian Far East is the future! Anadyr is already three times the size of Nome, Lavrentiya twice the size, not just in population but economically. The population of Nome is falling. *We* are investing in the North Pacific; the US is sleeping. Did you know they no longer have a single icebreaker of their own? The US Coast Guard rents Russian or Canadian ships to keep its sea lanes open! They have ignored development in Alaska for half a century, they have ignored Alaska's defenses, there has never been a better time for us to move!" Arsharvin grinned and raised his glass in a toast. "To the new Russian Panama."

Bondarev finished off the last drops in his glass and then reached forward tiredly. He poured a final shot for himself and his friend. "I salute your patriotism, but I don't share your conviction. America will not just sit still and let us create a new Panama Canal controlled by Russia. And our leaders in Moscow are not fools, they know this. You must have your orders but you are not telling me the whole story, Comrade Arsharvin."

Back at his quarters an hour later Bondarev lay in his bed, still wide awake. Were they insane? No matter how weak the backbone of the Americans when it came to intervening in other people's wars, they would nuke Moscow to glowing green slag before they would let Russia walk into Alaska. The thought convinced Bondarev this was about more than polar trade routes. Seizing Nome was the act of a desperate State that had decided it had nothing to lose.

There was a chance, just a small one, that the Russian action would be so swift, so unexpected, that the US would have no time to react. Arsharvin had revealed the broad strategic strokes to him. First, they would take Saint Lawrence, which would send the US politicians into apoplectic fits. They would mobilize their reserves, of that there was no doubt. But the bulk of their expeditionary armed forces were engaged in the Middle East and Asia – so the reserves they could call on at short notice were less effectual National Guard units with older equipment. If the American politicians bought the cover story of a crisis over international shipping rights, they would spend most of their energy on pointless diplomacy. By the time they realized they were dealing with an invasion, Saint Lawrence would be in Russian hands.

Alaska was a barely populated State, with a token military presence. The Russian plan relied on surprise. Using the emergency in the Bering Strait to justify pre-positioning forces and raising its alert level, Russian troops would in short order leapfrog from Saint Lawrence to neutralize US military installations in Alaska and secure the westernmost city in the USA, Nome. The critical point, the one on which the plan would stand or fall, was the ability of Russian air and sea transport to land sufficient ground troops in Western Alaska to enable them to control events on the ground.

Moscow would not threaten the major Alaskan population centers of Juneau, Fairbanks or Anchorage, it would not use nuclear weapons, and it was banking on the weak, indecisive US leadership to blink before resorting to its own nuclear arsenal, both out of moral weakness and out of the fear it would be killing its own citizens.

Within a week, perhaps two, Russia would have secured Nome and the Bering peninsula and would be negotiating a ceasefire.

Bondarev cursed, switched on his bedside lamp, and sat up. He pulled his tablet over and turned it on, calling up the latest report on the disposition of his Snow Leopards. On a screen in Moscow, it no doubt looked formidable – under President Navalny the Russian military was as strong on paper as it had been at any time since the cold war. The report in front of him told a slightly different story.

His command comprised several regiments, but one was a rotary-winged command transport unit, and another was a strategic bomber 'graveyard' – a parking lot for obsolete Tu-22M Backfire bombers.

Of the other six, one was a regiment of 48 Sukhoi Okhotnik drones attached to his personal command based at Kurba. The Okhotnik or 'Hunter' was a stealth drone based on the same platform as the piloted Su-57 but with an avionics suite optimized for ground attack. In that role it was designed to be operated by 'near-line-of sight' communications, in which radio signals from a ground station were relayed to the drones via an orbiting Airborne Warning and Control System, or Airborne Control aircraft. Only in the case of loss of the Airborne Control link would an Okhotnik fall back on slower satellite links. It meant they had an operational radius of only 600 miles from their base, but it also meant their pilots could control them manually with almost no input lag. Theoretically the drones could be used in air-air combat, or beyond a range of 600 miles if executing an autonomous AI-directed attack, but these applications fell outside Russian drone doctrine orthodoxy. The Okhotnik was a close air support platform, and close meant close.

Bondarev had a further 78 ground-attack aircraft in three Aviation Regiments, but these were fourth-generation Su-34s, lacking any stealth capability.

His primary air defense units were the aircraft of his two fighter Aviation Regiments, comprising 30 Su-57s and 32 of the newer Mig-41 air superiority fighters respectively, and he had just given orders to move these to the new base at Lavrentiya, from where they could cover all of Western Alaska as needed. The remaining unit was a strategic airlift squadron comprising twelve An-124 transport aircraft and four Beriev Airborne Control aircraft.

The reality was that his Brigade was designed to fight and support a ground defense of Russia in a time before the current detente with China, and not an operation like LOSOS which would require him primarily to fight his enemy air-to-air. For that, he had only 62 Sukhois and Migs, and could press his Okhotniks into an air-air role if needed, but their weapon bays were optimized for air-to-ground ordnance; they could carry only four air-to-air missiles to the piloted fighters' six.

There was another problem.

While his personal battalion of 48 Okhotniks was nominally at full strength, the Russian drones required two men to fly each. Unlike the US drones, several subordinate drones could not be slaved to a master drone flown by a single pilot. Each Okhotnik required one pilot *and* a weapons and systems officer, flying them from ground-based stations. Unlike the weaker command and control system of the US drones, which was over-reliant on vulnerable satellite communications for command inputs, the Russian drones were highly mobile – they could fly off almost any strip of dirt and be transported easily by train or truck – and they used encrypted digital shortwave for communications. His men and aircraft could be dispersed across hundreds of kilometers of front, and yet still be coordinated as a single attacking unit. It was a difference in strategy that had proven itself in combat on multiple occasions – it was easy for Russian forces to find and disable enemy airfields or depots, but almost impossible for their enemy to do the same, so widely dispersed were the Russian pilots and their drones.

If he had the pilots and weapons officers he needed, that is. His Hunter Regiment was still in a build-up phase. Its aircraft were all on line, but only 80% of its aircrew were. He could use almost any pilot certified for one of the Russian fighter marques, but the weapons and systems used by the new drones were not widely used and the all aspect air-to-air missile system in particular was barely more than a prototype, its rotary launch system jamming if deployed at high speeds or high Gs. Too few systems officers had been certified to operate the Okhotnik and training was taking far too long. Too long by peacetime standards, impossibly long if they were going to war. Bondarev had only 38 crewed drones ready for what was to come.

It was why he had asked Lukin if he could call on the resources of Central Command, which he knew numbered at least 80 fighter aircraft, both Su-57s and Mig-41s. As importantly, he wanted access to its Okhotnik crews.

Bondarev was a realist, not an optimist, and that had served him well in his career so far. He would always try to under-promise and over-deliver, ensuring he had more than enough assets at hand for the task he was given. Right now, yes, he had the assets he needed to secure the airspace over Saint Lawrence for a few days. But to achieve air superiority over Western Alaska, if that was the long game? That, he did not.

That thought led him to speculate on the long game; occupying Western Alaska. He could see why Nome was the key, and the strategy for taking Nome included denying the small airfield at Saint Lawrence to the Americans. Built to service the US communications base at Savoonga, it was capable of landing both fighters and heavy aircraft and one to two squadrons could easily stage out of there. Denying it to the Americans meant they would need to fly out of their Eielson or Elmendorf-Richardson air bases, each 600 miles from Nome. And if the ultimate plan was to knock out Eielson and Elmendorf-Richardson, which is what Bondarev would do, then the US fighters would be forced back to mainland USA, with their nearest Air Force bases 1,800 miles from Nome in Washington State, making it almost impossible for them to contest the airspace over Western Alaska against Russian forces that were flying less than a couple of hundred miles to cover the same operations area.

The US might react angrily to events on Saint Lawrence, and Bondarev expected to lose good men as it lashed out. But when Russia moved against Alaska, personally he had no doubt the American Grizzly would wake from its recent hibernation and strike back with nuclear claws.

His hand jerked and he nearly dropped the tablet. He closed it down and laid it back down on the bedside table. Sleep. He should sleep while he could.

There would be no time for sleep a few days from now.

THIS IS YOUR WAKEUP CALL

On the deck of a carrier, everyone knew their place, and aircraft were launched amid the roar of jet engines in an elaborate dance of colored shirts, hand-arm gestures and precision movements. Under the Rock, they relied on tightly choreographed commands over their headsets.

Rodriguez stood in the trailer, looking down on the flight deck at her crew crouched around the Fantom.

"Flaps, slats, panels, pins!" she intoned.

The reply from the deck came immediately. "Green."

"Man out." Referring to the hook-up petty officer who attached the drone launch bar to the catapult shuttle.

"Man out, aye."

"Visual."

"Thumbs up." A last check to be sure there were no leaks of fuel or hydraulic fluid. Her shooter turned, held his hand in the air, thumb up.

"Cat scan." Asking her shooter to make a last visual check of the catapult. No foreign objects, foreign object damage or people where they shouldn't be.

The cavern filled now with the roar of the Fantom's twin jet engines.

"Cat clear!"

"Cat to 520 psi."

"520, aye."

"Pilot, go burner."

"Lighting burner, aye," Bunny replied, spooling up the Fantom's jet engine and lighting the afterburner.

"Launch launch *launch*."

Rodriguez watched with satisfaction as the big aircraft shot along the deck and down the rails, flung through the chute like a rock from a slingshot. She had started her career as a shooter on huge, roaring steam-powered catapults, crouched on the flat top, ducking under the wings of aircraft blasting along the deck.

The electromagnetic Cat system had had a troubled birth, and had nearly been scrapped. But it was one thing to fire a steam catapult on an open deck in a windswept sea. In the confines of the cave under Little Diomede, it would never have worked. They would have had to find a way to capture the steam or vent it out over the sea without it being visible for miles in the Arctic air. The hugely powerful magnetos driving a Cat didn't need a steam compressor, but they did suck a ton of juice. On a US carrier that power came from the ship's own nuclear power plant, and nothing less was capable of pushing out the wattage needed. Which was why they had a repurposed *Ohio*-class submarine reactor buried deep under the Pond. Little Diomede was made possible by kludges.

Rodriguez bit her lip and watched as the flight systems aboard the Fantom stabilized it and it transitioned from kinetic to onboard hydrogen fuel power from its Scimitar engines. This was the moment most prone to disaster. The drones had to kick in full afterburner at the moment of launch or they would simply drop into the sea outside the chute.

Bunny had her hand on the stick and her eye on her simulated cockpit flight screen, but Rodriguez knew for all her bravado about flying her drone out of the chute, she was pretty much a passenger at this point. The drone's onboard AI could react to its environment and adjust its flight envelope a hundred times faster than Bunny and her redundant flight stick could. By the time she could twitch her stick a millimeter, the drone had already decided it had enough power for a successful launch, and aimed itself at the open air above Little Diomede. But AI could glitch, which was why she had her hand on the stick in case she needed to take back manual control while it was still in range of their undersea transmission array.

Bunny was controlling her Fantom through a virtual-reality helmet, with Rodriguez relegated to watching it in 2D on a bank of screens that simulated cockpit views, tactical overviews and a heads-up display of instrument readouts. Flicking her eyes to the forward view screen, Rodriguez saw the hulks of the old fishing fleet flash past underneath the drone and then it began to climb into the night sky. Before she had even exhaled the breath she didn't realize she was holding, the roar of the drone had died away and the cavern was suddenly quiet, and empty of all motion but the swirling water vapor from the drone's Scimitar engines. Until a huge cheer went up from the personnel ringing the dock. Rodriguez couldn't help but smile, and heard the relief in Bunny's voice as she calmly announced, "Fantom 4-1 successful egress. AI has control. Turning to 150, altitude 200." She leaned back from her stick, letting it go and flexing her fingers. She pulled up her virtual-reality visor, turned to Rodriguez briefly, flashing her a quick thumbs up, before turning and pulling the visor back down.

"Cat return to launch readiness. Recovery team to standby," Rodriguez said into her comms, and watched with satisfaction as the members of the red-shirted crash and salvage crew returned to their rest stations and changed their shirts to green in anticipation of recovering the aircraft after its mission.

The only other person in the trailer was the CO, Halifax. He patted Rodriguez on the shoulder. "Nice launch, Boss. Almost be a shame when it becomes routine."

"If shooting 80 million dollars' worth of warplane through a hole the size of a barn door underneath a billion tons of rock ever becomes routine, sir, you can hand me my discharge slip."

"Now you've got that Cat working again, you'll be firing three next time, then six, then twelve, Lieutenant Commander. And you'll be doing it at a pace you never thought possible. Your people ready for that?"

She watched as Lieutenant Severin, her catapult officer, went around high fiving everyone on the flight deck. "They were *born* for it, sir," Rodriguez said, sounding as confident as she felt.

The trailer was quiet for a moment as they watched Bunny at work, pulling data from the drone and tweaking its flight path as it settled in for its flight down the Alaska coast, skimming the sea at not much more than wave-top height. It would be an hour before it went feet dry over Alaska's southern coast near

Anchorage. Rodriguez had plenty to do outside, giving props to her people for a picture-perfect launch.

"Permission to hit the flight deck, sir?" she asked Halifax.

"Granted. Lieutenant Commander, before you go?" Halifax asked. "A question?"

"Sir?"

"How you and your pilot run this mission is entirely your call, but the coast facing Russia is probably the most watched piece of sky outside of Atlanta International Airport. I know the Fantom is fifth-generation stealth, but what radar can't see, thermal and magnetic imaging satellites can. No disrespect to Lieutenant O'Hare, but I'd like to know you have a plan so that Air Force won't be laughing their asses off at us for the next five years."

Bunny was listening. She lifted up her visor and gave Rodriguez a wink, then went back to work.

"Well, sir, firstly, you have to remember Air Force has been staring at that piece of sky for seventy years, without seeing anything but the occasional lone flight of Russian bombers acting like they accidentally got lost. Stare at nothing long enough, you start seeing nothing." She held up two fingers. "Plus, I checked and it's two years since the Pentagon put Eielson through an unannounced exercise like this. Whoever is on duty at this time of night is sitting over there right now, sucking back lukewarm coffee and probably sneak-watching porn on a tablet. They have no idea what kind of shitstorm is about to hit them. Plus, Lieutenant O'Hare there has a cunning plan for not getting my very expensive warplane shot down. Tell the Commander, O'Hare."

O'Hare turned around and took off her helmet. Her bleached white cropped hair topped a brown freckled nose and piercing green eyes that were never at rest. She opened her mouth to answer, but Halifax tried to prick her balloon. "Let me guess. You're going to circle south and blast up some river valley or mountain range at Mach 1.5 at treetop height, then pop up within cruise missile launch range, get a GPS lock on the target and call it mission accomplished before you high-tail it south again on afterburner."

Bunny grinned. "It's called the Tanana River Valley, sir, and maybe that's the way *you'd* do it. That's the way most folks would do it and the radar operators at Eielson would have wargamed that a hundred times. So yeah, I'm going to come at Eielson from the south ... or south-southwest actually. But on the *commercial* flight path that goes between Anchorage and Fairbanks. And I'm going to be flying at 10,000 feet, with my landing lights on, wheels and flaps down, at a stately 200 miles an hour. Every long- and short-range radar and every infrared satellite in the northern hemisphere should be able to see me."

Halifax looked at Bunny like she had completely lost her marbles, and then at Rodriguez, who couldn't hide how much she was loving it. And he could see clearly neither of them was going to tell him any more right now.

"With your permission, sir," Rodriguez said to Halifax. "We have work to do."

"Permission granted, Boss," Halifax said, his frown turning to a slight smile.

Airman E4 Dale Racine first saw the blip on his screen and heard the chime of the audio alarm as it came into the air traffic control zone for Fairbanks, 120 miles south of Eielson Air Base. His eyes flicked to his screen as his system analyzed the flight profile of the unidentified object and compared it to civil and military flight plans. By its size, speed and altitude the system identified it as a probable light passenger aircraft, but it didn't match any logged civilian flight plan. Plus it was on a direct heading for Eielson. Had he missed it earlier? He quickly checked the data logs for that sector, but came up empty. Air traffic control at Anchorage should have called it in then handed it off, but there was no record of them having pinged it. He sighed.

"Sir, I have an unidentified aircraft 100 miles out approaching from 185 degrees, altitude ten thousand, speed 226 miles an hour," Racine called out to the officer of the watch, Staff Sergeant Elmore Bruning. Bruning and the other Airman in the tower at Eielson were busy planning how they were going to land both a C130 transport flight and a flight of drone-modded F-22s 20 minutes from now with only one functioning runway and one man short up in the tower because Airman E3 Scarlatti had just reported sick again, the lazy bastard.

"Who do you have on station?" Bruning asked.

Racine checked his screen, looking for patrolling fighters. "Filial 3 and Filial 4, about 20 minutes from an intercept. Sooner if they light their asses."

Bruning looked up from his work. "No rush son, sounds like a civilian flight, probably hunters or trappers that didn't file a plan."

Another chime sounded in his ears and Racine looked down at his screen. The unidentified aircraft was descending now, moving through nine thousand nine to nine thousand eight. "It seems to be descending slowly now, sir, moving through nine eight zero to nine seven."

Bruning was tempted to give the guy an earful, but it was only his second week and he needed him sharp and motivated in about an hour when that C130 was coming in. He put on a patient tone. "Do the math, Airman. On that heading, at that airspeed and rate of descent, where might it be landing?"

Racine frowned. It was still a hundred miles out, so it could be making for FAI, Fairbanks' civilian airfield. Racine zoomed his screen out and started looking for commercial airfields on the bearing of the unidentified aircraft. FAI was the logical destination for sure, but it was too far to the northeast. So, on a hunch, he called up national park cabins that had dirt airstrips alongside them. *Bam.* He put his finger on the screen. "I got the Harding Birch River Cabin strip right about where that glide slope would bottom out, sir," Racine announced.

"Poachers," Bruning spat. Bruning was a hunter too, but he was one of the dumb ones who paid his license. "Cheeky sons of bitches, think they can just sneak in at dawn, bag a moose or bear, get out again at dusk and no one will know.

Make me sick." A thought suddenly crossed his mind. "Those fighters doing anything critical?"

Racine called up the mission orders for Filial 3 and 4. "Night flight instrument checks, sir," he said.

"Good, let's give them something more interesting to do. Tell them there is an unauthorized civilian flight approaching Eielson and give them an intercept. Once they get eyeballs on it, I want them to scare the shit out of whoever is in that plane."

"Sir?"

"Tell them to turn it around, Racine," Bruning explained. "Back to wherever it came from. With prejudice."

Rodriguez checked her watch. It was go time. There wasn't anything more she could do to get her people ready to recover the drone when it splashed down, so she walked over to the trailer and opened the door, stepping into a tight atmosphere of sweat and adrenaline.

Listening, she soon heard why.

O'Hare wasn't the one sweating, even though she was flying both as pilot and systems operator. What made US drone tactics possible were the huge advances in data compression of the last few years, which had reduced satellite comms lag from seconds to milliseconds, while also increasing a hundredfold the volume of data that could be flung through the ether. But even a lag time of milliseconds meant leaving most of the actual flying to the drone AI once it was out of 'line of sight', and Bunny still had a half-dozen screens to watch as they fed her tracking and targeting data, plus a hundred combat software routines at her fingertips ready to feed down the line. It troubled her not at all. As a child of the 'continuous partial attention generation' she had mental bandwidth she hadn't even tapped yet.

"Being painted by long-distance ground-based radar again, sir," Bunny said.

"Those fighters still closing?" Halifax asked.

"Yes, sir. Can't be precise with passive array, sir, but I'd say 110 to 120 miles out. Still only at cruising speed, they're not in any hurry. They'll be in weapons range in five minutes."

"Damn," Halifax said. "They're onto you."

Rodriguez smiled. Halifax was worried he was about to get 80 million dollars' worth of drone shot out of the sky but to Rodriguez it sounded like Bunny's mission was going exactly to plan.

"Light your IFF as soon as those F-35s get into weapons range," Halifax told Bunny, referring to the Identify Friend or Foe system that told the US and NATO aircraft and ground defense systems they were looking at an ally, not an enemy.

"But then we lose, Eielson wins, sir," O'Hare said. "With respect, I got this."

Halifax ignored her. He was leaning over O'Hare's shoulder, looking intently at a screen. "One minute ten to missile launch point," he said.

"Yes, sir," O'Hare replied.

"Those F-35s are three minutes from weapons range," Halifax said.

"Said I got it, sir," O'Hare said calmly.

"The window is too tight, Lieutenant," Halifax said through gritted teeth. "Pull up your wheels, light your tail and start squawking, this mission is a bust."

"Still seeing daylight, sir," Bunny said, not at all phased by having her senior CO riding shotgun on her. "I'm entering max range. It will be so much more convincing inside the 90% certainty zone."

"Best leave the pilot to do her work, sir," Rodriguez interjected gently.

Rodriguez could see Halifax wanted to say more, but he bit his lip and turned to Rodriguez, looking worried. "I really wanted this scalp, Air Boss."

Rodriguez winked at him. "Fat lady hasn't sung yet, sir."

"Who you calling fat, ma'am?" Right on cue, Bunny started a running commentary. "GPS and inertial targeting locked. Twenty seconds to air-ground standoff missile release."

Bunny's fingers danced across her keyboard like a pianist playing an arpeggio as she cued up a simulated hypersonic High-Speed Strike Weapon. "Cuda air-to-air missiles in passive mode, also locked on targets. Ten seconds." Her hands lifted from her flight keyboard to her weapons system console. "Get ready on the comms, sir," she said over her shoulder to Halifax. "Opening bay doors."

Rodriguez noticed for the first time that Halifax had a hand-held comms unit in his hand and he held it up to his mouth. She wouldn't have been surprised to see it shaking a little, with the amount of tension there was in the room.

"*Three-two-one ... standoff missile away,*" Bunny said coolly, punching some keys. "Initiating egress. Wheels and flaps up, going to Mach speed. Engaging red fighters!" The screen in front of her, her simulated cockpit, was completely dark, no horizon, not even a star showing to help her orient herself. But the ghostly green circle of her heads-up instruments display spun giddily as she ordered the drone to come around and pointed it at the incoming fighter patrol.

Bunny's virtual-reality heads-up display was made possible by a combination of quantum computation and AI imputation. The advances in data compression technology in the last ten years had enabled drones like the Fantom to squirt an almost real-time video and data feed from their onboard cameras and instruments up to a lurking satellite or Airborne Control aircraft and down to their ground station. This technological leap had been coupled with advances in data processing and imaging which meant that the Fantom could take what its cameras were seeing and then, based on the inputs sent to it by the pilot on the ground, project the effect of those inputs onto the cockpit virtual-reality simulation the pilot was working with and show them what the Fantom would be seeing and doing when their control inputs were acted on. It was a little like low-tech time travel but it meant that, for all intents and purposes, the control system lag introduced by pilot and drone being hundreds of miles apart was 'virtually' eliminated. Not enough for real-time air combat, but more than enough for recon or ground-attack work. It also meant that for observers not sitting with their heads inside a virtual-reality helmet, seeing what the pilot was seeing, a 2D tactical view of any engagement could be projected onto a screen showing low-res simulated recon imagery, targeting video, battlefield events and friendly and enemy dispositions in near real time.

"Light them up, Lieutenant," Rodriguez ordered, giving O'Hare permission to engage the two F-35s on an intercept course for what they probably still thought was a civilian light plane.

"Yes, ma'am, lighting up active targeting radar. I have a lock on two targets. I have tone. Permission to fire?"

"Kill them dead, Bunny," Rodriguez said grimly.

"*Fox one through four* ... Cudas away! Bugging out," O'Hare said. "Turning on IFF. IFF squawking." On the tactical screens they watched the simulated missiles track and then wink out as they reached their silicon designated targets and kill probabilities were calculated. Bunny couldn't keep the satisfaction out of her voice as numbers flashed on the screen. "Ground target kill confirmed, air target kills confirmed. All yours, sir!" Bunny said to Halifax.

Rodriguez watched Bunny's heads-up display spin again as she rolled her drone on its back and bullied it down to treetop height at a speed sure to rip the crowns off the trees it was blasting over.

Halifax sucked a big breath through his cheeks, then winked at Rodriguez.

"Eielson tower, this is US Navy Commander Justin Halifax of Navy Experimental Unit A4. You have just been put through a Pentagon-authorized exercise. My Fantom strike fighter just successfully fired a nuclear-armed hypersonic missile at your control tower. You are dead. Everyone within a twenty-mile radius of your base is dead. The two pilots wandering through the sky toward an intercept with my Fantom, wondering what the hell just happened, are also dead. I'm terribly sorry, Eielson. I have a hard time imagining what s-hole they might post you to that's worse than Eielson Air Force Base, so let's just agree I did you a favor. Please acknowledge."

"This is Eielson tower. Message received. Screw you, Navy."

"Confirmed, Eielson, my respects to your commanding officer. Rest in peace. Halifax out." He grinned and patted Bunny on her shoulder. "Nice job, officers. I'm going topside. The fun is just starting."

Airman Racine, like everyone around him, was staring dumbfounded at the gray dawn sky as if it had answers for him.

He was still trying to process what had happened. It had seemed like everything had happened at once, so trying to remember it was like trying to recreate a crime scene.

First, the screaming warning tone coming out of his command console. He had taken a second to realize what it was before he half stood and turned to Bruning with a frown. "Missile inbound?" He looked back at his screen. "*Simulation, sir!*"

"Oh shit," Bruning said, going pale. His tablet fell from his fingers.

"Attack Radar!" the voice of the flight leader of the F-35 patrol screamed over the tower audio system. "Eielson, we are being actively tracked by radar. *Missiles inbound!* Filial 4, deploy countermeasures! Break low!"

Racine bent to his screen, looking for the missile tracks on his monitor. There! "Simulated, sir!" he yelled. "It's all a simulation!"

Bruning put his hand to his forehead and reached for the comms button at his throat.

On the screen in front of him, nothing made sense to Airman Racine. He watched as the blip designating the civilian light aircraft suddenly changed color and flashed a US Navy IFF code, accelerated to Mach 1.5 and then… disappeared.

"Filial Leader, stand down, I repeat, stand down, you are seeing *simulated* launches," Bruning said. "I repeat, this is Eielson tower, you have been subjected to a simulated attack."

"Sir?" Racine asked, looking from Bruning to the other Airman at his console and not seeing any answers. He heard heavy breathing over the tower audio from the fighter pilots as they regained control of their aircraft and their composure. "That civilian flight, it was a Navy…" Racine tried to explain.

"Eielson, you better explain," came the tight voice of the F-35 flight leader.

Bruning almost spat the words, "Eielson tower to Filial Leader; an unknown *Navy* aircraft just fired an air-to-ground missile at us, and then attacked you with air-to-air missiles. Our systems show all launches were executed in simulation mode. That is all I know at this point, Captain."

There was a moment of silence, then the voice of the F-35 flight leader came through again. "Give me a vector for an intercept, Eielson," he demanded. "We owe this prick some payback."

Bruning clicked his fingers at Racine but he just shrugged. "I have nothing, sir," he said. He looked back at his monitor to be sure, but it was gone. "Can't even confirm an aircraft type, only that it was stealth. It launched, flashed a Navy IFF code, went Mach 1 and then disappeared."

"Eielson tower to Filial Leader, no business for you, sir," Bruning said, sitting down at his keyboard and screen. "The attacking aircraft has gone dark. Got nothing on radar. I'm pulling satellite infrared but that will take time."

They never heard the fighter pilot's acerbic response because right then a voice came over the encrypted interservice channel.

"Eielson tower, this is US Navy Commander Justin Halifax…"

In their trailer, Rodriguez watched as Bunny used terrain-following radar to pick her way out of the target area and head for the coast. It would soon be light enough for optical satellites to pick her up and track her using high-speed motion detection algorithms but she no longer cared. The main reason she was trying to stay low and stealthy was to make sure she didn't get two extremely pissed off Air Force F-35s on her tail. She had nothing on her passive sensors, but she wasn't taking any chances. She had a suspicion those Air Force jet jockeys could be so mad they would even consider putting a missile up the tailpipe of her drone and claim fog of war later.

Once her kite went 'feet wet' south of Anchorage she turned it back up the coast toward Little Diomede and gave the AI autonomous control. She leaned back, pulled up her virtual-reality visor and blew air out of her cheeks.

"Are all Australians as crazy as you, O'Hare?" Rodriguez asked, letting a little admiration leak into her voice.

"Oh yeah, comes from growing up swimming with sharks, ma'am," O'Hare grinned.

"If the Russians don't find this base and wipe it out, then the damn Air Force will, you just made sure of that."

"They can try, ma'am," Bunny said. "But by then you'll have twenty Fantoms online for me, right?"

Her adrenaline-fueled smile was infectious and Rodriguez let her enjoy it. "We'll do our best to keep up, pilot."

Bunny reached her arms above her head and cracked her fingers. "Thank you, ma'am. But that was the easy part. I still have to fly that bugger through a hole in a cliff the size of a car park entrance and land it in a Pond smaller than the lake in Central Park. There's no AI alive that will fly itself straight at a hole in a wall."

"My newly won admiration will be sorely tried if you break one of my Fantoms," Rodriguez warned.

"Define *break* for me, Boss," Bunny quipped.

The recovery was almost as nerve-wracking for Rodriguez as the attack had been for Halifax. Using the low-energy radio array buried in the sea floor off Little Diomede, O'Hare could assume manual control of the drone as it made its final approach toward the island. For the last mile the autopilot voice kept intoning, *Terrain warning, pull up! Terrain warning, pull up!*

"Can't you shut that off?" Rodriguez asked her.

"You stop hearing it after the first hundred times," Bunny replied. The virtual-reality visor in front of her eyes had her full focus. Through the nose camera on the drone and the picture it was throwing up on Rodriguez's 2D tactical screen, the cave entrance looked impossibly small.

The main reason Bunny was co-located under the Rock was to teach the drone AI how to take off, but more importantly, how to land a Fantom at sea level through a hole in a cliff face. It wasn't a flight maneuver you could code; in fact, the act of flying straight at a hole in a solid wall at sea level was something the AI had been taught specifically *not* to do. The Fantom's prototype AI was a learning system, but it needed to be taught and Bunny was the teacher.

The engineers had looked at various ways to try to hide the water-level cave entrance, but in the end, they decided that as it had been there for hundreds of years, it would arouse more suspicion if it suddenly disappeared. So they had made do with widening the diameter enough that it was two Fantom wingspans, or about 120 feet wide. They had blasted away about four feet of the floor at the mouth of the cave but they were worried about the integrity of the rock above if they went too hard, so the water at the cave entrance was too shallow to take the impact of a Fantom landing on skis.

So what Bunny had to do, what she'd spent all that simulator time practicing and had managed to do for real on a couple of test flights before the Cat was taken off line, was to glide the Fantom into the maw of the cave, float it over the rock ledge at the entrance to the Slot just above a stall, and then drop it hard into the water so that it had almost as much downward velocity as forward, and hope it wouldn't dig in a ski and go cartwheeling across the Pond to explode in a hydrogen-fueled fireball. The drone automatically dropped a small drogue into the water on landing to stop it from yawing and to provide extra drag – so if she did it right, the two hundred feet of water in the Pond should be more than enough to pull up in. She had reverse thrusters if she needed to pull up fast, but they were just as likely to send the Fantom ass-first to the bottom if she hit them too hard.

This would be her fourth real-life landing. The software engineers had told her the AI would need to sample from a hundred landings in order to be able to take over the job itself. And the occasional non-terminal screw-up would actually also be useful, so they didn't want her being *too* careful. Which was another thing that made Bunny just perfect for her job.

As the Slot loomed closer on Bunny's simulated cockpit view, Rodriguez knew better than to disturb her again. Even if it did look like she was bringing the Fantom in a little…

"Low and slow, dammit," Bunny said to herself, her left hand pushing forward a little on the throttle. "Come on, baby. Time to come home." She hit a key combination. "Skis down and locked."

Rodriguez pulled her eyes away from the screens inside the trailer and fixed them on the gray-white Slot on the other side of the Pond through which the Fantom was about to appear.

It was after dawn now, and the outside light was getting brighter. Inside the cave, they had switched on the low-intensity green light-emitting diode or LED lighting that was used for landing. Anything else caused the cameras on the drone to flare, and the pilot risked losing orientation as they adjusted for white balance. The low luminosity of the green LEDs meant that if all went well, Bunny saw a brief half-circle of complete black, and then the green wall lighting of the Pond and the dock sprang into view ahead of her. If all went well.

"That's it, mate," Bunny was purring to herself now, as though she was coaxing a racehorse into a starting gate. "Don't be scared."

Then Rodriguez saw the silhouette of the Fantom framed in the circle of light two hundred feet away and before she could react it was thumping down onto the water, hydraulic cushioned skids jumping as they soaked up the energy of the landing. Too fast! Bunny popped her air brakes, tapped a key to give the drone just a touch of reverse thrust, and it dipped its nose alarmingly, but not enough that it risked what Bunny called 'a face plant'.

From the back of the drone, a drogue parachute exploded, acting like the sea anchor on a yacht in heavy seas and pulling it up so sharply it slowed to a stop with fifty feet of Pond to spare. Bunny cut the engines, pulled off her helmet and leaned back in her chair, hands on her head, looking at the Fantom through the trailer windows like she couldn't actually believe she had really landed it.

As she watched her green-shirted crew get the recovery crane and sling rolling to lift the drone off the water and into a recycling bay, Rodriguez could see that every human-piloted landing on this base was going to be two parts art, one part terror.

"Someone needs to buy me a damn beer," Bunny said, turning around. "If I do say so myself, ma'am."

Rodriguez smiled. "How about breakfast, Lieutenant? Once we've got that Fantom squared away."

"You have a deal, Lieutenant Commander," Bunny said, standing and stretching her compact frame. "Got to stay sober anyway. So I can pull the logs and write up the mission report, doing justice to how totally awesome I was."

In her quarters that night, Rodriguez lay on her bunk staring at the raw rock ceiling. Above her was a hundred thousand tons of rock and bird droppings. She should be basking in the afterglow of their first successful combat exercise, but instead she lay on her back in the dark, going over the hundred small things that could have gone better. She hated this side of herself but knew she had no hope of changing it. It was how she had earned her handle – "Hammer" – early in her career, from chewing out subordinates for the smallest mistakes. She had no doubt her people called her less complimentary names, but it was her attention to detail and obsession with being the best that had got her this commission. "They are giving you two years to do what should rightly take four," her CO on USS *GW Bush* had told her. "Someone wants that facility ready for World War Three in a hurry," he said. "And the only thing that gives me peace of mind about that is they're putting you in charge."

World War Three? Their catapult software was still acting up, their complement of regular Navy aviators hadn't been assigned, a stiff wind could block the Slot with ice, and they weren't even ready to put *two* birds in the air in rapid succession, let alone six. Forget World War Three; right now, they couldn't fight their way out of a wet paper bag.

She drifted off to a fitful sleep, dreaming of storm clouds rolling toward her.

A RUN IN THE SNOW

While Alicia 'The Hammer' Rodriguez was dreaming of storm clouds, Yevgeny Bondarev was freezing his ass off in the melting snow of a Khabarovsk autumn. He'd asked for a few minutes of General Lukin's time and had been told he could meet with him at 0630 when the General was taking his morning run.

Fifty-nine years old and he was still taking a morning run in the subarctic temperatures of Khabarovsk? Bondarev sincerely hoped he would be dead before he had to even think about keeping up that kind of discipline himself.

He waited outside the General's quarters in his running gear, hopping from one leg to the other to keep warm. He knew it was dumb at these temperatures to blow warm air into his mittens, because it would condense, turn to water and freeze his fingers. Same for the balaclava around his face – blowing warm air into the mouth and neck would be as self-defeating as pissing in his pants to keep warm. There was nothing for it but to keep moving, but he also knew Lukin was the type who thought five minutes early was already late, so he wasn't too worried he'd be kept waiting.

Sure enough, at 0625 he saw the General come thumping down the stairs, fling open the doors from his quarters and take a deep breath. "Bondarev," was all he said before nodding and pointing up the single road out of the base and then padding off down the road. Once he might have been a sprinter or a hurdler, but Lukin was slower now, thank God. He pounded down the road like a heavyweight boxer and Bondarev jogged by his side, wondering who should speak first. It was a little awkward, because quality time with the most senior officer in the 3rd Command of Air Force and Air Defense was not something he got that often, and spending that time running through the snow in the dark with him was something he'd never had to do before.

Luckily Lukin broke the silence. "That shifty bastard Arsharvin has brought you into the circle, then?"

"Sir?" Bondarev asked, not wanting to throw his friend under the bus.

Lukin was the annoying type who could apparently talk and run without panting. The only sign he was exerting himself was that he spoke in clipped sentences and timed his words with his exhalations.

"You don't have to cover for him," Lukin said. "I know you two served together in Syria. You asked my staff for an urgent meeting with me and I can't believe it's because you misunderstood your orders from yesterday. It's a pretty simple combat air patrol cover role, no matter the context. You take your machines to Saint Lawrence, scare away anyone who gets in the way, and make sure by the end of two days our troops are boiling tea and cooking pork and potatoes on the ground below you without any bombs or missiles upsetting their appetites."

"Yes, sir," Bondarev agreed. "The Saint Lawrence objective is clear. But I have a suspicion that this is just our first move in a larger maneuver."

"Suspicion, Colonel?"

"Unfounded suspicion, Sir," Bondarev said carefully. "But if I'm right, I'd like permission to bring my Okhotniks up to full readiness. It's not the weapons platforms, sir, they are already on trucks, moving to Anadyr. I'm short of pilots and systems operators."

They had left the base now and were headed up a hill to a tree-lined horizon, dark on dark. As though to test him, Lukin perversely picked up the pace when they began the climb. Bondarev easily matched his pace, but was glad to see the older man at least begin to breathe more heavily.

"I can't confirm your 'suspicions', Colonel," he said. "But I am concerned to hear your brigade is not at full readiness already. It is intended to be a front-line unit. No one has told me anything about pilot or systems officer shortages."

Bondarev knew that was not true. He had been warning of the personnel shortages monthly in his reports to the General Staff for nearly eighteen months and knew these were read personally by Lukin. He had been told that Russian Aerospace Command was prioritizing combat operations in the Middle East and Africa and that the Eastern Military District was too far down the list for anyone to listen to him. He had accepted that, but hadn't stopped flagging the shortages in his monthly reports, or in fact, at any opportunity. He had personally had a conversation with Lukin about it six months earlier.

"The Comrade General is not expected to be across such details," Bondarev panted. "But it is the case that I am currently 20 crew short of being able to field my full regiment of 48 Okhotniks."

Bondarev half expected criticism from Lukin for his not keeping him informed, or at least something about the incompetence of his staff. Instead, he was silent. They jogged side by side, Lukin apparently in thought, Bondarev in stasis, until they crested the hill and began the curving downhill part of the run that would take them through a small village and then back toward the base.

"Twenty crew, you say," Lukin said finally.

"Yes, sir. For full operational capability I would require 24 to allow for … rotations."

Bondarev had hoped that Lukin would ease off his pace as they jogged through the darkened, quiet town. Only one or two houses were lit, with early risers who no doubt had duties somewhere on the military base. A dog barked off in the distance, highlighting to Bondarev how still the early morning was. There was no traffic, neither foot nor wheeled. In his soul, Bondarev hoped to hear at least a cock crow, but he knew that was a thought dredged up from a semi-rural childhood and not likely here in the middle of the icy wind-blasted desolation of Khabarovsk.

"You are not to commit your Okhotniks to the operation over Saint Lawrence," Lukin said finally, as the lights of the base appeared over a rise. "I expect a limited reaction from the

Americans. They are weak and indecisive but if your fighter regiments suffer losses, you will bear them, Colonel."

"Yes, sir."

If Bondarev had hoped for Lukin to share any of the grand plan with him, he was disappointed. They ran in silence for the rest of the distance back to the base, threading their way through the main gates, around a dead circle of hedge rustling in the early morning Arctic wind, and then back to the front door of the General's quarters.

Bondarev expected a curt dismissal, but was a little surprised as Lukin stopped on his steps, stretched out a leg and bent over it, warming down. "I am a fighting pilot like you, Bondarev," he said. He was looking at his foot, grabbing the toe as he pulled on his hamstrings.

"Yes, sir," Bondarev said.

"Did you know I am still current on the Yak-130?" he asked, pulling in his right leg and stretching out his left, still not looking at Bondarev directly.

Bondarev smiled. Of course he knew. The whole of the 3rd Air and Air Defense Forces Command knew that Lukin had his own Yak-130 trainer – a red two-seater light ground-attack fighter and trainer that had hardpoints for weapons and drop tanks and was painted like an Italian Ferrari. He flew himself and his adjutant from base to base for inspections, to observe exercises and join staff meetings.

"Yes, sir," he replied simply.

"You do your job," Lukin said. "Keep those skies clear. And I'll look forward to flying my Yak into that American airfield at Savoonga. You join me, and we will toast a job well done. Deal?" The General held out his hand, looking directly into Bondarev's eyes for the first time.

Bondarev took his hand. "A deal, General."

The General held his hand a moment longer than necessary. The gesture had a feeling of finality about it that unsettled Bondarev. It was as though they were saying a final goodbye. But Lukin dropped his hand and smiled. "You will also ensure your Okhotnik drivers are trained and working

78

together like the cogs in a Swiss clock," Lukin said. "I will see about that personnel shortage, Colonel. The fighting in Syria is more or less over now, from what I hear." He patted Bondarev on the shoulder and pulled open the door to his quarters, and Bondarev watched as he bounded upstairs for a shower. Something about Lukin's tone was less hearty than his words, though.

He's sending us off to die, Bondarev was thinking. He knows it, but he won't say it.

"You don't know your history," Arsharvin was telling him. It didn't quite come out that way, though. It was more like, "Youdunnoyahistry."

Bondarev was nowhere near as far gone as his friend. He was aware of, and spat upon, the clichéd Western images of Russians as big drinkers. He came from a family of teetotalers, in which he was the first in many generations who had ever taken a drink, and, recent anniversaries aside, it was rare he took more than two. His grandfather had been head of the entire Russian Air Force and he had never seen him touch a drop, even on the day he had turned up at a family dinner, pale-faced and quiet, clearly shocked over something that had happened. Yevgeny's mother had plagued him to know what had happened, but he had told her not to worry, it was just a military matter, not something he could share with her. Bondarev remembered his thirteen-year-old self watching the gray-haired, box-jawed older man sitting at the table, staring into his cold tea for nearly an hour without moving. A week later they heard an entire Russian air base inside Syria had been overrun by Turkish forces, with dozens dead and the rest of the personnel taken prisoner.

The old man had seen the worried look on his grandson's face and had pulled him over to the table as he sat there. "There will be war now, Yevgeny," his grandfather had said. "Not like you have seen before. I will be called away, and you will ..." He had patted his shoulder. "You will do your duty too."

His grandfather had been right. Following the Syrian civil war, Turkey had refused to yield Syrian Kurdish territories it had overrun, ironically with Russian military support, and after several years of cross-border skirmishes, Syria and Russia had declared war on Turkey. Attacking that country from the south in Syria, from the Black Sea, and from airfields in the Caucasus, Russia's action served several goals. To show the West that it was once again a military power to be reckoned with, and to show its allies or those in its shadow that they would need to choose sides for the second part of the 21st century, as divided loyalties were no longer an option. And, Bondarev realized now, to test the resolve of the United States when it came to meeting its many treaty obligations.

Russia had achieved all of those objectives and more. Turkey alone was never going to be a match for the Russian Navy, Air Force or special forces troops. And Turkey was very quickly left alone to deal with Russia. After years of antagonizing its European neighbors and throwing their overtures of friendship back in their faces, it had metaphorically burned all bridges across the Bosporus leading to Europe. Neither could it rely on US support, having been unilaterally expelled from NATO by the US after continued aggression against US Kurdish allies. Turkey quickly found that its own push toward independence from Europe and the West, and embrace of Islam, made it very vulnerable. Cut off from Europe, faced with an angry Russia bearing down on it, it cried for help and found itself in an echo chamber.

But Turkey was no military lightweight and Russian overconfidence had seen early victories in Syria and Turkey met with some unfortunate reverses: a war that planners had foreseen might take one year to eighteen months before Turkey was forced to capitulate was still raging two years later. While the fabled Blue Mosque in Istanbul was shown on Russian television still standing, as proof of both the discipline of Russian forces and the precision of its missiles and bombs, it stood almost as the only surviving building amongst the rubble of Istanbul.

By the second year of the conflict, the young Yevgeny Bondarev had earned his fighter wings. Bondarev's first combat mission had been in the skies over Istanbul, as he followed his flight in for a strike on anti-aircraft positions along the river dividing the city between Asia and Europe. They had blasted in at sea level, popped up over the first ruined bridge at Besiktas, and loosed their anti-radiation missiles at the targets that had been identified by high-flying Airborne Control aircraft and drones. Yevgeny had not seen the missiles strike. His flight had headed for the nap of the earth again as soon as their missiles were away and they were headed back to Sevastopol by the time they detonated. Russia had no need, nor appetite, for losing valuable pilots over enemy territory.

It was also the first time Bondarev had seen Okhotnik drones in action. As he had followed his flight leader away from the release point, he had seen a flight of nine Okhotniks, like small triangular darts, sweep in from his nine o'clock high to deal with the inadequate Turkish Air Force response to their attack. Turkish air defense satellites and radar had identified Bondarev's flight as it had popped up, and two outdated but well-armed F-18 Superhornets had been directed to pursue it. He was picking up their search radars as they tried to get a lock on the fleeing Russian flight and watched as the Okhotniks flashed past his wing, loosed two missiles each at the Turkish jets, and then immediately transitioned into an impossible full-thrust vertical climb that would have turned a human pilot's brain to mush. Within seconds the entire flight of Okhotniks was gone, surfing the stratosphere and no doubt looking for new targets even as their missiles swiped the Turkish Superhornets from the sky.

Bondarev saw the kills confirmed on one of the screens in his Su-57, and heard a grunt from his flight leader. "This isn't war," the man said. "It's a video game and the other side is still in the Nintendo age."

"That silicon can sure as hell fly and shoot though, sir," Bondarev said.

"You looking for a transfer, Bondarev? Your idea of war is sitting on your ass in a trailer in Georgia looking at a video screen, where the worst thing that can happen is spilling your coffee if you get a woody?"

Bondarev had instinctively run his eyes from controls to instruments, across his wing, the sky high and low around him, and then back to his controls. A hill was rushing toward them and, as one, the flight rose and then fell to avoid it. He checked the position of his wingman and felt the machine respond as he pulled back gently on his stick, felt the pressure of his seat against his back as he slid back into formation, the hill receding quickly behind him.

"Not likely, sir," he'd said.

But with a fabled name like Bondarev he wasn't going to be allowed to live out his days as a simple pilot. And despite their technological superiority, Russian losses were mounting as the conflict. A quick campaign had turned into a problematic, drawn-out intervention and occupation facing an asymmetric enemy, with Turkish forces maintaining control of vital oil reserves and a newly guilt-ridden NATO coming in late with material support; if not with troops, then at least with weapons systems. Russia had abandoned its Turkish adventure, only to support an ill-fated Iranian and Syrian attempt to reclaim the Golan Heights from Israel. Bondarev had barely escaped that escapade with his life.

But with two air and fifteen ground kills against his name, Bondarev had been given a Nesterov Air Medal, promotion to Captain, and command of his own Su-57 flight of six fighters.

He wasn't ready for command, but he had learned quickly and the first thing he had learned was to build alliances with the right people, like the then Lieutenant Arsharvin of the GRU, Russia's military intelligence arm. Arsharvin had been head of a combat intelligence unit, but to Bondarev his greatest value wasn't intelligence about the Turkish enemy. It was his network within the Russian Air Army, which had meant there wasn't a single political maneuver Bondarev wasn't forewarned about. Posted together to staff roles in Moscow, he and Arsharvin had learned about a near insurrection about to erupt in Snow Leopards' 8th Air Regiment. Arsharvin had handed the names of the plotters to Bondarev, and he had taken them to Lukin personally, afraid of trusting the information to anyone else. When the recriminations died down, Lukin had demoted the commander of the 8th, and put the now Major Bondarev in charge of the unit's twelve fourth-generation Su-34s. It was an inglorious command, with none of the glamour of one of the new Okhotnik regiments, but it was based in Khabarovsk with high visibility. He leveraged his year there to eventually achieve command of the 5th Air Battalion, an elite unit composed of the latest Su-57 and Mig-41 fighters. From there it was just a matter of leveraging his famous name, his many connections and above all, not screwing up, and he was handed a Colonel's commission and command of the Snow Leopards Regiment: nine battalions, 200 fighters or attack aircraft, 100 rotary-winged attack and support aircraft.

After the heat and dust of Syria, the move to the Snow Leopards' base in the Russian Far East had been welcome. Bondarev was no stranger to snow and ice. Loved, in fact, the biting cold of a cloudless night, salt tears in his eyes, lips numb. His mother, dead five years now, had taught him there was no such thing as bad weather, only bad clothing.

His grandfather had been right about the war coming, but he hadn't been there to see it end. He had died of an undiagnosed heart problem visiting an air defense unit outside Tbilisi; but he had seen his grandson decorated and Bondarev remembered clearly his words as he pinned on the medal. He had held him by the shoulders and then tapped the medal. "Each one of these is forged with the tears of mothers who have lost sons and daughters," his grandfather had said. "Remember that, every time you wear it."

"Hey, I'm talking to you," Arsharvin said, punching Bondarev's shoulder and bringing him back to the present. Bondarev had just told Arsharvin it was his professional

83

military opinion that Operation LOSOS was going to be just like Japan's attack on Pearl Harbor. A fantastic military victory that would guarantee their ultimate defeat. "Saint Lawrence is not Pearl Harbor," Arsharvin was insisting. "The US will react to our move on Saint Lawrence, yes. That is the intention – to create a provocation they simply cannot ignore. We will incur losses, inevitably. In fact, we are counting on it. In the face of continued US military aggression, we will move on Alaska and declare our intention to secure the west of Alaska as neutral territory, a bulwark between a militant USA and a peaceful Russia. Traditional US lapdogs like the UK, Australia, South Korea and Japan may react, but they are too weak and too far away to offer anything but political support. Our diplomats assure us Europe will not mobilize – there is little love left for the USA in Europe."

"Europe will respond when American ballistic missiles start to fly," Bondarev said. "I guarantee you that."

Arsharvin took another glass. "It won't come to that. If we move with overwhelming conventional force, take Nome quickly, the US will find itself in a hostage negotiation, not a war."

"They would hesitate to use their nuclear weapons against targets on US soil, I agree," Bondarev allowed. "But sub-launched tactical nukes on our Far East airfields and ports would be my response. The battle for Alaska would be over before it started."

"And how would we respond to an attack like that?" Arsharvin asked.

"Massively, and irrationally," Bondarev sighed. "The sky would rain ballistic missiles. We would be looking at the end of all civilization."

"Yes. Or no. Say the self-absorbed US President and the weak-kneed liberals in the US Congress hesitate. The US does not *need* Nome, they do not care about Nome. America has 12% unemployment, its factories are rusting ruins, climate change has turned its farms from San Francisco to Kansas City into dust bowls, it relies on Chinese loans to fund a military on

84

the edge of collapse. They will fight, yes, but not with nuclear weapons."

"You've been listening to your own propaganda for too long. And what makes you think we can even win a *conventional* war?" Bondarev asked.

"Nothing, but what a glorious cause!" Arsharvin yelled, raising an arm in the air. "Let us toast to it! Victory over the main enemy, and a new age of prosperity for Mother Russia!"

Bondarev lifted his glass, but put it down again without draining it. He needed a clear head for tomorrow. He was about to send four thousand men and women to war.

SNOWFLAKES IN THE BREEZE

Seventeen-year-old Perri Tungyan would rather have been fishing. His father and brother had taken their boat out earlier that morning to try out the new echolocator that had finally arrived from Nome. They already had the best boat in Gambell; the 16-footer was swift, with a twin-screw outboard engine that meant it could fly through the tight spaces between floes in pursuit of seal or whale. But the deep sea echolocator, that was the key to them finding new depressions, valleys and rock formations that might be hiding a nice big halibut.

It had been three years since Perri's brother pulled in a 180lb fish and their father made him throw it back in because anything over 70lb was a female, he said. Since then, the biggest they'd landed was about 40 inches or 30lb. Still a good-sized fish, but nothing like that monster from three years ago.

He looked out from the shed in which he was sheltering from the wind at the sea beyond the runway at Gambell Airport. He should be out there on the water. Instead he was stuck here, waiting to unload the weekly grocery flight from America. He didn't do it for the money – the money was peanuts and there was nothing to spend it on here except cigarettes and liquor. He did it for the loot. A dropped case of canned peaches here, a missing box of chocolate there. Was it Perri's fault internet orders had a habit of getting screwed up? He kept his pilfering at a low level, though, so no one got too upset at him. Didn't dip into the cargo every flight, just when he saw a choice shipment; little luxuries his family would never see otherwise.

He clapped cold hands against his chest. He knew there wasn't much chance of getting fired anyway, not when he was the only one stupid enough to waste a great fishing day like this hanging around Gambell's deserted airstrip. This wasn't Savoonga; there was no control tower here, no baggage handlers, no gate agents or ticket offices. Just the long dirt strip sticking out into the Bering Sea with water glittering on both sides, and Perri, his four-wheeler and his sled.

When his older brother had worked here, there had at least been an aircraft maintenance engineer hanging around too, to refuel the light planes coming in, restock them with food or water, or attend to any mechanical issues. Pilots brought gossip with them, from Nome, Fairbanks, Anchorage. It had made America seem closer then. Now all the flights were automated, pilotless Amazon freight drones. They landed, he unloaded, plugged them into the grid with a cable that held itself on magnetically, and when they were recharged they just took off by themselves as long as he'd shut the cargo bay door properly – he didn't even need to be there. More reliable, sure (no drunken bush pilots to deal with), but so damn boring.

He looked at the time on his phone and walked over to his all-terrain ATV bike. The electric engine came to life on the second press of the starter and he left it ticking over while he checked the connector to the big sled hooked up behind it. All good. He checked the snow plow at the front was also pulled up – it had a habit of dropping into the dirt and sending him head over heels over the handlebars, stupid thing. He should just unbolt it. It was a long time since there was snow on the runway at Gambell this time of year. The last thing he checked was that his rifle was tied securely to the grill at the back of the sled. It had been seven years since any polar bears had been seen on Saint Lawrence, but he didn't want to be that guy who finally saw one again and wasn't armed with anything except a mobile phone to take a photo of it. Plus if the drone didn't show up, he could always set out a few cans along the runway and practice his distance shooting. There were markers every fifty yards along the airstrip so he could measure the distance pretty accurately. His best shot ever was with the rifle he was carrying now, his father's Winchester XPR .300. A one hundred and fifty-yard headshot on a reindeer stag, in a slight crosswind too. Throwing his leg over the saddle, he gunned the bike out of the old hangar and onto the spit holding the runway.

The drones were either on time, or they didn't turn up at all; there was nothing in between. The weather over Alaska meant they might get canceled, but no one bothered to tell Gambell about it, so Perri had to go out there every time and just look up at the sky for the tell-tale small dot to appear high in the sky or drop out of the cloud base and fog. He pulled up halfway down the runway, and shaded his eyes against the sun. Great visibility today, he should be able to see it coming a ways off. You could always see them before you heard them – their small electric twin turbofan engines were almost silent.

You never knew which direction they would come from, though; it was something about the wind, but it seemed pretty random to him. He swiveled around, looking east, then west. Yeah, there it was. A tiny speck in the sky about ten miles out, if he had to guess.

No. Two specks. As he watched, the single dot split into two. Then three. *What?* No one had told him to expect three delivery flights today. That sort of thing only ever happened in the holiday season. Except these weren't delivery flights. The planes were closing way too fast. He leaned forward on his handlebars, eyes glued to the approaching aircraft.

Could be Air Force, he guessed. Since the Air Force had rebuilt the radar base up at Savoonga ten years ago there were occasional overflights by US bombers and fighters which the Air Force said were using the base to test their navigation systems. Transport flights too; the big four-engined jets bringing in personnel and equipment occasionally overflew Gambell on their way in and out. But none had ever landed. The runway was probably too short for a jet like that anyway. Whatever these planes were, they were *booking*. Within no time the dots had grown to small dart shapes and were going to be over Gambell in another second or two.

When the Air Force started appearing over Saint Lawrence again, Perri had quickly learned to identify their aircraft. Seeing one of them in the skies over his village was a welcome break in the monotony. Hard to tell yet, but these had to be F-35 fighters or Fantom drones. His money was on the older F-35s –

the specks racing toward him looked a little too big to be the pilotless drones. One, two, three; he had barely finished confirming the count when the machines were blasting over the top of him, so low that the sonic boom nearly blew out his eardrums.

He put his hand up to his ears. *Shit that hurt! Assholes!* That wasn't funny.

He watched the three jets zoom into a climb, spiraling up into the blue of the sky in perfect formation.

They weren't F-35 *Lightnings*. They weren't Fantoms either. What the hell?!

Bondarev pulled his Sukhoi onto its back at the top of his climb then barrel rolled to level flight at 10,000 feet over Gambell with his two wingmen staying in perfect formation behind and slightly above him. His radar warning system was screaming at him as the radiation from the early warning station at Savoonga painted his aircraft. It took all of his self-control not to target one of his antiradar missiles at the US installation, but the same heads-up display that identified the US radar for him was also telling him it was not actively tracking. His threat warning system was silent too.

Which was what he was expecting, since the message had come through while his squadron was in flight that Russian special forces had been successful in taking the US radar facility at Savoonga without firing a single shot. Arsharvin had texted him a report saying they had fallen on the sleeping US forces in the night, finding only two dozy sentries, a duty officer and two radar operators awake. The other twenty personnel stationed there had been asleep and woke to find themselves the first prisoners of Operation LOSOS. The Spetsnaz had kept the radar station in operation so that NORAD wouldn't raise an alarm at it going off the air.

He cracked his knuckles and smiled. Against the wishes of his staff he had insisted on being in the first wave of aircraft over the target and he eased his Sukhoi into a lazy racetrack orbit over Gambell. "Swan 1 to Swan 2, I make it one civilian vehicle by the runway at Gambell airstrip, confirm?" The motorbike or buggy down below was too small for his IMA BK air-to-ground radar to pick up, but he pinned it with his optical targeting system. In the town itself, he could see a few people moving around, and something that was probably a pickup truck driving toward the small harbor.

His wingman came on the radio within a couple of seconds. "Confirmed, Swan Leader, no military vehicles or signals identified."

Theirs wasn't a reconnaissance flight. Operation LOSOS was already supported by intensive satellite and drone surveillance and the whole of Saint Lawrence was being monitored in real time by every eye and ear in the Russian Eastern Military District inventory. But Bondarev hadn't survived 57 combat sorties over Syria and Turkey by trusting someone or something else to be his eyes and ears.

That was why he was leading this initial sortie himself, and had split his squadron of twelve Su-57s into four sections, sending one over Savoonga in the north, two to the eastern end of the island where they expected the inevitable US response to materialize, and he took the remaining element in over Gambell to reassure himself that the US hadn't moved any mobile air defense assets there to give him a horrible surprise.

Phase I of LOSOS was rolling. As he watched Gambell disappear under his wing for the second time, he canceled the lock on the small vehicle below, leveled his machine out and pointed it east, toward Alaska. "Swallow 1, this is Swan 1. Clear skies over the target, you are cleared for ingress."

"Swallow 1 acknowledges, beginning ingress," came the reply.

Perri was getting a crick in his neck from watching the fast-moving jets circle overhead. He was still trying to work out what they were. They'd had an Air Force officer come to Gambell school a couple of years ago, and he had played a game with them, showing them silhouettes of American fighter planes, bombers and drones and having them guess what each of them was from a small recognition chart he had handed out. Perri had won the quiz and got himself an Aircraft Control and Warning Squadron patch to sew on his anorak. You can bet he did; it was one of his coolest possessions – a large hand-sewn cloth emblem with an image of a polar bear holding a globe of the world in one paw. He reached absently for his sleeve and fingered it now.

As soon as he turned eighteen he was going to enlist. Get himself off this island and see the world. He'd already been sent the papers and filled them out.

As the three aircraft overhead stopped circling and sped away to the east, Perri had convinced himself these planes were not on the recognition chart he had at home. He watched them go. Some new sort of top-secret Air Force plane maybe? They could certainly move. In seconds they were gone.

Or had they just circled around and come up behind him again? Damn, that was fast. He heard a sound in the air to the west behind him and swiveled his head. This time he saw a flat line of what looked like five or six large fat flying insects closing on the airstrip. As they got closer, the sound in the air resolved itself into the thud of rotors. A little like the sound made by the Amazon drones as they switched from horizontal to vertical flight for landing. But that was more of a buzzing sound, whereas this was a chest-pounding syncopated *thump*.

There was no doubt in Perri's mind that these machines were planning to land. They went from a staggered line abreast formation into line astern, each one lined up five hundred yards behind the other, and they snaked toward the airstrip with unmistakable intent. Perri fumbled for his phone. He should call someone. This was too weird. But who the hell should he call? Mayor Pungiwiyi? He was the closest thing Gambell had to a law officer, but the guy was definitely still sleeping off his birthday party from last night. His father? He and his brothers would be well out to sea by now, well out of range of the small cellular bubble around Gambell.

He still had the card for the Air Force officer from Savoonga in his wallet. He'd call them. They'd know what the hell was going on. Fumbling with his wallet and phone in the cold air, he punched in the number and waited. It came back with a busy signal. He dialed again – same thing. It wasn't unusual, cell coverage between the two towns was often patchy. Damn.

So he put his phone away, bit his lip and stayed glued to the saddle of his ATV. But he turned it on again, kept the engine running. He wasn't sure why, it just seemed the smart thing to do.

As the fat black insect shapes converged on the airstrip, Perri suddenly realized what he was looking at. Just six months ago, one of the men from the village had got into trouble in the seas northwest of Saint Lawrence when his outboard gave up on him. He'd drifted toward the Russian coast and been spotted by a freighter headed south. The ship hadn't stopped, but the crew had radioed the Russian Coast Guard to report the Yup'ik fishing boat as a shipping hazard. The man had been plucked from his boat and dropped back on Saint Lawrence by a huge Russian Mil-26 heavy chopper. The whole of Gambell had gone down to look the chopper over, and Russian media had made a huge deal about it on the internet, telling how they had rescued an American citizen because his own Coast Guard hadn't responded to his call for help. A call he hadn't actually made, of course, but that wasn't the point.

So Perri pretty quickly worked out the bug-like shapes of the choppers now flaring over the runway a hundred yards away were Russian Mil-26s. And he was old enough and quick enough to realize that was Not A Normal Thing. Before the first machine had settled on its wheels and the rear cargo bay doors began opening, Perri had opened the throttle on his ATV and was racing back down the runway toward Gambell!

Out of the corner of his eye he saw men dressed in white and brown camouflage suits come tumbling out of the door of the chopper and fan out before throwing themselves down on the ground, facing out. More men jumped out behind them.

Perri cursed. He was still halfway along the spit, because the Amazon drones usually put down midway along the runway. He had his throttle turned all the way back, but the old ATV couldn't do more than 40 mph, and that was with a good tailwind.

If there was any warning shouted, he couldn't hear it above the clatter of helicopter rotors and whine of his engine, but there was no mistaking the crack of a heavy rifle and the sideways shove he felt as the round from a Spetsnaz AMR 12.7mm rifle slammed into the rear of his ATV and his engine shat itself. He felt the bike and sled scissoring dangerously and turned into the skid, trying desperately to avoid flipping over, but even as he tried he could sense the ATV begin to tilt and realized with a lurching stomach it was going over. He launched himself into the air so that he didn't get two hundred pounds of rolling metal and plastic landing on top of him, hit the dirt beside the runway in a welter of gravel and rolled with his hands over his head. The ATV flipped twice and stopped, the sled behind it cartwheeling free and flying over Perri's body to land on the other side of him with a scraping crunch. His first thought as he looked at the wrecked ATV was that he was so, so busted. Then he saw Russian troops up and running along the runway toward him and realized that was the least of his worries. They had shot at him!

The Russian soldiers were still a hundred yards away, and he saw one of them waving at him to lie down. Or that's what it seemed like. They all had guns, and at least two were down on one knee with rifles pointed at him, with another laying on his stomach, feet spread wide, a huge long-barreled rifle on a tripod pointed right at him.

Forget this, Perri thought. He scrambled to the sled and threw himself over it, putting it between himself and the Russian troops. The sled was on its back, so he quickly felt underneath it for the rifle wrapped in a sealskin blanket that had been tied to the grill at the back. Thank God, it was still there! He took a quick look over the sled and saw the nearest soldier was fifty yards away now, and sprinting hard.

The guy had his rifle in his hands, but it was on a strap across his chest, not pointed at Perri.

Perri looked desperately down the runway. It was a hundred yards more of open ground. He knew he wouldn't make it twenty yards before he was crash tackled, or worse, got himself shot. Looking behind him, Perri saw that the crash of the ATV had thrown him across the ground beside the runway toward the rocks lining the spit. On the other side of them was the bay, and on the other side of that, Gambell township. Perri put a loop of the rope tied around the rifle around his neck.

His thick fur-lined jacket was shredded, but it had probably saved him from getting his hide scraped off in the crash. It hung in tatters from one shoulder, so he pulled it off. Without hesitating another second, he rose into a crouch and then sprinted for the sea. He ignored the shouting behind him, shoulders hunched, expecting to feel a bullet slam into his back any second as he jumped from the shore onto one rock, then another, hopping like a demented Arctic fox, and then threw himself into the waters of the bay.

Private Zubkhov of the 14th Special Purpose Brigade, 282nd Squadron, covered his comrades with the anti-material rifle until they gave up chasing the man who jumped into the bay. He had been the one who had fired the shots that had brought the guy down. When it was clear there was no other target, he ran over to where the man jumped into the water and, resting his barrel on one of the rocks the man had used to make his escape, he sighted down at the figure splashing through the water. The man was a strong swimmer, but he hadn't made it across the bay yet. It was an easy shot.

A hand pushed up the barrel of his rifle and he lifted his face away from the sights to see his commanding officer, Captain Demchenko, standing beside him, also watching the man swim away.

"Let him go, Private," the officer said. "Minimal casualties, either military or civilian, remember?"

"Yes, sir," Zubkhov replied, folding up the bipod on his barrel and slinging the rifle across his back. He watched the man slice through the water. *Shame.* Zubkhov looked back at the runway. He saw the other men of his unit doubling down the runway in the direction of the road to the village. They had estimated it would take fifteen minutes to reach by foot.

"Permission to rejoin the squadron, sir?" Zubkhov asked.

"You won't catch them," Demchenko said. He looked back at the ATV. "You made that mess, you can clean it up. Pull that wreck further away from the runway and check the compartment under the seat for anything useful. Papers, maps, whatever you can find."

Zubkhov looked ruefully at the backs of his comrades as they reached the road at the bottom of the runway and wound around to their right and out of sight. "Yes, sir," he said, disappointed to already be out of the fight. Such as it was.

"When you're finished you can make yourself useful unloading the choppers," his Captain said, adding insult to injury. He saw the private's face fall and clapped him on the shoulder. "Cheer up, man. That was a nice takedown you made there. If it makes you feel better, I suspect it will be the only shot this whole squadron will fire today," he said.

Bondarev joined his second section at 50,000 feet over Eastern Saint Lawrence and they fell into formation briefly behind him, while he reviewed their dispositions and then ordered three of the six Su-57s to set up a combat air patrol to the northeast while he took the southeast, the most likely direction from which enemy fighters would approach. He expected a probing reaction from the Americans at first, giving him time to scale his response.

The leader of his second flight was a combat veteran, but his other pilots were not battle tested, whereas all three men in Bondarev's flight were veterans of Syria, men who had flown with him for years. He set up a combat air patrol that gave them control of a two-hundred-mile bubble of airspace, and then contacted the Beriev early warning aircraft that was coordinating the airspace over Saint Lawrence. Its Active Phased Array Radar could detect airborne targets out to 600km and warships out to 400. Although Russia bragged the Beriev was capable of detecting stealth fighters, Bondarev knew from experience that at best it could give a general vector, not a precise lock. The Beriev was supplemented by ground-based long-range radar and saturation satellite coverage as well, though, so Bondarev was not worried they would get jumped without warning.

"Raptor Control, this is Swan 1, we are on station and available for tasking," Bondarev reported.

"Acknowledged Swan 1, we see you, hold station," the controller onboard the Beriev responded. "All quiet here. We are moving to Phase II. Out."

This was war, Bondarev reflected, running his eyes across his instruments and checking them against what his heads-up display was showing him. Hours of total tedium, interrupted by moments of sheer terror. But his old grandmother had once said to him, "May you never live in exciting times." Unfortunately, her wish hadn't come true in the past, but he fervently hoped it would at least hold for today.

"I have Foreign Minister Kelnikov on the line for you, Ambassador," Devlin McCarthy's assistant said over the phone. McCarthy was in the back of her car, on the way out to a dinner with the Canadian delegation in Moscow.

She sighed. *More bluster about that lost ship, no doubt*, she thought. What Russia hoped to achieve with it wasn't clear. "Put him on," she said. She heard static on the line, and coughing in the background. "Minister Kelnikov," she said. "How are you?"

"Rather busy, I am afraid," the man said. "I am calling to advise you we have another nautical emergency in the Bering Sea, this time off the coast of your island of Saint Lawrence."

McCarthy leaned forward in her seat and tapped her aide on the shoulder, motioning him to get the car to pull over. "What emergency, Minister?"

"One of our *Kazan*-class submarines has suffered a flash fire and as a precaution, the Captain has chosen to scram the vessel's reactor. We have lost contact but his last report said he was unable to surface. We have mobilized rescue assets from Anadyr and Lavrentiya and air-sea rescue reconnaissance units are over the submarine's last known position."

McCarthy thought quickly. "Are you requesting our assistance?"

Kelnikov grunted. "No, Ambassador. We have the matter in hand and have notified your Coast Guard in Alaska. But I am advising you so that you can pass the message up your chain of command that they should not be alarmed to see Russian military vessels and aircraft in the area of Saint Lawrence while we stabilize this terrible situation."

"I will advise our military attaché and the Pentagon immediately," McCarthy said. "But I suggest your President also contact my President to open a channel of communication if the situation worsens. There will be concern about the risk of nuclear contamination."

"He is already doing so, I believe," Kelnikov said. "Our Ambassador in Washington is also on his way into your State Department."

"We stand ready to assist in any way we can," McCarthy said. "I imagine a nuclear sub reactor scram is not a small matter, Minister. I suspect our military chiefs will want to move emergency response assets to Saint Lawrence just in case they are needed."

There was hesitation at the other end. "That may be prudent," Kelnikov said. "Can you please arrange to give us the contact details for whichever officer you put in charge, so that we can speak with them directly? It would be best to let our two militaries manage this event between themselves so that no confusions arise."

"I'll personally see that you receive those details," McCarthy said. "Was there anything else?"

"No, that will do for now. I will keep you advised as best I can, but I do not expect any new information in the next hour or so. As I said, we have lost contact with our vessel; our military command will decide how to respond."

"Our thoughts and prayers are with those men," McCarthy said. "Can I ask what the name of the vessel was? It was a *Kazan*-class submarine you said?"

"That is all I know at this point," Kelnikov said, clearly dissembling. "Which of our *Kazan*-class vessels is involved, I am sorry I cannot say."

She hadn't expected him to identify the vessel, but it was worth a try. 'Cannot say' was not the same as 'do not know', but in a similar situation, US Pacific Fleet Command wouldn't rush to identify to the Russians which of their nuclear missile-capable vessels was currently bottomed out on the seabed off a foreign coast. It was probably already a breach of about ten different nuclear disarmament treaties that the submarine was even operating in the sea off Saint Lawrence.

"I had better start making some phone calls," McCarthy said. "If you will excuse me, Minister."

"Certainly, goodbye for now."

She cut the connection and leaned back in her seat. "Get us to the compound, stat," she told her aide, and he pulled up a list of destinations and tapped it in. This wasn't the sort of thing she could discuss over a cell phone, even an encrypted cell. As the car accelerated into traffic she made a mental list of who she should call and in which order. As she tapped her fingers on the window pane nervously, she bit her lip. *You lying sack of dung*, she thought. *Nuclear sub reactor scram off Saint Lawrence my broad ass.*

First the *Ozempic Tsar*, now this. What the hell are they up to?

IN COMMISSION

Air Boss Alicia Rodriguez was deeply asleep, dreaming of lying on a field of warm green grass staring up at a blue sky filled with rolling white clouds. There was someone beside her and they were playing games finding shapes in the clouds.

"That one is an ambulance," the mystery person beside her was saying. "Or a fire truck. It sounds like a fire truck."

"Sounds like a fire truck?" Rodriguez was about to respond in her dream when she suddenly realized she wasn't dreaming. There was an emergency siren ringing out through the base. At exactly that moment, the phone charging at her bedside began to buzz. She grabbed it.

"Lieutenant Commander, this is Commander Halifax. We have a situation, get down to the flight deck," he said. "I'll brief you when you get there. I'm calling all hands to action stations." He hung up.

Confused, Rodriguez stared at her handset for a second before her adrenaline kicked in. Within two minutes she had pulled on her flight suit and boots, pulled her black hair into a ponytail and was running at full pelt from the officer's quarters at the back of the docks and up metal stairs toward her command trailer – her position when action stations were sounded. There were men and women also swarming up the steps and she shouted at them to stand aside and let her through, pulling at a couple of shoulders as she bustled past, taking the steps two at a time.

Halifax was already in the trailer when she pulled the door open and jumped inside, and she saw Bunny at her pilot console, punching buttons and bringing her systems online. Which was kind of pointless since they didn't have a drone on alert…

"Lieutenant Commander," Halifax barked. "How quickly can you get a Fantom onto that Cat?"

Rodriguez didn't hesitate. If the station had been at readiness, there would be a Fantom hanging in the loading crane on alert, able to be dropped onto the Cat with five minutes' warning. But it wasn't. She did have a hex of Fantoms pre-flighted and loaded into their cartridges already fueled. They could be fitted with ordnance for a range of mission types from the auto-loading magazines with the tap of a few keys.

"Seventeen minutes, sir," she said. "Ten to load mission ordnance package, five to get flight systems online, two to verify system status and spool up for launch."

Halifax looked at her. "You have ten minutes. I want a drone headed out the chute in ten minutes tops and a second Fantom loading as soon as it is away, is that clear?"

"Mission profile from the Operations Order, sir?" she asked.

"The OPORD says unarmed reconnaissance," he replied tersely.

She grabbed a tablet from the rack over her desk and powered it on, bringing up her inventory screen. Unarmed recon meant no weapons other than guns, and a recon pod in the ordnance bay. Immediately she saw a problem – recon pods were not part of the auto-load system, they had to be fitted manually, and that would take additional time.

"Sir, is this another exercise?" Bunny asked, pulling her virtual-reality helmet over her platinum stubble.

"No, Lieutenant," Halifax said. "A Russian nuclear sub has declared a reactor emergency off the coast of Saint Lawrence Island. Alaska NORAD indicates the sky over the island is swarming with Russian aircraft, and the Russians are actively jamming. The situation with that sub is clearly worse than Ivan is letting on. With all the jamming we can't get through to our radar station base at Savoonga, so we need eyes over Saint Lawrence an hour ago. NORAD is repositioning satellites and scrambling a drone out of Eielson, but we can get over Saint Lawrence before anyone else can." He looked at Rodriguez. "So we need to launch stat."

"Then we can either go with the birds I have on the rack, which can be launched with a multirole loadout, or take an extra 30 minutes to fit dedicated recon payloads."

Halifax considered briefly. "Go with what you have ready."

"Rules of engagement, sir?" Bunny asked. "Standing rules?"

"No," Halifax said clearly. Standing rules of engagement allowed a pilot to fire back if they were fired upon first. "You will *not* engage Russian aircraft, even if fired upon. That's why NORAD has tasked us – they don't want to risk piloted aircraft, or create an international incident. And we do not want to give away the existence of this base. Set your waypoints so it looks like your origin is Nome."

Rodriguez didn't need more encouragement. She called up two fighters and authorized them to be delivered on the conveyor belt from the magazine to the catapult bay.

"Permission to go down to the flight deck, sir?" Rodriguez asked, clear that she would need to be close to the action if they were to shave precious seconds off every step of the regimented launch process.

"Granted," Halifax said.

Her crews were milling around down by the flight deck; aircraft handlers, catapult crew, ground equipment trouble-shooters… half of them looking like she felt (tumble dried and freaked out) and the other half just standing around ready to be told what to do. She headed out of the trailer and before she had even finished running she was barking orders.

"Ladies and gentlemen, this is not an exercise, this facility is now officially open for business!" she said, and couldn't help grinning. "I've dialed up two Fantoms – we'll launch immediately. You have eight minutes to get the first machine onto that Cat, systems online and ready to fire. Five minutes for the machine after that. Questions?"

"Bring two reserve machines into the bays, just in case we get a dead boot, ma'am?" one of the crew quickly asked. He was a young, pimply plane captain she'd seen at work on the *GW Bush* under one of her aircraft handling officers but in the flat structure they'd adopted under the Rock he had no qualms about speaking up.

"Good idea, Collins, I'll pull two machines into the reserve bays, you get them prepped with recon pods. Now, lock and load, people!" She stayed as long as it took for the conveyor belt to deliver the first Fantom and watched as a robot arm lifted it out of its cartridge and dropped it onto the guide rails of the catapult. Two crewmen got to work dropping the wings, locking it to front and rear bars and tensioning the launch wire. While they were doing that, two electronics technicians booted up the drone's AI system and began speeding through the pre-flight checklist. There was a 'fast boot' mode made for combat environments that gave the AI enough resources to get itself in the air, and left it to run its own 'pre-mission' checks during the first few minutes of flight. They didn't have to check with Rodriguez, it was obvious this was the mode they should load given the urgency in her voice.

After five minutes the two Cat crew members backed away and each raised an arm in the air. Almost simultaneously, the two electronics techs closed and locked the drone's system access panel and stepped away from the machine, raising an arm in the air.

"Outstanding!" Rodriguez said into her mike. "Launch stations. Prepare to retrieve cartridge and load Fantom two!"

Crew members a good distance from the deck crouched and turned their backs, while those who had just been working on the drone jumped over blast barriers and put their helmeted heads down.

"Flaps, slats, panels, pins!" she called.

"Green."

"Man out?"

"Man out, aye."

"Visual?"

"Thumbs up."

"Cat scan."

"Cat clear."

"Cat to 520 psi."

102

"520, aye."

Rodriguez reached for her throat mike. "Light her tail, O'Hare," she said.

She looked at her watch. Eleven minutes. Damn, they had to get faster. A hand tugged at her trousers. "You're not in the trailer now, ma'am, get down please," Collins said with a grin, pointing to a spot beside him behind one of the blast barriers. The engines of the Fantom began to spool up and blue-white fire burst from the rear exhaust.

"Launch launch *launch!*" she said, giving 'Lucky' Severin, the launch officer, the order to punch the drone out of the rock.

She had just ducked down behind the concrete blast barrier when the Scimitar engines of the Fantom fired in earnest and the delta-winged drone rocketed down the catapult, riding the rails to the end of the flight deck and flying straight and true down the chute and out of the cavern. There was no cheering this time. Rodriguez was glad to see two crew members already pulling the used cartridge off the line and putting it into the reloading bay, while the loaders got to work again fitting and configuring the second Fantom for launch.

"Bunny, I'm loading your second Fantom, with two more in the queue," Rodriguez said as she crouched. "We'll get them in the air, you can decide how to use them."

"Good thinking, ma'am, I'll add two more machines to the mission package."

She imagined Bunny in the trailer, playing her keyboards like a concert pianist, punching in coordinates for the drones to follow once they were outside the chute. In a situation like this, she would send the drones away in pairs, not wait for all four to form up.

Rodriguez nodded to Severin and pointed at herself, then back to the command trailer, indicating he should take over down on the deck while she went back to her real job. Ordinarily she would only come down to the deck if there was an issue, but what the hell … her first operational launch under the Rock?

She wasn't going to stand up on the island and just hope it went right!

"Five minutes to feet dry," Bunny said calmly a short while later. "Wedge is data-linked and all birds are singing."

A six-plane formation of Fantoms was a 'hex' but a four-plane flight was called a 'wedge'. Rodriguez marveled at how the pilot could control four combat aircraft at once, even if onboard AI was doing the real-time flying. It was a completely new type of combat pilot the Navy needed for drone combat. Bunny had been headhunted for drone testing because she had exactly what it took: a solid diagnosis of ADHD and excellent continuous partial focus skills. She had the heads-up display for each of the drones on a separate virtual screen, and flicked between them at will. She didn't try to control them in real time at such distances due to the satellite-induced communication lag; she could only do that when they were in direct 'line of sight' of the undersea comms array buried in the sea floor outside Little Diomede or hot linked via an Airborne Control aircraft. But she had memorized all of the literally hundreds of offensive, patrol and defensive sub-routines programmed into her keyboard. Combined with the mission waypoints and orders laid out on the tactical screen, which she could also change on the fly, it gave her tactical control of her drones without having to worry about little things like trying not to fly them into the dirt.

And then there was the force-multiplier that set US and Russian drone doctrine apart. The semi-autonomous combat AI. The first Fantom that had launched was Bunny's LMV or lead mission vehicle, and she had slaved the second Fantom to that one. Fantom 2 was in support mode, providing cover for the primary drone and feeding it with sensor data. The third Fantom was her SMV, or secondary mission vehicle, with orders to join the wedge and hold formation, while the fourth Fantom flew cover for the SMV. All machines were programmed with the Rules of Engagement or ROE, ordered to identify but not engage any potential threats and evade enemy fire if fired upon. In this way, switching from the lead machine in each two-plane element to the other, changing their orders on the fly, Bunny flew the four drones with keyboards and a mouse, her head nestled inside a virtual-reality helmet, just like a gamer on a console. She could manage up to six drones at once in this way – even when the lead started flying.

"How long to Savoonga?" Halifax asked, for about the third time.

"Seven minutes, sir," O'Hare replied in a deadpan voice, fingers dancing over the keys. Although on organization charts A4 was listed under Naval Network Warfare Command, in practice due to its covert nature it was anchored under the Headquarters of Commander, Naval Air Forces with a direct line up to the Navy's main 'Air Boss'. Its mission was to 'develop future weapons and tactics for the defense of the Continental United States'. And that meant that today they took their tasking from Alaska NORAD Region.

Bunny keyed her mike, reaching out to the controllers at NORAD. "NORAD, this is A4 flight of four inbound Saint Lawrence, targeting overflight of Savoonga. I have good feed on passive arrays, I see six, repeat six Russian fighters at 50,000 feet over the east coast, three over Savoonga, three over...uh...Gambell. I'm also picking up Russian encrypted radio traffic on electronic intel further west, probably also Gambell. Confirm?" The Russians might be trying to jam electronic surveillance of their sub rescue operation, but between satellite-mounted synthetic aperture radar and infrared sensors, the long-distance radar at Elmendorf-Richardson Air Force Base, and now the data being fed to them by Bunny's Fantoms, NORAD should be able to burn through.

"NORAD confirming. You are clear to ingress. Get eyes on the prize, A4. We have F-35s en route. They'll try to pull the Russian fighters east of Saint Lawrence, give you a window."

"Roger, NORAD," Bunny said. "Starting ingress."

Bunny was flying nap of the earth, counting on wave and ground clutter to hide her fifth-generation stealth aircraft from Russian naval or air radar.

It was the first time in her career Bunny had the chance to face off against real Russian radar and weapons platforms and operators.

She was looking forward to it.

"Raptor Control to Swan Leader, we have business for you," Bondarev heard the voice of the controller on his Beriev say in his helmet. "Sending data to you now."

Bondarev tightened his hand on his throttle and saw his heads-up display flicker before it switched into targeting mode. Immediately he saw six arrows on the screen with target identifier icons underneath them. F-35s moving out from Eielson Air Force Base, and they were not trying to hide. They were being tracked either by the Airborne Control aircraft circling back over the Russian mainland at Provideniya, or by satellites overhead. The data lock looked solid, which meant that Bondarev didn't need to risk confirming his own strength and position and could track the incoming American aircraft with passive systems.

But he had learned over Syria and Turkey to assume that if he could see the enemy, then they could probably see him. He had no faith in Russian electronic countermeasures against sophisticated US weapons systems; they had failed him too often.

"I have them, Raptor Control," Bondarev confirmed. "Orders, please."

"Swan Leader, you are to fly within visual range of the bogies but do not cross the Alaska coast. Repeat, you are not to cross the Alaska coast. Warn the American aircraft to stay outside of a fifty-mile radius around Saint Lawrence Island while our submarine recovery operation is underway. You can tell them this has been agreed *personally* between the US and Russian Presidents."

Bondarev smiled. He knew how he would react if he were one of the approaching Americans. He'd think twice before pushing through the Russian perimeter without checking first. It should buy the troops on the ground below some precious minutes, maybe even hours.

"Roger, Raptor Control, Swan 1 moving to intercept," he said. "Raptor Control, can you please scramble Eagle flight from Lavrentiya to my current position. I'm going to have to burn some fuel; I want overlapping combat air patrol coverage in case the US pilots do not respect our kind request."

"Scrambling Eagle flight, roger."

"Element 1, stay with me, Element 2, top cover please, Element 3, go low and maximize stealth profile. All elements, passive tracking only."

Bondarev lit his tail and felt his spine sink into the backrest of his seat as he accelerated toward the incoming Americans. He didn't want them to think they were being attacked, yet, so he kept his wingmen in tight formation and switched his radio to the Guard international communications frequency as soon as his system indicated he should be in range of the Americans, which was about fifty miles and closing rapidly.

"US aircraft approaching Saint Lawrence, this is the commander of Russian Air Force operations over our rescue zone. We kindly request you to hold station at least fifty miles back from Saint Lawrence Island so as not to compromise our submarine rescue operation," Bondarev said in slightly accented English. He had learned from a British teacher at the fighter academy, and then polished his language working with Syrian pilots and ground controllers in combat in the Middle East. Not to mention the American girlfriend he'd had when stationed briefly in Moscow, but that was another story.

"Unidentified Russian aircraft," the American fighter commander immediately replied. "You are ordered to depart US airspace immediately or risk being fired upon." At that moment, a threat warning sounded in Bondarev's helmet and his heads-up display showed that his flight was being tracked with active airborne targeting radar.

"Stay in passive mode," Bondarev said to his pilots, "but unsafe weapons and prepare to engage on my orders." The six Russian machines were linked via a data net that coordinated their targeting so that two long-range and two short-range missiles were allocated to each American aircraft. Satisfied they were bracketed, Bondarev turned his attention back to the radio. The Americans were twenty miles out now and within reach of medium-range missiles but he was not seeing missile-targeting radar warnings, so they had not armed their missiles yet. They would soon be within short-range infrared missile range, though – which was the equivalent of airborne knife fighting – and any short-range missile launch warnings would give him milliseconds to react.

"US aircraft, we cannot comply. I am advised this safety perimeter has been agreed personally between the Presidents of Russia and the United States. I ask you to check with a senior officer and to respect the safety perimeter." Bondarev did not say 'or else', but suspected he did not have to.

There was an ominous silence on the Guard frequency as the two flights continued to converge at supersonic speeds. Bondarev's infrared tracking system suddenly kicked in, picking up the incoming American aircraft before he could see them. They were two thousand feet below him, five miles away and rising to meet him head-on.

"Element 1, break left, Element 2, break right, Element 3, hold station, all elements prepare for defensive maneuvers," Bondarev ordered and hauled his own three-plane element into a sweeping and nonthreatening banking turn that presented their broadside profiles to the incoming Americans. Splitting the formation would force the enemy to do the same, though, so it wasn't a completely defensive move. Bondarev felt his gut tighten as he saw the US squadron split into two flights of three aircraft each, matching heading and speed with the Russian fighters, but staying behind them in a superior firing position.

Bondarev relaxed a little, or as much as was possible with an armed enemy on his tail.

"US flight commander, this is Colonel Ivan Smirnov of the Russian 3rd Air and Air Defense Forces Command," Bondarev lied. "I ask again for you to stay with us here, outside the agreed perimeter of rescue operations. You can see I am taking pains to convince you we are not interested in a hostile engagement."

"Is that right, Ivan?" came the drawl of the American behind him. "Then you wouldn't mind ordering the three-plane flight you have low on our six to break away, would you?"

Bondarev chuckled; so the Americans could see his fighters down low and they didn't like it. Well, let them stay worried about that. "I will happily do so when you confirm that US aircraft will respect the no-fly zone agreed between our two Presidents for the duration of this rescue operation."

There were several minutes of silence again. Bondarev pulled his element around slowly in a wide racetrack circle, the US aircraft trailing behind him, staying in a firing position. All it would take was an American with a twitchy trigger finger and he would get a missile up his backside. He checked his fuel state. He could keep this up for another thirty minutes, by which time his second in command leading Eagle flight, a further six Su-57s, should arrive to replace him on station over Saint Lawrence and he would have to withdraw to refuel. The arrival of new Russian aircraft was certain to make the Americans even more nervous.

"Swan 1 from Raptor Control, I am showing another 12 bogies headed for your operations area. Preliminary analysis indicates F-22s, probably Air National Guard. They will be within missile range in 15 minutes."

Right then the US commander came back on the radio. "I have been authorized to advise, Colonel Smirnov, that we will temporarily accede to your request. You are currently at the limit of the authorized incursion area, please do not stray closer to US territorial airspace. We will be holding station here until you withdraw." With that, the US fighter formation throttled back and settled a more comfortable distance behind Bondarev's fighters – not so close as to provoke any hasty reactions, but still in a perfect firing position if their orders should change. Bondarev also noted they had not switched off their targeting radars.

The submarine ruse had worked – for now! "Acknowledged, US aircraft commander," Bondarev said. "Your cooperation is appreciated." Bondarev smiled, ignoring the radar warning tone still chiming in his ears. They had the overconfident American pilots exactly where they wanted them.

While Yevgeny Bondarev was managing the first interception of the air war, Perri pulled himself from the freezing water at the opposite side of the bay and threw his rifle up onto the rocks. His fingers were numb and he struggled to get a grip on the stone. All the way across the bay he had expected to hear the crack of rifle fire and feel the thud of a bullet between his shoulder blades. Stroking fast, zigzagging in the water, he couldn't see where the Russian soldiers who had been doubling down the runway toward Gambell had gone, but he hoped they had better things to do than chase him down. Finally he got his hands working and hauled himself over the sharp rocks to the cover of some old shipping containers that had been dumped there. Pulling open a rusting door, he crawled inside, stripping off his freezing wet clothes. Naked now, he unrolled the sealskin blanket from around his rifle and shook the worst of the water from it. The wrapping had done what it was supposed to – the rifle was dry. Perri turned the blanket inside out and wound it around himself. He let himself shiver inside the blanket, body heat returning to the surface of his skin. After several minutes he gathered up his wet clothes and rung them as dry as he could. August on Saint Lawrence, middle of the morning, it was only about 40-45 degrees out of the wind. He needed to get somewhere warm. Staying outside in the ever-present wind would mean he could be hit with hypothermia. Wincing, he dropped the blanket, pulled on his wet clothes, then wrapped the blanket around himself again. He began shaking uncontrollably and squatted, letting the tremors settle and pass. He had to keep moving!

When he felt able, he stood, took up his rifle and slung it over his shoulders. Peering out of the door of the container, he saw nothing unusual. Shouting? He thought he heard some shouting from the center of the village, about two miles away. He looked in the opposite direction. Across the harbor road and a few hundred yards up a slight hill was the town's old abandoned gas station. When everyone had finally gone over to hydrogen fuel cells and renewables, the old gas station and its diesel generator were stripped bare and then forgotten.

It would do, for now.

Private Zubkhov wasn't cold, but he wasn't much happier than Perri. He knew his comrades were in the village, rousing the small local population out of their houses and into the big village school gymnasium. There were no police, there should be no fighting, he knew that. But *that* was his mission, not this... salvage duty. Behind him, the Russian military machine ground into action, fat-bellied helicopters disgorging the men and materials they would need to secure the airfield. He saw pallets of tents and food being unloaded beside crates of arms and ammunition. From one helicopter, troops in the green overalls of load crews were pulling out crated parts for an anti-aircraft missile system. Down the runway, Zubkhov saw two or three crews throwing down sandbags and preparing portable Verba-C surface-to-air missiles, but despite their advanced multispectral optical seeker – ultraviolet, near infrared, and mid-infrared – he knew they would offer scant protection against stealth fighters or stealth cruise missiles until the air defense unit got a satellite dish up and networked the Verba into the data feed from longer-range airborne radar and satellite surveillance. He heard shouting from the direction of one of the choppers as a crate threatened to tip and fall and men struggled beneath it. *Forget that,* he was in no hurry to help with the grunt work. He was Spetsnaz, dammit.

He looked with professional interest at the wrecked ATV and wondered briefly exactly where he had hit it. He had aimed for the bulbous engine housing behind the man's legs, and one of his two shots had apparently connected. He looked it over from the side he was standing on, and saw nothing. Then he walked around the ATV and saw with satisfaction the big black hole his bullet had made, leaking some sort of engine fluid. He pulled the machine back upright – no easy task, it felt like it weighed a ton – and did what his commanding officer had ordered him to do, checking the compartment under the seat for maps or papers.

It wasn't a wasted effort. Inside there were some American cigarettes, a large hunting knife with a razor-sharp edge on one side and a serrated saw on the other, and a broken fishing reel. The knife had a delicately carved whalebone handle. He hefted it, feeling the balance. A fine souvenir from his first ever 'kill' – even if it was only a glorified motorbike he had shot. There was no map in the compartment, nor did he expect there to be. The locals had all grown up on this wind-blasted rock in the middle of the Bering Sea and there were no roads between the only two villages anyway, so why would they need a map?

Shots! Zubkhov threw himself flat, scrambling to keep the wrecked bike between him and the sound of the gunfire. He kept his head down, trying to identify the weapon. It was Russian, a light anti-air gun. Sticking his head up, he saw one of the hastily erected gun emplacements by the runway open fire again at a target barely visible above. It looked like a light four-rotor commercial freight drone, not much more than a teardrop-shaped bulb the size of a car with wings. The second burst from the anti-air gun hit it as it was descending toward the runway and it tumbled from the sky to smash into the sea about a hundred meters offshore. There was some sardonic cheering from the gun crew but Zubkhov shook his head as he stood up. The first anti-air kill of the war was a glorified shopping trolley. Hooyah.

Something flapping off to his right by the overturned sled caught his eye. He hadn't noticed it before. It looked like a jacket, torn to shreds. The man must have been wearing it when he was thrown from his bike, and cast it off before he jumped

112

into the sea. It occurred to Zubkhov there might be something in the pockets; another 'souvenir' perhaps, or maybe even some US dollars? He walked over and picked it up, searching it for pockets. There were two deep external pockets which contained only a box of matches and an old piece of candy, stuck to the lining of the pocket. There was an inside pocket that held about twenty dollars and a piece of paper with what looked like a shipping consignment, but other than that it was empty. Disappointing.

That was when he noticed the patch on the arm of the jacket. He held it up to his face so he could see it better. A polar bear, holding a globe in its claws. Around it were the words, *Aircraft Control and Warning Squadron.* It looked military. Zubkhov felt his heart jump. No wonder the man had fled. He was US military! Their briefing had been clear on this, there was no military presence expected at Gambell, and only a token force manning the early warning station at Savoonga.

Well, the bloody briefing had been wrong! There was at least one US serviceman on the loose in Gambell.

Zubkhov looked around for Captain Demchenko, eyes searching among the dozens of men swarming over crates and boxes on the runway as dust and gravel were blown around by the rotors of the transports. His eyes landed on his CO, and he started running.

He knew it. He *should* have shot the bastard!

OPENING VOLLEY

"NORAD, I see rotary-winged aircraft on the ground at Savoonga. AI indicates they are Russian Mil-26s, are you getting the feed?" Bunny's voice didn't bely her shock. Russian troop transports at a US air defense facility?

Nuclear submarine incident be damned.

"We copy your feed, A4. We are showing clear airspace to your south, pull back twenty miles south of your current position, stay out of sight and await new tasking."

Bunny made a new waypoint, dragged it across the tactical map with her mouse, then watched as her four machines began moving south from Savoonga, using terrain-following laser to hop over hills and into depressions to stay off Russian radar. They hadn't picked up any targeting radar over Savoonga, so if Russian aircraft or ground-based radar was operating there, they didn't get a return off the small profiles of Bunny's Fantoms.

"Russian *ground* forces? What the hell?!" Rodriguez said, saying out loud what O'Hare and Halifax were both thinking.

"I can't think of any maritime rescue scenario that would require Russian troops to put down inside the perimeter of a US military installation," Halifax said. "But it explains why NORAD can't raise Savoonga on comms."

"Sirs and Ma'ams, I'm no expert on geopolitics," the Australian aviator commented. "But I do have two heavily armed Fantoms at the end of my kite string. You might want to ask for a review of the rules of engagement."

While the intel from Bunny's report was being processed back at Elmendorf-Richardson Air Force Base, alerting NORAD about the presence of uninvited Russian troops on US soil for the first time in history, Colonel Yevgeny Bondarev was playing cat and mouse with the US Air Force in the Bering Strait between Saint Lawrence and the Alaskan coast.

His own rules of engagement were anything but standard. He was free to do what he felt necessary to ensure the undisturbed operation of Russian ground forces in the theater, including pre-emptive attacks on American Air Force targets if he deemed them a threat. Right now, he could imagine USAF officers were frantically checking with their superiors in the Pentagon to validate Bondarev's claim that their two Presidents had agreed to a temporary US no-fly zone over Saint Lawrence. Bondarev himself had no idea whether the Russian President had even made a call to his US counterpart, but assumed that if the cover story was to be credible, he would need to have done so.

The only warning that Bondarev was likely to get if the US high command didn't buy their cover story was the high piercing chime of a missile launch warning in his ears before his combat AI seized control of the aircraft and sent it into a screaming spiral earthward. Bondarev didn't plan to be caught at a complete disadvantage, though.

"Eagle Flight, please assume a position above and behind our American escort." On his tactical display he saw his newly arriving reinforcements peel up and slowly slide to starboard, wedging the US aircraft between two formations of Russian fighters. It was a classic 'Mexican standoff' and would require the US commander to react. *How* he reacted would tell Bondarev if he was dealing with an American with an aggressive or defensive mindset. An aggressive commander would decide he still had a perfect firing solution on the bulk of the Russian fighter force, even though he was threatened from the rear. A defensive mindset would mean the American was more worried about his own planes and pilots than about challenging the Russian fighters, and he would break away to try to re-establish a tactical advantage, probably by withdrawing to long-range missile distance.

A few tense minutes passed, then Bondarev heard a voice drawl over the Guard channel, "Ivan, your trailing element is so far up my tailpipe that I have to assume you Russians are all a bunch of ho-mo-sexual ass bandits. Please confirm." Checking his tactical display, Bondarev saw no sign of the US flight breaking position. He smiled.

Very well. An aggressive commander. Let us see who blinks first.

"Raptor Control, please scramble a further nine Mig-41s from Lavrentiya and vector to my position."

Alicia marveled at how cool Bunny remained. She had her wedge of four drones hidden in ground clutter in a shallow valley south of Savoonga. She had a combat AI system that was filtering all the inputs, making sure she didn't drown in data and only had her attention directed to critical information, but Rodriguez knew her own head would have exploded trying to keep track of it all, at the same time as sending orders to her machines and being ready to execute any one of a hundred tactical options if needed.

"A4, this is NORAD," a cool voice broke in over the radio. "We are showing nine more Russian fast movers inbound to Saint Lawrence, bearing 268 degrees, altitude 40,000 feet. Designating enemy flight Beta. We have six F-22s inbound from Eielson to join aircraft already on station over Saint Lawrence... A4 we need you to..." There was a pause. On one of Bunny's screens Rodriguez saw the icons for the new Russian fighters appear, speeding toward Saint Lawrence from the Russian mainland. To the east, she saw six icons marking the US reinforcements. There was a massive furball building, and all it would take would be one slip of the trigger finger to turn things deadly serious.

Rodriguez felt the situation unraveling, and heard a new tone of urgency in Bunny's voice as she broke in on the air controller. "What do you want me to do, NORAD? Head east to help our fighters there, mix it up with the Russian beta flight or stay where I am?!"

"A4, you are to stay in the weeds but prepare to engage enemy flight beta approaching from the west," the voice said. "Lock them up and await orders. You are not authorized to engage. Repeat, you are *not* authorized to engage. NORAD out."

"Acknowledged, NORAD, lock up enemy B flight, do *not* engage. A4 out," Bunny said and pulled up her targeting interface. "Thanks for making up your freaking mind," she muttered, sending orders to her primary Fantom to turn 180 degrees, going from tracking east to tracking west in the blink of an eye. Unfortunately, the radical maneuver meant there was a risk she had popped up on the radar of a Russian air defense system if it was monitoring the combat area but she needed to get in position to lock and engage the approaching Russian reinforcements. The Russian reserve flight was soon in Cuda air-to-air missile range and she drew target boxes around them based on the data feed from NORAD's long-range radar.

There was no need to activate her own tracking radar and give herself away, yet.

Rodriguez turned to Halifax. "Sir, do you want us to launch more Fantoms? We have two more in the queue."

"Easy, Boss," Halifax murmured. "They'll call for more cavalry if they think they need it."

Rodriguez had launched the first two Fantoms with mixed air-to-air/air-to-ground ordnance. That gave Bunny eight of the multirole intermediate to short-ranged Cudas, and nine targets to fire them at. All four of her birds were armed with laser-targeted guns too. Her fingers tapped at her keyboard and touch screens, selecting targets and dedicating a single missile to each in case she was ordered to engage. The new Cuda had seen limited use over Turkey, but Bunny had read reports showing that at intermediate range it had a less than 75% kill ratio against the Su-57. Her plan was to disrupt the Russian reserves approaching from the west, and that meant distracting as many of the Russian pilots as she could in the first wave of her attack, hoping for a kill or two, and maybe the others would bug out.

First wave? If she was forced to fire off her full inventory of Cudas, she didn't have a second wave!

Bondarev's situation had gone from dominance to a knife-edge balance in a matter of minutes. His nine Su-57s had been facing off against six US Air Force F-35s, but six older National Guard F-22s were also now on the way. Another nine Mig-41s had been scrambled, but the approaching Americans would be within missile range first. In fact, they already were. And their missiles could home on the targets given to them by the fighters on his tail.

It was time to test his adversary's mettle. He turned his flight west, closing the gap toward his own approaching fighters, moving toward the east coast of Saint Lawrence Island. As expected, the Americans followed. He opened a Guard channel. "American flight leader, you are entering the safety perimeter for Russian rescue operations, agreed with your superiors. You must turn back, or you could be considered hostile."

"Negative, Colonel 'Smirnov'. Hostile is what I call a Russian fighter over US airspace," came the reply.

"Nonetheless, we are conducting a high-risk rescue operation in the seas off Saint Lawrence and we cannot allow any interference. If you do not respect the rules of engagement agreed by our superiors, you *will* be fired upon."

The USAF pilots were either foolish, or suicidal. They must know they were being targeted by Russian passive infrared systems on the aircraft, both in front of them and behind them. Not to mention the long-range radar on Bondarev's A-50 Airborne Control aircraft, which was able to burn through their stealth countermeasures using the data from Bondarev's flight to enhance the weak returns from its own radar. A tense minute went past. Bondarev tightened the webbing of his G-frame over his chest, expecting at any moment to hear the missile launch warning that could be the last thing he ever heard.

He realized he was holding his breath, and let it out all at once when he saw a flicker on his tactical heads-up display, spun his head around, and saw the glint off the canopies of the American fighters as they peeled away, moving back toward the Alaskan coast.

"Don't worry, Ivan," said the voice of the American flight leader, in the clear. "We're not going far. Try coming a bit further east, we'll be ready to welcome you."

"With respect, this is bulldust," Bunny said, watching the icons for the Russian and American fighters diverge. "Russian fighters over US territory and *we're* bugging out?"

"What are our options here?" Rodriguez whispered to Halifax. She was the only other pilot in the room. Theoretically, she could help fly the drones in an emergency, but she wasn't certified on these platforms and was from an older generation of pilots: strictly one girl, one machine. What Bunny was doing now, she couldn't dream of matching.

"You heard," Halifax said. "We are not to engage."

The Russian B flight had moved into a racetrack orbit over Gambell township on the east of the island, just behind the main Russian fighter force. "I could blow a big-arse hole in their B-team right now, ma'am," Bunny said. "I have a wedge of Fantoms right underneath them." Rodriguez saw the icons for the second flight of Russian fighters sweep over the top of Bunny's Fantoms without even realizing they were there.

"I think the Russians might react poorly to that, Lieutenant," Rodriguez said. "If our President did spit-swear a deal with theirs." A thought occurred to her. "But make a run over Gambell, will you? I'd like to know why the Russians have parked a flight of Migs right on top of a small Yup'ik fishing village."

"Yes, ma'am," Bunny said happily. "I'll throw the feed up here." Without taking her eyes off her virtual-reality visor, she pointed up to the two 2D screens showing the feed from the drones screaming toward Gambell. They showed two different views of the town, as Bunny had programmed two of the Fantoms to come in from the south, at wave-top level, while the others approached from the north and would be popping up to 5,000 feet to get a good look at the village and surrounds.

She gave them a rendezvous south of the island, over the Bering Strait and out of harm's way.

Rodriguez didn't know where to look. On one 2D tactical screen the heads-up displays of the Fantoms were still showing the target boxes for the two Russian air groups, one in the east, one in the west. On the screen Bunny had just pointed at, the view was split into four, showing the nose camera feed from the four drones approaching Gambell in near real time. They showed various versions of rushing water with a smudge of land on the horizon. Suddenly the ground vanished and then there was nothing but gray sky as the Fantoms popped up at the start of their recon run.

"F1 and F2 coming up on Gambell," Bunny said, and Rodriguez glued her eyes to the screen showing the feed from the four recon drones as the land slowly came into focus and the small village grew larger as they rapidly closed. Suddenly one of the four squares flashed with static and went black.

"Damn," Bunny said. She started tapping her keys, but the screen stayed black. She jabbed her touchscreen and dragged a finger across it. "Breaking off!"

"What?" Rodriguez asked. "Did we lose the feed?"

"No," Bunny replied, her voice ice cold and angry. "We just lost a damn Fantom!"

Perri Tungyan shivered uncontrollably. He needed to get warm, but that would have to wait. He was watching an invasion unfold right in front of him. He'd scurried up the hill to the old gas station and kicked in the door. It wasn't locked, just stuck. He'd been up there with other kids a few years back, looking for anything that could be salvaged and sold, but the place had been stripped clean. There was a shop and cashier area with broken windows looking out and down on the town, and Perri crouched behind the cashier desk with his wet blanket around him, his body heat warming the seal fur just enough to stop him going into shock.

The clutter of buildings that was the village of Gambell hid from view what was happening down there, but he could clearly see the military transports and soldiers down at the airstrip unloading crates and vehicles from them. As each chopper was emptied, it would take off and head west, and a new helicopter would fly in and take its place.

He almost missed the Verba ground-to-air missile leap into the air and zoom toward the horizon.

From the corner of his eye, at the far end of the runway across the bay, he picked up a flash and then a blossom of white smoke. A finger of light, almost like a laser, flashed across the sky and disappeared in a second, leaving a trail of wispy vapor in the air behind it, showing where the missile was headed. Looking at where it had come from, Perri saw soldiers standing around some kind of tripod by a small trailer, struggling to lift another missile out of a crate and fit it to the rails of a launcher mounted on the tripod and connected to a small antenna.

Suddenly he saw them look up, and then punch their fists in the air. They began clapping each other's shoulders until one who must have been their officer slapped one across the head and they bent to the task of reloading their missile launcher again. Whatever they had shot at, they must have hit it.

"Shit's getting real now!" Perri heard a voice say behind him, and he spun around.

"NORAD, my systems are reporting the destruction of one of my drones by possible enemy fire over Gambell!" Bunny said. "Can you parse the data and check for Russian ground-to-air missile radar signatures?"

"Roger A4, parsing," came the reply. "Pull back to your former waypoint."

Alicia Rodriguez had her eyes glued to the video feed from the remaining Fantoms. They had dropped back down to wave-top level and were pulling out to sea south of the island.

"Acknowledged, NORAD, completing egress," Bunny said. "I've got enemy flight B moving down through 20,000. They're wide awake now, it must have been a missile strike." Her threat display was not showing either ground or air radar with a lock on her remaining three drones but that couldn't last, with a flight of what looked like at least nine Mig-41s headed her way.

"Got your feed, A4, copy your analysis," the air controller said. "We are showing a ground-to-air missile launch at the time you lost contact with your bird. Break off one bird and give us a high-speed pass over Gambell please, we want to get a sniff of the ordnance Ivan has on the ground there. We'll have a satellite in place in twenty minutes, but for now, you are the only eyes over that island."

"Roger, NORAD, do we have any assets in the ops area capable of jamming Russian anti-air systems?" Bunny asked.

"Negative, A4," the controller said. "You have the only electronic warfare-capable platform in the operations area."

"Request permission to suppress enemy air defenses if identified," Bunny asked. "I have already lost one bird."

"Negative, A4, you are not to open fire on Russian ground or air units, understood?"

"Understood, NORAD. A4 out," Bunny said through gritted teeth.

An alarm sounded as one of her Fantoms parked south of the island reported a radar sweep by one of the Russian fighters bearing down on her. Rodriguez expected Bunny to react, but she ignored it, staying focused on the one drone that was fast approaching Gambell.

"Your Fantoms are being hunted by the Russian fighters," Halifax said.

"Yes, sir," Bunny said. "But all they're seeing are ghosts right now. If they had a fix, you'd see them light me up for real. And as soon as they light up their fire control radars, I'll have a solid Cuda lock. See if we can bluff them into breaking off."

"Don't push it, Lieutenant. It's too soon in this little catfight for us to be throwing more hardware away," Rodriguez cautioned.

"Yes, ma'am," Bunny said, pushing her master throttle forward. "Fantom 1-3 going Mach 1.5. Feet dry in five!" she murmured, then a few seconds later, "I have eyes on the target. Jamming." The Fantom had limited radar-jamming capability but it wouldn't help at all against optical or infrared guided missiles.

Six eyes glued themselves to the video feed as the Fantom popped up, swept in over Gambell airstrip and banked hard, curving over the village itself.

"Missile launch!" Bunny called. Her combat AI deployed flares and chaff then threw the Fantom into a wrenching 180-degree turn, sending it out over the sea again. After a couple of seconds it was clear the missile would miss, and Rodriguez caught her breath again. Bunny spooled the recon data backwards on a screen.

"A4 to NORAD, I am showing multiple aircraft on the ground, AI is calling them rotary-winged heavy transports. From the vision, I'm going to guess more Mil-26s." She replayed the video from the overflight. "At least five, with two more inbound, one moving west, about ten miles out. I have ground target heat signatures, probably motor vehicles, mostly stationary ... and ... *bingo*. I got an optical and electronic signature lock on a Russian Verba ground-to-air mobile missile unit. Probably networked given the range at which the swine brought down one of my Fantoms. You got enough, NORAD, or do you want another pass? I'm showing those Migs moving in for a closer look."

There was a moment of static before the controller came back. "Reviewing now... A4 we need another pass, further east. Sending you coordinates."

"*Damn*," Bunny said to herself. "One dead Fantom not enough?" Her console chimed as another short-range air search radar swept across her machine. With every passing minute headed north out to sea she was increasing the separation between the patrolling Russians and her recon bird, but they were decreasing the separation to her two drones orbiting uselessly in the south.

"Coming around. Lighting burner. Four minutes to objective," Bunny announced, her eyes flicking from screen to screen as she monitored both the threats to her two parked fighters and the ingress of the recon drone. The newly enhanced Russian Verba man-portable missile system was now able to link up with other ground and air radar data sources to track its targets, turning it from what had once been a nuisance into a deadly threat.

"Air or ground radar will pick you up at that airspeed," Rodriguez pointed out.

"And that Verba will swat me if I go in subsonic, ma'am," Bunny replied.

Rodriguez had to leave the mission execution to her pilot, but she couldn't help pointing out the obvious. The Russian fighters had begun moving with intent toward the two orbiting Fantoms.

Rodriguez looked over at Halifax and caught his eye.

"If those Russian fighters engage, Lieutenant, you are to evade and withdraw," Halifax said.

"Yes, sir," O'Hare replied. Rodriguez couldn't help noting the pilot was biting her lip now…

"Jeez, you scared me, man," Perri said, turning to see fifteen-year-old Dave Iworrigan looking at him with wide eyes from under a mop of unwashed black hair, his little fat cheeks red with either cold or excitement. "What are you doing up here?"

The other boy looked embarrassed, and shrugged. "I hang out up here a lot," he said, pointing into the storeroom out back where there was an old sofa and a table. "For the peace and quiet, you know?" Perri knew. Dave came from a big family, who were legendary in Gambell for their all-out brawls. Dave's brothers were as peaceful as lambs toward strangers, but

124

brutal toward each other. As the youngest, Dave had apparently decided flight was a better survival strategy than fight. He looked out the broken windows of the gas station again. "Sound of the choppers woke me up. I saw you run for it, then total your ATV and dive into the bay."

Perri looked past him into the dark storeroom. "You got a sleeping bag back there?"

"Not there, someone would find it," the boy said. "I've got it stashed."

"I'm freezing here, Dave," Perri said impatiently.

Dave looked at him as though deciding whether to let Perri in on his secret, and then sighed. "OK, follow me."

They went outside to a hatch in the dirt. It had an old padlock on it and Dave pulled out a key and undid the lock, putting it in his pocket.

"Welcome to my crib," he smiled, pulling up the hatch.

Perri saw a ladder going down a narrow shaft and a weak light below, and looked at Dave doubtfully.

It smelled and it was dark.

"Go on, it's bigger at the bottom," he said.

It wasn't like he had much choice. He'd die of hypothermia if he didn't get warm, and soon. He went down the ladder, his eyes adjusting to the weak light, and at the bottom found himself inside what must have been an old gasoline tank. It was about the size of a small fishing hut, and Dave had moved in a mattress, some small boxes for furniture and storage, a folding chair and some bedding. Perri sniffed; it stank of teenage boy, but not the gasoline smell Perri expected. The light was coming from a construction light hooked up to a car battery, sitting beside some solar cells and a cable which Dave obviously used to keep it charged. A 20-gallon plastic bladder of water sat beside them.

"I figure it's like twenty years since there was gasoline in here," Dave said. "Don't worry. I dropped a burning rag in here just in case there was fumes or something, but it didn't even get a flash. It's just a bit rusty is all."

Perri walked over and grabbed the sleeping bag on top of the mattress.

"Oh man, you'll get it wet," Dave said, but he helped Perri unzip it, took his wet sealskin blanket and wrapped the bag around him. He sat Perri down in the chair.

"What else you got in the boxes there?" Perri asked when he finally stopped shaking.

"Got a gas stove, some packet soups, instant oats, that kind of thing," the other boy said. "I was about to make some breakfast when those choppers rolled in."

"Got your phone?"

"Yeah, but…"

"Got a gun?" Perri asked.

"Of course I've got a gun," Dave answered, pointing at a long fish packing case, like it was the dumbest question in the world.

"Ammo?"

"Yeah. Couple boxes I guess."

"What caliber?"

"Got some .300 for this rifle, some 30 oh six for my other rifle. Why?"

Perri pulled the sleeping bag tighter around himself, and then heard the unmistakable sound of a sonic boom coming from the direction of the village. He pointed up toward the rolling thunder. "Because I think we're at war, is why."

"Air-to-air missile launch!" Bunny said as her Fantom swung around to start its second approach and was immediately picked up on radar by the approaching Mig-41 flight. "Jamming active. Countermeasures deploying." She was talking to herself as much as to the people in the room with her. She turned her helmet to look at data on a virtual screen on her right, then back to the heads-up display for the Fantom. "K-77s. Four. We're *dead.*"

She pointed up at the missile tracks, spearing in from the Russian fighter icons, spread in a fan with Bunny's Fantom at its point. "Question is only whether we can uplink the recon data before they splash us."

The K-77M was a new short-range phased-array, all-aspect missile that used infrared, optical and radar guidance to home on its target. Rodriguez knew the best way, maybe the *only* way, to survive a volley of K-77Ms at this range was to kill the fighters shooting them before they could even fire. And it was too late for that.

With nothing to lose, O'Hare pushed the Fantom higher to get the best possible imagery. They all watched the video feed intently as the town sped toward them, seeing choppers lifting off, men scurrying about and light transport vehicles lined up along the side of the runway like the Russians were holding a Gaz Tigr-M truck fire-sale.

Hammering through Mach 1.6 the Fantom flew over the top of the town just as the tracks of the incoming K-77M missiles on the tactical screen crossed its flight path. The video feed went dead. "A4 to NORAD, we are out of the fight," Bunny told her NORAD controller. "Tell me you got that feed!"

"A4, I confirm recon data package received. You are clear to return to base with your remaining birds. Nice job, A4, NORAD out."

Rodriguez started as Bunny punched the desk next to her joystick. "NORAD, those bloody Russians just shot down *two* of my Fantoms. I have mapped a Verba missile crew in at least one position on that isthmus and the electronic signature is telling me it is networked, not just some random guy with a missile launcher on his shoulder. My two remaining birds are carrying both air-to-air and long-range anti-surface ordnance. I am in a position to engage both Russian air and ground defenses. In accordance with standard rules of engagement I request permission to engage hostile enemy air defense assets!"

There was a tense moment of silence. Halifax stepped forward and put his hand on Bunny's shoulder, just as the radio crackled to life again. "Negative, A4, you are not to engage. You will return to base and await further tasking."

O'Hare pushed her keyboard away from her. "Roger, NORAD, A4 out." Then she lifted Halifax's hand off her shoulder without taking her eyes from the vision and data from her remaining drones. "Permission to indulge in profanity, sir?" she asked.

"Patience, O'Hare," Halifax said. "Russians keep this up, payback *will* come."

"Not soon enough, sir," Bunny replied. The only good news was that the Mig flight had been drawn to the recon drone, allowing the other two drones to escape without detection. Even as she checked on the status of her returning Fantoms and keyed in the dogleg return journey, Bunny was rewinding the vision her machines took over both Savoonga and Gambell and getting her AI to quantify the visual and signals intelligence it had gathered.

For the first time in an hour, she pushed back from her desk, pulled off her helmet, blew her spiky fringe from her eyes and took a long pull on the warm soda that had been sitting at her elbow since the catapult had fired her first drone through the chute.

She looked at the data from her overflights as it flowed across multiple screens. "So tell me, sirs and ma'ams," she asked, staring up at the numbers. "If you were reacting to an unexpected maritime emergency in foreign waters, even one involving a nuclear sub, is it likely you would be able to pull together at least 23 Mil-26 choppers, a Beriev Airborne Control aircraft, a squadron or two of front-line Su-57s and Mig-41s armed with the nastiest air-to-air missiles in the Russian arsenal, *plus* at least two battalions of special forces troops supported by fully networked Verba ground-to-air missile systems?" She spun her chair around and looked at them both. "Because personally, I don't think it's very likely at all. I think it's more likely Russia has just invaded your US of A."

STANDOFF

As Bunny was bringing her Fantoms home, Bondarev was finishing his mission debrief. It had been an entirely successful mission – on paper. US fighters were patrolling impotently up and down the Alaskan coast, but so far had not dared to test the exclusion zone around Saint Lawrence. The Russian President had persuaded his counterpart they were doing their utmost to contain the sub emergency but needed unfettered access to ground staging facilities on Saint Lawrence and undisturbed freedom of navigation in the sea and air around it.

Russian troops had rounded up the few hundred residents of Gambell and Savoonga without great drama. They had found fewer than fifty US military personnel at the radar station at Savoonga, only twelve of whom were security personnel. A short firefight had broken out when one of the radar station personnel at Savoonga who had camped out overnight hunting reindeer in the hills to the south had returned and decided to engage the encamped Russian troops, but he had been subdued with a non-lethal gunshot injury. The brief firefight had not impacted the operation. In Gambell they had herded the residents into the school gym. The population of Savoonga, including the military personnel stationed there, was considerably larger, so they were being kept in barracks inside the US military cantonment.

It couldn't have gone more smoothly, but Bondarev was not happy, and he was letting Arsharvin know it.

"I want to know how the Americans managed to get a flight of drones under our long-distance radar, through our Verba coverage, and fly them right down the damn runway at Gambell!" His voice was so loud it rattled the windows of the hut and he saw men outside look in, before deciding it was probably better they found somewhere else to be.

"We shot two of them down, Comrade Colonel," Arsharvin pointed out, carefully. "A Verba unit claimed one, your pilots the other."

"My pilots reported possible returns from at least four, and up to six different stealth aircraft operating at a low level while we were engaged," Bondarev continued. "We were just lucky they either weren't armed or didn't have orders to put a fistful of missiles up our asses." He took a breath, tried to speak more slowly. "I have reports of American drones overflying both Savoonga and Gambell. We had a brief window of time on Saint Lawrence to get our troops and aircraft down and out of sight before the Americans got satellites in position to see what was happening, but those drones got it all! There is no value in a no-fly zone that the enemy can penetrate with impunity!"

"With respect, Yevgeny," Arsharvin complained. "You should be chewing out the air defense commander, not me. If he'd got his Verbas networked quicker..."

"I have chewed him out," Bondarev said. "But now I'm looking at my head of operational intelligence, and I'm asking him to tell me how American drones managed to get into position over Saint Lawrence so quickly. The nearest US military airfields are Eielson or Elmendorf-Richardson, 600 bloody miles away! My strategy was based around identifying and protecting us from threats from that quarter and we succeeded. So *where* did those drones come from?!"

Arsharvin was struggling. He put his hands behind his neck, looking up at the ceiling. "Nome is the most likely launch point, but we have no reports of military aircraft or personnel being stationed there. We know they have been experimenting with truck-mounted launchers. It's possible they have positioned several of these at Nome, I suppose. Or at the Coast Guard station at Port Clarence? They are both only a hundred and fifty miles away," he offered.

Bondarev calmed a little. It did make some sort of sense. Drones, truck-mounted or otherwise, could easily be hidden in a hangar at the civilian airport, maybe even launched remotely if they were unarmed. And the Coast Guard base at Port Clarence was a US Navy facility – he probably hadn't paid it enough attention. "Then check that Port Clarence is on our targeting list for the first ground strike," he told Arsharvin. "And before we go in, get me some updated imagery. Show me some truck-mounted drones refueling, or empty truck-launchers lined up on the side of a runway in Nome, and I will relax."

If Bondarev was unhappy, Rodriguez was even more so. Bringing their birds home had not been a smooth process this time. One of the Fantoms had lost forward vision as it approached the Rock, meaning Bunny had to bring it in blind. A software kludge had been needed to get it to ignore its collision warning system as it autopiloted itself towards the Slot, and they had wasted precious time and fuel while O'Hare and a programmer hammered out the workaround, debugged and uploaded it. But it had made them realize they needed the software update applied to all of their drones, because any one of them could end in the same situation and they had to have a way to tell it that it wasn't about to wipe itself out on a cliff face. As the Fantom had glided into the opening, Bunny had grabbed manual control as soon as she had a visual, but it was rough. The drone had slapped onto the water hard, bending its ski support gear. Rodriguez figured two days, maybe more, for her small maintenance crew to replace the supports and forward video system and get it airworthy again.

There was not a lot of jubilation under the Rock that night, even though they had delivered on their mission objectives. It had cost them two Fantoms down, one damaged and out of play. Halifax picked up on it as he walked into the ready room that doubled as a duty galley down by the deck. He looked around him, seeing a distinct lack of laughter and teasing, and a whole lot of tired people slumped on their elbows spooning food into their mouths and not really even talking with each other. He walked over to Rodriguez, who was going through an inventory checklist with one of her ordnancemen.

"Officer on the deck!" she announced as he approached, and she snapped to attention.

"As you were, Boss," he said. "Can we have a word?" She dismissed her aircrewman and looked at him expectantly.

"Why the glum faces?" he asked.

"Two dead, one wounded, sir," she replied simply.

Halifax blinked. "They're *machines*, Rodriguez."

"And we know that. But if we have this attrition rate on every combat mission, this base will pretty quickly be out of business. It's supposed to be a covert center of operations, so we can't be flying new drones in here every few days or we'll get found pretty quickly. Could bring in the airframes by submarine, put them together here again, but that would be too slow for combat conditions. And we'd need double the personnel. The ambition is for this facility eventually to be fully autonomous if we can one day solve the problem of how to automate the aircraft recovery – right now we can't even guarantee to keep it operational when manned."

She was right, Halifax knew that, but he had expected to see a little more optimism among his people. They'd lost two drones, yes, but they'd also gotten vital intelligence and showed what they were capable of under combat conditions. He'd told them they needed to launch faster than they had, but O'Hare and Rodriguez's people had managed to get four drones into the air averaging five minutes between launches, off a single catapult. They needed to shorten the time from a launch order to the first launch, but he couldn't fault their performance once they got the first cartridge on the Cat.

O'Hare. He just realized she wasn't here and he hadn't seen her since the mission debrief. "Where is our pilot?" Halifax asked Rodriguez.

"She's DARPA's pilot, sir, and she's probably resting," Rodriguez replied. "Theirs or not, she's the only jock on the Rock. She knows you could be calling on her again anytime and she has to be mission capable."

"I've asked naval air forces command Coronado to get those reserve pilots here stat," Halifax said. "Some pencil head
132

told me we had to wait for the base to be certified before I could request more personnel. I told him we just certified the base under enemy fire and he'd better put me through to someone who realized the Russians had just invaded US territory." He bit his lip. "The problem is how to get them in without Ivan noticing."

"Can't you just chopper them in, topside? You must have personnel going in and out of the radar station all the time. We're facing off against the Russians a hundred miles south, no one is going to be surprised at some extra traffic on Little Diomede."

"That's exactly the problem. Damn Russian no-fly zone has Coronado rattled; they don't want to risk a shootdown even if we are fifty miles north of the perimeter. We lose anyone, even in an accident, it could start a shooting war. No ships or subs available, I tried." Halifax looked around the room and back to Rodriguez. "For now, your crew here and that hot-headed contract pilot are it." He put a hand on her shoulder. "So I need you to get your people off their mopey asses and ready for war, Boss. Clear?"

"Yes, sir," Rodriguez said. "You're right." She turned to the people scattered around the canteen and raised her voice. "Listen up! Simulated Fantom hex launch in ten minutes. One-zero. Get moving!"

"I'm freezing," came the whining voice for about the fifth time.

"Shut up, Dave, I'm cold too," Perri said through clamped teeth.

"I'm telling you, we should go down there, join the others," the younger boy continued. "At least they have heat, food."

"They're *prisoners*, Dave, do you want to be a Russian prisoner?" Perri asked. He shifted on his stomach, trying to get comfortable, and peered through the scope on his rifle again. The Russian patrol circled the village about every fifteen minutes in its jeep, about a hundred and fifty yards away down the hill. He'd thought about how easy it would be to shoot out one of its tires as it passed in front of them, maybe make it flip – but that trick only worked in movies. He was a good shot, but not Hollywood good.

It was the third day since he'd escaped from the invading Russians. He and Dave had spent the first night and day up in the abandoned gas station, watching what was going on down on the airstrip and in the town. It had been pretty uneventful after they'd seen the Russian anti-aircraft batteries firing off their missiles and then that spy plane had rocketed down the runway from two different directions and got splashed by Russian fighters, missiles slamming into it just as it cleared the town. So the US Air Force, or whoever it was, knew what was going on. The Russians had started piling sandbags and icy dirt around their emplacements on the runway, the last choppers had lifted off, and there had been a lot of shouting down in Gambell, but no shooting.

The next day they saw Russian troops going from house to house in Gambell looking for residents. Anyone they found, they bustled out of their houses or businesses and into jeeps and drove them all to the school at the eastern edge of town.

"Just a matter of time before they check up here," Dave had said. "We are so screwed."

"We could hike out to Savoonga," Perri had said. "I did it with my brothers once, this time of year. It's OK if the weather holds. Takes a few days along the coast track. Or we could steal a boat."

"What makes you think Savoonga will be any different?" Dave asked. "You tried calling but it's like the tower is down. Savoonga is probably full of these guys too."

"Yeah, in the town. But the Air Force has that base up there," Perri pointed out. "Maybe they're holding out. If we could make it there…"

That was as far as the conversation got. Right then, they'd seen a jeep heading out of town coming straight for them.

"In the tank!" Perri had said, pushing Dave out of the gas station office. He looked around him. Coffee mugs! They'd brought a couple of mugs of coffee up with them from Dave's hideout. He grabbed them by their handles and bustled out behind Dave, who flung the hatch open and waited until Perri was on his way down before climbing in himself and locking the hatch from the inside with a lock he'd put there to keep his brothers out in case they came looking for him.

At the bottom of the ladder they waited and listened. It was only six feet from the tank to the ground above, and the hatch didn't have an airtight seal anymore. They heard the crunch of tires on gravel and then at least two voices. The voices didn't sound worried or urgent. In fact, they sounded like they were having an argument.

"That's Russian," Dave whispered and Perri put a hand over his mouth to stop him saying anything else. But he was right. It was easier to pick up Russian radio in Gambell than stations from Alaska, so everyone listened to the Russian pop stations, even if few people spoke more than a few words.

Then they heard boots and the hatch rattled. There was some discussion, and a huge bang as something was hammered down on the hatch cover, maybe a rifle butt. Rust flakes filled the air. Perri was glad it was late summer, because the snow on the ground was mostly melted and their footprints would have been clearly visible. After a bit more rattling, it seemed the troops overhead lost interest in the hatch and moved off.

In another five minutes, they heard the jeep starting up and pulling away.

Dave put a hand on the ladder to head up again, but Perri grabbed him and pointed to the mattress. "Let's wait," he said quietly. "There's no point going up too soon."

While they'd waited, they'd agreed they had to get into town and see what was happening. They'd wait until nightfall, then sneak in through the old fish processing plant that bordered the school. So they had. And if Perri had been pissed at getting his ATV shot up and chased into the sea, he was doubly pissed at what he saw from the windows of the fish plant. Inside the school, they could see the Russians had gathered the whole town, young and old, and crammed them into the school gym. There were no windows in the gym they could look in, but every two hours they saw groups of people being led out of the gym and through the school to the toilets, then back again. Russian troops patrolled around the outside of the school and were stationed on the doors. In one of the groups was his mother and one of Dave's brothers.

That was all he'd needed to see. He'd grabbed Dave by the collar and led him back to the gas station on the outside of town. Down in the tank, he'd started loading his rifle and checking Dave's ammunition.

"What are you doing?" Dave had asked him. "There's hundreds of them. You can't take on a whole army. We might as well just give ourselves up."

"You can give yourself up," Perri said. "They have our families. They tried to kill me. I'm going to start killing them."

But the more they talked, the more Perri realized he would need help. He'd seen a fantastic movie once, about an army sniper team. You had this idea that snipers were these lone wolves who just headed out onto the battlefield with their gun and a bit of dried meat and hid in a bush until some African warlord came past, and then capped him before melting into the bush. But it wasn't like that. Snipers worked in pairs, with one person acting as a spotter with binoculars and the sniper keeping his vision protected and his rifle ready. You couldn't see shit when you were looking down a scope, so you needed a partner to be your wide-angle vision and spot targets for you. The best place for them to set up was on the slopes of Sivuqaq Mountain, looking down on the town from behind. He'd explained this to Dave.

"Yeah, we could do that," Dave had said. "Or, we could just cozy on down here until the US Navy comes steaming into Gambell harbor with one of its big missile destroyers and a few hundred Navy Seals and starts killing them for us."

"You think *America* gives a shit about a couple thousand dumb Yup'ik in the Bering Strait?" He pointed east. "They'll be

136

lining up their tanks and fighters, for sure, but over there in Nome, to protect Alaska. I've got news for you – the cavalry isn't coming, Dave."

"OK, but what's the plan here?" the boy asked. "You kill one of them, ten come after us. Maybe they don't catch us, we kill another one. A hundred come after us. Maybe they get mad, start executing the people in the school. None of this gets our families out of that school."

Perri knew that, but he was too angry to care. "It's called 'asymmetrical warfare', man. A smaller force can keep a bigger force unbalanced, distract them, tie up their troops so they can't do whatever they came here to do."

"You read that in one of your Army recruiting books?" Dave asked. "We aren't a 'smaller force', Perri. We're just two kids hiding in a hole in the ground."

"You aren't a kid anymore, Dave," Perri said, gesturing around him. "Look at this place. You already moved out of home, you just didn't tell anyone yet."

The young boy had seemed to straighten his back when Perri said that. After a bit more talk, he'd decided to help, but they'd agreed just killing Russian troops was pointless and just as likely to force the Russians to start killing their hostages in retaliation. So they'd spent their second night creeping through the town, raiding people's larders and dragging bags of canned or dried food back to the gas station and stashing it in the tank. There had been a couple of near misses and the most dangerous was about 3 a.m. when they'd broken into the rear of the general store. They'd wanted more ammunition, camping gear, water bladders for storing drinking and cooking water, stuff like that. They'd hoped to find guns there too, but while they had left plenty of ammo behind, the Russians had cleaned out the gun lockers. Anyway, Dave and Perri were in there filling big shopping bags with whatever looked useful when there were flashlights and voices outside. Dave ducked down behind the store counter, but Perri was stuck right near the window, reaching for a rainproof jacket on a dummy. Anyone looking in would have seen him. He'd frozen behind the dummy as two soldiers walked past, swinging flashlights from side to side. But they weren't really searching for anything. They walked past the window without a glance and in a few seconds were gone. It freaked Dave and Perri so much, though, they decided they'd pushed their luck far enough for the night and humped their loot back to the tank.

Perri had no idea what had happened to his father and brothers. They'd been out at sea when the Russians arrived. He had to assume they'd come back to the harbor to find themselves hostages like everyone else, but he hadn't seen them being walked to the toilets while he and Dave were watching, so he couldn't be sure.

Now it was the night of the third day, and Dave and Perri had crept out of the gas station and climbed up the slope that led up to Sivuqaq Mountain. Only 600 feet high, it was more like a bluff than a mountain, but it towered over Gambell like a stone guardian. It had been a pain in the ass getting to a position where they could look down over the town, within range of Perri's rifle, but not down amongst the nests of the crested auklets which infested the slopes of the bluff this time of year. Their alarmed chattering would have given the two boys away in moments, so they'd stayed above the nests and then moved downslope when they saw a clear space without too many of the little red-beaked birds sitting on their eggs.

They'd found a perfect spot between and behind some rocks, looking straight over the school, down the road that went through town and out to the airstrip. Their plan was just to try to identify some static targets on this trip, and maybe pick a few good hides they could shoot from.

"Stop moaning and tell me what you see," Perri said, looking through his scope. They had a thick gray tarpaulin pulled over them, the same color as the gritty dirt and sand around them.

"OK, well, I see a bunch of guys pulling nets over some boxes, and there are two jeeps there."

"Where?" Perri moved his scope around, but couldn't see anything in the small circle of glass, and could see even less with his bare eyes.

"To the left, this side of the school."

"I told you, man, you have to use the clock," Perri said patiently. "Straight ahead is 12. Left is 11, 10, 9, right is 1, 2, 3, OK? And tell me high, or low."

"OK, OK. Say 10 o'clock. And it's all low from here," Dave said.

Perri swiveled his sight and picked up movement. His .300 Winchester had a long barrel which he had resting on a rock to keep it steady. He had grabbed a new scope in the general store, one he'd had his eyes on ever since it came in, but would never have been able to afford. It was by a company called Precision Scopes, and overlaid on the glass viewer was a small 'heads up' display showing Perri the range to the target once he had it framed, the direction and strength of the wind, the degree of bullet drop, and a bunch of other stuff Perri wasn't sure about, like 'incline' and 'cant'. Having read about it in a hunting magazine, what Perri *was* sure about was how it worked. You put a red pip on your target and, with your thumb, pressed a button you mounted down back of the trigger of your rifle. Then the sight calculated a firing solution and a crosshair appeared, showing where your bullet would go if you fired it. You put the crosshair over your target and ... boom.

That was the theory anyway. Perri couldn't risk test firing to zero the sight, which he'd normally want to do. He'd just entered the make of the rifle and its ammo into the scope's settings, and had to hope it would do. He knew his rifle, though, and he knew it shot pretty true.

Now he saw what Dave had been talking about. At the edge of town, under an old carport, Russian troops were piling up cases. They were wooden and looked to be about the size of a 36-pack beer case. The writing on the outside was Cyrillic, and as Perri couldn't read it he had no idea what might be in them. Besides those there were some crates already stacked up three deep and he had no trouble guessing what was in them. The top one on the leftmost stack was open, and he saw what looked like missiles. While a couple of the soldiers were piling up the ammunition, another group of about four were building walls of sandbags up around the carport. At the rate they were going, Perri figured it would take maybe another day, and they would have created a nice little ammo bunker well away from any other building.

"You seeing what I see?" Dave said, looking through his binos.

"Missiles," Perri replied. "Maybe the ones we saw them firing on that first day? So the other stuff is probably ammo for guns, maybe grenades, wire-guided bazookas, that kind of thing."

"No, I mean, they're piling all those sandbags around it. You're never going to get a shot, once they're done."

Their plan, for what it was worth, was not to try to kill Russians, not directly anyway. They wanted to find fat, soft targets and take them out, making life on the island a real pain for the invaders. So far, they'd identified a few good ones: an electricity generator, the electricity junction that connected the town to the big pumped hydro plant, not to mention the pump itself, up on the bluff above them, and a vehicle park full of jeeps and small trucks. There was also a choice target in the hydrogen fuel tanks down by the harborside catalytic processor, but Perri figured he would need more than his little .300 Winchester to set them off and he knew if he did the town would really suffer, with winter approaching.

Anyway, he wasn't looking to blow stuff up. A bullet in the engine block of a generator or the radiator of a jeep would do the job nicely. If they could find one of those missile launch sites, he was pretty sure they would be connected to radar antennas or computers. A few .300 magnum rounds into one of those would probably mess it right up.

But an ammo dump? Maybe he *should* be thinking about blowing stuff up. He watched the men below at work for a few minutes more.

"Would they cover the roof in sandbags too?" Perri said, thinking out loud.

"Sure," Dave replied. "What's the point of protecting the sides if you don't protect the top? You could drop a bomb right through the roof."

"I don't think the sandbags are meant to stop a bomb," Perri said. "I think the sandbags are just in case there is an accident. So the whole town doesn't go up if some dumb ass throws a cigarette on top of a crate of explosives."

"Oh yeah. Then probably you don't want to sandbag the roof. You got to have somewhere for the explosion to go, so you probably want it to go up, not out the sides."

"Exactly what I'm thinking, man," Perri said. "And we can get a nice angle on the roof of that carport if we move back up about fifty yards, wouldn't you say?"

Dave looked behind them to where the bluff rose up dramatically. "For sure."

Perri rolled onto his back, looking up at the young boy sitting beside him. "That's enough for today," he said. "I want to get back to the tank and check that ammo we took from the general store. I'm hoping there's some steel tips there to get me through the aluminum roof of that carport. And I have to clean the barrel."

"When are we coming back?" Dave asked.

"Later tonight," Perri said. "While most of the bad guys are asleep."

"I *knew* you'd say that," Dave said glumly.

TÊTE-À-TÊTE

It was neutral territory. An unprepossessing single-story building at 9 Prechistensky Lane in the Khamovniki District, with a peeling yellow-painted facade, white trim around the doors and windows, and a small Danish flag hanging over the doorway.

"This is the place, ma'am," Ambassador McCarthy's aide announced as her security detail stepped out of their cars and took position on the deserted street. It was five in the morning, and they had gone to great pains to be sure there were no media or Russian FSB security service goons tailing them. Devlin had been ordered by her Secretary of State to deliver a message to the Kremlin, just in case they hadn't got the message from the President's phone call to the Russian President, or the multiple other channels through which the US was screaming in outrage at the Russians.

Devlin looked dubiously out the window at the modest building. "Have I been here before?"

"Yes, ma'am," her senior aide, Brent Harrison, said. "Six months ago; dinner with Frederik, King of Denmark, and his wife, Princess Mary." The man had a memory for every engagement and had memorized just about every street in the city too, so if he said she had been here, she must have.

She gathered up her things. "It seemed bigger at night."

She was met at the door by her junior aide, Lucy Sellano, who had come out earlier to ensure arrangements were in place. "Foreign Minister Kelnikov is here, ma'am. He had a military attaché with him – there was some confusion about who should be present for your discussion."

"I hope you told them it was a four-eyes meeting," she said. She wanted to be able to speak frankly to Kelnikov, even though he would assume the conversation was being recorded. They had both agreed on the venue, but that didn't mean

Kelnikov trusted the Danes not to eavesdrop. It was Devlin's experience that Kelnikov trusted no one.

"Yes, ma'am," Sellano said, a wispy brown strand of hair across her forehead bobbing up and down. As they turned a corner they nearly walked into a large, square-shouldered man in his fifties, with thin blonde hair and round-rimmed glasses. He held out his hand. "Ah, Ambassador Vestergaard, ma'am," Sellano said. "I think you know each other?"

"A pleasure to welcome you to our humble abode again, Devlin," the Danish Ambassador said warmly. "But under less convivial circumstances than last time."

"Yes, sorry about the intrusion, Jørgen," she replied. "I hope it wasn't too inconvenient."

He smiled. "I have told the staff there is a security sweep being conducted this morning and they are not to arrive until eight. I myself have a breakfast appointment," he said, and indicated the empty corridor with a sweep of his hand. *"Mit hus er dit hus,"* he said. "The place is yours. Your guest awaits." With that, he bowed slightly and left them alone in the corridor.

"So, their military attaché is…"

"Sitting with the Russian security detachment in the kitchen having coffee," Sellano said. "We'll join them…" She stopped and opened the door to another corridor. "When you are ready to come out, just text me; the arrangement is that we will leave first." She looked at her watch. "We have plenty of time. The Danish embassy staff won't be here for another two hours at least."

"Good," Devlin said, handing the woman her coat. As she did so, Harrison handed her a file. She looked at it. Printed across the top of the folder in letters almost big enough to be visible from space if she stepped outside with it was the title 'OPERATION LOSOS'. She was going to make sure Kelnikov could see it clearly too. It was an unsubtle message to the Russian Foreign Minister that US intelligence was not blind to the Russian plan to take over Saint Lawrence as a permanent maritime base. She opened the cover. Okay, it was a pretty thin file, but Kelnikov didn't need to know that.

"You talked to the analyst?" she asked Harrison as they walked. "Williams?"

"Carl Williams, yes," Harrison said, pointing to the NSA designator on the first page. He smiled. "CIA head of station wasn't very happy about us going straight to 'the Ambassador's new pet' as they describe him…"

"Then he should try giving me more than open source wire reports I could just as easily get from one of the TV news networks," Devlin said.

"Right … well, most of what Williams pulled together is signals intel, plus some human source stuff from CIA, but not much. He said he figured due to the situation you wouldn't give him enough time to task any of our assets for primary intel collection, and you'd want something you could hang over Kelnikov's head, so he directed his NSA crypto-bots to focus on trying to identify at least the code name for the Russian operation." Harrison's finger was resting on what looked like a Russian GRU military intelligence bureau memo, with the code word LOSOS marked clearly across the top. Devlin's rudimentary Russian wasn't good enough for her to be able to read it, and she didn't even know if it was real. "He figured if we had the code name, the Russians might assume we had it all."

"Smart guy," Devlin said. "I like how he thinks. At worst, they'll wonder how much we know; at best, they'll assume we know it all and might have to modify their plans on that assumption."

"Good luck, ma'am," Harrison said, stepping aside so her security detail could get past him into the waiting room.

"It's the red door at the end of the corridor, ma'am," Sellano said, pointing.

Devlin put the file under her arm and straightened her jacket. *Except we know virtually zip about why they're there.* All we know is that the Russians are swarming all over Saint Lawrence, they've declared they're acting under the authority of an Arctic treaty we never signed up to, and they're putting enough firepower on that island to create a no-go zone for US aircraft

144

and ships over the whole of the Bering Strait. Devlin sighed and wiped her teeth with a fingertip in case there was any lipstick there. *And they don't look like they're planning to leave anytime soon.*

Kelnikov rose and buttoned his jacket over his expansive waistline. He didn't smile, but gave her a small and almost ironic bow. "Madam Ambassador."

Without any ceremony, she sat the LOSOS file down on the table between them and sat down opposite him. "Minister Kelnikov."

They looked at each other for a moment or two. There was no protocol to cover this. Devlin saw his eyes flick to the folder, but saw no immediate reaction. *Give him time,* she thought. *He's not the sharpest knife in the drawer.* The challenge now would be for her to reveal a little of what she knew, without giving away just how little.

"I believe you have a message from your government," Kelnikov said. "Perhaps you have reconsidered your position and are willing to enter into negotiations for a new treaty guaranteeing free passage for all nations through the Bering Strait?"

It was all she could do to contain herself from swearing. The Russians had sunk one of their own ships, either themselves, or through a proxy. They had invaded US territory under the guise of a nuclear reactor emergency aboard one of their subs, and then they had made wild allegations in the media about a US cyberattack on their sub, before declaring that they were taking control of the sea lanes and airspace over the Bering Strait to 'guarantee freedom of navigation for all' in the name of the Barents Euro-Arctic Council of Nations. Williams' NSA report also stated that they had shot down two US reconnaissance drones. They had warned that any US military ship or aircraft breaking their no-go zone would be considered a threat to international shipping and dealt with 'accordingly'.

"Minister, we are under no illusions about your real purpose on Saint Lawrence," Devlin said. She reached down and took up the file, opening it to the first page as though she was referring to a briefing document. "Your Operation LOSOS? Is that how it is pronounced? It is nothing less than an old-fashioned land grab."

That got a reaction. Kelnikov's eyes narrowed. "The United States sinks one of our freighters and disables one of our submarines, risking hundreds, perhaps thousands of lives from possible nuclear disaster, and you accuse us of an 'old-fashioned land grab'?"

"It is only you and I in this room," Devlin reminded him. "So can we cut the hyperbole and discuss whether there is any way we can resolve this peaceably? Because I can tell you, Roman, we are at about one minute to midnight on this one," she said, referring to the infamous Doomsday Clock. Any student of history would know the last time it had been at one minute to midnight had been during the Cuban Missile Crisis.

"If the US is willing to negotiate a new Arctic treaty, this can be resolved very quickly," he said equably. "Why could you possibly imagine we have any interest in taking control of a tiny island full of Eskimos and whale bones?" He was fishing now, she could feel it. Trying to see how deep her intel ran.

She pulled aside the first page of her dossier and ran her eyes over the list underneath.

"Let me tell you what I know, not what I imagine," she said. "You have more than 500 ground troops on the island, four portable anti-aircraft systems capable of shooting down aircraft over US airspace, one submarine with a miraculously repaired reactor..." she paused and raised her eyebrows, "...and five littoral naval vessels, armed with ship-to-ship and ship-to-air missiles." She looked up, seeing a slight smile on the man's face. "You have a three-ship naval task force en route to the island from Vladivostok, you have activated almost every unit in your Eastern District Air Army, moved a squadron of Hunter drones to Lavrentiya and are staging continuous patrols up and down the Strait with manned Sukhoi and Mig fighters ..."

"All in order to secure the waterway for international shipping..." Kelnikov began again, but she held up her hand.

"And..." she said loudly, interrupting him, "and, you have the entire population of the island in the villages of Gambell and Savoonga under lock and key. They are being held hostage."

"No," Kelnikov insisted. "Clearly your intelligence is unreliable. The local inhabitants have been moved to safe locations so that there will not be any civilian casualties if you are foolish enough to respond militarily to our intervention." He tapped the table. "They are being given food, shelter and even advanced medical care. Which I understand is more than their own government has given them for decades. When the situation is stable, we will allow the International Red Cross access to the residents to verify they are safe and well."

"It is not your place to *allow* anything!" Devlin protested. "These are US citizens, being held against their will by the armed forces of Russia."

"Protected," Kelnikov corrected, leaning forward. "Against a rogue nation which has already demonstrated a reckless and violent disregard for the rules of international diplomacy and commerce."

"You would be wise not to treat us like fools, sir," Devlin said. "This aggression has one purpose, and that is to achieve Russian control of Saint Lawrence Island. This we will not abide."

The minute she spoke, Devlin saw her assertion was somehow wide of the mark. Kelnikov smiled and sat back in his chair, relaxing visibly. His eyes, which had been flicking between her file labeled LOSOS and her face, settled now on the sleeve of his jacket as he picked lint from it, as though he had suddenly lost interest in the meeting. Struggling to maintain her outrage, Devlin continued. "Our demand is simple," she said. "All Russian military forces and any other Russian nationals will depart Saint Lawrence within 48 hours, that is, by 1800 hours Tuesday, Alaskan Standard Time..."

"Please," Kelnikov interrupted her. "Don't tell me. You were about to say ... 'or there will be grave consequences'."

"No," Devlin replied. "That is what our President is saying to the world press and to your President. The message I have for you is a little more direct." Now she had his attention again. Good.

"Go on."

"I have been authorized to tell you that if you do not withdraw by this deadline, Russian forces on Saint Lawrence will be wiped from the face of that island with a fire and fury unlike any seen this century." She drew a breath. "And the United States will hold Russia entirely responsible for any and all civilian casualties that result from your refusal to comply."

As she walked to her car, Devlin glowered. She had delivered her message, but there was no victory in that. Kelnikov would pass the message to his President, of that she was sure. But the State Department's theory that this entire affair was about creating a conflict over Saint Lawrence to test US willingness to defend its interests in the Bering Strait waterway had fallen flat on the floor. Kelnikov had smirked, as though by accusing them of it she was just showing how ignorant she was. Dammit.

Her aide Harrison knew her well enough not to hit her with a barrage of questions as they climbed into her car. As it pulled away from the curb, he let her gather her thoughts. Finally, she spoke.

"This NSA Russia analyst, Carl Williams," she asked, patting the file on her knees. "Tell me he's on station here in Moscow, not in some bunker in Virginia."

"Yes, ma'am," Harrison said. "NSA secondment. He's attached to IT Support in the Environment, Science, Technology and Health section."

"But he's a spook?"

"Yes, ma'am, undeclared. Just arrived in country, I believe," Harrison said. In fact, he knew exactly how long Williams had been in Russia. Forty-two days.

"Get him on the phone," Devlin said, holding out her hand. "Encrypt."

Harrison pulled out his phone, and then tapped on the app that gave him an encrypted connection via a US Embassy VPN to other Embassy staff. He looked up and dialed Williams, then handed it to Devlin. "I asked him to stand by his phone, just in case," Harrison said.

"That's why I love you," Devlin smiled and heard the ringtone stop, to be replaced by a deep bass voice.

"Hello? Williams speaking."

"Mr. Williams, this is Devlin McCarthy, I don't believe we've met," she said.

"No, ma'am," he replied. No fumbling, fawning chit-chat. She liked that.

"When I get back to Spaso House I'd like to see you there. I need your thoughts on something," she said.

"Yes, ma'am," he replied. "But can you come to me instead?"

She blinked. "I beg your pardon?"

"Ma'am, there's someone you should meet," he said. "But I can't bring him to Spaso House. You have to come to my office in the New Annex. Or under it, actually."

She put her hand over the telephone and turned to Harrison. "What do you know about this guy?"

Harrison shrugged. "Crack analyst, earned his stripes in China before being sent here, an expert in neural networks…"

"Neural what?"

"Artificial intelligence," Harrison explained.

She put the phone back to her ear. "OK, Mr. Williams, your office it is. We'll be there in about thirty minutes."

"You'd better allow a bit more time, ma'am," Williams said.

She smiled. "Are you going to tell me your computer is showing heavy traffic on the ring road, Mr. Williams?"

"No, ma'am," he replied. "For the paperwork. I'm pretty sure you don't have the code word clearances for what I want to share with you."

Roman Kelnikov was also finishing a phone call from his car, but it was a much more straightforward one. His call was to the Defense Minister, Andrei Burkhin. They discussed the American threat and whether it was possible that the words 'fire and fury' were meant to convey a willingness to use tactical nuclear weapons.

"I can't rule that out," Kelnikov said. "But we knew it was a possibility. She mentioned civilian casualties."

"It won't be a disaster if they do use tactical nukes," Burkhin responded. "They would become international pariahs."

"We could lose thousands of front-line troops, aircraft and ships," Kelnikov said. "Not to mention the civilian casualties. Surely..."

"Show some spine, Kelnikov. The troops on Saint Lawrence are ... expendable," Burkhin said. "And they number in the hundreds, not thousands. The ships are cold war relics, *Albatross*-class corvettes. Aircraft losses would be limited to those directly over Saint Lawrence at the time. Civilian losses are a US matter. I'd almost *welcome* a nuclear strike. We could probably march into Alaska with the whole of the UN at our backs."

"All we need is a military response of some sort, preferably conventional," Kelnikov said, a part of him recoiling at the thought of nuclear weapons being used so close to the Russian mainland. "Could we not just have our ships sink a..."

"There *will* be a US military response, that is guaranteed now," Burkhin said. "And it will be executed with the typical American aversion for risking the lives of its troops – a blizzard of cruise missiles is most likely. All we need is for America's allies in Europe and Asia to baulk at entering the conflict when we announce we are creating a demilitarized zone in Alaska.

Two to four weeks, and we will control the entire Bering Land Bridge to the Yukon River basin."

Kelnikov couldn't help noticing the uncertainty in his colleague's timeline. "You said two to four weeks? I thought this was supposed to be a lightning attack, over in days."

"Relax, Roman," Burkhin said. "You get the United Nations behind us, leave the battle plan to me."

Williams had been right, Devlin had to admit. Of course there were areas of her own embassy that she was not able to waltz in and out of – high-security communications or intelligence collection areas on the 'Tophat' restricted access floors, for example. But she hadn't been aware that an obscure office of the Environment, Science, Technology and Health section in the basement of the New Annex was one of them. Mind you, she'd never had occasion to go there. It had taken Harrison a frustrating two hours on the telephone; first to find out which wheels he needed to grease to secure the necessary above-Top Secret clearances so that Devlin could be briefed directly by Williams, and then to get the clearances approved by Washington, where it was still the middle of the night and no one seemed to want to take responsibility for letting a lowly Ambassador into what was apparently a very closed circle of Need To Know.

As she followed Harrison and a security guard through the maze of corridors in the New Annex, it struck Devlin that they should find a new nickname for it. Built at the turn of the century, it had the working name 'New Annex' when people moved in, before later being officially called the 'Mueller Wing' after a former head of the CIA, in a move intended to irk their Russian hosts. The new name came too late, though. To everyone working at the Embassy, it would always be the 'New Annex', just as the additional secure floors of the Chancery were called the 'Tophat'.

"In here, ma'am," the security guard said, keying a door. "Mr. Williams' is the third office on the left." He held the door

151

open to let Harrison and Devlin through, but Harrison stayed in the doorway with a shrug. "I'll wait here. I could only get clearance for you, ma'am."

She didn't have to worry about where to go once the door swung shut behind her. A portly, bearded and bespectacled man in his thirties with disheveled salt and pepper hair and a spot on his white shirt which looked distinctly like pasta sauce stepped out into the corridor and gave her a small wave.

She walked down and held out her hand. "You must be Carl Williams?"

"In the flesh, Ambassador," he said, shaking her hand then turning to open the door behind him.

"Call me Devlin, please," she said, stepping inside and looking around. "OK ... disappointed." It just came out, without her thinking. She had expected to walk into some sort of supercomputer center, huge mainframes in liquid nitrogen-cooled towers behind hermetically sealed glass, sucking power from a small nuclear reactor buried under the floor of the New Annex. What else could have required such an effort to get her cleared?

Instead, Williams' office was about the size of her walk-in wardrobe in Spaso House, with just enough room for a desk holding a laptop and a coffee cup, a file safe and a chair for one visitor. Looking at the chair, she could see it hadn't had much use. Although Carl Williams had a bit of the mad professor look about him, his office wasn't as disheveled as his person. There wasn't a piece of paper, stray paperclip or even a pen on his desk; just a few rings from coffee cups that hadn't been cleaned off. The only personal item was a photo of a seascape that looked like it had been taken on a Pacific Coast somewhere.

"I know, right?" he said, clearly not offended. "They asked what kind of office I would need and I said as long as it had an encrypted 1.5 terabit fat pipe both up and down, I didn't care." He looked up. "At least it has high ceilings. You want a coffee?"

"Thanks, do you even have..." she asked, looking dubious.

He held up a finger and then pulled out a drawer. Inside was a kettle, which he switched on, and a container of instant coffee. "You take cream and sugar?" he asked, pulling a paper cup full of small sachets out of the drawer. "I don't myself, but I still have the stash I stole on the plane flight over." The water boiling was very loud in the small space.

"Black is fine," she said. She looked up at the seascape photograph on his wall. "You grew up on the coast?"

"No, ma'am ... Devlin," he said. "That's where I'm going to retire. La Jolla, San Diego. You know it?"

"Can't say I do."

"I've been putting away every spare dollar I made in China, and now here. Should have enough to buy into a condo by the beach in a couple of years, and then I'm going to learn to surf."

She looked at him dubiously. Despite the mop of gray speckled hair he didn't look old enough to be thinking about retiring, nor fit enough to think about surfing.

He held up a hand, little finger and thumb outstretched. "Sick idea, right?"

"California dreaming," she said. "There are worse retirement plans. But it takes a lot of money to retire."

He pulled out the kettle and poured two cups of coffee. "Oh, not completely retire. I'll still do consulting and stuff to pay the bills. There are only about twenty people in the world who can do what I do."

"And what is that, exactly?" she asked. "I'm told I've been cleared now."

"Yeah, I got the paperwork. Well ... I program natural scenes and natural language on recursive neural networks," he said.

"Again?"

"I teach machines to speak and understand plain English and interpret images," he said.

"OK, and what do you do for the NSA?" she asked. "Here at my Embassy?"

"Oh, I work with HOLMES, keeping him fed, debugged, and reporting on any intel he finds interesting," he said.

153

"HOLMES?"

"I know, you're wondering, is it an acronym or something?" he said. "It's kind of. It's like, I'm Dr. Watson and he's…"

"Sherlock Holmes?"

"Yeah, the someone I wanted you to meet," Williams said, opening his laptop and typing in a long password that he supplemented with a DNA thumb swipe. The laptop was hard-wired to the wall by something Devlin hadn't seen in a long time – a long, thin optical fiber Ethernet cable. "I couldn't just bring him to your office – it's best if he's hard-wired so his comms can't be intercepted. And you don't have the bandwidth up there anyway for me to show you what he is capable of." He turned his laptop around and Devlin saw a window that looked like a simple video conference window. She saw an image of herself captured by the laptop camera on one side of the screen, and a Japanese manga-style image of Sherlock Holmes on the other.

"Say hello to the Ambassador, HOLMES," Williams said.

"Pleased to meet you, Ambassador Devlin," a British accented voice said from the speakers of the laptop. "That's a nice necklace you're wearing. Australian South Sea pearls from Broome, correct? A present from the Australian Foreign Minister."

Involuntarily, Devlin's hand went to the pearls at her neck. She looked at Williams. "That's creepy. I was given this about six years ago, when I was leaving Canberra."

"There must be a photo of it on a State Department server somewhere," Williams said, sounding unimpressed. "Ignore him, he's just trying to show off. HOLMES, the Ambassador met with the Russian Foreign Minister today. She is going to ask you some questions."

Devlin stared at the manga detective on the screen, not sure where or how to start.

"Just ask," Williams prompted. "Start your questions with his name, like you do for Siri or Alexa. If I need to rephrase your question, I'll chime in."

154

"OK... HOLMES, do... what do you know about the current political situation between Russia and America over Saint Lawrence Island?" She leaned forward, but Williams spoke before the AI could.

"Parse it, HOLMES, ultra-brief download, specific answers only from here," he said, then looked at Devlin. "I'm guessing you don't want to know *everything* he knows. That could take hours."

"Yes, Carl," the British voice said. "At 0400 hours last Monday Russian ground, air and sea forces invaded the US territory of Saint Lawrence Island in the Bering Strait and have occupied the territory claiming they are doing so to protect commercial shipping from, quote, 'unprovoked US aggression'. They have demanded that the US enter into negotiations on a new treaty guaranteeing freedom of navigation in Arctic waters. The incursion followed the destruction at sea of a Russian-owned merchant vessel and an alleged cyber-attack on a Russian nuclear submarine, both of which Russia has blamed the USA for. Is this summary sufficient?"

"Ah, yes, sure. State Department has a theory that this is just a pretext, and the Russian occupation of Saint Lawrence is a feint, intended to test our willingness to go to war over control of the Bering Strait. The first step in a possible attempt to redefine maritime boundaries. But when I put this to the Russian Foreign Minister this morning, he looked... I don't know..." Devlin petered out.

"Confused, relieved, guilty, happy, sad..." Williams offered.

"Smug," Devlin said after thinking about it. "He looked smug."

"Thank you, Ambassador, that is very valuable input," HOLMES said. "I was able to take the audio file of your meeting off the Danish Embassy server but I had no video with which to put your discussion into emotional context."

Devlin looked at Williams. "The Danes recorded us?"

"Of course," Williams said. "Wouldn't we have?"

"I guess," she said. "But you hacked..."

"Their server, yeah. We already had a backdoor into most of the missions in Moscow. Those we didn't, we do now thanks to HOLMES. Except for the Chinese. Those Unit 61938 guys are good. What do you want to ask, Ambassador?"

"You worked out it was a Finnish submarine firing one of our missiles that sank that Russian robot ship," she said to Williams. "You warned in a briefing note to NSA of a scenario in which Russia would use that attack as a pretext for political or military action of some sort in the near future and you were right."

"That was HOLMES," Williams said. "Scenarios are his thing. He runs them night and day. He has access to every single data point collected by the NSA, CIA, FBI, Homeland Security, Border Force, DIA, Aerospace Command... you name it... going back twenty years. Once he lands on a scenario, he tests it against the data and then refines it as new data comes in. He's good at it, aren't you HOLMES?"

"I love new data," HOLMES said.

Devlin raised her eyebrows.

"I didn't program that," Williams said defensively. "He's decided that himself. He means 'like', he likes new data. I give him broad areas of investigation. Then he builds scenarios and he's programmed to seek data out, use every new datum point to refine the probabilities in his scenarios. Once they reach a threshold of 30% probability, I write them up."

"I don't like new data," the voice from the laptop said, sounding piqued. "I *love* it."

"Still working on that," Williams said to Devlin. "Sorry. He's only supposed to respond when you page him, but he's always listening so he's started to anticipate verbal cues. You want him to share the scenarios he's building on the Russian invasion of Saint Lawrence?"

"Yes," Devlin said. "That's exactly..."

"OK, HOLMES? What's the highest probability scenario you are working on the Russian invasion of Saint Lawrence?"

"I currently have a scenario with 83% probability, Carl," the voice said.

"HOLMES, describe that scenario, parse, ultra-brief summaries until further notice, please."

"Yes, Carl. The Russian government plans to create the pretext for a nuclear attack on the United States of America which will result in assured mutual destruction, massive radiation fallout, climate change and potential human extinction," the voice said calmly.

Devlin felt the hairs rise on her neck, but Williams just sighed.

"OK, HOLMES, let's just assume for now that isn't their plan. What is the second highest-rated probability?"

"The Russian government is trying to create international sympathy for its next move, which is likely to be an invasion of the United States mainland."

"Supplement. Supporting evidence?" Williams asked, ignoring the shocked look on Devlin's face.

"In the two weeks prior to the invasion of Saint Lawrence Island, Russian military command ordered elements of the Eastern Military District to high readiness, totaling 120,000 troops. Ordered to active combat duty was the 3rd Air Command, the Snow Leopards, and the special forces Spetsnaz Brigade, which was the unit that conducted the initial ground operation on Saint Lawrence. Further Special Forces units ordered to active combat duty but not yet deployed include one Spetsnaz Brigade and two Airborne Brigades. Do you want me to continue?"

"Yes."

"In the Russian Central Command, the following units were also activated. The Yekaterina Communications Brigade, a Guards Spetsnaz Brigade, a Guards Airborne Brigade and the 14th Air and Air Defense Forces Army."

"Uh, HOLMES? How do these 'activations' support your hypothesis of a ground invasion of mainland America?" Devlin asked.

"In the last two years the Snow Leopards air brigade has been built up significantly and almost exclusively with squadrons and pilots returning from the Middle East and it now

157

comprises the most combat-hardened Air Force unit in Russia. It is a composite force of fighters, ground attack, airborne refueling, command and control, electronic warfare, transport and close air support rotary-winged aircraft. It would be ideally suited to the task of achieving air supremacy over a battlefront, while the Air Army of Central Command filled in for its continental duties. Continue?"

"Yes please."

"The ground units ordered to active combat duty in the Eastern Military District are too numerous for the occupation of Saint Lawrence alone and are almost exclusively rapid deployment units: Spetsnaz and airborne troops. These are the forces that would be used in the initial phase of an invasion to quickly eliminate threats and secure high-value targets…"

"Stop, HOLMES," Williams said. He had a pencil twirling between his fingers and tapped it on his teeth. "HOLMES, have you seen any evidence of major ground forces of battalion strength or greater being brought to readiness?"

"No, Carl."

"Supplement. Wouldn't that be necessary if Russia intended a full-scale invasion of the US mainland?"

"Yes, Carl. In 2019 the US Army War College in Carlisle, Pennsylvania wargamed a major conventional war in Europe between Russian and NATO forces. Russia initially made significant gains in Eastern Europe before the intervention of US forces on the Western Front. 'Russian' commanders then decided to try to alleviate the US pressure by attacking the USA through Alaska in order to threaten the major population centers of the US northeast. The Alaska invasion required the initial commitment of 80-100,000 Eastern District ground troops and, if successful, would have required up to 620,000 troops."

"It wasn't successful," Williams guessed.

"No. However, Russian airborne forces nullified and captured the key US Air Force bases at Elmendorf-Richardson in Anchorage, and Eielson in Fairbanks, as well as the port of Anchorage, and used them to land ground forces via an air and

158

sea bridge. From there, they attacked through Canada, reaching Vancouver, where they paused to consolidate before attacking Seattle. Two US carrier task force groups were deployed and together with attack submarines began interdiction of Russian sea and air supply lines across the Bering Sea and Alaskan airspace. A Russian attempt to land troops of its 35th Army in Anchorage by sea through the Aleutian Islands was intercepted by the US Pacific Fleet. US ground forces attacked Russian forces in Vancouver from the south and then Canadian and US ground forces attacked their eastern flank through the Canadian Yukon Territory, recapturing Fairbanks and Anchorage and causing the Russian attack to collapse. The total irrecoverable personnel losses of the Soviet Armed Forces, frontier, and internal security troops in the US came to 14,453. Soviet Army formations, units, and HQ elements lost 13,833, FSB security service subunits lost 572, Internal Affairs formations lost 28, and other ministries and departments lost 20 men. US and Canadian losses were, however, double these numbers."

"A full-scale invasion makes no sense," Devlin said to Williams. "They couldn't invade the USA with a few brigades of special forces troops, no matter how powerful their Air Force."

"HOLMES, thoughts?"

"I concur with the Ambassador. But my scenario does not consider that Russia intends a full-scale invasion of the USA," HOLMES said.

"What, then?"

"In this scenario, the forces assembled are too numerous for Saint Lawrence Island to be the main objective. However, they may be sufficient to take and hold Alaska."

"Thanks, HOLMES, let us think about this," Williams said. "Stand by."

Devlin reached for her coffee cup. "No wonder that bastard Kelnikov looked so smug when I accused him of designs on Saint Lawrence. If your silicon friend is right, I couldn't have been further from the mark." She sipped. "I accused him of a border skirmish. But, *Alaska*?"

"I know, right? They have a billion acres of unoccupied land in Siberia they could build on if they were looking for icy wasteland real estate, so it isn't living space they're after. HOLMES, list the main natural resources of Alaska."

"Yes, Carl. Alaska has commercially developed or potentially viable deposits of oil, copper, silver, mercury, gold, tin, coal, iron ore, borax, chromite, antimony, tungsten, nickel, molybdenum, sand, gravel, and limestone," the British voice intoned.

"Supplement. Does Russia have significant shortages of any of these resources?" Williams asked.

"No, Carl. Russia is either an exporter or is self-sufficient in all of these resources."

Williams dropped his pencil on his desk. "Nah. This scenario doesn't make sense, HOLMES. Russia needs a reason to want to mount a ground invasion of Alaska. You've got all the other pieces, but you're missing *motive*, my man."

"Thank you, Carl. I will weight motive higher in future analyses," HOLMES said. Devlin couldn't help smiling, despite how she felt. The voice of the great detective sounded distinctly miffed.

"HOLMES, continue speculative analysis with full focus on the broader implications of the Russian Saint Lawrence operation please, disregard all other tasking," Williams said. "Find me a motive, HOLMES."

"Yes, Carl."

Williams reached out and pulled the lid of his laptop down.

"He's annoyed," Carl said. "That *is* programmed. It forces him to revisit all of his analyses and broaden his search for data to support high probability scenarios."

Devlin stood. She had called in a report of her conversation with Kelnikov but still had to write it up and include some of what Williams and his silicon sidekick had shared with her. She sat down again.

"How reliable is this AI of yours?" she asked.

"Only as reliable as the intel he can access," Williams said. "But don't worry, he's not the only one working this on our

160

side. NSA has three systems like HOLMES. All of them are learning systems and they share their analyses and test hypotheses with each other. When they agree on something, it's usually rock solid."

"They *talk* to each other?" Devlin asked, sounding dubious.

"In code, yeah. At quantum speeds. They're like brothers, argue a lot," Williams said.

"Brothers."

"Yeah. And HOLMES is the big brother," Williams said proudly. "He was the first, and he's learned more. I've got him doing stuff the other two systems are years away from being able to mimic."

Devlin shook her head. "Look, can you send me a report on the top three most likely scenarios you are working on and the intel you have backing them? I am going to send a note to State saying Kelnikov's reaction makes me think their theory about 'testing our mettle' is bogus, but I need to be able to put an alternative or two forward."

Carl laughed, enjoying hearing an Ambassador talking about a concept being 'bogus'. He was starting to get a feeling she was going to be his kind of Head of Mission.

"Bogus, right. Like invading Alaska for no reason we can see?" he asked, and Devlin realized as he spoke that HOLMES' scenario also sounded a long way from plausible.

"Like that," Devlin said. "Thank you, Carl." She stood to leave, then hesitated. The man intrigued her. The whole setup with the NSA AI system did too. "Can I ask you something?"

"You're cleared for it, ma'am." his whiskery Father Christmas face smiled at her.

"Not for this. If all you need is broadband and a laptop, you could probably work from anywhere in the world, but your last posting was China and now you're here in Russia. Why?"

Williams looked around him at the bare walls and sparse furniture and shrugged. "I like to travel to exotic locales?"

SIGHTSEEING

"We're going back in," Halifax said. "Target identification." He had called a meeting in the trailer to brief Rodriguez and O'Hare and get their thoughts on how to execute the mission he'd been given.

"What targets?" O'Hare asked.

"Gambell," Halifax said. "We know the civilian hostages at Savoonga are being held in the radar station cantonment at Savoonga. Don't ask me how we know, probably signals intel. But we don't know where they're being held in Gambell." He saw the look on Bunny's face. "I know, it's where we lost those two Fantoms. They got lucky, but this time we know what we're up against."

"Don't we have satellite coverage now?" Rodriguez asked.

"Thick cloud down to 1,000 feet for today and expected into the next week," Halifax said. "We have synthetic aperture coverage but that will only let them triangulate what they already have. Plus Ivan is trying to blind our satellites with ground-based lasers."

"They can do that? I didn't know they had the capability," Rodriguez said, surprised.

"Me neither. Seems they had a few surprises up their sleeves. Satellites are functioning at one third nominal, I'm told."

"Infrared?"

"As well as the laser interference, Russians have lit fires all over both Savoonga and Gambell; probably just smudge pots, to mask the heat signatures of their emplacements and any buildings they're using. You'll go in tonight with recon pods, low-light, infrared and synthetic aperture radar. There are nearly two hundred people in Gambell, they must be using some sort of heat to keep them warm. If nothing else you can identify those smudge pots and decoy fires and we'll locate the hostages by process of elimination."

"We are 24 hours out from the deadline we gave the Russians to withdraw," O'Hare said. "Is there any sign they are packing up and bugging out? Signals intel, air traffic, that kind of thing?"

"I haven't been advised. But if they are, you get a Fantom over Gambell, we should be able to see it. Primary objective, though, is to identify the location of the hostages at Gambell."

"We're going to send in a Seal Team, try to get the hostages out before we hit the Russian positions?" Rodriguez asked hopefully. She hadn't been briefed, but she had a good idea of what was coming, and if she had family on Saint Lawrence she wouldn't want them covered by Russian guns when it happened.

Halifax shook his head. "I haven't been told, and probably wouldn't be. But I'd doubt it. By the time we get the intel back to NORAD, it would probably be too late and, in any case, there are hundreds of Russian regular troops on that island with some heavy-duty air cover. It's not like Seal Team Six can just buzz in there in their helos, take out a bunch of jihadis and save the day."

"Speaking of which, I'm going to need someone to pull that air cover away somehow," Bunny said. "We got in underneath them last time while they were distracted. We try the same this time and I'm going to get swatted from above again, and that's assuming I can blow through that data-linked Verba anti-air coverage."

Halifax smiled a grim smile. "Oh, I can promise you they'll be distracted."

After the tense first 24 hours of the takeover of Saint Lawrence Island, during which Bondarev had flown three sorties with his men, the last few days had been surprisingly quiet. US aircraft had kept to their coastline, respecting the Russian-imposed no-go zone, even though it technically crossed into US airspace. As far as he was aware, there had also been no US recon flights over the island since the first intrusion, in which the Americans had lost two of their drones. Bondarev wasn't naive; he knew the Americans would have satellite coverage and may have managed to sneak one of their smaller recon drones in under his nose.

American recon drones weren't his big concern. His real worry was if they managed to get a flight of unmanned *combat* aerial vehicles, or drones, in under his fighter and radar screen. Six of the compact Fantom fighters, loaded with the new US Small Advanced Capabilities Missile, nicknamed the Cuda, could bring down an entire squadron of his Su-57s if they were lucky. He had argued with General Lukin about even putting piloted aircraft at risk in the air over the Bering Strait once the initial need was past, but Lukin had turned it around and pointed out to Bondarev that his Okhotnik drones were still missing trained pilots and system operators and it would be at least another two weeks before crews moved from other units could fill the gap.

Modern Russian air war doctrine called for the use of piloted aircraft for critical operations. While Russia had matched the US in the capabilities of its piloted fighters and weapons in recent years, it had chosen a different strategy on drones than the USA. The winning designers at Sukhoi had successfully argued that Russia needed a drone optimized for air-to-ground operations to match the capabilities of the US Fantom, and, given the limitations of the Okhotnik platform, that meant two crew sitting in a trailer on the ground – a pilot and a systems officer. The US, however, was more advanced in terms of combat AI, meaning that a lot of the tasks of the traditional systems officer could be handed off to onboard AI, freeing the US pilot to both fly and target weapons.

Combat experience in the Middle East had shown that Russian human-crewed fighters still had a higher kill to loss ratio than American unmanned fighters. But America had dramatically increased its use of armed drones much earlier than Russia and had run into exactly the same problems as Bondarev was faced with now around crew availability. That had forced a major revision of US drone doctrine and the requirements

164

issued for the competition to design the platform that would become the Fantom had included the capability for 'autonomous AI' in combat and an ability to 'slave' the Fantom to any compatible NATO system so that one pilot could fly up to *six* drones at a time – the now infamous US drone 'hex'. Once the bugs had been ironed out of this system, and faced with both a resurgent Russia and an assertive China, America had put its energy into optimizing drone pilot training and aircraft production capacity so that it could field enough pilots and drones to support a 'two-front' doctrine again: the ability to once again fight a major war in two theaters at the same time, just as it had done in World War II.

Bondarev and his men had only seen American drones in small numbers over Turkey and Syria, though, and even then, usually only the unarmed reconnaissance version, the Fury. NATO air forces in the region had not been armed with the latest US frontline drones and the US had not been willing to commit, and risk losing, its much-hyped Fantom. The Russian pilots assured themselves it was because the pilotless robot planes were not the threat the US made them out to be, and they were afraid to lose face by committing them against battle-hardened Russian fighter squadrons.

All of this was going through Bondarev's mind as his squadron wheeled through the sky in the narrow air corridor between Saint Lawrence Island and the Alaskan mainland. Yes, he could have stayed warm and safe on the ground in Lavrentiya, but he was the kind of commander who liked to fly the front himself. And he wasn't so vain as to think himself irreplaceable. If he died up here, there were a hundred men able and more than willing to take his place.

His eyes flicked across the threats on his heads-up display without alarm, as the situation had not changed greatly since day one of the operation. The US was moving a huge number of aircraft into Eielson and Elmendorf-Richardson air bases and had mobilized its National Guard to protect those bases and the population centers of Fairbanks and Anchorage. Centers which Bondarev knew Russia had no designs on. It was

Nome Russia was interested in, and so they would be drawing a red line across the state of Alaska from Fort Yukon in the northeast to Bethel in the southwest, just short of the bigger Alaskan cities.

If all-out nuclear war did not erupt (and that was a big 'if' in Bondarev's book), the US was expected to focus on fortifying its population centers against an attack that would not come. Nome would be taken – Russia needed *some* geopolitical leverage after all, and would need an administrative capital in its new Yukon territory. But to the outside world, it should look exactly like Russia had kept its word. Its stated intention in the attack on Nome would be that it simply wanted to create a buffer zone, a demilitarized area between Russia and the USA – a response that had been forced on it by rampant US aggression in the Bering Strait.

By the time the US realized that Nome was in Russian hands, it would be too late.

To Bondarev, what had seemed like a suicidal gambit a week ago was suddenly looking like it might, just possibly, pay off. Confusion clearly reigned in Washington about how to respond to the Russian intervention. NATO was crippled by an indecisive European Union, not interested in going to war over a 'minor border shipping dispute'. The US military was being held in check by an administration that was full of bluster, but no bite.

"Gold 1 from Gold Command, vector 045 degrees, altitude 35,000 please, we have business for you," he heard as the voice of his Beriev airborne warning air controller broke his reverie. At that moment he cursed his overconfidence, knowing it had almost certainly jinxed him. "Patching through data now," the airborne warning aircraft said. "Vectoring all available support to your sector."

He looked down at the threat screen in his cockpit and took a deep breath. The airborne warning aircraft was sending through data from ground and air-based long-range radar sources. The screen showed huge numbers of US aircraft forming up over Eielson and Elmendorf-Richardson. The

166

numbers beside the swirling vortex of icons indicated he was looking at two elements of at least fifty aircraft in strength, each.

"Gold 2 to Gold Leader," his wingman called, a slight note of panic in his voice. "Are you seeing this!?"

"Roger, Gold 2, standby." His first reaction was that it didn't make sense. This had all the hallmarks of the prelude to a major attack, but there were still nearly 24 hours until the US deadline for Russian troop withdrawal from Saint Lawrence. Were they trying to take Russia by surprise, by moving early? It was hard to see what the tactical advantage would be, and there would certainly be no political advantage. It would only serve to confirm how hawkish and erratic the US leadership was. But if this was the 'fire and fury' that the US had promised, surely Bondarev would have already received warning that the US had also scrambled elements of its strategic bomber force or moved naval assets within missile range?

Of course, if the US stealth bombers had sortied from Guam several hours ago, they may not yet have been detected.

Perhaps it was just a feint, to test Russian readiness in advance of the real attack. Or a PR stunt, intended to reassure a restive US media and public that its armed forces were ready for action. He checked his watch. It was 0200 at night in Alaska, which made it 0600 in Washington. That made sense – perhaps this was just smoke and mirrors, timed to make the morning TV shows on the US East Coast. He watched carefully as the circling icons over Eielson and Elmendorf-Richardson coalesced into a single 'aluminum cloud' of at least one hundred aircraft that no stealth systems in the world could disguise. Definitely a PR stunt or feint. Multiple smaller attacks would have been much more effective.

The Russian command and control system throwing data onto Bondarev's screens sorted the electronic signature and radar returns it was getting from the enemy formation and assigned different icons to each aircraft type to let its pilots know what they were looking at. As his eyes scanned the screen, a chill went over him.

The spearhead of the huge enemy formation comprised almost exclusively aircraft with the designation Fantom.

Fantoms. These were not National Guard reserve units. As one, they began moving toward Saint Lawrence Island.

This was no feint.

If Dave was cold before, he was both cold and *tired* now. They'd retired to the tank to warm up, eat and get some rest. Perri had cleaned the barrel of his rifle. He was still annoyed he hadn't been able to zero the new sight on his Winchester, and he hadn't been able to find any army surplus armor-piercing rounds in the loot they'd taken from the general store. On the other hand, they had hundreds of steel-tipped 180-grain magnum rounds with an anti-fouling coating, and even at a couple of hundred yards range he was sure they would slice through the aluminum carport roof without trouble. The steel-tipped, copper-jacketed Winchester rounds were popular for hunting reindeer stags – anything less risked not being able to penetrate the animal's thick skull, and the less confident hunters could aim at the shoulder or haunches, the steel tip letting the bullet slice through the thick hide while the copper jacket and lead core would spread on impact and shatter a leg or hip joint.

It also left a smaller entry hole in the valuable reindeer hide.

A little metal on metal probably wouldn't hurt for his upcoming 'hunt', as he was trying to trigger an explosion in the ammo inside the carport. He wanted some friction or sparks to set the ammo off. He was pretty sure that even without having zeroed his rifle, he'd be able to hit something as big as a carport roof with his new precision-guided scope. Hell, just using iron sights he could plug a seal in the head from a hundred yards as it was coming up for air, and that in a raging blizzard, so he had no excuses for missing a stationary carport.

Dave had tried to argue he wasn't even needed on the trip. But Perri had insisted he needed to come along to keep an eye out for Russian patrols. Perri wanted to be sure there were no foot or vehicle patrols near the dump when he set it off. He was pretty sure any buildings near the ammo dump were empty now, with all the residents being held at the school a few hundred yards away, but he didn't want to accidentally kill any Russian soldiers and give them an excuse to retaliate against the townsfolk.

Not yet, anyway.

Once again, they'd navigated their way around the nesting auklets. Finding their previous position in the dark hadn't proven as easy as they'd thought, but eventually Dave spotted the two upright stones they had hidden behind while scouting out the town, and using them for reference they scrambled up the side of the bluff to give themselves about another twenty feet in vertical distance, without adding too much to the lateral.

"What about the flash from the barrel?" Dave asked. "Won't it be like a big old strobe light saying hey, up here, come up here and kill us?!"

Perri looked up at the sky. The cloud had come in thick and low, and Dave was right, it was a dark night, with only a faint diffuse glow from the moon making its way through.

"Maybe," Perri agreed. "If anyone is looking in exactly this direction at exactly the right time. I'm going to put ten rounds into that building as quickly as I can, then we'll run for it. Nothing blows up, then they'll arrive tomorrow morning and wonder who the hell used their ammo dump for target practice and maybe we at least put some holes in some of their missiles." He smiled, teeth white in the dark night. "But if that shed goes up, I don't think they'll be looking up here amongst the rocks and birdshit for the reason. They'll probably think it was a cruise missile or something."

He sounded completely confident, but Dave wasn't buying it. "Yeah, right. We are so going to die tonight."

During the cold war, lone sorties by strategic bombers or surveillance aircraft from both sides of the Bering Strait had 'strayed' into opposition airspace and provoked a response.

Sometimes deliberately, to test enemy capabilities and response times, other times innocently, due to navigation failures. As the newly reinvigorated Russian Air Force had shown in the Middle East that it was more than a match for its old foe, it had also begun to be more brazen in its provocations in the Pacific Far East, more than once resulting in the US threatening to shoot down wayward Russian aircraft, though they never had, and Russia had not chosen to push them that far.

Never, though, had one side put so much air power into the Pacific Far East theater as the US was doing right now.

Bondarev's eyes flicked from his tactical display to his instruments to the night sky around him in a constant circle. His heads-up display was showing that two other squadrons from his Brigade were forming up as ordered, above and beside him. But this still gave him only 54 aircraft to nearly double that number of US fighters. The Beriev airborne warning aircraft's AI was still designating the bulk of the approaching aircraft as American Fantom drones, flying out front like a silicon shield – no doubt armed with the newest Cuda missiles – with piloted F-35s behind them, probably carrying the long-range engagement weapon which was too large to fit into the drones' weapons bays.

Against these his 54 Sukhois and Migs were each armed with two long-range and four short-range missiles, but only about a third of them were carrying the new KM-77 phased-array missile because Operation LOSOS had come in the middle of an upgrade cycle. The KM-77 had a slightly greater range than the Cuda, otherwise they were an even match. Not for the first time, he regretted Lukin's direct order not to field his Okhotniks. It would have been advantageous to be able to put his own drones out in front of his piloted aircraft to meet the incoming US armada.

In any case, they might be about to see how the vaunted American Fantom performed in air-to-air combat against a real flesh and blood enemy. And they would know in about 30 seconds as the American force reached missile range!

"Gold Control to Gold Leader, enemy aircraft approaching standoff missile range in *five, four...*" the airborne warning aircraft announced. The first test would be to see whether this was a direct attack. If it was, the US F-35s could launch long-range air-to-ground missiles aimed at targets on Saint Lawrence from within Alaskan airspace, and then turn around and flee under the protection of the cloud of drones surrounding them.

"Silver Leader to Gold Leader, Silver airborne and en route," he heard a voice say over the radio. Having seen the size and apparent intent of the US attacking force, he had scrambled the 36 remaining Sukhois and Mig-41s he had at readiness in Lavrentiya. It had taken them a precious 20 minutes to get airborne and formed up. Too slow. Someone would have to get their butt kicked for that. They wouldn't be able to climb to altitude in time for the coming engagement.

"Roger, Silver Leader, vector zero three zero, nap of the earth please. Passive arrays only. Take your targeting from the data net," Bondarev ordered, telling his reserve flight to stay low and try to hide. He would use them as a surprise attack force, hoping if he kept them down at wave-top level the enemy aircraft wouldn't know they were there until their missiles started tracking. "Gold Leader out."

"...*two...one...mark*," the air controller continued to count down the range to possible standoff munitions launch. Bondarev had his eyes fixed to the threat display, listening for the warning tones indicating enemy air-to-ground missiles were on their way. The KM-77 was also an efficient standoff missile killer and he knew the pilots fielding it would be prepared to switch their targeting from the US aircraft to US missiles if they appeared. But the board stayed clear, there were no tones.

"Gold squadrons, hold station," Bondarev ordered his pilots. On his heads-up display he saw that while they might not have fired any missiles, the US armada was still boring in, straight at Saint Lawrence. "Flight control, ROE update please?"

"Rules of engagement unchanged, Gold Leader," the controller replied. "You are free to fire if US aircraft cross the no-fly perimeter."

Bondarev cursed under his breath. Their rules of engagement hadn't changed since day one of Operation LOSOS. They were hemmed in behind an invisible line in the sky, giving the US fighters a clear tactical advantage because they could choose the time and place of their attack.

"Enemy aircraft approaching US air-to-air missile range in *ten, nine, eight...*" the controller stated, unnecessarily. His pilots would soon be within range of the US long-range air-to-air missiles. So be it.

The Americans might get the first missiles away, but they would not go unanswered.

"Gold aircraft, lock up targets but hold your fire," Bondarev told his pilots. "Keep your heads, people. Anyone who fires without my express order will be court-martialed."

"*Two...one...mark...*"

Once again, the missile threat warnings stayed clear, but the US aircraft pushed forward, hitting the Alaskan coast now. They would be on top of Bondarev and his men within minutes. Could it be they were going to try to overfly Saint Lawrence, just to test Russian resolve? To prove they were masters of their own skies still?

"Gold Control, requesting permission to engage with K-77s before enemy aircraft reach Cuda missile range. Please advise."

Tactically, the US full frontal attack was insane. Dozens of their aircraft would be swatted from the sky within minutes if Bondarev was the first to engage. Could they be that stupid?

Stupid like an Arctic fox, perhaps. Politically, it wasn't so crazy. Let Russia be the aggressor. Force them onto the diplomatic back foot. Create the rationale for a major assault to retake Saint Lawrence on the basis of Russia invading and then shooting down American aircraft over American soil? Maybe that explained why the bulk of the approaching force were politically expendable drones.

"Gold Leader, we have orders from General Lukin directly," the voice of the Beriev controller said. "Only if US fighters cross the no-fly perimeter are you free to engage, repeat, you cannot fire until the perimeter is breached."

"Gold Control, if we wait that long, we will be within Cuda range," Bondarev said. "We will have no tactical advantage. That may be exactly what they are trying to achieve."

The voice that came back was stone cold, and Bondarev recognized it immediately. He should have known General Lukin would be monitoring comms and he flinched as the man broke in on the radio traffic. "Are your orders unclear, Gold Leader?"

"No sir, perfectly clear. Gold Leader out." Bondarev hammered the perspex over his head in frustration. It was a typical political compromise. His life and the life of his men put in the balance so that politicians or diplomats could claim a moral high ground, before abandoning it completely. "Gold and Silver flight leaders, keep your targets locked, await my order."

Bondarev rolled his shoulders in the tight confines of his cockpit, and flexed his fingers. He had a feeling the dying was about to begin.

Perri sighted down onto the town below.

It was damn dark. The glowing display in the scope showed very little wind, but a surprising amount of elevation if he was going to put any rounds through the roof of the car park below. He had to check what the scope was telling him against his own instincts. The copper-clad bullets were heavier than the polymer-tipped varmint rounds he usually used, but would the bullets really drop that much over this distance? He'd had to input the rifle and ammo type into the scope manually – had he screwed it up?

He cleared the target and put the small glowing red pipper over the dark black rectangle that was the carport roof, and pushed the button near his trigger again. It showed the range as

230 yards, wind at about 3 feet a second from the northwest, but the crosshairs telling him where his bullet would go were way under the roof. He lifted the barrel until the crosshairs were centered on the middle of the roof, and it felt to him like he would be shooting into the sky.

Damn. He'd rushed it. He should have been patient, should have hiked up into the rocks on the bluff, out of earshot of the town, fired a bunch of test rounds with the new ammo and the new scope until he was satisfied he had it zeroed.

Damn damn damn.

"What's the matter?" Dave asked him. "Shoot already! Let's get out of here."

Perri bet on his instincts. He was the best damn shot in Gambell, he knew that. He had a sense, a feeling for wind and elevation, for the movement of his target. He had a way of knowing just when a seal or walrus was going to breach, when a bird was going to dip right or left. And right now what the scope was telling him – the windage felt right, but the elevation didn't.

He took a breath and held it.

He steadied the crosshairs just above the outer lip of the roof. If he saw his shots hitting the sandbags, he could correct.

OK, Perri. Ten shots, as fast as you can pull the trigger, or until the damn carport blows up.

And then run like hell.

"Every Russian aircraft in the sky near Saint Lawrence just lit their burners and headed east," Bunny said, visor down, nestled inside her virtual-reality helmet inside the trailer. "Care to share why, sir?"

"Well, you're going to see it on the morning news anyway," Halifax said. "The media name for it is Operation Resolve. The idea is to show the Russians just what will happen tomorrow if they don't start withdrawing."

"Whatever it is, it's giving us clear air over Gambell," Rodriguez noted. The late-night launch of their two recon

Fantoms had been a routine affair, and she'd been locked in the command trailer with Halifax and O'Hare for nearly an hour as Bunny got her one of her drones into position to make a run over the target while the other stayed in reserve. Satellite synthetic aperture radar images had shown a lot of hardware lining the side of the landing strip, and intelligence analysis had identified at least four Verba sites, two bracketing Gambell and two bracketing the facility at Savoonga. The way the Verbas had engaged outside optical range showed they were fully networked, pulling targeting data from Airborne Control aircraft, satellite and aircraft overhead. There were also older, less lethal SAM systems on the Russian navy ships circling the island, but Rodriguez had a feeling their crews would be looking east right now, because whatever 'Operation Resolve' was, something big was brewing there. The imaging also showed concentrations of vehicle traffic in a couple of places in the township, one that had been identified as the 'town hall' and was speculated to be a military command post, and the other identified as the John Ampangalook Memorial High School. If the 200 plus townsfolk were being held anywhere, it was probably there, but the tell-tale heat bloom that would come from a mass of people packed into the school buildings there was being confused by a number of other heat sources burning in and around the school and the outskirts of town. This was what Bunny had to investigate. It was possible Russian troops were torching houses to drive people out, but more likely they had just lit fuel-oil 'smudge pots' to confuse infrared imaging.

Bunny's Fantoms were carrying no weapons except guns this time. In the load bay were dedicated reconnaissance pods that sported a suite of low-light, infrared and radar imaging capabilities. If she could just get one good run the length of Gambell, they would get a wealth of data. If she could get two, they might have a real chance of identifying where those hostages were being held so that they had a hope of surviving the coming metal storm.

"Starting ingress," Bunny said. She had a suite of recon flight routines at her fingertips, leaving the AI to run the surveillance systems using a low-level full-spectrum target ID algorithm that directed it to both map the entire target area at wide angle and zoom in to try to identify military equipment and targets based on their physical or electronic signal properties. "No nosy Sukhois around," she observed. "Thank you, Operation Resolve!"

"Gold Leader to Gold flight commanders, prepare to... hold! *Safe your weapons, repeat, safe your weapons!*" Bondarev nearly yelled into his mike.

He had just gotten a report from both his Airborne Control aircraft and the ground-based air defense commander that the enemy armada would be crossing the no-fly perimeter any second. He had been straining his eyes, looking for any tell-tale light or exhaust trail to show on the horizon, while flicking back and forth between his instruments and the threat display showing the mass of icons that was the American aircraft headed straight for him and his fighters. He had six missiles, and a target locked for each of them. He knew his pilots would also have their targets designated, the offensive assault distributed across all of his aircraft so that every US plane had at least two or three missiles allocated to it, arrowing at it from various angles, both high and low.

If that gave him any confidence, then the knowledge that the enemy had nearly a quarter as many missiles again targeting the Russian aircraft took that away. There would be very few aircraft left flying a few minutes from now.

But why hadn't they engaged at long-distance missile range? Why weren't they trying to jam Russian radar? What were they waiting for?

Bondarev got his answer just before he ordered his fighters to engage. In one smooth movement, as it crossed the Alaskan coast into the waters of the Bering Strait, the US force split into two, half swinging north, and the other half swinging south.

They were no longer approaching Saint Lawrence. And they were still outside the Russian no-fly perimeter.

Bondarev quickly split his own force, suspecting that was exactly what the US planners were trying to force him to do, but he had no other option. Within moments he had 27 aircraft flying parallel to and about twenty miles apart from 50 US fighters headed north, and the other 27 tracking the US southern group, with the 36 aircraft of his Silver battalion staying low in the clutter of the Saint Lawrence landscape.

He told his flight commanders to stay alert. There was still a chance this was just a pincer movement, and the US force would swing toward Saint Lawrence again to slam shut the jaws of the pincer. His eyes flicked frantically from threat to threat on his heads-up display, his fingers hovering over the missile launch buttons on his stick.

But then the US fighters turned away, back toward Alaska. One group set up a lower racetrack circuit along the coast to the south, the other took a high cover position, but also set up a racetrack position along the north coast. Bondarev let out a huge breath and ordered his people to do the same to the north and south of Saint Lawrence.

He moved his thumb away from the firing button for his weapons. "Gold Leader to Gold and Silver Commanders, weapons safe, but stay alert. Gold Control, do you see any other enemy air activity? Could this be a decoy for an attack from another quarter?"

"Gold Control to Gold Leader, the board is clear," the air commander replied. "The enemy force did not cross the no-fly perimeter. It looks like they are just rattling their sabers."

"Roger that, Gold Leader out," Bondarev said. *Roger that.* If this was saber rattling, he could only imagine what tomorrow would bring when the US deadline ran out!

"OK, they're around the corner at the next block now," Dave said. He'd been following a jeep that was making a regular circuit of the town, waiting for it to get well clear of the ammo dump. There were no foot soldiers near the dump that he could see, and no lights in any of the nearby houses.

Perri ignored the guidance of the digital scope, settled the crosshairs on the furthest edge of the carport roof, took a breath, waited for the small trembling circular motion of his gun barrel to steady itself, and then squeezed the trigger. The report from the Winchester sounded impossibly loud in the still night air, and caromed off the rocks around them. But before it had even registered, Perri worked the bolt and fired again, and again.

Down in the dark, he saw a spark.

"Holy hell!" Bunny exclaimed as the surveillance feed from the Fantom that had just started its run over Gambell flared bright white. In an instant it looked like she had lost both low-light and infrared camera coverage and was suddenly flying blind. She quickly ordered the drone to level out, and saw with relief that it was responding to inputs. She wasn't showing a missile launch. It hadn't been hit.

"Laser jamming?" Halifax asked.

"I don't think…" Bunny muttered. She flicked her fingers across her keyboard. The drone should have passed the airstrip by now and be making its run over Gambell harbor. She reached for a small toggle and, taking back control of the drone's low-light camera, she swung it around, seeing the green-white flare fade and some solid imagery emerge again. As she pointed the camera toward the drone's starboard aft quarter, it became clear what had happened.

"Explosion, down in the township," Bunny said, pointing at a screen above her head. "Big mother. Look at that cloud. Showing secondaries too."

Rodriguez and Halifax leaned forward. On the 2D screen they could see a small mushroom-shaped cloud rising over a brightly burning building at the edge of the town. Smaller explosions within the building seemed to send phosphorescent arcs of smoke out in all directions, starting other fires.

178

"Operation Resolve, sir?" Rodriguez asked Halifax. "That looks like a cruise missile strike timed exactly with our ingress. Is that what we were supposed to record?"

"No, I..."

"With respect, sir, we should have been briefed," Bunny said, turning her drone out to sea. "Target identification and bomb damage assessment, those are two completely different missions."

"I wasn't... I didn't..." Halifax was stammering.

Rodriguez got the distinct idea that he had no idea what had just happened!

"Holy hell!" Dave yelled, at almost the same time as Bunny O'Hare, 200 miles away. He hadn't counted, but it seemed to be on about the sixth or eighth shot from Perri, just as Dave was deciding nothing was going to happen, that the Russian ammo bunker exploded in incandescent white light.

"Run!" Perri yelled, scrambling to his feet. "We have to get down among the rocks before anyone looks up here."

The light from the burning pyre that had once been the sandbagged carport was as bright as a dozen stadium lights. It threw crazy, dancing shadows over the slope of the bluff and the noise and light sent hundreds of auklets squawking into the night in fright. Perri found himself running through a cloud of birds in what felt like the strobe from a nightclub light show.

They came to the edge of a group of rocks, with a large open patch of ground ahead of them. Dave would have kept running, but Perri grabbed his jacket by the shoulder and pulled him down. "Wait, let's see if it's safe." He looked down toward the town.

Soldiers had spilled out of the town hall. He should have realized that's where the bulk of them would be. Some jeeps were moving cautiously toward the ammo dump. Other soldiers were spilling out of the school, surrounding it, maybe worried about a breakout? Or with something else in mind.

No one seemed to be headed toward them.

"OK, let's go," Perri said, getting to his feet again.

"We did it!" Dave was saying. "We actually *did* it!"

"Celebrate when we're back in the tank," Perri grunted.

Right then, he saw a missile lift off from an emplacement beside the airstrip and arc away toward the sea, aimed at some unknown target.

"Missile launch!" Bunny reported. "Not tracking. They're firing blind. I won't jam unless they get a lock."

"Are we the only aircraft in the target area?" Rodriguez asked Halifax. "Or are there others we aren't seeing?"

"As far as I know, we are the only unit over Gambell," he said vehemently. "No one told me anything about a missile strike. We have set up patrols over the Alaskan coast, that's Operation Resolve. Not specifically to give us cover, but that's why our mission was timed now, while the Russian combat air patrol was focused east."

"Beginning second pass," Bunny said. "We aren't going to get a third."

Halifax reached for a comms handset. "Make the pass and then get to a safe distance and hold. I'm going to try to get some clarity on this."

At that moment, a voice came over the trailer loudspeaker, "A4, this is NORAD. We are showing one or more ground-to-air missile launches or major explosions near Gambell. Can you confirm?" Rodriguez and Bunny stole a *no shit Sherlock* glance at each other, and left Halifax to respond.

"Gold Control to Gold Leader, we have reports of a ground strike on an ammunition dump at Gambell," the airborne controller said in Bondarev's ear. "Air defense command at Gambell has reported returns from at least one aircraft in the area, probably stealth, but they cannot get a lock. We are assessing the situation, you are to prepare to engage the

US airborne force over Bering Strait on our order. Standby. Gold Control out."

"Hold position please, Gold flight leaders," Bondarev said with calm dread. "Weapons free. Prepare to engage US aircraft on my mark."

Please, he said to himself. *Please just let us fire first!*

As they scrambled down the slope at the outskirts of town toward the safety of their underground bunker, Perri saw another missile lift off from the airstrip and speed out to sea. The Russians were shooting at something, but what? Whatever it was, it made it less likely they suspected a kid with a Winchester had blown up their ammo dump, and Perri was glad about that.

"OK, down down *down*," Dave said urgently as he hauled open the trapdoor to the tank and waved at Perri to jump in.

Feet on the rungs, Perri took one last ground-level look at the boiling white column of smoke rising up over Gambell.

Now the shit really got real, he thought to himself.

Bondarev knew the crew of the Beriev Airborne Control aircraft. He had hand-picked them. He had seen them at work over Syria and Turkey, seen them stay calm even in the face of a direct attack intended to bring their aircraft down. He knew the scene inside the aircraft right now would be one of frenzied efficiency, plotting targets, handing them off to the AI to assign to his aircrafts' targeting systems, confirming and reconfirming that every US aircraft had been triangulated to maximize the chances of a kill while they awaited orders from Lukin's staff.

Still, he wanted to scream at them to hurry the hell up and decide.

"Gold Leader, you are free to engage. Repeat, weapons free, you may engage."

"Gold and Silver Leaders, engage!" he said. Even as he spoke, he swung his own machine east-northeast, seeing his wingmen follow, and one by one the six missiles in his ordnance bay dropped out and raced away east. Soon the night sky around him was a tracery of white smoke and bright fire, leaping ahead of his fighters like the bony white fingers of death. He looked away so that he didn't completely burn his night vision.

There was no time to even register the kills. On his heads-up display he saw the icons of US aircraft scattering as their threat warning systems reacted to the missile onslaught. Several winked out, and at the edge of his vision he thought he saw bright flashes in the night sky, far away. Then his own threat warning alarm sounded.

"Evade!" he called, "and re-engage." If he survived the next two minutes, if any of his men did, the next phase of this battle would be fought with guns.

At night. Against robots, piloted by a generation of video gamers safe in trailers that could be anywhere in the world.

She heard the feet running down the corridor toward her office before her security detail burst through the door.

"Madam Ambassador? Come with us, please," the senior Secret Service officer said, holding the door open as she jumped to her feet. Somewhere in the building an alarm began to sound and her stomach fell. She felt her feet going from underneath her and had to grab the doorway as she went through to stop herself from falling.

It was the Critical Incident alarm. A terrorist attack. Or worse.

"New Annex safe room, ma'am," the officer said, confirming her worst fears. "Stairs, this way. We can get there inside two minutes, just take it easy."

"What's the alert for?"

"Just follow us, ma'am, you'll be briefed when we're in the secure area."

Two minutes to safety. It seemed like such a short time. But she knew that 'safety' was an illusion. A sub-launched ICBM starting from the Baltic Sea would take less than 20 minutes to reach Moscow, but a hypersonic cruise missile launched from an aircraft over Germany would take only ten. Say she did make it to the bunker under the Embassy. Say she did survive the nuclear strike.

Then what?

"No!" she said, stopping in her tracks. She knew the protocol; the bunker was equipped with a pulse shielded landline to the Kremlin. In the case of a nuclear attack, she was supposed to ride it out and then seek to establish contact with Russian authorities and either negotiate their surrender or await further instruction. She also knew how insane that idea was.

"Ma'am!" the Secret Service officer said, grabbing at her elbow. "Please."

"Let me go. Make sure our people are safe. I'm getting on the line to Washington," she said, in a voice that made it clear she was not interested in discussion.

"Yes, ma'am," the officer said, exchanging a look with the others in the detail before ordering two of his men to stay with her and running off down the corridor.

"Not good, not good," Bunny said, horrified. She had zoomed out the tactical map and patched in a feed from NORAD as she watched the map light up with hundreds of missile tracks over the air east of Saint Lawrence, not to mention another lancing out from Gambell but falling away behind her drone as it scooted to safety. The missile had obviously been blind fired at a return the Verba crew had picked up from her Fantom, but they might as well have fired at a random arc of sky. Without a solid lock from the ground or another data source, the radar and infrared seekers on the missile were just sniffing empty air.

"NORAD, this is Colonel Halifax of A4, please confirm upload of data from Gambell recon, and I request update on the full disposition of blue and red forces over Saint Lawrence."

"Upload confirmed, A4," a voice replied. "Data request denied. You are directed to return your aircraft to base and await further orders."

"It's bloody World War Three up there," Bunny said, pulling off her helmet and pointing at the air-to-air missile tracks on the 2D screen. She quickly punched in a return course for their Fantoms that would skirt around the hell over Saint Lawrence and get them back up north to the Rock. It would take at least an hour.

Halifax didn't respond to her exclamation. He picked up a handset and called up to the commander of the Naval Computer and Telecommunications Area Master Station inside his radar dome.

"Sound general quarters, Captain Aslam," he said. "When the men are assembled, I want everyone not on active duty inside the station to get down here under the Rock. Meet me at the elevator topside."

Rodriguez looked at him, and he turned to the threat display. "This little cold war just got real hot, Boss," he said. "Russia may not know we're down here, but they sure as hell have seen our radar dome up there and it wouldn't take more than an old Mig with a bunch of dumb iron bombs to scrape my nice white radar installation off the top of this rock and into the sea – and everyone up there with it." He turned and took a step toward the door of the trailer. "I'm going topside to make sure only essential personnel stay behind. You get this place organized – and find bunks for everyone!"

Having been bustled down unfamiliar corridors on the way to the bunker under the New Annex, Devlin found herself taking one wrong turn after another as she tried to move against the flow of people running for the illusory safety of the New Annex basement. It wasn't entirely irrational. The same alarm was used for a terrorist or chemical weapons attack, and the airtight, radiation-shielded and self-contained secure rooms below the New Annex were adequate to protect staff against threats that were slightly less dramatic than a direct hit by a nuclear weapon. As the panicked traffic thinned out, Devlin found herself standing in a corridor that looked familiar, and yet...

"You lost, ma'am?"

She turned and saw the analyst, Carl Williams, with his head sticking out of his office.

"You should be in the bunker," Devlin replied, pointing up at the wall where a loudspeaker blared.

"Shouldn't *you*?" he asked, looking at her security detail, who both gave him pained looks. He himself clearly wasn't in a hurry to go anywhere.

She didn't have time for this. "I need to get a secure line to Washington. What is the quickest way to the Chancery from here?"

"You can do it from my office," he said.

"But it's a dedicated..."

185

"No problem," he insisted. "Trust me."

"Sorry," she said to the Secret Service officers, "there's only room for two." Carl stood aside so she could get into his little cubicle of an office and he closed the door behind her. The critical incident alarm was still blaring outside and she winced. It would make holding a phone conversation a real pain.

Williams read her mind. "You want me to turn that off?"

She hesitated. "I don't think you should."

"There's no threat to the Embassy," he said calmly. "A little skirmish in the air over Saint Lawrence, but that's all. Nukes aren't flying, yet. Triggering a critical incident alert based on that is a complete over-reaction by someone in State."

Devlin was about to ask him how the hell he knew that, but she was learning that with Carl Williams, for deniability purposes it was probably best she didn't ask.

"Can you shut off the siren without pulling everyone out of the bunkers quite yet?" she asked.

"HOLMES? Can you kill the critical incident siren, but leave the alert in place until it is canceled by State?" Williams spoke toward his laptop.

"Yes, Carl," the cultured British voice replied.

"Do it please."

The alarm cut instantly, an eerie silence replacing it. No heels on the floors, no voices in the corridor.

"Just sit there, ma'am, tell him who you want to call," Williams said, pointing to his chair behind the desk and laptop. "Once you connect, I'll leave you alone."

Devlin sat, then leaned forward over this laptop. "OK, HOLMES, this is Ambassador Devlin McCarthy…"

"Confirmed, ma'am, I have facial recognition," HOLMES replied.

"Right, well … I want to speak to Secretary of State Gerard Winburg, please, on his direct encrypted line."

"Yes, ma'am. He is airborne in Airforce 1 at the moment. All communications are encrypted. Putting you through," the AI said.

Williams pointed at the door and moved toward it, but Devlin reconsidered. There was probably no point in secrecy, and she might be able to use Williams' help. She motioned to him to stay put.

"That line is busy, ma'am," the AI said. "We are on hold. Do you want me to put you through to the President's direct line instead? He is on Airforce 1 with the Secretary of State."

Devlin hesitated, but before she could answer there was a click on the laptop's loudspeaker. "Winburg here."

"Mr. Secretary, this is Ambassador McCarthy in Moscow," she said. "The critical incident alarm has sounded here."

"Yes, I authorized it," the harried voice at the other end said, clearly under pressure. "I don't know how much you know about current developments over Saint Lawrence, McCarthy."

Devlin looked at Williams. He came around to her shoulder, tapped a couple of keys on his laptop, and Devlin saw he had been preparing an intelligence report when she had interrupted him. She put her finger on the screen and started reading.

"Sir, I know that at 0200 Alaskan time this morning explosions were reported in the township of Gambell, cause unknown. Local Russian anti-aircraft missile batteries, however, responded to an unidentified threat, indicating the source of the explosion was possibly an attack by US aircraft, or they simply panicked. Following this, Russian aircraft stationed in the eastern no-fly zone around Saint Lawrence engaged US aircraft on patrol along the Alaska coast." She hesitated, looking at Williams in disbelief, but he nodded. "And as of ... five ... minutes ago, data from NORAD and Airborne Control aircraft in the combat area indicates the destruction of 17 Russian aircraft for the loss of 23 US aircraft destroyed, eight damaged." She had to read the last part again. *That was nearly as many aircraft lost in one engagement as had been lost in the entire Middle East conflict, and the battle was still going?*

There was a silence at the other end before Winburg came back on the line. "Dammit, how are you getting that intel in

Moscow?! You have real-time data on kills and losses over Saint Lawrence? That's more than I have!"

"I have an NSA analyst on station here, Secretary," she winked at Williams. "He's very ... resourceful."

"Apparently. Anything else?"

"No, sir, we are working to identify Russia's strategic aims in this conflict. I hope to get back to you soon on that," Devlin said. "Sir, I am not CIA head of station, I know that, but I wanted to report that we have seen no signs of military preparations on the streets here in Moscow, we have heard of no evacuations or civilian warnings, and as far as I am aware key senior politicians and bureaucrats are still in Moscow and behaving normally. Russian TV and radio are also running normal programming."

"OK..."

"Sir, I have seen nothing today, or in the last week, to indicate the Russian government is about to conduct a nuclear strike on the USA or that they are anticipating one from us."

"Which could, of course, be part of their strategy," Winburg said. He was the former CEO of a major defense contractor, and Devlin had heard him say his policy was to trust no one, in business or politics. "Look, this was a good call, Ambassador. Good context. Make sure you share what you have with CIA. And you feel free to call me again when you have anything to add."

"Will do. Goodbye, Mr. Secretary."

She looked at Williams. "How do I hang up?"

The British voice replied, "I have disconnected the call, ma'am."

Looking at the data onscreen again, she whistled. "That's what you call a 'little skirmish'?"

Williams shrugged. "In the big picture, yeah. I mean, it's not nuclear war."

"Yet. You heard the man. Can you be sure to copy your report to CIA?" she asked the analyst.

Williams looked a little uncomfortable. "Sorry, ma'am, no."

Devlin looked surprised. "No?"

"No. I mean, someone will. The data is all there. HOLMES is pulling it from servers inside NORAD, DIA, CIA, Pacific Command and so on. I was just putting that report together for NSA to show what he can do in these types of situations. I can't share data on HOLMES capabilities with anyone outside NSA." She was clearly not impressed, because he stammered on. "I mean, except you, because, like, you have clearance now."

"So sanitize it, include the information I gave the Secretary and then send it as soon as the dust settles. Can you do that?"

"Sure, I guess, but aren't there other people who…"

"Carl, right now, the only people above ground here are the two guys outside your door plus you and me, and to be honest only one of us seems to know what the hell is going on out there, and that's you."

To Yevgeny Bondarev, it was no 'little skirmish'. It was a tooth and nail fight to the death! The melee over Saint Lawrence had degenerated into a knife fight. Most of the remaining aircraft, about 20 Russian and 40 US fighters, were engaged in one on one, gun on gun combat.

Bondarev had survived the first blizzard of US missiles, registered one, maybe two kills of his own, but was now twisting and turning above the sea with a very determined Fantom on his tail. He had no more short-range missiles left, but apparently, neither did his opponent. As tracer fire flashed over his canopy for the third time, he put his machine into a fast roll, then flicked into a climbing starboard turn to try to gain a little separation from his attacker. He needed altitude for what he had in mind, but it was a desperate last chance roll of the dice. If he screwed it up, he was dead.

The Su-57 was a magnificent airplane, but it was big and intended to kill airborne enemies at long range. It was not optimal for close-range combat. The smaller American Fantom was less deadly at range, but much more maneuverable in a knife fight because there was no pilot to black out. The thrust-vectoring nozzles on his Sukhoi, however, gave him one spectacular trick for an opponent who was close on his six o'clock, and he was willing to bet that whether he was up against a drone commanded by a ground-based pilot or operating on autonomous AI control, he'd catch it unprepared. As he leveled out at the top of his turn, he could almost feel the gun pipper on the heads-up display of the machine behind him settle on his tail. He bunted the nose of his Sukhoi down, keeping his speed at 450 knots, trying not to give the other pilot too easy a shot. Tracer blasted over his wing.

He checked his airspeed. Good. *Now!* He hauled back sharply on his stick, pulling it all the way back until it rammed into the stays and couldn't go any further. To the American behind him, man or machine, it must have seemed as though the Sukhoi had simply stopped in mid-air and pointed its nose at the sky. The American machine nearly lost control as it tried to avoid colliding with the Sukhoi that was skidding through the air on its tail, like the cobra the maneuver was named after.

"Come on you fat-assed bastard!" Bondarev yelled at his Sukhoi, pushing the nose down before it pitched over backward and, increasing his engine to full burner, regained forward momentum. This was the moment Bondarev was most vulnerable. Recovering from a virtual stall, hydrogen fire pouring from his afterburner like a small sun, he knew he was a sitting duck if there was more than one Fantom behind him. He hunched his shoulders waiting to die, but grunted as he saw the exhaust flames of the American fighter wallow through the night sky ahead of him, having failed to keep the Sukhoi in its sights, fighting against a stall itself. It pulled an ugly looping turn across Bondarev's nose and his guns fired automatically as soon as they had a radar lock on the American. The machine fell apart in a glittering rain of metal shards.

Bondarev had control over his own aircraft again, and scanned his threat display for another target. He tried desperately to get a grip on the situation. Where were his pilots, where was the enemy? He was at ten thousand feet again, swinging wildly around the sky to avoid the trap of being the legendary sitting duck. "Gold squadron, report your..."

At that moment he heard a missile launch warning scream in his ears. The enemy must have been close, because even as his automatic countermeasures of flares and chaff fired into the sky behind him, the Sukhoi's combat AI took control of the machine from him and flung the Sukhoi into an inverted dive that pulled all the blood from his head. His pressurized combat suit inflated, trying to keep the blood flowing to his brain, but it wasn't enough! He was pulling too many g's, and his world went black.

What happened next wouldn't matter to Yevgeny Bondarev. He was out cold.

It was designated 'Hunter' for a reason. Like the Fantom, the unmanned Okhotnik drone was a multirole platform with a range of more than 4,000 miles. It could stay airborne for 20 hours at cruising speed, carry a payload of two tons, and while it was able to pull data from multiple sources to assist its own air-to-air targeting and engage enemy aircraft with both long- and short-range missiles, its real talent was stealth delivery of air-to-ground ordnance.

Like the 1,500kg thermobaric fuel-air explosive precision guided bomb. Comprising pressurized ethylene oxide, mixed with an energetic nanoparticle such as aluminum, surrounding a high explosive burster, when detonated it created an explosion equivalent to 49 tons of TNT. That was why it was unofficially called a MOAB – Mother of All Bombs. It couldn't be mounted on a cruise missile – an aircraft had to penetrate enemy air defenses to be able to deliver it, which was a drawback. But just one could flatten a small town, render a harbor unusable and sink all the ships in it, or destroy every hangar, aircraft and living person on an airfield inside a radius of about 1,600 feet.

Stealthy delivery of the MOAB was a talent that had been honed in the deserts and mountain ranges of Northern Syria by pilots and systems officers of the Lynx Air Brigade, and they were exceedingly good at both the stealth and the delivery. Further, while Bondarev's Snow Leopard Okhotniks had been held back from the battle for Saint Lawrence, no such restriction had been put on the Okhotniks of the Lynx Brigade.

At the same time as Bondarev received his order to engage, a squadron of Okhotniks in a low-level holding pattern in the middle of the Bering Strait split like a starburst, with four three-plane elements departing to attack US ground targets within the no-fly exclusion zone. One flight headed for targets around Nome and Port Clarence. Two flights headed for Saint Lawrence, to be ready for tasking should close air support be needed against US ground targets on the island.

The fourth flight headed for the only other US installation inside the no-fly zone. It wasn't a target on which you'd usually use thermobaric bombs — something much less powerful would have been sufficient, but sometimes you just had to use what you had to hand.

And at least there was complete certainty they would no longer have to worry about that annoying US long-range radar installation on Little Diomede Island.

Alicia Rodriguez had trained her whole adult life to go to war. But now that she was, she found all that training suddenly futile. The world under the Rock had descended into a noisome chaos, turning her perfectly ordered flight deck into a mass of personnel from the 712th Aircraft Control and Warning Squadron all looking for somewhere to park backpacks or backsides, and for someone to answer their big and small questions. That person should have been their CO, Captain Ali Aslam, but Aslam was still topside with Halifax getting his men down from the station above in the goods elevator that held only fifteen personnel at a time. Men and women were also pouring out of the emergency stairs beside the elevator shaft.

Bunny wasn't helping either, trapped in her 'cockpit' growling at anyone who came within twenty feet. Her recon
192

drones had been parked in a sea-level orbit ten minutes south of Saint Lawrence and hadn't been retasked or recalled. She only had about ten minutes of fuel left before she would have to call them home anyway. Rodriguez had just finished ensuring her recovery team was ready to recycle them when they landed, despite all the chaos in the cavern.

Rodriguez pulled open the door to the trailer and stepped inside, closing the door behind her and taking a breath. She pressed her forehead to the door. Come on, girl. You can get a pair of drones into the air through a hole in a rock inside ten minutes, you can land a measly two kites and deal with a hundred worried base personnel and their stupid questions. Right?

Right. Question of the moment. The head of base security, Master Sergeant Collaguiri, had been ordered down under the Rock by Halifax, but insisted his place was topside with the CO. He had tried appealing the case to Rodriguez, and Rodriguez had promised him she would call up to the CO and see what he wanted to do about it.

She sighed and picked up the comms, punching in the number for the radar installation control room, assuming that was where Halifax would be. It wasn't a long call.

"Rodriguez, we are currently tracking about a hundred friendly and enemy aircraft in combat over the Bering Sea. Tell the Master Sergeant he can..." The line went dead.

Then a second later the entire island shook as though the God of Thunder himself had spoken.

The effect of a thermobaric blast against living targets is gruesome. First, the pressure wave from the fuel-air explosion flattens anyone caught unprotected. If you are within the kill zone and unlucky enough to survive the pressure wave, the vacuum created collapses your lungs so that you suffocate. Not all of the fuel in the bomb is guaranteed to go off, so if the fuel deflagrates but doesn't detonate, anyone still left alive will be severely burned and probably also inhale the burning fuel. Since the most common Fuel Air Explosive or FAE components, ethylene oxide and propylene oxide, are highly toxic, undetonated FAE is as lethal to personnel caught within the cloud as most chemical warfare agents.

Luckily for Halifax, he was at ground zero for the first of the three MOABs that hit the Naval Computer and Telecommunications Area Master Station on Little Diomede. As he was talking with Rodriguez he just had time to register the sound of an explosion and a sharp kerosene-like odor before he and every man, woman and bird on the surface of the Rock were obliterated.

It was like two or three earthquakes hit them in quick succession, followed shortly afterward by a thundering series of booms. Spreading outward from the point of impact on top of the rock dome, a series of pressure waves pushed the sea surrounding Little Diomede down and outward. The pressure waves passed quickly, and the displaced seawater came flooding back.

Little Diomede was ultimately supposed to be fitted with blast doors and airlocks at the mouth of the Slot that could withstand a tactical nuclear strike and enable the base to keep functioning. There had been no urgency; they had not yet been installed.

The gantry over the submarine docking bay rocked and a part of the reinforced roof over the small harbor collapsed. Seconds later a huge wave flooded in through the entrance of the cave and instantly submerged the entire dock area in waist-deep water.

Anyone there fifty feet below the trailer who had kept their feet through the first round of violence was knocked down by the force of the water and as Rodriguez got to her feet, she saw the harbor was a maelstrom of churning water and flailing personnel. Her mind raced.

A nuke, we must have been hit by a nuke! But shouldn't there have been a flash? Wouldn't a nuke have evaporated the seawater, turned it to steam? The cave was open to the sea, so if they were at the center of a nuclear explosion, even here under the Rock they should have been toasted to a crisp.

Not a nuke, then.

She saw Bunny struggling to her feet, cursing as usual.

That was as far as thinking got her. Outside the trailer people were drowning. She jumped for the door and ran down to the still rising waterline.

IN YOUR FACE

Bondarev woke with a headache like he'd dropped an entire bottle of whiskey in a single sitting, then realized he was still strapped into his cockpit. His vision was blurred and graying out, alarms were sounding in his ears, and he could smell the distinct ozone-tinged smell of fried wiring. An instant of panic rose in him, the most basal fear of all fighter pilots – *fire!?* With one hand he reached for his ejection handle, with the other he fumbled for the oxygen dial that supplied air to his mask, turning it to full rich, and breathed deeply.

Almost immediately his vision cleared, his headache dropped to a dull throb, and he could see he was flying straight and level, about a hundred meters above the sea. His heads-up display was dead, but his instruments still worked, if they could be trusted. A quick scan told him he had taken a hit from either missile or gunfire. His right wing was perforated and the control surfaces there jammed, but his engine was running within normal operating ranges. No fuel or fluid leaks being reported. His combat AI had saved his life and gotten him out of the fight, putting him on autopilot and setting a course for Lavrentiya. He was about twenty minutes out.

He knew better than to take manual control. *If it's broken, don't try to fly it.* Cutting out the autopilot now, without knowing the state of his aircraft or how the AI was compensating for flight damage, could send him into an irrecoverable spin and he didn't have the altitude to risk it. Just like when he was in his passenger car at home in Vladivostok, he was putting his life in the hands of the AI.

He should never have looked down at the floor of the cockpit. But something felt wrong and he realized his right foot felt wet. That was when he noticed the noise, the high whistling sound of air rushing past and into the cockpit. He looked down. There were holes in the wall of the cockpit where no holes should be. And a pool of blood on the floor by the pedals where no blood should be.

Between the two of them, Rodriguez and O'Hare had pulled ten people out of the water before anyone else around them had reacted. Being up in the command trailer a good distance from the mini-tsunami had helped them get their wits together faster than most people, but pretty soon there were twenty or thirty people down at the waterline, hands grasping limbs, heaving bodies out of the water.

Most were alive.

Some weren't.

It seemed to Rodriguez they were just starting to get on top of things – there were more people up above the waterline than there were still foundering in the water.

Suddenly there was an almighty crash from the direction of the topside elevator as the plane lift and a few hundred feet of cable crashed to the floor of the cave. Then, as though in sympathy, the loading crane by the submarine dock gave a forlorn groan and, with majestic gravity, fell across the Pond, its heavy crown smashing into the transformer room on the other side of the dock. The last thing Rodriguez saw was Master Sergeant Collaguiri and a group of men disappearing under dust and rubble.

And then the cave fell into total darkness.

Perri fell to the bottom of the ladder and just managed to get out of the way before the hatch above slammed shut with a clang and Dave and his rifle fell in a heap right where he'd landed.

"Screw this," Dave grunted.

Perri looked up. "Did you lock it?"

"No, I didn't freaking lock it," Dave swore, looking at him like it was a totally unreasonable question. "I came in head first. *You* can lock it."

Perri didn't argue. Pulling himself up off the floor, he climbed the ladder and pulled the combination padlock through the eyelets that Dave had drilled into the wall, clicking it shut. He slid down the ladder, using just his hands to slow himself, and landed lightly. He had so much adrenaline in his system he felt he could have flown down.

He looked at Dave and the two of them burst out laughing. It was a hysterical, uncontrollable kind of laughter and they let it roll all the way out and back again before they both fell onto their backsides.

Perri gasped. "That was insane."

"Asymmetrical, you said?" Dave said, wiping his eyes. "That was totally asymmetrical, man!"

"I know."

"I thought maybe you could hit it, maybe a bullet would get through the roof, but I never thought..."

"I know."

"Did you see those missiles blasting off? Was that us?"

Perri remembered the missiles arcing into the sky and heading out to sea, definitely hunting something out there. "Don't think so."

Dave wiped his face. His hand was shaking, and he sat on it.

They were both quiet a while.

"That was one mother of an explosion. You don't think..." Dave asked.

"Think what?"

"You think we killed anyone? I mean, the school..."

"The school was five hundred yards away, no way."

"No. What about Russians?"

"I don't know. I didn't look. I was too busy running and getting crapped on by auklets." They laughed again.

"Yeah, at least someone was more freaked than us," Dave said.

Perri reached over and checked the rifle he'd thrown down the ladder ahead of him. It had landed on its stock, but he quickly checked the scope, turning it on to see if he'd damaged it. No, it was okay. It was built to take some tough love.

"They're going to start hunting us now," Dave said, watching Perri as he jacked out the remaining ammunition and started pulling the rifle apart to clean it.

"For sure."

"We should stay down here a while, eh? Stupid to go out the next couple of days."

"Like we agreed."

"I know. We have to pull that old sheet of tin across the hatch cover, though." They'd found an old sheet of corrugated iron and worked out how to lean it up and over the hatch covering the tank and then pull the hatch down so the tin covered it over. It was light enough they could lift the hatch and the tin at the same time from below, but heavy enough it wouldn't easily blow away. It wasn't much, but it hid the hatch from plain view and looked like the hundred other pieces of junk lying around the gas station.

"So do it," Perri said. "Better to do it now while it's dark, then we can bunk down."

"Yeah, right." Dave disappeared up the ladder again. Perri heard him fooling around outside and pulling the cover shut a couple of times before he was satisfied it was good enough, then he came back down and collapsed on a mattress next to Perri. He grabbed a water bottle off a shelf and took a long pull. "Damn, I should have taken a whizz while I was up there," Dave said, and Perri laughed again.

After a few minutes Perri laid the parts of his rifle aside. He heard heavy breathing and looked across and saw Dave with his head cradled onto the crook of his arm, asleep.

Perri suddenly realized he was exhausted too. He drank some water, then reached over Dave to cut the power to the lights. Blackness consumed their small, cold cell deep under the dirt and he lay down, pulling a sleeping bag over himself.

"Sniper team," Dave said somewhere to his right. "Deadly, eh?"

"You did great, brother," Perri told him.

"I did, right?" Dave said. "You too."

"Sleep, Dave."

Private Zubkhov had rolled out of his bed and found himself crouched on the floor beside it before he'd even realized he was awake. From somewhere outside, maybe out by the airfield, he heard the unmistakable whoosh of a ground-to-air missile.

Then as a second explosion rocked the air, he realized what had woken him. A few blocks away, it sounded like a full-on war was raging. As the men around him had tumbled out of their bunks, he'd grabbed up pants and a jacket, found his anti-materiel rifle against the wall, and staggered out into the freezing dark night.

Across the other side of town, explosions lit the night sky.

"What the hell?" he asked no one in particular.

Captain Demchenko took control, sending half of the men to the airfield where they'd been digging sandbagged emplacements all afternoon. He pointed at Zubkhov. "You, and the rest of you, with me." And with that he'd started running *toward* the explosions, which seemed to Zubkhov to be the complete opposite of what they should be doing. That opinion was confirmed five minutes later as their squad rounded a corner to see half of the houses on the next block on fire and, at the end of the row, a volcano of white fire spitting shrapnel and 7.62mm rounds at them.

"They hit the ammo dump," Zubkhov said to himself.

"Who did?" asked the man next to him.

Zubkhov looked at the dark sky around him as another ground-to-air missile leaped off its rails and sped away into the night.

"Who you think, dumbass?" Zubkhov replied.

The other soldier had a quick comeback ready, and he was about to throw it back at Zubkhov but never got that far. Something whizzed past their ears.

Zubkhov watched in horror as the smile on the man's face was replaced with a gaping hole through which Zubkhov could see his brains. Then he crumpled to the ground.

The emergency lighting kicked in, bathing the cavern below the Rock in a ghostly red light. People had frozen in place, with the exception of the few still in the water, kicking to keep their heads above the freezing waves.

Bunny pulled another woman out of the Pond and hauled her up onto the dock. The water was flooding out of the cave again now, dragging debris and bodies with it as though it was pouring into a bottomless hole somewhere outside the cave.

Tsunami, Rodriguez was thinking. She'd seen a movie once about a tidal wave hitting Asia. One thing she remembered – the water pulling away, leaving fish flapping on an empty beach. Then it came back. She realized people were standing watching in fascination as the Pond emptied.

"Everyone! Up to level two, higher if you can!" she yelled. She bent to help up an aircrewman beside her and pushed him up the dock.

"I have to get to the trailer," Bunny panted beside her. "I have to bring those Fantoms down somewhere."

"If the trailer has power."

"I'll try the backup generator," Bunny replied. "Or we can patch it into the emergency grid."

"I'll get everyone up above the old waterline," Rodriguez said. "I don't care if you get those Fantoms down in one piece or send them to Nome, but I want you to get vision of whatever the hell happened topside."

"Yes, Boss," Bunny said before sprinting away.

From the direction of the cave entrance she heard a sound like a steam engine blowing, and felt the air pressure inside the cave start to build. A boiling wall of water appeared in the darkness at the other side of the Pond.

Her stomach fell as she realized it was twice her height and still fifty feet away.

She had just turned to run when it hit her.

The US Air Force Pacific Command did not hesitate when the shooting started. Their President had promised 'fire and fury', and though Operation Resolve was intended to be a simple show of force in advance of the approaching deadline for Russian withdrawal, they were prepared for belligerence.

Analysts had rushed Bunny O'Hare's recon images into strike planners who added her data to satellite imagery and then quickly identified the likely location of the hostages at the school in Gambell, the Russian HQ and anti-air emplacements there, and the presence of Russian troops, air defenses, US personnel and civilians inside the US cantonment at Savoonga.

The 36th Air Wing had already pre-positioned six of its B-21 Raider stealth bombers at Elmendorf-Richardson and two of them were on patrol east of the US base when the first of Bondarev's air-air missiles left its weapons bay east of Saint Lawrence. Each of them carried 12 second-generation Joint Air-to-Surface Standoff – Extended Range missiles, capable of putting a 1000lb warhead onto a target the size of a minivan. It had a range of nearly 300 miles and it didn't matter that Russian laser weapons were effectively jamming satellite coverage over Saint Lawrence, the joint standoff weapon had its own inertial and optical-based navigation and onboard target identification system.

There had been a lot of talk in the early part of the century about whether the strategic heavy bomber still had a role in the age of the drone, but no US drone or attack fighter could field the larger standoff stealth weapons and it took eight drones to match the payload of a single B-21 Raider. By the time the first US fighter pilot was ejecting from his F-35, 24 of the deadly stealth cruise missiles were on their way to targets at Saint Lawrence.

Gambell could be hit cleanly. The civilians there were judged to be outside the blast radius of the inbound cruise missiles. Six missiles were allocated to Gambell, three to

202

Russian positions and stores identified at the airfield, one to a Verba emplacement near the town hall, one to a Russian transport ship that had recently arrived in the harbor, and one to the town hall itself. Savoonga was another matter. Bunny's initial recon and limited satellite data showed that Russian troops there had quartered themselves in buildings all over the US military cantonment, and had distributed their military and civilian hostages like human shields, scattered throughout the complex. At least two potential Verba air defense systems had been identified, but planners had little or no intel on the specific disposition of Russian forces and equipment at the site.

There was no way to avoid friendly casualties at Savoonga, but the order had come from the very top. The 712th Aircraft Control and Warning Squadron Savoonga base and its top-secret tech were to be denied to Russian forces. Eighteen cruise missiles were allocated to targets in and around Savoonga. The facility would be leveled.

Private Zubkhov had dived for the ground and lay there until it seemed the secondary explosions from the ammo dump were done. The fire still burned like a small volcano, lighting up the whole town and the body of the faceless man beside him.

Udinov, that had been his name. They'd served together nearly a year. He liked American country and western music. *Had liked.*

Zubkhov had taken off his jacket and laid it over the man's head. A few other men had hit the dirt around him, and they were slowly picking themselves up, checking to see if they still had all their arms and legs.

Captain Demchenko had disappeared. Literally. Usually he would have been there shouting at them to pull themselves together and do … something. Zubkhov looked around him. He counted seven other soldiers like himself, saw a jeep roaring toward them from the other side of town. But the captain was nowhere.

He found himself looking at the dirt, expecting to see a bloody smudge somewhere, but all he saw was dirt, ground ice and debris.

That was when he'd looked up at the bluff that towered over the town and had seen the black clouds of birds lifting into the night, like a small squawking storm cloud, lit by the lightning in the town below.

He watched them swirl into the sky in panic, circle once or twice, and then land again.

And beyond them, barely more than shadows flashing between the rocks, he could swear he saw two men, running.

The water smashed Rodriguez face first onto the concrete of the dock and then rolled her across it. It seemed to Alicia just a question of *how* she was going to die, not *whether* she would. Her head collided with something solid and her arms flailed around her trying to grab a hold of something, anything. A leg appeared out of nowhere and gave her an almighty kick in the chest, forcing what little air she had left out of her lungs, and she kicked back reflexively, legs slamming into something. She sucked in water, then foam, then blessed air, coughing and heaving before her head went under again. But she'd got a glimpse of where she was, and which way was up.

Kicking out, she sought the red light that must be the surface and broke out onto the top of a wave just as it hammered into the seawall above the submarine dock, then rolled back onto itself. She rolled with it, calmer now, seeing the man who had probably kicked her in the chest floating past, his head and neck bent at an impossible angle.

"Got you, Boss!" she heard a voice yell as a hand grabbed her collar and pulled her over to where she could throw one weak arm around the rungs of a ladder and the other around someone's legs.

It was her arresting gear officer, Lieutenant 'Stretch' Alberti. His small frame clung doggedly to the ladder with one hand while the other held her collar in a titan's grip and refused to let the sucking water pull her away.

The broken man who had floated away floated back again, dead eyes looking up at her with an accusatory expression as the ebbing tide carried him past.

Could have been me, she thought, then looked across the Pond at the smashed cranes, collapsed elevator shaft and blocked stairwell. *I wonder who's luckier.*

A fighter pilot in Bondarev's Snow Leopards had to land one out of three sorties himself, without autopilot, in order to remain qualified for combat operations. Most of Bondarev's pilots had too much pride to let the AI land their kite even once. Right now, Bondarev had no choice. It wasn't just that he didn't dare touch the stick and throttle, it was also because he couldn't seem to lift his arm to even touch it.

A shell, or parts of a missile warhead, had hammered through the skin of his fighter beside his leg, sliced across his calf, opening up his great saphenous vein, and then spent the last of its energy as it buried itself in the floor beside his foot.

By the time he'd realized what was happening, he'd lost about a half liter of blood. He'd stared at his leg, asking himself why his foot felt wet, why he was having trouble moving it, why he could hear wind blasting around the cockpit. Finally something in his mind clicked, or some of the years of training kicked in, and with his good arm he pulled a cord from a utility pouch in his flight suit and tied a tourniquet tight around his leg. By then, blood was pooling on the floor.

He spent the next fifteen minutes watching the instruments as the AI steered him down the glide path toward the airfield on the horizon, trying to remember how many liters of blood a human body had in it. Wasn't it five liters, and you could afford to lose 20%, right? So that was, what, a liter? Or was it twenty liters, and you could afford to lose five? No matter how he turned it around, the answer wouldn't come.

The lights of the airport approached.

Definitely five liters. You gave blood, they usually took a third of a liter, maximum, right? So more than that must be dangerous. He looked at the floor. *That down there, that is way over the permitted maximum, Yevgeny.*

He laughed, and then laughed at himself laughing.

Two green lights. Wheels down.

That was good. Assuming there *were* wheels and tires at the end of the struts and not just broken stumps.

Like his leg down there. Maybe that was just a stump as well.

He laughed at that too. He'd change his call sign to 'Stumps Bondarev'.

The ground rushed up. His head jerked as the Sukhoi hit the deck once, bounced, and then settled into a hard three-point touchdown.

Useless bloody AI, bouncing all over the field. He tried to reach for the stick again, saw his arm flop to his side as though it belonged to someone else, and saw the flashing red lights of emergency vehicles speeding across the field.

Damn. Not good. Someone must be in trouble.

Perri woke to feel the ground shaking. They were ten feet below ground, but he could feel the mattress beneath him vibrating. Then a sound like muted thunder rolled overhead, penetrating even the hatch cover and the shaft down to their tank. More sonic booms from fighters maybe.

He reached over and turned on the battery-powered lamp. Dave had been woken too.

"What was that?"

"I don't know."

Another rumble shook the tank and some cans fell off one of the makeshift shelves.

"We have to look," Dave said.

"Or we could stay here and wait it out," Perri said. "Which would be smarter."

"It's our families out there," Dave said. "I'm going to look."

Perri rolled into a crouch and handed Dave the binoculars, taking up his rifle and scope. "You're right. Here."

Dave opened the hatch cover slowly and quietly, lifting it just a few inches so that he could look for any sign of Russian troops nearby. When he was sure they were still alone, he eased it a few more inches up and pushed the sheet of rusted tin aside before crawling out onto the cold ground. It was still dark.

They hadn't slept long.

Crouching, they ran into the gas station office through the back door and peered out through the windows, onto a scene from hell.

Rodriguez wasn't sure when she had passed out, but it must have been somewhere between when Stretch Alberti had pulled her up onto the flight deck and when they laid her out on the padded bench inside the command trailer. It wasn't necessarily because she was the ranking officer under the Rock they thought she should be laid out in the command trailer. It was because there was no other space. Every bit of dry ground up above the high water mark was littered with the drowned and half-drowned, bent, broken or shattered bodies of the personnel of A4.

Levering herself up onto an elbow and looking out the windows of the trailer above her head, she saw in the red-lit cavern maybe half of the complement had been taken by the surging water, caught in the fall of the crane or the explosion of debris triggered by the falling elevator. The other half were tending to them as best they could, with supplies from the flight deck sickbay.

Someone had apparently bandaged her head and decided Rodriguez just needed to sleep it off. She touched her head, feeling the bandage and the swelling on her face.

"It's still all there, ma'am," Bunny said, leaning into view from the bench beside her. She held Rodriguez's head gently, put a hand on her shoulder to stop her getting up, and lowered her back down onto the bench. "Your nose is a bit flatter now, but it's actually prettier."

"Screw you, O'Hare," Rodriguez managed, wincing.

"Yes, ma'am," Bunny smiled.

"What's our status? Collaguiri? I saw him…"

"He took five tons of elevator to the head, he's gone, ma'am. We've got about thirteen dead, ten with serious injuries, fractures and the like." She held up a bruised hand. "Dug two out of the stairwell, might be more in there. Another dozen walking wounded but still in the fight, twenty uninjured."

Rodriguez remembered something. "Topside, did you…"

"Yeah, no. I couldn't bring the Fantoms in and I couldn't land them outside and risk they would be seen if the Russians did a bomb damage assessment overflight. I sent one straight to Nome. Had enough fuel left in the other for a few passes over the Rock before I sent it off too." She took a breath. "I can replay the night-cam vision for you but it's like…everything up there was just scraped into the sea. The dome is gone, and everything inside it. The cabins and huts down by the water are just ashes and splinters, floating around in the water with a hundred tons of wrecked boats and pontoons."

"No survivors?"

"None moving that I could see," Bunny shook her head. "No IR signatures."

"Do we have comms?"

"Drone comms, yeah. The cable to the undersea array survived, just like it was designed to do. But we'll need someone to find a kludge if we want to use it to contact Coronado without putting a drone in the air."

"What was it? Tactical nuke?"

"I don't think so," Bunny said. "I'm no ordnance expert, but the snow is only melted on top of the island and down by the accommodation, which makes it look like whatever hit us, hit the top of the island and the harbor at the same time. The rest of the island still has some snow and ice on it, though. I'd have thought a nuke would melt it all."

"I didn't see a flash," Rodriguez remembered. "Did you?"

"No lightning, just thunder," Bunny agreed. "I'm thinking more thermobaric than nuclear."

She looked down on Rodriguez's frown. "You're thinking what I'm thinking, right Boss?"

"That this attack wasn't about us?" Rodriguez said.

"Right. If they knew about this place, they'd have used some kind of deep penetrator, a bunker buster. Or flown a cruise missile straight into the mouth of the cavern. But they just wanted to scrape a barnacle off the Rock, so they went with thermobaric," Bunny said. She waved a hand at the destruction outside the trailer. "This was all just collateral damage. They got lucky."

Rodriguez looked at her watch, then closed her eyes. 0330 hours. So tired.

"Get me some drugs, will you?" she said. "Painkillers and stimulants. We've got to tend to our dead and wounded, send a party out the cave entrance and check for survivors topside, then restore comms with Coronado and see if we can get this base back online." She looked across the dock to the intact loading bays next to the catapult. "That was a classic 'first strike' if you ask me. We've still got hangars full of hardware capable of kicking some serious Russian ass and I would dearly love to get some orders and get it in the air."

Bunny looked at her admiringly. "Hoo-bloody-yah, Boss."

As the boys watched, a huge mushroom cloud was rising over the town where the town hall was. Over by the airfield there were three or four fires burning and what looked like fuel exploding. Several houses in the town seemed to be on fire too. Their eyes went immediately to the two-story gym at the school.

It was untouched. There were fires just a block away, a huge crater where the town hall had been, but the school gym and its outbuildings were still standing. If they could feel the bombs down in the bunker, he could only imagine what it had been like for their families, holed up in the steel-walled gym just a block or two away.

Perri looked at the town through his scope. He had expected to see Russian troops running around the streets, jeeps, maybe ambulances or something. But apart from a couple of soldiers standing around or picking themselves up off the ground, there was nothing except for flickering flames and rising columns of smoke.

"Our own side bombed us," Dave said unbelievingly. "They bombed Gambell."

"They never cared about us before," Perri said bitterly. "Why should they start now?"

"Yeah, but… this is like, this is US territory. They bombed their own territory!"

Perri tapped Dave on the shoulder, pointing back to the tank. "Let's get back down. Any Russian out there left alive is going to be looking for blood after this. Lying low is looking like an even better idea now." Even as he said it, a shadow streaked across the harbor, straight for a Russian ship that had berthed there the day before. It struck with a muffled thump, a half second passed, then the ship, the harbor and everything around it lit up in a boiling, black and red ball of fire!

Private Zubkhov had been caught out in the open when the cruise missiles hit. He knew they were cruise missiles because he saw one of the bastards curl around the bluff at the end of town and head straight for the harbor.

It hadn't even been an hour since the ammo dump had gone up. They were still looking for the Captain. It was kind of strange. Not like there was some big explosion there on the street that could have vaporized him. The guy next to Zubkhov had been hit with the base plate of a field mortar – that was what took his face off. And another guy, he took a ricochet in the leg. So they'd all ducked behind cover and waited until all of the ammo had cooked off and it was just a red smoldering mess down there, and then they stuck their heads up again.

But the Captain was missing. The Sergeant who had been sent to the airfield had finally come back after about thirty minutes, wondering why he hadn't received any further orders and the Captain wasn't on comms. He'd told them to start searching through the town, block by block.

"Could have been freaking partisans," Sergeant Penkov said. "They blew the ammo dump, took the Captain hostage maybe."

Zubkhov thought about the frightened Inuit families he'd helped herd into the school building, and didn't think so. They were fishermen and women with kids. Grandmothers and grandfathers. He didn't see an armed resistance in their faces, more like weary resignation. But then he remembered the flickering shadows of men running up on the bluff, and he wasn't so sure. He was thinking about that as he rounded a corner behind some sort of warehouse and found the Captain.

The man was standing and staring out to sea. Just standing there, staring. He didn't react when Zubkhov called out to him, and didn't turn when he came up behind him. "Captain Demchenko?"

He was just standing with a strange smile on his face, watching the sea.

"Comrade Captain?"

Now he turned, eyes semi-glazed, looking at Zubkhov, or looking *through* him. Zubkhov couldn't tell.

"I love mankind," the officer said. "But I find to my amazement that the more I love mankind as a whole, the less I love man himself."

Zubkhov stared at him. Demchenko stood there, as though he was waiting for an answer. Zubkhov was used to the vagaries of the officer class and took the observation in his stride.

"Well, yes, sir. There's not a lot to love." Zubkhov looked around himself. "Especially in a shithole like this, sir."

The Captain frowned, like that was not the reply he had expected. "The mystery of human existence lies not in just staying alive, but in finding something to live for," he said, looking out to sea again.

The voice was so dead and even, it chilled Zubkhov. He stepped in front of his CO. "Sir, I think maybe we should just…" Then he stopped talking, because he saw a thin line of blood running down the man's cheek, from the corner of his eyeball to the corner of his mouth, pulsing with every beat of his heart. The man's tongue darted out of the corner of his mouth, licking at it.

"Sir, why don't you just come with me," Zubkhov said. He took his arm and started to lead him, unresisting, back to the poorly lit, smoky streets.

"You can be sincere and still be stupid," the Captain said, conversationally.

Finally Zubkhov realized where he had heard the words before. It was Dostoyevsky. The man was standing out in the ruined night quoting *Dostoyevsky* to himself. He stopped and took a flashlight off his belt. He shone it in the face of the Captain; the man flinched, but he didn't ask Zubkhov what the hell he was doing. He just screwed his eyes shut.

Zubkhov looked carefully at the line of blood leaking from the man's eye. It was still pulsing out of the eye in a tiny red stream. On an instinct, he reached his hand up to the opposite side of the Captain's head and felt the hair there. There was blood there too.

"Man is sometimes extraordinarily, passionately in love with suffering," the Captain pointed out.

"Yes, sir," Zubkhov agreed. "He most certainly is. This way if you please."

And as they'd emerged from between buildings, with Zubkhov wondering where the hell in this chaos he might find a medic, the first cruise missile hit. It exploded with enormous force across the other side of town near the town hall, bracketed almost immediately by two more strikes out by the airfield.

Not partisans then!

Zubkhov had shoved his damaged Captain back behind a wall and then dived for the dirt. As he watched, he saw a dark deltoid with a tail of fire come screaming around the bluff, over the bay, and head straight for him.

Bondarev seemed to exist in a twilight of blurred gray light for eternity. Was this death? Just as it seemed it must be, features around him started to come into sharper relief. A window showing a bleak snowy landscape outside, a bed with rails on both sides, curtains around him. A hospital, then, not quite the Valhalla he had been hoping for.

"Welcome back. It is a miracle you didn't go into cardiac arrest," the base physician said as he realized Bondarev was awake and watching him. "You lost more than a liter of blood."

"Yes. I was trying to do the math on that," Bondarev admitted. He looked up at the IV bag next to his bed, then down at his bandaged leg.

"Otherwise, it's not too bad." The doctor moved down to the end of the bed and pulled the bed cover aside. "Wiggle your toes for me."

He did so, wincing as something felt like it was tearing in his calf. "OK, that's enough, stop now," the doctor said. "Just rest." It sounded like a grand idea.

He was wide awake the next time the physician called past.

"Good, you're looking more alert now. The shrapnel sliced through your gastrocnemius muscle. It opened up a vein but didn't sever the Achilles. We've stitched you up. You just need to rest."

"How long?"

"Six weeks," the doctor said. "Maybe five if you can stay off it. Then you can start physiotherapy."

"No, doctor, I need to fly," Bondarev said.

"Not with that leg. Not happening."

Bondarev sighed. "Comrade Doctor, in World War Two the British had an ace, Douglas Bader, who had no legs *at all*. He flew Hurricane fighters; big, stinking, gasoline-powered metal and wooden beasts without fly-by-wire, without dynamic control surfaces, without the help of a combat AI." Bondarev lifted his leg off the bed, trying not to wince. "So put a splint and a bandage around it, give me a crutch and sign me out. I need to find out what is left of my 4th and 5th Air Regiments."

The physician held Bondarev's foot and lowered it back onto the bed. "There is no rush, Comrade Colonel. Your men won the air battle, but American cruise missiles exterminated almost all of our troops along with half of their own citizens on that island. Our governments have agreed a ceasefire. The genie has been put back in the bottle. For now."

Despite Bondarev's bravado, his leg was throbbing and his vision blurring again. He laid his head back on the pillow. "Tell someone I want to see Lieutenant Colonel Arsharvin, please." The man did not instantly react. "Now!"

He needed to find out how many men and machines he had lost. This hiatus wouldn't last long, of that he was sure. The American attack had been expected, had in fact been needed. With or without him, Operation LOSOS would be moving into Phase II by now. Leveraging global outrage over the US attack on Russia, on its own citizens, the invasion of Nome would soon begin.

SUBTERRANEAN

"There is no way to sugarcoat it, Colonel. We got a lesson in air power," Arsharvin said. He watched as Bondarev put his hands on the wall in front of him, one leg straight and heel to the ground, then crossed the other leg in front of it and stretched until it seemed like his Achilles would snap. "I bet that exercise gives you buns of steel."

"Air power?" Bondarev stretched again. "We faced an enemy greater in number and claimed two of theirs for every one we lost."

"We claimed two *aircraft*, not two pilots," Arsharvin pointed out. "Most of the machines you faced were drones. This was the first real test of Russian fighter doctrine against American and the results were not ... compelling."

"Two for one is not compelling?" Bondarev asked bitterly. "Tell me, comrade, what is compelling? Three for one? Five for one?"

Arsharvin held up his hands, trying to calm his friend. "Let's just talk numbers. I've sent you the report but perhaps you didn't read it. I wrote it, so I know the math." He held up his hand and started counting off his fingers. "Firstly, the Americans sent up a force of 97 fighters, 80 of which were Fantoms, 17 of which were piloted F-35s. You faced them with a force of about 54 Su-57s and Mig-41s. You fired first, though that was moot, as the enemy drones reacted with counterfire as soon as they detected your missiles launching. I'll save you the blow by blow commentary and get straight to the final result. You lost 14 aircraft destroyed and eight damaged. The Americans lost between 30 and 35 machines destroyed and 15 damaged."

"Better than two for one then," Bondarev grunted.

"In *machines*, yes," Arsharvin said. "But not in pilots. We lost 12 pilots! The Americans lost just six, killed or captured! Six men! That's two to one in *their* favor!"

Bondarev was quiet a moment. He was well aware of his losses. He'd been sitting in his hospital bed writing to as many widows and parents in the few days after the battle as he had in three years over Syria and Turkey.

"A human pilot will beat a machine every time. We have proven it in testing against our own Okhotniks over Armavir, we proved it again in combat over Syria," Bondarev insisted.

"But not in these numbers, not against Fantoms armed with their new Cuda missiles. And you aren't just fighting machines, Comrade Colonel," Arsharvin said, clearly frustrated. "Their 'hex' data-linked combat formation means there is one pilot to every six drones. They can choose to fly and operate weapons systems, or let their drones operate semi-autonomously. *One pilot to six drones, Yevgeny!*" Arsharvin threw his hands in the air. "Every one of our drones requires two crew and we can't train them fast enough to keep them fully manned."

"I was fighting with my hands tied," Bondarev pointed out. "Not allowed to commit my Okhotniks, not allowed to engage until we were almost at guns range. The odds were all in the Americans' favor. They won't be next time, I promise you."

"If there is a next time," Arsharvin said. "Lukin is in Vladivostok with a bunch of other generals and politicians looking at the same numbers I sent to you."

Bondarev frowned. "The way I see it, we're committed now. It's not like there's anything to talk about," he said. Getting down on his haunches, he tipped forward, balancing on his toes. His right calf muscle screamed in protest, but he embraced the pain. When the time came to return to duty, he would be ready.

Arsharvin winced. "If you're a politician, there's always something to talk about, my friend. We haven't yet moved on Nome, so for now it's still just about Saint Lawrence. Moscow aren't just spooked by the capabilities of the US air forces. They aren't getting the sympathy or even the neutrality they expected from the UN after the US attack. And my sources in the Kremlin tell me President Navalny is personally rattled by the brutality of an opponent who apparently had no qualms about the mass murder of fifty of their troops and several hundred of their own citizens at Savoonga."

It was to be Devlin's third meeting with the Russian Foreign Ministry in as many weeks, but the first with their Foreign Minister since a ceasefire was declared, the day after the 'Battle of Bering Strait'.

Whether her superiors had really expected Russia to fold in the face of a demonstration of US airpower and withdraw from Saint Lawrence, she couldn't say. But she did know they had been fazed by the unhesitating Russian willingness to defend their 'no-go' zone. Just as she was aware the Russians were fazed by the US willingness to do whatever it took to defend its territorial rights.

Devlin had been shocked too. She had emerged from Carl Williams' office to the news that US Pacific Command had ordered the effective destruction of the Savoonga cantonment, accepting that with that decision there would be inestimable loss of civilian life. Russia was claiming that in addition to 200 of their own troops who died in Gambell and at Savoonga the attack had resulted in 80 US service personnel and 1,000 civilians dead or wounded. Russian media had been quick to broadcast video footage of shocked civilians being treated at a medical center at Savoonga, asking *why?* Why had their own government attacked them? Some couldn't believe it, but one Yup'ik elder was more sanguine. "America hasn't given a damn about us the last two hundred years, and this just proves it still doesn't give a damn."

In the court of international opinion, the US had tried to hold Russia responsible, claiming it had provoked the attack by opening fire on "US aircraft patrolling inside US territory, outside the illegal Russian no-fly zone." Russia in turn had claimed that the massive US provocation that was 'Operation Resolve' had been timed together with a stealth missile or aircraft attack on its "legitimate peacekeeping forces" in

Gambell, and followed by the massive cruise missile attack on Russian and civilian targets spread across Saint Lawrence Island.

The US had made no mention of the Russian attack on Little Diomede.

International sympathy had split across traditional lines, current allies siding with the superpower they were aligned with, and no neutral states stepping outside their comfort zones to get in between the two combatants. The UN Secretary-General had called for urgent de-escalation, while the Bulletin of the Atomic Scientists' Science and Security Board had moved their 'Doomsday Clock' to thirty seconds to midnight, the closest it had been set since 1953 when the US and Russia both tested hydrogen fusion bombs. Devlin's Russian counterparts had one clear goal in any conversation she had with them – to find out whether the US was willing to use nuclear weapons to defend its territory. If Russia still refused to withdraw from Saint Lawrence, even after the scorched earth approach the US had taken with non-nuclear weapons, would it truly consider using tactical nuclear weapons and risk planetary-scale nuclear destruction?

Devlin had been ordered to reply that the US demand for the remaining Russian troops to withdraw from Saint Lawrence was still valid, and that any attempt to reinforce the island would be met with "the necessary force."

But the same thing still puzzled Devlin now as had puzzled her before. Would Russia really risk nuclear destruction just to test American resolve in the Bering Strait? It remained the only theory the State Department could anchor the Russian aggression to, and the people inside State who propounded it were arguing now that Russia had gone too far to back away, that the loss of nearly 200 ground troops on Saint Lawrence and numerous front-line aircraft could not be ignored, and domestic political pressure would stop them from backing down.

It was a stalemate. Russian forces remained in control of the island's population centers of Gambell and Savoonga.

Russian aircraft still patrolled overhead and Russian warships plied the seas up and down the Strait, turning away any US shipping or aircraft that approached. They were letting the much-reduced trickle of internationally flagged ships through, but any US flagged or owned ship was being warned and, if it did not turn back, boarded and forcibly turned around. There were no more viable military targets on Saint Lawrence for the US to attack and attacking Russian warships in the waters of Saint Lawrence would have been a major re-escalation.

What Devlin was going to the Foreign Ministry to tell her Russian counterparts today was that a US carrier group centered around the latest (and in fact probably the last) of the US supercarriers, the USS *Enterprise*, had just departed San Diego. Its objective: a 'freedom of navigation' transit through the Bering Strait.

Devlin had always thought of herself as a peacemaker. So she was surprised by the emotion boiling in her chest. A peacemaker should be feeling dismay, sadness, or perhaps resignation. She felt something very different. It was outrage. As she sat in her car looking out at a rainy gray Moscow afternoon, she had one defiant thought.

Try to turn the USS Enterprise around, you bastards!

In the days since the thermobaric bombs had dropped on Little Diomede, the Rock had been left to fend for itself. Coronado had not wanted to draw any attention to its top-secret facility, so Little Diomede had been included in general US protests about Russian aggression, without specifically calling out the attack there.

With the death of the CO, Lieutenant Commander Rodriguez had found herself suddenly in command of the Naval Computer and Telecommunications Area Master Station, Alaska – both her own people and the personnel from the radar station. The chief petty officer and search party she had sent topside had found no survivors. In fact, they hadn't even found any bodies. It was as though the officers and personnel

219

manning the radar station had been scraped from the rock like barnacles from the hull of a ship. The radar station itself was nothing but melted metal and plastic, twisted rebar and foundation concrete. One of Rodriguez's fears had been that the large elevator shaft down to the cave below, which had been hidden by the radar dome, would lie gaping and open for any prying Russian eye to see.

She needn't have been concerned. The walls around the elevator shaft had collapsed over it, leaving only a small rubble-filled depression.

Dealing with the wounded had been her first priority. She had a Marine medical officer and two corpsmen still alive, and they quickly and efficiently triaged the injured personnel and treated the most severely wounded. Several urgently needed to be evacuated.

So communication had been her next priority. She needed to organize transport for the wounded, and let Coronado know that they had been hit hard but were in the fight. By patching into the undersea drone command array they'd re-established voice and data contact. Their launch infrastructure had come through the attack largely undamaged. They could still hit any target within 300 miles, they just needed to be told what, and where. Without the heavy lift crane on the dock, though, they couldn't recover and recycle their drones from the Pond. Any drone they sent out the chute would be on a one-way trip to the target and, if it survived, onward to an airfield in Alaska. Rodriguez still had a loaded magazine and a burning desire for payback. A4 was still mission capable.

That was what she pitched to Pacific Command anyway. They didn't see it the way she did.

Rodriguez had called a meeting of her 'command staff': a grand word to describe Bunny O'Hare, her arresting gear and catapult officers Stretch Alberti and Lucky Severin, and Chief Petty Officer 'Inky' Barrows, the senior ranking seaman from the radar station, so named because he got a new tattoo every time he hit a new port and, at thirty-two years of age, was fast running out of real estate to place it on.

"We're being decommissioned," Rodriguez announced. "Navy is sending a sub with medical facilities. We can't get it into the dock here, so it will have to moor outside the harbor debris field. We are to rack all aircraft, power down all equipment, and rig charges to bring the roof down by remote detonation just in case Ivan discovers it and tries to breach. The sub will take off all remaining personnel, not just the wounded."

Their faces said it all, but Alberti was the first to speak. "They can't decommission us, we haven't even been commissioned yet," he commented dryly.

"Speak for yourselves," Chief Petty Officer Barrows, the radar station electrician, said.

"I don't think they're too worried about protocol, Stretch," Rodriguez said. "Informally, I was told they need to do an assessment of how it was we got hurt so badly by a few lucky bombs that weren't even aimed at us."

"Those MOABs are like mini-nukes," Barrows protested. "And the whole point is they *did* get lucky, the Russians still don't know we're here."

Severin was chewing on a thought. "A few weeks later, give us blast doors behind the Slot, we would have been fine. The seawall was rated for a category 4 hurricane and storm surge, not for a bloody thermobaric blast. We just need to re-engineer the cave entrance, create some baffles, fit that pressure door..."

"They're not in the mood for re-engineering right now," Rodriguez told them. "If we aren't part of the solution to this standoff, we are apparently just part of the problem. They're pulling us out."

Rodriguez looked over at O'Hare; she looked angry but was suspiciously quiet. Rodriguez had expected her to explode. They discussed what needed to be done to decommission or destroy their equipment, how long it would take to rig explosives enough to bring the reinforced roof of the cave down if needed, and whether there were any personnel too badly wounded to move. When they were done planning, Rodriguez dismissed them to start work.

"Lieutenant O'Hare, can I have a word?" Rodriguez said as they all rose to leave the trailer. When the others closed the door behind them, she looked at the woman who in the last few days had become just as much a friend as a junior officer. "OK Bunny, what's up?"

"Sorry, Boss?" O'Hare raised an eyebrow. "Don't know what you mean."

"Yes you do. I know you want payback. You're choking for it. But I tell you we're packing our bags and pulling out and you don't say a word. Alberti and Barrows both erupt, even Severin is coming up with ideas, but you're an Easter Island statue."

Bunny sat down again. "I won't lie, Boss. I do want payback. But I'm not Navy, I'm DARPA. They pull us out of here before I can even blink, I'll be on a plane back to DARPA in California watching this war on CNN. It isn't even *my* war. Hell, after this debacle they will probably cancel my green card and ship me back to Aussie."

"Yeah," Rodriguez said. "About that…"

Perri and Dave had grown bolder. Over the last three days they had set up a lookout 'nest' under an upturned satellite dish on the gas station roof that gave them a clear view down onto the town, and as long as there was no fog, they could see all the way across to the airfield. And they'd been out nearly every night, watching and listening to the town below.

They had been relieved to see the school buildings in Gambell had somehow escaped the destruction that had rained down on the town in those few short and terrifying minutes. They were worried about reprisals, but it seemed that those Russians left alive had other concerns than revenge on the local civilians.

They saw them bring their wounded to the school on stretchers and the hoods of jeeps. Then they saw them bring out their dead and line them up in bags on the road outside.

Some of the bags clearly didn't hold a whole body. Perri counted fifty-nine body bags.

On the third day, Perri got a good count of the number of Russian troops left in Gambell when they held a funeral service for their dead comrades.

There were twenty-seven Russian soldiers still combat ready – physically at least – and maybe ten badly wounded inside the school somewhere.

What Perri couldn't understand was why no help arrived for the Russian troops. The air had been swarming with fat-bellied helicopters that first day, and a few came and went in the days following, but the skies were completely empty now. There were no warships moored off the breakwater anymore, just the wreck of a transport ship that had been hit by a missile three days ago and exploded in a liquid hydrogen-fueled fireball that had flattened all the harborside shacks and broken windows hundreds of yards back. With at least three missiles hitting the town and more out at the airstrip, Perri doubted there was a window left intact in the entire town. But the Russians should have been able to get new men and supplies in. There had been plenty of days with clear skies but it had been foggy the first two days after the attack, if they had wanted to sneak people in or out. And he had clearly seen Russian aircraft overhead, flying back and forth across Saint Lawrence, apparently unmolested. So why no choppers?

Whatever the reason, whatever their new orders, Perri and Dave could see the soldiers left in Gambell had little interest in keeping up patrols around the town, and even less interest in sitting in sandbagged bunkers out by the airstrip. The only semblance of their former routine were the guards posted at the doors of the school buildings and the routine trips from the gym to the toilets with groups of hostages. Which was good, because it meant that at least once a day, Perri and Dave could see their families were still okay, even though they must be worried sick not knowing what had happened to their two boys. Perri had been able to confirm his parents and brother were among the people in the school, so at least they hadn't been

223

stupid enough to pick a fight or try to run for the American mainland in their little fishing boat. Which, by the way, had been destroyed in the American strike just like every other boat in the harbor.

He lowered his scope. "I'm sick of just watching and doing nothing."

Dave clapped his hands together to keep the blood flowing in the cold late summer air. "Isn't anything left for us to blow up or shoot holes in man, you know that."

"I have another idea," Perri said. "I don't believe the whole world forgot about us. We need to remind them we're still here."

"Americans bombed the shit out of us," Dave pointed out. "You expect their sympathy now?"

"Not them," Perri said. "I'm thinking about those guys we met at the Pow Wow in Canada that time."

Dave knew what he was talking about. The last time both of them had gotten off Saint Lawrence. Two glorious weeks on Vancouver Island in Canada for a meeting of indigenous youth. It was the first time Perri had realized there was a world of kids out there going through exactly what he was going through, and he'd stayed friends with a bunch of them over the years through social media.

"We've still got no internet," Dave pointed out. "So the only calls we can make here are local and there's no one to call. How are you going to get a message out?"

Gambell's connection to the outside world was through a satellite internet router and dish up on the town hall roof that used to hook up to their cell network. It was the first thing the Russians took down, and then the Americans sealed the deal when they took out the whole block on which the town hall sat. They might have killed half of the Russian troops in Gambell, but they also made sure it was cut off from the world for good. Or had they?

"Those guys down there, they must have some way to contact their base back in Russia, right?"

"You're going to call Moscow, ask them for help?" Dave joked. "Hey, come and save us from those crazy Americans? Oh wait, you were already doing that? My bad…"

"No, you dick. I'm thinking whatever radio they have, it must hook up to a satellite somewhere. Maybe we can use it to get online. Like a mobile hotspot."

Dave stood and winked. "OK, let's just go ask them, eh? Excuse me, shithead invaders, got a radio we can borrow?"

Perri stood too. "Sure. Or, how about we just go out to the airfield where there are about a dozen smashed-up Russian trucks, cars and ATVs and see what we can find?"

It turned out a razor-sharp, needle-thin fragment of shrapnel had entered the Spetsnaz Captain's skull just beside his eye, traveled right through his brain, and then left his head at the back, making a pinhole-sized exit wound.

It had turned him into a walking Dostoyevsky quotation machine, but that was about all he was capable of. Sergeant Penkov had talked more than once about just shooting him to put him, and everyone around him, out of their misery. But in the end they settled for locking him in a classroom and guiding him to the toilet twice a day.

Sergeant Penkov had managed to contact 14th Squadron headquarters within a few minutes of the first American strike, and was told to bunker down and ride it out. When the cruise missiles hit, Private Zubkhov and the poetic Captain Demchenko were groveling under the foundations of one of the houses two blocks from the town hall. The explosion as the ship in the harbor went up was the loudest, nearly blowing Private Zubkhov's eardrums out. So it was that he hardly heard the town hall strike which had killed most of his comrades.

He'd waited until things stopped blowing up, and then waited some more. He'd learned a few lessons since the ammo dump went up. When he finally emerged from under the house, it was starting to get light, and he was cold, hungry and pissed off at the world. His pique lasted until he found the first body part out on the street. He found his way through the wreckage of the town to the sound of someone shouting orders, and found Sergeant Penkov organizing search and rescue parties.

So much for food and warmth. He spent three days digging out the wounded and bagging the dead. When he ate, it was cold soup or ready to eat rations. When he slept, it was on the floor of one of the school buildings, shivering under a thin blanket because the bastard engineers had all been killed and no one left alive could get the damaged pumped hydro powerplant up and running. None of the Russians, anyway. The locals had refused to help – they seemed impervious to the cold and apparently liked to see their captors suffer. They were probably used to the damn thing punking out on them.

Sergeant Penkov had sent urgent requests to 14th Squadron HQ for evacuation. Denied. Resupply. Denied. Reinforcement? Denied. He was given orders to do what he could, where he was, with what he had.

Private Zubkhov was there when he got this last piece of good advice.

"This stupid village doesn't matter anymore," Penkov spat, putting down the satellite radio mike. "If it ever did." He looked around him at the beaten men who had given up looking at him with hope. Now they just looked at him with resignation. "We're on our own, boys. Ideas?"

"We need to get across the island to Savoonga," someone offered. "Join up with the 308th, consolidate our strength."

"We can't just abandon our post, Private," Penkov told him. "I need an operational imperative."

"What about the civilians?" another prompted. "The American missiles took out our supplies and we aren't being resupplied. We can't feed them – either we shoot them or transport them to Savoonga."

"Can't drive, we'd have to walk out," another pointed out. "The locals say there's no road between the towns, only reindeer trails at best."

"We can't take our wounded out that way. We need air transport. Or a boat."

"You're right about the civilians and the supply situation. But we've got no transport," the Sergeant pointed out. "And it isn't going to magically appear. We're walking out, or we're going nowhere."

Private Zubkhov spoke up. "What is the situation in Savoonga? Do they have supplies?"

"I spoke with the commander of the 308th yesterday," Penkov said. "The airfield is still in our control and the air force is starting to build up, big time. If the Americans are coming we'll be better off combining our strength and fortifying Savoonga, for sure."

Zubkhov laughed at that. "Strength? Yeah, right."

"Can it," the Sergeant grunted at him. The man was a Muscovite and seemed to have a hate on anyone born east of the Urals. "This is what we're doing. We're walking out. We'll take the locals with us, to show the way. The walking wounded come with us. Those too badly hurt to walk can stay here, with any of the locals who are too old or too weak to make the walk."

"They'll cut our guys' throats the minute we leave town!" Private Zubkhov said.

"If our guys get their throats cut by a bunch of old women and geriatric men, they bloody deserve it," Penkov said.

"We can't just leave the wounded behind," Private Zubkhov protested.

The Sergeant looked at Zubkhov for a long moment. "You're right son. It can't look like I just abandoned this post. So you'll stay here with the wounded and the elderly civilians to make sure they're properly looked after. How's that?"

It was the first vehicle they looked in. A big Humvee-like jeep with a long aerial on the roof, it had just seemed natural to start with that one. It had been blown onto its side by a missile strike, and its underside was a tangle of gutted metal. The fuel tanks had caught fire, apparently without exploding, the tires had burned away, and the underside was covered in an oily soot. Someone had been through the inside of the vehicle and emptied all of the lockers and compartments lining the interior. There wasn't even a stray packet of cigarettes or random piece of paper left behind.

But they hadn't taken the radio receiver out of its mount under the dashboard.

It took Perri twenty nerve-wracking minutes to free it and uncouple the cables leading into the engine compartment. While he worked, Dave was under the hood, pulling out one of the hydrogen fuel cell batteries. They weren't sure if the radio would run off the same voltage as the battery they had down in the tank, so while Perri lugged the surprisingly heavy radio with him, Dave dragged the battery on a makeshift sled fashioned from a truck door and some electrical cables he'd scrounged from the wreckage around the airfield.

Back inside the tank, Perri had hooked the battery up to the radio, guided by photos he'd taken of how the wiring had been organized when it was still connected inside the jeep.

It was dead, and stayed dead, no matter what he did.

"Russian piece of crap," Dave decided after about an hour of watching Perri mess with it. "Can't even take a hit from a bomb and keep working." He reached down to Perri's feet and held up something that looked like a small pair of tweezers with one blue arm and one red. "Better keep all this stuff together, we might be able to use it for parts if we find another one."

"Give me that," Perri said, taking the clip and turning it around. "Did this fall off it?"

Dave looked at him strangely. "No, you took it off, together with a bunch of wires, and you put it down on the ground. You're the techie, I figured you'd decided you didn't need it."

Perri held the small metal clip in one hand and began turning the radio over with the other, looking for somewhere to fasten it. On the backside of the radio he found two copper studs that looked just the right distance apart. He slid the clip onto them to see that the blue arm was held by one stud, and the red arm by the other. He clipped the power wires to the battery again.

A small hum filled the tank as the radio sprang to life.

Someone else springing to life was Senior Lieutenant Bunny O'Hare.

"Please say again, ma'am," Bunny said slowly. "I was almost sure you said you wanted me to stay behind in a cave full of explosives after everyone else has left."

"I'll stay as well, of course," Rodriguez said. "We'll wire the base for remote detonation before we pull people out, but I've asked Coronado for permission to fly our aircraft out rather than leave them in situ. There are two billion dollars' worth of hardware in those hangar bays, so I'm expecting to get a yes rather than risk Russia walking in and taking it. When the last Fantom is on its way home, they'll pick us up and seal the base."

"Two people can't launch 24 drones," Bunny pointed out. "You'll have to keep a bunch of people back."

"Actually that's not right. One person has to fly them out. But it only takes one person to load and launch them. This system was designed for truck-mounted launch using a crew of one driver/mechanic, and one launch officer. It's fully automated, from fueling to pre-flight checks, loading the cartridges and firing the Cat." She grinned. "And I'm the best damn shooter in the Navy."

"So if you only need one person to run the launch system, why do you have two crews of 12 people each?" Bunny insisted. "What am I missing?"

"Speed," Rodriguez said. "With more people we can do things in parallel rather than in sequence, shorten the time between launches. Plus, I'm only talking about launch; recovery is completely different. Truck-mounted launchers are 'one and done'. They can launch, but they can't recover and relaunch – a truck-launched drone has to land at an airfield after its mission. Down here it takes several people to recover the drone, do the

229

post-flight system and damage check, reload ordnance, slot it into a new launch cartridge and port it back to the launch bay."

"Are you serious, ma'am?" Bunny asked, close to exasperation. She lifted her nose in the air and sniffed. "You smell that? This place reeks of death now. It would be different if we were going back up there, getting some payback, but we're not, we're bugging out and rigging the roof to blow. You're talking 24 drones. How fast do you figure we can pre-flight, load and launch, all on our own?"

"Twenty-three – we don't have time to fix the bird with the bent leg. I don't know... say one airframe every two hours?"

"So we fire one out the chute, I set it on its way to either Eielson or Elmendorf-Richardson and program the AI to bring it home." Rodriguez saw Bunny was at least thinking it through now. "We've got to eat and sleep or we'll screw up. So 23 kites, 12 hours on, six hours off, that will take us ..."

"Three days, if we push through," Rodriguez said, having already done the math. "They may not be able to turn around a sub or surface pickup that quickly, though. So we might be down here a week or so."

Bunny looked out the trailer at the gray concrete and rock walls. "All just to save your Great American Taxpayer a few dollars' worth of hardware."

"It's not the money. I just figured that's what might appeal to NORAD strategists. I'm actually thinking if this fight heats up again, we are going to need every one of those machines or the next generation of kids in Alaska might be learning Russian instead of English." Rodriguez let a little desperation creep into her voice. "I know this isn't your fight. You aren't American, you aren't even Navy. So, you want to get on that sub when it docks, I won't stop you."

Bunny leaned forward, elbows on her knees, her face just a foot away from Rodriguez's face. "Ma'am, my great-grandfather was Royal Australian Navy. He stood on the deck of the HMAS *Napier* in Tokyo Harbor when the Allies took the Japanese surrender. He told my father, and my father told me, that if it wasn't for the US Navy, I'd have grown up speaking Japanese. So I guess I owe you one." She reached out and grasped Rodriguez's fist in hers, pulled it toward her and held it there. "Besides, when people drop thermobaric bombs on my head, I tend to take it personally."

THE PHONY WAR

There were times when it was right to ask for permission, and times when it was better to ask for forgiveness. Devlin figured this was one of the latter. She knew that Carl Williams' intelligence report was on its way to NSA. She'd made sure it was also copied to the CIA and FBI heads of station in Moscow, and her own channels in State. She wanted it widely read, and well understood. HOLMES' analysis had convinced her this wasn't a fight about the *Ozempic Tsar* or a small island in the mouth of the Bering Strait. It was just the first move in a plan to take western Alaska.

That was a whole other war than the one they were preparing to fight. Devlin wasn't privy to the plans the Pentagon were putting together, but she was pretty sure they just involved putting a few hundred Rangers or Airborne troops in the air, landing them on Saint Lawrence, and taking the island back. It wouldn't be easy. They'd have to win air superiority to get the troops in, which also meant dealing with Russian naval assets in the Strait. But that was the purpose of the *Enterprise* task force, now on its way north from San Diego. At the same time she was due to meet with Kelnikov, a media announcement would be going out proclaiming the task force's intention to reinforce 'freedom of navigation' in the Strait, but the signal to Russia should be clear: 'We are going to take back our island.' Knowing what she knew, Devlin realized Russia was not likely to be spooked by the approach of the *Enterprise*. They probably already had a plan for how they would deal with it.

If HOLMES and Williams were right, then Russia was already at war. It just hadn't declared it yet.

Foreign Minister Kelnikov had organized to meet Devlin at an office inside the Foreign Ministry building on Moscow's Smolenskaya-Sennaya Square. As with everything in Devlin's world, such meetings always had an element of predictable theater. The Minister had kept her waiting an unreasonably long time, even given the state of relations. The seating was arranged so that she was uncomfortably perched on an ornate 18th-century chair that seemed to have been stuffed with porcupine quills. It was mid-morning by the time the Minister arrived, a bright sunlit day, so she was of course arranged with the sun in her eyes and his face in shadow. He had insisted she come alone, while he was flanked with a phalanx of Foreign Ministry officials. It was so predictably pathetic.

But he wouldn't have taken the meeting if he didn't have something to tell her. She doubted he was there to listen, but she hoped to change that.

Adjusting himself behind a long low desk, Kelnikov smiled expansively. "Madam Ambassador, I am terribly sorry to have kept you waiting. I was in a tiresome meeting with the Prime Minister of Burundi." *Translation: this business with Saint Lawrence is not top of my agenda.* Devlin smiled back at him. "Julius? Yes, I met with him yesterday." *Translation: screw you.*

"To the business at hand," Kelnikov said, one of his aides handing him some papers. "It is good our ceasefire seems to be holding. Great powers have great responsibilities. A slip now by either side could have global repercussions neither of us wants."

"Indeed," Devlin replied carefully. "And on that point, I have been asked by our Secretary of State to convey to you once again our very simple demand that you liberate the citizens of Saint Lawrence and withdraw your remaining forces."

"Yes." He affected to sound bored. "And is there another deadline accompanying this ultimatum?" He looked at the top page of the papers he had been handed. "I see you have just announced you are going to try to send an aircraft carrier task force through the Strait. A 'freedom of navigation' exercise, you call it. We might see it differently."

"Oh, no, you misunderstand," Devlin said, and paused. She was supposed to communicate that the *Enterprise* task force would not be dissuaded from transnavigating the international waters of the Strait, Russian objections or not. After the devastation of the US cruise missile strike it was to be seen as an unsophisticated attempt to force Russia's hand and give them the opportunity to withdraw their meager force without any further combat. Looking at Kelnikov, even in the half shadow caused by the light behind him, she could see something of the same smugness in his eyes as she saw all those weeks ago. He radiated it, and her blood was boiling.

She had decided. She was going to go seriously off-script.

"That's just media spin," she said. "The *Enterprise* task force is actually moving into position to be able to take back Saint Lawrence and protect us from any likelihood you might be stupid enough to attempt to invade Alaska."

Now she had his attention. Oh, she would have paid a million dollars for video of his face as she said it. That insufferable smugness vanishing in an instant, to be replaced by a horrified uncertainty.

"I am sorry?" he said. "You accuse us of…"

She reached for her own briefcase and took out the printout she had made of HOLMES' analysis of Russian troop activations and air force dispositions. She handed it across the table, and one of Kelnikov's aides took it, studying it with a frown before handing it to the Minister.

"You have a serious leak at the highest levels of your defense ministry," she lied, maliciously. "Clearly not everyone in your government agrees with the insanity of its leadership."

"What is this?" Kelnikov demanded, turning the page over and back again.

"Your timetable for war. A timetable in which Saint Lawrence was the first move, and Nome will be the next."

He threw the paper down on his desk. "This is fiction."

"As you will," Devlin said, standing. "Minister, the *Enterprise* is not sailing to the Bering Strait for a 'freedom of navigation' exercise. And we are doing more than preparing to take back Saint Lawrence Island, which we soon will. We stand ready to defend the sovereign State of Alaska against invasion, with every man, woman *and* weapon at our disposal." She delivered a small, mocking bow. She had rehearsed her next lines in the car and took a breath to make sure she delivered them properly.

"You seem to have forgotten that the last 'great power' that attacked a US territory was Japan. That decision ended for them in ruin and nuclear fire."

She turned to leave, the sound of voices arguing with each other in Russian behind her as Kelnikov's aides broke their silence. He said nothing himself.

On a whim, she turned to face the Russian delegation again but fixed her eyes on the Foreign Minister, speaking only to him. "Minister, there is a way out of this. Russia will find it humiliating and the compensation terms will not be favorable. But it could save millions of lives. Just put your troops back on the helicopters they rode in on, and bring them home."

His glare burned through her back as she closed the door behind her. She hadn't actually lied. Not really. She was pretty damn sure that as soon as Carl Williams' report started circulating inside the State Department and Pentagon, everything she had just said was about to be true.

As she reached the end of the corridor outside, her aide Harrison fell into step beside her.

He wasn't able to contain himself this time. "How did it go, ma'am?"

"Not well, Harrison," Devlin said. "Not well at all. I'm terribly afraid I nearly lost my temper."

Life in the age of 'always on' had its advantages. Perri had found that if he ran a copper wire from the antenna input on the radio up the ladder to the sheet of tin covering the hatch, his Russian radio connected automatically to some sort of satellite communications network. So far so good. He could read just enough Russian from years of watching Russian TV to see the display was asking him to input a code word to link into a Russian military network. That wasn't an option. But the radio also had a guest device connection capability, and it was more than happy to hook up to his telephone and connect him to the unencrypted world wide web. "Warning," said the text scrolling across the display. "Communications on this channel are not secure."

The person he had called was a kid they met in Vancouver, who actually lived in Whitehorse, Yukon Territory, Alaska. He was a member of the Ta'an Kwach'an first nations tribe, called Johnny Kushniruk. Perri and Dave had agreed Johnny was the best person to call because his old man was a Mountie in the Royal Canadian Mounted Police at Whitehorse, and they needed someone with a few stripes to help get their story out and tell them what the hell they should do.

When they'd convinced Johnny they weren't messing around, and then convinced him to get his father on the line, the conversation got very serious very fast. Johnny's father's name was Dan Kushniruk, but he told the boys to call him Sarge.

"Are you guys safe?" was his first question.

"Yeah, no one is looking for us," Perri told him. "Not since the missiles. They're pretty much occupied with just staying alive now, I think."

He got the boys to walk him through what they'd done the last few days, and their attack on the ammo dump. His main concern was for the townspeople still being held hostage.

"I've got photos of everything," Perri told him. "Most of them are from long distance, up on the bluff, but we did a run to the airstrip yesterday to get this radio, so we have some photos from there too. I could upload them?"

"I can give you a website to send them to," Sarge told them. "Send me everything you've got. Look, you have to assume that using that Russian radio isn't safe. Someone in Gambell could be listening in next time, or someone in Russia. When you're online, it will be pretty easy for them to track your signal down, triangulate you. If the place you are in is safe, you need to keep it safe."

"OK."

"So once you make that upload, I want you to cut this connection and never call me from your base again."

236

"What?"

"Don't call me from your hiding place. Never make a call from the same place twice. Keep the calls under three minutes, less than a minute would be even better."

"Got it. Should we have a schedule or something?"

"Good thinking, son, but not a fixed schedule. What's your birthday?"

"My birthday? January 7, 2012."

"And your friend?"

Dave leaned forward toward the phone. "November 19, 2014."

"Right, so for the next few days you will connect only once a day at 1 p.m., 7 p.m., 8 p.m. and 12 p.m., got that? That's the numbers in your birthday. Then you follow your friend's birthday: 11 p.m., 7 p.m., 8 p.m. and 2 p.m. You get me?"

"Yeah, I get it: 20 is like 20:00 military time, so that's 8 p.m.," Perri said.

"Right. It's a pretty random pattern but easy to remember and hard for anyone to predict. We get through the next few days like that, then we'll come up with a new schedule."

Sarge took them through what he wanted them to report on in their next call later that day: how many civilians were being held hostage, where they were being held, whether any appeared sick or injured, and then the Russian troop numbers, how many were still in Gambell, how many body bags they had seen, how many injured, what uniforms they were wearing, what equipment they appeared to still possess.

"Can you get word out to the press? We want to let people know we're still here, we're fighting back," Perri told him.

"I get that," Sarge said. "And it's amazing, the two of you holding out this long, doing what you've done. But that would be suicide. Right now the best thing you have going for you is no one knows you are there."

Private Zubkhov had joined the Spetsnaz three years ago on a dare. His buddy in the 18th Artillery Division had applied and Zubkhov had told him he was crazy. A scrawny stick like him would never get through. They only took men who were totally hardcore, like Zubkhov.

"OK, so, you apply too, we'll see who gets through," his friend had said. "I bet you get booted out in your first week. Mental resilience, that matters more than brawn." He was wrong, of course. You needed both. Zubkhov qualified, but his buddy didn't.

He had brawn, and he had brains. So why was he being left behind to babysit a bunch of grandparents, seven wounded Russian troopers too sick to walk and too tough to just die, and one lobotomized Captain? It wasn't fair. He was Spetsnaz! *From any height, into any hell!* The motto had stirred his blood when he first heard it. But if it hadn't been for the dare, he probably wouldn't have made it through. The physical tests were nothing for a boy who'd grown up on the steppes, nursed from a frozen teat. But the gung-ho idiocy of his squad members made his teeth grind – there wasn't one of them who had recognized it was Dostoyevsky the Captain was spouting. He doubted any of them had ever read anything longer than a weapons manual.

Technically, his contract had already expired. He was waiting for his release papers to come through when they'd shipped out; he'd already decided he was done with the special forces. No re-up for him. He'd saved a little money and he had a buddy in Anadyr with a fishing trawler who wanted a partner who could throw in some cash to help upgrade the boat and join the business. He figured he'd probably meet cod who were smarter than some of the guys he was serving with.

So the attraction of being Spetsnaz *really* started to wear off the moment the enemy started landing goddamn cruise missiles on his head. And when Sergeant Penkov had singled him out to stay behind, that was the last straw. *From any height, into any hell?* He didn't realize hell could be a job as a nursing assistant in a schoolhouse on a windy little island in the Arctic. To make things even more enjoyable, it was the rainy season on Saint Lawrence, with day-time temps in the low forties and night-time temps close to freezing.

238

Sergeant Penkov had every remaining soldier out fossicking through the town and over at the airfield for the supplies they would need for the overland trek. They had to feed twenty soldiers and nearly 200 islanders for up to a week. Zubkhov suddenly became worried there would be nothing left for him, let alone the wounded and his elderly captives.

Looking for the Captain the night of the attack, Zubkhov had stumbled across a small shack down on the dock that looked like it was used by the local supermarket to store dry goods. Rice, pasta, sugar, flour, canned fruit and vegetables, packet soups and bottled water. So he'd spent a morning with a wheelbarrow ferrying it over to the school while no one was looking, and hiding it in a utility cupboard.

It would keep him fed for a few weeks. But it wasn't anywhere near enough for all of them.

Right now, he had his feet up on a desk in what must have been the schoolmaster's office, which was a grand name for a little hideaway at the back of a classroom with a desk and a filing cabinet. They'd put a transceiver dish on the roof, run a cable down to the transmitter on the desk beside his boots and wired it into one of the undamaged wind turbines. The transmitter was a United Instrument Manufacturing Corporation M01 base set, through which field units could send and receive signals at distances up to 600km. Until they were able to patch directly into the comms network in Savoonga, it was their lifeline to Russia, and their link to their comrades on Saint Lawrence.

But it wasn't portable. It sucked too much juice.

"This is your order of priority," the Sergeant had told him. "Your own well-being is your *last* priority. The well-being of the wounded is your *second* priority. And the well-being of this radio base station is your *first* priority. If it comes down to it, the last thought in that thick head of yours, as you die, should be, 'Thank God, the radio is safe.' Clear?"

He looked at it resentfully. They had of course taken the only working field handsets with them. Penkov didn't want him moaning to anyone up the line about being left behind. For a moment he'd fantasized that if he had a second handset, he could just put a call through to his buddy the fisherman in Anadyr and get him to sail over and pick him up. His papers had probably come through while he was over here – technically, he wasn't even a member of this damn unit anymore anyway. He sighed.

But he decided that since the useless piece of junk was now his responsibility, he'd better refresh his memory on how to use it because he hadn't looked at one since the early days of his training. He pulled out the manual, flicked through it, and tossed it aside. The base station featured a large LCD screen with a menu and he paged through that. OK, yeah, most of it he remembered. There was a menu that showed connected field units. It showed the type of unit connected, and the signal strength, and a submenu enabled him to select a particular field unit and boost the gain to improve the signal if they were in a hole somewhere.

But did it have any way he could hook up a basic microphone handset? Could he get a signal out himself?

No. Useless piece of junk.

He looked up at the wall where the ten mobile field handsets were normally racked. Empty. Tapping the screen, he checked and saw the only working unit, the one being used by the Sergeant, was there on the connections menu. It was at max signal strength, which was to be expected as the column of soldiers and refugees had only left about a half hour ago, so they hadn't gone far.

Strange. There was a *second* signal showing.

It didn't have the same designator as the other field handsets, it was showing a different 'friend or foe' code. Zubkhov picked the manual off the floor and turned to the back where the designator codes were listed.

He frowned. The code for the second radio signal was the one listed for an ATOM Infantry Fighting Vehicle comms unit. The only ATOMs they had brought with them had all been destroyed in the attack, two out by the airfield, and one that had been parked outside the town hall. He checked the signal strength. It was showing a distance of 6 to 10 kilometers. Unfortunately, it didn't show direction. But 6 to 10 kilometers, that would be right if, by some quirk, one of the radios in an ATOM out at the airfield was still switched on.

But after three days? The battery should be dead by now.

As he watched, the signal disappeared and didn't come back.

Ah, right. Faulty connection, cutting in and out. That explained why it hadn't completely drained the battery yet.

Suddenly, life didn't seem so hopeless after all. If there was a working radio out there somewhere, all he had to do was salvage it, call his buddy to sail over, pick him up, and then he could say goodbye to this stupid unit, this stupid army, and this stupid windy rock in the Arctic, forever!

General Lukin and his staff were walking into the briefing room at Lavrentiya at the same time as Bondarev. Lukin put an arm on the Colonel's shoulder. "So, how is the leg?"

Bondarev dropped into a squat and stood again, ignoring the tearing feeling in his calf. "Stronger than ever, General. I am grateful you arranged a ceasefire to allow me to recover without missing any combat."

"Anything for the Commander of my Snow Leopards," the General chuckled.

"General," Bondarev asked. "Just quickly. Is LOSOS still on track? I can assure you..."

"Patience, Comrade Colonel," Lukin said. They were walking into the room now and Bondarev greeted the commanding officers of the three other Air Regiments, together with its nine subordinate group commanders, most of whom reported to him. He fell back and let the General step ahead and take his seat. Lukin looked serious. Very well. The news was either going to be very good, or very bad.

The General wasted no time on pleasantries. "Gentlemen, I have just returned from Moscow after high-level strategic discussions about how we should respond to the American threats to our troops on Saint Lawrence." He looked around the table. "As you know, Operation LOSOS troops are on the island lawfully, under the mandate of the Barents Council of Nations."

There was a folio of maps in front of each participant in the meeting, and a cover sheet. Lukin nodded to the intelligence officer Bondarev remembered from their first LOSOS briefing. Lieutenant Ksenia Butyrskaya.

She stepped beside a screen on the wall and brought it to life, showing a map of the Operations Area. "Comrade officers, as you know, following the sinking of the *Ozempic Tsar*, we succeeded in our objective of peacefully taking control of the island of Saint Lawrence. Not a single civilian or military death was recorded, and only minor injuries to our own or enemy troops. Under the auspices of the Barents Council of Nations, a no-go zone was declared around the island affecting only US military aircraft and shipping, and freedom of commerce was restored." She took a breath and brought up a table of figures on the screen. Bondarev didn't need to look at it, he knew the kill/loss ratio numbers by heart. She continued. "Unfortunately the USA did not respect the no-fly zone and responded with a major act of aggression in which it attacked our peacekeeping troops on and above Saint Lawrence with fighter aircraft and cruise missiles." She glanced briefly at Bondarev. "Although outnumbered, we inflicted significant losses on the US air element, but we sustained considerable losses ourselves both in the air and on the ground. With the viability of our defensive position on Saint Lawrence threatened, a ceasefire was negotiated and is still in force."

She clicked a button in her hand and an overhead satellite image appeared on a wall behind her, showing a group of ships, at the center of which was clearly an aircraft carrier sailing on the open sea.

"Yesterday, a US aircraft carrier task force centered around the USS *Enterprise* and comprising at least three guided missile cruisers, five guided missile destroyers and two supply vessels left San Diego naval base for what the US Navy announced was to be a 'freedom of navigation' transit of the Bering Strait. Such carrier strike groups are usually accompanied by at least two attack submarines, not visible in this image."

She zoomed the photograph in on the supply vessels. "These are not normal supply vessels. They are in fact amphibious assault vessels, each capable of carrying 2,200 US Marines and landing 36 amphibious assault vehicles, supported by two to four manned vertical take-off transport aircraft or six drones. Their inclusion in this strike force is an unambiguous declaration by the Americans that they plan to land troops in the theater." She clicked the screen off. "The carrier strike force will arrive in theater within five days." She stepped back against the wall. Bondarev noted with interest she had said "land troops in the theatrer," not that they planned to "land troops on Saint Lawrence."

"Gentlemen," General Lukin said with gravity. "Operation LOSOS is moving to a new phase, dictated by the continued irrational and irresponsible behavior of the USA. The cruise missile strikes on Saint Lawrence, mere miles from Russian territory, are a provocation we cannot ignore. The willingness of the crazed politicians in Washington to sacrifice their own citizens to their missiles is also something the world community cannot ignore. Today, the Council of Ministers in Moscow agreed to a plan to establish a neutral geographic zone as a buffer between the USA and Russia, to secure against future attacks and to mitigate the threat of any land-borne invasion of Russia by the USA." Bondarev looked around to see he was not the only one who was unsurprised by the news. Good. At least he knew his fellow officers were not fools either. Before anyone could speak to ask questions, Lukin waved a finger to Butyrskaya again.

She flashed up a map of Alaska, showing what were clearly landing zones and directions of attack. The ultimate objective was shown to be a diagonal line of control stretching from Fort Yukon in the north to the fishing town of Bethel in the southwest. It was almost entirely uninhabited country. The nearest US military facilities were the air bases at Eielson and

Elmendorf-Richardson, hundreds of miles outside the line of control. The only population center of any note was Nome, population 2,300.

"Speed of action will again be the byword of Phase II of Operation LOSOS," the Lieutenant said. "However, there are no passable roads or bridges in the target area east of Nome. Because of this, support by even light armored vehicles and mobile anti-air defenses will be limited to zones of control around key airfields in Nome and Port Clarence. The first objective will be to secure the Nome airport and position logistical units, forward air units and heavy air defenses there. Second phase objectives will be the airfields at Port Clarence, in the west at Wales, south at Bethel, in the central region at Galena, and in the far north at Deadhorse. Airborne and special forces will secure the airfields and any police, paramilitary and urban weapons depots in these small population centers."

Urban weapons depots? Bondarev realized she was talking about hunting and fishing stores. What kind of 'invasion' was this? Focused as he was on the coming air war, he hadn't considered the challenges of controlling a huge wilderness area with only a few scattered population centers.

Hands were starting to be raised around the table, but Lukin waved them down. "You all have questions. Please let the Lieutenant finish, then you will be directed to new rooms for tactical briefings where you can ask questions to your hearts' content."

Butyrskaya continued. "A report from the Foreign Ministry in Moscow today indicates that the US anticipates an attack on the Alaska mainland. This isolated report, however, is not backed by other intelligence, which shows the US has been slow to bring its ground forces to readiness. It has activated National Guard units in Alaska and Washington State, but not in the nearby states of Oregon, Idaho or Montana, as would be expected. Reliable information indicates that the Alaska National Guard is preparing to defend its major population centers only: the capital Juneau, and the cities of Anchorage and Fairbanks. Even this will stretch its capacity and it does not have the strength to counter-attack our beachhead at Nome as well as defend major urban centers." She threw up a map showing the expected track of the US carrier task force. "We believe the true objective of the USS *Enterprise* task force is not to retake Saint Lawrence, but to protect US civilian and military assets in Anchorage and Fairbanks."

She clicked the map and showed big red arrows arcing up toward the line of control from Anchorage in the south and Fairbanks in the center. "If we succeed in taking Nome, the strategic pivot points for any counter-attack by US ground forces would usually be from these two centers, Anchorage and Fairbanks, but again, the lack of roads leading into the Yukon River catchment makes major ground-based assaults impractical. The US, like us, will be forced to rely on airborne and special forces units to retake its territory, so the 3rd Air Army will play a critical role in maintaining air superiority in the theater." She left the map on the screen for them to absorb. "That concludes this preliminary briefing. Unit briefings will now be held in the meeting rooms indicated in your folders."

Lukin folded his hands in front of him. "Gentlemen, this is a winnable war. We will not be threatening US population centers, we will make that clear. We will simply be establishing a non-militarized zone in the Alaskan wilderness for the protection of international air and sea traffic in the Bering Strait. The US cannot attack us by land; it can only threaten us by sea and by air. Nome is the key. If we can take and hold the airfield there, together with our base at Lavrentiya and the airfield at Savoonga, we will have a nexus of control over the entire Strait." He looked around the room in case there were any dissenters, but saw none. "Very well. You are dismissed. Colonel Bondarev, you will remain."

That got Bondarev some sharp looks from the other regimental heads. Unfortunately, most of them were of sympathy. Arsharvin had told him the engagement over Saint Lawrence was not seen in Moscow as a tactical success, even though losses had been expected. He wondered if he was about to be relieved of his command. He stayed nervously sitting as

Lukin made small talk with a couple of his officers before the room was suddenly empty and the General sat down again. He knew by now it was best to see how the dice would roll, so he said nothing.

"So, you are fit for combat again?" Lukin asked.

Bondarev noted he did not say 'fit for command'. *So, his days as commander of the Snow Leopards were done.*

"Yes, Comrade General. By week's end I will have restored the 4th and 5th Air Battalions to full strength. Thanks to your intervention, I am also now able to report that my Okhotnik ground-attack regiment is also fully crewed and ready for offensive operations." He wanted Lukin to know that if his command was to be taken from him, he was leaving it at optimal readiness.

"Good, good. I thought I should tell you this myself," Lukin began, and Bondarev's heart fell to the floor. He steeled himself for what was coming. Lukin continued. "The operation to take Nome will depend entirely on your ability to establish air supremacy over the Bering Strait and the target area around Nome."

Bondarev started to speak. "General, if I could just…" Then he heard what the General had said. He wasn't being relieved, he was being given a pivotal role! Perhaps *the* pivotal role.

Lukin misinterpreted his interjection. "Yes, whatever you need this time. I want any requests on my desk tomorrow morning. I am releasing your drones for use in support of operation LOSOS and the Okhotniks of the Lynx Air Brigade will also operate under your command. This gives you 60 fighter aircraft and 110 drones. I want you to keep a regiment of Mig-41s in reserve, to be released only on my command." Lukin leaned forward. "You will not be outnumbered next time, Yevgeny."

"Thank you, sir. We will not fail."

"You cannot," Lukin smiled thinly. "Our masters in Moscow were wavering. The ferocity of the US attack, their willingness to sacrifice their own people … it shocked President

Navalny. He was not willing to commit further ground troops to Operation LOSOS unless I could guarantee complete air supremacy."

"Our losses will be considerable," Bondarev warned. "Are they aware…"

"Yes. But the Americans may find they suddenly have other problems to deal with in coming days. You won't be facing the entire US Air Force."

"And the *Enterprise?*" National Guard units did not faze Bondarev. Neither did regular USAF units. Against human pilots, his men were more than a match and this time they would not allow the enemy drones to close to dogfighting range where they could use their maneuverability advantage. If Russian ground-attack units were successful in suppressing the US ability to operate out of Eielson and Elmendorf-Richardson air bases, the enemy would have to fly from further afield in Washington State, Oregon and Idaho, so they would have no home ground advantage. But the approaching supercarrier, with its 75 F-35 and Fantom fighters, could change the balance. It was a headache he didn't need.

"You needn't worry about the *Enterprise*," Lukin assured him. "It is a big stick the Americans rattle at small nations. The Navy will take care of the *Enterprise*. Admiral Kirov assures me the Americans will soon learn how vulnerable their capital ships are."

Vulnerability was something Perri knew all about.

How to feel it in yourself, how to see it in others. It wasn't an easy life on Saint Lawrence. You had to earn your living from the land and sea around you, no one was going to give it to you. And sometimes you eat the bear, sometimes the bear eats you.

Right now he was staring at that damn radio again, knowing it was like a homing finger of death that pointed straight at him and Dave. He wondered whether he should turn it on and tell the Sarge what he was seeing.

247

Because something was happening down there in Gambell and it didn't look good. All yesterday, they'd watched the Russians go house to house with sacks, looting. Not televisions or computers or jewelry, though they probably didn't hesitate to help themselves to anything shiny that was lying around. They saw one guy with a shopping trolley and it looked to Perri like they were loading up on food. OK, so there hadn't been any helicopters flying in supplies for weeks now, they were probably running low, but what had been low-level scrounging the last couple of weeks seemed like planned pilfering now.

Then they heard shouting down by the school. Perri and Dave were up on the bluff and looked down on the town with scope and binos.

"They're pulling people out of the schoolhouse," Dave said. "Lining them up."

"I see your brothers," Perri said. "Shit. I think they're going to shoot them."

"Do something, man!" Dave said. "You've got the gun. You're the sniper!"

"Shut up!" Perri hissed. He knew he was too far away to take a shot. Sure, he could spray a few downrange, and he might disturb whatever was going on, but he wouldn't be doing any more than making the troops down there aware he was up here. Maybe a few of their people could get away, though…

"Wait, no. The Russians all have backpacks. Our people have got packs on too, coats and boots! Would you load people up and then take them out to shoot them?" Dave asked, confused.

Perri watched down the scope a minute more. "They're moving them somewhere. They're all heading out."

"Where the hell…"

"I don't know, but everyone down there is kitted out like they're going cross country," Perri said. As he spoke, he saw his family in the lines of townspeople. His brothers and father, his mother. She looked so small. And pissed. She was yelling at a Russian soldier who was trying to push people into line. Yeah, that was his Ma.

248

When they finally had the 200 townspeople lined up in two long lines, the Russian soldiers formed up ahead and either side of them, with a few at the rear, and they headed off down toward the road out of town that went along the airstrip and then skirted the bluff. After that it went nowhere in particular. Only bird watchers and hunters, or berry pickers, used the tracks out that way. In ten minutes, though, it was clear they were quitting town.

"I can't see my grandma," Dave said, running his binos up and down the line of hostages. "I can't see your grandparents, either. None of the elders are with them."

"Kids are with them, though," Perri said. He ran the scope back through town and stopped at the school, where he saw a solitary Russian soldier standing on the school steps, watching everyone leave. He didn't appear in a hurry to join them. Perri watched as he finished a cigarette, ground it out under his boot, and went back inside the schoolhouse.

"They split them up," Perri said. "I bet they left the elders back in Gambell, took the adults and kids with them."

"Human shields," Dave said. "That's what they call it, right? Can't get a missile up your butt if you're walking next to a bunch of civilians."

Perri thought about it. "Yeah, but walking where? We've got to decide; do we follow the group or stay here, see if we can somehow get the kids and elders out."

They looked at each other. Without speaking they knew what they had to do.

Ask Sarge.

Devlin also knew what she had to do. She had to have a shot of bourbon.

Just a little one. Medicinal.

She swirled it around her mouth. It was a John J Bowman single barrel and five-time winner of the World Whiskey Best Bourbon award. A fine example of American craftsmanship, and every glass she poured for a guest was trade promotion, right? She put the bottle back on the tray beside the gin, which was the favored end-of-day tipple among the diplerati. And it was the end of a very long day.

Her people had been working their networks in embassies and consulates across the city, testing support for a coming UN Security Council resolution rescinding the recognition of the Barents Council of Nations. It couldn't succeed, not with Russia and probably China abstaining, but it was the first step to a full vote in the UN chamber to have the Council delegitimized so that Russia could no longer hide its aggression behind a veil of international probity. State wanted to get that done to take one of Russia's threatening pieces off the chess board.

They were also drawing up a 'skins and shirts' list of who would be with them, who would be with Russia, and who would try to stay neutral, if the shooting war started again. It didn't look good. The US had its traditional steadfast allies behind it: the UK, Australia, Canada and New Zealand. Also looking like it would fall behind Team USA was Turkey, still worried about continued Russian influence in neighboring Syria. Russia could be sure of the support of its newly won Baltic ally, Finland, and the 'Stans': Uzbekistan, Kazakhstan, Turkmenistan. Russia could also muster Middle East support from Syria and Iran. But there was a depressingly long list of countries declaring this was a bilateral 'maritime dispute' between Russia and the USA, including most of Europe.

Devlin had spent the morning with the Swedish Ambassador, impressing on him in diplomatic double-speak that if he wanted to keep selling Volvo motor cars in the USA and Swedish arms like Gripen fighters and Bofors cannons to US allies, the US would be expecting Sweden to get off the fence and vote in the UN to de-accredit the Barents Council at its next meeting in two days. "Abstaining again is not an option," she'd told him. "I suspect it would annoy Volvo's Chinese owners mightily if they weren't able to sell their cars in the US anymore because of a political miscalculation?"

The reason she needed a drink was not because it was the end of a hard working day – she'd had plenty of those. It was because she feared all her efforts, all her people's efforts, were like firing buckshot at a hurricane. She had called Washington at midnight the night before to follow up on her report about the imminent Russian attack on Alaska, only to be told it was regarded as "interesting but unlikely." It did not concur with intelligence from other sources, or reports from other embassies. Russian military movements were consistent with defensive preparations or the proposed 'no-fly' zone over Alaska, but not consistent with what would be needed to mount a full-scale invasion. That would require the mobilization of hundreds of thousands of troops, as well as the transport of armor and materiel, and there were no indications that was taking place.

"They're mobilizing their Far East fighter brigades, air defense batteries, airborne troops and special forces, Ambassador," a State Department analyst in the Secretary of State's office had told her in a patronizing tone. "Not the divisions of troops, main battle tanks and the ships they'd need to land them. They're getting ready to defend themselves and their position on Saint Lawrence, not go on the attack."

She didn't have the stripes to be able to ask anyone in the Pentagon what specific preparations – beyond sallying forth with the *Enterprise* strike group – the US was making to either challenge the Russian occupation of Saint Lawrence or defend against an attack on Alaska, so she had turned to an alternative source. An old Canadian friend from her days as a junior officer in the embassy in Ottawa. He sat on the Canadian Foreign Ministry Joint Intelligence Committee now, and she asked him if her communique had reached his desk, or had it been buried.

"Oh, I got it," he said. "Or a filtered version. Under the five-eyes agreement they couldn't exactly bury it, they had to share it, but they 'contexted' it with five other reports indicating this business was all about Saint Lawrence Island and needling the USA, and nothing to do with trying to land troops in Alaska."

She had blown her top. "*Needling* the USA?" she'd asked him. "Why the hell would Russia risk nuclear war just to 'needle' the USA?"

"No one believes you'd start World War Three over Saint Lawrence Island," the man said, with untypical directness. "The Ukraine, Syria, Finland ... this is Russia once again testing how far they can push you."

She saw how you could look at it that way if you bought into the bill of goods Russia was selling. "OK, but look. You've seen my report. What is Canada's play here? If Russia marches into Alaska, you have to react."

"We're not worried, but we're ready," he'd said. "Army is activating the 3rd Division, moving all four brigades into British Columbia. And in the unlikely event of an invasion, our Prime Minister would probably be open to discuss US air and ground forces staging out of BC if he received a formal approach."

"Oh, he'd be open to *discuss*," she'd sighed. "That's so kind."

She sat down in her chair and swung her tired legs up on her desk. At her elbow was a pile of papers and she picked from the top of it a book Carl Williams had sent her a few days before. *The Man Who Saved Britain*, by a Harvard history professor. She had read the blurb on the inside cover. The professor had come across a trove of papers in Germany written by the impressively named Friedrich-Werner Graf von der Schulenburg, the last German Ambassador to the Soviet Union before Operation Barbarossa, the battle which signaled the start of the German war on Russia. In his personal letters, written communiques and personal diaries von der Schulenburg had relentlessly pursued a campaign to persuade the Reich Chancellor, Adolf Hitler, and his trusted coterie that if they embarked on an invasion of Britain, their Russian 'allies' would take advantage of their distraction and immediately stab them in the back, marching into Poland, Czechoslovakia, Albania, Yugoslavia and, most importantly, the precious oilfields of Romania. He cited numerous conversations with Russian politicians, bureaucrats and military officers to back his claims, he sent translated clippings from newspapers, and he made three trips to Berlin to personally brief the Nazi party hierarchy about the threat. He also cited conversations with the US Ambassador in Russia indicating the US had no intention of entering the war in Europe.

In the end, he prevailed. Hitler postponed his plan to invade England, shored up his defenses along the Atlantic front, and sent his tanks and Stukas east. He was mostly right – Russia would have stabbed Germany in the back, postwar documents confirmed that. But the US did enter the war and, together with Russia, gave Nazi Germany a spanking.

The small handwritten note in the front told her what Williams was thinking when he sent her the book.

To Devlin von der McCarthy,
Sometimes the voice of one person is enough. Keep at it.

In the early part of the century, the US became very concerned about the threat to its ability to project sea power from Chinese and Russian hypersonic anti-ship missiles. In testing, the scramjet-driven missiles proved capable of speeds up to Mach 8 – eight times the speed of sound. Russia had shown that a missile like its Tsirkon DM33, fitted with double-core fragmentation warheads, could achieve a terminal velocity of 5,800 miles per hour, making it impossible for even state of the art counter-missile defenses to track, let alone intercept it.

With a range of about 250 miles and the ability to cover 100 miles in less than a minute, able to be launched from multiple platforms on, above or under the sea, the missiles risked not only making aircraft carriers and larger surface combatants vulnerable, they could make them *obsolete*.

In addition to accelerating its own hypersonic missile program in the face of advances by China and Russia, the US invested billions into research on how to counter such missiles. How could they even be tracked? The problem wasn't designing a radar that could detect them, but whether the software could keep up and what type of algorithm was needed to solve the problem of target 'ambiguity'. What type of processing capabilities would be needed to react and activate countermeasures when reaction time was measured in milliseconds? Could they be spoofed by decoy strategies? Could they be jammed? Could they be destabilized with simple air cannons fired by perimeter vessels?

Quantum computing and dedicated radar and processing software solved the detection problem, and the answer to intercepting hypersonic missiles was found not in ballistics, but in optics. The only defensive system able to target and fire quickly enough was a high-powered laser. After successful testing, the Gen 5 High Energy Liquid Laser Area Defense System (HELLADS) was deployed on all US Navy ships and other military and industrial targets which were deemed vulnerable to hypersonic or ballistic missile attacks. In the Syria-Turkey conflict it had proven able to intercept eight out of ten conventional ballistic missiles before they reached their targets.

Seen to be politically akin to a weapon of mass destruction, no hypersonic missiles were used in the Syria conflict and it was widely perceived that the first nation to use them in war would be opening a new Pandora's box.

Of course, HELLADS just triggered a new arms race, on the premise that the best way to defeat HELLADS was to overwhelm it with multiple missiles, and all the major armies started stockpiling scramjet missiles at the same time as fitting their surface warships, submarines and aircraft to be able to field them, while arguing strenuously in public that the use of hypersonic missiles by any nation would be akin to using a tactical nuke.

Still, it remained the case that a hypersonic weapon had never been used in war, and the HELLADS system on the USS *Enterprise* and its escorts had never actually been tested in combat.

Perri Tungyan was feeling pretty combat tested.

"I'm looking at him right now," Perri said down the line to his new friend Sarge in Canada. "Through the window of the headmaster's office. Got my scope on him."

"For God's sake, don't do anything stupid!" Sarge said urgently. "You don't know what the situation is inside that building."

"He's on his own in there, just smoking a cigarette, scratching his butt," Perri said. "I could take him down, then we could check out the school. If he's the only one, I could get our people out."

"And if he's not, they could all be dead," Sarge said. "Did the Russians take any wounded with them? Did you see stretchers, people being carried?"

Perri looked at Dave, who shook his head. "No."

"Then if they're alive, they're still in there and they're probably still able to hold a gun on your people. Or they could have wired the place with explosives in case they are attacked, take out your entire town with a flick of a switch. Just *relax*, son."

"I am relaxed," Perri said to him through gritted teeth. "But I have about ten minutes to decide if we do something about this guy and try to get our people out of that school, or whether we go after the others who are getting further and further away the longer we talk."

Sarge gave him a moment to calm down. "They are probably going to an evacuation point, to meet a ship or submarine," Sarge speculated. "If they are, we need to know."

"Why would they be heading out of town?" Perri asked. "A ship could pick them up here."

"I thought you said the harbor was destroyed," Sarge asked. "It looked like it in the photos you sent."

"Yeah, I guess."

"They could be going down to Kavalghak Bay," Dave said. "You could get a small ship in close to shore there."

"If the Russians are quitting Gambell, if they're pulling them *off* the island, that's critical intel," Sarge said.

"Oh *man*," Perri groaned. There had been no activity in the town, so he and Dave had climbed up to the roof of a building two streets back from the school and he had perfect line of sight down into the schoolmaster's office and the Russian soldier sitting there, drinking his coffee and enjoying his cigarette while he stared at some sort of screen. Dave was dragging the car battery and the Russian radio and complaining all the way because he'd had to leave his rifle behind; he couldn't carry it all. They'd worked out that they could wire the radio to any old TV aerial or satellite dish and get a good signal, so they'd hit the general store and stolen one of those folding portable TV and radio aerials and it worked just fine.

"I could knock this guy out now, and then we could head out after the others," Perri insisted. He'd zeroed the scope with a few shots at a target a good distance out of town a couple of days ago, and the crosshairs in his electronic scope were indicating very little windage, and minimal bullet drop. He put the red dot right on the temple of the Russian soldier, with the crosshairs sitting on his ear. He told himself it was a shot even Dave could make.

"What you're doing there is bigger than those elders, Perri," Sarge told him. "I've passed your intel to our military here, and they've passed it to the Americans. Yeah, maybe you could free your old people from that school, or you could stay cool, and maybe help to free your whole island. The US just announced it is sending a carrier task force your way. The Marines are coming, Perri, and they need your intel."

Perri felt his finger tighten on the trigger, saw the crosshairs quiver on the head of the Russian soldier. Then he rolled onto his back and swore up at the lead-gray sky.

Private Zubkhov scratched his temple, not realizing how lucky he was. To still *have* a temple, that is. But he wasn't exactly focused on the world outside the school office window. He was focused on that damn ghost radio signal, because if he was reading the screen right, the damn thing was transmitting again and it had gotten *closer*. The screen showed range rings in bands of five kilometers, and he could see the last remaining field handset, taken by the Sergeant, had just moved from the 5km ring to the 10km ring as his unit hiked out of town with their captives and headed north around the bluff toward the coast.

The ghost signal, the one with the icon that said it was coming from an armored personnel carrier, that one had just popped up on the screen again, and it was showing *inside* the 5km ring now! He tapped the screen, in the way of all the non-digitally inclined through the ages, and as he did so, the icon disappeared. He was still seeing the portable handset taken by the troops, but the APC radio had winked out.

Maybe he'd read it wrong. There was that wrecked APC down by the town hall. That must be the one transmitting, not one of the ones out by the airstrip. The screen he was looking at only showed range, not direction, so he must have been mistaken thinking it was coming from way out at the airstrip.

It was right down the street!

He stood up, ground out his cigarette, finished the cold coffee in the bottom of his cup and pulled his thick padded jacket on. It was still about 12 degrees outside, but the wind out there could freeze a man's tits off. He picked up a 39mm AS VAL rifle, stumped down the corridor and looked in on the wounded. There were seven of them lying on makeshift beds laid across desks. One had an IV drip in his arm that Zubkhov had to change every day. Two of them had abdominal wounds that couldn't be treated, so they couldn't be moved. One of them had a fever. He wasn't expected to make it, so all Zubkhov could do was make him comfortable. In reality, the ones with abdominal wounds were already dead, but luckily none of *them* were fully conscious; they were on big doses of intravenous painkillers. There were several with leg wounds, including one soldier who'd lost his entire lower left leg. They were doped up on painkillers and antibiotics, sleeping or reading. One gave a small wave to Zubkhov and indicated that he wanted a smoke with a sign so that he didn't wake the others. Zubkhov nodded back to him to show he had seen him.

Sitting in the corner, mumbling to himself, was Captain Demchenko. He was loaded up with antibiotics too. Zubkhov had expected him to contract some sort of encephalitis and clock out sooner or later, which, if you asked Zubkhov, would have been a mercy. But the red-hot metal splinter that had sliced through his head had apparently been surgically sterile. The guy didn't even have a temperature and looked perfectly normal, for a man who had just had accidental brain surgery, that is.

It was only thirty minutes since he'd asked the civilians if anyone needed a toilet break, and an hour until he was supposed to go around and check on them, and hand out some rations for lunch.

But during his first morning of playing combined nurse and prison camp guard, Private Zubkhov had decided. Screw being left behind to play nurse and prison camp guard. Screw the 14th Spetsnaz Squadron. He'd been near-drowned in interrogation simulations, beaten on the soles of his feet with an ice hockey stick for coming last on a cross-country march, and had to take a solid shotgun slug in his protective vest just to get through basic training. Hell, he'd survived a US cruise missile landing less than a block away from him, without even a scratch.

He was technically a free man. So, he was going to find that damn radio, call his buddy the fisherman in Anadyr, and get off this dogpile.

A high-value unit like a supercarrier is very well protected indeed. Two hundred miles out from it, covering all quarters, are the 'picket' ships, combat air patrol aircraft and airborne early warning drones. Inside that is the outer screen of ships anywhere from 10 to 20 miles from the carrier, positioned to provide anti-missile and anti-air defense. The ships making up the outer screen for the *Enterprise* were primarily there for anti-submarine defense – 'delousing' as it was called – and maintained a constantly patrolling swarm of drones around the formation using thermal imaging and towed sonar, looking and listening for any sign of a subsea intruder.

And inside that, the inner screen. This was the dedicated anti-air warfare screen. For the *Enterprise*, nothing but the latest HELLADS armed anti-air frigates, supplemented with more conventionally armed anti-air missile destroyers fitted with close-in ballistic defenses. The entire group was tactically data linked; if one of the pickets detected an inbound missile, it was engaged if possible, and simultaneously handed off to the outer screen and inner screen to engage if needed. With a hypersonic missile able to get from detection range outside the pickets to its carrier target in less than two minutes, it was unlikely the pickets would be able to successfully engage, but at quantum computing speeds, the inner screen would theoretically have ample time to lock a target and bring it down. Even a target moving at 5,000 miles an hour.

That was the theory.

Russia was well versed in the theory, and in the practice. It had led the race to develop hypersonic missiles and aircraft for decades, and was also aware of the countermeasures developed against them. It had had many years in which to wargame a hypersonic missile attack on a carrier strike group, and had done so in secret using dummy missiles sent against its own (and only remaining) carrier, the TAVKR *Admiral Flota Sovetskogo Soyuza Kuznetsov*. These exercises had revealed that penetrating the multilayered defenses of a carrier task force even using multiple sub-launched hypersonic missiles fired from inside the picket screen had a less than 50% likelihood of success against HELLADS-armed carrier defenses.

Attacking a US supercarrier was also an unambiguous declaration of full-scale war. Which is why Russia's chosen strategy for taking the USS *Enterprise* out of the Battle for Bering Strait was ... a rowing machine.

Of course, Aviation Electronics Technician E-3 Thomas Grayson was, as far as he was concerned, just applying an operating system update to the exercise machines on one of the hangar decks. It was probably the most exciting thing he'd been

259

given to do that day, not because it was technically challenging, but because it involved real risk of bodily harm from the fitness fanatics he had to kick off the equipment so that he could patch and reboot it. Like everything else on the *Enterprise*, even the fitness equipment was networked. A seaman scanned in their ID, did their workout, and the results were uploaded to a server, then to the cloud, so that they could set goals and track their progress. Some of them were on compulsory scheduled workouts due to weight issues, and the data was used to assess their fitness for service. So yeah, he got a lot of grief when the machines had to be shut down, but life sucks, as he told the grumblers.

The order for the patch had come through a day out of San Diego and landed in his inbox looking like every other routine piece of shit job he had to handle. They were sailing into a war zone, and he was patching the OS on fitness equipment. No irony in that, at all. He pulled the patch down from the attached link, validated it, then called up the interface for the equipment in question and applied the patch. The reboot had to be done manually, pulling the power and restarting the machines one by one, which meant him trekking all over the damn ship, from deck to deck. By the time he rebooted the last machine at about 1500 Pacific West Coast time, *he* was the one ready to hit someone.

But he got it done. And tomorrow was sure to be another fun-filled day.

The Russian virus was elegant but complex and it had never been used before. It had been created specifically to attack the USS *Enterprise*. Once it had gained access to the *Enterprise*'s local network via the exercise machines on multiple decks across the ship, it copied itself to every available server and networked device, and then went to work. Perhaps not surprisingly, Seaman Grayson was one of the first to notice something was wrong. Back at his station, he turned on his tablet and went to enter the day's activity in his duty log, only to find he couldn't connect to the ship's wireless network. It was there, his tablet just couldn't log into it. Piece of shit tablet. He grabbed another one, entered his ID and tried to log on with that. No deal. He went over to a stationary computer and was about to try and turn that on when the general quarters alarm began to sound and total chaos broke out!

Grayson was already at his 'combat station' and didn't need to go anywhere, but throughout the ship he heard people yelling, feet running, compartment doors being slammed and locked tight. He waited for an announcement – was it a drill, or 'vampires' – enemy missiles – inbound?! There had been a lot of talk that they might even see action on the way up to the Arctic if Russia had parked an attack sub on the seafloor ahead of them. But there was no announcement, nothing at all but the blare of the alarm. And that was almost worse than the fear that there were missiles on their way.

The first thing the virus did was take down the ship's internal communication links. Within minutes, nothing on the ship could talk to anything else, whether it was Grayson's rowing machine, or the primary flight control center, the bridge, combat direction center or the carrier intel center. The only way anyone or anything could communicate was suddenly, and critically, by yelling. Which there was a lot of. The next thing it did was cut the carrier's links to the outside world: shortwave, longwave, digital radio, radar, satellite up and downlinks, they all went black. In minutes the most sophisticated ship in the navy had been reduced to the status of a steam-driven World War Two vessel, with its only communication options the infallible battery-backed Aldis lamps, flags and Morse code.

And just like a 'fly by wire' aircraft, the *Enterprise* was 'steer by wire'; its two 700 megawatt Bechtel A1B reactors drove four shafts which took their orders from the bridge computers, just as the rudders did.

So the only communication channel on the ship that the virus left open was the link from the bridge to the steering and propulsion system. And the last thing it did before locking those down was to push the *Enterprise*'s speed up to 35 knots and order full right rudder.

Seaman Grayson didn't have to worry for very long why there were no announcements. As the USS *Enterprise* slowly but horrifically *accelerated* into a wide skidding turn, it began to lean over 20 degrees and the contents of a high filing cabinet that Grayson had been using emptied themselves onto his back, knocking his head forward into his desk and taking all his worries away.

If he'd still been conscious, he would have heard the sound of metal tearing and, worse, the sound no seaman or officer on an aircraft carrier wants to hear – the sound of inadequately secured aircraft sliding across hangar decks to smash into each other.

Followed by the smell no seaman anywhere, on any vessel, ever wants to smell.

Smoke!

Bunny O'Hare was smoking, but only in the metaphorical sense. She'd gone from fuming, when Rodriguez had told her she'd be left behind in an explosives-filled cave to fly out their complement of drones, to incendiary as she watched the navy launches shuttle her fellow cave dwellers out to their waiting submarine. But now … now she was smoking.

As in, smoking *hot*. As in the most smoking hot drone aviator in the whole damn US Navy because over the last two days she and Rodriguez had just set a personal best, single-handedly flying 15 Fantoms out the chute over a 30-hour period without one hitch. Of course, if they'd had Rodriguez's full launch team working they could have got a hex of drones out the chute within 35 minutes, but it was just her and the Lieutenant Commander doing all the heavy lifting.

They'd worked out that Bunny wasn't needed in the trailer between launches. Once she had a Fantom airborne and set its course for Elmendorf-Richardson or Eielson, she was basically a free agent because it was flying itself on full auto until it entered air traffic control range where the Air Force controllers at the other end took over to make sure it got down safely without bumping into anything.

So once her Fantom was out the chute and on its way, she went down to the flight deck and helped Rodriguez bully the empty cartridge off the Cat and into the reloader, then dropped the next cartridge and drone onto the Cat, locked and loaded it, and helped with the pre-flight check. She learned it wasn't as hands-off as Rodriguez had made it out to be. The damn things didn't always come out of the cartridges clean, they tended to stick, and sometimes the only solution was a good old-fashioned kick in the ass with the heel of a boot to shake them loose. The launch bars and locks on the Cat that secured the airframe to the catapult shuttle, the carriage between the two catapult beams that flung the aircraft forward, were damn fussy and even when you were sure you had a good lock, they refused to give you a green light and you had to reseat the damn thing. Finally, every drone was loaded inside its cartridge with wings folded, and an external hydraulic pressure system had to be connected to unfold and lock the wings in place. Only then could the pre-flight physical and digital inspection be carried out.

The launch schedule wasn't exactly regular, either. Unless they wanted to blow their cover completely, they could only launch when NORAD was showing cloud or mist cloaking Little Diomede and no nosy Russian aircraft overhead. Luckily most of the Russian air activity was centered further south.

With 12 hours on and six off, at the end of their second 12-hour shift Rodriguez had lost track of whether it was night or day. Her watch was telling her it was 1430 in the afternoon, but her body was ready for food and bed. They could afford to take it a little easier now. With 15 kites away, they only had eight remaining Fantoms to get home. Their lift out of here was the same sub that had ferried the walking and the walking wounded out of here two days ago, and it would be back six days from now to pick them up. Rodriguez wanted to get the job done, but they didn't have to kill themselves doing it. They could fall back to their planned six launches per day, take two

263

days to launch the rest, and spend the last four days making sure there was no accessible data left on any of the local systems and the demolition charges were set to blow.

Rodriguez slumped down at a makeshift mess table in one of the empty hangars, where Bunny was flicking through a digital girlie magazine on a tablet. She smiled. "Sorry to interrupt."

"Just checking out the competition, ma'am," Bunny said. "They got nothin' on us."

"Speak for yourself, O'Hare," Rodriguez said. "I've got bow legs and a big ass and everything topside is heading south."

"With respect, I'm calling bullshit on that, ma'am. Anyway, these girls, it's all silicone and implants – me and you are the real deal." Bunny ran her hand over the fuzz on her head. "I am a bit jealous of their flowing locks, though." She turned her head like she was looking for something. "You think anyone left their hair dye behind in this joint? I'm thinking of dying my stubble black."

Rodriguez lowered her head onto one arm and looked up at her. "You seriously have the energy to worry about what your hair looks like?"

"We've finally got the place to ourselves, no damn men spraying their testosterone everywhere? Hell yeah. I'm thinking a hot bath, paint my fingernails and toenails black and dye my hair to match. Might even do the next shift naked, just because I can. What do you say, ma'am? You in?"

Rodriguez laughed at the image that popped into her head; a huge, exhausted laugh.

Devlin got back to her apartment in Spaso House, threw her keys on a table near the door, dumped her bag, kicked off her shoes and poured herself a glass of cold white wine from her refrigerator.

She had unanswered messages and texts to deal with, the US West Coast was just waking up with worried business people and Congress members wanting to talk with her, and in her bag was a pile of code-word paper ten inches thick that people wanted her to read by morning. She turned off her phone.

Five minutes, just five minutes. She would have a glass of wine, and then get back to it. She sat on her sofa and turned on the TV news.

She saw the tickertape across the bottom of the news anchors' desks first – 'FLASH update...' – and expected it to be about Alaska. It wasn't. She watched with horror as she read the text rolling across her screen. "Syrian troops enter Lebanon. Government ministers arrested. Hezbollah seize power. Israeli armed forces placed on high alert."

It was a strategy as old as time. Use your alliances to occupy your enemy with a crisis on two fronts. No ally could demand US support in a crisis like Israel, and providing military support to Israel would mean committing, or at least reserving, significant assets that could otherwise be brought into play against Russia. So creating an existential threat to Israel through Syrian intervention in Lebanon was a masterstroke. It divided focus in Washington, in the Pentagon, in the armed forces, intelligence and security services, and in the State Department.

It told her with certainty this intervention in the Bering Strait had not just arisen out of the sinking of a single autonomous freighter. The speed with which Finland jumped into bed with Russia on the Barents Euro-Arctic Council and their probable involvement in the sinking already told her that. But mobilizing an ally, even a vassal state like Syria, to effectively invade a neighboring country and depose its government, on *your* timetable, not theirs ... that took long-term planning, and significant negotiation, pressure, compromise. Syria would have seen an opportunity while the US was distracted by events off Alaska, but it must have been offered something big, and it wouldn't surprise Devlin if they saw Iran weighing in soon too. With Saudi Arabia and the Emirates weakened by the collapse of oil prices, with Turkey licking its wounds after a bruising border war, suddenly the whole power balance in the Middle East was at risk.

She stood, and found herself in front of her hall mirror, just staring at herself. She was going to break. In two, right down the middle. She felt like she was standing outside herself, watching someone in crisis. She wanted to help, but there was nothing she could do. The woman in front of her was drowning but there was no life preserver to throw, no ladder to help her up. She imagined the water closing over her head, and herself disappearing without a ripple.

She put a hand on the mirror and pushed her image away.

SUPPRESSION

As Syrian tanks rolled across the border into Lebanon, Bondarev's 110 Okhotniks reopened the air war over Alaska. The machines themselves staged out of roads and highways around the large air base at Lavrentiya on the Russian mainland, but Bondarev didn't need to collocate his pilots and aircraft – in fact, it was wise not to do so. They had to be within 200 miles of the target area, but otherwise he was free to place their container-sized trailers anywhere with fast data links, a good supply of juice, and enough food and water for 200 plus crew.

So while he had the drones based at Lavrentiya, he had positioned his Okhotnik pilots, and their command trailers in Anadyr, well back from the Operations Area but still within operational range when linked to their drones by Airborne Control aircraft.

Two days after the briefing at 3rd Air and Air Defense Forces Command HQ, 60 Sukhoi-57s and Mig-41s took off from Lavrentiya as though moving into what had become routine patrol positions in the air over Saint Lawrence and the Bering Strait. What was not normal was the high number of aircraft Russia had scrambled.

When they reached what would have been their normal stations inside the Russian no-go zone, they pushed east toward the Alaska coast.

Waiting for them just outside the air exclusion zone were the F-35s and older F-22s of the Alaska Air National Guard. Behind them, at five-minute readiness, were two regular squadrons of the US Air Force under the control of an Airborne Control aircraft. As soon as it detected the large Russian formations approaching Saint Lawrence, the Airborne Control aircraft scrambled its Air Force fighters. Within minutes, the US force facing Russia numbered 36 fighters, and 20 more were another 20 minutes out. Pulling data from a combination of its own radar, NORAD and satellites, the US Airborne Control aircraft handed off targets to its flock of defenders and put ground-to-air defenses around Elmendorf-Richardson and Eielson on alert.

NORAD was also tracking a squadron of nine Russian Blackjack strategic bombers that was returning from what had now become routine trans-polar 'provocation' flights.

Ceasefire or no ceasefire, there was no ambiguity in the US aviators' orders. If the Russian fighters closed on Alaskan coastal airspace, the US fighters were cleared to engage.

Bondarev had no intention of letting his piloted aircraft get within air-to-air missile range of the Americans. Not yet. Before the US fighters were within range, he turned his Sukhois back west and they withdrew to the Russian mainland.

The US air commander fell for the ruse. He misinterpreted the move as a failed attempt to provoke US aircraft into following and breaking the terms of the ceasefire. Now he had machines he needed to get down and refuel, and pilots who had been living on edge for weeks who needed their rest. He pulled half of his force back to Elmendorf-Richardson and Eielson once it was clear the Russian fighters were withdrawing too, and ordered the rest to keep station until they were at bingo fuel.

Timed to coincide with this, to the north and south of Saint Lawrence, Bondarev had scattered 60 Okhotnik stealth drones, configured for ground attack. He had ordered his drone pilots to fire at the extreme limit of the range of the Okhotniks' Brah-Mos supersonic cruise missiles. With two missiles per aircraft, as the last of the sortied US fighters was landing, within minutes there were 120 cruise missiles on their way toward Elmendorf-Richardson and Eielson!

The last time Eielson had faced a cruise missile attack it was from Bunny O'Hare, and that had not gone so well. But this time its HELLADS systems and crews were ready. They might not have anticipated when Russia would strike, but the two US air bases were targets too strategically vital for Russia to ignore and US war planners knew it. So additional units had been flown in from Stateside to ensure the critical US airfields in Alaska were bristling with anti-air systems.

Sixty vampires inbound? *No problem.*

"Ma'am, turn on your laptop!" Williams' voice said over Devlin's telephone line. She had just been getting ready to go to bed when the phone had rung. "I'm going to push something through to you."

"Okay, just give me a minute," Devlin said, cradling her telephone on her shoulder and pulling her laptop out of her bag. She hit the button to boot it up. "Always takes a couple of minutes, this old thing."

"Two minutes and it may be all over," Williams said.

"What's up? Lebanon?"

"No. Russia just broke the ceasefire," Williams said. "HOLMES is tracking multiple cruise missile launches over Alaska toward our air bases at Fairbanks and Anchorage. I'm sending you the feed, you can follow the attack real time."

"You can do that?"

"Already doing it. When you log on, you'll see an icon of a pipe on your desktop. Click on that."

"What?"

"Don't ask me, HOLMES installed it. I think it's an Arthur Conan Doyle thing. You'll see what NORAD is seeing."

She shook her head and clicked on the icon as it came up. A screen expanded showing a map of Alaska. It took her a moment to make sense of what she was looking at. A spider web of lines was lancing out from small icons that looked like inward-facing double triangles with the letters A above them, while a bunch of other triangle icons milled around in the air over Alaska. "OK, I've got the computer open, but what am I looking at?"

"The icons with an A over them are Russian attack aircraft, HOLMES is saying mostly drones. They've already fired their payloads and are heading back to mother Russia on afterburner. The icons over Alaska, they're our boys. Most are not close enough to take a shot at the retreating Russians, but they're trying to engage the cruise missiles. Not much chance, their radar cross-section is too small, but they'll try."

"The missiles are headed for our Air Force bases?"

"Yep. They're scrambling everything they can so that the fewest possible machines get caught on the ground if any missiles get through. But apparently we were caught refueling after a major defensive action."

"HOLMES, what are the odds?" Devlin asked, knowing HOLMES would have already calculated them. "Of the missiles getting through?"

"Twenty-three percent chance of one to six missiles getting through, ma'am," she heard HOLMES' voice say on the line.

"How long until they hit?" She saw the lines seemed to be extending toward their targets very quickly.

"At 2,000 miles per hour with just fifty miles left to run, one minute thirty, ma'am," the AI replied. "I am showing 47 missiles still tracking. Correction, I am now showing *101 missiles inbound*. Fifty-three seconds to first HELLADS interception."

"What?!"

Williams peered at the screen. "Uh, a squadron of Backfire bombers in international airspace north of Alaska just fired their full payload of six missiles each, ma'am," he said. "A suicide shot. They were being tagged by a flight of US F-35s out of Eielson. They've engaged the Backfires, and they're unescorted. Those Backfires are toast."

"Twenty seconds to HELLADS interception of the first wave," HOLMES said.

Devlin watched in horror as the blue lines tracked toward the two US air bases. One by one, the lines winked out. Then red dots began to appear underneath the airfields. Inside five seconds, all the blue lines were gone and a row of red dots appeared under each airfield.

"The red dots are strikes?" Devlin asked.

"Yes, ma'am," Williams said. "Four on Eielson, three on Elmendorf-Richardson. Damn good performance by the HELLADS." He sounded pleased.

270

"There are dead Americans under those dots, Carl," Devlin said gently.

"Yes, ma'am, sorry," he said.

"Thirty-three seconds to the impact of the second wave of missiles. There are no air assets in position to intercept," HOLMES said. "HELLADS batteries recycling."

"Recycling?! What does that mean?"

"A single HELLADS battery can track and shoot down as many as five missiles simultaneously, with a half second between volleys. There are probably four or five batteries around each of those airfields, so they can target twenty incoming missiles all arriving at the same time, and handle multiple waves of missiles for up to five minutes, but working that hard overheats the optics. They need time to cool down – recycle. The second Russian launch was deliberately timed to coincide with the HELLADS' recycling phase. They'll be arriving just as the laser defenses are coming back on line, so until then the base will only be defended by last-gen anti-air missiles and ballistics. It's going to be close," Carl said, pulling anxiously at his beard.

"Two batteries on line. Five seconds to impact," HOLMES said. "Three batteries. Firing. Impact." A blood-red bloom of dots appeared across the map at both airfields.

"I'm coming in to the Embassy," Devlin said hurriedly. She put down her telephone and reached for her robe. She was in no doubt that what she had just witnessed was a declaration of war.

Between 2015 and 2022 Russia launched a series of small satellites it designated Kosmos-2499 to Kosmos-2514. Radar tracking of the small 100kg satellites showed they were highly maneuverable and, shortly after arriving in orbit, they executed what seemed to be a range of test maneuvers, darting away from and then matching orbit with various pieces of circling space junk including their own launch vehicles. They were also detected by amateur radio enthusiasts communicating with the ground using burst radio transmissions. At a year-end press conference, the head of Roskosmos, Tomas Olapenko, denied speculation that what Russia had launched were 'killer satellites'. Olapenko said the satellites were developed in cooperation between Roskosmos and the Russian Academy of Sciences and were used for peaceful purposes including unspecified research by educational institutions. After two years of apparent testing, the satellites were parked in permanent orbits and went silent.

Five of the satellites were in orbit over the North Pole. In the intervening years since 2022 they had been quietly mapping all known US and Chinese space-based military objects in their quadrants.

Olapenko had not lied. The Kosmos satellites were not intended to kill other satellites.

They were made to blind them.

Alicia Rodriguez was blind. Her bedside alarm was ringing, she had to get to school, but she couldn't see it to turn it off. She panicked, flailing around her, trying to find her alarm clock. She was going to be late for school again!

She opened her eyes. Same dumb dream again. But there *was* an alarm ringing somewhere. She swung her legs out of bed and hit her bedside light. It was the comms alarm – an incoming call. She fumbled for the handset on her bedside table.

"A4," she replied, rubbing her eyes. She looked at her watch. She'd been asleep three hours. It was 0400. She and Bunny had planned another three hours' sleep, then breakfast and another day flying their drones out. As the voice on the other end spoke, she realized that wasn't going to happen.

"A4, this is NORAD control," the voice said. "Major Del Stenson. Who is speaking, please?"

"Rodriguez, Lieutenant Commander. What's up, Major?"

"Ma'am, I need to bring you up to speed with events and then check your operational status," the Major said.

"Our operational status? We are decommissioned, Major," Rodriguez told him. "We are four days from bringing the boom down on this base."

"Negative, ma'am. I have a new Operations Order for you. The situation is that Russian air forces have attacked Eielson and Elmendorf-Richardson air bases. Damage was limited, but both airfields are going to be offline for at least the next 48 to 72 hours. We have moved air assets south to Kingsley Fields, Portland and Lewis-McChord." He paused. "We have nowhere to receive your drones right now, ma'am, and besides, we need them back in the game."

"Major, there are only myself and one aviator remaining on this base. We can launch, but we can't recover, refuel and rearm those drones at anything like the speed that would be needed for combat operations. If you are asking us to go to war, I need the full complement of base personnel back here stat."

"That's also negative, ma'am," Stenson said. "All available naval units have been retasked. We are responding to multiple simultaneous threat vectors, Lieutenant Commander. You are on your own. A mission package is being sent through as we speak. You are to review it and respond. Questions, ma'am?"

"Plenty," Rodriguez said. "But let me look the package over. I'll get back to you on what we can do."

"Yes, ma'am. NORAD out."

Rodriguez cut the connection and hit the button that connected her to O'Hare's quarters.

"O'Hare speaking. Yes, ma'am?"

She sounded like she was already awake.

"We have new orders, Bunny," Rodriguez said.

"Yes, ma'am," the pilot replied. "I heard the comms alert. Briefing in the trailer?"

"Five minutes," Rodriguez confirmed. "And O'Hare?"

"Yes, ma'am?"

"You will be wearing more than just black nail polish, understood?"

"Aw, you are such a buzz killer, ma'am," O'Hare said. "As you wish." She cut the line.

Rodriguez smiled and reached for her trousers. Then she thought about what they were being asked to do, and the smile faded from her face.

Yevgeny Bondarev had a broad smile on his face as he stood in his own operations room, eyes scanning over reports of the morning's operations and bomb damage assessments. Around him, his staff were going about the business of destroying the US armed forces' ability to respond to the planned landing in Nome.

He had been ordered to achieve air supremacy, not just air superiority. Air superiority meant temporary control of the airspace over an operations area. Supremacy meant the effective destruction of the enemy's ability to oppose the operations of friendly forces. The Russian commanders were not dreamers, they knew Lukin's 3rd Air and Air Defense Forces Command could not defeat the entire US Army, Navy and Air Force once it had been completely mobilized. But it had to establish dominance of the air for the duration of the invasion and that meant creating an effective air-front over Alaska all the way to the Canadian border so that any attempt by the US to penetrate Alaskan airspace resulted in the complete destruction of American aircraft in the combat area.

The airfield denial operations against the two major US Air Force bases in Alaska had been a spectacular success, with the first wave of missiles being intercepted but performing their task of overwhelming the American defensive systems so that the second wave of mine-laying cluster munition armed warheads would be able to penetrate. Russia had learned through many wars that blowing holes in enemy airfields was a pointless exercise, because even a twenty-foot crater blown in a concrete runway by a deep penetrator bomb could be filled in a matter of hours and overlaid with metal mesh patches so that flight operations could quickly resume.

So the Brah-Mos III missiles that had made it through the defensive perimeter of Elmendorf-Richardson and Eielson air bases had streaked across the airfield scattering thousands of area-denial anti-personnel and anti-vehicle mines. Within seconds each airfield was littered with 5.5lb RDX explosive-armed proximity-triggered submunitions. Once the mines were scattered, the missiles buried themselves in their terminal targets – usually hangars, radars and control and command facilities. It might only take a few hours to fill a crater or get a new mobile command center up and running, but it would take days to clear all of the unexploded mines at the two air bases.

Bondarev had lost none of his Su-57s or Okhotniks, but all six Backfire bombers had been quickly shot down. That had been expected and their pilots and crews had been volunteers, knowing the mission would likely result in their deaths. Bondarev wasn't sentimental, but the sacrifice of such men in the service of their nation stirred his blood. He would use their example to encourage his own men to do their utmost.

With no US carrier task force within range, that meant that unless Canada allowed the US to base its aircraft out of British Columbia, America had to fly its combat aircraft from airfields in Oregon, Washington State and Idaho, and ten years of US bullying over trade and tariff disputes meant that without evidence of an actual invasion yet, Canada wasn't looking disposed to choose sides. That meant US aircraft could only reach the combat area with the help of in-flight refueling, which gave Russian radar and satellites precious time to detect them and respond. It was time Bondarev planned to use well.

The second prong of the initial attack had not been Bondarev's responsibility but belonged to the Russian Aerospace Forces. Their small 100kg satellites parked over the pole had maneuvered within range of eight critical NORAD surveillance satellites and were blasting out radio signals at frequencies calculated to jam the ability of the American satellites to send or receive. If they were working as planned, the US 213th Space Warning Squadron based at Denali Borough in Alaska – the eyes and ears of NORAD – should be blind and deaf.

His staff advised it would take at least six and up to 18 hours before the US could retask other nearby satellites to fill the void or find workarounds to mitigate the jamming.

That gave Bondarev a solid window in which his Okhotniks could roam the skies over Alaska seeking out and destroying US land-based radar and air defense units, while his Su-57s ran combat air patrols overhead. Several of his units were actively engaged in combat with the US fighters that had managed to get airborne before the missile strikes. He had lost nine aircraft, with two pilots dead and six down, but his intel indicated 23 enemy combatants destroyed, both fixed and rotary-winged aircraft. After trying to engage the incoming cruise missiles, most of the airborne US aircraft were low on fuel and ammunition and were retiring to US mainland air bases or inadequately equipped civilian fields. The Americans had not yet marshaled aircraft for a major counter-attack, but Bondarev was certain it would come, probably in the form of another blizzard of cruise missiles launched from naval vessels or strategic bombers.

But at what targets? Thanks to the air and sea picket Russia had established around the Bering Sea, his own frontline airfields at Lavrentiya, Anadyr and Savoonga were out of range of anything but a ballistic missile strike, which the Americans would only conduct as a last resort. Strategic bombers launched out of Guam, or attack submarines, would also have the range and ability to launch cruise missiles, but not in the numbers needed to completely overwhelm his defenses in the way he had been able to do against Eielson and Elmendorf.

Savoonga, however, as his southernmost air base, was the most exposed. Twelve hours earlier he had begun airlifting heavy anti-air and anti-shipping missile defense systems to Savoonga to reinforce the airfield. A Russian Navy destroyer flotilla was also en route to add its radar coverage and firepower to the island's defense. That was why he was now able to move the bulk of his unmanned aircraft to Savoonga, just 150 miles from Nome. They were ideally suited to flying out of the limited facilities at the forward base, because their pilots and system officers could be based at Anadyr, hundreds of miles away. They didn't need to be quartered with their planes and he didn't risk losing valuable pilots if the US, against all odds, successfully targeted Savoonga for another cruise missile attack.

The bulk of his precious 4th and 5th Air Battalions, his critical Su-57 fighters and pilots and ground crews, he would keep at Lavrentiya. To reach him there, even if it did have the range, the enemy air force would have to fight its way across the skies of Alaska or the North Pacific and back again, and its navy would have to brave ring after ring of Russian anti-submarine defenses.

The American situation looked hopeless. But Bondarev wasn't a man to take the enemy for granted. So he also had a surprise or two up his sleeve in Lavrentiya and Savoonga for any US aircraft or missile that did make it through.

Perri and Dave had been following the column of hostages for a couple of hours now, and it was clear they weren't going down the coast to Kavalghak Bay. Once they had cleared the road out of town to the south of the bluff, they had turned northwest and started hiking up an old hunting trail that would take them over the bluff to the deserted inland of the island. It was harsh, windswept terrain that didn't offer much in the way of game, berries or shelter, so the Islanders rarely ventured inland. The sea and the ice around the island were their home, not the rocky interior. They decided the destination must be Savoonga.

"Why would they be going to Savoonga?" Perri asked. "Wouldn't it have been just as badly hit as Gambell?" He could have kicked himself. While they were online last time, he should have downloaded some news videos to see if there was any information about what had happened to Saint Lawrence. All they knew was what Sarge had told them, and that wasn't much. He'd spent most of the time they were online asking questions, not giving out information.

"Where else could they be going? There's nothing else in this direction except vole turds and bird droppings," Dave said.

"It's going to take them days."

"And us. Oh man." Perri settled the straps of his backpack on his shoulders. "I hope we've got enough food."

"Yeah? Well we could have carried about another 20 pounds except you've got me lugging this damned battery and radio," Dave complained. He was carrying the same big backpack that Perri was carrying, with the difference being the bottom two-thirds of his pack was the car battery and on top was the Russian radio they'd liberated.

"You keep telling me how you're the strongest of all your brothers," Perri said. He was looking at the ground, seeing the scuff marks in the snow and dirt from hundreds of feet. Following the column wouldn't be hard; they were leaving tracks you could probably see from space. He looked up to test the weather, saw low cloud, but no sign of rain. At least they'd be dry the next day or so. As he watched, he heard the now familiar sound of jet engines crossing the island from west to east. They hadn't heard or seen any more signs of combat, so he had to assume the aircraft overhead weren't American.

They trudged on. "Sarge said there were Russians in Savoonga as well as Gambell. Maybe the ones in Savoonga were dug in better," Perri speculated. "The ones here were pretty dumb, just hiding out in the town hall, waiting to get bombed. Maybe the guys up there were better prepared." He thought about the radar station at Savoonga, the Air Force officer who'd come to talk to them. "I'm going to call Sarge tonight if we can get a signal," he said. "Ask him does he know what's happening at Savoonga. If we get that far, I've got cousins we could hide out with."

Dave grunted. "I can tell you this for free. If we can't get a signal on this stupid radio, it's going in the nearest creek!"

There had been no working radio in the wrecked APC near the town hall, so Private Zubkhov had hiked out to the airfield.

Two of the APCs out there were total write-offs, just burned out, half-melted hulks. The third had taken a hit that had flipped it on its roof, shredded its tires and filled it full of holes before its fuel had caught fire, but the fire had burned upward, through the chassis, and the cabin was still pretty much intact. Except that the radio and handset were gone.

And Zubkhov had a pretty good idea where.

He leaned back in his chair inside the school master's office, watching the display on the base station for it to pop up again, just to be sure. His orders were to keep the wounded comfortable and the prisoners fed until reinforcements arrived from Russia or the unit returned to Gambell. But if Russia had really intended to hold Gambell, it would be swarming with choppers, anti-air batteries and new troops. He wasn't seeing anything like that. There weren't going to be any 'reinforcements' for Gambell.

Air cover or not, a US Navy Seal team could sneak in here on a sub and who could stop them? Zubkhov and his team of gut-shot and crippled comrades? They were all going to end up dead, or as prisoners, probably be tried for war crimes. And once he started thinking about those Navy Seals, climbing out of the water in their wetsuits to cut his throat in the middle of the night, he couldn't stop.

If he was going to get off this island, it had to be *now*. But he couldn't just leave his comrades here to starve to death, so he had to work something out for them. Luckily when he'd been searching for the radio, he had found the solution.

Most of the wounded Russian soldiers were sleeping, which wasn't surprising given firstly their injuries and, secondly, that he had crushed quite a lot of sedative tablets into their food earlier in the day. One of them was awake, a young boy who had lost most of his foot and who had said he had no appetite. He had joined the unit after Zubkhov and Zubkhov hadn't really bothered to get to know him. Zubkhov looked at the chart at the end of his bed – Kirrilov, that was his name.

"I need some painkillers," the guy said. "My foot hurts like hell."

"OK, I got something for you here," Zubkhov said, pulling out a syringe he had taken from the back of a wrecked field ambulance out at the airfield. "It's pretty strong, though."

The man lifted his bedsheets to reveal a bloodied bandage. Zubkhov pulled it gingerly away and saw the man had lost the two leftmost toes from his foot, a strip down the side, and most of his heel. "If all I did was sleep between now and when they airlift me off this bloody island that would be fine with me. So don't hold back," the boy said. He was propped up on one elbow, watching.

"OK," Zubkhov said. "This will make you very drowsy." He dialed up two units of the sedative, did an air shot and then injected the rest into the man's thigh.

"Man, that was one big needle," the guy said through gritted teeth, an arm covering his eyes. "It better work."

Zubkhov had little doubt it would work. The sedative was a pH-modified version of the tried and true anesthetic fentanyl, created to help overcome issues with addiction, but the effects of an overdose were identical. He had just given the man three times the recommended dose per kilo. As the man closed his eyes and sighed, it was just a question of how long until he either had a heart attack or just stopped breathing.

He sat back to watch.

SUPERIORITY

Bondarev paced the floor of his operations room at Lavrentiya airfield like a caged animal. The day's operations had gone to plan, that wasn't the problem. The problem was that as long as he was in command of this part of the air war, he was tethered to the ground. He preferred to lead from the air, but that wasn't practical. Instead, he was here, barking orders and watching his men move icons around on the huge screens mounted on the walls.

Bomb damage and combat assessments of the opening battle the day before showed 24 US fighters destroyed on the ground and 11 in the air, for the loss of 13 of his own. Since being driven back to Oregon, Washington State and Idaho the day before, US forces had only engaged in squadron strength probing patrols at the southernmost part of the front, the extreme limit of their range. Their satellites and ground-based radar inside Alaska blinded, they were no doubt ruing the decision to abandon their own anti-satellite offensive program. It meant they needed to rely on vulnerable Airborne Control aircraft to fill the gap. In these contacts over the last 12 hours he had claimed five American aircraft destroyed for the loss of none of his own and had brought down one US Airborne Control aircraft that had wandered too far northeast trying to map the Russian presence over Alaska. Fixed and mobile US anti-air units inside Alaska were being dealt with by ground-attack configured Okhotniks across the State as quickly as they appeared, but he had lost three of the drones to ground fire. His losses were within acceptable parameters and he was close to being able to demonstrate that he could repel any attempt to challenge the airspace over Alaska – the definition of air supremacy.

Despite Russian submarine and surface naval pickets 300 miles out from Saint Lawrence, the US still had formidable naval firepower and the ability to unleash a rain of cruise missiles on Saint Lawrence or Russian mainland targets like the Pacific Fleet base at Vladivostok or the Northern Fleet base at Severomorsk. It would be a logical response to their attacks on the US strategic air bases in Alaska, but beyond moving a carrier strike group from the Atlantic through the Panama Canal into the South Pacific the US naval response since the crippling of the USS *Enterprise* task force had been muted and it appeared to be trying to avoid a major naval confrontation. The US response would come, of that he was sure. The question was only how, and when.

What troubled him most in this respect were the aircraft from the *Enterprise*. Details weren't clear, even to Bondarev, but Lukin had delivered on his promise that the *Enterprise* wouldn't be a factor in the conflict. The carrier strike group had stopped dead in its tracks, and the US media was reporting that there had been fires reported on board the carrier, perhaps even a collision with an escort vessel. They were speculating that the carrier had been sabotaged, or had struck a mine, but Russia was denying any involvement. The carrier was being ignominiously towed back to port in San Diego.

The *Enterprise* task force might have been taken out of play, but its aircraft weren't. Russian satellite surveillance showed more than 50 of the carrier's aircraft had been flown off after it was put under tow. Bondarev wanted desperately to know where those aircraft were. His big fear was that Canada would give the US permission to use not just its airspace, but also its western Yukon airfields. They were mostly gravel, not paved, and couldn't support intensive operations, but the navalized versions of the US F-35 and Fantom carried by the *Enterprise* had Short Take-Off Vertical Landing capabilities and may be able to operate out of Canadian bush or civilian airstrips or even paved highways if they needed to. If the Canadians had been reluctant to give the US permission to use their facilities, Bondarev was pretty sure that as longstanding members of NATO, they would sooner or later be compelled to.

He desperately wanted to know where those carrier aircraft were, and brightened as he saw the man he had tasked to find

282

out, the GRU intelligence chief Arsharvin, walking quickly through the crowded operations room toward him.

"You have news, I hope," Bondarev said, as Arsharvin put a tablet down on the table in front of him and turned it on.

"Not good," Arsharvin said. "Look for yourself."

The screen showed a small table, listing the aircraft types which had been flown off the *Enterprise*, and how many of each type were estimated to have been repositioned. Beside them was the base they had been flown to. Bondarev expected that column to show him the names of the now familiar Air Force stations in the US Northwest States.

"Naval Air Station Leemore?" he asked, looking up at Arsharvin. "Where is that?"

"Fresno, California," Arsharvin said. "Three thousand miles from Alaska."

"What? The range of an F-35 is 1,500 miles. A Fantom is 1,800. Even with airborne refueling they can't fight a war in Alaska out of Fresno, California!"

"No."

"Are they under repair, or taking on ordnance?" It was all Bondarev could think of. Perhaps the Americans were worried their aircraft had been damaged by fire, or US logistics were taking time to get ordnance into place further north, so the Navy planes were having to repair and load up further south.

"Satellite intel shows them parked, with not much activity around them," he said. "We thought it might be some interservice political problem preventing Navy aircraft using US Air Force bases in the north, but our human sources say that wouldn't be it." He pointed at the screen. "The US is keeping them back. And the US Navy is holding all of its visible assets south of our naval picket line. They might sneak a few submersibles through, but not enough to mount a significant counter-attack in the Operations Area. My people think that can only mean one thing."

"It's a good sign," Bondarev said hopefully. "They are leaving Alaska to its fate, as we hoped."

"No," Arsharvin said. He leaned forward and dropped his voice. "We think they could be preparing a tactical nuclear strike."

"What? Why? We haven't even moved on Nome yet," Bondarev said.

"No, but the loss of their two key air bases in Alaska is a pretty obvious precursor."

"The fact they are holding their air and sea assets in reserve is hardly proof they are preparing a nuclear strike. Are their ICBM silos or mobile units on alert?"

"No, but they don't need to be. Our undersea surveillance line in the Bay of Finland picked up a trace today. Not definitive, but the acoustic signature fits with one of their new *Columbia*-class boats." He didn't have to say more, his voice said it all. Bondarev had been friends with the man for many years, and this was the first time he had heard him sound truly frightened.

The *Columbia*-class nuclear stealth submarine was the newest and quietest in the US fleet. Even bringing one close to the borders of Russia would have been regarded as an act of war in more peaceful times. If the US had managed to get one of their doomsday machines within a few minutes' missile flight time of Saint Petersburg, it could mean either they were being prudent, or they were preparing for nuclear war.

Bondarev scowled. "We need to initiate the attack on Nome *now!*" he said. "Get it underway before the Americans stop dithering and do something stupid." He grabbed his uniform jacket off his chair. "Where is Lukin today?"

Arsharvin looked at his watch. "Right now? He'd be airborne, en route to Anadyr," the man said. "I was told he has a meeting with the commander of the Lynx Air Brigade. What are you thinking?"

"I'm thinking I have to persuade him the air supremacy window is open now. We need to act before it closes. I'm flying to Anadyr."

If she was flying a jet off the deck of a carrier at sea, Bunny would be engaged in a carefully choreographed dance right now. As Air Boss, Rodriguez would have cleared her for take-off and she'd be watching her yellow-shirted flight deck controller as he directed her with hand motions up to the catapult. She'd be holding up her hands to show she wasn't touching the controls while checking the red-shirted ordnance guy as he loaded weapons or drop tanks. Then she'd be looking back at one of the yellow shirts again as they pulled her machine forward and into the shuttle. As he swept his arms back and forward and they ratcheted up the tension on the Cat, she'd be applying full power, putting her stick to all four corners and cycling the rudders to show the deck her controls were free and clear. The yellow shirt would then point her attention to the shooter and her life would be in his or (in the case of Rodriguez, her) hands for the next few vital seconds as she waved you off the deck.

Down under the Rock it all had to be much simpler. With a full crew, Rodriguez would have had her green-shirted technical crews under the command of Stretch Alberti, yellow-shirted plane handling crew and launch officers under the command of Lucky Severin, and a few red- and blue-shirted fuel and ordnance personnel working away from the flight deck in the storage hangars. With just the two of them under the Rock now, she and Bunny had to do all the grunt work getting their Fantom's wings down, locked into the shuttle for launch and booted up; once that was done, Bunny ran to the trailer for the launch.

They already had one Fantom in the air. They'd prepped two of the machines the night before when they'd got their orders and had taken just 20 minutes doing a final pre-flight check and launch of the first drone. Now they were ready with the second. Rodriguez had told NORAD there was no way the two of them could get a hex of six drones in the air in anything like the time needed for combat operations, but a flight of two – that they could manage. Bunny had set the first to hold position at wave-top height about ten miles north of Little

Diomede. They were both terrified it would be spotted by overflying Russian aircraft, but so far the little fighter's stealth defense was holding.

They'd also had to come up with a new version of the standard launch checklist, with only Rodriguez down on the flight deck and Bunny up in the trailer.

"Flaps, slat, panels and pins," Bunny called over the internal comms.

"Green," Rodriguez replied, roles reversed. Usually it would be her running the checklist.

"Man out." Referring to Rodriguez, crouched down at the catapult shooter's panel behind a blast protector.

"Man out, aye. Thumbs up." Rodriguez did a visual check to be sure there were no leaks of fuel or hydraulic fluid. "Scanning the Cat, Cat clear." She bent to the shooter's console. "Cat to 520 psi."

"520, aye," Bunny replied, confirming the catapult launch power from a readout on her heads-up display.

"Ready for launch."

When she was satisfied, she gave Bunny the green light. "Pilot, go burner."

"Lighting burner, aye," Bunny replied.

"*Launching!*"

Rodriguez punched the button to fire the Cat. On full afterburner the Fantom leaped off the catapult, down the chute and out of the maw of the cave. It sped north to link up with the first drone, and soon the two of them were outbound.

In the belly of each Fantom were two 'mini-mothers' or Massive Ordnance Air Blast bombs: GPS-assisted iron bombs filled with 40% RDX explosive, 20% TNT, 20% aluminum power and 20% ethylene oxide. Cut down to fit the weapons bay of a Fantom, they were a smaller but still deadly version of the bombs that had wiped the radar station off the surface of Little Diomede. The mini-mother had been designed to destroy large concentrations of enemy vehicles or troops, or in this case the large number of enemy transport aircraft, fuel, anti-air defense emplacements and command and control facilities at the Russian forward airfield at the port of Anadyr.

Anadyr had been chosen by US war planners for political shock value – an air strike so deep behind the Russian air perimeter that it might cause them to re-evaluate their strategy and pull assets back to protect their mainland bases. It was also intended to give Russia pause for thought – the US fighters were armed with conventional weapons, but what if they had fielded nukes?

Bunny and Rodriguez knew their chances of successfully charging directly across the Bering Strait and down the throat of all the radar energy Russia would have pointed eastwards was almost zero. So Bunny would be sending the Fantoms at nap of the earth height along the coast of Russia northeast to Polyarny, then take a sharp southerly route along a river valley and across rolling hills and low ranges to Krasnero, about 50 miles inland of Anadyr, in the direction of Moscow. The Fantoms would then bank hard to port to follow the contours of the Anadyr River, coming up on the Russian airfield at the height of about 100 feet from a vector the Russian defenses would, hopefully, least expect.

For a human pilot, dropping a bomb that didn't have a timed fuse from that low an altitude would be suicide, but for these Fantoms it wasn't an issue. Theirs was a one-way trip. The long loop northeast and then south would be a journey of about 1,000 miles; it would take a couple of hours and the route Bunny had plotted had 132 distinct waypoints. It was a route no cruise missile could possibly execute. And there wouldn't be fuel for them to make it home.

But with luck, they could give the Russian commanders a shock that would set them back on their heels.

If they pulled it off, it was a fitting payback mission – one Russian base in exchange for the attack on theirs. The only thing Bunny could have wished for was a full crew and a hex of drones instead of just two.

But she would make do.

Oh, yes.

Private Zubkhov looked at the syringe in his hand with a little surprise. The soldier with the wounded foot had taken less than ten minutes to go from injection to a gasping death. It seemed he had the man's bodyweight about right — he'd just looked up a dosing guide online and tripled it.

He lifted the man's sheet and covered his face with it.

Then he walked around the room to each of the other seven men, injecting each with a freshly loaded syringe. For some — those who had untreatable abdominal wounds, already in the grip of fever and delirium — it was a pure mercy. For the others, well, if they had ever made it out of here it would be to a life as crippled and limbless outcasts, so Zubkhov didn't actually feel that bad about it. One had woken from his drug-addled sleep and watched in confusion as Zubkhov injected him, but he didn't protest. Zubkhov had simply placed a hand under his head, lowered him back down to his pillow and held his hand until he fell asleep. It was very peaceful, actually.

That only left the Captain, who Zubkhov hadn't thought it necessary to sedate. He sat in a corner in a chair, watching events as though he was watching a mildly interesting TV show.

As Zubkhov approached him and held the needle up to do the air shot, the Captain smiled. "Right or wrong, it's very pleasant to break something from time to time," he said.

Zubkhov hesitated, then lowered the syringe.

He realized then what he was feeling. It wasn't pity, not exactly. It was the feeling that they had some sort of bond, he and the Captain. The two of them had been knocked down by the ammo dump blowing up, taken a direct hit from an American cruise missile, and they were both still here. Both of them had been left behind by that bastard Sergeant who had pissed off for Savoonga without a second thought.

They were survivors, the Captain and he.

He dropped the full syringe into a soda bottle with the others, then put that into a plastic bag with his gloves and sealed it tight. Then he clapped the Captain on the shoulder. "Back soon, sir."

Giving his comrades an overdose of injectable sedative had been a simple and pragmatic solution to the problem of leaving them behind without anyone to care for them. He wasn't a monster, he didn't want them to spend their last days in agony, starving and thirsty and in unbearable pain. It wasn't a solution he could use for the twenty or so Yup'ik town elders, though. He didn't have enough sedative for starters.

So he had taken some of the oral opioids he'd used to sedate the wounded Spetsnaz and mixed them in a saucepan with some melted chocolate he'd scrounged from the ruins of one of the town's grocery stores. He couldn't be sure all of the old people would eat the chocolate, though, so he had also added the sedative to the huge pot of onion soup he'd cooked up for their lunch.

Outside the school administration building, Zubkhov picked up two jerry cans of diesel that had survived the cruise missiles and walked over to the gymnasium building. Early that morning he'd piled packing crates and wooden building debris around the outside of the sports hall and started singing to himself as he went around soaking the wood in diesel fuel. The walls of the nearly twenty-year-old gym were wood framed, clad in light aluminum and painted with an oil-based paint so that the paint would flex in the extreme cold. Zubkhov had no doubt it would burn nicely and leave a big smoking wreck that looked just like every other burned building in town.

He dribbled a line of fuel through the dirt to a safe distance and then threw a match on it. The piled-up diesel-soaked wood went up with a whoomph that he could feel against his chest, and in minutes the blaze had really taken hold. Between the chocolate and the soup, he was pretty sure everyone inside would be having a nice nap by now, but just to be sure, he sat on a nearby ATV with his pistol in his lap and waited in case any of the old people ran out.

No one did. He didn't even hear any cries for help.

He waited until the gym roof collapsed, sending bright orange sparks into the late afternoon air. One more job done. Now he just had to drag his comrades' bodies into the grave he had dug with a small bobcat he had found and give them a proper Spetsnaz burial – they deserved that, after all – and he was free to start executing his exit plan. It was a very simple plan: find that 'ghost' radio handset, deal with whoever was using it, call his buddy in Anadyr, and start a new life as part owner of a fishing trawler.

There was just one problem, but it didn't trouble Zubkhov. In fact, he was blithely ignoring it.

That offer from Zubkhov's buddy in Anadyr? That had been eight *years* ago. The guy had gone broke, sold his trawler, and was a bank clerk in Vladivostok now. Private Zubkhov hadn't spoken to him for about five years, but in Zubkhov's shattered mind, it was like it had been yesterday.

Everyone deals with the brutality of war in their own very individual way. Private Zubkhov had seen a man decapitated, a town obliterated, his Captain lobotomized, and his fellow soldiers killed and wounded before being abandoned by his own NCO and the men he had believed were his comrades in arms.

He had dealt with this by going completely and irrevocably insane.

Devlin was also losing her mind. She had warned her colleagues in the State Department that Russia was not interested in Saint Lawrence and polar sea routes; it was going to go after Alaska. They had replied officially with "Thank you but that doesn't fit our internal narrative" and unofficially with "Russia is going to attack Alaska? Has McCarthy been hitting the vodka a little too hard?" Now Russia *had* attacked ground targets in Alaska, so of course her detractors had come crawling back to her saying "We are so sorry, Devlin, you were right all along, we were fools not to believe you."

Like hell they had.

The massive Russian air offensive over Alaska and the fact they were shoring up defenses in Savoonga were being used to further support the theory that Russia intended to permanently occupy Saint Lawrence. The new State narrative went like this: We have entered a cycle of escalation. Russia hit us in Saint Lawrence, so we responded with a massive air and missile attack. Russia cannot withdraw from Saint Lawrence without losing face, so it hits back at the only US facilities in reach – Eielson and Elmendorf-Richardson. In this through-the-looking-glass view, the cyber-attack on the *Enterprise* was actually taken as further proof Russia was trying to limit the conflict. *De-escalation* is our best response, said the majority voice in State. No one wants full-scale war. Let them have their little island in the Arctic for now, we'll leverage the outrage to get concessions in Western Europe and besides, we have bigger problems in the Middle East.

The Russian attack was highlighting how internally divided her administration was. On the one hand, she had her colleagues in the State Department preaching de-escalation in the face of massive loss of civilian life and challenges to US air and sea power. On the other hand, you had Defense in a rage over the attacks on its air bases and the crippling of its supercarrier and they were in no doubt what was behind that. Air Force had lost personnel in the air over Saint Lawrence and on the ground at Elmendorf-Richardson and Eielson and had been sent packing from the skies over its own territory. The Pentagon didn't care *why* Russia was on the offensive, it only cared that it was, and it had no intention of playing some BS cat and mouse game of airborne 'tit for tat'. The Defense Secretary had pushed the margins of his power to the limit, moving nuclear first-strike resources to within a few hundred kilometers, or a few minutes' flying time, of key military targets within Russian territory. Unlike the State Department's de-escalation proposal, the Pentagon narrative went like this: *They took our territory in Bering Strait, they attacked our airfields in Alaska. We need to lay a tactical nuke on the Russian Northern Fleet home base at Severomorsk or the Baltic Fleet at Kaliningrad and put Ivan back in his box. De-escalate my ass.*

For once, as horrified as she was at the thought of anyone starting a nuclear shooting match, Devlin found herself siding with the hawks in the Pentagon instead of the doves in her own State Department. And she had heard that the Pentagon point of view was prevailing with the US President, who had refused to take a call from the Russian President after the attacks on Eielson and Elmendorf-Richardson.

Which is why she found herself in a dilemma for her next meeting with the Russians. It wasn't with Kelnikov this time. The crisis had moved beyond the stage where a lowly Ambassador could get face time with the Russian Foreign Minister, when even heads of State were not talking with each other. In fact, it had moved beyond the stage where she was able to have official contacts of any sort. Instead she had been invited to a back-channel meeting with a Russian industrial magnate, Piotr Khorkina, who was an old school friend of the Russian President's son. Officially, he was interested to hear if the current military 'situation' would pose problems for a multi-billion-dollar deal he was about to sign to supply lithium batteries to a US car maker. Unofficially, he had said he also wanted to pass on a message to the US administration from his friends in the Kremlin. She had chosen to receive him in her office at the Chancery and her aide had organized a nice tray of tea and delicacies.

The thing was, Devlin was supposed to pass a message back to the Kremlin from the bureaucrats in State. We will let you pull your aircraft back from Alaska to the ceasefire zone of control. We will not allow your continued presence on Saint Lawrence, but we would be open to a new Arctic freedom of navigation treaty. This may be your last chance to achieve a negotiated outcome because the hawks in our administration are arguing for a resolution by force of arms.

Devlin had full faith in her bucolic NSA analyst and his eccentric AI. HOLMES had been monitoring Russian military signals traffic and troop movements and had increased his assessment of the likelihood of Russian airborne troops moving on Nome to 99.7%. And knowing what she felt she knew about Russia's true intentions, the words she was scripted to say were already sticking in her craw. It made no sense to offer to re-establish the ceasefire terms when she knew Russia was already preparing to move ground troops into Alaska.

There was a knock on the door and her assistant showed the man in. He wasn't your standard oligarch – fat, feted and fetid. He was in his mid-forties, played tennis to keep fit, and had a wife, three kids and no mistresses, according to his embassy file.

"Peter, welcome," she said. "Tea?"

They dealt with the small talk up front. Some days small talk was all she had. Today was not one of those days.

"So, to business ... I have to say, the climate at the moment makes it difficult to progress any major business deals," she said. "As you know, Congress is in emergency session debating sanctions."

"I understand, Devlin," he said, looking troubled. "We have written off any sales to the USA for this year, and for next year we've put in a six-month delay as a downside. But our base case is still that the deal will progress."

Really? she thought. *In your world, war between Russia and the US is a downside? And global nuclear annihilation, is that also a downside?* It was clear the US State Department weren't the only ones out of touch.

"Do you have any special reason to be optimistic?" she asked, giving him an opening to pass on the message from his government.

"Well, you know I have no special information, but people in the circles I move in..." (such as the President's family) "...insist this situation can be contained. It's not like Russia wants a full-scale war with the USA."

"No? Because it could look like that," Devlin observed. "When Russia invades our territory, starts an air war and bombs our airfields."

The man smiled and brushed an imaginary crumb off his trousers. "You are refreshingly direct as always. Of course, there are different views around who started this shooting match. There are those on our side who would say you sank our freighter, disabled our submarine and then bombed our rescue personnel on Saint Lawrence."

Ah, to hell with the script, she decided.

"Peter, listen to me, and listen well. Russia may not want full-scale war, but it is about to get it. Your political masters don't seem to understand that we know what their end game is here. Russia plans to invade Alaska."

If she expected him to look surprised or confused, she was disappointed. He simply stared back at her and responded, "I was told you would say that. And I understand that you are alone in your State Department in thinking it."

She scowled. "Do not bet on that."

"I hope to persuade you that war is the last thing we want. I'm told by my contacts in the government that the Barents Arctic Council will propose a demilitarized buffer zone between our two States, given your general belligerence. No military aircraft, no navy ships will be allowed in or near the Strait."

She laughed. "Seriously? A military no-fly zone over our own State?"

"Initially, yes. And not the whole State, just Western Alaska."

"Ah. Well that's alright then," she said sarcastically.

"Here. I have drawn on a map how I understand the no-fly zone would work." From his pocket he pulled a folded piece of paper. It hadn't been drawn, someone had printed it for him. Probably someone in the Russian Foreign Ministry. It showed a map of Alaska with a diagonal line drawn across the middle from top right to bottom left and the proposed 'buffer zone' shaded in red. She saw that Nome was inside the zone; Juneau, Fairbanks and Anchorage were not.

Later, looking back, Devlin thought she took it pretty well, considering.

"Have you people lost your goddam minds?" she asked. "How about we create a 'no-fly zone' *inside* Russia, say from Lake Baikal in Siberia to the Pacific Coast, taking in Lavrentiya and oh, say, Anadyr as well? How about that instead?"

"You can keep the printout," Khorkina said. He wasn't fazed. "Would you like to consult with your superiors and get back to me, or is 'have you people lost your goddam minds' your last word on the matter?"

Devlin collected herself. She would actually land the meeting close to the wording State had given her after all, just not quite with the tone they had probably hoped for.

"No, here is my last word on the matter," she said, taking up the page he had pushed forward. "I will pass your message on to my 'superiors' in State along with this map, but you should tell your friends in the Kremlin that Russia is courting nuclear oblivion. If Russia doesn't pull back, and immediately, I expect to spend my final hours in the bunker under this building wondering what more I could have done to save the world from atomic annihilation."

Bunny collected herself too. She was totally hyped but she had to channel full focus. She had just flown two Fantoms along the northeast coast of Russia, literally. So close to where the sand and gravel met the icy sea that she could have told you where the good beaches were, in case you wanted to buy real estate for the coming climate-change boom. Then she had pushed her Fantoms down a frozen river valley, across rolling hills and mountains, and just about clipped a cliff face as she wheeled her drones east up the Anadyr River toward the Anadyr airport at Ugolny. She had picked up the air traffic control radar signature of Anadyr, but hadn't been locked up by a single military search radar along the way. Of course she couldn't rule out that she'd been spotted by satellite infrared or motion detection, but no fighters appeared to have been vectored to intercept her.

Through the low-def forward scanning wide-angle camera on the Fantom, sending its feed up to one of the only functional Air Force satellites over the Operations Area, the river below was a 660mph blur of brown water and gray gravel. Occasionally her machines flashed over a small leisure or fishing boat, but she had to figure it wasn't too likely they were patched into the Russian military command network.

As she got within 50 miles of Anadyr, she started picking up the skeleton fingers of a search radar brushing across the skin of her drones every 20 to 30 seconds. It was like the touch of a creepy guy at a Christmas party. It slid across her sensors and then was gone again. But like at a Christmas party, the only touch you cared about was the one where solid contact was made, a true butt cheek clutch. So far, the search radar was in the annoying but not lethal range. Which is what she had planned for. If she was a Russian anti-air battery commander set up to defend a forward air base against the USA, she'd have 90% of her energy pointed north, east and south – facing the enemy – and configured to look for cruise missiles first and foremost. Anything to the west, any threat coming from their rear quadrant, would get lower priority.

She hoped.

She only had two shots on goal. Four, technically, but she had set the two bombs in each drone to release in salvo, so as soon as they had punched the 'mini-MOABs' out of their guts they were done – there would be no go-around.

"Starting ingress," Bunny told Rodriguez. It was a courtesy. Rodriguez could follow the mission on a tactical 2D screen over Bunny's head, but with it just being the two of them under the Rock now, Bunny felt the need to share.

"They aren't smelling you?" Rodriguez asked, rolling her shoulders and massaging the back of her own neck.

"No, ma'am," Bunny said. "I am chamomile and roses right now."

Sure enough, as soon as Bunny spoke, a red alarm started flashing on her heads-up display.

"Damn. I'm picking up radiation in the higher-frequency C, X and Ku bands. I think they've got an S-500 system pointed at us."

"Which means?"

"Means they have a low 30% chance of seeing us with this attack profile," Bunny said. "And I'm already low and slow — if I got any lower, I'd be sucking river water."

"Long way to go to get swiped out of the sky," Rodriguez commented.

"Swiped my ass," Bunny said. "I've got a 70% chance of getting through any S-500 without even needing to jam, and I'll take them odds."

Rodriguez knew better than to bet against the aviator who had laid a hurt on Eielson by faking the flight profile of a civilian light aircraft. She watched intently as Bunny flew her two Fantoms within minutes of the Russian base.

"Five minutes to release," the pilot said. Rodriguez saw that the newly dyed black stubble at her neck under her virtual-reality helmet glistened with sweat.

"SAM radar alert," Rodriguez warned, seeing Bunny's threat screen flash.

"No lock," Bunny replied tersely. "Three minutes."

Bunny was a good pilot, but she knew her limits. With only simulated real-time vision and an input lag of a half second, for the last two minutes flying into an uber-hot target zone there was no human who could fly it better than the combat AI with its instantaneous reactions. She punched a last command through to her Fantoms and lifted her hands into the air. "I'm out!" she called.

They both watched as a large airfield appeared in the split-screw view of the forward nose cameras of the two Fantoms. Anadyr was made up of two long parallel runways, late summer grass and half-melted snow between them. One of the Fantoms broke slightly left, the other slightly right. Their targets were the stationary aircraft and related command and control facilities. Bunny was counting down under her breath. "Three, two, one, *release...*"

The last thing they saw was a couple of parked aircraft on one screen, and on the other a control tower; behind it several other aircraft and what looked like a container park. One of the drones dropped its bombs and made a kamikaze dive straight at the parked aircraft. The other did the same and made straight for the control tower.

In what was an inevitable anticlimax after such a tense mission, both of the screens in front of Bunny O'Hare flashed momentarily white, and then went completely blank.

"Holy hell's bloody bells," Bunny said, her hands still in the air where she had left them when she took her hands off the controls. "I think we actually did it!"

But she didn't celebrate, not yet. Their primary objective had been to catch as many Russian fighters on the ground at Ugolny as possible. But, it seemed to Bunny, for a forward airfield it had contained a heck of a lot of trucks and containers, and *not* a heck of a lot of Russian aircraft.

Strange, though, one of the fighters parked on the airfield had been painted bright red.

The briefing room for the Lynx Air Brigade was in the basement of the control tower building at Ugolny air base, Anadyr. It had been a combined civilian and military air base before the war had started, and CO of the Lynxes, Colonel Artem Kokorin, had commandeered the baggage tracking center in the lower level of the control tower building for his operations facility. There was of course a perfectly functional operations room on the military section of Ugolny field, but the reality was that the former civilian facility, having long ago been privatized, had far superior comms links than his long underfunded military infrastructure. It also had the advantage of being two levels below ground, with multiple exits to the surface, so it was also better protected than the military command center up on the ground floor of the control tower.

Nevertheless he looked around at the peeled-paint walls and cursed. It was bad enough his group had been pulled out of their base at Khabarovsk to support LOSOS – an operation whose political logic he didn't fully grasp – 2,500 miles here in the northeast. He had protested that it had left Russia without ground-attack aircraft in the critical Sea of Japan border area. He had protested even louder when he had learned his regiment was to be made subordinate to Bondarev's Snow Leopards. The man was a commander of fighters, with only one of his five squadrons made up of attack aircraft, whereas Kokorin led a dedicated ground-attack unit comprising both Okhotnik drones and rotary-winged close air support aircraft.

The reason he had been given for the fact his machines and men had been put under the nominal command of the CO of the Snow Leopards was that he might be asked to commit his aircraft to an air-air defense role over Saint Lawrence if heavy fighter losses were sustained over Alaska. It was a role for which his machines were not suited, and his men not adequately trained.

Now that he had been repositioned to Anadyr, within range of Saint Lawrence, he *should* be getting ready to react to any attempt by US naval or airborne forces to retake the island and flying sorties over the island terrain to familiarize his men. Instead, he had been ordered to drill them in air-air combat. He had dispersed his aircraft and their maintenance techs to nearby roads and freeways but he was deeply uncomfortable that all of his pilots had been collocated at the same airfield. He had been told there was no excess capacity at Lavrentiya, and no other facility that could service his 50 crews and provide them with the bandwidth and electricity they required to function. It made a mockery of the ability to disperse his force and protect it from attack with his pilots crammed onto a single airfield, but he had been reassured by Bondarev that the risk of attack this far behind the air front was less than none. In the event of a cruise missile strike, he would have warning enough to get his men to safety.

Maybe, unless the Americans decided the situation warranted *hypersonic* missiles, he had mused uselessly.

And now he had Lukin dropping in. A snap inspection by General Lukin would normally have had him in a panic, but this time he had welcomed the news. No, of course his unit wasn't at full readiness yet. He had just settled in all of his pilots and systems officers. He had one-third of his Okhotniks still in maintenance in hangars at Ugolny, with only two-thirds deployed to Savoonga and combat ready. But his men had done an admirable job getting their drone command trailers off the IL-77 transports, sited and linked into the base network. In anticipation of the General's arrival, he had ordered all pilots to their stations, either running simulations or commanding the squadron of 16 operational Okhotniks he had scrambled. He had put them in the air over Ugolny a half hour in advance of the General's arrival, patrolling overhead to give Lukin something to look at as they made their circuits, landed and were recovered. No, he wasn't fully ready, but the inspection would give him the chance to make his concerns clear to the General again.

On top of everything, he had just learned that Bondarev was crashing the party! Damn him. He must have people inside Lukin's staff keeping him informed. To make things worse, Bondarev had contrived to arrive about twenty minutes *before* the General, so Kokorin had lost the chance to put his views to Lukin in private.

Despite being theoretically of equal rank, and with a longer service record, Kokorin had no illusions about who was the senior officer as Bondarev walked into the briefing room in his flight suit. Even without his dress uniform and service medals, the son of the hero of the Russian Federation reeked of privilege and that most critical of all attributes – political momentum.

As he reached out his hand to greet his fellow officer and girded himself for the meeting ahead, he saw Bondarev hesitate and frown, looking up at the ceiling as a jet aircraft boomed low overhead, the noise penetrating even to their position two floors underground.

"Your men need not show off for my benefit, Kokorin," Bondarev said.

Kokorin frowned too. "That was *not* one of mine."

Only one of Bunny's Fantoms delivered its bombs with total accuracy – the other missed by more than 100 yards. The deviation was significant. The first Fantom dropped its two bombs right on target on the apron of the long concrete runway right near the maintenance hangars where three Okhotniks were parked on alert status, ready to give a demonstration to the General of how quickly they could get airborne. Two more were in the process of being refueled. Another three were in the hangars having engines and electronic systems maintained, but unknown to US planners, most had already been moved or were on their way to Savoonga. The air blast bombs from the first Fantom detonated together 50 feet above the hangar complex and the blast wave spread out over a radius of about a mile. Anything and anyone inside a few hundred yards was vaporized. Anything from 500 to 1,000 yards was atomized. Everything from 1,000 to 1,500 yards was pulverized. Everything flammable was set on fire. In the space of a millisecond the eight drones and their support personnel were no more. Bunny's first drone added its fuel and momentum to the chaos as the pressure wave from its own bomb flung it into the maintenance complex and it detonated.

The second strike, however, missed its target. An extremely unfortunate observer, in their last few seconds of life, might have seen the approach of the Fantom. If they had, they would have seen two fat cylinders at the end of tiny parachutes tumble end over end out of the Fantom's weapons bay just as it swept across the egg blue and yellow striped administration buildings at Anadyr. One of the cylinders floated briefly down right in the middle of the road between two large apartment buildings commandeered for military personnel. As it reached fourth-floor level, it detonated. Every window in the street was blown in and the buildings, which had been made to withstand Arctic

301

storms but not the thunderous pressure wave of a mini-MOAB, collapsed instantly, killing nearly all of those inside.

The other bomb completely missed the administration complex that was its target and landed in the field beyond.

A field that normally would have been empty except for the hulks of a dozen abandoned cold war Su-15 Flagon interceptors deemed too far gone to salvage when they were decommissioned in 1993. A week ago, however, these had been towed aside and piled together in a corner of the field, while the cleared space was turned into a parking lot for the 24 drone command trailers of the Okhotnik pilots and systems officers of Lynx Air Brigade. Plus a centrally located commissary wagon serving coffee, tea, hot soup and bread.

The timeline Bondarev had been given for LOSOS didn't allow for optimal dispersion of the Okhotnik crews. The trailers holding the precious pilots, whose aircraft were now flying out of Savoonga, had been camouflaged and hidden among rusted shipping containers, so that the park looked like it had gone from a dumping ground for obsolete aircraft to a dumping ground for empty containers. They had been spread as widely as practical, but so many trailers and crew drew down a lot of power and needed hardwired data links so that they didn't fill the sky with radio energy and give themselves away that way.

The camouflage was ingenious, and the trailers hadn't been spotted by NORAD's strike planners. But camouflage was no defense against an errant MOAB.

The parachute on the last of Bunny's mini-mothers deployed a half second late; it overshot, and then detonated right on top of the commissary in the middle of the drone trailer park.

And in its last act, the Fantom that delivered the weapons zoomed into the sky, onto its back, and then speared back down on full afterburner toward the small control tower at the side of the air base.

It impacted at the base of the tower, two floors above Colonels Artem Kokorin and Yevgeny Bondarev. And, as he walked toward the control tower building pulling off his flight gloves, right beside Lieutenant General Yuri Lukin, who had stopped to watch in horror as the fireball of the first strike, across the airfield, lit up the sky and rolled toward him. He was dead before the thunder of its detonation even reached his ears.

SUPREMACY

The building above Bondarev and Kokorin collapsed as the pressure wave from the 'mini-mother' exploding above them flattened it like a boot landing on a house of cards. However, the command and control complex was in a concrete and rebar reinforced basement two floors under the ground, and luckily the bomb that hit them was an airburst, not a bunker buster, or the Colonels would have suddenly and violently lost all personal interest in the future conduct of the war.

Their comms to the outside were not completely cut, however, and once emergency crews had restored power, Bondarev managed to direct help to their location and get them shifting rubble and bodies so that they could be dug out.

He emerged after four hours to learn that the runway at Ugolny Air Field had survived the American attack completely unscathed. Using massive ordnance air blast munitions indicated the Americans hadn't intended to shut the air base down, even though they had flattened some above-ground infrastructure. As long as the paved runways were intact, mobile air traffic control, radar and communications could easily fill the gap. And most of the Okhotniks that were airborne at the time of the attack thanks to Lukin's impending inspection also came through unscathed. Lacking command inputs from the ground, they had reverted to AI control, maintained a safe separation, and kept circling until they were low on fuel before calmly landing themselves and taxiing to preassigned holding positions.

The lack of material damage was not relevant. The use of air blast munitions, coupled with the targets of the attack – the hangars, administration buildings, accommodation block and the drone trailer park – indicated that the US attack had the inhuman intent of achieving the maximum possible loss of life.

And among those lost was the commander of the 3rd Air and Air Defense Forces, Lieutenant General Yuri Lukin.

It was hard not to conclude that the US airstrike, carried out as it had been by what seemed to be two stealth drones sent on a one-way mission, was a straightforward assassination attempt. Arsharvin had told Bondarev it was being treated as such, and there would be brutal repercussions for anyone found to have been careless regarding Lukin's schedule. Bondarev could only imagine what machinations were going on back in Khabarovsk and throughout the Air Force as other officers jockeyed to replace the dead Lukin as commander of the 3rd Air Army.

To Bondarev, the loss of a good commander like Lukin was tragic, but the politics were a sideshow and no one was irreplaceable. What was especially problematic was the strike on his drone crews. Among the 225 Russian armed forces personnel who died or were seriously wounded in the attack were all 54 primary and reserve aviators and systems officers of the Lynx's Okhotnik ground strike regiment.

His stomach churned and he resisted the urge to vomit. He also had to resist the thought, the primal urge, that was telling him he should step outside the ambulance in which he was lying, ask someone there for a sidearm, and shoot himself in the head. It was a number he simply couldn't comprehend. Had any Russian officer since World War Two lost *two hundred and twenty-five lives* in a single attack?

Yevgeny Bondarev suddenly grabbed his shirt, tore it open and howled in mortal pain at the ceiling of the ambulance.

Dave was moaning again about the pain in his shoulders from carrying their radio, but he wasn't getting much sympathy from Perri. They'd managed to catch the column of hostages because it wasn't traveling as fast as they were. Sure, there weren't any old or infirm hostages among the prisoners, but there were some pretty young children and people couldn't carry them on their backs the whole way.

Now a chill night had fallen and Dave and Perri had found the column easily, because it was winding its way along the 'coast track', the barely traveled west-east coastal path that led from Gambell to Savoonga along the cliffs and rocky beaches of the serrated northern shore. As the day had worn on and the route the column was taking became more obvious, Perri had to admit Dave was right. They *were* headed for Savoonga. He could only assume it wasn't hit as hard as Gambell had been and the Russian survivors from the Gambell attack had decided to link up with their buddies in Savoonga.

As they had coasted a rise, Dave and Perri had been forced to drop to a crouch as they saw the circle of prisoners about a mile ahead, huddled around a couple of lamps. Somewhere in there were Perri and Dave's mothers, fathers and brothers. There was no fuel for them to start any sort of fire, so they were pressed together in a circle like emperor penguins, using their body heat to keep each other warm, with the kids in the middle of the press. It was a survival tactic as old as time, and though the temperature wouldn't drop much below freezing tonight, it was just a good idea to keep your body heat up and stay out of the drying wind. People who died of exposure often died of dehydration as much as they died of the cold. Every hour the people at the outside of the circle would hand over their blankets and sleeping bags, move into the center, and a new group would take their place on the outer circle. Perri figured that with about two hundred people in the huddle, that meant most would get five or six hours of nice warm sleep.

Which was more than he and Dave would get in their crappy little sleeping bags on the rocky ground.

They couldn't turn on a lamp or even shine a torchlight, or they'd risk giving themselves away to the troops in the distance, so Perri had to fumble his way to getting power to their radio and tuning it so that they could fang the receiver in Gambell and get a signal through to Sarge. While he worked in his sleeping bag in the dark, Dave stood up in his sleeping bag, holding their makeshift antenna aloft until they got a lock on the Russian base unit in Gambell.

"Perri calling Sarge, do you read me? Hello? Perri calling Sarge."

The Mountie had told them he would be sleeping by the radio and waiting for their call, and he was true to his word. Perri only had to call three times before he got a bleary voice on the other end.

"Sarge here, Perri, just wait, OK? Out."

"OK, Perri ... um ... waiting," he said, shrugging to himself.

He didn't have to wait more than about twenty seconds before the Sergeant came back on the line. "Perri, hey. Are you guys OK?"

Sarge had taught them how to use a 'duress signal' in case they were captured and the Russians forced them to make contact. If they were safe, they should reply, "We are just fine, Sarge." And if they were not, they should say, "Couldn't be better."

"We're just fine, Sarge," Perri said. "We caught up with the Russian troops and the people from Gambell. We figure they're headed for Savoonga."

"They're walking them out?"

"Yeah, they made about 12 miles today. Savoonga will take them another three or four days."

"OK, look, Perri, the Russians are moving some heavy hardware into Savoonga and you are our best chance to get some up close and personal intel on exactly what they're doing there. Are you safe where you are? Can you talk for a few minutes?"

Perri looked up at his friend. "Dave's arms might fall off if he has to hold the antenna in the air too long, but yeah, shoot."

The Secretary of State *had* to listen to Devlin once she scanned the map that Piotr Khorkina had given her and uploaded it. To make sure it didn't risk getting stranded on some analyst's desk, she took the Secretary at his word and called him directly on his cell. Even he had to admit the map clearly showed that the Russians planned to cauterize Western Alaska and separate it from the rest of the USA, at least by air. All this supported by the ridiculous fiction of establishing a 'demilitarized zone' to protect the shipping in the Bering Strait and the scared and huddled masses of the Russian Far East (all 290,000 of them) from the rampaging bald eagle across the ditch.

He also had to listen to her when HOLMES was able to show through accessing Moscow traffic CCTV systems that the car driving the rather handsome oligarch who had been the government's intermediary had traveled directly from inside the Kremlin to the gates of the US Embassy compound, without even a minor detour. It removed the likelihood that he had come up with the map himself in a fit of geopolitical creativity.

And if there was a single doubter left in Washington after those two little snippets of intel, they couldn't keep faith in their misguided de-escalation fantasy after Carl Williams' highly motivated AI was able to pull down an intercept of the Russian Foreign Minister, Kelnikov, traveling with an unknown Foreign Service employee on a car trip to the Bolshoi Ballet the previous evening. Devlin had asked Williams and HOLMES to keep her apprised if there were any intelligence reports appearing on his radar involving Kelnikov, and they had struck gold.

The conversation had been captured using a Type 4193 Bruel and Kjaer software-enhanced infrasound microphone mounted on a French intelligence microdrone paralleling the ring road beside him. The little microdrone was a bug in all senses of the word. About the size of a finch, it used pressure-field measurement to read the conversation in the car by picking up passenger side window vibrations, digitally filtered in post-processing for the rumble of the road. And it went a little like this:

Kelnikov: (Translator Comment (TC): indistinguishable, could be cursing) be there? And we are sure of his vote?
Unidentified Male (UIM) 1: He will support you.
308

Kelnikov: This is slipping out of control. That (expletive) submarine. Now that (expletive) woman is threatening nuclear war.

UIM 1: The Minister of Defense says this is the moment in which we will either secure the future of the *Rodina*, or we will throw it away.

Kelnikov: Burkhin is a fool.

UIM 1: I am not qualified to say.

Kelnikov: Then you are a fool. Did you read that situation report? An entire ground-attack squadron out of action?

UIM 1: We still have the resources of the 4th, 5th and 7th Air regiments.

Kelnikov: I told Lukin it was folly to trust the air war to the same man who had his ass handed to him by the Americans over that shitty island.

UIM 1: We have air superiority over the operations area. The loss of the Okhotnik regiment was a temporary setback. The LOSOS landing at Nome is still on schedule.

Kelnikov: On schedule? The Americans are building an air armada south of Canada where we cannot reach them, and they will reach out and swat us like bugs when they are good and ready.

UIM 1: Let them hide behind the Rocky Mountains. Nome is ours, Minister.

Kelnikov: Driver! Pull this heap over. Get this idiot out of my car.

UIM 1: Minister! I...

(TC: Sound of car doors opening and closing and more cursing from Kelnikov. Silence until end of journey.)

The conversation told Devlin a lot, and it had sealed the deal in Washington too. It told her the Russian council of ministers was split. Kelnikov, it seemed, was afraid the Americans were about to tip the conflict over into nuclear war. Devlin was afraid of this herself. She didn't know what submarine Kelnikov was talking about, but it made sense to her the Pentagon would be preparing for the worst and positioning its stealth submarines within first-strike range of Russia. The conversation also told her that there had been a major US attack on Russian air assets and it had shaken their confidence. Finally, the French intel had shown the NSA and thus the whole of the US military intelligence apparatus that the next target for a Russian ground operation would be Nome.

There were of course things which Carl Williams wouldn't, or couldn't, tell Ambassador Devlin McCarthy.

The first was that it seemed his AI had fallen completely and totally head over silicon heels in love with her. Or what passed for love to HOLMES. One of Willams' breakthrough coding efforts had been to program HOLMES to experience 'pleasure' and to seek it out. He had defined pleasure for the AI as the ability to satisfy the intelligence needs of individuals of high rank, and of course he had weighted the various bureaucratic positions in the US government to ensure HOLMES knew who outranked who. Their satisfaction was measured by the number of times one of his reports was cited or forwarded by them. It was a simple algorithm and HOLMES had taken it to his silicon heart. Williams had programmed HOLMES to derive intrinsic 'pleasure' from providing intel perceived of value to high-ranked individuals. Few individuals came with a weighting as high as the US Ambassador to Russia.

The conflict was this. One of the only individuals in HOLMES' universe who currently had a higher status rank than Ambassador McCarthy was the head of the NSA, Levy Cohen. But Cohen was a cheerleader for the 'de-escalation' strategy. HOLMES derived little or no pleasure from providing reports which were routed to Cohen because he saw they were always 'qualified' by other analysts and assigned a low 'truth and reliability' rating. HOLMES was finding himself outplayed by the human analysts in the NSA who also derived their pleasure from satisfying individuals of high rank but who were much more sophisticated than HOLMES in realizing that success was driven by feeding Cohen with the intel that supported his worldview, and discounting the intel which did not.

In the face of this dichotomy – a first-ranked stakeholder who showed no interest in his intel, and a second-rank stakeholder who accepted and championed his analyses – HOLMES made the very rational and almost human decision to down-prioritize data requested by the NSA and focus on the intel requests of Ambassador Devlin McCarthy.

Williams saw this happening and was powerless to interfere. And he was caught in a catch 22. He could of course at any time rewrite the code and pull HOLMES back into line. But he was seeing his AI behave with a level of intuition and sheer bloody-minded genius that had him gasping with exhilaration. Common to many successful artists was that they had a muse – a huge, heartbreaking love that inspired them to greatness.

Fifty-four-year-old Devlin McCarthy was serving as five-year-old HOLMES' muse. And it was a relationship Williams was not inclined to disrupt.

Carl was sleeping in his broom cupboard in the New Annex, with his head in the crook of his arm. It was good, solid sleep and he deserved it to not be interrupted. Therefore, of course, it was.

The small rippling alarm was both soothing and irritating, designed by HOLMES to wake him gently but insistently. Without raising his head he hit the space bar on his laptop to wake it, and mumbled into his arm, "This had better be on the scale of imminent global nuclear war."

"Hello Carl," HOLMES said. "I need to speak with Ambassador Devlin and she is not answering her telephone."

He didn't lift his head. "What is the time?"

"Three a.m."

"That is why she is not answering her telephone, HOLMES."

"Yes, but I need to speak with her."

"No. And besides, you shouldn't be calling the Ambassador on her direct line. That's not protocol, my man. You go through me."

"In war, protocol goes down the toilet," HOLMES quoted.

"Is that so?"

"According to former five-star general and Secretary of State Colin Powell, yes."

Williams sighed. "HOLMES, she is sleeping, like other normal people. What do you want me to do?"

"I need you to go to her residence and wake her," HOLMES said. His calm British voice radiated patience.

"Spaso House is five blocks from here. She might not be there. That's probably why you couldn't reach her. People do strange shit at the end of the world. She's probably out bonking her fitness instructor."

"She is in bed at Spaso House. She uses a sleep tracking app with inbuilt GPS locator and it is currently reporting that she is in a deep sleep cycle, which is why I cannot wake her."

"You hacked her fitness bracelet. That is beyond creepy, HOLMES."

"Will you wake her?"

"Give me one reason why I should," Williams demanded.

There was a millisecond pause, and Williams knew it was because HOLMES was thinking, in his quantum-core brain, *ooooh, should I tell him?* Apparently the answer was yes.

"I need you to wake her so that I can tell her I have identified the Russian Air Force officer who is leading the offensive against US forces in Alaska."

Carl shifted his head to be more comfortable. "So what, he's probably put it on his online CV already. 'June to December, leader of air offensive against USA.'"

"The leader of the Russian air offensive, Colonel Yevgeny Bondarev, is the father of her grandchild," HOLMES said. "Will you wake her now?"

Private Zubkhov had a grandmother. She was a lovely, wrinkled old woman who lived behind a church in Irkutsk. She had an apple tree in her backyard and made the best apple pie you ever ate in your damn life, and it was so simple. You took the apples, and you peeled them, then you stewed them in sugar and cinnamon water. When they were soft you mashed them and ladled them into a baking dish. Over the mashed apples you spooned a thick layer of oats, and more cinnamon sugar. Into the oven, and bake for 30 minutes until the oats had soaked up the juice of the apples and turned crisp on top. Oh, but you weren't finished. You took it out of the oven, and across the top of the crisp oats you spooned thickened whipped cream. And on top of the whipped cream, a sprinkling of almond flakes. Soaked in orange liqueur.

On top of all the other surprises in that baking dish, it was the orange liqueur almonds floating on the whipped cream which turned it from an ordinary apple crumble into a work of culinary art.

He had been thinking about that pie as he said goodbye to the old people in the school buildings. They didn't know he was saying goodbye, of course. They thought he was giving out their rations, and although a few of them had acted like they were suspicious, most of them had reacted with muted delight when he had handed out the big blocks of chocolate alongside the soup.

He liked the thought that the old people had gone to their next life with the taste of chocolate on their tongues.

Once he had dragged the bodies of the Russian wounded outside and covered them up with the bobcat, he had retired to his office. From a pill bottle on his desk, he tipped out two sleeping tablets and drank them down with a glass of water. He leaned his chair back and put his feet up on his desk. He needed to sleep. Tomorrow he had to get a read on that second radio, try to work out where it was. He had a pretty good idea it was that damn American soldier using it, but he had to find him first.

And as the pills kicked in, he played a mind game and gave his report to Sergeant Penkov up there somewhere on the coast. He imagined Penkov asking him for an update on the wounded and Zubkhov telling him (truthfully, if not in a complete way) that one of the wounded had died.

"Who?" the NCO would ask, like he cared.

Hmmm, who? Zubkhov thought to himself. A name came to him. "Kirrilov, the boy with the sheared-off toes and heel."

"How did he die?" Penkov would ask. "He was the least wounded of them all."

"I don't know," Zubkhov would lie. "Infection?" *Or perhaps he died from an overdose of painkillers.* An unfortunate mistake but, after all, he wasn't a trained medic.

"Your job was to keep those men alive, Private!" the Sergeant would say. "If you see infection, clean it and make sure the men are taking their antibiotics and antibacterials. We left most of the medical supplies with you."

Most, right. Thanks so much. "Yes, sir!" he would say earnestly. "I will not lose another!"

"You had better not, or I'll have your balls."

"Yes, sir."

"We are making good time. The locals say we are four days from Savoonga. I will call again tomorrow at this time. I will need to get instructions from whoever is in command once we reach Savoonga. Keep this channel open," the Sergeant would tell him.

"Yes, sir."

"The civilian hostages?"

"I gave them chocolate, sir," he would say.

"What?"

"I found some chocolate, so I gave them that, with their rations."

"OK, well, that's OK, I guess. I'm signing off now. Keep the base station online and stay on top of those wounded, Private. Penkov out."

"Yes, sir. Out."

Not that he *could* give the man a report, as he had left him without any way to communicate. But as he played the conversation through in his head, there was a beep from the base station and he looked at the rangefinder screen. It was showing *two* handsets now, both at a range of about 20km, one of which was probably the column of troops and townspeople. He tried to zoom the display, see if he could separate the two signals.

Yes! That goddamn ghost radio!

It was showing bright and clear on the rangefinder, but now it was almost right on top of Penkov's field radio. He stared at the two dots for five minutes, but they stayed right next to each other.

Until the ghost blip winked out and was gone again.

So, the American was following the column? Private Zubkhov loved it when a plan came together!

He wearily clicked the base station to standby.

Sleep. It had been A Big Day.

In the morning, he would gather supplies and ammunition. Catch up to that column, find that ghost and deal with him, get the radio handset off him, then call Anadyr. He'd be back in Gambell before his buddy arrived to pick him up. With luck, the Captain wouldn't go more than a day without a meal. Let the US send its black-clad assassins to Gambell to try to take it back. All they would find would be charcoal, ashes and graves.

He'd added something to his plan too. The Captain? He was going to bring him along on the boat to Anadyr. Teach the guy to fish. It got boring out in the Northern Pacific at night. You could really use a guy who could recite Dostoyevsky by heart.

"A4, this is Commander Naval Air Forces Coronado, stand by for a message from Vice Admiral Lionel Solanta," the radio in the trailer under the Rock said. After their mission against Anadyr, Rodriguez and Bunny had prepped two more Fantoms and loaded one on the Cat in an air-air configuration, with the other in its cartridge loaded for ground attack with standoff missiles, fueled up and ready to roll. They hadn't received new orders, but they had just stuck a stick into a hornet's nest and wanted to be ready to defend the base if they needed to. The air-air loadout would let them defend themselves against another small-scale strike by attack aircraft, while the ground-attack loadout would be useful if they were given a land-based target or something on the water. Rodriguez wasn't under any illusions – if NORAD kept sending them combat tasking, it was just a matter of time before Ivan worked out where they were hiding and came for them.

"Standing by, Coronado," Rodriguez said.

Once they had their two drones locked and loaded, there was nothing more Rodriguez and O'Hare could do. So they had shared a pot of coffee, grabbed some food, and dropped into exhausted sleep. Both were awake and on station again at 0400 and the order to stand by their comms had come through at 0430.

Bunny was sitting at her pilot's console with two booted feet up on her desk beside the coffee cups, joystick and throttles and keyboards. True to her word two nights ago, she had dyed her cropped white-blonde hair black and painted her fingernails to match. As Rodriguez watched her, she was a study in intense concentration, painting small white skulls with crossbones on her black nails. Rodriguez was willing to bet she had painted her toenails black too. She found herself thinking how Bunny had never mentioned a boyfriend. She'd never mentioned a girlfriend either, for that matter.

"Vice Admiral, eh?" Bunny stopped painting her nails and smiled. Then she said in a high sing-song voice, *"Bunny go-ing to get a me-dal…"*

"Or court-martial," Rodriguez said, smiling too. "You probably hit the wrong target. Took out a fish factory."

"Fish factory workers in Russia go to work in Okhotniks do they, ma'am?"

"Maybe." They hadn't seen a bomb damage assessment yet, but they'd rerun the nose cam footage from the two drones

316

and had counted at least a handful of Russian fighters on the base before they hit it. Pending the BDA, the strike had made Bunny a 'ground ace', a pilot with five or more ground kills. And she had been pointing it out to Rodriguez at every opportunity.

"There's probably a promotion when you get ground ace status, right?" Bunny asked. "He's probably calling to tell me I've made Captain."

"You're on DARPA secondment, O'Hare, any rank you have is honorary. Besides, you don't even know those bombs exploded," Rodriguez pointed out. "They could have been duds."

"All four? No way, ma'am, those eggs hatched," Bunny retorted. "They..."

"A4, this is Admiral Solanta. Can I speak with Lieutenant Commander Alicia Rodriguez, please?"

Rodriguez took a deep breath. "Speaking, Admiral."

"And is Lieutenant O'Hare there with you?"

"Yes sir, Admiral," Bunny replied.

"Good. Look, I wanted to speak with you in person to let you know I've been following what happened to A4. I know you got hit, and hard. I heard how you got your people out from under that rock, Rodriguez, and I also know the two of you volunteered to stay behind and close the base down, and you've managed to keep it operational despite all that."

"Yes, sir," Rodriguez said. "Do you know how my people are?"

There was a pause. "I'm told all the wounded are recovering well. One is still in a critical condition, but stable," Solanta said.

Bunny leaned over and gave Rodriguez a high five. "Sir, this is Lieutenant O'Hare," Bunny said. "Do we have a damage assessment from our strike on Anadyr yesterday?"

"That's why I'm calling," the Admiral said. "Our intel ... and we have multiple-source confirmation on this one ... says you have rendered the Russian 573rd Army Air Force drones totally non-mission capable."

Bunny and Rodriguez looked at each other. "Sorry, sir, can you repeat?" Rodriguez asked in shock. "Did you say we NMC'ed a whole Russian fighter regiment?"

"Yes, Lieutenant Commander, you heard me right. I don't call active duty personnel on a whim. You whupped some serious Russian ass, ladies." Right then you could have lit a skyscraper from the wattage coming from Bunny and Rodriguez's smiles. Admiral Solanta knew how to motivate his warriors. He also knew how not to. He hadn't made mention of the massive casualty tally his intelligence staff had handed him. He also made no mention of the unconfirmed report the attack had killed a Russian general. He gave a cough and continued. "Now, I have to keep moving, but I wanted to give you a sitrep. It's not good. While you've been trying to stay alive and get a little payback up there, Ivan has knocked us on our can. Eielson and Elmendorf-Richardson are out of action, at least for another three days, maybe longer. We've got some mobile anti-air fighting back, but just as soon as they put up their radar dishes, Russia hits them. We've decided we aren't going to fight Ivan's fight on this one, not on his terms. We're preparing a joint services counter-offensive on a scale that is going to blast him back to Siberia, and we're looking at ... other options." The Admiral paused to let those last two words sink in. "Which we hope will never be needed. But here's the other reason for my call. Right now, A4 is the only offensive air unit I have in the Operations Area. I'm going to be asking you two to hunker down under that rock, and you'll be flying day and night until you drop dead with fatigue, or you run out of drones, whichever comes first."

Rodriguez gulped. *The only offensive air unit in the Operations Area? Holy hell.* "Yes, sir. Understood. We'll do our best."

The Admiral laughed. "You telling me I haven't seen your best yet, Lieutenant Commander? Well, I look forward to that. You two are rewriting the book on how to fight a modern air war. Keep it up. They'll be teaching the next generation of aviators at Annapolis about the 'A4 model for bare bones kick-assery', I guarantee you that."

"Yes, sir!" they both chimed at the same time, bumping fists.

After the Admiral logged out, Bunny swiveled twice around in her seat, and then fixed Rodriguez with a fierce glare. "Ma'am, we get out of here alive, you and me have *got* to get tattoos."

Devlin McCarthy had a tattoo. And she was willing to bet none of her staff had ever even entertained the thought their graying stress cadet of an Ambassador had a tattoo on her right upper arm. Even less that it was a tattoo she'd gotten recently. When she was wearing light shirts, she covered it with a skin-toned plaster. It was only a little tattoo, just a name really, in a nice curly font. It said 'Angel' and there was a story behind it, of course.

Devlin's daughter Cindy had been thirty when she announced to her mother she was pregnant. She'd moved in with Devlin in Moscow a year earlier after a long-term relationship ended in disaster. A lawyer in a private practice in DC, she'd told her bosses she needed time away from work and rather than let her quit, they'd told her to take a few months and get her head together. They knew it was a better option than losing her for good. A few months had turned into a year, and Cindy had based herself in Moscow and traveled all over Europe. She and Devlin had talked about the breakup she'd been through, and how the one thing that had kept her daughter together with her partner for so long was the hope they'd have kids together one day. She'd waited and waited and then started suggesting it, more and more insistently – she was thirty, dammit, and she wanted kids! But it turned out he didn't, and that was that.

Devlin remembered every detail of the afternoon Cindy told her she was pregnant. It was a Sunday. Cindy had been in Saint Petersburg with a 'friend' she'd met in Rome, she said. A friend she'd been seeing a lot of lately, but hadn't brought back home.

She'd come in from the airport, dumped her bags in her room, and Devlin had made her a pot of tea. It was raining, but not in that drab, melancholy way it often rains in Moscow. They were sun showers, fresh and brisk, and Devlin had the windows open because she liked listening to the patter of the raindrops on the green copper of the roof above. Cindy came in, sat on the sofa with her cup of tea, one leg tucked underneath her. She was beautiful, of course, and not just because Devlin thought so. She was a young, bright, competent and together young woman with style and as Devlin walked into the lounge room and looked at her daughter sitting there in a ray of sunshine, framed in raindrops, her heart near burst with pride.

"I'm pregnant," Cindy had said.

Devlin sat next to her, taking it pretty calmly. After all, the girl wasn't fifteen years old.

"OK, wow," Devlin said. "You sound ... actually you sound OK about it."

"I wanted it," Cindy said. "I didn't know how to tell you. But I've kind of been shopping while I've been here."

"For a husband?"

"No, for a ... man," she said. She laughed. "I didn't want to just go bonking random guys until it happened. I wanted a love affair, with someone I liked, but not so much I couldn't say goodbye."

"And you found one," Devlin said. "I've been wondering who you've been traveling with, all these places. I thought maybe ... I thought you maybe had a girlfriend and were afraid to tell me."

Now Cindy really laughed. "A lesbian rebound? Oh *Mom*." She sipped her tea. "No. I just figured it wasn't worth introducing him because he's not going to be a part of this."

"What do you mean?" Devlin asked.

"I mean, he's Russian and I'm going back to the States to have my baby," she said. "I'm not sure I'll even tell him."

Devlin clutched her hand, gave her a hug and, yes, she cried a little. While her daughter had been talking, she had suddenly had this image of the two of them, living in Moscow,

320

a little baby in the residence, Devlin suddenly and wonderfully a grandmother. But, no. Apparently not.

"When I'm finished here, I'll get something back in DC," Devlin said, sniffling. "Maybe I could get out of the posting sooner, say next year."

"It's OK, Mom," Cindy said. "We have a whole lifetime to work this out. I want you there for the birth, though," she said, holding her mother's face. "You promise me that, OK? I wouldn't want anyone else there."

And that night, the two of them had gone for drinks – mocktails for Cindy, a dozen different variations on a vodka theme for Devlin – and then the two of them had gotten tattoos. And their tattoos said 'Angel' because Devlin had decided that's what her grandchild was going to be and it was small enough it wouldn't hurt too much and she could cover it with her sleeve and Cindy said 'whatever', she couldn't believe she was getting a tattoo with her fifty-four-year-old mother, the US Ambassador to Moscow.

The way she felt then, waking up the next morning with a hangover and a throbbing pain in her arm, was exactly how Devlin McCarthy felt now, having been woken in person by Carl Williams and his ever-present laptop-based lifeform, HOLMES.

"You woke me to tell me what?"

"Ma'am, there's no way to sugar-coat this, so I'll let HOLMES tell it and you can decide what you do with it," Williams said. He sat his chubby bearded self down on the end of the sofa outside her bedroom. She sat at the other end in a bathrobe, slippers, and with a confused expression on her face. He took out a smartphone, turned on the speaker and sat it on the table in front of her.

"I thought you needed him hooked up to your 'fat pipe'?"

"For analytical work and data exchange. Right now he's just in conversation mode."

She nodded. "OK, sure. Go ahead, HOLMES."

The tinny British voice was loud in the small room. "Hello Ambassador, do you remember saying to me that the Russian

Air Force officer behind the attack on Saint Lawrence must be someone they really trust? 'A party insider' was your exact phrase?"

Devlin had by now had dozens of conversations with HOLMES, and she didn't share his perfect recall. "No, HOLMES, I have to admit, I don't."

"Well, ma'am, you did. So, working on that premise, I have been looking at officers of the Eastern Military District 3rd Air and Air Defense Forces Command and building a database of the sons and daughters of prominent political and military leaders who would be of the right age to be leading a Russian air unit of at least brigade strength. The interrogation of pilots downed and captured over Alaska identified they were from the Russian Snow Leopards Air Brigade, and the commander of this unit fits the profile you described. He is Yevgeny Bondarev, the grandson of the former Commander in Chief of the Russian Aerospace Forces, Viktor Bondarev. He is an active member of the Progress Party, served with distinction in the Middle East, and on his return to Russia his unit, the 5th Air Regiment, was attached to the 3rd Air and Air Defense Forces Command. When the commander of the Snow Leopards retired, Bondarev was promoted." HOLMES was talking like a military search engine, and Devlin had trouble assimilating all the detail, being as it was 0330 in the a.m. and she was still waking up.

"Yes, so ... so, what?"

"I have examined every single piece of data currently held in US intelligence databases related to Colonel Bondarev," HOLMES said. "I have also obtained access to his GRU personnel file and an FSB intelligence dossier compiled on him as part of his vetting for the position of brigade commander."

Now Devlin came awake. "You hacked GRU and FSB servers?"

"Not personally, ma'am," HOLMES replied, his voice conveying no irony. "But you don't need to know more."

"No, I don't," Devlin agreed. She turned to Williams. "Where are we going with this?"

Williams squirmed awkwardly. "We found something in the files, related to you."

We found something in the files, related to you. This was a sentence no Ambassador ever wanted to hear from a spook.

"Tell me," Devlin said.

"In the FSB file, there was a US birth certificate recording a Russian national, Yevgeny Bondarev, as the father of a child born two years ago," HOLMES said. Devlin went cold. HOLMES continued. "The mother of the child was listed as your daughter, Cindy McCarthy. The child's name is..."

"Angela," Devlin said quietly. "Angela McCarthy."

"What I want is simple," Bondarev was telling Arsharvin. He had just reviewed imagery from the US attack on Ugolny. His voice was low and dangerously quiet. "I want to know how the Americans managed to get two Fantoms, which have a range of only 1,500 miles when carrying a full payload of ground-attack ordnance, through our long- and short-range air defenses and underneath a cloud of circling drones and then hit my air base, bury me alive, and kill every damn crew member of that Fighter Aviation Regiment, when the nearest US airfield out of which they could have flown is Lewis-McChord in Washington State!" He took a breath. "Which is twice the range of a Fantom, or in case you need reminding, two thousand, five hundred freaking miles from Anadyr."

"We're working on that, Comrade Colonel," Arsharvin said. There were other officers present, so he was sticking to formalities. He was also being very careful because he knew his friend, and he knew what he was going through. This was not a time for being defensive. "Our first theory was mid-air refueling. But they would have had to refuel over Alaska, or the north coast of Russia, and we have not been able to identify any likely radar or satellite data indicating the US managed to get a refueling aircraft into the theater, manned or unmanned."

Bondarev was staring at him, waiting. They were seated across a table from each other in his temporary operations center in the harbor at Anadyr, a former harbormaster building commandeered because it was the only building with enough connectivity to support their data communication needs without choking. "You have other theories, then," Bondarev stated, not asking.

Arsharvin nodded to one of his junior officers. "The most likely is still that the US at some point managed to position mobile drone launch units in Alaska State and, since the outbreak of the conflict, has moved these west, so that they are now in a position to threaten our rear," the man said. "They have had the capability to launch their Fantom aircraft off the back of a heavy hauler since..."

Bondarev cut him off. "We already discussed US mobile drone launch capabilities." His eyes narrowed. "However, my intelligence chief has not identified any such units operating within this theater. Or was there a report that I missed?"

"No, Comrade Colonel."

"But you have information to that effect now?"

"No, Comrade Colonel," the man said. "Only speculation."

Bondarev stood abruptly, and Arsharvin flinched. "I cannot target 'speculation', Lieutenant Colonel Arsharvin," Bondarev said. "I have an immediate and existential threat to my ability to maintain air supremacy in the Bering Strait theater, and that threat is currently unknown, unquantified, and..." Bondarev slammed a hand down on the table, "un-*located*!" He was not finished. He held up a sheaf of papers Arsharvin had delivered earlier in the day. "The enemy is not playing our game, you tell me. He is putting nuclear submarines into firing positions off our coastline. He is moving a significant part of his Air Force to the US northwest, but holding it in reserve. Currently, I have five regiments facing his three. Within a week we will probably be evenly matched. Within two, we will be outmatched, and then he can come against us. We need to get our troops safely on the ground in Alaska before then, but ..." He slammed the table again. "Instead! Instead I am being bled by an asymmetrical interdiction force of insignificant strength able to inflict significant losses because my intelligence unit was apparently deaf, dumb and blind to this threat!"

Arsharvin had taken all he could. Yes, his friend was a superior officer. Yes, he was hurting. But he could not place the blame for the deaths of 200 men on Arsharvin and his officers. Not alone.

"With respect, Colonel," Arsharvin said, standing as well. "There were only *two* stealth aircraft used in this attack. However they got through, they got lucky." There was a map of Alaska on the table, and Arsharvin span it around. His finger stabbed down on the rugged western coastal region. "If they have mobile launch units in the theater, there are very few areas they could operate from. We have standing patrols over Nome, so they didn't come from there, and east of Nome there are no roads, only logging trails. There are no suitable airfields, only dirt strips used by light aircraft flown by bush pilots. If they are there, we will find them." He took his hand away and stood. "I promise you, Comrade Colonel."

"The rest of you are dismissed. Lieutenant Colonel Arsharvin will remain," Bondarev said. When the other officers were gone, they sat again.

"I share the burden of those deaths too, my friend," Arsharvin said quietly. "Wherever this attack came from, we will find them. You have my word."

Bondarev span the map of Alaska thoughtfully. He stopped, pinning it with his finger on Nome.

"General Lukin gave me two weeks to show we have control of the airspace over Western Alaska," Bondarev said. "He said he was being pressured by a faction in the Council of Ministers to abandon the plans for a ground assault and consolidate our presence on Saint Lawrence as a bargaining chip."

"Bargaining chip for what?" Arsharvin asked, frowning.

"That is what I want you to tell me, Tomas," he said. "I deserve to know the *real* reason 200 of my people died."

Arsharvin stared at him for a moment, then stood, went to the door and locked it. He returned to the table and sat.

"Alright. This *isn't* about us monopolizing the polar shipping route," Arsharvin said.

"No new Panama Canal? Give me some credit, I already guessed that much. What then?"

Arsharvin leaned back in his chair. "To answer that, I have to take you back to a meeting I attended a year ago in Vladivostok."

Bondarev groaned. "You're going to tell me how you met President Navalny again."

"Yes and no. I told you I met him, I didn't tell you why."

"A briefing on Far East resources, I think you said. 'Pivot to the Pacific' blah blah blah. Sorry, I fell asleep while you were explaining."

"And you thought the President would travel all the way to Vladi-bloody-vostok for a boring briefing on Far East resources?"

"I don't recall thinking much at all except how tiresome it was listening to you name dropping about your top secret Far East intelligence committee meetings again."

"Russia is dying, my friend," Arsharvin said. And he said it with such surety that Bondarev stifled the laugh that was forming in his throat.

Bondarev waved his hand dismissively. "Moscow is corrupt, yes, but it has always been. Our economic partnership and trade pacts with China mean our economy has not been stronger for a hundred years. Chelyabinsk is now the third biggest city in Russia. Anadyr will soon be bigger than Vladivostok. What do you mean, 'dying'?"

"This is different, Yevgeny. I'm not talking about trade, I'm talking raw human survival." Arsharvin reached over Bondarev's desk, picking up a bottle of water. He uncapped it and held it out to Bondarev. Bondarev picked up a glass, confused. Arsharvin filled it, poured one for himself, and then clinked his glass against Bondarev's before drinking the water down. He held his glass up to the light. "Enjoy it. Because it's soon going to be more precious than your 25-year-old whiskey."

326

"I don't get you," Bondarev admitted.

"Remember at military college, you and I, we used to argue about peak oil?" Arsharvin asked.

"Sure. You said the next world war would be over oil, and I said that renewables would solve the problem before it got that bad," Bondarev said. "And I was right."

"You were. But we were arguing about the wrong thing," Arsharvin said.

"So what's the right thing, if it's not peak oil?"

"Peak *water*. And Russia passed it ten years ago without the world even knowing it."

"This country is covered in snow, rivers, lakes. Plus..." Bondarev pivoted and pointed out the window. "Head that way to the coast. You'll hit the Sea of Japan. East of there is the biggest body of water on the planet, the Pacific Ocean. Follow that far enough, you'll hit the Atlantic. This planet is 70% water, Tomas."

"Russia has poisoned its lakes and rivers. The snow melts into empty aquifers. And the sea is saltwater, my friend. *Salt*. I am talking about peak *freshwater*."

Bondarev reached over and poured some more water into Arsharvin's glass. "You never heard of desalinization? What do you think you have been drinking the last twenty years? Mountain-fresh spring water? Every city lives on desalinated water – Moscow pipes it from Saint Petersburg since Lake Kljasma dried up, but so what?"

"That's the whole point!" Arsharvin said. "We can supply the big cities, but the smaller cities and towns, they have been living off whatever they can pull out of poisoned rivers and lakes, or suck out of the melting permafrost. The meeting I was at, it had the title, *Coming water shortages*."

Bondarev scoffed. "Since I was a boy there have been water shortages. Then they bring another desal plant online, and everyone relaxes again."

"Not like this. Within ten years, Yevgeny, 40 million out of 150 million Russians will be facing water rationing. If we built a new desalination plant every month for the next two years, we couldn't provide for that many people, and that's if we had the time and money to build all those plants and pipelines, which we don't."

"There was talk of a pipeline from Scandinavia," Bondarev said, trying to absorb what Arsharvin was saying. "I thought that…"

"Will buy us five years, and is already accounted for. Plus it puts us at the mercy of Europe, which could bring us to our knees just by turning off a tap. The Middle East is already tearing itself apart over water. Did you think we were immune?"

Bondarev was quiet, staring into his glass. Water? Seriously? "Wait, what does the Bering Strait have to do with this? Polar ice or something?"

Now it was Arsharvin's turn to laugh. "Polar ice? What polar ice?" he asked. "It's melting at an exponential rate. That's why we can sail the northern route even in winter now. But you aren't completely wrong."

"What, then?"

"As that ice cap melts, all that beautiful freshwater goes somewhere. Into the sea, most of it, raising the sea level. Some into Canada, a little into our northern territories – not enough of it, though, we are too far from the pack ice now. But there is one place where the glaciers reach down from the pole into mountains and valleys and canyons and become huge raging rivers and lakes of pure, fresh water."

"*Not* Saint Lawrence Island, I'm guessing," Bondarev said.

"No, but close. Alaska accounts for more than 40% of US freshwater reserves. The Yukon River alone delivers six *thousand* cubic meters of fresh water into the Bering Sea near Nome every second! That's close to the flow of the Volga, three times the flow of the Nile River. With a dam on the Yukon feeding our Far East expansion, we can save Russia *and* rule the north."

Bondarev felt his fist tightening on his small glass, and realized he was in danger of crushing it before he relaxed his grip.

Arsharvin saw his white knuckles. "That's why your men are dying, Yevgeny. Nothing less than the survival of their homeland." Arsharvin shifted in his chair. "Now, Lukin is dead. You are the most senior commander in the 3rd Air Army until a new general is named. For all intents and purposes, you are leading this air war now. What is our next move?"

Bondarev sighed, tapping his finger on the map of the region around Nome again.

"I leave for Savoonga tomorrow to see if the airfield there can be used to stage a squadron or two more for the attack on Nome. I can't afford to have so many aircraft concentrated in Lavrentiya, and Anadyr will take precious days to rebuild. My two weeks are running out, my friend," Bondarev said. "I have only days now to show Moscow that the Americans cannot repeat what they did in Anadyr. And from today, it gets harder. They have moved new satellites into position." He reached over and patted Arsharvin on the shoulder. "I can keep the two US air bases in Alaska out of commission, even without the Okhotniks we lost at Anadyr. My Sukhois and Migs can fend off their probing patrols and my remaining Okhotniks can degrade their mobile anti-air capabilities as fast as they get them up and radiating." He fixed Arsharvin with a cold gaze. "But I need *you* to find whoever killed my people at Anadyr, so that I can kill *them* before they hit us again."

SOME DAYS YOU EAT THE BEAR

Private Zubkhov couldn't bring the base radio and its rangefinding scope with him, so he had to track the ghost radio the old-fashioned way. He knew whoever was carrying it was following the column of prisoners along the coastal track to Savoonga. So he would do the same. They had a one-day start on him though, so he had to hustle.

He had moved the Captain into the relative comfort of the schoolmaster's offices, sat him in a chair, and set him up with a bottle of water, cold tea and biscuits with some cheese. The man was now able to eat and drink, find the toilet and lie down when he needed to sleep. Anything more complicated seemed to befuddle him. But he would be okay for a couple of days.

The Captain sat in the schoolmaster's chair, watching as Zubkhov got himself ready.

Zubkhov had decided to travel light. A half-sized backpack, water, dry rations, his Makarov sidearm, a knife and a folding stock VSS Vintorez silenced sniper rifle with a few magazines of 9x39mm. He had his winter camouflage uniform on, mottled brown and white, with just a utility belt across his waist and the backpack strapped tight to his shoulders. The Captain was watching him as he pulled on his gear and adjusted the strap on the rifle so it sat comfortably on his back.

"I know what you're thinking, Sir. I should be taking the Dragunov," Zubkhov said, talking as much to himself as to the Captain. "Better range, hits harder. But I need to move fast to try to catch up with this guy, and the Vintorez is lighter and quieter."

The Captain actually appeared to be considering. "When there is no God, everything is permitted," he quoted.

"Amen to that, sir," Private Zubkhov said. He checked his sidearm and ammunition one last time, holstered it, and headed for the door. He had a damn good idea who was out there, following that column with a stolen Russian radio. He'd shown the guy's jacket and Air Force patch to the Captain when the man had gotten away from them, their first hour on the island. And that shadow he'd seen on the hillside just after the first missile hit? That was no coincidence. The US soldier must have called in the strike.

Zubkhov should have shot the bastard when he had the chance. He wouldn't make that mistake twice.

The last remaining officers of the last remaining US offensive air asset in the Operations Area were trying to work out what the hell had just gone wrong.

They had been tasked to hit a Russian supply depot at Lavrentiya where it looked like the enemy was stockpiling a significant cache of supplies outside the military airport for some sort of offensive. The base itself was assumed to be heavily defended, but their target was a warehouse and munitions depot on the outskirts of town.

It was an industrial town with a small harbor and what was now a disproportionately large airport. A single five-story administrative center and, not far from it, a six-story hospital. Four or five factories belched foul black smoke into the air over the town.

It was a perfect target for the Joint Air-to-Ground – JAGM – missiles they had already loaded aboard one of their Fantoms. They had a drone already on the Cat configured for air-to-air escort, so put that into the air first, then bullied the second Fantom into place and sent it up the chute.

The JAGM had a warhead similar in hitting power to its predecessor the Hellfire, and the four missiles carried inside the weapons bay of the Fantom were more than sufficient to destroy the weapons dump at Lavrentiya. The only problem with the JAGM was that the Army and Navy had never been able to agree on its final design, with the Navy in and out of the program a couple of times over the years. In the end, it was a compromise between the longer-range standoff weapon the Navy wanted and the shorter-range missiles preferred by the

Army. Guided by semi-active laser and multi-band radar, the JAGM was a fire and forget weapon, but with a range of only about ten miles.

There was no back door into Lavrentiya as they had found for Anadyr. The city lay abreast of a wide sweeping bay on a flat permafrost plain. Low hills skirted the city to the north, but they weren't suitable to provide any sort of radar cover. Electronic intel showed the base was covered by short-range surface-air missiles, but stealth and the Fantom's onboard electronic warfare suite should enable them to get in under the base defenses.

"We blow in low from the south with the sun behind us, pop up, jam, lock and shoot, then bug out," Bunny had decided while they were planning. "We've got no intel on what missile systems they have in place, but it's the main Russian offensive air base, so there must also be some ugly-ass anti-air protecting it. Fantom 1 goes in first, tries to draw any fire, helps me identify what they have hiding there. I can use one missile for suppression, two for the depot, which still leaves me one for a target of opportunity, if we're lucky."

They were going to try to bring their drones home this time. Neither Eielson nor Elmendorf were ready to receive them yet, while Nome and Port Clarence were covered by standing Russian fighter patrols. They had gotten an auxiliary heavy lift crane working, and decided they could land the drones on the Pond, tie them up, then pull them out by crane and refit them when they got a chance. Yes, it increased the chances of their being discovered twofold, but with only ten aircraft left, they couldn't treat every mission as a one-way trip.

They made a careful plan. But they didn't get a single missile away.

What Rodriguez and O'Hare couldn't have known was that, unlike at Ugolny, Bondarev had made very sure indeed that his front line base at Lavrentiya was well protected.

Sitting on a low-rise overlooking the bustling town was a Nebo-M anti-aircraft/anti-missile system and it was just about to come online. Mounted on four 24-ton trucks, it featured a

332

command module and three radar arrays, arranged to provide 360-degree area denial defense of the airspace around Lavrentiya. The Nebo-M battalion at Lavrentiya controlled 72 launchers over a 100 square kilometer area, fielding a total of 384 missiles. In 'circular scan' mode the Nebo-M battalion could track up to 200 targets at a distance and at altitudes of up to 600 kilometers. In 'ICBM killer' sector scan mode, a Nebo-M could track 20 ballistic targets at ranges of up to 1,800 kilometers and at an altitude of up to 1,200 kilometers. They were Russia's equivalent of the US HELLADS system, but based on older, more proven technologies.

If Bondarev had had such a system at Anadyr, the Americans would never have gotten through, but he'd seen his assets at Lavrentiya, closest to Alaska and Savoonga, as being the higher priority and the Nebo-M was a precious resource. Although Russia had once had grand plans to install Nebo-M systems all over the country to provide an effective anti-missile shield, teething problems had delayed their introduction and they were only now being deployed, with a focus on providing protection to the major population centers. Thus it had taken a bureaucratic catfight and the personal intervention of General Lukin for Bondarev to get the only two Nebo-M systems in the Eastern Military District moved from Vladivostok and Khabarovsk to Lavrentiya and Savoonga to protect his fighters for LOSOS.

The Nebo-M was a system specially designed to detect stealth aircraft, but even it would have trouble picking up at long range the small profile of the two Fantoms Bunny was sending toward it. For this, it relied on a shorter-range array radiating at the lower-frequency S and L bands, which had a range of less than 30 miles.

With Bunny able to fire her missiles at a range of 10 miles, and fly at 1,300 miles an hour at sea level, assuming she could get close enough, that gave the Russian system a window of about one minute in which to lock and fire at the Fantoms before she could fire herself.

Even if she had known the Nebo-M was sitting there waiting for her, she would probably still have taken those odds. But because it had just arrived in theater and hadn't got up and radiating yet, it had not been flagged by electronic signals intel and there was nothing on her threat warning system to tip her off it was even there.

It was no ordinary anti-air battalion either. Painted on the door of the command module of the Lavrentiya array were the silhouettes of six fighters, two ICBMs and four rotary aircraft that the unit had 'destroyed' in exercises. It had never fired a shot in actual combat – the Nebo-M was a home defense system and hadn't been deployed in the Middle East – but the personnel staffing the unit at Lavrentiya were the best in the Russian Armed Forces at what they were paid to do.

So when an Airborne Control aircraft picked up a couple of ghost returns to their south, battalion commander Lieutenant Colonel Alexandr Chaliapin had ordered his technicians to get their array online and do it *now*, dammit. The Airborne Control aircraft didn't have a firm fix on anything, but a fighter patrol was dispatched to scan the sector – and still that hadn't made him relax. He'd heard what had happened at Anadyr, everyone had. But Anadyr wasn't defended by his Nebo-M. And he had no intention of letting what happened at Anadyr happen to him at Lavrentiya.

Getting the battalion flown in and physically into position had taken precious days. Getting it networked and able to link with other air, sea and ground defense units was even more of a headache. Now they were in the middle of their first live test cycle and they had a threat on the board? Other commanders might have panicked or, worse, been lulled into complacency by the next forty minutes without any further contact being reported, either by the Airborne Control plane or by the fighter sweep. But Chaliapin let his men work and, when they declared the system ready, he played a hunch and sent a narrow beam of low-frequency energy down the bearing of the previous contact and hit gold! Another faint return bounced back, then was gone. Now he had a validated threat and a vector on it. He put three launchers armed with low-level active homing 9M96J missiles on high alert, bringing them to instant readiness. He fed the numbers to his AI, shut down his active systems and stopped radiating. If he was wrong, he had just condemned the city to an attack from an unknown quarter, but he had never before been wrong.

In her virtual-reality rig on Little Diomede Bunny's radar warning flashed for the briefest of moments. Too short for her to identify the source or type of defensive system that was sniffing after her. She logged it, then ignored it.

The Nebo-M's AI ran the numbers on the two ghost returns, calculated a speed and bearing, and waited with silicon patience for the identified threat to enter S and L frequency range. At exactly 32 miles estimated, it brought its radar arrays back online and blasted energy downrange toward the expected position of the unidentified aircraft.

As her threat indicator showed a targeting radar lock on her heads-up display, Bunny just had time to yell, "Radar lock!" The combat AI on Bunny's Fantoms reacted before she could, sending one Fantom in a hard banking right turn, while the other broke left, but it was too late. Missile launch warnings screamed inside the trailer. With the 9M96J missiles flying at two and a half times the speed of sound, the missile alert warnings sounded almost at the same time as the two screens she was using to pilot the drones flashed suddenly white, then went blank.

They had just lost *two* of their dwindling complement of Fantoms!

An hour of tense anticipation had ended with disbelief. If Rodriguez and O'Hare had been last-gen aircrew, they would both have been dead, not sitting around trying to analyze how they had screwed up. But this was a new world, and that's what they had spent the hours after reporting their failure to NORAD doing.

They had pored over the mission data and uplinked it to NORAD for analysis. The answer that had come back had not been the one they wanted to hear. They had hoped they had been skewered by an older S-400 or even a ship-based missile system that had gotten lucky. But NORAD's analysts had pegged the system that killed them as one of the newest Russian Nebos, and that meant a simple stealth air attack wasn't going to cut it. Neither was Lavrentiya a likely target for cruise missile attacks. The US was not in a position to get overwhelming numbers of missiles on target, and at the distance they would have to launch, Russian satellites and radar would have ample time to bring up their defensive systems and fly their aircraft off. A ballistic missile attack on a Russian mainland target? Tensions were on a knife edge now and that was exactly the sort of thing that could tip the conflict over into nuclear war.

"There has to be a way," Bunny was saying. "There has to be."

"We don't have any long-range standoff missiles in our inventory, and they'd be detected anyway," Rodriguez replied.

"This is why we still have humans behind the stick," Bunny told her, determination in her voice. "An AI can't think its way out of this, but we can."

"The Ambassador did not appear pleased with my report," HOLMES said.

"No. Well, she was upset, but that doesn't mean she didn't want to know," Carl replied. Sometimes he had to pinch himself over the 'conversations' he was having with his natural voice neural network.

"My report made her cry," HOLMES observed. "Now she will not like me."

"You can't conclude that. Humans cry for a lot of reasons, and she may be crying at the information, without being annoyed at you or me for giving it to her. You should watch more films and see what sort of things make humans cry and how they react to those situations."

"Yes, Carl. Can I ask the Ambassador to rate my report? If she rates the source as 'reliable' still, I will know it has not impacted her assessment of me."

336

"No, not right now, HOLMES. Let her process it."
Process it? How do you process the knowledge that the father of your grandchild is leading the air war against your country. You could write it off and deal with it later, that would make sense. Or pass it up the chain, let people know it might affect your judgment.

"Carl, I have been running scenarios on the intelligence opportunities posed by the link between the Ambassador and Yevgeny Bondarev," HOLMES said. "They are immature but I would like to discuss them with the Ambassador."

Williams clicked his tongue. "No. You can discuss them with me first, and when they are mature we can decide who to discuss them with." He took a pull on his coffee, feet up on his desk. What he needed in this little broom closet was a nice big poster of a beach in Hawaii. His parents had taken him and his sister to Hawaii once and he would never forget it. That would help take his mind off ... end of civilization kind of stuff.

"Yes, Carl. I will send you the list of opportunities and risks I have created with associated probabilities, projections and exploitabilities."

"HOLMES, what's top of the list, ranked by 'exploitability'?" he asked, suddenly curious.

"Assumption: Bondarev knows about the child or can be persuaded the child exists. Assumption: Bondarev has feelings about the child and/or the mother. Opportunity: threaten to kill the child and/or mother if Bondarev does not agree to work as a US agent-in-place."

Carl nearly spat his coffee out of his nose. "HOLMES, let's keep these exploitability scenarios to ourselves for now. Confirm, please."

"Yes, Carl. Your eyes only, no uplink to NSA."

"And they are definitely not to be discussed with the Ambassador. Repeat."

"Yes, Carl, exploitation scenarios for discussion with you only," HOLMES said.

"Thanks. Log me out, please," Carl said, and closed his laptop. Was it his imagination or did the synthetic voice actually sound a little disappointed?

Following the column was an agony for Perri. It was mid-morning now after a fitful night of little sleep. Sarge had kept the call short, but he was pretty keen to tell them what to do.

"You both have to keep safe," he'd told them. "Remember this, okay? If you can see them, they can see you. In fact, they might be carrying infrared vision, so they might even be able to see you *before* you see them. If you are too close, you could go to sleep and never wake up because you got a 9mm Spetsnaz sleeping tablet."

"You want us to go back to Gambell?" Perri had asked, confused. "We could get our elders out, maybe you could arrange for someone to come and pick them up?"

"No," Sarge had said firmly. "They'll be okay until the US lands troops to rescue you. I need you to keep tracking those Russians. We figure they're going to meet up with the rest of their force, but we need to know where. We need a troop count. Images of defensive positions. They could be in Savoonga town, or maybe out at the Northeast Cape cantonment," he had said. "What's left of it."

"The Americans bombed Northeast Cape too?" Dave had asked.

"They did."

"Some of our people worked there," Dave had pointed out.

The Canadian Mountie was quiet. "Yes, I know. I'm sorry." He wasn't about to tell them the Russians had moved everyone in Savoonga town to the cantonment before the Americans had hit it. They would learn that soon enough. "Look, how easy would it be for you to fall back out of line of sight of the column, but keep following it?"

Perri thought about it. "Pretty easy. There's only one track along the coast, and no reason for them to go inland. There's
338

totally nothing south of here. And there's two hundred people in that group. They're leaving tracks so obvious even Dave could follow them." Perri winked at the other boy, who took one hand off the antenna and gave him a finger back.

"Then that's what I want you to do," Sarge had said. "Hang back where you're safe. Don't take any risks. Once they get where they're going, you call me again and let me know. Then we're going to really need your eyes and ears. There's heavy weather moving in, fog and rain for the next few days. We've got satellites over the top of you but they'll only be able to use synthetic aperture radar and heat imaging. Your Mark 1 eyeballs and that radio you're carrying will be the best intelligence we can get."

"Rain," Dave had said. "Great."

That had been last night. So they had waited until mid-morning before setting out after the column again, following the trail of boots and shoes scraping across the stone and ice and gravel of the coast track. It was about 11 a.m. when they came across Susan Riffet. It was Dave who saw her first, sitting a short way off the track to their right, her back propped against a rock.

"Hey," he said, grabbing Perri's arm. "Hey!" And he put his gear down on the ground, running over to her and dropping to one knee beside her. "Hey, Mrs. Riffet? You OK? Mrs. Riffet?"

As Perri landed next to him, he saw her eyes were closed and her lips were blue. Dave was shaking her shoulder. "Mrs. Riffet?" She was one of their teachers; a new one who'd come from Saint Paul, Minneapolis, about two years earlier. She was short and round and jolly and for some reason she thought being on Saint Lawrence was the coolest thing that had ever happened to her. She used to go for long walks with a camera, take close-up photos of plants and animals, and come back and show them to the kids as though every little vole or fox was a natural wonder. In summer she'd take them out with the elders, combining hunting and gathering trips with nature lessons. At times it had seemed she loved the island more than they did.

"She's dead, buddy," Perri told Dave, stopping him from shaking her any more. Her head had fallen down onto her chest and lay there like she was sleeping. Which, in a way, she was.

"Bastards," Dave said, and Perri realized he was crying. "The *bastards*."

Perri lifted her head and looked at her face. He lifted her arms too, looked at her hands, then let them drop. It didn't look like she'd been beaten up or been in a fight or anything. Then he remembered something. "She had a heart problem, didn't she?"

"Yeah," Dave said. "She used to take pills."

"Right. So it was a heart attack or something…"

"Why didn't she take her tablets with her?" Dave asked. "They wouldn't have stopped her, would they?"

"I don't know," Perri shrugged. "Maybe she ran out. The drug store got smashed, remember? She might not have had any for days."

Perri laid the woman out. He thought about burying her, but the ground was too hard for them to dig with their bare hands or the butts of their rifles.

"We can't just leave her," Dave said. "Foxes will get her."

"What about the beach?" Perri said, looking back toward the coast. Where they were, there was a low cliff that led down to a gravel beach. "We could dig there, if we can find a place above the water line."

"I guess," Dave said. "If we can find a way down with her. I don't see a choice."

Getting Mrs. Riffet down the short cliff face hadn't been easy. Dave had suggested just throwing her, because it was only about 20 feet, and soft gravel at the bottom, but Perri couldn't stand the thought of that. He'd suggested lowering Dave on a rope and Dave could carry her over his shoulders, but Dave said no way was he carrying a dead lady down any damn cliff on his back. So they compromised and lowered Mrs. Riffet down first, tied off the rope, then climbed down after her. It was a good beach for a burial, with a high portion of gravelly sand up above the tide line. As long as they came and got her again

340

before the next big storm, it should be easy enough to find her again. They'd put a pile of rocks over her body and a cairn of rocks up on the cliff line to make it easy to find their way back to her.

Using the butts of their rifles, they started digging a hole deep enough to cover her easily. Dave decided burying Mrs. Riffet on some random beach was easily the most messed up thing he had ever had to do in his whole life, and Perri told him if *that* was the worst, then he should consider himself damn lucky.

And while they were down at the base of the cliff, arguing about how bad life could get, Private Zubkhov caught up with them. They had dumped their gear well off the track, though, and Zubkhov wasn't stopping to peer over every little hill and cliff. He was jogging, an easy loping pace he could keep up for hours. The tracks of the column of hostages and Russian troops were easy to follow, and somewhere in its wake was that damn radio. As he drew parallel to where Perri and Dave were digging, he stopped and pulled a water bottle from his pack. You had to stay hydrated even though it was cold, because the humidity was so low. The wind was blowing from the northeast and he watched some seabirds surfing the uplift over the cliff, fascinated at how they hung in the air without even flapping their wings. Maybe he should have brought the Dragunov after all. It would be good practice to see if he could bring any of them down in mid-flight, bobbing and soaring like that. He thought about having a crack at one with his sidearm, then gave himself a mental slap. *Head back in the game, Zubkhov!* You have a radio to find and a radio operator to kill. You can get in some target practice later. He wondered if the Captain could still use a rifle. He seemed to be able to do stuff that was mostly instinct, like eating and going to the toilet, so why not shooting? Shooting should be second nature to a Spetsnaz Captain. Zubkhov would have to check that out when he got back.

Putting his bottle back in his backpack, his eyes sought out the scuffed dirt and ice of the coastal trail, and he set off again.

"Check this out!" Bunny cried, running into Rodriguez's quarters. She had gone to bed only a couple of hours earlier, after making her suck of a report to Coronado and then throwing around the problem of how to tackle Lavrentiya for hours. Coronado was worried about their attrition, with them now having lost four of their precious twelve drones on two missions, only one of which was successful. NORAD was re-evaluating its targeting list, they were told, looking for lower-value, less well-defended targets. They had called it a night. Or Rodriguez had thought they had. Apparently Bunny had said goodnight, and then kept combing through the intel on Lavrentiya.

It wasn't cold under the Rock. With no direct wind, and still mild days outside, the temperature at night inside the cave with all the equipment still powered up was a pretty reasonable 58 degrees, even without any heating on. Rodriguez was near naked under a light sheet and remembered this suddenly when Bunny snapped on the light, saw Rodriguez sit up, then quickly turned around. "Comportment, ma'am," Bunny said, a smile in her voice.

Rodriguez lifted a shirt from her bedpost and pulled it on. "Don't comportment me," she grumbled. "You're standing in *my* damn quarters at 0300. This had better be good, O'Hare."

The aviator sat down on the bed beside her commander. She had printed several satellite photographs and a table of data downloaded from NORAD. She spread them out for Rodriguez to see.

The images appeared to be bird's-eye views, enlarged, of some sort of Russian transport aircraft, flying over the water, and then in a landing or take-off circuit near the Lavrentiya airport. A final image showed two of the behemoths parked nose to tail on the newly built concrete apron beside the runway.

"Ilyushin IL-77s," Bunny said, excitedly. "Codename, White Whale. I was thinking, Ivan has to be getting all that material into Lavrentiya somehow, right? And if they're moving

342

it in, they must be planning to move it out the same way. Arctic roads in and out of Lavrentiya suck, and shipping would be too slow for the speed this war is moving at. Vulnerable too. So I started looking for intel on big transport aircraft at Lavrentiya. I figured they'd be taking the polar route from Murmansk, or a nice safe inland route out of Tiksi or Alykel..."

"Slow down, Lieutenant," Rodriguez said. "Let me catch up. We can't take down the base, so you propose we intercept a few big fat Ilyushins? It's a good compromise, but I can't see us impacting the war that way."

"Boss, we can *totally* take down that air base," O'Hare said, a big grin on her face. She shoved the printout of the table under Rodriguez's nose. "Ivan is moving a mountain of supplies into that base. Six flights a day, four hours apart. Like clockwork. And most of the flights are out of Murmansk, like I guessed." She dropped a map in Rodriguez's lap. "Northern polar route. They take off from Murmansk loaded with 200 tons of fuel, food, ammo and hardware, fly 3,000 miles, five to six hours. It's a single straight-in NW-SE runway so, depending on the wind, they approach from either the top of the gulf in the Northwest or the open sea between Saint Lawrence and us."

"You're going to shoot one down and take its place?" Rodriguez said, still trying to get onboard. "You'd have to fake their radar signature, IFF codes..."

"No, we don't need to do that. We can skate a couple of Fantoms in under its radar shadow. These freight flights aren't escorted, as far as I can see. Ivan is pretty confident right now, what with our Air Force 2,000 miles south and keeping to itself. So with that, and their big ugly Nebo on overwatch, they're sending in those Ilyushins fast and loose."

Now Rodriguez saw it. The IL-77 was a beast of an aircraft. In essence just a big flying wing, it was originally boasted that it would cruise at just over 1,000 miles per hour carrying a payload of up to 200 tons and had a range of more than 4,350 miles, meaning it could easily reach Lavrentiya from anywhere in Russia without refueling. Western analysts scoffed.

But when it eventually took to the air, the boasts weren't far wrong. It could indeed lift 200 tons, had the range that Russia had boasted of, and a cruising speed fully laden of 600 miles per hour. It made sense that if Russia was moving war materials into position within easy reach of Alaska, it would use its IL-77 fleet and not slow, easy to intercept shipping. "I smell you now, Lieutenant," Rodriguez said. "The IL-77 is going in on the glideslope, a few thousand feet up, and we put a couple of Fantoms down low in its radar shadow. If that damn Nebo picks us up, it will just read the return as something bouncing off the IL-77. A phantom return."

"Yes ma'am!" Bunny said. "Freaking genius or what? At *best* we lay some hurt on Lavrentiya Air Base and, if we include a couple of Cudas in the loadout, at *worst* we can take down a White Whale."

Rodriguez swung her bare legs out of the bed and reached for her flight suit. It was a little like the play they had used with success at Eielson, Bunny sneaking into missile range dressed as a light aircraft; the kind of play only Bunny O'Hare could have thought of. "Don't get ahead of yourself, O'Hare," Rodriguez said. "You can't pilot manually at that range so you have to come up with an AI kludge that will glue your Fantoms to one of those Ilyushins and keep them right where they need to be. You also have to sneak through a swarm of Russian fighters. And I still have to convince Coronado and NORAD this screwy idea is worth them committing a couple hundred million worth of hardware to!"

BARE BONES KICK ASSERY

"These photos are from the attack on Lavrentiya, you say?" Bondarev said, reviewing the report Arsharvin had just put on his desk. He had moved his 4th and 5th fighter regiments to the former US airfield at Savoonga to free up facilities at Lavrentiya for his heavy airlift and Okhotnik ground-attack aircraft. Both were equidistant from Nome, but Lavrentiya was his best-protected airfield, with standing fighter patrols and heavy ground-air missile defenses.

Wary of being buried alive again, Bondarev had put his new operations center on the ground floor of the modern Hogarth Kingeekuk Sr. Memorial School in the Savoonga township. With fast communication links and its own wind turbines supplying power, plus a field medical clinic already set up inside to treat the local townsfolk, it made a surprisingly suitable headquarters.

Ordinarily he'd say it was also an advantage that the 200 remaining townspeople of Savoonga were being held in the school meeting hall 'for their own safety', as it *should* dissuade the US from attacking the school for fear of killing their own citizens. But they had already shown a callous disregard for such humanitarian considerations.

"Yes. The photos show wreckage recovered off the coast from American drones downed by the Nebo-M array before the Americans could get their missiles away," Arsharvin said. He didn't sound happy, because he knew his commander wouldn't be.

Bondarev glowered. "More of your damn 'mobile Fantom units'? You still can't find the trucks they're launching off?"

"Analysis of the wreckage confirms they were Fantoms," Arsharvin said. "But they weren't truck launched."

"What the hell? The enemy has an operational airfield somewhere in this theater and we can't find it?"

Arsharvin had a photograph on his tablet. He pulled it up, pinched to expand it, and showed it to Bondarev. "We've solved the mystery. They aren't flying them off the ground."

"What is this?" Bondarev peered at what looked like a bent ski attached to a piece of aircraft fuselage.

"Landing ski-floats," Arsharvin said. "This is a Fantom variant we haven't seen before. Some sort of top-secret prototype, I imagine."

"A seaplane?" Bondarev frowned. "The Americans haven't fielded a combat version of a seaplane since... when?"

"The 1950s, the Martin P6M Sea Master," Arsharvin said, having expected the question. "But it makes sense, yes? You could launch it off just about any ship the size of a destroyer or bigger, land it alongside when it returned, and recover it by crane. They're already doing it with recon drones – this gives them a strike or air defense capability, extends a ship's eyes, ears and teeth by hundreds of miles. You don't need static airfields or a big carrier to fly them off – the smallest guided missile destroyer could carry it. Same concept as putting them on trucks, just sea-borne."

Bondarev had to reluctantly give his enemy credit. They were a generation ahead of his own country not only in the capabilities of their drones, but also in their application.

"Very well. Find me the damn ships these things are launching off," Bondarev said. "Compared to finding a few trucks hidden in the Alaskan wilderness, finding a ship launching drones in the open sea south of here has to be easy, right, Comrade Intelligence Chief?"

Arsharvin gave a wan smile. "If you say so, Comrade Colonel." He stumped out the door again.

Bondarev called out to his retreating back. "And attack options! I need a way to disable or sink that damn ship without starting World War Three!" He swung around in his chair and looked out of the window as one of the ubiquitous local four-wheel electric bikes that had been commandeered by his security group hummed past. They were slowly getting Savoonga airfield organized for the upcoming operation to land troops in Nome. The American cruise missile attack had devastated its long-range radar facility, no doubt because they were worried about what Russia could learn from it after it had fallen so easily and so intact into their hands. It was a state of the art long-range early warning facility, with radar arrays dotting the hills of Saint Lawrence all the way down the spine of the island to the site of the old Northeast Cape base it had abandoned nearly half a century earlier. With the improvements in communications achieved in the intervening years, the Americans now no longer had to have their command and control facility located right next to their radar arrays, so they had chosen to build up the airfield at Savoonga and create a small base comprising about fifty personnel just outside of the new village.

The base had given a big boost to the island's economy, provided civilian jobs, and made a posting to Saint Lawrence a little less like a prison sentence than it had been when the facility had been located hundreds of miles to the southeast. The US Air Force Savoonga Aircraft Control and Warning Squadron had been recommissioned under NORAD, a strike-hardened cantonment was built, with the command center and personnel barracks inside. New businesses and infrastructure sprung up in Savoonga to service the small Air Force detachment – a bar, a supermarket, a new school with fast satellite internet links, and even a new hotel to serve the needs of families flying in to visit the personnel stationed there. Savoonga had pulled younger people from Gambell, which is why there were more than 500 residents there when the Russian airborne troops arrived.

And why the most secure facility in the area to hold the residents had been the Savoonga cantonment, which US forces hit with enough high explosive to decimate the facility. And a large proportion of the personnel in it, including their own troops, who they knew would be there. And the civilians, who they claimed they didn't.

Bondarev couldn't imagine what the scene had looked like as the Russian troops who were left unscathed at the Savoonga airport had made their way into the ruins of the cantonment. They were only able to recover about 200 of 500 civilians alive, fifteen with serious wounds and five with minor wounds. Since then five more had died. The Russian airborne commander had estimated nearly 600 dead, including civilians, his own, and US troops caught inside the cantonment. Bondarev shuddered at the thought. The Americans had been lucky at Gambell that they had not hit the civilians there too. What sort of nation was it that would treat its own people with such callous disregard?

One to be feared, Yevgeny.

And yet their air forces were happy skulking down south, leaving their population in Alaska at the mercy of Bondarev and his pilots. They couldn't know he wasn't interested in attacking their population centers and had been reading reports of the National Guard ground forces in Fairbanks, Anchorage and Juneau hastily building defenses against a Russian ground attack that would never come. Bragging, in fact, about the fact they had downed several Russian aircraft, trying to bolster morale, when in fact Bondarev wasn't even flying missions over populated and defended areas like Fairbanks, Juneau or Anchorage. His only interest was to keep the Western Alaska skies clear of US fighters and attack aircraft, not to terrorize the local population.

Let them pile their sandbags as high as they wanted, let their anti-air missile sites ring their cities. Right now, there was only one threat to his dominance of the skies over Alaska and that was these damn pinprick attacks by sea-launched Fantoms. Anadyr had cost him both in men and material, and serious political capital. The Kremlin didn't seem to care about the numerous US probing attacks he had stopped in the south and east and they were ignorant of the strike on Lavrentiya that had been thwarted. All that seemed to matter to them was that the Americans had gotten through at Anadyr and that had been enough to cause political knees to further weaken.

The Americans had been lucky once, and not since, and Bondarev intended for it to stay that way.

All he had to do was hold them back for another two days. Looking out the window he couldn't help a small swell of pride at the activity he saw. These were *his* forces, these aircraft, these men and women.

With the death of General Lukin he had lost a patron, but he had not been relieved from his position – yet. Gathered at Savoonga and Lavrentiya under his command now were more than 150 aircraft of the Russian 3rd Air and Air Defense Forces Command of the Eastern Military District. In Lavrentiya, and dispersed through nearby towns, were nearly 10,000 airborne and special forces troops, and the material needed to support the operation to take Nome.

He realized he shouldn't let the pinprick attacks of the American drones bother him. A major air or ship-launched cruise missile strike was a greater threat and the one which his 14th Air Defense battalion at Lavrentiya was in place to prevent. Then there was the overhanging risk of a tactical nuclear strike, either against a target in the Operations Area, or against an unrelated target on the Russian mainland. The US had the assets in place to effect it, and Bondarev had the strike on Anadyr and the command vacuum it created to thank for the fact he was able to convince his superiors they should move on Nome as quickly as possible before it came. They may not care about the lives of a few hundred citizens on Saint Lawrence, but with the 4,000 citizens of Nome under Russian control, the US would *have* to start negotiating.

When the war had been about sea commerce, his attitude had been cynically professional. But now he knew he was fighting for the very survival of his nation, the fight had become personal.

The call from the State Secretary showed he was still an old-fashioned Southern gentleman, in the best sense of the concept. Devlin had always known that he would never break good or bad news to her in a communique or text. It always came in person. So when she was told to expect a call from the

349

Secretary in ten minutes, she knew it would be one or the other – either very good, or very bad news.

She paced her office nervously, ordering her assistant to stop anyone else from coming in or calling in, no matter how urgent they insisted it was. She knew she wouldn't be able to concentrate on a single thing until the call was out of the way, and any decision she made while distracted like this would be totally random.

Her mind raced. She was being recalled, that was one possibility. Perhaps Foreign Minister Kelnikov had complained one too many times about the directness of her language and approach, and had demanded she be called home. Or her own people had turned on her, called her out for running her own foreign policy agenda independent of State. That much was true – they had been pursuing a pointless appeasement agenda while she had been dealing with the reality of imminent invasion and trying to persuade her Russian contacts that the consequences of going down that path would be catastrophic.

And then there was this whole business of the Russian commander of the Snow Leopards being the father of her grandchild. She had *not* called her daughter about it. Like, how was that phone call supposed to go? *Oh, hello darling, yes, fine thanks. Tell me, did you have a child with the man who is leading the war against the USA?* No, but she was convinced HOLMES' discovery would not remain confidential. Whether or not it had already been leaked by him or Williams, it would be leaked, inevitably. That's what this call must be about. The Secretary would be nice about it, but he would expect her to understand they couldn't have someone in Moscow representing US interests who had such an obvious personal conflict.

When it came, the ringing of her encrypted comms unit nearly made her jump out of her skin. She took a big breath and lifted the handset.

"McCarthy," she said.

"Devlin, this is Gerard Winburg. How are you holding up?"

"Fine, thank you, Mr. Secretary. What's up?" she asked, and in the background she could hear the sort of burble of conversation that indicated to her that Winburg was in a room full of people.

"I have to keep this short, Devlin, I'm sorry. It turns out you were right. I have to advise you our satellites are showing a huge amount of air and ground traffic indicating military mobilization in the Russian Far East. We estimate at least one airborne division. Russia has now moved considerable air power onto Saint Lawrence in what we assume is preparation for a major airborne landing and offensive. The President is about to go public with this information and issue a warning to Russia to withdraw from Saint Lawrence and to cease its military build-up in the Bering Strait, or there will be 'catastrophic consequences'." He paused. "Between you and me, the President has asked the Secretary of Defense to draw up plans to conduct a demonstration of a nuclear-armed hypersonic cruise missile over the Pacific Ocean, east of the Russian Kuril Islands. He wants it ready to execute in 23 hours."

The world fell out from underneath Devlin. She'd had her own theories about the way the political winds were blowing, but she'd hoped she was wrong. "An *atmospheric* nuclear test off the coast of Russia?"

"Yup, and they should be thankful we're just vaporizing a few billion tons of seawater and fish. The President thinks Russia needs reminding why it should stay the hell out of Alaska."

"My God..." Devlin had no idea what to say. "What do you need from me?"

"Real-time readout on reactions. I'll get back to you with exact timing when I have it, but I want your people face to face with Russian key stakeholders when the news of the test drops. I want you getting their unfiltered reaction and then feed it with a single message – that we *will* use the nuclear option if they escalate further."

"We'll do our best here, Mr. Secretary," she said.

"I know it. In the meantime, get onto all of our so-called NATO 'allies'. Tell them now is the time for them to shit or get off the pot. We are calling in our markers and if they are on the wrong side of the next vote in the UN Security Council or General Assembly – and neutral *is* the wrong side – there will be hell to pay for them too!"

Bunny had checked the weather and calculated the best IL-77 flight for their shadow play would arrive at the top of its glide path over the Bering Strait southwest of the Rock at 0630 the day after she dragged Rodriguez out of bed. That gave them the night and most of the morning to prep two Fantoms with ground-to-air ordnance and get them in the air and on station in time for the low-level game of shadow puppets.

The Fantom didn't have passive detection systems like many Russian fighter aircraft, but NORAD had managed to get two new satellites on station over the Operations Area. One of them was National Reconnaissance Satellite L-70, launched in 2022 with the specific mission of tracking Russian and Chinese military aircraft in real time through their digital, infrared and visual signatures. Satellite L-70 could track up to 100 individual targets at any one time, and by AI interpolation could predict the flight path of 1,000 different objects simultaneously.

For the mission that had been assigned to A4, Satellite L-70 dedicated a small part of its considerable attention span to one aircraft, an Ilyushin IL-77 'White Whale' flight out of Murmansk it designated as 'flight IL-203'. It was tracking all IL-77 flights out of Murmansk, and tracked flight IL-203 in real time as the aircraft made its way across northern Russia. About halfway through the flight, the AI monitoring L-70 calculated a 73% probability, based on signals intelligence and the aircraft flight path, that it was headed for Lavrentiya, and it alerted NORAD, which alerted A4, or to be specific, Lieutenant Commander Alicia Rodriguez.

"You have a 'White Whale' incoming," Rodriguez told Bunny as her fingers tapped her touchscreen. "I'm patching the flightpath through now, plus coordinates for intercept."

"Roger that, ma'am," Bunny said, voice tight. If she was tired, then, like Rodriguez, she wasn't feeling it right now. "I'll be on them like a leech."

"You mean remora," Rodriguez told her.

"Sorry ma'am?" Bunny frowned, head lost in her multiple screens.

"*Remoras* attach themselves to whales," Rodriguez told her. "Leeches attach themselves to mammals."

Bunny didn't break her stride, just shot back at Rodriguez, "Isn't a whale a mammal, ma'am?"

"Land mammals then. You ever hear of a leech attaching itself to a whale, Lieutenant?"

"No, ma'am. Would I be correct in guessing the Air Boss is a little tense right now?" she asked, without looking over.

"Yes, O'Hare," Rodriguez told her. "Yes, you would."

"Chill, ma'am," Bunny said. "I have a vector to the target. Uh, eight minutes to intercept. Entering Nebo low band range in ten."

On a big screen in the middle of Bunny's weapons and navigation system heads-up display, Rodriguez was watching as the icon for the Russian transport plane appeared on the screen and began to track toward Bunny's two Joint Air-Ground Missile JAGM armed Fantoms. She had managed to flit above the wave tops over the Strait without being detected by Russian land, air or satellite-based systems so far, but the same threat vectors applied to this mission as previously. She could be spotted by any random Russian fighter flight that happened to look in her direction and get a lock, and within 30 miles of Lavrentiya she was at the mercy of the Nebo-M array which had so easily batted her out of the sky last time.

The go/no-go for Bunny had been whether she could come up with a combination of AI routines that would allow her Fantoms to lock onto the incoming Ilyushin and then hold position underneath it at wave-top height. To do it, she'd rewritten and combined the code for an optical targeting algorithm with a nap of the earth formation keeping algorithm meant for use with air-to-ground radar, but it had been impossible to test, so it would either work or ... the Fantoms would die. Most probably by plunging into the ocean as the Ilyushin began its landing descent.

"Got a visual lock. AI matching course and speed," Bunny said, eight minutes later. Rodriguez saw the two icons merge – the Ilyushin at 20,000 feet and descending, and the two Fantoms below it at wave-top height, flying in train, nose to tail, making them nearly the same total length as the monster above them but with a much smaller radar cross-section.

The communications between the tower at Lavrentiya and the IL-77 were encrypted, but the L-70 satellite could read the inherent pattern in them and reported to NORAD-NORAD-A4 that comms appeared normal as Bunny's Fantoms began gliding toward Lavrentiya directly underneath the track of the transport flight.

Inside the command trailer of Russia's undisputed ace Nebo-M unit – the only unit now with two confirmed combat kills – Lieutenant Colonel Chaliapin listened to the chatter of Lavrentiya air traffic control and watched on his own display as the 0640 transport flight from Murmansk began its approach. There was no enemy air activity in the Operations Area, and he reflected with some satisfaction that the US appeared to have given up any idea of trying to hit him in retaliation for the destruction of their aircraft two days earlier. Normally he would expect a 'wild weasel' air defense suppression attack or a cruise missile strike intended to target his radiation signature, and local air patrols had been increased in anticipation. But personally, he doubted the US had the resources in place for another strike this deep behind the forward line of control. The drone attack of the day before had probably been made with fighters piloted by an autonomous AI and sent on a one-way trip from a base

1,000 miles distant, which is why it had been so dumb, and had failed.

He could see no activity around the incoming IL-77, and there were no reported contacts from either Airborne Control or any of the 3rd Air and Air Defense Forces Command fighter patrols currently blanketing Western Alaska. This particular White Whale was safe.

But he had not become the leading Nebo-M unit in the Air Force through complacency. If the enemy planned to take this particular flight down, it would be getting in position to hit it now, when it was in its vulnerable landing phase, wheels down, flaps up, flying close to a stall and unable to maneuver.

"Low-frequency sector scan on the IL-77 now, 30 seconds," he ordered. Any stealth aircraft sneaking in behind the White Whale thinking it was going to make an easy kill was about to get a serious dose of radiation poisoning. He smiled. He freaking *loved* his job.

"Nebo in narrow beam search mode," Bunny said suddenly. "They're looking for us."

"They can't be," Rodriguez said, pointing at the NORAD feed showing the Russian fighter combat air patrols following routine patrol routes. "They'd be sending fighters your way if they were."

"OK, maybe not for us, but they're suspicious bastards," Bunny said. "No lock. Yet."

"Sir, I have… I'm not sure…" the systems officer of the Nebo-M said. "Here, look…"

Chaliapin bent over his system officer's screen. It showed an icon for the White Whale and, overlaid on it, the icon for a potential unidentified contact. As they watched, the system's AI wiped the unidentified contact from the screen due to 'low return, low probability'.

"OK, get ready to override AI," the Nebo commander said.

"But the UI contact has been wiped," the man pointed out. "It was a false return."

"You might trust your life to an AI system," the Russian commander said. "I don't. If you get another return like that, override and lock it manually."

He turned to another officer. "Keep all arrays in circular mode. The bastards could be using the IL-77 as a distraction, trying to jump us from a different direction." To himself he muttered, "It's what I'd do."

"Five miles to release point, ma'am!" Bunny said. "Goddamn, I never flew a combat mission so damn *slow!* Any slower, our birds will have to drop flaps and we'll lose stealth..."

"Easy, girl," Rodriguez said, letting all formality go. "Can you show me the White Whale?"

"Sure," Bunny said, swiveling her head to look at a virtual screen inside her helmet, tapping a touchscreen and then pointing to one of the overhead 2D viewing monitors. "Topside cameras." The view on the screen flicked from a forward view, showing water and a smudge of land, to the sky above the Fantoms. The transport swam into focus and looked like it was about to drop right on top of the Fantom.

"*Shit...*" Rodriguez said, holding herself back from grabbing Bunny's shoulder. "What's the separation?!"

Bunny looked down at her virtual-reality instrument panels. "Five hundred feet," she said. "If they evacuate the in-flight toilets, we're going to get wet, ma'am."

"Sir!" the systems officer called. "I have another return. Manually locking unidentified object. Entering 30-mile inner-ring range. Shall I bring the S-500 missiles up?" He sounded

356

unsure. "Whatever it is, it is congruent with the approaching aircraft. The Ilyushin will be at risk if we fire."

"No, that's the last resort. We can order the Whale to abort and go around for another landing, see if that shakes anything loose." He picked up a handset and prepared to call Lavrentiya air traffic control.

"It's on final approach," his operator said. "A go-around now would bring it nearly overhead anyway."

Lieutenant Colonel Chaliapin squinted hard at the screen. Overlaid on the IL-77 icon was a 'UI aircraft' icon. The two were blinking alternately, indicating the returns were completely aligned. The AI had decided the two returns were both from the same aircraft, not unsurprising given how close the huge transport plane was to water level. They were probably getting a double return – refraction of their radar energy off the aircraft onto the surface of the water and back. It happened.

But almost never.

"Dammit. Bring the missiles up and give me a full burst sector scan of that Ilyushin!" the battalion commander said. "I really don't like this."

If he was wrong, he might be about to blow away one of the biggest aircraft in the world, its crew, and 200 tons of war supplies. But it was the kind of call he relished.

"JAG-ems one through six away!" Bunny called. *"Air-to-air missiles one and two away!* Bugging the hell out."

From the weapons bays of her two Fantoms, six JAGM air-to-ground missiles dropped and accelerated toward Lavrentiya, just visible on the horizon. Right behind them, two Cuda missiles fell free, lit their burners, turned 180 degrees to clear the tail of their launching Fantom, and then sped over the top of it, headed straight for the White Whale wallowing along above them. It didn't stand a chance. Bunny's fighters spun on their wingtips, went to full burner and began active jamming to spoof any missiles that might be fired their way.

Chaliapin had done everything a human could do to defend the airspace over Lavrentiya. He had his sector scanning radar pointed directly at the source of the coming attack. He had his missiles online. He had his people on the edge of their seats expecting an attack.

As soon as he heard the systems officer call a warning, he knew all of this wasn't going to be enough.

"*Vampires inbound!*" the man yelled. "UI aircraft maneuvering. AI engaging!!"

Outside the trailer, from three sites around him, missiles leaped off their rails. But prioritized by the combat AI, they weren't aimed at Bunny's Fantoms, which were heading as fast as they could out of range of the Russian missiles. The Russian AI had sensed the existential threat and stopped tracking the two stealth fighters to focus on intercepting the smaller, self-guided JAGMs, speeding downrange at 600 knots. The firing inclination of the S-500 launchers meant that as they were mounted on the elevated hills behind Lavrentiya, their missiles had to begin diving radically almost as soon as they were fired if they were to have any hope of intercepting the JAGMs speeding in at wave-top height.

"Mayday from the Ilyushin, it's going down!" his operator called. He turned in terror, looking to Chaliapin for hope, but seeing none.

One S-500 missile made a proximity detonation and took out a single JAGM. Two others detonated behind their targets, to no effect.

Five JAGMs made it through.

The first and second hit in the center of the truck park and container yard outside Lavrentiya township. The yard contained mostly food and clothing, and the explosions were less than impressive.

The third and fourth hit targets that had been identified as probable fuel storage sites, and these caused an altogether more impressive conflagration, with a single huge fireball rising a hundred feet into the air. The explosion also rained burning debris over the town, causing spot fires in multiple buildings including a row of containers holding anti-aircraft artillery ammunition. One of them was in the process of being unloaded and the exposed AA shells exploded in a fan-like spread of armor-piercing anger, detonating one by one the other containers alongside them in a ripple that caused the air to quiver and sent out a blast wave that took out the windows of the five-story administration center two miles away. The final shed to detonate was at the end of the Lavrentiya airfield runway, and it sent shrapnel slicing laterally through three of the five temporary hangars housing Okhotniks of Bondarev's Fighter Aviation Regiment which were in the middle of being fueled and armed for the upcoming operation.

The fifth missile wasn't intended to cause massive destruction. It had been programmed by Bunny O'Hare to identify and home on the communications signature of a Nebo-M command hub, and the subsonic scream of its solid-propellant engine was the last sound that Lieutenant Colonel Alexandr Chaliapin, commander of Russia's premier anti-aircraft defense battalion, ever heard.

The last thought to go through his mind was, "I was *right*."

Bunny O'Hare had no time to celebrate.

She had nullified the threat from the Nebo-M, but it had not gone quietly into the night. Even as it fought to intercept the JAGMs closing on Lavrentiya, it was sending targeting data on the two Fantoms to a combat air patrol of two Su-57s circling overhead. Between the data from the Nebo and her own radical maneuvering, the Sukhoi pilots had no trouble locking up Bunny's Fantoms.

"Missile launch!" Bunny grunted. "Jamming, firing countermeasures." Rodriguez watched as she handed off countermeasure control of the Fantoms to their autonomous defensive AI, and tightened the grip on her mouse. The virtual-reality helmet around her gave her a near 360-degree view, simulating the view out of a cockpit. The two Sukhois were high on Bunny's starboard quarter and she ordered her Fantoms around to face them, staying low to the water, trying to force the Russian missiles to overshoot.

They did, missing her lead aircraft.

Checking the other Fantom she saw that the AI had spoofed the other pair of missiles too, either through jamming or by drawing them away with chaff and flares. The fact her machines were still alive told her the pursuing fighters weren't carrying K-77s – they were probably fielding older R-77s. She still had a chance!

She had two units in the fight. They weren't armed with anything but cannon, but that would have to be enough.

"I'm sorry, baby," Bunny said, taking her support drone off of defensive subroutines and commanding it to attack the nearest Sukhoi. "We all have to die one day."

It was the only chance she had. If one of the drones could engage and distract the fighters now dropping down on her rear quarter, the other might just have a chance of escape. In her downtime under the Rock, Bunny had 'tweaked' her drones' offensive AI settings, creating what she called '*berserker mode*'. When initiated, the AI would only execute maneuvers intended to give it a firing solution on an enemy. It would take no evasive action whatsoever, no matter how imminent the threat. And even after all ordnance was expended, unless she canceled the 'berserker' command, the drone would try to destroy its target by ramming it. With each drone costing upward of 80 million dollars, it wasn't surprising the designers of the Fantom's combat AI had not considered implementing anything like Bunny's berserker code. But Bunny hadn't felt bound by budget constraints.

"It would totally suck to lose both drones again," Rodriguez said, before she could stop herself.

"Understood, ma'am," Bunny said, dragging a waypoint across her touch screen and ordering her lead drone to bug out by scooting under the noses of the approaching enemy fighters. "Will try to avoid total suck scenario." The two Sukhois were dropping on her like sea eagles hunting salmon. She locked them up with her missile targeting radar, knowing it would set alarms screaming in their cockpits, even though she had no missile to fire. Her ploy was psychological. Their own AI would have told them by now that they were facing two drones. Human pilots *hated* drones. A drone like the Fantom had only a silicon life to lose, it could pull g's that no human pilot could, and it knew no fear. US air combat orthodoxy said that if you couldn't kill a drone with your first missile salvo, you should do everything possible to avoid getting in range of guns and short-range missiles. Bunny was banking that at least one of the Sukhoi pilots would lose his shit at the sight of her Fantom closing on him with a missile warning screaming in his ears.

There was no sign of that yet, though. As she tried to extend at least one of her Fantoms away from the oncoming Sukhois and let the other take the fight, a warning alarm filled the trailer and the Russians let fly with their *second* salvo of short-range off-boresight missiles!

Carl Williams of course knew about the planned nuclear strike before the Ambassador did. HOLMES didn't spend all of his time gathering intel for the Ambassador; he also had a considerable portion of his bandwidth devoted to keeping Williams up to date with military developments, with orders to break in on whatever Williams was doing (including sleeping) with a flash alert for any event involving actual or potential losses to either side.

Well before Devlin took the call from the Secretary of State, a small buzzing alarm from Williams' laptop was the signal of just such an alert. Carl had dragged a mattress down to his office, and had taken to showering in the gym and eating in the Annex's commissary. He hadn't see his own apartment for nearly two weeks. Nowhere else had the connectivity he needed to keep his uplink to the NSA HOLMES platform operating at full capacity.

He groaned, reaching an arm up from the mattress on the floor and batting the spacebar on his laptop. "Yes, what?"

"The time is 0100 hours," HOLMES announced. "I have a military sitrep for you."

"Go ahead," Williams said, rubbing his eyes. He could have HOLMES copy it to NSA, and the Ambassador if it was material. He'd probably insist on doing so anyway. HOLMES was still trying to get back into her good books after the Bondarev thing.

"Satellite, electronic and human source reporting from Saint Lawrence indicates that further elements of the Russian 3rd Air and Air Defense Forces Command have moved into Savoonga. The aircraft based there include both piloted and unmanned aircraft. DoD analysts conclude this has been done to extend their flight time over the southeastern area of operations."

"They've got Alaska pretty much to themselves then," Williams observed.

"I have seen no reports of anything except reconnaissance flights from US mainland bases in the last 24 hours," HOLMES confirmed. "However, there is a Navy covert air unit which has conducted two successful strikes on Russian mainland facilities in the last three days."

"What covert air unit?" Williams asked, his ears pricking.

"I only have the code name," HOLMES replied. "Its designation is A4. I am unable to find any other information about this unit. But I can confirm that three days ago it carried out a strike on Russian military targets at Anadyr which caused significant damage, including the incapacitation of a drone squadron of the Russian Snow Leopards Air Defense Brigade. I have just picked up a report from NORAD that about 30 minutes ago, the same unit apparently struck a Russian supply depot at Lavrentiya. Damage assessment has not yet been conducted, and I have no details yet on the fate of the attacking Navy aircraft."

"Get some, Navy!" Williams said, punching a fist in the air. "I'm guessing those Russian planes at Savoonga are going to be next on their Christmas list."

"That may be planned but is unlikely to be effected," HOLMES said. "I believe a US *Columbia*-class nuclear submarine has been ordered to a position off the coast of the Kuril Islands."

"*Believe?* Expand."

"I have used comms traffic pattern analysis to isolate transmissions to and from Pacific Fleet nuclear submarines and identified two signals I believe indicate a boat is moving toward the Kurils."

"*Columbia*-class subs carry long-range hypersonic cruise missiles, right?" Williams said. He could imagine tempers in Washington getting short. They might want to send a high-explosive ultimatum toward one or more Russian military targets.

"Yes. I have indications that other US nuclear submarines have also been ordered to readiness, although their posture appears more defensive than offensive. I have assigned a 78% probability to a tactical nuclear attack using hypersonic cruise missiles on a Russian military target by the nuclear submarine located off the Kurils." Williams was not sure he heard right.

"A nuke?!"

"Yes. I have a conventional weapons attack with subsonic cruise missiles or ballistic missiles at 54% probability."

"What .... what target?" Williams said in a strangled voice.

"Repeat your question please, Carl."

"Assume this is a political attack, not an attempt to start an all-out nuclear war. Assume the submarine is only going to target a single Russian base, or location. What are the likely targets for a submarine-based off the Kurils?" He had to believe that whatever this was, it was intended as a 'shot across the bow'. He couldn't believe his own country wanted to trigger Armageddon. Not over Alaska.

But then he realized, he was hoping exactly what the Russian planners were hoping, and hope was not a sound military strategy.

"Weighted for combined geopolitical and military impact – Iturup anti-ship missile facility 91% probability, Matua

Northern Fleet replenishment facility 73%. I also calculate a probability of 34% that the warhead will be detonated over a remote area in the Northern Pacific; however, this probability is low due to the limited military value of such an act."

Williams swore. He was shaken to his core. He had grown up in a world where the use of nuclear weapons in conflict was simply inconceivable. It hadn't happened since 1945. Sure, the world had come close to calamity a few times – the Cuban missile crisis, the Russian submarine malfunction, a US strategic bomber shot down by its own escort when it received a nuclear launch order by mistake. There were probably other events he didn't know about, but they were all accidents. Even in the heat of the proxy wars in the Middle East, when US-backed Turkish forces were being forced back out of Syria, nuclear weapons had never been considered.

But the world had let itself become complacent. Nuclear arms reduction treaties had lapsed and not been renegotiated. Politicians had more focus on the dangers posed by new technologies – hypersonic missiles, cyber warfare, AI systems, unmanned combat vehicles – and had all but forgotten about the first doomsday weapons. The number of nations with nukes had proliferated uncontrollably because no nation was willing to go to war over them before it was too late. North Korea had been the first example, then Iran and Saudi Arabia. Afraid of being left in the cold by weakening US commitment, Taiwan joined the nuclear arms club. And after the bruising it took at the hands of Russia and Syria, Williams had seen reports that Turkey was now starting its own underground weapons program, with the US turning a blind eye.

"Assume a hypersonic cruise missile strike. Have you run the numbers on how soon the sub will be within launch range?"

"No, Carl. Exact nuclear submarine location data is inaccessible even to me. But priority tasking orders are rarely issued more than 24 hours in advance."

"So it's going to happen *today*?" Carl whispered, still not believing it.

"There is still a 22% probability my analysis is wrong," HOLMES said. "It requires that I assign motive and intent to numerous human actors on both sides, but I have calibrated for the recklessness of past strategic decisions and, I believe, weighted the role of the US President appropriately."

Williams knew what HOLMES was saying, even if he didn't mean to say it. The current US President was a cowboy, in many senses of the word. Short in stature, short on temperament, inclined to shoot first and think later. *If* he had enough support in DC and the Pentagon...

He thought fast. "Copy your analysis to NSA," Williams said. "If you have been able to identify a possible nuclear submarine launch by analyzing signals traffic, Russia or China could have too. And copy the report to the Ambassador. She might be able to do something to calm down the hawks in Washington."

As much as it terrified him, it made a dark kind of sense. The US had been pushed ignominiously out of its own territory. Its most powerful supercarrier had been crippled by cyber-sabotage and its other carrier groups were out of position. It could fight a conventional war that would cost tens of thousands of lives, or it could threaten nuclear retaliation. And potentially cost millions of lives.

An idea came to him.

"HOLMES," Williams said. "I have a new priority-A task for you. Find all possible contact details for Yevgeny Bondarev: landline, cell phone, sat phone, encrypted chat, Savoonga bloody post office, whatever you can pull down." He had to stop his voice from shaking as the reality of what was about to happen starting building inside him. "Send everything you can find to the Ambassador's cell phone and mine."

"Yes, Carl."

"OK, keep updating your data on those subs and send that report. You can log off for now. No, wait!" he said, suddenly remembering something. It had been niggling at him. Not an important thing, just a question he'd meant to ask. "HOLMES, about the Russian forces at Savoonga… you said you had seen human source reporting?"

"Yes, Carl."

"We have special forces on Saint Lawrence?" Carl asked, impressed. "Right under the noses of the Russian 3rd Air and Air Defense Forces Command?"

"No, Carl," HOLMES said. "The human source reports are being generated by the Canadian Security Intelligence Service. It is their agent on the ground, not one of ours."

Canadian Security Service agent Perri Tungyan literally had his ass on the ground. He and Dave were camped on a low hill west of Savoonga, overlooking the town and the new base that the US had built nearly ten years ago, which, okay, you couldn't really call new.

Or more correctly, they were overlooking where the base *had* been. All they could see were the still smoking ruins of the cantonment. At least here, the Americans had spared the township.

Earlier that morning, they had watched as the weary column of townsfolk from Gambell and their Russian captors had trudged into Savoonga. Just as in Gambell, the townspeople had been herded into the Hogarth Kingeekuk Sr. Memorial School, which already looked like a stockade, so Perri figured there must be local Savoonga people in there too.

He didn't know how few.

About mid-morning, they had contacted Sarge. For a very long fifteen minutes they reported everything they could see from outside the town, from the number of troops and vehicles, their locations and apparent patrol routes, to the number and type of aircraft down at the airfield.

And that, in particular, had taken time, because they had to count them three times to get it right. In the end they made it about 45 fighter aircraft, mostly all Mig-41s and Su-57s as far as Perri could tell. There were some aircraft without cockpits that Sarge said were probably recon drones, not the bigger Hunter drones. And transport aircraft were coming and going almost continuously. There was one big one too. A huge, white flying-wing thing Perri had never seen before. It needed drogue chutes to slow it down so that it didn't run off the end of the airfield when it was landing, and when it took off again a couple of hours later it only lifted its nose at the very last minute before it ran out of runway. For what it was worth, he took some photos with his phone and uploaded those too.

"OK, that's good, that's good," Sarge had said. "Now, are you two safe where you are?"

"I guess," Perri said. "We're under a rock overhang, so you can't see us from the air. We can stay pretty dry. Without a fire, it's pretty cold though, eh."

"Pretty cold, or dangerously cold?" Sarge asked. "You guys know your country better than me. It's your call."

Dave was making signs like he wanted them to head back to Gambell, to their nice warm bunker under the gas station.

"Nah, we'll be OK," Perri said. "We can stick it out a couple more days at least. Then we'll be out of food, and probably battery too. It will take us three or four days to hike back to Gambell, or we can try to sneak into Savoonga. I've got people there." He looked through his scope at the Russian troops in the streets and realized he couldn't see any locals. "Maybe."

"OK, you'll be calling in reports like this for me every four hours, but you shut down and lie low for now," Sarge said. "You guys are doing awesome, you know that, right?"

"Awesome, yeah," Dave said, unconvincingly.

Perri disconnected the radio and started to pack it away so it wouldn't get wet. The wind was picking up and the sky looked like rain was coming. The small overhang they were sitting under wouldn't offer that much protection. Dave had been sitting with his rifle across his knees, but put it down and picked up Perri's, switching on the scope. He waved it around a bit, then settled it on some far-off target. He squinted. "What's these numbers across the bottom?" he asked.

"Uh, by memory? I think left to right it's like compass bearing, then elevation, then windage," Perri answered.

"Uh huh, and you got it zeroed in, right?"

Perri was winding up the battery cables. "Yeah."

"So, if I was going to shoot something, I wouldn't use the red dot in the middle of the scope, I would use these crosshairs off to the side. The ones that move around a bit?"

"You're not going to shoot anything," Perri told him.

"I said if I *was*," Dave said.

"Sure," Perri said. "You'd use the crosshairs, not the red dot. The bullet goes where the crosshairs are. That's the theory."

Dave got up on one knee and pointed the rifle downhill toward the town. "Like, if I wanted to shoot that Russian soldier who is coming up the hill, straight toward us?"

Perri grabbed the rifle off him and stared down the scope. At first he saw nothing. "Ha ha, very fu..." he said, then stopped. A movement in the corner of the scope caught his eye. He swung it slightly to the right.

"Shit. It's that guy from Gambell," Perri said. "The one we saw in the school office."

"No way."

"Way," Perri said. He lowered the rifle, then lifted it again. The soldier was too far away to see with a naked eye but in the scope he could see he had a large rifle strapped to his back, was moving fast and staring intently at the ground. "How did he get *ahead* of us?"

"Quad bike or something?" Dave said. "Maybe a boat or chopper, eh. But he's walking back along the track from Savoonga. So he's already been there, and now he's going back to Gambell? Why?"

"Maybe he's hunting."

Dave laughed. "Freaking idiot. What, he thinks he's going to get bear or walrus? Nothing out here this time of year except birds."

Perri put his own rifle back up to his cheek. "No, Dave, I got a feeling he's hunting *us*."

368

Private Zubkhov was cold too. But no one was giving him any praise. He'd followed the trail of the column of hostages all the way to Savoonga, but he hadn't come across whoever it was that had been carrying that ghost radio. If he'd gone on any further, he'd have run a risk of bumping into one of his old comrades, or a sentry outside of Savoonga, and he wasn't ready for that. So there was nothing for it but to double back. His quarry must have turned off at some point and he missed their tracks.

Suddenly he got this funny feeling. He dropped to one knee and looked around him. Nothing. He saw nothing but scrub, rock and seabirds in any direction. He felt like slapping himself. *Come on boy, you're getting spooked now. But you're right, that American is around here somewhere, he must be. You just have to be patient, move slower, stay more alert and wait for nightfall. He'll probably light a fire to stay warm, and you'll have him.*

Zubkhov didn't hear the shot. The shooter must have been upwind. He felt something punch him in the chest, just below his right shoulder. It spun him around and knocked him to the ground.

Bunny's berserker routine had done its job. The attacking Fantom had locked up one of the enemy Sukhois, spooking it into thinking it was about to face a US all-aspect short-range missile at point-blank range, and the pilot choked. He threw his machine into a twisting dive, firing off chaff and flares as he headed for the deck. The Fantom meanwhile centered its gun pipper on the other Sukhoi, which was following its missiles downrange. One Fantom was able to dodge the missiles fired at it, but her kamikaze Fantom did not even try to evade. At maximum range, it opened up with its 25mm cannon. It was a lighter version of the aircraft and ship-mounted heavy attack cannon that it had been based on, but the only thing 'light' about it was that it used 25mm ammunition instead of traditional 30mm. What it lacked in hitting power it made up for in accuracy – it had its own laser targeting system, making the system accurate out to 12,000 feet.

Which coincidentally was its exact distance from the Sukhoi at the moment it opened fire. In a head-on attack situation, against an unswerving enemy target confidently barreling in behind his missiles at 1,000 miles an hour, it was hard for the 25mm cannon to miss. In the three seconds before the two Russian missiles slammed into it, the Fantom put nearly 200 shells into the Sukhoi.

Its pilot was dead before his missiles hit their target, taking Bunny's sacrificial drone off the board.

With his flight leader off the air, and his threat warning alarm telling him there was still one enemy drone out there, the second Sukhoi pilot decided to get while the going was good. One on one with a human pilot, he would back himself any day. Down on the deck, out of energy and facing a damn robot, those weren't odds he liked. Bunny watched with satisfaction as he bugged out and she regained stealth status. She gave her surviving Fantom a dogleg route home to try to confuse any satellite surveillance that might be lucky enough to pick up her heat signature along the way, and leaned back in her chair.

"Permission to declare myself freaking *awesome*, ma'am?" Bunny said, grinning widely but keeping her eyes on her monitors.

During the dogfight, Rodriguez had hovered behind the pilot's chair, biting her bottom lip so hard she could taste blood now. It was ridiculous. *Not like my life was on the line.* But it felt like it. And that was the way O'Hare was running her drones too – as though her life depended on it.

"Denied," Rodriguez said. "You don't get to do that. *I* get to do that. That was simply awe-inspiring, Lieutenant. From ingress to egress."

"You know, ma'am, I agree with you," Bunny said. "What was it that inspired the most awe, in your personal opinion? Was it the way I snuck in under that IL-77 like a freaking ninja and blew it out of the sky, or was it the four solids I laid on

Ivan at Lavrentiya?" She spun her chair around, giving Rodriguez a deadpan look. "*Or* was it the way I burned that Nebo, evaded like a hundred missiles and bagged myself a Sukhoi-57 in the process?"

Rodriguez knew better than to say something that would bring her ace pilot back down to earth. It was O'Hare's moment, and she had earned it.

"Honestly?" Rodriguez smiled. "None of that. The most awesome thing of all is that all that hurt was laid on the Russians by an Australian pilot whose handle is 'Bunny'."

Perri saw the Russian soldier drop and roll, then he disappeared from view behind some low scrub.

"Did you hit him?" Dave asked, scanning the ground in front of them with binoculars.

"Yeah, I hit him," Perri said. Crouched on one knee, the Russian was not a big target. He'd aimed for the guy's center mass, not taking any chances. The shot had knocked him down, he hadn't ducked, of that he was sure.

"I can't see him," Dave said. "Should we go look for him? Make sure he's dead?"

"No, we should not go look for him, we should get the hell out of here. He might not be the only one looking for us. Someone could have heard that shot."

"You want to go back to Gambell?" Dave asked, hopefully.

"Shut up, I'm thinking." He and Dave were on a small rise, about two miles out from the southwest end of the long runway. Savoonga town was a ways off, on the other side of the runway. The bombed-out radar facility cantonment was south of it, about two miles southeast of the runway. It wouldn't have as clear a view over the town and airport as they had now, but they couldn't stay here, and they had to hide out somewhere. "Saddle up," Perri said, pointing at the ruins in the distance. "There's our new home."

He expected Dave to argue, but the guy just shouldered his rifle, lifted his pack onto his other shoulder and stood there waiting. "What?" he said, when he noticed Perri was staring at him. "You want me to congratulate you for taking down that Russian?" He walked off in the direction of the cantonment, muttering. "*I'm* the one spotted the guy. Shooting him was the easy part. I've shot sleeping walrus that were harder to shoot than that dumbass Russian..."

That dumbass Russian was having trouble breathing.

Lying on his back, looking up at the sky, Zubkhov had clawed his pistol off his belt and had its butt propped against the ground, left hand with a finger inside the trigger guard, ready in case the bastard who shot him decided to come and finish the job. He had almost no chance if he did. Zubkhov's right arm was completely numb, and he couldn't even lift the pistol, let alone hold it steady and point it properly.

The American was good, Zubkhov had to give him that. The way he'd escaped back in Gambell, diving straight into the water instead of being stupid and trying to run for it along the runway. Found a Russian radio and got it working. It had to be the same guy. He'd tracked the Russian troops all the way to Savoonga, somehow realizing Zubkhov was on his tail, got around behind and set him up for a hit at a range so great Zubkhov hadn't even heard the report of his rifle. Guy like that, he *couldn't* be a simple radar technician. He had to be at least base security or something more, maybe special forces – just happened to be in Gambell. Yeah, you had to give him credit.

But not too much credit. Zubkhov was still alive, for now. He waited, expecting every second to be his last. But the kill shot never came.

When he was sure the guy wasn't coming to confirm his kill – which either made him very cocky or very careful – Zubkhov let his pistol drop and felt around under his uniform. His shirt was soaked in blood: not good. But he could feel an entry wound at the front of his right shoulder, and a pretty damn huge exit wound at the back, which was where most of the blood was coming from. From a pouch on the leg of his uniform trousers he pulled a small field first-aid pack. Ripping open the foil with one hand and his teeth, he pulled out the sterilized gauze bandage, shoved the wrapping between his teeth, and then jammed the bandage as far into the wound in his back as he could. He had to stifle a scream, but he got a fair wad of gauze in there, and then rolled back onto it to try to keep some pressure on it.

He'd told Sergeant Penkov he was no medic. Zubkhov had basic combat medical training, though, so unfortunately he knew enough to realize he was hit pretty good, but his wound wasn't sucking air, so he hadn't suffered a punctured lung cavity. Hurt like hell, though, and it was bleeding pretty good. If the shoulder blade wasn't broken, the slug had taken a big chunk out of it. He could see blood pulsing out of the entry wound. He fumbled with the first-aid pack, trying to find the large plastic adhesive wound patch he knew was in there. Finally his fingers grabbed the thin film and he ripped the back off it with his teeth. Luckily he was one of those semi-neurotic guys who were terrified of battlefield wounds so he shaved his chest, arm and legs to get rid of hair. And yeah, some of the others had given him shit about it, but right now, right *now*, who was the smart guy, huh? Who was laughing now? He laughed out loud.

He realized his mind was wandering. The patch. He pulled the plastic film off the back of it and slapped the patch over the entry wound, then remembered something. Something, something. He was doing something wrong. He needed a pressure bandage on there too but was it supposed to go over the patch, or under it? Whatever. He put a wad of gauze over the patch and bound a bandage around his arm and shoulder as best he could with one hand.

Then he just lay back again. No point sticking his head up and flagging to anyone he was still alive.

Actually it was quite nice down here out of the wind. He closed his eyes.

BERSERKER ALGORITHM

Bondarev knew it was going to be an interesting day when the Savoonga tower called him to let him know that General Vitaly Potemkin's aircraft had entered Saint Lawrence airspace and would be landing in 15 minutes. Unannounced.

Potemkin was the commander of the Central Military District, 2nd Command of Airforce and Air Defense, so a courtesy call on a 3rd Air Army unit was not part of his normal remit. Bondarev sincerely hoped it wasn't the attack on Lavrentiya that had prompted the visit. Although it was the second time American aircraft had gotten through his defenses to hit a mainland Russian target, the actual damage caused by the American attack was inconsequential. Casualties had been light. Materiel losses were replaceable. The crippled Nebo unit had been restored to full capability within hours. It was a pinprick, nothing more.

He realized not everyone in the Air Army or back in Moscow would see it that way. Bondarev's Air Army network had told him the rumor was Potemkin was the one taking over after Lukin's death. Potemkin had been a junior officer under his grandfather and reported directly to him at one point. But he had served almost his entire career within Russia's borders and Bondarev knew almost nothing else about him. Once again he found himself walking a tightrope across possibly hostile seas. He could almost hear sharks snapping in dark waters beneath him.

Unlike Lukin, Potemkin did not fly himself around. As Bondarev waited for his Ilyushin 112 to taxi to a stop on the apron outside the old terminal building, he reflected it would be interesting to see who Potemkin had brought in the aircraft with him. A couple of staff lackeys would be normal – a GRU guards unit would not. He held his breath.

As the General and his retinue stepped out of the cabin and down the stairs, he saw someone he recognized. So, the indomitable intelligence officer, Lieutenant Ksenia Butyrskaya, had survived the transition from Lukin to Potemkin. But why had he brought her? Bondarev stood with hands behind his back and waited, his mind racing.

As he stood there, Arsharvin came panting up beside him. He looked at the man, busily adjusting his uniform and trying to catch his breath.

"You need to exercise more," Bondarev told him, still watching the General dismount with assistance from a ground crew. "You're getting fat."

"Easy for you … to say … Comrade Colonel," Arsharvin said. "You aren't answering your phone. I just sprinted … two kilometers."

Bondarev patted his pocket; he hadn't noticed the telephone ringing, but with the ever-present Saint Lawrence wind and the noise of aircraft out on the flight line, that wasn't surprising. "Why?" he asked.

"We found where the Fantoms are launching from," Arsharvin said. "Or actually *I* did, but I bet she's going to try to take the credit," he continued, pointing to Butyrskaya. "That's why I wanted to get to you first…"

Butyrskaya reached him before the General did, and saluted. "Comrade Colonel," she said. "I have a gift for you."

Bunny had flown her remaining Fantom into the maw of the cave and splashed it down onto the Pond. They had secured it to a wrecked handrail and left it there for now. Recovery, refueling and rearming was a time-consuming chore that would have to wait. In the meantime, they had locked another Fantom onto the catapult and had another prepped, queued and ready to go. The bomb damage assessment from Lavrentiya had showed significant damage to infrastructure, but the airfield was still in operation and they had made no discernible dent in Russian air strength. In a conventional war, it was a target they would be required to go back to again and again before it was considered non-mission capable – ideally before Russia got another Nemo command and control system in place.

But this was not a conventional war.

It had become clear to Rodriguez their job was only to keep the enemy off balance. To strike them where it hurt, and show them they were vulnerable. In the absence of a major US air counteroffensive, Bunny was providing a taste of their capabilities that should be giving Russian military and political commanders pause for thought. Rodriguez knew they wouldn't be the only pressure point in play, but she was determined that they would give Russia more than just a headache.

Their new tasking order, however, posed more than a few challenges. The first was that A4 was down to eight fighter aircraft, not including the one floating out on the Pond, and they couldn't afford to lose another. The second problem was the target they had been assigned.

"Savoonga? No problem," Bunny said, looking at the intel they had been sent on her tablet. "OK, so the Russians have moved in some heavy anti-air. Another Nebo system, multiple close defense anti-missile batteries." She looked down at the map and printouts on the planning table in the trailer. "And sure, they have two fighter brigades, totaling 60 plus aircraft on station now. Round the clock combat air patrols protecting the airspace for 200 miles around. That's all?" she asked ironically.

Rodriguez shoved another of the photos over toward her. "You forgot these." It was a satellite photo of a formation of ships underway.

Bunny frowned. "Oh, right. Sure, that's what, a *Lider*-class destroyer?"

"Arrived off the Savoonga coast in the company of two older *Sovremenny*-class destroyers yesterday."

"S-500 missiles?" Bunny asked, checking what anti-air systems the destroyers were fielding.

Rodriguez read the briefing file. "Fifty-six S-500 launch cells on the Lider, 24 missiles each on the Sovremennys. You know, it's like they don't *want* visitors."

"I know, right?" Bunny said, pulling at her lip thoughtfully. "I guess the David and Goliath trick won't work again."

"You can fool Ivan only once," Rodriguez said. "Fuel and ordnance is mostly coming in on smaller transports, and there's a big fuel freighter on the way from Anadyr, should arrive tomorrow." Rodriguez didn't mention it, but she could see from the source reporting on the intel that at least some of it was coming from a human source. They had a *spy* on the island feeding them real-time intel on airport traffic? Whoever it was, they had real cojones.

Bunny looked up. "Hit the fuel transports? All those combat air patrols they're flying, that's got to burn a ton of hydrogen. No fuel, no fly."

"That tanker will basically be sailing under fighter and naval anti-air cover the whole way. We won't get near it."

"Try their own strategy on them? Hit them with a slew of cruise missiles, overwhelm the air defenses, we ride in on the slipstream while they're shocked and confused?"

"I'm told we are on our own with this one, no available support assets."

Bunny tapped a pen on her teeth. "Cool. Way I like it." She moved some map printouts around like she was playing with a Rubik's cube. A long time went past without anyone saying anything. Finally Bunny stepped back from the table. "Shit, ma'am. There's simply no way to get in there with two measly Fantoms. I got nothing."

"Coffee," Rodriguez said. "I'm buying. You keep thinking."

Carl Williams was thinking too. Mostly, he was thinking about imminent global nuclear war. He was also thinking about a girl in Idaho called Kylee Lee who he had started building a real relationship with about two years ago. And how Kylee had asked him not to take the posting in Moscow, to leave the NSA and just come and do 'some sort of IT stuff' in Boise, because that's what normal couples did. In Kylee's world, normal

378

couples didn't just give up everything and move to China and then Russia because their country asked them to, even if they were one of the world's leading experts in machine learning.

And then he thought how he had asked for some time to think about it and how Kylee had said *"whatever,"* and things had just gone more and more wrong after that and now he found himself in Moscow, still with the NSA, and with no Kylee.

And he couldn't help thinking how, when you sat here at what might just be the end of civilization, you realized how freaking dumb you were.

He was still sitting there beating himself up about it when he saw an embassy Marine security guard stick his head around his door. "Carl Williams? That you?"

He stuck up a finger. "Present."

"Can you come with me, sir?" the guard asked.

Carl levered himself up and followed the Marine's back through a maze of Annex corridors and then up some stairs. "Can you wait here, sir?" the man said, leading him into an empty office. The Marine was young, maybe twenty. Carl found himself hoping the man made it to twenty-one.

"What's this about?" Carl asked him. "Just curious."

"I don't know, sir," the man said, and left him standing there. Carl looked around the office. He was in the commercial section, that much he could guess. Someone's office, family photos on the wall, a few pictures from European holidays. Brochures from US companies sitting on a small coffee table. OK, no clues here.

A minute later, Devlin McCarthy walked in.

"Hi Carl," she said simply.

"Hi ma'am," Carl said. He always felt like he was in the presence of one of his old school teachers when he was with her, and he'd gone to a very strict school.

From the pocket of her jacket she fished out a telephone and held the screen out to face him. "What is *this*?"

Carl looked and could see it was the list of contact numbers for Yevgeny Bondarev that HOLMES had sent to McCarthy before the lockdown.

"It was just an idea," Carl admitted. "I thought you might..."

"You seem to know everything before I do, so I guess you know how freaking busy I am right now," Devlin said. "I can't even call my own daughter. Why would I call this guy?"

"I didn't really think," Carl said, shrugging. "But the guy is leading the Russian air offensive over Alaska. I was thinking, what if someone were to call him and warn him that if he doesn't pull his planes back to the other side of the Bering Strait before three o'clock, we're going to nuke Kaliningrad?"

"A call from his *enemy*? If he even picked up, which I doubt, he would hang up in a flash," Devlin said. "Besides, we're not going to nuke Kaliningrad," Devlin continued, frowning. She worked on the assumption now that she could share any intelligence she had with Carl, because he had clearances she didn't even know existed. "But we *are* going to conduct an above-ground nuclear detonation in the Pacific off the Kuril Islands."

"You're sure of that?"

"It's what I've been told."

"And State wouldn't lie to you."

"Why would they lie to me?" she asked.

"Oh, I don't know, maybe because if they told you the truth you would tell everyone in the Embassy to take the rest of their lives off, call their mothers or see their priest before the world ended?"

"What are you talking about?" she asked.

Carl laid out HOLMES' analysis of nuclear submarine movements and signals traffic for her. "It adds up to more than just a test. We are getting ready in case Russia wants to take this all the way. All it would take is a tiny miscalculation."

Devlin realized he was right. "Dammit, Carl!" she said. "What do you think *I* can do about it?!"

"Call Bondarev, tell him unless he pulls his aircraft back, he's courting Armageddon."

"And he'll take my call because why?"

"Duh. You're Ambassador to the Russian Federation *and* grandmother to his child?"

She shook her head. "I can't. It would be treason."

"Is there still a death penalty for that?"

"I assume so."

"Vasily Arkhipov," Carl replied.

"What?"

"Commander of a Russian missile sub flotilla. Risked a death penalty but single-handedly prevented one of his captains from firing a nuclear torpedo during the Cuban missile crisis when he refused to authorize the launch. Saved the world, faced a court martial."

"Is this supposed to encourage me? Because it isn't working."

"He was found not guilty, returned to service and eventually received a medal. Posthumous."

"Still not helping," Devlin said.

"It's a phone call! You call the guy, you tell him who you are, maybe it works, maybe it doesn't. Best case, it does, and you go to court. Worst case, global nuclear Armageddon!"

"I'm going to call an officer of the Russian Air Force currently on frontline duty and somehow sweet talk him into surrendering because of some fling he had with my daughter two years ago and a child he probably doesn't even know he has?" she said.

"No, of course not, but it might mean he'd take your call. And if you tell him the consequences are global nuclear Armageddon?" Carl pointed out. "Maybe he's another Arkhipov."

She thought about it.

"Every word I say on my phone, anything on any Embassy line, is monitored. Can you set it up through HOLMES? If we do this I can't waste time leaving messages on his cell or with his damn secretary. I need to know I'll get through."

"If he's contactable, we can get the guy on the line," Carl said.

Devlin paused. "I can't believe I'm about to give our war plan to our enemy," she said.

"If it helps," Carl said, "blame me later. I'll blame it on HOLMES."

She was still holding up her phone and a tinny British voice interrupted them. "I heard that, Carl."

The smell hit Perri before he saw the first body. He'd seen dead Russian soldiers through the scope of his rifle lying on the streets of Gambell after the attack there, but not decomposed like this. It wasn't actually a body, it was a leg, buried under some rubble, that he assumed belonged to a body somewhere. This body must have been too hard for the surviving soldiers to recover, so they had been forced to leave it there and had just covered it with a tarpaulin. In the middle of the compound they found what looked like a mass grave, with smaller graves beside it. The smaller graves had small wooden crosses with a double horizontal bar on them and Russian names written in the middle. Most of these had small metal dog tags with rounded corners and Dave cupped one in his hand, reading it. It had a bunch of letters across the top, and numbers underneath. He dropped it and looked across the burial site.

"If these smaller ones are military graves, what are those big ones?" he asked, pointing to two long scars in the earth, each about a hundred feet long, with soil two feet high heaped on top.

"I have a bad feeling those are … non-military," Perri said, unable to say what he was really thinking.

"It's like they were dug with an earth mover," Dave said, looking up and down the rows of earth. "They just piled the bodies in there and pushed the dirt on top?" He started walking along the grave and saw a sneaker toe sticking out. He pulled at it, and it came free. It looked like a child's size. A bit further down, he bent down and picked up a telephone with a busted screen. He tried to turn it on, but it was dead. All along the graves were other small items – a plastic bead necklace, a single walrus ivory earring, a man's jacket turned inside out, a bloodied shirt. "Who *did* this?" Dave asked.

Perri's face showed nothing. "Does it matter? Russia, America ... neither of them gives a damn about us, man. Come on..." He pulled at Dave's sleeve.

Dave jerked away. "It matters. These are *our* people!"

Perri pointed at the Russian graves. "And those are theirs."

Beyond the graves, Perri saw what looked like a water tower that had somehow survived the bombing. It was about ten feet high and sitting on four wooden legs, one of which was shattered. The round water tank on its platform had been perforated in a hundred places and the water inside had long ago emptied itself out. But climbing up the ladder on the side, Perri pulled aside the manhole on top and saw that they could both fit through it and get inside.

He called down to Dave. "Hand me the gear. I found our hiding spot."

Private Zubkhov woke, remembered what had happened to him and pried himself up from his hiding spot. Which wasn't really a hiding spot, more just the bush he'd fallen behind after he got shot. He'd fallen asleep, or passed out; one or the other, or both. His uniform shirt and jacket were stuck to his back, but the blood was mostly dry. The entry wound had also stopped bleeding. His right shoulder was frozen and any movement of his right arm sent a stabbing pain up his side and neck, so he had to hold the arm in tight against his chest. He picked up his Makarov, put it in his belt and looked around. While he'd been lying on his back and before he'd gotten up, he'd decided on a new plan. He needed medical help, and the only place to get it was Savoonga. But he'd been ordered to stay in Gambell. OK, so this was his story now: he'd spotted the ghost radio signal, realized the Russian column was being followed, suspected it was US forces. Remember the radar unit jacket he'd found at Gambell? He felt responsible. He'd let that American escape, he felt a duty to try to capture the American again. Except he got ambushed and wounded – that much was all true. What about the wounded back at Gambell, what about the civilians? Yeah, that was the tricky part. But that is where the Captain came in, and it made Zubkhov so glad he hadn't killed him along with the others. He'd just say the Captain had seemed to recover, mentally at least. He'd given Private Zubkhov permission to go track the American, said he'd look after the wounded and the civilians.

What happened after that Private Zubkhov couldn't explain. He'd act shocked. They were *dead?* All of them? Wow, it must have been the Captain's work.

Maybe they'd buy it, maybe not. It was his only choice now. The fishing trawler, that would have to wait until he was well again, but a wound like this? They'd *have* to evacuate him.

Every step was agony, but he began picking his way down the hill toward the town below.

And that was when, silhouetted against the sun behind the bombed-out cantonment south of the town, he saw a figure, climbing up a ladder.

In the office he'd cleared for himself in a building beside the Savoonga airport terminal (a grand name for a big, roughly partitioned shed), Bondarev was standing with Arsharvin up against a cold side wall, while General Potemkin sat at the only desk. Potemkin had advised them he was now taking over the 3rd Air Army after the death of Lukin, as Bondarev had expected, but that was not the main reason for his visit. Butyrskaya had laid a map out on the desk.

"Little Diomede?" Bondarev asked skeptically. He'd flown over the tiny island a dozen times, and there was nothing there but a small American radome. Now even that... "We hit that on the first day," Bondarev said. "I've seen the damage assessment. There's nothing left on it but a black smudge."

"Not *on* it, Comrade Colonel," Arsharvin said. "Under it."

Butyrskaya looked annoyed that he had taken her thunder. "As you know, commercial shipping through the Bering Strait has been halted during the current conflict, but smaller coastal fishing vessels have defied the restrictions. Three days ago we got a strange report from one such vessel, which advised the Coast Guard it had seen an aircraft flying out of the cliff face on the eastern side of Little Diomede."

"The report was ignored," Arsharvin said. "By Eastern Military District. I never saw it."

"Yesterday, Comrade Arsharvin asked for any reports we may have received of American commercial shipping north or south of the Strait large enough to launch a drone from. I asked him why. He shared with me his theory about the drones that hit Anadyr and Lavrentiya being amphibious..."

"And you remembered the report from the fishing boat?" Bondarev asked.

"I told her, the drones didn't have to be ship launched. They could maybe also take off from a harbor. A boat yard or something," Arsharvin said.

"I pulled satellite surveillance for the three weeks since your Okhotniks hit Little Diomede. I only have digital still imagery, no infrared or synthetic aperture. It hasn't been a priority surveillance zone, and a lot of the days were foggy," she said, reaching for a folder on the table. From it, she pulled a single image. "But this is from yesterday."

The image showed a jelly bean-shaped island from above. It had a flat, plateau-like top and in the middle of the plateau was the cratered radome that Bondarev had mentioned. A number of wrecked fishing boats lay submerged in a shallow harbor on the concave side of the island, and just to the east of these a small blurred shape was clearly visible. Something shaped like an arrowhead, moving fast.

Bondarev peered at it closely. It could be a Fantom, caught in the act of launching.

Or it could be nothing.

He looked at Butyrskaya, arching his eyebrows. "You must have more than a drunken fisherman and a blurred photograph to have dragged the General all this way?"

"Oh, she does, Comrade Colonel," Potemkin said, enjoying the reveal. He nodded to the intelligence officer. "Show him."

Now Arsharvin stepped forward. "Allow me. It was *my* drone that took the photograph."

"At my request," Butyrskaya pointed out.

Potemkin sighed. "If you don't mind…"

Arsharvin raised his hands in defeat and stepped back as the photograph was placed in front of Bondarev. It was the same island, taken from above, but from a much lower altitude. The time and date stamp showed it had been taken mere hours ago. It took him a moment to see the difference.

Floating on the water, hidden among the smashed and sunken fishing boats, was a US Fantom drone.

The decoy had been Bunny's idea. Of course.

Rodriguez had returned with two steaming mugs of coffee to find O'Hare sitting with her feet up on her console desk and a big smile on her face.

"We can't hit them on the ground, so we have to take them in the air," Bunny said. "I think Sun Tzu said that."

Rodriguez sat and handed her a mug. "I'm pretty sure they didn't have air warfare in ancient China," she said. "Unless he was talking about kite fighting?"

Bunny leaned forward. "Or that von Clausewitz guy. Anyway, if we try and go anywhere near Saint Lawrence, we are going to get swatted, right?"

"Correct, whether we go for them on the land or in the air," Rodriguez said. "So?"

"So the biggest problem isn't the 50 enemy fighters, it's the damn ground and ship-based anti-air. But what if we lure them up *here* to Little Diomede, out of range of their anti-air cover?"

She looked at Rodriguez like she had just laid a golden egg. "Snap. Problem solved."

"Two brigades of enemy fighters still sounds like a big problem to me," Rodriguez said. "When we can only launch two fighters at a time."

"Sure, *if* we only launched two at a time," Bunny said. "But we have to lift our ambition level, Air Boss."

"Even three, or four," Rodriguez said. "Against 50?"

"Yeah, what I'm thinking – we launch them *all*," the pilot said. "How many do we have?"

Rodriguez thought about it. "We have nine Fantoms, including the one docked on the Pond."

"Ordnance?"

"Plenty. We could go with Cuda loadouts on all of them if we wanted to."

"We don't," Bunny said. "Say seven carrying Cudas, two configured for electronic warfare."

"That's nine in total, O'Hare. Every machine we've got. Even with two full crews down here, we couldn't pre-flight, load and launch any faster than one machine every five or ten minutes. We've been averaging two prepped and launched in an hour, you and me. A Fantom only has a one-hour duration at combat airspeeds, so by the time we got the next two up, the first two would have to come back down again."

"I know, but what if we *weren't* bringing any down? And what if we weren't doing any pre-flight or quality? What if I programmed every drone to autonomous flight, set it to mount a combat air patrol overhead, and you and I are out there on the catapult, pulling down drones, locking them into the Cat and just firing them into the air as fast as that conveyor belt can deliver them? Two Fantoms set to jamming mode, make life hell for Ivan's targeting systems, alert him that something is up so he comes sniffing around – the others are loaded for bear, with aggressor code activated. They'll kill *anything* that comes near us."

The words 'no pre-flight, no quality' were just not in Rodriguez's lexicon. She was an Air Boss; her job was to ensure

387

the aircraft got off the ground and back down again safely. She bit down on her natural instincts. "The Cat can fire and recharge every five minutes, theoretically. I've never pushed one that hard. Something is going to fail – the shuttle, the power supply, hydraulics, something mechanical say – it's inevitable," she said.

"Best guess, then, how many can we get up, inside an hour?" Bunny persisted.

"Say 60%, about six of nine," she said.

"Good enough. So we get a couple electronic warfare Fantoms in the air on overwatch, and then we start firing off the Cuda-armed Fantoms, set them to form a fighting hex. Any Russian comes near us, it will be like flying into a wasp nest. I tell you, ma'am, if we can get them here, and if you are willing to commit *all* our hardware, we can give Ivan a kicking. A lot worse than if we try a ground attack on a heavily defended air base."

"Eyes in the air won't be enough," Rodriguez said. "You need a way to attract their attention, get them to sortie against us in squadron strength. If they pick up the radar noise of a couple of Fantoms buzzing around overhead they'll respond proportionately – just send a few fighters over to take a look."

They both sat thoughtfully. Perhaps Bunny's plan was all holes and no cheese.

The only sound came from the wash of water on the dock below, and the occasional slap of one of the painters holding the Fantom from the Lavrentiya mission, tied up below.

Bunny snapped her fingers and pointed at it. "That's it. We pull that Fantom outside and tie it up in plain sight. Unless he's blind and completely dumb, Ivan is going to see it sooner or later, probably sooner, all the trouble we've been making. I can set up a data link, set it up to radiate – use it like a mini-radar base station. Two Fantoms in the air pushing out energy, and one on the deck acting like a ground radar… that's got to get them *real* curious."

For the first time, Rodriguez started to believe it might work. It would cost them everything they had, but it could set

388

Russian ambitions back on their heels. If they could destroy just two Russian aircraft for every Fantom they lost, it would be a significant loss for Russia. Pilots lost over this part of the Strait would probably not make it back, even if they survived the destruction of their aircraft. It was a big sea, and cold.

"It's a plan," Rodriguez said. "It might even be a damn good one. I need to clear this with Coronado. We'd be burning this base for good."

"Navy already wrote us off, ma'am," Bunny reminded her. "We were decommissioned and on a sub to Nome a week ago."

"I'll make the call," Rodriguez said. "You start pulling that decoy duck down toward the cave entrance."

That had been in the morning. After Anadyr and Lavrentiya, Rodriguez had some credit in the bank, so when she argued they'd already pushed their luck beyond expected limits, Admiral Solanta had given them a green light for one last roll of the dice. He authorized them to commit all of their remaining aircraft and send any survivors east to Juneau's civilian field.

"I can't lift you out of there anytime soon, you know that, Lieutenant Commander?" he'd asked.

"We do, sir," Rodriguez had replied. "But using this base as a honeypot is our best chance of dealing some serious hurt."

Solanta approved because he knew something Rodriguez didn't. If her plan worked, she would be dealing a big blow to Russian air power in the Operations Area at the same time as it was being dealt a political shock by the test off the Kurils. Together, the double whammy might be enough to check Russian ambitions.

They had paddled the floating Fantom out into the bay and lashed it to the mast of a sunken fishing boat. It hurt Rodriguez sorely to leave it out in plain view, but that was the point. While Bunny set up the Fantom as a ground-based early warning radar, Rodriguez went into the automated launch delivery system and queued up every aircraft they had. She set up the launch sequence as Bunny had described, with two electronic warfare Fantoms, followed by six dedicated air-air Cuda-armed Fantoms. The aircraft would be automatically fueled and primed for engine start, loaded with either jamming pods and/or air-to-air ordnance. And Bunny had configured the electronic warfare Fantoms with her 'berserker' combat AI algorithm. They might be light on weapons, but on her command they would do everything in their power to lock up an enemy and destroy it, and once they were out of missiles and guns, they would become the ordnance!

BERSERKER ALGORITHM II

"This American covert base has cost you hundreds of men, dozens of aircraft, tons of supplies," General Potemkin said.

"Comrade General," Bondarev explained, "Lavrentiya was a mosquito bite. Unlike at Anadyr we lost only a few personnel, and no critical capabilities. Our Nebo-M unit was operating at full capability again within ten hours of the American strike. I have already given orders for a reorganization of our ground strike forces. There will be no impact on ground support for LOSOS."

Potemkin looked unimpressed and Bondarev could sense his second in command, Colonel Artem Akinfeev, shifting his weight nervously beside him. "You misunderstand, Colonel. First Anadyr, now Lavrentiya. These attacks have cost the Air Army political capital, and the respect of our peers. I want to see this American base dug out from under that island and obliterated."

Arsharvin was looking at the map of Little Diomede. "If they can fly a drone out of a hole in that cliff face, then we can put a missile down their throats, General."

"It would be better to land a detachment of special forces," Lieutenant Butyrskaya said. "They could deal with US security, secure the base. There may be valuable intel, not least examples of these new amphibious drones."

General Potemkin coughed. "I commend the Comrade Lieutenant for her professionalism. However, we can glean whatever intelligence can be gleaned from the burning sunken wrecks of these American floatplanes. I do agree, though, that special forces will be needed to ensure the complete destruction of this base. We don't know what is in there, or how it is defended." He turned to Bondarev. "Colonel, I authorize a combined-forces attack on Little Diomede immediately. You will use whatever assets are required to eliminate the threat and achieve the complete destruction of the enemy base."

"Yes, General," Bondarev said. "I'll lead the air attack myself."

Potemkin appeared to think carefully. "Ordinarily I would say your place is here, overseeing our operations over Alaska. But within these walls, Comrade Colonel, a newsworthy victory wouldn't hurt you right now. No one is blaming you directly for the losses these US aircraft have inflicted behind our line of control, but..."

"But they are..." Bondarev finished for him.

Potemkin gave him a wry smile. "We move on Nome in three days. These pinprick attacks have not impacted the schedule for LOSOS, but they must be stopped."

"I'll see to it," Bondarev assured him. He turned to his second in command, Akinfeev. "You know what to do, get the wheels in motion." He turned back to Potemkin. "And if the Americans dare come north against us, I *will* hold them back."

"Good, good. Tell me, Colonel, is there anything you need?" Potemkin asked, expansively. "I can't magically make a replacement squadron of Hunter pilots available, but how about fuel, weapons, food?"

"Yes, Comrade General. I do have one request," Bondarev said. "A squadron of Fantoms."

Potemkin glowered at him. "Very droll, Colonel." He nodded toward the others. "Comrades, would you leave us for a moment?"

Butyrskaya smirked as she left the room, Akinfeev looked mildly panicked, and Arsharvin shot him a look of sympathy, none of which reactions were particularly helpful. "Sit, sit," Potemkin said, indicating the chair opposite him and pulling his coffee cup closer. He watched as Bondarev seated himself, and waited a beat longer, looking into his eyes. "I served under your grandfather. You don't look much like him."

"I'm told I get my looks from my mother, Comrade General," Bondarev replied, carefully.

Potemkin raised his eyebrows. "Really. And how about your loyalties, Bondarev? From whom do you take those?"

"My ... what?" Bondarev replied. "I'm sorry, I don't understand the question, General."

Potemkin looked out a window, as though regarding the dark sky. "I've followed your career from afar. Progress Party darling. Lukin's protégé. But the Party is not what it once was, and Lukin is ... no more." He waved his hand at the window. "A storm is gathering. When it breaks, where will your loyalties lie?"

Bondarev frowned. "My loyalties are with our homeland, with the *Rodina*, Comrade General. Is that in question?"

"Ah. But the *Rodina* is many things, is it not?" Potemkin said enigmatically, turning in his chair to drill Bondarev with his gaze again. "Not just one thing. It is the earth beneath us, the sky above, the songs we sing and food we eat. But what Russia really is, *who* we are, depends on who leads it. Would you agree?"

If there had been witnesses to this conversation, Bondarev would be suspicious he was being led into a trap, to committing an error of speech that could be used against him. But only himself and Potemkin were present. This was something else and he decided neutrality was his best play until he could work out what.

"My grandfather frequently used a quote to sum up how he felt about serving in the Air Army, General," Bondarev said. "I have lived my life by those words. With your permission?"

Potemkin raised an eyebrow. "By all means."

"He used to say, '*Duty, Honor, Country. Those three hallowed words reverently dictate what you ought to be, what you can be, and what you will be*'."

Potemkin smiled. "Yes, I think I remember him saying that. A quote from Lenin, was it not?"

"No, Comrade General, it was Douglas MacArthur, I believe. If there is nothing else, I must attend to the matter of Little Diomede."

"Something big is going down," Perri said. "Hook up the radio, will you?" He had taken the scope off his rifle and was peering through a shrapnel hole in the water tank, which was easier than looking through one lens of the binoculars. He and Dave had made themselves a pretty cool nest, spreading out their sleeping bags on the bottom of the tank so they could sit in relative comfort. They'd been through the cantonment and salvaged a couple of wooden boxes that they could fit through the manhole, along with bottled water, canned fruit and vegetables and unspoiled dry food like breakfast cereals they'd recovered from the larder of a destroyed mess hall. They had a big juice bottle for pissing in, so the only time they had to leave the tank was if they needed to crap, and they had even found a few rolls of dry toilet paper for that.

What Perri was seeing was a whole bunch of activity on the airfield. He had been counting aircraft, but it was hard, because they were parked out not only beside the airfield or on the apron, but also under camouflaged canvas shelters behind walls made of barrels and sandbags. He figured there were at least fifty jets and maybe six propeller-driven transports, plus three helicopters, distributed around the airfield. The jets had been taking off and landing in pairs, about every thirty minutes to an hour, with the largest a single flight of three which had departed about a half hour earlier. That had also been a little strange, because they had seen a large airliner-style aircraft circling overhead, and then the three jets had taken off, fallen into formation with it, and then all of them had headed north.

But now he saw a large number of trucks and aircrew running around, and about ten jets were taxiing out, forming a line on the single runway, clearly getting ready for take-off. He could see the engines had been started on another four or five, and even more were being pulled out of their hangars by towing trucks.

Even from inside the tank, two miles away from the airfield, the building roar of jet engines was palpable.

"Here you go," Dave said, handing him up the radio handset. "Have you seen anyone we know out there?" They

394

hadn't seen the hostages from Gambell since they had been taken into the town, and both boys were wondering how they were doing. Their families were over there. And it was hard to shake the image of those mass graves, the small shoes and gloves lying half buried in the dirt.

"No, nothing," Perri said, then squeezed the button on the handset. "Hey, what was that stupid codename Sarge asked us to use instead of our names?"

"White Bear?"

"Yeah, thanks." Perri clicked the button on the radio handset. "Sarge, are you there, this is White Bear, come in?" He had to repeat the call a couple of times, but that was normal. Sarge always answered eventually.

"Sarge here, White Bear, how are you doing?"

"Doing just fine thanks, Sarge," Perri said. He put his eye to the hole in the tank again. "Sarge, I count about fifty or sixty different aircraft on the base here. I can give you a run-down later, but I need to tell you, something big is happening."

"Tell me exactly what you see, son," the man said calmly.

"I see about twenty aircraft getting ready to take off, maybe more," Perri said. "I think they're mostly combat drones, Hunters, and Sukhoi-57s."

"When you say 'getting ready', exactly what do you mean?"

As Sarge spoke, the first of the jets roared down the runway and lifted into the air. Perri held his hands up to his ears, then lowered the mike to his mouth again. "Did you hear that? I mean, they are *all* taking off, that was the first one!"

"OK, got that. Anything else? Do you see rotary aircraft, transports, anything like that?"

Perri watched as another pair of jets took off. "No, just the fighters. Oh wait, it may be nothing, but about a half hour ago there was a big airliner type of aircraft up high, circling over the island. Three jets took off, met up with it like an escort, you know, and they all headed north."

Perri heard a noise like paper rustling at the other end. "Can you be more precise? What did the big aircraft look like, exactly what direction on the compass did they go? Not east, or southeast? Definitely north?"

Perri knew why he was asking. East was Alaska. Southeast was the US mainland. North was … nothing. Big Diomede, Little Diomede. Open sea. "Yeah, north," Perri said. "The big plane was way up high, just a little white shape. Maybe it had a glass nose. It seemed to catch the light, you know. And I didn't check the compass, I just know they went north," he said. He looked at Dave in case the boy had anything to add, but he just shrugged. Another aircraft roared off the runway outside.

"I'm going to have to log out," Perri said, the pitch of his voice rising. "I don't want to be yelling, and it's getting noisy here. You've got about twenty Russian fighters taking off *right now!*"

"OK, White Bear, keep the radio close. Call me in thirty. I'll have more questions. Sarge out."

Perri sat down, hands over his ears. The metal of the perforated water tank was like an echo chamber and the noise of the jets came in through the walls and shrapnel holes and bounced around, assaulting them from all sides. There was nothing they could do except grit their teeth and ride it out.

Admiral Solanta had come through for Rodriguez. He sent word that he was committing two anti-air-capable submersible fast-attack drones to the defense of Little Diomede. The *Manta-*class drone was a particularly potent weapons platform. A trimaran design, with the vast majority of its hull and superstructure built of lightweight and radar-translucent carbon-composite materials, it had a length of around 130 feet and a long and streamlined center hull. Originally designed to be able to hunt and kill anything from nuclear to the newest near-silent air-independent diesel subs, it soon became evident the platform was capable of being adapted to field multiple weapon systems, including sea-launched ground or air attack missiles. Lurking beneath the waves, with only a cable-buoy mounted Naval Integrated Fire Control Counter-Air data link

396

to air and land radar, and satellite tracking systems, each anti-air Manta carried 12 cells capable of firing the latest over-the-horizon, networked SM-6 (Enhanced) anti-air missile with active seeker autonomous terminal interception capabilities.

Solanta had gotten four of his stealth submersibles successfully through the Russian naval picket and sent them north in support of the *Enterprise* carrier battle group. Two had already reached station in the Bering Strait when the *Enterprise* was forced to turn back, so he had kept them on station and in reserve. It was a platform that had demonstrated an ability in testing to intercept everything from fast-moving fighters and bombers to satellites or ballistic missiles. But it had never been used in combat, until now.

Rodriguez's operations order was simple: draw the enemy to Little Diomede and identify targets for the Mantas. With a projected shoot-kill ratio of 70% against fifth-gen Russian fighters, the two Mantas between them should be able to account for about 16 Russian aircraft. He'd just seen human source intel indicating Russia was sending around 20 aircraft against Little Diomede, leaving Rodriguez and Bunny to mop up the remainder and then put their drones down in Juneau. The Admiral hoped with a bit of luck they may even be able to avert a direct strike on the base, and if the ploy off the Kurils worked, the shooting match might be over before Russia could gather itself and mount a new attack on the island base.

It was a calculated risk. And his officers on Little Diomede had already proven Lady Luck was their personal friend. But they would need all the help they could get.

Admiral Solanta was a deeply religious man. As he looked at a map of the Russian control zone, and the tiny dot right in the middle of it that was Little Diomede island, he crossed himself. "May God protect you, ladies."

Perri's frantic warning from Savoonga had been relayed by Canadian intelligence to NORAD immediately. The FLASH alert from NORAD was received at the Rock simultaneous with a contact alert from the Fantom out in the harbor flashing onto Bunny's threat warning screen. She scanned both reports.

"We better get down to the deck, ma'am!" Bunny said. They had both been lying on makeshift bunks inside the trailer, trying to doze, saving their strength. "NORAD has received human intel indicating Russian aircraft are scrambling from Savoonga. Estimated 20 plus bogies, and radar confirms they are headed this way. Skippy outside has just detected what looks like a Beriev Airborne Control aircraft, with escort, taking up station about fifty miles south of us. We need to get our electronic warfare birds up there, jam that sucker and get those Mantas networked." She looked over at Rodriguez. "This is *it*, Boss."

"Skippy?" Rodriguez asked.

"The Fantom out in the harbor. I gave it a name," Bunny shrugged. "It's earned it."

Rodriguez smiled. "OK, Lieutenant, let's get this production line rolling…"

They had a Fantom locked and loaded on the Cat and had it on standby power, ready for a five-minute power up and launch. The rest of the drones were queued, fueled, armed and programmed – two with electronic warfare pods and the rest with air-air missiles. They had disarmed the explosives in the cave, but were acutely aware that a lucky Russian shot through the cavern mouth or down the chute could trigger one of the charges and bring the roof down on them. It would have to be extremely lucky – the chute was only 100 feet wide and putting a missile all the way through it would be like Luke Skywalker's Hail Mary shot at the Death Star cooling tower. The only way to attack them within the cave would be from water level – a missile fired straight into the mouth of the cave – but all that would do, unless it was a nuke, would be to take out the dock and command trailer. Bunny would lose her cockpit, and they would be deaf and blind (perhaps literally), but the flight deck was shielded from a direct hit for exactly that reason, and as long as the Cat kept working, the chute was clear, and at least one of them was alive, they could keep launching.

One last precaution they had taken was to create a 'castle keep' – a fortified position deep inside the network of racks and belts serving the catapult feeder system, with light, food and water, arms and ammunition, and a low-frequency radio linked to the subsea array in the Strait so that they could stay in contact with Coronado. Bunny had wryly observed that they could hold off an army from inside the 'keep', so they were more likely to die from boredom rather than any other cause.

They sprinted down to the flight deck and pulled on helmets, as much for communication as for protection. The first drone was ready to rock and roll, so Bunny waited behind the blast shield while Rodriguez went to the shooter's chair, just like in her former life aboard carriers. The console showed a lot of different readouts, digital and mechanical, but in the end it came down to just two buttons, really: charge and launch. She hit the first, and the Cat started humming. It was already on reserve power, and needed only a few minutes to reach full charge, drawing on only a small percentage of the power that could be generated by the nuclear power plant buried deep under the Rock. As it charged, it triggered the engine startup sequence for the Fantom and the liquid hydrogen Scimitar engines whined into life. A slipstream exhaust fan sucked most of the displaced air down into vents for distribution around the cave, but not all, and dust and small particles started swirling while a small ripple began dancing on the surface of the Pond. Green lights began showing on the shooter's console, telling her the Cat was fully charged and ready to deliver the required thrust, the drone was locked to the shuttle, its engine was at full power, ready for the afterburner to be lit, and its combat and autopilot systems were up.

They rushed through the launch sequence.

"Preparing to light the tail," Bunny said into her helmet mike. "Clear?"

"Clear, aye," confirmed Rodriguez, crouching lower.

"*Launching!*"

The Cat fired and the afterburner roared, hurling the Fantom along the catapult, flinging it down the chute and out into the open air. They both watched the shrinking silhouette to see that it flew true, turning away and slowly pulling up until it was gone from the small letterbox view they had of it.

"Electronic warfare 1 away," Bunny said. As she spoke, the catapult shuttle returned to its start position while the automated delivery system lifted a new drone cartridge off the conveyor belt and dropped it on the catapult rails. Bunny hit a release and the two halves of the cartridge fell away into pits on either side of the catapult and were ejected into the Pond, like bowling pins at the back of an alley. While Rodriguez fixed a hand-held system diagnostics unit to the newly arrived Fantom, in essence 'booting' the drone to life, Bunny was rocking it back and forth to lock it into place on the shuttle and fitting the holding rods.

Rodriguez felt the Fantom thud into place and counted off precious seconds as hydraulic rods pushed the wings down.

"Locked!" Bunny said, arms in the air, stepping away.

"Booted!" Rodriguez said a moment later, seeing the go-codes on her handset and pulling the magnetic connecting cable off the access point on the drone's skin.

Bunny jumped over the blast protector again as Rodriguez ran for the shooter's chair. Every minute now was literally life or death. The Russians scrambling from Saint Lawrence would be forming up, waiting for guidance from their Airborne Control aircraft. If they formed up in the usual Russian formation of two flights of three, the first fighters could be on their way already. Flying time from Saint Lawrence to the Rock was about 20 minutes for an Su-57. They needed to get at least six Fantoms in the air by then. What they were trying to do had never been done before. Launch two electronic warfare birds then a hex of air-to-air Fantoms inside thirty minutes? With only two people? It was crazy.

As she waited for her shooter's console to light up green, Rodriguez looked over at Bunny and saw the woman looking across at her too.

They could be hit at any moment but Bunny was grinning like a fool. "Are we having fun yet, ma'am?"

400

"Spruce Leader, this is Spruce Control," Bondarev heard his airborne controller say. "We are experiencing heavy jamming. Intermittent signal loss on several frequencies. Status over the target is unchanged, no activity."

Bondarev cursed. The observation from the airborne controller was contradictory. If the enemy had started active jamming, then the situation over the target *had* changed, obviously. It showed they had detected or anticipated Russian activity, they had spotted or suspected the presence of the Airborne Control plane, and were targeting it with electronic warfare aircraft. It was unlikely to be ground or satellite-based jamming, therefore there was at least one US stealth aircraft in the Operations Area that the Airborne Control and mainland-based radar had not yet detected. Probably more than one.

He had taken off in the lead formation from Savoonga. Spent ten frustrating minutes forming up. Was still 15 minutes from Little Diomede. His flight of six aircraft would set up a combat air patrol over the island. If there were any enemy aircraft in the air near the island, he would deal with them. And he didn't need the airborne controller to tell him they weren't picking up any returns, he could see that on his empty threat warning screen. The only upside was that the jamming confirmed beyond doubt that there was a significant enemy base on the island.

It was an interesting tactical challenge. Recon photos showed a small cave at water level, with an opening not much higher or wider than the profile of one of his Okhotniks. It was conceivable you could fly a drone through it, but it would require skill. And there was no flight path cleared along the water outside the cave. Several fishing boats were wrecked in the shallow harbor lying in front of the cave, so while it was possible a ski-equipped drone could land in the mouth of the cave, taking off would be problematic as there wasn't enough 'runway' to get an aircraft up to take-off speed. Once he had dealt with any threats, he needed to get a low-level look at the mouth of the cave himself before he sent his special ops team in.

Following behind him were ground-attack armed Okhotniks, four carrying deep-penetrating precision-guided bombs with 1,500lb warheads that could punch through 10 feet of hardened concrete, or 20 feet of soil. The rest were armed with short-range ground-attack missiles designed to take out enemy armor. Their warheads were smaller, but their guidance systems more precise. If he was to have a chance of getting a shot inside that cave mouth, it would most likely be with an Okhotnik, flying in at wave-top height and delivering its ordnance at point-blank range.

An icon Bondarev had rarely seen on his heads-up display threat display started blinking as the Airborne Control aircraft broadcast again. "Spruce Control to Spruce Leader, we are blind. Total signal failure. Interference on all frequencies, anti-jamming measures ineffective. Sorry, Spruce Leader, we could give you a vector to the likely source of the jamming, but you are already headed there. We will update if status changes."

"Spruce Leader, understood, out," Bondarev replied.

He quickly scanned his heads-up display, the skies, his wingmen's positions. The passive and active sensors on his Sukhois should be able to burn through any jamming once he arrived over the target, but that meant long-range missiles were virtually useless, reducing his effective payload from eight to four missiles per aircraft. He was not concerned. The jamming aircraft were likely just unarmed drones. And if there was a significant force of drones in the target area, the Airborne Control aircraft should have picked them up before it went off the air.

"Spruce Leader to Spruce flight," Bondarev said, speaking to his wingmen. "Radars up, arm short-range ordnance, take your targeting from your flight leaders. We are probably facing stealth drones, stay sharp!"

He flicked his eyes around the skies and across his instruments again. That familiar combat operation tension was building in him. He didn't believe the BS from pilots or commanders who tried to sound like a combat mission was just another day at the office. Any flight had the potential to cost you your life if you weren't careful, and a combat mission put all the odds against you. And different thoughts went through your head. You couldn't shut them out. He had no wife and he didn't think about his mother or father at times like this. He thought about his grandfather, hero of the Russian Federation, former commander of the Aerospace Forces. The man who had taught him to fly, nearly thirty years ago, sitting on his lap in the cockpit of a Yak-152 turboprop, his feet working the rudder pedals while Bondarev flew with stick and throttle. The man who had taught him how to fight – not the combat maneuvers, but the mindset he needed. "Kill without thought," his grandfather had told him. "Without regret. The enemy pilot has made a choice to fly, to fight, and to die if needed. No pilot in modern war is there against his will. If he wanted, he could object, refuse to fight, and take the consequences. But if he fights, he also accepts the consequences." His grandfather had died ten years ago now, but Bondarev imagined the man watching his every move when he was in the air. Looking out for him? No, that was his own job, but perhaps guiding his decisions, yes.

His lessons applied to a bygone era, though. Bondarev and his men were almost certainly going into combat against soulless robots, not flesh and blood men or women. There were no moral dilemmas in the destruction of silicon and steel, only tactical ones. In a ritual that never varied, Bondarev crossed himself and muttered under his breath, "Be with me, Dedushka."

"Fourth Cuda bird away!" Rodriguez called, bent double and panting. She was ready to collapse, had no idea how Bunny was still standing. The stocky, well-muscled aviator had stripped to her singlet, uniform trousers, gloves and boots. Her black, short-cropped hair glistened with sweat which ran in rivulets down her back between her shoulder blades. As they watched the sixth Fantom depart, Bunny arched her back. Rodriguez handed her a bottle filled with electrolytes and high-dose caffeine and she chugged it hungrily.

Bunny looked over at the command trailer. "Ivan will be overhead any minute," she said. "And my babies will still be trying to form up. I want to get into that trailer and get them through the shitstorm they're flying into."

"If those Mantas don't do their job, and Russian ground-attack aircraft break through, the shitstorm will be in here, not out there," Rodriguez reminded her. They both watched wearily as the loading crane lifted another Fantom cartridge off the belt and dropped it on the catapult rails. So far, the only mechanical failure had been a catapult-locking mechanism on the second Fantom that didn't want to engage. They had talked through what they would do for nearly every possible failure scenario, and for this one their only option was to push the malfunctioning drone down the rails and into the Pond at the end of the deck, losing not only a machine, but precious time. Just as Rodriguez was about to call it, the Fantom shuttle had clunked into place. "I've seen your code in action," Rodriguez said. "Your 'babies' can look after themselves."

Of course Bunny wanted to be at her desk, head in her virtual-reality helmet, guiding her machines through the engagement, but she couldn't be in two places. She had been forced to launch them in autonomous mode and leave them to fight or die on their own. The algorithm she had plugged in was hyper-defensive at the merge, though – her electronic warfare birds and her fighting hex would seek altitude and try to 'spot' targets for the Mantas, which would be pulling data from the drones, their own targeting systems and NORAD to triangulate the Russian aircraft. Only when the Mantas reported they were weapons dry and disengaging would Bunny's drones engage, and even then they were programmed to only engage with missiles, evade, and then bug out for recovery at Juneau.

That's what she'd told Rodriguez, anyway. It wasn't exactly dishonest, but she might have omitted to tell her CO that she had also programmed her berserker algorithm into the two electronic warfare drones. It would be triggered if they were engaged and were in a guns dry state. Her logic was that if the engagement got to the state where her electronic warfare machines were still engaged after the Mantas had done their work and her fighting hex was out of the fight, things were desperate enough to justify a little suicidality.

"Well, they're going to need all the friends they can get," Bunny sighed, looking at the next Fantom in line. "Are we just going to stand here doing the girl talk thing, or are we going to get this hex launched?"

The first Cuda-armed Fantoms formed up north of Little Diomede and started creating a fighting hex. Their neural networks linked to share data, their passive and active targeting systems scanned the sky for targets to feed to the submersibles. The two electronic warfare Fantoms already airborne were sending data to the hex and the Mantas about both the Airborne Control aircraft and its escort, but also a new group of aircraft entering the combat area that were radiating fearlessly, clearly confident and bent on detecting the US stealth aircraft. The two electronic warfare Fantoms had reached 30,000 feet and were climbing for 50. Bunny had programmed the flight waypoints for the electronic warfare Fantoms to be staggered between the Russian Airborne Control plane and Little Diomede, and Fantom electronic warfare 1 was jamming the Airborne Control aircraft undetected from a distance of only ten miles. It had a perfect lock on the Airborne Control plane and one of the Mantas designated it as a priority target, allocating secondary status to the approaching Russian fighters.

As Bondarev's flight of six Sukhois flashed by underneath it, the Manta flooded its missile bays and launched. Fired from below the surface using high-pressure steam, the launch canisters of seven missiles broke out above the water and the SM-6/E booster engines fired, accelerating the missiles to three and a half times the speed of sound. One launch canister failed to release, sending its missile into a cartwheeling death across the surface of the sea. The other six missiles arced straight into the sky. Pulling on the data from three remote sources, coupled with their own active seeker systems, they took just over ten seconds to cover the 30,000 feet to their targets.

The Beriev Airborne Control aircraft was able to detect surface ships out as far as 300km and had registered no US warships in the target area, or even within surface-to-air missile range. The first Bondarev knew that his Airborne Control crew was under attack was a brief radar tone, the appearance of an enemy missile icon on his heads-up display showing a contact below him, then the flash of light and ball of flame on the horizon behind him that signaled the 160-million-dollar aircraft's destruction.

Before he could even react, his combat AI took control of his aircraft, automatically fired flares and chaff, and began to maneuver radically.

His formation split like a starburst, every pilot looking desperately for the source of the attack, threat warning HUDs ominously empty of enemy aircraft, but Bondarev's blurred vision could see the threat marked on his heads-up display. *Ground launch!?* His head swiveled quickly, looking for the tell-tale contrail of a missile to tell him where it had been fired from. He was over the open ocean, so whatever ship had killed his Airborne Control aircraft must be close. He felt as much as saw a missile scream past his port wing and explode overhead. Simultaneously, left and right of him, he saw four of his wingmen hit, dissolving in bright yellow balls of fire.

As his machine pulled out of a near vertical dive he saw what must be the wreckage of the Beriev spiraling down to the sea, trailing ugly black and brown smoke behind it, while around him was nothing but clear blue sky. Far below, a parachute bloomed, then another. That meant little. The aircrew still had to survive landing in the freezing sea below. Bondarev cursed and took back his stick. His threat display was only showing a general vector to a jamming signal over the

Diomede islands. Threat display empty, sky clear! He flipped his radar to ground scan mode. Nothing! Where had the attack come from?! He flung his machine around the sky, bullying it down toward the relative safety of the waves below.

For the first time in multiple missions, Bondarev was at a loss. "Spruce Leader to Spruce flight, report!"

"Spruce 5," a single voice replied. "Forming up, Colonel. Orders?"

Bondarev checked his tac display. "I have a strong lock on a stationary radar signature by Little Diomede," he said. "Do you copy?" The only threat on his board was an American radar broadcasting by the eastern side of the island. His AI had tagged it as a Fantom signature, but it was not moving. Perhaps it was the aircraft Arsharvin's drone had photographed, either landing or preparing to launch? It didn't feel right. On the edge of his display he saw his follow-on flight entering the combat area, another six Su-57s followed by 12 Mig-41s. Behind them should be six ground-attack-configured Okhotniks.

"Acknowledged, Spruce Leader," his remaining wingman responded. "Orders please?" The man sounded on the edge of panic.

Bondarev didn't even have time to reply before his missile threat warning sounded again and the stick was ripped from his hands as his machine desperately inverted and dived.

The first Manta loosed two more missiles in the direction of Bondarev and his wingman but they were now moving into the optimal kill zone for the second Manta so it handed them off and turned its attention to the next wave of incoming Russian fighters. It had claimed five kills with its first seven shots, had two SM-6/E missiles in flight and three left. Based on solid and unconfirmed returns combined with standard Russian flight doctrine, it estimated at least 12 Russian aircraft in the approaching wave. It had a firm lock on only four, but that was more than it had missiles for anyway. It sent its remaining three SM-6/Es downrange then, closing its cell doors, reeled in its targeting comms buoy, cut off all emissions, and began a silent glide toward the bottom of the Bering Strait.

One, two... five! Bondarev quickly counted five missile icons, and within the blink of an eye they detonated. His wingman, Spruce 5, had broken high, managing only to attract both of the missiles launched at them, and his machine disappeared in a maelstrom of metal and fire. In horror, Bondarev listened as voices full of controlled terror filled the air and the icons of his follow-on wave began to wink out. Five missiles, four kills this time. The remaining nine Su-57s scattered wildly, looking for the source of the attack in vain.

Bondarev was down on the deck, back in control of his machine, still screaming toward Little Diomede but with nothing at which to aim his rage than the loudly emitting Fantom still stationary next to the island and the vague vector he had to the jamming aircraft now high above him. He'd led his men into a trap and could see nothing for it but to call on them to disengage. He thumbed his comms.

"Spruce Leader to all Spruce aircraft..." he called. His time had run out. With a sickening feeling of finality he heard a new missile launch tone, saw the icons of a dozen enemy missiles appear right in front of him, and closed his eyes.

Ignoring the virtual surrender of its pilot, the Sukhoi's AI took control of the aircraft, rolled the machine hard to starboard, using thrust vectoring to put it at a radical angle of approach to the incoming missiles, punched flares and chaff, and Bondarev felt his vision going red. An explosion, behind. *Safe.* A second, right below his damn *feet!*

His aircraft shuddered and began to wing over toward the sea. He grabbed the stick, disengaged the AI, tried to keep his machine level, felt it falling away to starboard underneath him. Tried to roll level to port, and it was like trying to roll a damn airliner upright, so he took a crazy risk, flick rolled to starboard instead. The Sukhoi responded normally to the stick for a starboard roll, and he stopped the roll as the aircraft came level.

Warnings were flashing in his heads-up display and in his ears. He realized he was pulling back on the stick, but the nose was still dropping slightly. He had one engine dead, the other was still online, but temps were redlining. He eased back on the throttle, pushed the stick forward. Engine fire! Extinguishers fired automatically and that warning went out, but he could hear his remaining engine slowly spinning down. Heads-up display was down. Tac display was down. He could hear the comms of his remaining pilots, tried to order them to break off and return to base but got no response; he was deaf, blind and dumb, shooting over the sea still aimed at Little Diomede, not much more than 1,000 feet above the waves. If his Okhotniks began their ingress now, they would be decimated. His nose dipped as his engine began to spool down.

The Su-57 wasn't a glider. But it wasn't a brick either. He still had electrical power and the dynamic control surface modulation system did its best to optimize his wings for low-speed flight as he fought to keep some altitude, avoid a stall, avoid the fighter tipping over onto one wing and going into a death spiral. He desperately scanned the sky around him, checked his altitude. He was already down to 800!

He should punch out.

Up ahead he saw a broad channel of sea, coasts on each side, too far away, and, straight in front, the twin islands of Big Diomede and Little Diomede. Big Diomede was Russian territory. Uninhabited, but Russian. Little Diomede was, he now knew for sure, an enemy base. An enemy base that had survived an attack with Fuel Air Explosive or FAE munitions, hit and hurt Anadyr and Lavrentiya, and had now claimed at least eight of his own aircraft, probably significantly more thinking of that last volley of missiles. Out of the corner of his eye he saw several parachutes. Drones did not need parachutes, they could only be his own men. Destroyed by what? Ground-based anti-air defenses on Little Diomede? It couldn't be – they had hit the island with iron bombs, overflown it a hundred times in recent weeks without incident, scoured satellite and electronic intel data for any sign of anti-air defenses. Arsharvin had concluded its only defense was a solid cap of basalt.

As much as they were friends, it was an unforgivable mistake.

He was dropping toward Little Diomede from the east and could feel, without looking at his instruments, that he was not going to clear it. Choices flashed through his head like items on a menu. Steer a little to starboard, punch out over the water between the two islands, swim for Big Diomede and Russian territory. Or punch out either near or over Little Diomede and wait on the enemy island until the Spetsnaz or a rescue unit arrived, assuming they could even get through. But he had no idea what the currents were like between the islands, could just imagine himself being caught and swept north or south into the open sea where he would die in minutes from the cold, despite his insulated flight suit. His nose dipped further ... no way to get over Little Diomede now. It was decision time. He scanned the rocky shore ahead of him. He could jump in or near the small wreckage-strewn harbor at the base of that cliff there. Worst case, swim to the mast of one of the sunken ships; best case, make it to shore. But what if he jumped right in the middle of all that wreckage, or got blown past? Once again he was wracked with indecision. *Dedushka! Why can't I think!?*

What the hell? In the middle of the cliff face ahead of him he saw a small rectangular aperture, not much wider or higher than his aircraft. He wouldn't even have noticed if he hadn't been pointed straight at it, and even then might have missed it, except that out of its black maw an American Fantom blasted into the air and, turning right in front of him, began a fast climbing turn to port.

A cold calm came over him. Suddenly his path was clear. He would aim his Sukhoi at the opening in the rock and fly his machine straight into it.

"This is Spruce Leader," he called on his radio, just in case anyone could hear. "I have been hit, lost engine power, going down. Oak Leader, get the job done, you are in command. Good luck, Akinfeev. Bondarev out."

410

"No response!" Rodriguez called out. She had the boot unit connected to the hull of the Fantom they had just dropped onto the catapult and hit the command to initiate engine start-up, but got nothing. Even the boot unit was showing a blank display. It was their last drone. They had managed to get seven up, this would be the eighth, and the last Cuda-armed fighter if they could only boot it to life.

"Try another boot unit!" Bunny yelled back. "It might not be the drone."

Running back to her shooter's console, Rodriguez pulled out a reserve boot unit and turned it on. For safety's sake she took a spare magnetic connection cable too, in case it was a cable problem. Bunny took the chance to swig some water. They had gotten seven Fantoms into the air now, but had no idea what was going on above them. What they were doing was the equivalent of firing arrows blindfolded into the air, one after the other, at a target they weren't even sure was still there. Except of course that the arrows had brains and reflexes of their own. And if the enemy was out there, they would find them. What happened after that – that was a question of man against machine.

Rodriguez slapped the magnetic connector onto the port on the side of the drone and hit the boot command. An error code flashed up.

"Fault in fuel cell, access port 23a!" she called. "Where the hell is access port 23a!?"

Bunny put her water bottle away and ran toward their engineering supply room. "I'll get another fuel cell!"

"Goddamit…" Rodriguez said, going back to her console and pulling up the drone service schematics. "Port 23a, 23a … where are you?" She punched in a search string and a wire diagram came up on her screen, the battery port highlighted in pulsing blue. It was on the port side fuselage, under the wing root. Grabbing a pistol grip screwdriver she ran to the drone, ducked under the wing, located the port and screwed it open.

The hydrogen fuel cell inside was held fast in a metal brace and she had to free it before she could pull it out. As she turned to drop it on the ground, Bunny jogged up, holding a new cell, and she jammed it into the bracket, closed the port door and Rodriguez screwed it into place.

They had wasted valuable time. Bunny turned to Rodriguez, about to say something, when a huge explosion threw them off their feet and fire roared out of the chute.

Bondarev never saw his machine hit the cliff. He had centered the nose of the Sukhoi just above the hole in the cliff face to allow for the last few feet of descent. He'd judged it was 500 feet above sea level, or about 500 feet below his safe ejection height. About a hundred feet from the cliff face, he pulled the ejection lever. His canopy flew away and the ejection gun hammered his seat out of the cockpit, then a rocket booster blasted him into the cold air at 200 g per second. In any ejection there was a one in three chance the pilot would break their back, but when the alternative was to end as a red smear on a cliff face in the middle of the Bering Strait, it wasn't something Bondarev had even thought about. His immediate problem was whether his chute would even deploy in time to retard his fall at this low altitude. The Sukhoi was equipped with a 'zero-zero' ejection system, designed to be safe even if the pilot ejected at zero altitude, zero speed, but while he was about 500 feet above the sea he was still ejecting below ground level if you counted from the top of the cliff face.

The solid fuel rocket boosters on the bottom of his chair burned white hot for 0.2 seconds, lifting him 200 feet into the air over Little Diomede. Having taken altitude data from the dying Sukhoi, the seat computer calculated it should dump the chair immediately and deploy both the drogue and main parachutes. Bondarev was still moving forward at about 500 miles an hour as he started to drop!

He felt himself being jerked out of the chair – if his back hadn't been broken by the kick out of the cockpit, there was

412

another chance it would be snapped by the chute deploying – and saw the lip of the cliff face disappear below him in a blur. He was still wearing his helmet, so he registered the explosion of his aircraft as a bright flash somewhere below his legs, but didn't hear it. Then his chute opened and swung him forward like a child on a swing. His legs kicked out in front of him and then he swung back down, the black rock and ice of the island rushing up to meet him. He braced for a hard impact, but the ground was a little further away than he had first sensed. A second went past, then another, then he hit … hard!

Colonel Artem Akinfeev, Bondarev's second in command and leader of the Mig-41 Oak Squadron, had heard his CO's shouted missile warning as he came under attack over Little Diomede but he hadn't acted on it. It wasn't that he doubted the sanity of the order, questioned the tactical wisdom of committing his aircraft before the source of the threat was identified, or was arrogantly overconfident about the capabilities of his Gen-6 Mig stealth fighters.

He hadn't heeded Bondarev's warning because, by the time he could have reacted, he was already dead.

Having dispatched most of Bondarev's squadron, the remaining Manta had immediately moved to engage the incoming Sukhois and Migs. An American missile had struck his machine from a low portside aspect, detonating inches from his fuel tanks, causing an explosion that incinerated both the Mig and Artem Akinfeev in milliseconds. Akinfeev's wingman, Lieutenant Igor Tzubya, had also heard Bondarev's warning but luckily he had time to respond and had evaded the missile that had been aimed at him.

"Oak 4 to Birch Leader, we are engaged over target," he said to the Okhotnik commander, pushing his machine down to sea level to try to recover stealth capability as his sensors showed American Aegis ground-air and Fantom air-air radar sweeping across the skin of his fighter. "Hold your current position, do not approach the target. Repeat, do not approach."

Igor Tzubya's call sign was 'Yeti' because of his coolness under fire, and he showed it now, his voice giving no sign of the stress he was feeling, either mental or physical. As he recovered his stealth profile he swung his aircraft around toward the source of the Aegis radar and was looking for a surface ship when, far ahead of him, he saw two sea-launched missiles leap from the empty water. A submersible anti-air system! He had no air-ground weapons other than his guns, but he knew exactly how to respond. He locked the rough position of the Manta on his nav system and sent the data to the other Russian aircraft.

"Oak Squadron, get down on the deck," he said. "We're being targeted by sub-launched missiles. Converge on my coordinates!" Tzubya commanded. Tzubya and his men were trained in how to counter a Manta attack. The Manta had to be stationary to launch and the trick was to stay as close to the launch point as possible. After clearing the surface of the sea and being kicked out of their canisters, the SM-6/E missiles would accelerate straight up and then start homing on their targets, but if the targets were below them and close, the American missiles would be forced to try a radical 180-degree reverse to get back down to sea level to hit a circling aircraft. It was a maneuver they weren't optimized to achieve and the chances of a miss were greatly improved.

Assuming there was only one Manta out there firing at them, of course!

He had no option. In moments he was joined by the remaining five fighters of Oak Squadron and they began tight banking turns over the last known position of the Manta. He tried desperately to get a visual on the submersible drone but that was impossible. The water below glittered with sunlight, the reflections blinding.

"Missile launch!" one of his men called and he saw to port one of the missile canisters exploding out of the water, the rocket booster igniting and sending the missile out of sight overhead.

"Hold your positions unless they get a lock!" he called sternly, knowing the pressure to break away would be almost irresistible to many pilots.

He counted the aircraft swimming through the air behind him. So few. But that must mean the enemy Manta was growing short on missiles.

He just had to hold his nerve!

If Rodriguez and Bunny had been in any doubt about whether there was a war going on outside, it disappeared in the gout of flame that spewed out of the chute at the end of the catapult. As they had been standing off to one side, locking the wings of the disabled Fantom, the flame spewed out of the chute between them and they scrambled aside, Rodriguez on all fours, Bunny almost comically crabbing backward on her butt.

What saved them from almost certain immolation was that Bondarev's Sukhoi had struck the cliff face about six feet over the chute. Smashing into the rock, its fuel tanks had ruptured and spewed flaming fuel into the chute, but the plane itself had simply pancaked into the cliff above the chute, exploded with huge force as its ammunition and fuel detonated, and then dropped to the rocky beach below.

Ironically, the smoking wreck served to obscure the chute from anyone who might have been looking for it from the air or sea.

When the fire subsided, Bunny stuck her head up and peered down the chute, still seeing unobstructed daylight ahead. "Missile, you think?"

"Had to be," Rodriguez agreed. "But they missed. Come on, we can't expect they'll keep missing. And you can bet it's just a matter of time before they'll be dropping some heavy harm on that cave mouth. Let's hustle!"

Having installed the new fuel cell and locked it down, they booted up their last drone without any further drama and got it ready to launch. Rodriguez had no way of knowing how many of their fighters out there were still operational, but they had now put two electronic warfare aircraft and five armed with air-to-air missiles in the sky overhead. If the Mantas had done their job, and each Fantom just killed two Russians each, they would have accounted for the best part of a full enemy squadron. That would have to hurt. She checked her panel. *Oh what now!?*

She deciphered the data on her screen. "Cat is overheating," she told Bunny. "We can push it, risk that it seizes, or wait and let it cool."

"How long?"

"Ten … nine minutes."

At that moment they heard a mighty crash outside as something, probably one of the combatants, smashed into the water in the harbor outside the cave mouth.

"We might not have ten minutes," Bunny said. "I say take the shot, even if the damn thing blows up." Her words were all fire and brimstone, but Rodriguez could see the woman was about to pass out if she didn't kill herself with overexertion first.

"I'll see if I can bypass the Cat safety lock," Rodriguez said. "You run up to the trailer, try to get a read on what is happening out there. Grab some electrolytes, then get back here."

"Yes, ma'am," Bunny said, without hesitation. She wanted to know what was happening above the Rock just as much as Rodriguez did. Rodriguez noticed she didn't run over to the trailer, but moved with a shuffling jog.

With a heavily armed enemy circling outside, the cavern under the Rock seemed smaller to her now than it ever had before, the wet stone ceiling lower, the rippling water in the Pond more threatening. She realized screens full of menus and commands were just cycling unheeded in front of her on the shooter's control panel and she forced herself to focus. They just needed to get their last Fantom away. Then they could rest … forever if need be.

Bondarev hit the hard ice-covered rock and rolled. As he tumbled he tried to keep his head and arms tucked in, but his head took a heavy blow that made him see stars even through the helmet. When he stopped rolling, he tried to stand but found he couldn't balance, even to get up into a crouch. *Brain injury*, something told him. *Concussion. Take it easy. No one is shooting at you down here.*

He decided to lie still where he had landed, knees curled up to his chest. He pulled his parachute up around himself to keep warm, felt down to his trouser leg and triggered his emergency beacon. No rescue could come until the area was secure, but at least aircraft above would know he was down and still alive!

Which, miraculously, he seemed to be. He gingerly rolled one foot, then the other, to test for a broken ankle. The same for his wrists and hands. He knew he might not feel any pain for a few minutes, the amount of adrenaline that had to be flowing, but it seemed he had gotten down in one piece. He still had spots in front of his eyes when he opened them, and a massive headache, but no pain in his back, no splintered bones.

He was, however, lying on the stone and ice roof of an enemy air base in the middle of a shooting war, and if his pilots could secure the airspace over the island there would be an air strike blowing in any minute now.

Gathering himself, he rolled into a crouch. About two hundred feet to his left he saw what must have been the remains of the American radome. It was nothing more than blasted metal stumps and rough foundations but it offered the only potential shelter on the whole rock, in case any of the incoming Russian munitions went high.

He looked up at the clear blue sky, could see some contrails and, far away, a burning machine falling from the sky. He had no idea if it was American or Russian. But judging by the first ten minutes of the battle, he wasn't hopeful. It was the first time he had ever gone up against an autonomous sub-launched air defense system.

And it had kicked his human ass.

Yevgeny Bondarev might have been more cheerful if he could have seen the data Bunny was running as she chugged a bottle of non-carbonated energy drink. The screen told its story in a format she could digest in seconds, but she kept looking at it for as long as it took her to finish the pint of fluid she was throwing down.

Skippy, the Fantom in the bay, had been linked into the hex data feed and was tracking the aircraft overhead. It had faithfully recorded every kill and loss. She looked at the data in disappointment. The Manta ambush had claimed just 14 aircraft for its 24 missiles. There were still four Russian fighters, all sixth-generation Mig-41s, reforming south of the island. They were not giving up.

She put down her empty bottle, reached to take one for Rodriguez, and saw a group of new icons appear on the screen at the absolute limit of Skippy's range, about twenty miles out. They flickered in and out, indicating they were stealth aircraft, but the AI was confident enough it could identify them from their radar and signals cross-sections.

Nine Su-57s in the company of Okhotniks. Six of them! They were spearing straight toward Little Diomede, and that could only mean one thing. She touched the comms button on her helmet. "Boss, I got mud movers inbound! I'm going to stay in the trailer, make sure my formation has its head in the game, OK?" she called urgently.

"Acknowledged. Keep them out of our backyard, O'Hare. I'm still working on this Cat."

"Yes, ma'am." Bunny pulled off her plane captain helmet, jammed on her virtual-reality rig and plugged it in. Bunny's hex, holding low and optimized for stealth north of Little Diomede, was programmed with priority targets and a 20-mile defense perimeter around the island it was tasked to defend. Knowing that pilot kills hurt more than drone kills, Bunny had programmed her Fantoms to seek out and attack Su-57 or Mig-41 aircraft first and foremost. Each Fantom was armed with eight Cuda medium-range missiles – 40 in total. Her aggressor

418

algorithm gave the three lead aircraft in the formation the role of engaging first, and as soon as Tzubya's reformed flight of four Mig-41s entered the kill zone south of Little Diomede – their own radars marking their place in the sky like neon lights – they were immediately locked with eight Cudas, two per aircraft.

No! She needed to retask them to stop the ground-attack Hunters! Right now they were the biggest threat to Rodriguez and O'Hare.

She was too slow. Homing on the Russian Mig targeting radars, her Fantoms let fly with a volley of Cuda missiles and the sky south of Little Diomede was suddenly a mosaic of contrails.

"Fantoms! Missiles inbound," Tzubya called in an emotionless voice. *One, two... five...* he quickly counted five drones and near twice as many missiles headed for his formation. The American aircraft were nearly 30 miles out, hiding down low in the wave clutter. One of the returns on his tracking screen suddenly turned solid and, quicker than he could think himself, a K-77M missile leaped off his rails toward the target. A second missile was fired by one of his wingmen, but his systems were showing heavy jamming and the Russian missiles lost their lock almost immediately. He had to get within optical guidance range!

At least two incoming missiles appeared to be targeting his aircraft. Damn, damn, *damn*. He looked to his right and saw he still had a wingman with him. Then he saw a flash of fire, the white cloud of a missile impact beside him, and he rolled instinctively away from the explosion as his wingman detonated in a ball of flying metal.

No, not a missile. The US missiles were still closing, two seconds to impact. A glint caught his eye and, looking to port, he saw a lone Fantom pull out of a screaming dive above the water and climb away, trying to regain altitude. Ignoring the missile warnings, he flung his own machine onto its wing and

419

tried to lock the US aircraft up. He had to override his combat AI as it fired countermeasures and tried to assert control in the face of imminent destruction from the incoming US missiles, but he grunted in satisfaction as he turned inside the fast-moving Cuda missiles and both detonated harmlessly behind him. As the enemy aircraft reached the top of its zoom climb he got an optical lock on the US fighter that had taken his wingman out with its guns. He got a firing tone. His thumb reached for the missile release...

As he was about to jab down on the button, tracer flashed over his wing. One of the damned winged hell-hounds had gotten behind him! Cursing, he broke hard left and dived for the sea.

"Oak 4 to Birch Leader, we are engaged over target," he said, wrenching his machine into a flick roll to avoid a line of tracer fire from the drone behind him. The missile warning screaming in his ears stopped. The inferior American missiles had lost their lock. He stopped his roll, reversed it, and pulled his machine into a screaming starboard climbing turn. He had little chance of outmaneuvering the American drone, but his Mig had a trick up its sleeve that set it apart from 5th-Gen fighters like the Su-57 or Fantom. *If* he lived long enough to use it. More tracer fire flashed over his canopy as he jinked. "How far out are you?" he called to the Su-57 pilot shepherding the Okhotniks to the target.

"Birch Leader to Oak 4, we are at ingress waypoint, twenty miles out," the voice of the commander of the Okhotnik flight replied. "We have Poplar squadron with us, ten minutes from release point."

"Spruce flight is down, Oak Leader is down, Oak flight of three remaining, I am lead," Tzubya said. "We'll occupy the American combat air patrol," he continued, rolling his machine on its axis and pulling it into a power climb. "I authorize ingress of Birch aircraft."

"Roger, Spruce 4," the Birch flight leader said. "We are merging. I am showing two to four bogeys over the target, confirm?"

420

In any other aircraft, pulling up into a spiraling climb with an enemy on his six would have been suicidal. He felt his airspeed bleeding away despite his powerplant being at full thrust. In his rear aspect camera view he saw the US Fantom closing, firing in short controlled bursts. But at that moment a laser tone sounded in his ears. The anti-missile laser mounted in the rear of his Mig had finally got a lock on the Fantom behind him. As soon as it locked it fired automatically, a noiseless, recoil-less pulse of focused energy that burned through the nose of the pursuing drone, melted vital components to slag, and sent it spinning out of control toward the sea.

"Splash one! Estimate four to six remaining," Tzubya said. As he tried to digest the data on his tactical display he heard a scream over the radio and saw another Russian icon disappear. He brought his machine around and tried to get a lock on another American aircraft, knowing in his guts that the approaching Sukhois would not arrive in time.

In her trailer, Bunny saw she now only had four birds in the air – three with Cudas, one guns-only electronic warfare machine. She had accounted for five Migs. Between the Mantas and her Fantoms, that gave about 19 US kills for three losses. The threat board showed a large Russian force of air and ground-attack aircraft moving in. It was time to get her babies to safety. But there was one Mig in range and she still had ordnance. She had to save some missiles for the ingress to Nome in case the drones were intercepted on their way home, but she issued a command to her remaining air-to-air armed fighters to volley half their ordnance and then head for the deck and bug out for Nome.

Igor Tzubya heard the alert and saw eight missiles on his heads-up display threat display, *four vectored on him*. His AI wrenched his machine into a tight banking turn, firing chaff and flares automatically.

But Tzubya took his hands from his stick and throttle and closed his eyes. He knew Death had finally come for him. *Goddamn robots.*

With her Fantoms out of Russian missile range and on their way to Nome, Bunny ran from the trailer. *"Ground-attack aircraft inbound!!"* she yelled. Rodriguez looked over from the flight deck. "We have about five minutes!" She ran up beside Rodriguez and grabbed her arm. "Forget that!"

Rodriguez did the math. Five minutes until the Russian attack aircraft were in position to launch missiles at the cave. One minute for their missiles to run. That was six. But it would take her two to boot the Fantom, two to run the emergency take-off routine, two to spool up the Scimitar engines, one to launch.

They were out of time.

Bondarev looked over the sea to the south and watched in anger as the last of his Migs was skewered by several missiles at once. The Mig-41 disintegrated instantly, scattering into a thousand parts, several of which were his pilot. Further out, a formation of US Fantoms wheeled in the sky and headed northeast.

They were withdrawing?

Despair turned to hope and he stood and cheered as nine Sukhois in tight formation appeared on the horizon, with no sign of pursuit. In seconds they were flashing overhead. Which meant his Okhotniks must be...

Sure enough, moving in just above sea level, he spotted a flock of small dark delta shapes spearing in toward Little Diomede. If he had a radio he would have yelled at them to divide their fire between the cave mouth and the small window in the rock high and to the left. But some well-placed munitions in the maw of the cave might be enough.

Sitting in their trailers in Anadyr, the pilots and systems operators of the Okhotniks had AI-enhanced, HD-magnified, simulated real-time vision of the cliff face ahead. They had lost true real-time control of their drones when they lost their Airborne Control link, but the remaining satellite links were good enough for them to identify the low mouth of the cave as a cold dark smudge above the water and to place the targeting crosshairs of their standoff missiles right in the middle of it. To do it they had to designate the target manually, because it was actually an absence of something, not an object in itself. But with no enemy aircraft to worry about, it didn't matter that they didn't have real-time control of their drones.

A further complication was that the half to one second of lag caused by sending their targeting commands via satellite meant a difference between what their pilots were seeing as the aircraft position and status and what its real position and status were. To allow for that margin of error, they had committed more than the usual number of aircraft to the attack and the Okhotnik drivers were taking no chances they would miss. They let the drones close to two miles out before Bondarev saw the tell-tale flash under their bellies as missiles dropped out of their weapon bays. Lines of smoke traced a path from the aircraft toward the island. Despite himself, he crouched lower. He tried quickly to count the contrails but they were moving too fast. As they disappeared from view under the lip of the cliff, he lowered his head to his arm and waited.

In fact there were *six* missiles tracking toward the mouth of the cave.

Targeting a post-box-shaped slit just above the water was no easy feat, even for a missile with a trimode target seeker, when the pilot firing it was giving his orders from a hundred and fifty miles away in Lavrentiya, a full second into the past. One missile malfunctioned when its stub wings did not properly open and curved wide. Two hit the water a few hundred yards out. One smashed into ice overhanging the cave mouth and another slammed into the cliff beside the Slot.

But *one* missile flew straight into the opening of the cave, straight toward the dock under the Rock.

A4 was designed to take a punch in the guts from a Russian cruise missile or torpedo and stay operational. The cave opening led to the Pond and the hardened concrete walls of the dock beyond. The 'flight deck' was set off to the left behind blast deflectors, so unless a missile could stop in mid-air and turn ninety degrees left, it would slam into the dock at the end of the Pond and any explosion would dissipate among the infrastructure of the dock, which was largely made up of personnel ready rooms, the lower galley and the heads. Fittings, cranes and loading gear were replaceable. The command trailer was set up high, with its own blast-deflecting armor. The single missile that made it into the cave slammed into the back of the dock at two and a half times the speed of sound.

The blast from its 90kg high-explosive warhead struck the already canted dock crane and cracked the concrete and wood dock fairings, while the pressure wave shattered the windows of the crew quarters, mess and ready rooms, sending glass, metal and rock flying around the cavernous space like a thousand small arrows. If Bunny and Rodriguez had been standing in the open, they would have been flayed alive.

But as soon as Bunny had screamed about the Okhotniks, Rodriguez had jumped from behind her console, grabbed Bunny around the neck and pushed her toward the iron door leading to the loading mechanism for the flight deck, barreling in behind the pilot and pulling the heavy blast door shut behind her.

The designers of A4 had calculated the base should be able to remain drone launch-capable through such a strike. But they hadn't planned for the roof of the cave above the Pond to be laced with demolition munitions when it got hit.

Even though they had been manually disarmed by Bunny and Rodriguez, the charges were still buried in the roof, positioned to bring it down on top of the dock and block the cave mouth. While it didn't penetrate the cave, the missile that had struck the ice at the cave mouth detonated with enough force to trigger a sudden and catastrophic ripple of blasts, from the mouth of the cave inward toward the dock as the demolition munitions exploded, dropping tons of concrete and rock into the Pond. The mouth of the cave had received special attention and the ring of charges there collapsed the mouth of the cave so thoroughly that within seconds it was completely sealed.

Not a chink of light shone through.

Bondarev could hear the detonations below him, but if he expected the Rock to shake and tremble with their force he was mistaken. Little Diomede Island had towered over the Arctic seas for tens of thousands of years and seen two ice ages come and go. Despite the outrages visited on it today, it would stand ten thousand years more.

He lifted his head and looked up again. The battle for the airspace above him was over. He saw his Sukhois make another pass over him and then sweep up into a steep climbing turn. He jumped up from the hole he had been crouched in and over to where he had left his parachute rolled into a ball, weighted down by rocks. He unfurled it and spread it out, using the rocks to hold down the edges. Then he stood in the middle of it and waved.

A Sukhoi circling overhead broke away and dropped low. As it passed, the pilot lowered a wing and Bondarev saw him clearly, waving from his cockpit to show he'd been seen. Bondarev watched as the fighter pulled around and made another pass, slower and lower this time. As he dropped his wing this time, Bondarev thought he saw the pilot hold up his fist and flash five fingers, twice.

Ten minutes, the pilot was saying.

Bondarev waved back to show he understood, and sat down on his chute.

The Spetsnaz quadrotor was on its way.

When the cacophony of sound on the other side of the door finally stopped, Bunny and Rodriguez tried the hydraulically operated blast door. It was jammed, the mechanism probably warped by the pressure waves from the blasts.

"No effing way," Bunny cursed, trying the door again. They could hear bolts sliding back, could hear the hydraulic system whirring, but the blast door stayed obstinately, firmly and depressingly shut.

They had an exit – out through the tool room to the hangar-level elevator shaft – but that only let down deeper under the Rock, not outside. Power to the base had not been lost – the reactor was of course not vulnerable to anything less than a nuke going off inside the base.

Rodriguez patted the door. "Well, I think it is safe to assume this place is a high degree of screwed," she observed.

"So are we, ma'am," Bunny added, nodding at the jammed blast door. "If that's jammed, the only way out of here is down."

Rodriguez felt a lump in her chest as she bit down on her despair. They'd prepared for a siege, laid in food, water, weapons. Booby-trapped the environment around them to give Ivan a few surprises. They hadn't prepared to be entombed.

"So what's the plan, ma'am?" Bunny asked. She looked around her. "It's possible the blast door into the aircraft elevator isn't jammed. We could access the elevator shaft, find a way to bridge the gap, get out that way." She tried to make it sound easy.

"The elevator shaft is a 30-foot-wide hole in the rock," Rodriguez said. "We still have power, so we still have comms. I think our best idea is to get a signal out to Coronado, tell them our status, wait here for a rescue."

"Yeah ... unless Ivan comes and 'rescues' us first," Bunny observed.

As Perri watched the last of the Russian jets lift off and light its burners, heading north, he pulled his hands down from his ears and then dropped on his backside, onto his sleeping bag beside Dave.

"About damn time," Dave said. "Seriously, they have the whole Russian Air Force out there?"

"Not anymore," Perri said. "I think we need to get onto Sarge, tell them they just put about everything they have into the air and sent it north."

Dave reached across his legs to haul the car battery onto his lap and picked up the cable connecting it to the radio. "Yeah, yeah, I'll just…"

From outside the tank there came three sharp reports. Three small holes appeared in the tank above their heads!

Both of them froze.

"Hey, American!" came a heavily accented voice. "You hear me in there?" There was another shot and another hole appeared in the tank, lower down this time, making them both duck. "Yeah, I think you hear me." There was a bitter laugh. "It's me, guy you tried to kill." Another shot, another hole in the tank, even lower this time. Dave and Perri both scuttled as far from that side of the tank as they could, but there was nowhere to go. "Hey!" the voice called. "I think you have radio in there. First thing you are going to do, you drop that radio down to me." Another laugh. "*Softly*. I have been looking for that radio."

BLITZ

Yevgeny Bondarev hadn't planned to join the Spetsnaz assault on the enemy base, so it was with not a little surprise that he found himself on the end of a rope, rappelling down the cliff face overlooking the collapsed cave, trying to find the drone-sized egress hole in the cliff.

The GRU Spetsnaz company commander was a Siberian Yakut, Captain Mikhael Borisov. He had grown up in the coldest region on the planet, Verkhoyansk, where the average winter temperature was 30 degrees below. The near-zero winds on top of Little Diomede were like a spring breeze to him, but he wouldn't have felt them anyway, because he was boiling with rage.

He had decided the operation to capture the US base was a basic airfield seizure, with the complication that he had no intel on the layout inside the Rock. Fresh Air Army drone imagery of the entrance to the base showed the cave mouth had collapsed. Ingress would have to be through the remaining cliff face tunnel unless his men could find a lift or stairwell leading from the destroyed US radome down into the base below. He had planned to take the US base using five 5-man squads in three quadrotors, a mix of rifle and weapons troops.

But one of his machines had developed engine trouble and had been forced to turn back, taking with it eight of his men including a number of their heavy weapon specialists. Their attack was timed to follow as closely as possible behind the Air Army missile strike on the enemy base. Borisov had decided to move ahead with the troops he had. That left him with 16 men, himself and the Russian Air Army Colonel who had been waiting for them on top of the rock, with further bad news. The aviator had scouted the ruins of the American base and had not been able to identify any sort of lift, stairs or shaft leading down from the dome of the rock into the base below due to the damage caused by the thermobaric bombs used in the first wave of the LOSOS attack. That didn't mean there wasn't one, just that he hadn't found it. It could be well concealed. Now Borisov would have to use valuable time and resources looking for and securing it to ensure they didn't find themselves suddenly flanked. He would also have to leave one of his squads on the surface to check the wrecked radar base and protect their copters while he took his remaining squad through the launch chute and down under the rock to probe the enemy's strength.

The observation had led to a heated exchange.

"You no longer have the strength to take his base," Bondarev said. "You should call in at least another platoon."

"With respect, Comrade Colonel," the GRU officer pointed out, "that is not your call to make. I am the ground force commander and this element of the operation is being led by the GRU, not the Air Army. Every minute we delay, the enemy can be recovering from your missile attack," Borisov continued. "Attending to their wounded, shoring up their defenses." He took a step forward toward Bondarev. "Perhaps the Air Army would like another week of rest and recreation before finishing its job, but we are Spetsnaz, and I say I still have enough men to secure this landing zone, penetrate that base, and assess the size and disposition of the enemy defenders, and only then will I make a decision about whether to call in reserves." Realizing he had taken his authority as far as it would go, he gave an insincere smile. "Now, perhaps you would care to equip yourself for climbing? Seeing you are here, your insights about this base could be valuable."

Borisov had created a defensive perimeter around the copter with one of his squads but Bondarev looked at the remaining ten or so soldiers standing behind their commander and could see that if they weren't going to be allowed to start killing some Americans, and soon, they might very well decide a coward of an Air Army officer would make a fine substitute. In reality, there was nothing he could do about it.

Which was how he'd found himself dangling on the end of a rope, trying to identify the American drone launch chute for the Spetsnaz team above. Bondarev had taken his best guess, looking at where his Sukhoi lay crumpled and still smoking at the bottom of the cliff, and with Borisov on a rope beside him, had dropped over the edge of the cliff and was easing his way down.

About a hundred feet down, and still 500 feet above the sea, he found it. It lay off to his left, so he had to kick and bounce his way over to it. He gave a hand signal to the Spetsnaz soldier on the other rope, and they took up positions on either side of the hole. It showed nothing but complete darkness. Bondarev had discussed with Borisov that it was possible the attack through the mouth of the cave had knocked out the base and everyone in it, but neither of them was willing to trust their lives to that assumption.

Pulling down the night vision device on his helmet, Borisov stuck his head tentatively around the rock and Bondarev half expected to see it disappear in a volley of fire and spray of blood, but the darkness remained silent.

"Long tunnel, some sort of low-intensity lighting at the end, so we can assume your attack didn't kill the power. Big enough to stand up in, slight incline. No cover I can see. Stealth is out, we're going to have to pop smoke, go in fast." He started relaying orders to his men above. Bondarev had borrowed one of the Spetsnaz helmets and took a look for himself. The NOD, or Night-vision Optical Device, on the helmets could be flipped between light-enhancing and an infrared mode that would penetrate dust and fog. He saw the tunnel was long. He could see only a faint glow at the end, and there was a guide rail set in the floor which must be used to keep the drones centered in the tunnel during launch. It was big enough for them to stand up in without crouching, and the roof and sides were shored up with steel beams, recessed into the rock. Bondarev whistled; the tunnel was a major piece of engineering in itself. He couldn't help but be impressed by what the Americans had done, right under their noses.

When the others had joined them, Borisov and one of his men took a position on either side of the tunnel entrance and pulled out smoke grenades. On a signal from Borisov they swung into the opening, threw their grenades and dropped prone with OSV-96 'Cracker' rifles extended in front of them. The others swung in behind them and rushed down the slight incline, also throwing themselves flat. Bondarev came in last, unable to see anything, with only the small Makarov he always carried in a trouser pocket on the leg of his flight suit. He smelled wet concrete, machine oil, salt air and spent explosive.

"No contact," the Spetsnaz commander said to his squad. "Move up!" They began crawling on their stomachs down the tunnel through the smoke. The walls of the tunnel were smooth, covered only by a black soot that Bondarev guessed was the remains of fuel from either drone launches or his own exploding Sukhoi. As they'd identified, there was no natural cover, so Borisov's men moved in overlapping teams of two down either side of the tunnel. All Bondarev could do was keep his eyes on the dark shadow of the man in front of him and try not to bump into anyone.

Suddenly up front there was a signal and everyone stopped.

"End of the tunnel," someone radioed back. "Three-meter gap. Continues on the other side."

Bondarev tensed. If the enemy was waiting in ambush, this would be the perfect time as they paused at the edge of the drop. Bondarev heard a splash.

"Water below," the man up ahead called back. "Still no contact. We can jump it."

"Coming forward," Borisov said and ran up to the lip of the chute in a crouch. He signaled to Bondarev to join him, giving Bondarev his first look inside the enemy base. Or what was left of it. He could hear heavy-duty exhaust fans working overtime to clear the dust, smoke and water vapor left behind by the cruise missile strike, but with his helmet on infrared mode he could see no movement inside. It appeared the cave had once been much bigger, but a huge rock slide had closed part of it off. He could see the outline of a trailer or comms room set up above the waterline, cables running from it to the roof where they were gathered into thick plastic tubes that ran over to what must be the drone flight deck and launch catapult.

"Tell me what we are looking at," Borisov said, coughing. Bondarev was also having trouble breathing but the American air filtration system was doing its job, the smoke was visibly thinning out.

Bondarev explained. "The Americans have basically recreated the deck of an aircraft carrier in this cave." He pointed. "That is the catapult, electromagnetic. They pull a lot of juice, so I would suspect they installed a nuclear power plant to drive it."

"Shit, we don't have anti-radiation gear," Borisov said. "We could be soaking up lethal doses already."

"I'd guess not," Bondarev said. "They'd bury something like that deep in the bedrock. It wouldn't be vulnerable to a simple missile strike." He pointed a finger in the air. "Listen, the air filters are still working, so they have power."

Borisov cocked his head to listen, then nodded to the rockslide that filled half the cavern. "That doesn't look like a simple missile strike."

"No, it doesn't," Bondarev agreed. "I'd say that was deliberate. Sabotage. Might even have been done before we attacked."

"They were launching aircraft right up until we moved in," Borisov pointed out.

"*Something* was," Bondarev said. He looked at the flight deck. The base was lit with emergency lighting and through his low-light vision he saw more clearly the feeder system that pulled the drones out of hangars inside the rock and dropped them on the catapult, where one of the American drones sat patiently, apparently ready to launch. Could the whole thing be automated? Was their enemy that far ahead of them that they had built an unmanned robot base to launch their robot warplanes from? "Automated feeder system," he explained to the Spetsnaz commander. "Pulls the drones out of hangars back there somewhere, loads them on the catapult." He looked more carefully. "But that's a standard catapult officer's chair

432

and console right there. And you'd need maintenance crew for recovery and repair even if the pilots were based elsewhere." Bondarev decided. "Whoever was launching those drones at us, they're still in here somewhere."

"OK," Borisov said quietly. "Give me an estimate of how many."

It's a fault in warriors consistent throughout history. If they are challenged in battle, it is always by a numerically superior force. Their pride lets them admit no other option. "I'd estimate we were up against as many as twenty drones," Bondarev said, "plus sea-launched anti-air submersibles, which might also have been based here. That would take a sizable base. The crew down on the flight deck there, say six people. Officers, two or three. Security detail perhaps, five or six. For the base to operate under combat conditions, every active duty crew member would need to be matched with one who was off duty. Logistics, intelligence and administrative officers. Cooks and maintenance staff." He did the math. "There would need to have been at least fifty people serving on this base, but it could be as many as one hundred."

Borisov lifted his rifle and used the scope to look around at what was left of Auxiliary Unit A4.

"So where the hell are they all, Comrade Colonel?"

"Where the hell is he?" Dave whispered urgently. "The next shot could be into our heads." He was holding the radio up to Perri. "Just give it to him!"

Perri was doing some panicked thinking. If the guy outside was the one he had shot, he was likely to be sorely pissed. Hadn't he said 'American', not 'Americans' plural? Maybe he didn't know there were two of them in the tank. A plan began to form. Their only chance was to try to kill him, before he was able to kill them. But all the Russian had to do was stand out there and fill the tank full of holes until Perri and Dave were dead. Or drop a grenade through the manhole and shred them. Their situation was multiple degrees of suck. Looking around

433

he saw the bullet holes, tried to guess where the guy had been standing. "You do it," Perri whispered. "Get up that ladder with a backpack, I'll do the talking. I'm going to try to get a line on the guy."

Perri lifted his rifle and waddled over to the side of the tank where he thought the voice and shots had come from. The tank was perforated in multiple places, a few of them big enough to get a rifle muzzle through, if he could just find an eyehole too.

"OK!" he yelled, motioning to Dave to start climbing the ladder. "Stop shooting! I'll bring the radio out. I'm surrendering!"

Dave looked at him like he had lost his marbles. But Perri gave him a *just do it* face and turned back to try to get a direction on the Russian soldier.

"Yes, first radio, then your weapons," the man said. "Then we take a nice walk to Savoonga and I get medal for capturing you."

Perri had guessed right. He could tell from the voice the man was standing right in front of him, somewhere below. He heard Dave start to climb the ladder to the manhole.

He found an eyehole and slowly put the muzzle of his rifle against a tear in the metal just below it. He couldn't sight it, just aim in a general direction. It was a Hail Mary play.

But he didn't believe for a minute the guy he had just shot was going to take them prisoner.

Rodriguez's call to Coronado had got her a 'message received, hold for further orders'. They were unable to confirm whether her drones had made it through the Russian combat air patrol and managed to put down at Juneau. They were unable to confirm Bunny's estimate of kills and losses in the dogfight over Little Diomede. The one thing they could confirm was that Russia retained air superiority over the Strait and that meant an extraction in the near future was highly unlikely, which increased the chances that Russian ground troops would get to them first.

While they had a number of surprises ready in case enemy troops made it into the base, Rodriguez had held Bunny back from booby trapping the drone launch chute.

"It's a perfect choke point," Bunny had told her earlier, squinting up the tunnel at the weak daylight beyond. "We blow the cave mouth, mine the floor or ceiling of the chute, the two of us down here with automatic weapons, we'd run out of targets before we ran out of bullets."

"You blow the cave mouth, this is our only way out of here," Rodriguez had pointed out. "Turn it into a kill zone, Ivan will just haul off and hammer it with a bunker buster, and with the stairs to the surface blocked, we're trapped in here forever."

The redoubt Bunny and Rodriguez had built for themselves was at the end of the service shaft that the techs used to get at the machinery that fed the drones onto the catapult. It was a narrow tunnel, two persons wide, one person high, that ran back fifty feet into the rock, then took a left-hand turn around behind the equipment another hundred feet. At the end of it was a tool room, which they had prepared for their last stand.

The enemy would first have to breach the blast door. It was three-inch hardened steel, hydraulically operated and set into the rocks with two-inch steel rods – built to stop a blast and pressure wave inside the cave penetrating the service tunnel and destroying the delicate machinery inside. In fact, given the scale of the explosions outside, Rodriguez doubted an enemy could open the door even if they tried. But of course, it could be cut out or blown off its frame with shaped charges.

Once through the door, their enemy would have to get down the first corridor, one or two at a time. She and Bunny had put three heavy chest-high barrels of graphite lubricant at the bend in the corridor to provide defensive cover and jammed them in place with timber reinforcing. Overhead pipes left only a small gap between the barrels and the roof, which

435

would provide some protection against anyone trying to lob grenades at them. But the gap was large enough to vault over, assuming you weren't under fire.

If they got pushed back from there, they would retreat to the tool room, which had a metal anti-flood door with a brace bolt they could shelter behind. It wouldn't hold long, but they had a little surprise in store for anyone who started knocking on the tool room door. Bunny had mounted a belt of 25mm Fantom fragmentation ammunition in the pipes in the roof that would fire mercilessly down into the corridor when triggered. The ammunition was fired by electrical primer, an innovation that completely eliminated 'lock time' when the single-barrel cannon of the Fantom was firing, but which also meant it could be ignited by the electrical primer cable Bunny had pared and clipped to the contacts on the belt and wired to a fuel cell with a simple switch. She'd set the detonation range to zero so that the slugs would immediately frag into lethal .50 cal-sized shrapnel, shredding anything in their path.

If they were forced to abandon the tool room, there was a service hatch leading to the 30-foot-wide aircraft elevator shaft. They probably wouldn't have time to ride the heavy elevator down so they had put it in maintenance mode and parked it at the top of the shaft, fixing ropes to a workbench so that they could slide down to the lower-level drone hangars and maintenance bays. The lower levels of A4 were wide and open with no obviously defensible positions apart from the ordnance storage facility, which was not a place you would want to be sheltering in a firestorm. They both knew that if they were forced down that elevator shaft, it could only end one way.

Bunny had a remote detonator switch in one hand and a sandwich in the other as she and Rodriguez sat with their backs up against the graphite barrels in the corridor.

Rodriguez was a little troubled by how careless she seemed to be with the switch. "Can you put that down?" she asked. "I don't want anything going off while we're out in this corridor."

Bunny held it in two fingers and showed her the light on the end, which was dead. "It's safe, Boss," she said. "But if it makes you feel better." She leaned over and put the trigger on the ground between the barrels, taking a bite of her sandwich and pulling her HK416 rifle closer to her. Suddenly she froze.

They heard muffled voices outside.

Russian voices.

One of the Spetsnaz troopers had jumped the gap over the Pond between the launch ramp and chute with a rope tied around him and had secured it on the other side. It was only a three-meter gap, but Bondarev had held his breath as the man sailed through the air, half expecting him to miss or hit the lip on the other side, but he cleared it with room to spare. The gap wasn't designed to prevent access, it was there so that defunct drones could be pushed off the catapult into the Pond and out of the way. On the other side he found a control that extended a bridge across the gap, and they all moved into the main chamber of the cavern. There were only a few wan red emergency lights still burning inside the cavern, so they kept their low-light visors down.

Bondarev was fascinated by the mini aircraft carrier flight deck the Americans had built under the island. It was simply amazing. And it was the first time he had seen one of the amphibious Fantoms up close and personal. It was bigger than it seemed in the air and seemed to have been able to ride out the missile strike further down in the dock without visible damage. Of course, its systems could be fried. He could get right under it, and saw the retractable ski-floats it used for take-off and landing. They would have to have been replaceable – even coated with graphite lubricant, they would have worn out after just a few launches. The aircraft was hanging from a claw that held onto three hardpoints on its upper shell and the claw ran on a belt that went back into the rock to where he assumed there were hangars and service bays.

And if there were service bays, that meant there had to be maintenance and ordnance crew access somewhere, probably on multiple levels. He passed his assessment on to Borisov as his men worked their way around what remained of the misty cavern, ensuring it was clear of threats.

His eye followed the wall away from the Fantom into the gloom in the corner of the base. "Can I borrow your torch?" he quietly asked a trooper standing beside him. The man handed him the light and they walked down into the darkness. At the end of the wall he came to the door he had *known* must be there. It was solid metal, and he had more than a hunch that it would be locked, but he took out his pistol, stood to one side, and spun the wheel that served as both a handle and lock. It turned freely, but did nothing. It was either locked from the other side or warped hard into place by the cruise missile blast. Walking along the wall the full length of the launch ramp, he found another heavy blast door further down. Judging by what he could see of the drone conveyor belt and loading system, he made an educated guess that the second door opened into the system of hangars that fed the drones up to the flight deck for launch, exactly as on an aircraft carrier.

Automated or not, machinery had to be maintained. The drones that flew out of here had to be stored, along with fuel, ordnance. He was certain that behind these doors had to be a network of hangar bays, maintenance floors and storage facilities.

He looked around for Borisov. "Captain! Over here."

As he called out, he heard a telephone buzzing. With a frown he looked around and realized it was coming from a pocket in his flight suit. He had been given a satellite phone by Borisov so that he could let his staff know he was down and safe and to get an update on the tactical situation before he went down into the base. He had given the number to his operations staff on Saint Lawrence and ordered them to re-route any urgent calls to his official cell number to this one, but he hadn't expected he could get a signal down here.

It seemed he could, even under 300 feet of rock. The Americans must have built a signal repeater into the base which a brace of thermobaric bombs and several air-to-ground missiles hadn't managed to disrupt. He shook his head. There was no end to the surprises this base held.

"It's ringing," said Devlin McCarthy.

The ringtone stopped and a gruff voice came on the line.

"Eto Bondarev, kotoryy zvonit?"

"Colonel Bondarev, please hold. I am putting you through to the Ambassador for the United States in Moscow, Devlin McCarthy," HOLMES' voice announced, like he was just any other embassy official.

For a moment she thought the man had hung up, then she heard him say in English, "Who are you and how did you get this number?"

"Connecting you now," HOLMES said. "Go ahead please, Ambassador."

Devlin took a deep breath. "Colonel Bondarev, this is Ambassador McCarthy. I hope you have a few minutes to speak."

There was another silence at the end of the line, then a caustic laugh. "Whoever this is, no, I do not. Thank you and goodbye."

Devlin jumped in as soon as she heard his tone of dismissal. "Yevgeny, I'm the grandmother of your child. The child you had with my daughter, Cindy?" Devlin heard a voice in the background and Bondarev barked at them. She had no doubt they were being told to shut up.

"Cindy McCarthy is your daughter?" he asked.

"Yes, Colonel, you are the father of my grandchild, Angela."

"I know my child's name. Why are you calling? Has something happened to the child?" he asked.

OK, so he wasn't taken by surprise, and maybe even cared. Good. She wouldn't have to convince him the whole story was some sort of psy-ops trick.

"Colonel, I know this call is highly irregular. Believe me, I know. I am about to commit treason. And you will ask yourself

439

why you should trust what I'm telling you, and I can only tell you I am calling you as the grandmother of your child, and not as the US Ambassador to Russia."

"Go on."

"Colonel, my country is currently preparing to conduct an above-ground nuclear missile test off the Russian Kuril Islands. We are also moving strategic nuclear assets into position to conduct a retaliatory strike on Russia should you continue your misadventures in Alaska. Following the test, our President will issue Russia with a final ultimatum to withdraw from Saint Lawrence Island, and I can assure you it *is* final. If you do not comply, there *will* be a full retaliatory nuclear strike by the USA."

"With respect, why should I believe you?" the man asked.

"We know the Bering Strait incident is a pretext. We know you intend to occupy Alaska. We know almost to the hour how and when you plan to invade. I can't tell you how we know, but I can tell you, we will not allow it. I have a Commander in Chief who would rather be known as the man who started World War Three than he would be known as the man who surrendered Alaska."

"I will pass your message to my superiors," Bondarev said.

"*No*, damn you!" Devlin said. "Your superiors already know they are risking nuclear war. They have made their choices. I am talking to *you*, on behalf of your child and her entire generation! You are the theater air commander – there can be no invasion without air cover. Ground your aircraft. Before it's too late." There was nothing but silence at the other end of the line.

Devlin held the phone out to Carl Williams. "I think the bastard hung up."

"HOLMES, can you confirm?" Carl asked into the handset.

"I can confirm, Carl, the line has been cut and that telephone is now offline."

440

Looking around the corner of the corridor, Rodriguez saw the wheel on the inside of the blast door spinning. It had been disabled when they had locked it from their side, but it still spun. She heard a shout, in Russian, and more muffled voices, then pulled her head back and checked her weapon.

"You got any last messages you want me to give anyone?" Bunny asked her. "You know, in case you don't make it out?" She had a mischievous glint in her eye.

"Oh, in case *I* don't make it?" Rodriguez responded. "Because of course you will."

"Of course," Bunny said. "Don't you watch war movies? The tough but likable kick-ass grunt always makes it."

"Really? And *you* are the tough but likable kick-ass grunt?"

"Yeah, mate. The commanding officer never makes it, though. Usually they sacrifice themselves so their subordinates can live, unless they are British, in which case their own troops shoot them first."

"You watch a lot of war movies?"

"When I was a kid. So anyone you want me to contact?"

"That's a very personal question, Lieutenant," Rodriguez said.

Bunny took a swig of water, then handed Rodriguez the bottle. "OK, I'll share first, shall I, ma'am? I've got no one."

"No one?" Rodriguez was surprised. "No family?"

"Mother dead, no brothers or sisters, father is a rolled gold shit," Bunny said simply. "Cousins plenty, none I ever cared about. When DARPA called, I took three seconds to say yes."

"No ... love interest?"

"Well, that's a very personal question, Lieutenant Commander," Bunny smiled. "No. I tend to piss people off if they hang around me too long."

Rodriguez could believe it. "I'm married," Rodriguez told her. "He's serving on Guam."

"Actually, I knew that," Bunny admitted. "But you don't wear a ring. So..."

"He wants kids," Rodriguez said.

"Fair enough."

"I don't," she said.

"OK. That's fair enough too."

"I do love him, though," she said. "It's complicated."

Bunny lifted her rifle and sighted along it. "OK, ma'am, tell you what. I'll make up some stuff at your funeral about how we were talking about him right before you sacrificed yourself to save my life. Happy ending for everyone." She drew a deep breath. "Shame, though, we never did get those tattoos."

Bondarev dropped the telephone back into a pocket on the leg of his flight suit. Borisov looked at him. "What was *that* about?"

"Misdirection," Bondarev told him. He slapped the blast door. "You have two doors and eight men, including yourself. We still have no idea who or what is behind them. What do you propose?"

"I propose, Colonel, that we plant explosives in that tunnel we entered through, go topside, and turn this cave into a tomb for whoever is in here," the Captain said.

Bondarev looked around him, his eye catching on the gleaming gray skin of the amphibious Fantom still poised on the launch ramp. It was generations ahead of his Okhotniks, he knew that now. Together with the other tech and software still intact inside the base it was too great a prize to seal away like a pharaoh in a burial chamber.

"No," Bondarev said firmly. "The mission is to take this base intact. If you are not capable, Lieutenant, call in additional troops as I proposed."

Borisov stiffened, was clearly about to reply, then realized it was an act he might regret. "The Comrade Colonel has miscounted. I have *nine* men, including himself." He turned and looked the blast door up and down. "A positive breach charge should ensure we get this door open and stun anyone directly behind it. Myself and five men will clear the facility behind this door, leaving two to cover the other door in case the Americans try to exit that way." He nodded to one of his men, who

442

unslung a duffel bag he was carrying over his shoulder. From within it he began pulling explosives and detonators.

Bondarev watched him. "Do you have a spare rifle?"

"No, Colonel," Borisov said, not sounding particularly apologetic. "That is why you will join the men watching that other door."

Bondarev looked down at his little Makarov. It suddenly seemed very small indeed.

It all happened in *seconds*.

Dave opened the manhole cover. He held a backpack over his head with one hand, the other hand hanging on the ladder as he moved up, then as he reached a step just below the lip of the opening he put both of his hands in the air, poking out of the manhole to show he wasn't holding a weapon.

Perri saw a movement below him, saw the Russian soldier. The same soldier he had seen in the schoolhouse in Gambell. The same one he had shot outside Savoonga!

The man was watching Dave's hands and arms emerge with the radio and he was grinning. His uniform tunic was soaked with blood on his right side and he held that arm tucked into his chest. In his left hand he held a pistol, and as Dave was opening the manhole cover, he lifted up the pistol and sighted on the top of the tank.

Perri didn't wait to see if he was just being careful or meant to fire on the area of the tank where Dave had to be. Crouched with one eye to a hole in the tank, the muzzle of his Winchester XPR sticking through a hole just beneath it, he racked the bolt on his rifle, made a guess at where he should aim, and fired.

He missed!

The soldier swung his pistol around, pointed at Perri, and fired three quick shots. The bullets hit the steel above his head. Perri had taken a custom-built 10-round magazine from the general store when they had looted it. As fast as he could, he worked the bolt again, fired, worked the bolt, and fired again. And again. The Russian soldier went prone, resting his pistol arm on the ground as he fired up at the tank. Perri saw spurts of dust beside the Russian as his shots went wide and corrected his aim, but the Russian's semi-automatic pistol shot much faster than Perri could fire with his bolt-action rifle.

Suddenly, they were both out of ammunition. Perri fell back onto his haunches, pulling the empty magazine out and scrabbling in one of the boxes for another one. Dave had jumped or fallen down from the ladder, but was standing there looking at Perri in shock.

Ammo! he wanted to yell at him. *Where the hell was that extra magazine?* He jammed the rifle into his crotch, pulled the bolt back with one hand as he felt around in the box with the other, except he couldn't feel anything in there now, let alone the ammo. Damn hand was numb. *Why was Dave looking at him like that?* He looked down at his waist where Dave was looking.

Ah, hell.

Rodriguez and O'Hare had been prepared for the blast. They had heard the sound of drills as the men outside bored holes into the rock either side of the door and placed their explosives. So just being left behind the door to starve or die of thirst was apparently *not* something they were going to have to worry about.

But neither of them was really trained for what was about to go down. A massive concussive blast, yeah, probably supplemented by grenades thrown in by the attacking soldiers. That was a no-brainer. They were waiting around the corner from the door, a good distance down the long corridor where they wouldn't be exposed directly to the blast, either from the door being blown away or from grenade shrapnel. The barrels of graphite they'd put across the end of the first corridor each weighed about 400 pounds. They had hammered timber support beams into the wall behind the barrels to reinforce them and had to hope the barrels would be able to take whatever was coming and still provide some kind of protection. Unless their attackers were armed with rocket-propelled grenades, in which case they could just stand off at a distance and reduce the barrels to piles of metal and black dust.

They also had a spotlight, one of the Pond landing lights, positioned above and behind the barrels shining right at the door. Bunny had observed that if it survived the breach, whoever was out there had better be wearing suntan cream because they were going to get burned.

They were identically armed. Both had HK416 rifles with flash suppression, and belts around their waists that held five magazines each. They had no grenades themselves. No body armor, no night vision goggles, so they had the LED lights in the corridor switched on. Some of the lights were sure to be knocked out by the blast, but they expected there would still be enough light for them to aim by. And for what it was worth, they had their flight deck helmets on. Not that they would stop a bullet, but they might just block some of the noise and protect them from flying debris.

As they sat with their backs to the wall, listening as the drills fell silent, and knowing what the silence meant, it occurred to Rodriguez they had never discussed surrendering. She knew why Bunny hadn't raised it. She still believed they could win this fight, get out there, and launch at least one more drone.

But Rodriguez hadn't considered surrender either. Not because she was a 'death or glory type'; not at all.

Maybe it was just that age-old feeling that she didn't feel like she could just give up, when so many others had given their lives – from Halifax and the others topside, to those who'd been crushed and drowned in the shockwave that followed.

Then suddenly the time for reflection was over. The world around her went white, then black, her eardrums caved in, and she found herself lying on her side with her rifle barrel jammed up under her armpit! Bunny was lying flat too, but looked like she had come through the explosion a little better, lying on her back with her rifle across her chest. Bunny rolled onto her stomach, swung around, and started crawling toward the corner, but Rodriguez grabbed her foot and pulled her back.

Sure enough, a further series of blasts went off around the corner as the Russians threw in fragmentation grenades. The graphite-packed steel barrels rocked against the timber braces holding them and some of the timber shattered, but they held, still blocking the corridor. It had taken a hydraulic dolly for Rodriguez and Bunny to get them into position, so it wouldn't be easy for any advancing troops to shove them out of the way.

Through the ringing in her ears, Rodriguez heard boots in the corridor around the corner.

"Now!" she called, and they ran to their prepared positions, Bunny up against the far wall, her rifle between barrels, Rodriguez taking the near corner, sighting between the wall and the first barrel.

Through the still-settling smoke from the explosions she saw dark shapes advancing down the corridor toward her. Rifle on semi-auto, she worked the trigger as fast as she could put the dot on a target.

Despite his bluster, Captain Borisov had never led his men in combat before. Police actions, yes. Anti-terrorist operations in Dagestan. But for the last four years he had been cooling his heels in Vladivostok, with the only real action outside training exercises being a bank robbery gone wrong in which three hostages had been killed before he was ordered to go in and end it.

In that situation, he had building plans, optic fiber and infrared intelligence on the location of the tangos and their hostages. He had multiple ingress points to choose from. His men had the advantage of darkness and night vision technology. They had hours to plan their action and more than enough personnel to execute it. In the end they lost one additional hostage, killed two of the armed robbers, and captured three. None of his men had taken a bullet. It was called a success.

There was no way to get an optical fiber camera under the blast door or around the frame, nor did he have time to drill a hole. Lacking intel, his only option was to breach and move in fast to clear the area behind the door, snake formation, two by two. He didn't like it. In fact he hated it. But he wasn't going to let that damn Air Army flyboy see a moment's hesitation.

O'Hare and Rodriguez, on the other hand, had chosen the field of battle and their strategy was pretty clear. Kill or be killed.

The naval officers weren't trained weapons experts, but they had both received the same basic firearms training as Marines and they drilled their targets with short, controlled bursts. The return fire was also rapid and controlled, but what came their way thudded into the graphite barrels without ricocheting. The hammer of heavy weapons fire filled the corridor.

"Reposition!" Rodriguez called as soon as the weight of incoming Russian fire stuttered. She was sure she had hit a target or two and with enemy soldiers down in the corridor in front of them, the Russians couldn't use grenades without risking their own men. She covered O'Hare as the woman pulled back out of the line of fire and threw herself down behind Rodriguez.

"*Reloading!*" Bunny called. "Did we hit anything?"

Rodriguez held a finger to her lips and looked around the corner. Heavy suppressive fire hammered the wall above her head but she'd seen enough. About twenty feet down the corridor, there was a dark form lying still. Behind that, another, being dragged away, and a cluster of black-clad troops falling back to the blasted doorway. She sent a few more shots after them, but then remembered her veteran father telling her a wounded enemy was more valuable than a dead one, because the wounded had to be looked after, while the dead looked after themselves. Gradually the suppressing fire died down.

The Russians would be hurting and angry now, of that she was sure. *Serious* harm was on its way.

Borisov cursed as he pulled his men, literally, out of the corridor. He had one dead, one wounded, and one stunned from multiple hits on his body armor and a blow to the helmet which had not penetrated.

"*Shooters*?!" he yelled to the only survivor out of the two troopers who had led the breach, a man who had taken a bullet in the ankle. "How many? Show me."

Borisov handed him a tablet and stylus and his hand shook as he drew. "Hard to see because of the bloody smoke and that spotlight. Four, maybe five shooters," the man said. "In cover. A corridor, thirty to fifty feet. Some sort of barricade. Barrels. Obstructing the corner, no way around. You could try to climb over, but it's a kill zone."

Bondarev had heard and seen the probing attack fail and ran over, listening. "Do you have an anti-tank missile?" he asked. "Blast that barricade and whoever is behind it."

"No, our heavy weapons were on the chopper that turned back," Borisov replied. He turned to one of his weapons experts. "You, load counter-defilade – you are to clear those barrels and disable whoever is behind them, then follow me in. You two – on my order we rush that barricade, get grenades around the corner so we can get over the top." He gave Bondarev a withering look. "Colonel, my men can watch that exit. Make yourself useful and help this man with his injuries."

Bondarev looked down and saw the man's lower leg was a bloody, shattered mess.

Rodriguez and O'Hare had pulled back to the tool room at the end of the second corridor. Nothing but a small dozer was going to move those graphite barrels and they had no desire to be near them if the Russians hit them with rocket propelled grenades. They hunkered down by the door of the tool room and waited. The tool room might be a dead end, but it was a very defensible one. Unless the Russians had gas, of course. Or just decided to pull back and blow the whole base to hell. There was nothing they could do but wait and see.

They didn't have to wait long. From the first corridor they heard the crack of suppressing rifle fire then more whip-crack explosions as shrapnel began flying around the barricade and rattling around the long corridor. The flying shrapnel took out their spotlight, making the corridor suddenly seem very dark.

"Defilade rounds," Bunny said, pulling her head back in case of a ricochet. "But no bazooka. They're not taking us seriously, ma'am."

"Men. Typical," Rodriguez grunted.

Developed in the first part of the new century, counter-defilade ammunition together with laser targeting systems on new generation combat weapons allowed ground troops to fire over obstacles and explode the round right above the head of defenders hiding behind them. The ammunition started as large-bore grenade rounds but grew progressively smaller until even heavy assault rifles could shoot counter-defilade ammunition.

Rodriguez watched cautiously as the end of the corridor a hundred feet away was filled with flying metal and the heavy graphite barrels were perforated, spilling the fine graphite slowly out onto the floor. Their barricade wouldn't last much longer after all.

The covering fire paused and Rodriguez heard boots thumping down the corridor again and bodies crash hard against the barricade as the Russians stormed it. Grenades would be next.

"Now!" she called to Bunny and pulled her head back behind the door frame.

The 25mm cannon ammunition belt Bunny fixed into the ceiling pipes was laser-guided fragmentary. Fired by a Fantom, it used the laser seeker on the cannon to determine when to explode the round to give the maximum chance of a kill even with a near miss. It could also be pre-programmed to detonate at a specific range if the pilot preferred. Bunny had overridden minimum safe distance protocols and set the rounds she had placed in the ceiling of the corridor above the barrels to detonate 0.01 seconds after firing.

As she pushed the button on her remote, 100 rounds of 25mm frag exploded simultaneously into the first corridor, ending the very brief and extraordinarily violent war of Captain Borisov and his three men.

Mercifully, they were already dead before the grenades they were holding exploded.

From his position ten feet back where he was putting a splint and bandage on the wounded trooper, Bondarev had a 45-degree angle view into the mouth of the corridor and it was like looking into a slaughterhouse killing floor. Neither Borisov nor any of his men made it out. Smoke poured from the corridor.

"*Idiot*," Bondarev cursed. Borisov's remaining two men were still stationed further along the flight deck, watching the second door. "Hold your positions!" he yelled at them. "Prepare for the Americans to counter-attack!"

Bondarev grabbed the wounded man by his combat vest and tried to drag him away from the door, but with the weight of his gear and the rifle he was still carrying he was too heavy. He pointed at a blast deflector further up the ramp. "Get yourself over there and get ready with that rifle. They'll try to break out now." The man started belly crawling, dragging his wounded leg behind him. Bondarev looked balefully over at the pristine blast door further down the deck, with only two troopers covering it. There was nothing for it. He lay on his belly at an oblique angle to the bloodied corridor, pointed his little Makarov optimistically at the entrance, and waited. He kept looking down at the other door. When they came, surely they would come from there too.

What he couldn't know of course was that Rodriguez and O'Hare had only one way out of their redoubt, and it was over the barrels and out the mouth of the first corridor, straight into the muzzle of Bondarev's Makarov!

They hadn't counted on the thick, choking smoke from the detonation of the 25mm shells, and had to slam the metal tool room door shut and jam cleaning rags against the crack under the door to keep the smoke out. It made the 20 foot by 30 foot tool room that was their last refuge seem even smaller.

"How many rounds in that belt?" Rodriguez coughed.

"About a hundred. Seemed like a good idea at the time," Bunny shrugged. "Now, not so much." She took a slug of water from a bottle and handed it to her CO.

"Good to go?" Rodriguez asked, putting down the bottle and lifting her rifle.

Their next move was Bunny's idea, of course. She was a fighter pilot. She didn't have a defensive bone in her body and the idea of waiting in a 20 by 30 sarcophagus for the enemy to come and finish them, that wasn't her idea of a plan. At all.

They'd agreed they'd ride out the first wave of attackers and then try to break out. It was possible the Russians had brought a whole company of airborne troops into the base, so they were fully aware it might be a very, very short counteroffensive.

"Yes, ma'am," Bunny said, giving Rodriguez a tight smile and holding out her fist for a bump. Rodriguez saw it was shaking, and she put her rifle against the wall and grabbed Bunny's fist in both hands. "We're getting out of here Lieutenant, alright?"

"Hell *yeah*, ma'am. Hooyah."

They moved silently back up to the remains of their barricade. Looking around it, Rodriguez could see virtually nothing, no movement, just dead bodies and blood. The cavern outside was silent. Could they have killed them all? Not a chance she would take.

"Round two, Lieutenant."

Bunny held up her remote and put a thumb on the toggle switch. Moving it in one direction had triggered the 25mm ammunition belt. Moving it back again would trigger the second surprise she had rigged up for any uninvited guests. She had placed home-made 'flash-bang' pipe bombs disguised as electrical conduit pipes running the length of the wall along the launch ramp forward of the docked Fantom. Simple plastic pipes filled with a mix of aluminum powder and potassium perchlorate, they weren't intended to bring enemy troops down, merely disorient them for a few vital seconds so that Rodriguez and Bunny had a chance to break out of the corridor and begin engaging their attackers.

With O'Hare at her back, Rodriguez put her head around the corner a few inches, checking one last time that the corridor was still clear. She gripped her rifle tight. "God help us. Light it, Lieutenant," she whispered. Bunny flipped the switch.

Outside the service tunnel there was a rippling series of explosions. Rodriguez vaulted over the remains of the graphite barrels and doubled down the corridor, expecting to feel the punch of heavy rounds slamming into her body at any second, but she made it to the shattered blast door and together with O'Hare broke left, dropping onto one knee and looking for a target as O'Hare ran across the deck for the cover of the shooter's chair blast deflector.

Rodriguez saw one Russian down, lying on his stomach about fifty feet away and crawling toward a safety barrier. She put four rounds into him and looked immediately for another target. Her eyes were met with a scene of devastation. The Pond looked like it had been hit by a landslide. Water had flooded the cave to just below the flight deck. Their command trailer and all of the crew accommodations had been crushed. A second Russian was crabbing backward on his butt and she fired at him, but missed, and he rolled onto his feet and ran for the cover of the shattered command trailer, Bunny's rifle fire chasing him all the way. Rodriguez noted he was wearing a Russian aviator's uniform, but then incoming fire from somewhere on her right started hammering the wall behind her and she half stumbled, half dived for the relative protection of their last unlaunched Fantom, still crouched on the catapult.

She saw two Russians another fifty feet away further up the ramp opposite the aircraft elevator door, spraying bullets toward her but not accurately – they were clearly still fighting the disorientation caused by Bunny's flash-bangs. One of them was crouched behind cover, but the other was dazed and standing in the open. Rodriguez sighted on his chest, squeezing her trigger in short two-round bursts. One of her bullets snapped the man's head back and he fell, unmoving.

The other trooper wasn't making the same mistake. He stayed behind the low safety barrier and his return fire slammed into the landing gear of the Fantom, which was Rodriguez's only cover. But O'Hare had him flanked from her position and seeing Rodriguez taking fire, she switched her aim from the fleeing aviator to the trooper up the ramp. It looked like at least one round from O'Hare hit home and he scuttled to his left, trying to keep some of the safety barrier between him and O'Hare, but that just exposed him to Rodriguez and she put two rounds into the barrier near his head.

He quickly decided his position was hopeless and threw his rifle away, holding his hands in the air.

"*Surrender!*" he yelled in English. "I surrender!"

Bondarev had put his arms over his head as the bright, deafening explosions rippled along the launch ramp wall. His vision flared, blurred, and his ears were ringing at the noise from so many concussive blasts in such a small space. As he pulled himself up onto his haunches all he could see was a blur of movement in front of him and he staggered to his feet. The only option open to him seemed to be to run from the direction of the attack and he staggered away, seeing the crushed control room further up the launch ramp which seemed to offer the only hope of cover. Ricocheting bullets spattered around his heels as he weaved toward the wrecked trailer and then dove behind it.

Bullets hit the rock wall and metal around him, then suddenly the incoming fire stopped. He could hear at least two

American rifles continue to bark, answered by the distinctive sound of at least one 39mm Vintorez as Borisov's men fought back. He risked a peek around the corner of the trailer.

He saw one American crouched behind the landing gear of the Fantom, another in the catapult shooter's pit. The wounded man he had been bandaging lay on the flight deck, unmoving. As was one of the troopers who had been watching the second blast door. From his slightly elevated position, Bondarev could see a large pool of blood around the man's head. The other Spetsnaz up by the bridge was still returning fire, and the Americans both concentrated their fire on him next.

Bondarev didn't have a clean line of sight to the two Americans from his position and even if he'd wanted to get into the fight, his little Makarov would have been near useless against assault rifles. The two Americans who had broken out of their barricaded defensive position were in cover, and Bondarev was both too far away and too damn smart to start taking pot-shots at them. He crouched back behind the crushed remains of the former command trailer and watched. As though to confirm his own thinking, one of the Americans spun suddenly and sent a few rounds his way, which sent him ducking even lower.

Caught in a crossfire, trading shots with the two Americans, it didn't take long for the remaining Spetsnaz trooper up on the bridge to decide his position was hopeless, and Bondarev found it hard to imagine, with all the fire that had been directed at him, that he hadn't been wounded. Sure enough, after a couple of seconds without returning fire, he put an arm in the air, and Bondarev heard him yell in English, "*Surrender!*" as he threw his rifle away from him.

"Drop your weapons!" the Americans yelled back.

The man stood up, holding his sidearm out by the trigger guard and the bag which Bondarev recognized as holding demolition charges in the air over his head. Slowly, he began walking – limping, in fact – back down the bridge toward the Americans at the end of the deck.

"I surrender!" the trooper yelled again in English.

"Drop ... your ... *weapons*," the Americans yelled again. Why didn't the Spetsnaz drop his sidearm and the backpack? Did he know Bondarev was still there? Was he expecting him to do something?

As the man approached the two Americans with his pistol and backpack held high above his head, he appeared to stumble and dropped the pack. It was a distraction. Lowering his sidearm quickly, he squeezed off two shots at each of the Americans. One dropped. The other returned fire with cold precision. Three flowers of blood appeared on the man's chest and he fell to his knees, then onto his face.

After so much violence, it was suddenly very quiet inside the cavern.

"Bunny!" yelled the voice from behind the Fantom. "Talk to me!"

A grunt came from behind the blast deflector and the American who had been hit rose to one knee and rested their rifle on the barrier, pointing at Bondarev. "Still here, Boss."

Women?

"You!" the first voice called. "By the trailer. Throw your weapons in the water, hands in the air, and approach."

Bondarev shrunk back behind the wrecked trailer. "Why should I?" he called back. "You will shoot me like you shot him."

"So don't be as dumb as him," the woman said. "Drop *all* your weapons, hands in the air, nice and empty, and move this way. O'Hare, cover!"

Bondarev watched as the American by the Fantom ran over to the dead Spetsnaz, grabbed his rifle and took grenades from a pouch on his belt, then moved to a new position back inside the doorway of the blasted corridor so that Bondarev would be flanked.

Yes, it was true. He was not as dumb. But with a copter and another squad of Spetsnaz still on top of the island, able to call in an entire airborne brigade to rescue him, he wasn't too worried about being taken prisoner either.

He threw his Makarov out in front of him, watching it skid down the slope and into the water with a splash. For good measure, he pulled his survival knife out of his aviator boot and threw that into the Pond as well.

"I am coming out," he said, putting his hands up and showing empty palms.

As he moved toward the woman crouched in the wrecked doorway, he saw the other American out of the corner of his eye, moving around behind him.

"Stop there," the first woman said. "On your stomach, hands behind your head."

He did as he was told. She stepped out from the door, her rifle pointed at his back, and she flipped up the visor on her flight helmet. He got his first good look at his captor. She was wearing a dirty US Navy aviation uniform. Stocky and well muscled, black hair, she appeared to be a Latino in her early forties, and a Lieutenant Commander if he was correct. As he lay, he twisted his head to look behind him. The officer coming up behind him was a woman as well, also in a Navy pilot's uniform. She also had her visor up now, had her rifle held loosely across her chest, and blood was dripping from her right elbow.

The way they were acting, they didn't expect to be joined by anyone else.

He lay his cheek on the ground.

"I am looking very much forward to hearing your story," Bondarev said. "And how you expect to get out of here alive."

"All nuclear submarines are now on station," HOLMES advised. "By my estimate the USS *Columbia* is holding in position at 49.411841 latitude, 172.854078 longitude, about two hundred miles south of the Aleutian Islands and 600 miles east of the Russian Kuril Islands, but I calculate a degree of error of up to 10%. Signals intel indicates the rest of the nuclear submarine nuclear strike force is also in position."

"What is the range of a nuclear-armed hypersonic cruise missile?" Carl asked. "Can they hit the Kurils from there?" It would be a logical form of payback. The Russians create a dispute over an island in the Bering Sea, America makes its point with an attack on an uninhabited island in the disputed Kurils chain, north of Japan.

"Five hundred and twenty miles. It cannot strike Russian territory from its current position with a hypersonic missile. It does, however, carry ICBMs which are well within range."

"The Ambassador says it's a 'shot across the bows' – a warning," Carl said. "They can get their point across with a nuclear detonation in the open sea."

"On the basis of her information I have upgraded that likelihood from 12% to 13.5% since yesterday," HOLMES replied. "But I still regard a full nuclear pre-emptive strike to be the most likely US response."

"I thought you liked her," Carl remarked.

"Please rephrase, I do not understand."

"I'm betting she's right."

"You have a 13.5% chance of winning."

"Forget it."

Carl reached his head behind his neck and scratched his greasy scalp. It had been how many days since he last showered? Too damn many, that was for sure.

"The President is about to make an announcement. Shall I bring it onscreen?" HOLMES asked.

"What? Yes please." Carl tilted the screen and leaned back in his chair.

He hadn't voted for the guy who was staring out at him from behind his desk in the Oval Office. But then, he hadn't voted for anyone, so he only had himself to blame that in the middle of the biggest military crisis of the century, their Commander in Chief was a seventy-five-year-old whose sole military experience was as a platoon leader for the 3rd US Infantry Regiment, guarding Arlington National Cemetery in Northern Virginia. He had demonstrated his temperament in the Turkey-Syria conflict, cutting loose the Emirates as allies when they refused to allow him to base US aircraft there – a decision which unfortunately moved them into the Russian sphere. Williams had to hope President Fenner had cooler heads around him, but if Ambassador McCarthy was right, it wasn't certain he did.

"My fellow citizens," Fenner began. He had a pinched, narrow face and long nose, atop which sat small round rimless glasses of a type that had been fashionable several years ago. His bushy silver hair was swept across his forehead and looked like it was held in place by solid epoxy. "At this hour, I have taken steps to free our citizens on Saint Lawrence and to defend the world from a grave danger.

"As you would be aware, for the last several weeks, under the guise of moving to protect the rights of international shipping in the Bering Strait, Russian forces have occupied the US territory of Saint Lawrence Island, to which we responded forcefully with regrettable loss of life on both sides. Russia has since escalated the conflict further and attacked US Air Force bases at Fairbanks and Anchorage. We have again responded to Russian military aggression in kind, with successful attacks on Russia's frontline offensive airfields at Anadyr and Lavrentiya."

The President paused as a graphic came onscreen showing the location of the Russian bases and grainy images of bomb damage, and Carl realized he was allowing this last news to sink in, because until now it had not been public.

"This escalation cannot be allowed to continue. It stops, *today*.

"At 0800 hours Eastern Standard Time I advised President Navalny of Russia that unless he gave a commitment to withdraw his troops from Saint Lawrence by 1200 hours, he would witness a demonstration of force the like of which the world has not seen for nearly 100 years. As there has been no indication that President Navalny wishes to comply with this demand, I have authorized our Navy to conduct the first-ever live demonstration of a hypersonic missile-borne nuclear weapon – the first atmospheric nuclear weapons test by the

United States since 1962. The test will take place in three hours over the North Pacific Sea.

"While it will pose no threat to humankind, it will wreak terrible environmental devastation, and we deeply regret it has come to this. But I am afraid that unless Russia is persuaded to halt its military misadventure over Alaska and the Bering Strait, even greater catastrophe awaits us." Fenner looked straight down the barrel of the camera. "President Navalny, withdraw your troops. The United States stands ready to use any and all of the weapons in its arsenal to defend its sovereign territory.

"My fellow citizens, the dangers to our country and the world will be overcome. We will pass through this time of peril and carry on the work of peace. We will defend our country and we will prevail.

"May God bless our country and all who defend her."

The camera faded to some shocked news anchors, mute for possibly the first time in their lives.

Carl turned down the sound, leaned back, and whistled.

There was a very strict NSA rule about not using the organization's bandwidth and resources for private purposes. Carl regarded it as more of a guideline. He wasn't a big investor, but he had all of his non-401(K) savings invested in stocks. So yesterday, he had gotten HOLMES to analyze the likely impact on the stock market of a US nuclear weapons test in the context of the current conflict.

When he'd finished reading HOLMES' conclusions, he'd gone straight online, sold everything he had, leveraged himself to the eyeballs and bought gold. Not gold futures, or gold mining stocks. He'd bought real gold: 535,000 dollars' worth of one-ounce South African Krugerrand coins from a bullion dealer in Moscow, which were now stashed in a duffel bag under combination lock in the filing cabinet of his office.

Because HOLMES' conclusion had been that while a US nuclear test in itself wouldn't necessarily mean Armageddon for the planet, it certainly would be the equivalent of a cosmic meteor strike on the stock market.

He sat and watched his screen for a few minutes as the Dow reacted to the President's address. Blood-red numbers started filling one window. A second window showed the spot price for gold heading skyward. *OK, so that's what the end of the world looks like.* He turned the screen off. By the end of the day, if HOLMES' projections were right, he'd be able to pay off his loans and still be a millionaire, even accounting for the spread when he tried to sell some of his 300 Krugerrand again. It didn't make him happy, because there was the small matter of whether anyone would be alive to trade with, but he'd deal with that problem when he got there. Or not.

ARMAGEDDON

When the President announced the American decision to give Russia a reminder of its nuclear capabilities over the North Pacific, Devlin McCarthy was sitting with the Russian Deputy Foreign Minister, Sergei Popov. She had requested an urgent appointment with Foreign Minister Kelnikov but had been told he wasn't available. At the same time as she was in the Foreign Ministry building, every single member of her Embassy staff with high-level contacts was also in meetings with their Russian counterparts, waiting for the media bombshell to drop.

Popov was one of those stereotypical 'ministry of anything' bureaucrats, who never added anything to a conversation, but who occasionally nodded, smiled or frowned, meaning his body language was usually more telling than what he said. He was very overweight and if he wasn't comfortable, began to sweat heavily. If he was angry, his round, smooth face would turn bright red. If he felt he was in a winning position in a discussion, he would audibly snicker like a vaudeville actor. And he had a very annoying habit of speaking in a derogatory way in Russian to his aides about the very people he was meeting with, knowing that some of them spoke perfect Russian and understood everything he was saying.

The excuse McCarthy had used to call for the meeting was the demand, made that morning by President Fenner, for the immediate withdrawal of Russian forces from Saint Lawrence. Devlin knew the deadline of midday was neither practical, nor reasonable – not least because Russia was not acting alone but on behalf of a so-called 'coalition of nations' in the Barents Euro-Arctic Council. Popov had spent the first few minutes of their meeting making her aware of this, before advising that in any case Russia had no intention of complying. He had then commented in Russian to his people, of whom there were three sitting like nodding Easter Island statues, that "perhaps these dumb Americans should have thought through the consequences before they sank the *Ozempic Tsar.*" The Easter Islanders agreed.

It was around then when her telephone began buzzing in Devlin's jacket pocket. "Excuse me," she said, looking at the screen. "I think I need to take this. The American President is about to make an address to the nation. Shall we watch it together?" She logged onto the video feed and sat her phone on the table between them so that they could all see.

There was sudden consternation among the Russians as one of them suggested they should break off the meeting and perhaps reconvene after the President's address. Another suggested to call off the meeting completely. By then, it was easier for them to remain and listen, out of fear of missing what the US President was saying.

As phrases like 'nuclear missile test', 'North Pacific' and 'all weapons in our arsenal' began to sink in, Devlin studied Popov carefully. She had seen the text of the President's address before going into the meeting, so she knew what to expect. The Russians listened in complete silence, but the shock on Popov's face was not just clear, it was palpable. It emanated from his every pore. Gone were his brash overconfidence, his dismissive asides to his aides. Beads of sweat peppered his forehead after the first few sentences, and by the end of the Presidential address he had reached for a handkerchief to wipe them away.

As the President concluded, Popov stood up. "I must consult with the Minister," he said and started gathering his papers.

"Please tell him that at this stage it is just a weapons test," Devlin said. "What happens next is in your hands."

"Just a…" Popov said, biting off his words. But he could not contain himself. "It is a declaration of world war! Nuclear war! Has America gone mad?!"

"It was not us who invaded your territory and attacked your Air Force," Devlin said, deliberately goading him.

"You… you sank our freighter, made cyber-attack on our submarine, launched cruise missiles at our legitimate peacekeeping forces. Now you threaten us with nuclear war!"

His hands were shaking as he stuffed papers into his briefcase, shaking so badly in fact that an aide took the papers and the briefcase from him.

He really believes it, Devlin realized. The Kremlin propagandists have done their job well. This is how war gets legitimized.

Now Popov's look changed from anger to … what? Sadness? "This meeting is over. Someone will show you out," Popov said. He walked to the door with his people. "Our military will not ignore this provocation. You have just doomed yourselves, and perhaps the entire planet."

"Lie down, just lie still," Dave said, kneeling behind Perri, holding him around the shoulders and easing him to the floor of the water tank. Blood stained his shirt just above his belt. "We have to get out. We have to get into town and get you some help."

"Check… the guy… outside," Perri said through gritted teeth.

Dave lay Perri down and he curled up on his side, knees to his chest. Stepping carefully to a bullet hole at eye level on the side the shooting had come from, he peered out.

There was no one there. He saw blood on the ground though. He walked slowly around the tank, as quietly as he could, peering through bullet and shrapnel holes. The Russian had disappeared.

"He's gone. I think you hit him."

"You have to get out," Perri said.

"We *both* have to…"

"Just go!" Perri said. "I can't move."

"I can't just leave you here. You're bleeding!" Dave said plaintively.

"Bleed worse… if I try to walk," Perri said.

Dave looked outside again. There was still no sign of the Russian. "I can't leave you lying here." *What can I do?* He crouched and reconnected the radio, fumbling with unfamiliar wires before it came to life.

"Sarge, this is uh, White Bear. Sarge, are you there?" he asked. "Come in, Sarge!"

He had to repeat himself three times, when finally the Mountie's voice came on. "White Bear? This is Sarge. Is everything OK?"

"Yes, everything is fine. Except it isn't. We ran into a Russian soldier and Perri has been shot. In the guts. What should I do?"

"Dave, are you safe?" Sarge asked. "First, you have to get to somewhere safe."

"I think so, I think the Russian is gone. Perri shot him," he said.

"Stay on the line, I am patching you through to emergency services," Sarge said. Perri listened in as Sarge called what sounded like a 911 number, explained who he was and told the paramedic he was dealing with a gunshot wound in a foreign country. He came back on. "OK Dave, putting you through."

It sounded like Sarge was holding the radio microphone up to a speakerphone. "Dave, is that your name?" a paramedic asked, sounding like he was talking from a fish bowl.

"Yeah."

"I'm going to ask you a lot of questions, Dave, and for now I just want you to give me short answers, OK?"

"Yes."

"Is your friend conscious?"

"Yes."

"Is he breathing?"

"Yeah."

"Can he speak?"

"Perri? Can you talk on the radio?"

"Hurts…" Perri said. "Thirsty."

"He can, but he says it hurts. And he's thirsty," Dave said, reaching for a water bottle on the floor of the tank.

"No! Don't give him anything to drink. OK?"

Dave put the bottle back down. "Yeah."

464

"OK. Tell me where your friend was shot."

"In the stomach, just above his waist."

"Can you see blood anywhere else? Look carefully." Dave checked Perri all over.

"I don't think so."

"Can you get his shirt open and have a look at the wound for me?"

"He's all curled up."

"You need to be careful, but I need you to have a look for the bullet wound and describe it to me, Dave. Can you do that?"

"Yeah. Just wait." He put down the radio handset and pulled aside Perri's jacket, then gingerly unbuttoned Perri's shirt, his fingertips slipping on the buttons because of the blood. Perri had his arms around his waist and Dave had to lift one away. He saw a small neat hole off to the left of Perri's belly button, leaking blood. "OK, he's been shot down near his belt," Dave said. "Between his belly button and his hip."

"Is it a hole or is it sliced open?"

"Hole."

"Is it bleeding?"

"A bit."

"This is important, Dave. Is the blood pulsing out, or is it just leaking out?"

"Uh, leaking I think. Not really pulsing," he said. "It's not really bleeding that much."

"Is it bright red or dark red?"

"Uh, a bit hard to see in here. Dark, I think," he said. "Wait." He reached into his backpack and pulled out a torch. Shining it on the wound he saw dark red blood leaking slowly out. "Dark. Is that good or bad?"

"Neither," the man said. "Can you check his back for me, see if there is a bullet wound there too?"

"OK." Dave checked Perri's back, rolled him over a little, peeled off one arm of his jacket and lifted his shirt. He winced. "Yeah. There's another hole, a bigger one, in his side near his hip." It looked like the bullet had expanded on its way through and the hole at the back looked like something that had been made with an ice pick. From the inside.

"Is he still breathing? Is he still conscious?"

"Perri? How you doing, buddy?"

"Still ... here," Perri said.

"Yeah, he is."

"OK, keep an eye on him, tell me if anything changes in his breathing or if he loses consciousness. You are going to put a pressure bandage around his stomach to get some pressure on those wounds, but not too much. Do you know how to do that? Do you have a wound dressing, or something you can use as a bandage?"

"I guess," Dave said. "I've got some clothes here."

The paramedic talked him through it as he tore up a shirt, wadded part of it into a pad to put over the bullet hole, and then bound it in place by tying the strips of shirt into a bandage and winding them around Perri's waist. As he did it, the paramedic had him check on Perri constantly and give him a better description of where the wounds were. When he was finished, he asked again, "Perri, how you doing, man?"

"Been shot, Dave," the boy replied with his jaw clenched, eyes closed.

"He's still with us," Dave told the paramedic.

"Right. You can't do any more right now. You need to get him to a hospital. He may have been shot in the intestines, or he may have been lucky and the bullet has just passed through his dorsal hip muscles, I can't say."

"I can't just 'get him to a hospital'!" Dave said. "Dude, I am hiding in a water tank in the middle of a bombed-out city surrounded by freaking Russian stormtroopers!"

There was a pause at the other end. "Dave, I understand. I need you to calm down and listen," the paramedic said.

Dave took a deep breath. "Okay, okay, I'm listening, but this is no normal hunting accident, you got that?"

"I understand. Your friend is losing blood. He might have internal bleeding too. He might stabilize, or he could go into shock and die. Even if he stabilizes, he will almost certainly

466

have infection, and that can kill him too. If you can't get him out, you need to bring medical help to him, urgently. Is there a doctor you can go to for help?"

"You *don't* understand! The whole town is being held prisoner!" Dave said. "If there is a doctor, he's *Russian*. Sarge, are you there? Sarge, what are we going to do?!"

The paramedic started to talk again, but Sarge broke in over the top of him.

"Dave, you have no choice," he said. "You have to go to the Russians and ask them for help."

"You are kidding me! We blew up their ammo dump in Gambell, we just shot one of their guys."

"They probably don't know that. You find them, you tell them you were hiding out in those ruins and you were scared and you shot Perri by mistake."

"And I'll be a prisoner, and he'll be dead."

"Or they'll help. There's a chance. It's his only chance."

"Damn, Sarge," Dave whined.

"Go...blubber brain," Perri said, listening to them.

Dave looked down at him. Perri was still lying curled up, eyes closed, breathing slowly. *"You're* the one got shot, blubber brain," Dave said. But Perri was breathing more raggedly now, almost panting in short, shallow gasps. "Okay, okay, I'll go." He logged off the radio, took off his own jacket, then worked Perri's arms into it and pulled it tight around him, zipping it up. With a grimace he pulled Perri's bloodstained jacket on, then put his rifle over his shoulder and patted Perri on the back. "Hang in, buddy."

"Water..." Perri said.

"I can't man, sorry," Dave said, moving the water bottle out of reach. "Doctor's orders." Then he put a foot on the ladder and began to climb.

Private Zubkhov watched as the hatch at the top of the water tank opened. He had heard what sounded like a radio conversation within the tank, but was too far away to hear what the American was saying. After the exchange of fire he'd crawled away from the tank and hidden himself in a destroyed building about fifty feet away.

That goddamned radio!

It was the second time the American had shot him. This time the slug had buried itself in his upper thigh, tearing through his leg muscle, but luckily missing his artery. He'd scrambled for cover, dragging himself into the ruins on his one good leg before he collapsed. Inside the ruin he'd tied a tourniquet around his leg to stop the bleeding and checked his ammunition. He had his rifle, five clips, but couldn't hold it to aim it for a damn. His sidearm and three clips. Not that he could do much with a sidearm from this far away, shooting with his wrong hand.

So he watched helplessly as the American climbed out of the water tank and started shinnying down the side, looking around him as he did. Smart guy. Sneaky guy. It had all gone sideways quickly but all he could remember was the guy coming up out of the hatch in the tank and then opening fire on him. He'd returned fire, but had had no idea where to aim and had been shooting with his bad hand so his aim had been wild.

As Zubkhov watched him, the only satisfaction he got was the sight of the blood on the man's shirt. So, he'd wounded the bastard. Not that he looked like it bothered him. The man reached the platform on which the water tank was mounted, threw his rifle down and then jumped down, without any apparent difficulty. Zubkhov lifted up his sidearm and sighted on the man as he picked up his rifle. "Bang bang, you're dead," Zubkhov said quietly as the man straightened up, looked around again, and then jogged off toward Savoonga township. Without the radio.

He lowered his Makarov. For the second time, Zubkhov watched as the American soldier escaped. The guy was a freaking Baba Yaga, some kind of unkillable spirit monster.

Yeah? Well, Zubkhov was still alive too. And in what was left of the decreasingly rational part of the mind of Private

Zubkhov of 14th Special Purpose Brigade, 282nd Squadron, he was still operational and his mission objective was in reach.

The American had not taken the radio with him.

OK, so he wasn't going to be able to make it back to Gambell, but his buddy could just as easily pick him up somewhere near Savoonga. Zubkhov was going to get that damned radio if it killed him.

Devlin's car was navigating itself through the streets of a city that had gone mad. People were running, everywhere. They were running out of their offices and workplaces. They were running toward supermarkets and kiosks. They were running down the road with bags heavy with canned food and bottled water. Devlin closed her eyes and swallowed the lump in her throat. She understood the people running home to be with their loved ones, but why were people queuing outside the shops? How did you shop for an apocalypse?

On the back seat of the limo, she began composing her message to State. It would be in short sparse sentences, as would the reports of all her people. There was no time for elegant prose, or making a collective report. State wanted raw, real-time feedback on the responses of the Russian nomenklatura.

Devlin's report looked like this:

Met with Deputy Foreign Minister Sergei Popov in his offices and watched the Presidential address in his company.

He appeared shocked.

He called the nuclear weapons test 'a declaration of war'.

He accused the US of starting the conflict with the sinking of the Ozempic Tsar and does not doubt the Russian version of the story that the US was behind this sinking.

He said the Russian military would be bound to respond to the nuclear test and that the USA had just 'doomed itself'.

He then terminated the meeting.

She was about to hit 'send' when the car swerved around a group of people in the street and she saw them putting a large pole through the window of a closed shop, smashing the glass. Up ahead, traffic was at a complete standstill.

She returned to add to her message:

Moscow's civil administration has declared a State of Emergency. There is panic in the streets, hoarding of food, looting of shops. On return to the embassy I will initiate a lockdown. Local staff will be allowed/required to leave, all US personnel ordered to return to the compound. All available security personnel will be put on the entrances with orders to admit no Russian nationals, whether civilian, police or military.

I will be authorizing armed security personnel to use lethal force to protect the embassy if needed.

"Ma'am?" her head of security said as the car jerked to a stop. Several people standing in the middle of the road were looking at the car. Even though they had removed the traditional US flags from the wings, it still carried diplomatic plates. "My GPS says traffic is gridlocked. Looks like the whole city is trying to evacuate. I suggest we go the rest of the way on foot."

"Very well." Devlin hit 'send', then grabbed her briefcase.

The driver reached over and handed her his black knee-length coat. "Take this, ma'am."

She smiled at him. "Thanks, David, I'll be warm enough."

"No, ma'am, to cover your clothes. This isn't a neighborhood you want to be seen walking around in a red power suit."

"You warm enough, mate?" Bunny asked Bondarev. "Sitting comfortably?"

"Enough, Lieutenant," Rodriguez said. She'd tied up Bondarev and attended to O'Hare's wounded right hand. The pistol round had smacked into the hand wrapped around the grip of her rifle, passing between the metacarpal bones in the middle of the back of her hand and spinning the rifle out of her hand. In the heat of the firefight she'd been able to grab the rifle again and get her finger into the trigger guard, but as every

470

minute passed the torn muscles in the hand had stiffened and Rodriguez had almost to pry the hand off the gun to be able to sterilize and dress the wound. She probably needed stitches to close the entry and exit wounds on both sides of her palm, but that would have to wait. Of course, Bunny had looked more pissed off than wounded as Rodriguez had given her a local anesthetic jab.

When she was done fixing up Bunny, they had dragged the bodies of the dead Spetsnaz troopers into a storeroom leading off the tool room that was their 'keep'. Bunny had searched Bondarev and confiscated a small first-aid kit, survival blanket, map and satellite telephone from the pockets of his flight suit.

Rodriguez pointed her gun at him. "How many men do you have up top?"

"Enough that you would run out of bullets before I ran out of men," Bondarev told her.

"The last bullet would be for you, tough guy," Bunny said. Bondarev looked at the young pilot. She still had her rifle slung over her shoulder, her wounded hand – trigger finger sticking out of the bloodied bandage – on the scarred grip. He had little doubt she was speaking the truth.

"You have no way out of here," Bondarev said to the senior officer. "You fought a good war. But your war is over. You can't hold me hostage forever. Let me contact my men. I will guarantee you are treated according to the conventions for prisoners of war."

O'Hare laughed bitterly. "Because you are so respectful of conventions," she snarled. "Like the convention against the use of massive ordnance air blast weapons, like the convention against the use of cluster munitions, oh, and the convention against invading foreign countries? How about that one?"

Bondarev ignored her, kept his eyes fixed on her superior. "The Spetsnaz overhead would have protocols if contact is lost with their recon squad down here. They would be preparing, right now, to react to this situation. You were lucky once, you won't be lucky again. And I don't want to get killed in the crossfire."

Rodriguez knew that what he was saying held a lot of truth. They had dealt with the first Russian force that had entered the Rock, but what about the next, and the one after that? She and O'Hare had not expected to survive the Russian assault; they certainly hadn't expected to find themselves back in control, and with a Russian Air Force Colonel as their hostage as well. She had no doubt the troops topside were preparing a plan to come in and find out what had happened to their comrades. And when they came, they would come in hard and hot. It would not be a recon force they sent.

The only option Rodriguez saw was to trade this Colonel for their own safety. Some kind of mutual swap that might get them off the damn Rock.

It was as though O'Hare could read her mind. She looked sharply at Rodriguez. "Ma'am, are you thinking what I…"

She didn't finish her sentence. They had emptied the Russian's pockets and Bondarev's telephone was in a bag at her feet. It started ringing.

"The telephone is still switched on and receiving," HOLMES said. "Would you like me to call again?"

"Yes please," Devlin said. She had arrived at the Embassy and got herself waved through by several nervous Marines to find Williams standing at the gates.

"Carl," she had said. "Whatever this is will have to wait. I have a million…"

"HOLMES says the Russians are scrambling two Tu-162 strategic nuclear bombers from Vladivostok," he said. "Their target is inside Alaska. Don't ask me *how* he knows. They'll be airborne in five minutes!"

Devlin had put her hands behind her head and looked up at the leaden gray skies. The world had gone mad. "Carl, what do you want *me* to do about that? If HOLMES knows, then NORAD already knows too, or they soon will. They'll probably try to intercept them."

"There is not a single US aircraft that can get there in time!" Carl had said urgently. "Russia has air superiority over the Alaska theater."

Her head was spinning. She had nearly yelled at him. "So? So *what* Carl?!"

"Call Bondarev again," he'd said. "Appeal to him. Maybe he can stop the bombers. He's operational commander in the Russian Operations Area."

"Carl, you heard him, he hung up on me. His fighters are probably *escorting* those bombers."

"Then he's in the perfect position to shoot them down. Fenner authorizing a nuclear test over the North Pacific was dumb, but Russia ordering a nuclear attack on a target in Alaska in response is totally *insane*. There's a chance he doesn't know or he doesn't support it." He looked at her like a man trying to talk a suicidal jumper off a rooftop, and that was more or less how she felt. "It's a *chance*, Devlin!"

Five minutes later she was standing in his office once again, listening to a telephone ring somewhere in the Arctic.

"Hello?" a voice replied. It was not Bondarev. It was a woman. "Who is this?" the woman at the other end demanded brusquely. *Speaking English?*

"Uh, this is Ambassador Devlin McCarthy of the US Embassy in Moscow," Devlin replied, unable to keep the confusion out of her voice. "I am trying to get in contact with Colonel Yevgeny Bondarev of the …"

"Uh huh. You're the US Ambassador in Moscow?" the woman asked in an Australian accent. "And I'm Nicole Kidman. What do you want with the Colonel?"

Australian? What the… "I need to speak with him urgently on State business," Devlin said. "Can you please connect me?"

"He's a little tied up right now…" the woman said. Then Devlin heard a muffled conversation and a new voice came on the line.

"This is Lieutenant Commander Alicia Rodriguez of the US Navy," the voice said. "Ambassador, you need to find a way to authenticate yourself before I can even begin to believe you are who you are."

McCarthy frowned. An American Navy officer on Bondarev's telephone? This was getting weirder and weirder. Devlin looked helplessly at Williams sitting across the desk from her.

He took a breath, put his hand on Devlin's to calm her, then spoke in a loud voice. "Commander Rodriguez, this is Carl Williams of the NSA. Please stay on the line and listen carefully. HOLMES, can you please pull up the service record of US Navy Lieutenant Commander Alicia Rodriguez and put it on my screen?"

"Yes, Carl. I have three possible candidates, putting the best match on screen now."

Williams scanned the screen quickly. "Commander, your current assignment is to a unit called A4 on Little Diomede Island, a Naval Air Forces Command black facility that is classified Top Secret Warling Orcon, your previous assignment was as mini-boss about the USS *GW Bush* and, uh, let's see ... sixteen years ago you were docked two weeks' pay for returning late from a shore leave in Hawaii."

The silence at the other end didn't last long. "Put the Ambassador back on."

Devlin leaned over the desk. "Lieutenant Commander, McCarthy here. I need to speak with Colonel Bondarev *urgently*, is he with you?"

"Yes, ma'am, but we are in a difficult situation here, we..."

"Commander!" Devlin barked. "Get off this damn phone and put Bondarev on. Now!"

Rodriguez held the phone away from her ear as the woman on the other end shouted, and then put it on speakerphone, moving it closer to Bondarev. "Ambassador Devlin McCarthy for you."

Bondarev frowned; he had no real choice but to listen. "Colonel Bondarev here. Is this about my daughter again?"

"No. Colonel, are you aware the US is about to conduct a nuclear weapons test in the North Pacific Ocean?"

Bondarev didn't react. "No, I am not. And I have no reason to believe you."

"It was announced about 30 minutes ago on worldwide media. But if you aren't aware, you may also not be aware that your Air Force has scrambled two Tu-162 strategic bombers and they are en route to conduct an attack on Alaska as we speak?"

Now Bondarev reacted. He paled, visibly. "I do not believe you."

"I am not asking you to," the Ambassador said. "But I am asking you to stop them somehow if it is true. For the sake of your daughter. For the sake of the *world*."

Bondarev thought quickly. "Will the US stop its nuclear test?"

"I can't promise that," Devlin said. "That is the honest truth. It isn't in my power."

"Assuming you are telling the truth, you are about to detonate a nuclear weapon, but you want me to stop our response to your attack?" he said, incredulously.

"We are about to conduct a *demonstration* out at sea," she said. "Your bombers are about to respond by attacking innocent people in a sovereign state. Only a monster could see that as a proportionate response and I can't believe my daughter would have chosen a monster to be the father of her child!"

Bondarev looked up at the faces of his American captors. They seemed as shocked as he felt. The appeal to his fatherly instincts had not moved him. But the near inevitability of all-out nuclear war following a Russian tactical nuclear strike... "How much time do we have?"

"HOLMES?" Devlin asked.

"Twenty-three minutes to release point, Ambassador," Bondarev heard an English voice intone.

To Rodriguez he said urgently, "I am going to give you a number. Hang up this line and then call the number as I read it to you."

"Ambassador?" Rodriguez asked.

"Do as he says, Lieutenant Commander," Devlin said. "You heard what's at stake. Good luck, Colonel Bondarev."

"I promise nothing," Bondarev said. As the call was disconnected he turned to Rodriguez. "Double zero, seven, nine zero two, four eight two, eight four one, four zero."

Before she hit the connect button, the American hesitated. "How do I know you aren't just calling those troops up above?"

"You don't," Bondarev told her. "But you are welcome to listen, if you speak Russian." He waited.

She connected him.

At Savoonga airfield it was one of Tomas Arsharvin's staff who noticed his telephone ringing. The sound went unnoticed among the clamor of voices in the air field's operations room until the telephone buzzed itself off Arsharvin's desk and onto the floor. One of his people picked it up and handed it to him. When he saw who it was, he took the phone and went out into the corridor to find an empty room.

He called back immediately.

"Yevgeny!" he said. "They said you'd been shot down! Why are you..."

"I was," Bondarev replied. "Listen, Tomas..."

"Yevgeny, it's crazy here. You lost nearly a full squadron up there! Sukhois, Migs... there is a total command vacuum with you gone. Akinfeev is missing too, so Captain Komarov is technically in command. Komarov! He..."

"Tomas, *shut up!*" Bondarev said. "Is it true the Americans plan to set off a nuclear weapon in the North Pacific? Yes or no?"

"Yes," Arsharvin said. "Their President announced it. The test takes place in twenty minutes in the sea off the Kurils if they keep their word."

"And we are planning to reply with a nuclear attack on Alaska?"

Arsharvin blinked. How could Bondarev possibly know? Where *was* he? "Yes. On Anchorage. Potemkin authorized the attack. Ilyushins of the 21st Guards will be on station in about fifteen minutes. We have no way of knowing the American missile isn't aimed at a mainland target. If the Americans do carry out their nuclear launch, the bombers will get the final release codes. The minute we confirm target destruction, our airborne troops and Spetsnaz will move on Nome. It is madness."

"Potemkin *can't* authorize a nuclear attack," Bondarev said.

"No, but Defense Minister Burkhin and Potemkin together can. There's some sort of shit going down in the Kremlin, Yevgeny. My people tell me President Navalny hasn't been seen or heard from since the American President went on air, and Foreign Minister Kelnikov is under security service guard."

Bondarev had a sudden flashback to his conversation with Potemkin about the difference between duty and loyalty. He'd had a feeling Potemkin was feeling him out about something more than just loyalty to his new commander. Now he saw what it was! And with that same realization came the certainty of where his duty lay. Bondarev's voice was cold and calm. "It's a coup, Tomas. This whole thing, sinking the *Ozempic Tsar*, the attack on Alaska, it's about more than just water resources. I knew something was wrong. It stank a mile away."

Arsharvin thought hard. "But ... they're going to nuke an American city? Why?"

"Think it through, Tomas!" Bondarev's voice was urgent. "The Americans set off their nuke, the General Staff demand a nuclear response, but President Navalny refuses, Kelnikov refuses. Of course they do! Burkhin has his excuse to take Navalny out and other Generals will back him. I guarantee as soon as our nukes hit, Burkhin will be consolidating power and negotiating a ceasefire. This is not just an attack on Alaska, it is a State coup."

"The Americans will not allow a nuclear attack on Anchorage to go unanswered," Arsharvin argued. "There will be all-out nuclear war."

"The coup plotters are gambling there won't," Bondarev said. "The Americans let us take Saint Lawrence. They gave up the airspace over Alaska. If they really wanted to make a point, they could have nuked the Baltic Fleet base in Kaliningrad, but instead they're going to vaporize a few square miles of seawater and fish. The political leaders of the US have become piss-weak and Burkhin is betting they'll take his ceasefire and give him Alaska. He gets the Presidency, and Russia gets its fresh water. He's suddenly President *and* a national hero."

Arsharvin pulled air through his teeth. "I see it now," he said. Arsharvin had no love for President Navalny or Foreign Minister Kelnikov and their faction of West-leaning, pro-democracy liberals. But neither did he want to bet his future on an insane roll of the dice by some power-crazed madmen in Moscow. "What the hell can we do, Yevgeny?"

"We fight for the *Rodina*, my friend, not for Burkhin and his cronies. Get ready to call in every favor everyone ever owed you," Bondarev told him. "And back me when the time comes, alright?"

"You know I will," Arsharvin said. The line went dead. *What had he just done?* He had agreed to be either a patriot or a traitor. And he wouldn't know how his country would judge him until tomorrow dawned. If there even was a tomorrow.

Private Zubkhov's dilemma was how to climb the ladder to the top of the water tank. But escape was so close now he could taste it. All he had to do was get that radio, call his buddy, and he could get off this pile of bird dung and ice. Get himself patched up on the mainland. A drunken argument between hunters, that would be his story. OK, it was a bit weak. He'd work on it while he was on the boat. He hefted the pistol in his left hand. As he remembered the sight of the American soldier jogging away again, he regretted that he hadn't at least tried to take the shot. But he probably would have missed. Nothing had gone to plan since Gambell, nothing at all.

As he stood at the bottom of the ladder, working out how he was going to get up there with only one arm and a bad leg, he heard a voice *inside* the water tank.

What?

Despite the pain, he dropped into a crouch and lifted his pistol.

"White Bear, can you hear me?" Perri heard a voice saying. "Come in, White Bear."

The voice seemed a long way away, but then he was listening to it through a curtain of pain. All he could think about was how thirsty he was. He'd tried uncurling a little, to see if he could reach any water, but the smallest movement had caused his side to feel like it was going to rip open, so he'd clenched himself even tighter.

"White Bear, come in please. Perri, let me hear your voice, son."

Perri cracked his eyes open. As his vision focused, he saw that Dave had left the radio switched on and the handset right in front of his face. It cost him, but he reached up for the handset and pulled it closer, closing his thumb on the transmitter button. "White Bear," he whispered with a dry mouth. Then slightly louder, "This is White Bear."

"Hey, good to hear your voice, son," the Mountie said. "How are you feeling?"

Perri thought about it. "Not so good, Sarge." Perri couldn't remember. Had Dave told him what had happened? It was too much to tell, so Perri just went straight to the bottom line. "I got shot."

"I know. But it may not be as bad as it feels," the Canadian told him. "You can pull through this, alright?"

"Yeah."

"You are one tough sonofabitch, you know that?"

"Yeah."

"Your friend is going to bring help. You just have to hang on. Can you do that for me?"

"I'll try."

"You'll do more than try. You *need* to stay alive, kid. Thanks to you boys we know everything Ivan has been doing on that island of yours. What, who, how many, where and when. They're going to want to pin a medal on you one day."

"Sarge?"

"Yes, son."

"It hurts to talk. Going to stop now."

"Sure, look...."

"Won't ... die on you."

"You better not," the man said. "I'm going to call you every 20 minutes and you better answer, alright?"

"White Bear out." Perri let the handset drop and returned his arm to his waist. It felt better just trying to hold everything in tight.

He thought you were supposed to pass out when you were in this much pain. Every book he ever read, right about here was when the writer would say about the guy who got shot or clubbed or burned, *'mercifully, at that moment, he blacked out'*. But every time he moved, every time a muscle even twitched in his leg or his stomach, a bolt of searing fire shot through him, jolting him right back into his screwed up reality. How did people manage to pass out with this sort of shit going on?

So he was wide awake when he heard a voice below him say, "Hello in there, American number two."

Rodriguez heard the line drop out and she cut the call. She kept her rifle on the Russian Colonel.

"Did you understand any of that?" Bondarev asked, looking at his captors.

"I had some language training," the Australian said. "I got some of it. Like the part about a coup."

480

"You heard your Ambassador. There has been a putsch in Moscow. We are on the brink of nuclear war," Bondarev told them. "I might be able to stop it, but you have to cooperate."

Rodriguez didn't take her rifle off him. "Keep talking."

"In the backpack of one of the men you killed is a radio. I need it to contact my pilots."

"How about you contact those Spetsnaz up there and tell them to stay right where they are?" Bunny asked. "How about that for cooperation?"

"I will, after I talk with my pilots," Bondarev said. "Don't you understand? We need to work together!"

"Contact your pilots and tell them what?"

"I need to stop the attack on Anchorage," Bondarev told her. "Those bombers will be overhead in ten minutes."

Rodriguez stared at him incredulously. "You are going to tell your pilots to shoot down their own bombers?"

"They wouldn't do that," Bondarev said. "It would be treason. But I *can* order them to return to base. That's an order they might follow."

"What good would that do?"

The Russian jerked his head toward the remaining Fantom, queued up beside the flight deck. "It would leave the bombers wide open." He gestured to the hands behind his back. "But they are going to launch their missiles as soon as the American atomic test is confirmed, which means they will only wait on station for the next fifteen minutes, so I need that radio!"

Carl had been listening to the BBC Russia Service on the radio in his office and turned it off. "HOLMES, give me an update on the Alaska situation," he asked.

Carl had to admit, he was almost as much in love with Devlin McCarthy as HOLMES appeared to be. She had walked back into her Embassy with the world outside going to shit, realized he wasn't insane and was offering her a way to save the world, had jumped on the line with the Russian Commander of air operations for the 3rd Air and Air Defense Forces

Command, and had then clapped him on the shoulder and told him, "You'll have to take it from here. When that nuke goes off, angry and frightened Russians are going to be looking for a target for their anger and this Embassy is going to be goddamn ground zero." Then she'd waded back out into the maelstrom of shouting and panicked voices outside Carl's office.

"US strategic nuclear forces are at DEFCON 1," HOLMES reported calmly. "However, I now estimate the likelihood of a US first strike at less than 9%. US CYBERCOM has just initiated a high-level denial of service attack on Russian defense, financial, security and police service servers inside mainland Russia, Georgia and the Ukraine. Russian and Chinese hackers have initiated the same against American cyber systems. Lebanese Hezbollah militia backed by Syrian regular army troops have crossed the Lebanese border into Israel. The nuclear submarine USS *Columbia* has just reported it is in position as ordered and ready to execute the planned hypersonic missile launch. It is awaiting final go codes for a launch in 18 minutes. The Russian strategic bomber flight and its escort has just crossed the Russian coast at Anadyr and is holding on a racetrack pattern in the Bering Strait over Nome, Alaska. Based on satellite, cyber, signals intel, and limited human source reporting, I show a high probability the Russian force is also awaiting go codes for its attack and that the attack will be timed to take place immediately after the US nuclear detonation is confirmed."

"Do you have intel on the payload the Russian bombers are carrying?" Carl asked.

"No, Carl. I have at 64% probability the payload is nuclear, 36% it is conventional."

"Do we have any chance of an intercept?"

"Zero. No available US asset is within strike range."

"Give me your prognosis on a US Strategic Command response to a Russian nuclear attack on any populated area in Alaska."

"Insufficient data," HOLMES responded.

Carl frowned. "What do you mean? I'm asking you to run the percentages on some pretty uncomplicated scenarios. Do you need me to spell them out?"

"No, Carl, the scenarios are not complex. They range from a full-blown retaliatory nuclear strike, to a limited escalatory response, to no response at all due to total US political incapacitation."

"Then why do you have insufficient data?"

"The US response in this particular threat scenario is entirely dependent on human personality factors. I do not have sufficient insight into the personalities of President Fenner and his military advisers or their past response to such situations to calculate the relevant probabilities."

"Make a wild-assed guess," Carl ordered. One of the things he had experimented with in relation to HOLMES was something he called 'WAG code'. It worked on the knowledge that HOLMES was constantly generating and updating scenarios, assigning probabilities to them and updating the analysis as more intelligence was received. When he reached a pre-determined certainty threshold, he would share the probabilities. But until then, he would report an 'insufficient data' condition. The 'WAG state' forced him to put forward the current scenario with the highest assigned probability, even if that probability didn't meet the threshold.

"Yes, Carl. My guess is that if Russia conducts a nuclear attack on a population center in Alaska, USSTRATCOM will respond with a full-scale nuclear attack on Russian military and civilian centers."

"Right," Carl said. "Thank you. Please continue monitoring the Alaska situation, and also throw a text feed on the desktop regarding any potential threats to the US Embassy in Moscow."

"Yes, Carl." There was an unusual pause from HOLMES. "Carl, I have just picked up a report from NORAD of the launch of a US drone from the A4 base."

"*What*?? Repeat, expand!"

"NORAD is tracking a Fantom drone launched from A4 on an intercept course for the Russian bombers. It will be within air-to-air missile range in eight minutes."

"Can you hear me in there, American?" Private Zubkhov called up to the water tank. "You still have radio in there. I want that radio."

There was no response. He had heard the American say he had been shot. So it was his blood Zubkhov had seen on the man who had left the water tank. It explained a lot. Firstly, it made perfect sense there were *two* American soldiers. It explained how they had been able to outmaneuver him. He had simply been outnumbered, that was all.

Now they had separated. They had a radio, so they could have called for help. The only explanation for not doing so was that the man's comrade had deserted him. Left him to die. That was something he could use.

"American, I know you are in there!" Zubkhov said. He lifted his Makarov and fired a shot into the air. "I am still armed, but I will not shoot you. I just want that radio. Bring it out to me, and I will get you help."

"Come ... get it," a weak voice inside the water tank said. "Already shot you twice. Happy to make it three."

Zubkhov looked up at the water tank again. It sat on a wooden and steel platform. The voice had sounded like it was coming from the bottom of the tank, so the man was probably lying down. If he was badly wounded, that made sense. But Zubkhov's 9mm ammunition wouldn't have much chance of punching through the wood and steel platform and the reinforced steel bottom of the water tank as well.

He slumped down against one of the legs of the water tank.

"Dumb ass American," he said loudly. "Your comrade has left you for dead. I can get you help. I am only one who can save you." There was no answer. Zubkhov stared out at the ruins around him. "They have left you all alone, comrade. No one cares for you. I know what that feels like."

Bondarev had made the radio call to his third in command, the incredulous Captain Komarov. "Comrade Colonel, with respect, what do you mean, *ground* all aircraft?!"

"I mean, issue the order to return to base," Bondarev said. "All air patrol, air support and escort missions are canceled. All aircraft are to RTB at Lavrentiya or Savoonga."

"Sir, I am relieved you have survived the destruction of your aircraft, but were you ... injured? Your orders would mean handing the airspace over the Operations Area to the enemy," Komarov said. "I would have to confirm..."

"You will confirm nothing, *Captain*," Bondarev said, his voice steel hard. "You will follow my orders to the letter, or you will be court-martialed." Bondarev softened his tone a fraction. "We have received new operational directives and there is no time for you to take your question up the line. If you want confirmation, you can contact GRU operations intelligence on Savoonga." *I hope. Be there for me, Tomas.*

"Lieutenant Colonel Arsharvin?"

"Yes, he will confirm the order."

"Yes, sir. I will have Lieutenant Colonel Arsharvin confirm your order and recall all patrols."

"Captain?"

"Yes, Comrade Colonel?"

"There is a flight from the 4th or 5th Air Regiment escorting two Tu-162 bombers from the 21st Guards on a classified mission. We will not be recalling the bombers..." *I don't have the authority over units of the 21st Guards Heavy Bomber Aviation Regiment,* he thought to himself. *Or we would.* "But you will recall their escort. Is that clear? The commander of the 21st Guards will deal with the recall of his own aircraft."

"Yes sir!"

The man cut the line. Bondarev had no way of being sure if Komarov would comply. But he knew the man, and he knew he had never counteracted an order in his entire career, no matter how facile, so Bondarev had to hope he would not start now.

The two Americans had kept their weapons trained on Bondarev the whole time he had been speaking, and the younger one lifted hers slightly now. "Spetsnaz," she said.

"You need to launch that Fantom," Bondarev told them, failing to keep the urgency out of his voice.

"Spetsnaz," the pilot said. "We won't be launching anything if someone sends some sort of sick chemical gas grenade down that chute."

He couldn't disagree with her logic. He quickly put through a radio call to the Sergeant in charge of the remaining Spetsnaz troops topside. The man was unsettled by the lack of contact with Borisov since they had breached the US base.

"Communications have been blocked by the depth of the rock," Bondarev lied to him. "The situation here is under control. The enemy force has been neutralized. We will soon be finished here. Maintain your positions until you hear from me again."

That satisfied the two Americans. They bound him hand and foot again and pulled him over to a side wall, within speaking distance and where they could easily keep an eye on him. He saw the pilot disappear into the blasted corridor in which they had been hiding, while her commanding officer moved to a console and hit a sequence of keys which triggered the drone loading system to extend the gantry holding the drone out over the launch catapult and lower it into place.

The two allied aviators soon began a ballet of activity that left the Air Force officer in Bondarev completely awestruck.

It wasn't foresight, it was pure bloody-minded optimism. One of the last things Bunny had stowed in the 'keep' was a mil-spec laptop, a portable set of flight controls, and a wireless uplink that could log into the central servers still running deep within the base. The servers were the last thing Bunny was supposed to blow if they were bailing on the base, but even with the Spetsnaz knocking on the door, she hadn't done it. Call her crazy, she just had this hunch if she got through alive, she might just need an uplink. And if she didn't, what the hell difference did it make?

As Rodriguez ran the boot sequence on the Fantom and checked that it wasn't reporting system errors after the beating it had taken, Bunny closed the catapult bridge, then, one-handed, pulled some crates and boxes behind the blast shield and created a makeshift cockpit for herself. With only the virtual screen real estate of her virtual-reality headset to work with, and with her joystick and throttle clamped to a stack of boxes, her ass parked on a collapsible chair and her feet on a pair of hot-linked rudder pedals held to the ground with two heavy iron bars lying across their plastic feet, she felt like a fourteen-year-old again, flying flight sims on a gamer rig in the basement of her parents' house. Those sims had been her refuge from all the BS happening upstairs between her parents, and she had to bite hard on the memories to hold them back as she got herself set up and online. It only took her about five minutes, though. It was a routine she could run in her sleep.

"Ready to boot!" Rodriguez called over to her. "You mission capable there, Lieutenant?"

Bunny gave her a bloodied salute with her mangled paw. "Let's lock and load, ma'am!" she called, putting her virtual-reality helmet down and running over to the Fantom. Between them they bullied the drone onto the catapult rail and got it locked into the shuttle.

Bunny headed back behind the blast shield and pulled on her helmet.

"Booted!" Rodriguez called. She dropped into the shooter's chair. The boot system told her the Fantom's flight and weapons systems were online and ready for launch. The boot system check had reported no faults. But there had been no time to check the Fantom's physical integrity. There had been a lot of metal and stone flying around the Fantom in the last few hours. It wasn't unlikely some of it had struck the

Fantom in its cradle. She just had to hope its hardened alloy shell hadn't been punctured anywhere fatal.

Or it could be a very short flight.

"Bridge locked and Cat clear?"

"Locked and clear, aye!"

"Man out?"

"Man out, aye!"

"Light her tail."

"Afterburner, aye!"

The Fantom's engines screamed to full power. Her shooter's console lit up green.

"*Launching!*" she called.

Despite herself, she flinched as the fighter rocketed down the catapult, across the bridge and out of the chute, expecting to see it explode into a spectacular fireball of hydrogen fuel and liquid metal at any moment. It was almost with disbelief that she watched its silhouette disappear out of the mouth of the chute and bank away south for the 120-mile, ten-minute journey to the bomber intercept point.

"Systems green, Boss, good launch," Bunny said from inside her rig. Her left hand flew over the keyboard but she winced as she stabbed down with her right index finger and thumb, the only digits on her right hand she could use for anything. "Hey, 'Skippy' is still on the air!" she said in surprise. "How you doing out there, little buddy?" It was an unexpected and welcome advantage. Linked to NORAD, its data-net covering an area two hundred miles around Little Diomede, the grounded Fantom was working like a seaborne-WACS. It would help bring down the lag time between Bunny's control inputs and the drone response dramatically.

Looking over at their Russian hostage, Rodriguez saw him watching them intently. OK, so A4 had no more secrets to keep. She walked up behind Bunny. She couldn't see on the laptop exactly what Bunny was seeing inside her virtual-reality rig, because it was showing Bunny both a virtual cockpit instrument panel and heads-up display, the view out of the drone cockpit simulation cameras and data being downlinked from NORAD satellite coverage. But Bunny had set the laptop to show the tactical map of the Operations Area, and Rodriguez could clearly see the icon for their Fantom heading south from Little Diomede. She also saw with some satisfaction the red icons of other enemy formations moving south and west from the Bering Strait and Alaska toward Savoonga and Lavrentiya. It seemed Bondarev's orders were being implemented after all. At least until someone further up the chain asked what in the name of Stalin's Sainted Son was going on.

Major Vasily Ivanovich Alekseyev of the 21st Guards Heavy Bomber Aviation Regiment was one of the first frontline pilots qualified on the new generation Tupolev Tu-162 strategic bomber. Essentially a large flying wing made of stealth composite materials, it was able to carry up to 88,000lb of fuel and ordnance, but its normal loadout was two rotary launchers each holding six hypersonic cruise missiles capable of carrying either conventional or nuclear warheads. The Tupolev itself was already a treaty breaker, because its development had specifically been banned under at least two bilateral US-Russia arms treaties. The Tsirkon 3M22 hypersonic missiles it carried were also banned by several treaties. So it mattered little whether they were armed with conventional or nuclear warheads.

Major Alekseyev knew exactly what warheads had been loaded on his Tsirkon missiles, but his crew and the crew of the other aircraft flying in formation with him did not. He did not consider it necessary that they knew. If they had known, several of them might not have been able to perform their duties. Alekseyev had no such issues.

He had known every time he took to the skies for the last twenty years that the day may come when he was required to fire nuclear weapons at an enemy of his motherland. He trusted that if he was asked to do so, it would only be in a situation of national survival. Literally of life or death, at the risk of total national oblivion. As he kept his flight of two Tu-162s on

489

station off the coast of Alaska and waited for the go codes that would confirm his mission, he couldn't help but reflect that he probably felt exactly the same right now as an American called Paul Tibbets had felt nearly 100 years ago.

When *he* had been asked to drop a nuclear bomb on 350,000 unarmed civilians.

In a city called Hiroshima.

Bunny had pushed the Fantom high, tail on fire all the way. She had to trust what her screens were telling her, namely that the Russian Colonel really was pulling all of his aircraft out of the Operations Area. Not just those escorting the Tupolevs, but every damned bird over the Bering Strait and Alaska. She knew NORAD would be looking at the same feed she was, and had no doubt hundreds of US fighters down south were currently getting airborne to fill the vacuum the Russians had left in the sky behind them.

Within minutes she was within Cuda missile range of the Russian bombers. For all their stealth technology, the bombers were too big to hide from satellites and ground stations that knew exactly where to look, and there wasn't a single inch of air over the Operations Area that wasn't covered by US eyes in the sky right now.

Bunny kept radiation from her Fantom to a minimum, taking data from NORAD and Skippy, and assigned missiles to each of the two targets, but held her fire. She had never taken on a Tu-162 bomber before, either in a sim or in real life, and had no idea what kind of countermeasures, physical or electronic, it had up its sleeve. So she planned to let her missiles go at the absolute inside of their effective range, giving the bombers the least possible time to detect and evade the active radar and laser guidance systems of the Cudas.

That window closed quicker than she would have liked, but as warnings began to appear within her heads-up display that she was about to breach the operational envelope, she lit up the targets with her own radar and launched four of her eight air-to-air missiles. Her voice betrayed her as she nearly shouted, "Target locked: Cudas away!"

One thousand eight hundred and sixty miles away, in the North Pacific Sea west of the Kuril Islands, the USS *Columbia* rose to launch depth. Only one of the hull doors for its 16 missile launch tubes was open, and that had only been opened after its escort of three SSN(X) *Virginia*-class attack submarines had ensured there would be no unwelcome visitors trying to disturb the launch.

At precisely four minutes to three p.m., US Eastern Time, 120,000lb of sea water was flash vaporized inside the launch tube, blasting the hypersonic Waverider missile out of the water and into the air above the sub. There it hung for a moment as its upward momentum faded and gravity tried to pull it back down into the sea. Until its first-stage MGM-140 ATACMS solid rocket booster ignited and drove the missile five hundred feet into the air on a diagonal trajectory that quickly took it to 3,000 miles per hour.

Unlike in an ICBM launch, it only burned for a few incandescent seconds before the rocket burned itself out, and the missile nosed back toward the earth. As it did, it ejected its outer shell, revealing a dolphin-shaped head fixed to a conical booster. Small, stubby wings sprang out of recessed grooves at the back of the missile, and its second-stage Pratt & Whitney Rocketdyne SJY61 scramjet accelerated it to 4,000 miles an hour.

It covered the 400-mile 'safe distance' to the west of the USS *Columbia* in just six minutes.

The Waverider was fitted with a 200-kiloton W89 nuclear warhead, otherwise known as a 'tactical nuke' for its relatively modest size. It was only twenty times the power of the bomb that had destroyed the Japanese city of Nagasaki. The W89-armed Waverider had never been tested under operational conditions and it was in fact the first ever such test of a nuclear weapon mounted on a hypersonic missile. A second missile had

491

been queued in case of a launch failure but it wasn't needed. It flew true.

When it detonated, the flash of light was clearly visible from the Russian city of Petropavlovsk on the Kamchatka Peninsula, and within minutes vision of the weapons test had been broadcast around the world.

When the Tupolevs' escort had radioed Major Alekseyev that they had been ordered to return to base, he had not been overly concerned. He knew the 3rd Air and Air Defense Forces Command had achieved total air superiority over the Operations Area since the early days of the conflict, when several older Tu-160 bombers had been lost in the successful attack on Elmendorf-Richardson and Eielson air bases. The men of the 21st Guards had drunk many a toast to the memories of those brave men.

Alekseyev was entirely focused on the small box mounted on his dashboard, right at eye level, that would light up with the go codes if his mission was authorized. He had a wingman with him for redundancy, but there had been no threat to their mission and he didn't expect one now.

"Captain, news outlets are reporting that the Americans have detonated their nuclear weapon!" his systems officer reported.

"Very well. Be alert."

He heard a tone in his ears and then saw six red figures appear on the box in front of him. He turned to his co-pilot. "Authenticate please, Lieutenant. One nine five four three alpha alpha."

His co-pilot tapped an icon on a tablet and read out the figures there. "Confirming. One nine five four three alpha alpha."

"Turning to heading zero nine seven. Weapons, you are clear to engage the target with a single Tsirkon missile," Alekseyev said.

"Yes, sir. Clear to fire Tsirkon."

492

The Tupolev's weapons bay doors opened and the rotary launcher lowered into the slipstream.

Alekseyev compensated for the drag by lifting the nose a little.

"Launcher down and locked. Missile system check complete..." his weapons officer intoned.

Alekseyev felt as though he should say something a little more momentous, given this was the first time in history Russia would be firing a nuclear weapon outside a test environment.

But the moment passed and, anyway, his crew wouldn't understand what he was talking about.

Until their weapon struck Anchorage in about 13 minutes.

Suddenly an alarm screamed in his ears. "Missile alert!!" his systems officer yelled. "Initiating defensive protocols!"

In an instant, Alekseyev felt the stick of the Tupolev rock to starboard as the defensive combat AI took control of the bomber from him!

"Never seen this before," Bunny muttered. Her missiles had been tracking faithfully toward the flight of Tupolevs when the bombers had suddenly broken port and starboard, accelerated dramatically, and fired clouds of decoy devices. The decoys spoofed two of her four air-to-air missiles, but the other two kept tracking. Until suddenly they went haywire and began spiraling through all points of the compass and lost their targets completely. They self-destructed, but Bunny could see they were nowhere near the bombers. Four shots, four misses. She only had four short-range all-aspect missiles and guns left.

"What?" Rodriguez asked, peering over her shoulder at the tactical display.

"Ivan has some kick-ass jamming rig on his new Tu-162s," Bunny said. "We can forget radar. Need to go optical and IR."

Rodriguez looked over her shoulder at Bondarev. "Anything else about these beasts you haven't told us?"

"I'm not an expert on the jamming systems of the Tu-162," Bondarev said. "They haven't been implemented on any other type. We have been told, though, they are very effective against both infrared and radar homing missiles."

"So, we're down to optical," Bunny said. "Great. Need to see the whites of their eyes."

"And they are rumored to have some sort of secret close combat defensive weapon," Bondarev said. "I have never seen it trialed. It may just be a rumor."

Bunny moved her bandaged hand off her mouse and tried to tap a key on the keyboard with her right forefinger but missed the keyboard completely. Cursing, she slammed her hand on a crate beside her and began kneading it with her left hand.

"You OK, O'Hare?" Rodriguez asked with concern.

"Yes, ma'am!" O'Hare growled back at her, a little too loudly. "Going to kill this bastard even if I have to unlace my boot and start typing with my right foot."

"Mayday, mayday!" Alekseyev's systems officer was calling on the radar. "This is Molotok Flight, under enemy air attack in sector 34 West, requesting immediate assistance."

The Tupolev was indeed a bastard. Its four Samara turbofan engines put out 245kn of thrust at emergency power, accelerating it from normal cruising speed of Mach 0.9 to Mach 2, or 1,300 miles an hour, in less than 15 seconds. The pressure from the sudden acceleration would have been enough to cause spinal injury if the seats and pressure suits of the crew hadn't been designed for it. Couple that acceleration with an inverted low banking turn as the combat AI sought to present a difficult targeting solution to the incoming missiles and it was no wonder his co-pilot lost his lunch into the space between his legs.

Alekseyev hated the feeling of helplessness more than he hated the nausea and narrow vision. Giving control of his aircraft over to a computer system because the designers didn't believe his own reflexes could save him and his crew left him impotent to do anything except try to keep his eyes on the threat warning screen and watch as the American missiles, for that was all they could be, speared toward him and his wingman.

Where the hell had they come from? A stealth fighter, obviously. But how had it penetrated so deep into Russian-held airspace? It was probably a drone sent on a one-way mission, but how could it have reached them so quickly, flying all the way from the US mainland? The answer was, it couldn't have. So either it was loitering, like a trapdoor spider waiting for an unlucky victim to wander past, or it was launched from close by. Which was also *impossible!*

Two of the four American missiles winked out. His systems were unable to pick up the fighter that had fired them. So, definitely a stealth fighter. There was no AWACs coverage available, so they had been relying on their now absent escort to scan the airspace around them and locate any threats. But they had become complacent.

The Tupolev reversed its roll and began a sweeping high-speed turn, dropping even lower. He heard a clunk as the missile launcher thumped back into place in the weapons bay. It had withdrawn as soon as the bomber started evasive maneuvers.

"Molotok Flight, this is Krolik flight of four Su-57s, we are the closest to your position, we will be within range in twelve minutes," Alekseyev heard a voice say in his ears.

"Acknowledged, Krolik flight," Alekseyev said into his mike, breathing heavily as he fought the g-force. "Please hurry, we may be dead by then."

Or maybe not, he thought with sudden optimism, as he saw the remaining two American missiles on his screen spiral out of control and self-destruct.

Bunny's mind raced. The two Tupolevs had separated now and were accelerating away from each other. She couldn't get within visual range of both of them, and unless she took her shot within the next few seconds, at least one of the bombers would have time to make a missile run again.

She decided. The optical targeting system on the all-aspect Cuda allowed for full 360-degree off boresight fire. That meant that she could have her aircraft pointed at one of the bombers and fire at the other, even though it was behind her, as long as she could see it and lock it up with her magnified weapons screen. She put a nav lock on the Tupolev in front of her, which was thankfully completing an evasive turn or it might have been able to outrun her. Leaving her flight AI to keep up the pursuit of that bomber, she concentrated her attention on her Cuda targeting system, swinging the crosshairs through the sky toward the now small delta-winged shape of the other fleeing Tupolev. As the crosshairs jerked over the bomber, she got a tone, and the white crosshairs turned red, indicating she had an optical lock. Before she lost it, she fired two of her remaining missiles at the locked Tupolev!

The missiles dropped out of her weapons bay and lowered their noses, turning 180 degrees before they accelerated to Mach 2.5. Even though the Tupolev was accelerating away at Mach 2, there was no question the missiles would catch it. So it just remained to see if it had any other tricks up its sleeve.

It didn't. Twisting like a snake, desperately firing clouds of tinfoil chaff to try to spoof the incoming missiles, one of the Cudas made direct contact with the Tupolev and detonated. The other found itself in what seemed to be a double cloud of foil chaff and also triggered its proximity fuse, without effect. One direct hit on the central fuselage of the bomber would have been critical, but this one hit just below the Tupolev's weapons bay. It disappeared in a flash of aviation and rocket fuel as its fuel tanks and ordnance exploded.

If missiles could think, the second Cuda would have had a single thought as it dived into that double cloud of chaff. And its thought would have been, '*This is not chaff*'.

"Splash one!" Bunny said.

"Yes!" Rodriguez yelled, unable to help herself.

"Closing on second target," Bunny said out loud. "Two missiles remaining. Guns up."

"You have Russian fighters closing from the south," Rodriguez pointed out. "ETA about eight minutes. I don't think you'll catch it before…"

"I see them," Bunny confirmed. "It's going to be close. Wait. *What?*" Rodriguez saw Bunny swing her head around as she looked at multiple virtual screens within her virtual-reality rig. "Oh shit, this is not good. He's decelerating."

"What? Why would he be doing that?" Rodriguez swung around and called over to Bondarev. "The second bomber is slowing down. It's stopped running. What is happening?!"

"The commander is doing what I would do," he said. "He is trying to complete his mission."

The Tsirkon missile could not be launched at speeds above Mach 0.9. Any attempt to lower the rotary launcher above that speed risked it being ripped off, damaging the airframe as it pulled away.

Alekseyev had already made his decision before he saw the ball lightning-like flash on the horizon that had been his wingman. Whatever was pursuing them, drone or human-piloted fighter, or fighters plural, it made no matter. He had survived their first attack, and he was still alive. For now. He had no way of knowing how many US aircraft were hunting him or where the next attack would come from.

He had disconnected the defensive AI and taken back control of his aircraft.

"What are you doing, sir?" his co-pilot asked.

In answer he keyed his internal mike. "Weapons. I am going to brake to launch velocity. Prepare to lower the launcher and fire."

The co-pilot looked like he wanted to protest, but whatever he was about to say, he bit it back. "Preparing for close-in decoy release," he said, flicking some switches.

"The enemy sent two short-range missiles after Molotok 2," Alekseyev told him. "Probably on optical guidance. Jamming was ineffective. The default countermeasure systems were ineffective." He cut the bomber's thrust and deployed the emergency air brakes. They were both thrown forward against the straps of their harnesses as the massive bomber began decelerating hard. "I want you to set the swarm for maximum spread and fire at the outside of the intercept envelope!"

"Setting swarm for max spread," the co-pilot confirmed. He crossed himself. "God help us."

"If we succeed in launching our Tsirkon missile," Alekseyev told him cryptically, "it is not God you will need to reckon with."

Bunny had been burning toward the huge flying wing at Mach 1.8. In a flat-out footrace, the Tupolev could have outrun her Fantom. But it had been dodging and weaving and had lost considerable airspeed before it decided to bug out, so her intercept calculator had put her on a track that should have given her a very short window in which she could attack the bomber before it reached the approaching Russian fighter flight that was clearly responding to its call for help.

She'd been gearing herself up for that engagement, so she'd been taken by surprise when the Tupolev suddenly swung east on a new heading and threw out its sea anchor. One moment it had been a silver sliver on the horizon, the next it was filling her forward camera like it had stopped in mid-air and decided to fly backward and attack the Fantom. She knew that was an optical illusion enhanced by the visual simulation system on the Fantom, and her threat screen told her the true story: it had just cut its airspeed dramatically and was falling from Mach 2 toward Mach 1 and below.

"Tracking target," she said, her voice calm, even though her heart was pounding. "Optical lock. *Firing one.* Tracking. *Firing two.*"

She chopped her own airspeed back so that she didn't overrun the bomber. It took what seemed like milliseconds for the missiles to close.

Rodriguez saw them as two small lines on the laptop's tactical screen, reaching between Bunny's Fantom and the Russian bomber. "Come on," she urged. "Let's get this done."

"No!" Bunny suddenly exclaimed. She had been watching the contrails of her two missiles reach out toward the bomber. Just as she expected them to strike, two black clouds burst from the back of the Tupolev like two huge swarms of bees, filling the sky. Her missiles flew right into them.

The black clouds flashed brilliant white, and her missiles disappeared.

The radical new drone-swarm defense that had been fitted to the Tu-162 bombers could indeed be compared to a swarm of bees. Dropped out of apertures lining the underside of the Tupolev, the swarm comprised two clouds of 1,000 miniature drones each, which could be programmed to take a set distance from each other once launched, forming either a dense or a loose cloud. Like tinfoil chaff, when concentrated they reflected radar energy and could attract radar homing missiles – with the advantage that they stayed in formation, unlike chaff, which quickly dispersed. But their real talent was that when they were dispersed, their eight gyro-stabilized rotors coupled with autonomous range finding could keep each drone at a maximum holding distance of 50 feet from all of its neighbors, creating two separately positioned clouds that were two drones thick and a half mile wide.

Anything flying through them, if it had a proximity fuse, might be fooled into thinking it had struck its target. If it was allowed the luxury of thought. Because the last trick the swarm had up its sleeve was that each drone had its own proximity fuse. And if anything that wasn't another drone or flashing a recognized IFF code came within 25 feet of it, it detonated, setting off a chain reaction among the other drones in the cloud that instantly vaporized anything inside or even near the cloud. Like Bunny's last two air-to-air missiles.

"What do you mean 'no'?" Rodriguez asked. "Tell me what you're seeing!"

"The bomber just spat out two clouds of decoys, the missiles flew into them, and they got toasted," Bunny said.

"Drone swarm, proximity detonations," Bondarev told them. "I heard it was being developed, I did not know it had been deployed."

"How many of those clouds can it spit out?" Bunny yelled.

"I don't know. A Tu-162 bomber can carry 40 tons of ordnance," Bondarev said. "You should assume it can launch multiple swarms."

Bunny cursed. "I'm down to guns. If I try to fly through a cloud of killer drones, I'll be dead before I can put lead on target and nothing will stop it."

Rodriguez turned and yelled at Bondarev. "How do we defeat this?!"

He was sitting with his back against a wall and lifted his legs, indicating they were still tied. "I need to see a tactical screen."

Rodriguez pulled a knife from her boot, ran back and cut Bondarev's leg-ropes. With the knife in her hand, she gestured at Bunny in the virtual-reality rig and the tactical screen sitting on the box beside her.

"Hurry it up!" Bunny yelled. "Radar cross-section just spiked. It's got its weapon bay doors open!"

Private Zubkhov wasn't in a hurry, but he wasn't a patient man either. He wasn't bleeding to death, though pushing himself too hard was out of the question for now; blood was still leaking around the tourniquet on his leg. And the American couldn't shoot him through the wood and steel platform at the base of the water tank that was his new roof.

He didn't really have any options. If he wasn't wounded, he could outwait the American, move on him when he fell asleep or passed out. But to do that he would have to get up that damn ladder. He had one last try at luring the American, with his radio, out of the stupid tank.

"Hey, American, wake up in there!" he yelled. "We both need help. You shot me, I shot you. No bad feelings, OK? I can get help for you." There was no answer.

With a shrug, Zubkhov pointed his Makarov at the platform above his head. The American wouldn't necessarily know he couldn't penetrate it. For a moment he hesitated, thinking how dumb it would be if he miscalculated and put a bullet through the radio he'd come all this way for. He aimed obliquely, fired two shots into the wood, listening with satisfaction to the crash from his gun and the thud of the bullets into the base of the water tank.

"Wake up, American!" he called out again. He put two more slugs into the base of the water tank. "Or I'm going to start aiming to kill."

He heard no movement above him. The guy was either dead, or playing dead. It was time to find out.

Bondarev stood with his hands tied behind his back and looked over Rodriguez's shoulder. "The only option is to get above and ahead of it. Make a frontal diving attack. The decoy swarms can't be fired forward, only backward."

"You sure?" Rodriguez asked.

"No," Bondarev admitted.

"Do it, O'Hare," Rodriguez ordered.

"Ma'am."

"No Russian drone could execute such a maneuver under autonomous control," Bondarev remarked quietly, watching intently as Bunny worked her keyboard.

"No ordinary US drone either," Rodriguez replied. "But ours are prototypes, personally coded by O'Hare. If she says she can do it, she can."

"Executing," the pilot said. She finished hammering in the maneuver codes with her left hand, went to tap 'execute' with her right ... and found her arm was frozen. It wasn't just her hand, her forearm and bicep had locked into place. The hand just lay on top of her mouse, useless!

"O'Hare!" Rodriguez jumped.

The first phase of a Tsirkon hypersonic missile launch was a booster which took the missile from its 600-knot launch speed to Mach 2.5 inside thirty seconds.

Once the first-phase boost was finished, the solid fuel booster rocket would fall away and the second-stage scramjet pulse engine would ignite, speeding the missile to an unstoppable Mach 4.5.

Like Elmendorf-Richardson and Eielson, Anchorage was defended by multiple HELLADS systems. In the first wave of the Russian air offensive, the HELLADS at Eielson had faced supersonic Brah-Mos II missiles, successfully bringing down a large number of the missiles before being overwhelmed.

The American strategists defending Anchorage had learned from that mistake. What they had learned was it was better to let a few missiles through and still have sufficient firepower to take on a second wave of missiles than to commit all your energy to the first wave and leave yourself defenseless against a follow-up attack.

Faced with a single missile, though, the HELLADS surrounding Anchorage, on paper at least, should have been more than capable of defending its 200,000 residents.

Except that the Tsirkon was not a *super*sonic missile like the Brah-Mos, and though the US had never admitted it, a HELLADS system had never actually successfully intercepted a *hyper*sonic missile like the Tsirkon. Which was why the US had concentrated considerable diplomatic efforts on treaties to ban any use of hypersonic weapons and declared that the use of hypersonic weapons in any conflict would be regarded in the same vein as the use of nuclear weapons, and would trigger a proportionate response.

A threat which, right now, was completely moot.

Reaching across herself with her left hand, O'Hare ignored her lunging CO and frantically slapped the 'execute' key on her right-hand keyboard, ordering the Fantom to light its afterburners and move into a spiraling climb over the Tupolev. Agonizing seconds passed as it eased ahead of the Russian bomber before it inverted and dived down toward it. In her virtual-reality view, the big wing zoomed up toward her.

"Target locked, guns on auto. *Guns guns guns!*" Bunny called.

Captain Alekseyev waited with one hand on his stick, the other on his throttles, threat warnings screaming in his ears. The American had accelerated above him, rendering his defensive measures useless. Seconds, he just needed seconds...

He listened to his weapons officer tersely reading from his screen, "Bay doors open. Rotary launcher down, locked and cycling up. Target locked. First phase ignition counting down. Launching in..."

Alekseyev's muscles tensed. As soon as the missile was away, he'd roll the Tupolev on its back and point it at the earth, leaving the enemy drone in his wake. He'd never tried to put a Tu-162 into a screaming Mach 2 vertical dive and had no idea if he had any chance of pulling out of it at this altitude, but he would soon find out.

"Five...four...*three*..."

The shells from the Fantom's 25mm GUA/8L cannon punched the Tupolev in its canted Concorde-like nose. Alekseyev actually had time to see the sparks of the detonations as the shells walked along the nose toward his cockpit. Had

time to hear his weapons officer say in triumph, "…
two…one…launch!"

Had time to take his hands off his stick, lean back in his
seat and pray as he died, *"Forgive me, God."*

"Missile launch!" Rodriguez yelled. She couldn't see it, of
course, but the tactical screen on the boxes next to her flashed
the warning and a new bright blue icon appeared on the screen
where the Tupolev had been and began tracking east.

"Got it," Bunny said calmly. She had seen the slightly
delayed vision of the Tupolev rolling on its side as her cannon
shells struck vital control cables, saw the missile tumble free of
its launcher and its rocket booster ignite, saw it begin to
accelerate. She locked the missile optically and ordered the
Fantom to intercept.

Rolling level again, hauling its nose up toward the horizon
at g-forces that would have blacked out a human pilot, the
Fantom got its gun pipper centered on the blazing light of the
fast disappearing Tsirkon missile and held its virtual thumb
down on the trigger.

The Tsirkon was still inside the two-mile range of the
25mm shells and with the Fantom traveling at near Mach 2, the
question was whether the added 3,000 feet per second velocity
of the 25mm would be enough to catch the missile before it
had reached its first-stage boost peak and went hypersonic!

The line of cannon shells reached out for the flaming
missile like grasping fingers.

It didn't explode. It was simply slammed in the rear, folded
in two, and tumbled out of the sky.

Bunny didn't explode either. She just took her left hand off
her keyboard as her right dangled uselessly beside her and held
it in the air, fist clenched. Eyes fixed on the screens inside her
helmet, watching as men in chutes tumbled free of the falling
Tupolev, Bunny O'Hare was smiling broadly as Bondarev
spoke.

"That was truly impressive," he said. "Now, shall we discuss your surrender?"

Private Zubkhov had taken nearly ten minutes to drag himself up the ladder on the side of the tank with his one good arm and one good leg, expecting to be shot at any moment. But he had made it, and now he trained his gun on the man lying in the bottom of the tank as he raised his head over the lip of the manhole cover and peered inside.

Zubkhov had waited a long time under the water tank, alternately haranguing the American, trying to goad him into speaking, and firing the occasional shot into the base of the tank to try to provoke him. He had even eased out from under the base of the tank and taken an angle which allowed him to put a round through the metal wall of the tank, near the top, just to remind the man that he was a fish in a barrel, in case he needed reminding.

But after nearly 30 minutes, with no reaction, not a sound, Zubkhov had decided to make his move. It was going to get dark soon, he was wounded, he couldn't keep a watch on the tank all night.

The man at the bottom of the tank was lying on his side in a fetal curl with his back to the manhole cover. A rifle was leaning up against the wall of the tank beside him, but of course he could have a sidearm hidden away. Private Zubkhov held his fist against the metal of the tank to stabilize it, sighted on the man, and fired twice.

The bullets thudded into him without any effect. He didn't jerk, didn't move. It was like shooting a side of beef.

Still, Zubkhov took no chances. He lowered himself down into the tank legs first, pistol pointed at the man as he slowly negotiated the internal ladder. The grenade on his belt bumped against the ladder all the way down – *clang, clang, clang*. But when he reached the bottom he saw with satisfaction the thing he had come for. The radio.

Bigger than he'd imagined. He didn't have to take the car battery the man had been lugging around but the radio set wouldn't fit in his light backpack. He'd have trouble getting that up the ladder with just one working arm. But here it was, at last. *His* radio.

"Thank you, friend," he said sincerely to the dead man's back. Then he realized that all this time, since their first meeting on the airfield, he had never really seen his face.

With a grunt, he took the man by the knees and rolled him over.

Not a man. A boy.

Zubkhov kneeled and looked at him closely. Somewhere between sixteen and twenty was all he could guess. By the look of his face, he was Inuit too. No wonder he had been able to move around the country like he owned it. Zubkhov looked up at the Winchester standing against the wall, with its big digital hunting scope. Blunderbuss like that could take the head off a polar bear. Zubkhov figured he had been very lucky indeed. He thought he'd been hunting this boy and his radio, and the whole time *he* was the one who had been hunted.

He reached down and closed the boy's eyes. He had fought well. Zubkhov felt like he should say something, so he tried to imagine what the Captain would say. Suddenly it came to him – a Dostoyevsky quote of course. "God gives us moments of perfect peace," he told the boy. "In such moments, we love, and we are loved."

Rodriguez looked at the Russian Colonel with a wry smile. "You forget I've still got a Fantom overhead," she said, jerking her thumb at O'Hare who had just flipped up her virtual-reality visor. "And a pilot who is very keen to give it a new target, correct, O'Hare?"

"Bloody oath, ma'am," the aviator said.

"And *you* forget," Bondarev countered, "that I have six fighters inbound which will make very short work of your Fantom."

506

"Before I destroy the chopper on top of this rock and any Spetsnaz dumb enough to be near it?" Bunny asked, pulling down her visor again and turning away. "I'll lock up the target ma'am, you just say the word."

"Your men are seconds away from death, Colonel," Rodriguez said. "So let's discuss *your* surrender, shall we?"

"I am Air Force, not Spetsnaz," the Russian said, his voice cold and even. "They are not my men."

Dave heard the shots behind him and skidded to a halt at the edge of the ruined cantonment. *Seriously?* That damn Russian was still alive? Or maybe there were more. He swapped his rifle from his left shoulder to his right. *Ah hell.*

It took him twenty minutes to get back to the water tower and, as he approached, he crouched low, using the rubble of the blasted buildings for cover, and found a spot where he had a good view of the water tower on its shattered base. Sure enough, he saw a Russian soldier climbing up the ladder to the platform on which the water tank stood. Scanning the ground below, he couldn't see any others. It appeared to be just the one.

Dave could see blood on the guy's uniform and he was holding his right arm in against his chest, climbing with his left arm on the rungs, dragging one leg up the ladder behind him. It must be the same damn guy. He pulled his rifle from his shoulder and settled it on the wood and bent iron in front of him. He was maybe fifty yards away. But Dave just had iron sights on his rifle, no scope. And he was no marksman. He tried to hold the sight at the end of the barrel steady on the back of the Russian soldier, but he was panting, his heart was pounding, and it kept moving around. That Russian was damn near unkillable. Dave had a feeling if he missed, he'd have given himself away for nothing and the guy would come for him.

Damn damn *damn!*

He slumped back down behind cover, feeling useless. The Russian was shouting something, but at least he wasn't shooting into the tank. Dave kept an eye on him through a crack in the debris, thought about a hundred times about taking a shot at him, even just to try to lure him away, but did nothing.

Then the Russian got to the platform, adjusted the pistol in his belt and started climbing the ladder up the side of the tank itself.

He was going for Perri. Now! Now Dave had to do something! He sighted on the Russian's back between his shoulder blades, took a deep breath. The Russian moved up the ladder … and Dave's shot was blocked by an overhanging sheet of steel. Oh come *on*. He looked around. He'd have to move around the back of the building beside him, see if he could get a shot from the other side. Quickly he scuttled through the rubble, couldn't get a line of sight on the tower, found his way blocked by a tumbled wall, backed out again and went around further, down the side of two collapsed huts, kicking up carbon and soot and ice. There! He could see the top of the tower now. See the Russian soldier climbing up to the manhole cover. He sighted down the barrel.

Two shots rang out as the Russian fired down into the tank and Dave ducked back down.

He was shaking. He felt like crying. The guy wasn't even shooting at *him*, he was shooting down into the tank, at Perri. Sticking his head up again, he saw the Russian lower himself into the tank.

OK, Perri is dead. You screwed up and now he's dead.

No. Maybe he isn't. Maybe you can still do something.

Do *something*, you cowardly piece of shit!

Dave crouched and ran over to the ladder. He was wearing a pair of basketball shoes he'd lifted from a sports store. Their soft rubber soles were silent on the metal rungs of the ladder as he climbed.

He reached the top of the ladder, under the manhole. It was cold. The wind was blowing hard. He reached the top of the ladder, pulled his rifle off his shoulder and, as quietly as he could, worked the bolt. OK Dave, this is it. Foot on the next rung, lift yourself up, aim and fire. You can do it.

508

He counted to three then stood, bringing the rifle up and aiming straight down the barrel. The Russian soldier was crouched beside Perri and he looked up in surprise at the sound of Dave's rifle barrel on the metal rim of the manhole. He started to lift his pistol, but Dave fired first and the bullet caught the guy in the middle of his chest and threw him back against the wall of the water tank, his pistol flying from his outstretched arm.

"I have the copter on the Rock locked, ma'am, in range in two minutes," O'Hare said. "Russian fighters are still five minutes out. Orders?"

Rodriguez had picked up her rifle again and pointed it menacingly at the Russian officer. "Decision time."

He stared at her, ice blue eyes unwavering. A minute went past.

"Beginning strafing run," O'Hare cautioned. "Guns hot and set for autofire."

A bead of sweat appeared above the Russian's brow. "*Abort!*" he said. "I'll guarantee you safe passage out of here."

"Abort, Lieutenant!" Rodriguez called. "Head for the deck, evade and retire."

"Roger that, ma'am," Bunny said, tapping at her keyboard. "Ivan never got a lock on me anyway. Going ninja."

Rodriguez lowered her gun but kept her gaze fixed on the Air Army officer. "She can call that Fantom back anytime," she warned him. "So what's your best offer?"

"I'll tell the troops above to return to base," he said. "My other patrols have already been recalled and I'll stand down the fighters overhead. If you let me depart with my men, I'll guarantee there will be no more attacks on this base."

"Oh, *now* they're your men?" O'Hare said, pulling off her helmet.

"Thank you, Lieutenant," Rodriguez snapped. She gestured with her rifle toward the chute. "Your exit is that way, Colonel."

Devlin McCarthy's office was chaos defined. There was an ugly mob at the gates of the Embassy compound, waving placards, throwing rocks and the occasional Molotov cocktail. Not a Russian police officer was in sight and the head of her Marine security detail was down there, asking her for permission to fire warning shots over the heads of the crowd.

She had three technicians trying to pull a built-in cabinet away from a wall to get at the wiring they needed to try to patch her into a new secure satellite uplink so that she could re-establish communications with Washington after someone, probably Russian cyber-intelligence services, cut all landlines and fiber in and out of the compound and jammed their usual satellite signal.

She had a dozen department heads either asking her what was going on or telling her what she should be doing, and on top of this, she had Carl Williams hovering at the door with his damned laptop trying to get her attention and arguing with her personal security detail.

"Let him in," she barked at them, then turned to the three technicians. "I don't care if that cabinet is three hundred years old, pull it off that wall and get me a link to DC. What is it, Carl?"

"NORAD has reported that the Russian bombers were destroyed, and I have Colonel Yevgeny Bondarev on the line for you," the analyst panted. Clearly he had run from the New Annex over to her office, laptop in hand.

"How do *you* have comms?" she asked, and then realized it was a stupid question. "Did you call him or did he..."

"He called NORAD," Williams said. He pushed the laptop across her desk and she saw he had a video feed running.

She looked for the first time into the face of the man who was the father of her granddaughter and, right now, her enemy in war.

"Hello Ambassador," he said. He seemed to be standing outside, wind blowing his hair. She could see a quadrotor helicopter in the background.

She took a deep breath. "Colonel Bondarev. Did you stop those bombers?"

He nodded. "I did. Or rather, *you* did. One of your pilots did. The immediate threat has passed but I need you to give some information to your political masters. Can you do that?"

She looked across at the three technicians, one of whom held up five fingers.

"We lost our uplink but I'm told it will be restored soon," she said. "What is the information?"

"There has been a coup attempt in Moscow. The attempted nuclear attack on Anchorage was not authorized by our President or Prime Minister but by the coup plotters, led by the Defense Minister and the head of the 3rd Air and Air Defense Forces Command, General Potemkin. The situation is currently highly fluid."

"Do these coup plotters still have access to your strategic nuclear arsenal?" Devlin asked, horrified.

"No," Bondarev told her. "Our military intelligence service is still loyal to the President and has secured the codes. They are currently in the process of determining which military and police units the coup plotters have turned, and which we can trust. It will take some hours."

"What do you want, Colonel?" she asked.

"I have ordered the arrest of the 3rd Air and Air Defense Forces Command Commander, General Potemkin. The aircraft and support units of our two active Air Brigades are being withdrawn from the Bering Strait area of operations as we speak. Ground forces should start withdrawing to their pre-conflict bases tomorrow. I just ask for time to get the situation under control, that is all."

"I'll pass that on," she told him. "Thank you."

"Ambassador," he said. "There may be men on your side who see this as the ideal opportunity to attack us, while we are riven with internal division." He leaned forward toward the camera. "Tell them that would be very unwise. The President of the Federation is back in control of our strategic rocket, space and submarine forces and will not hesitate to use them if necessary."

She swallowed. "I will be sure to make them aware of that."

Someone called to Bondarev from off camera and he looked away, then looked back. "I must go. There is one more thing. Your facility under Little Diomede Island will not be allowed to operate so close to our border. You have 48 hours in which to evacuate any personnel there, after which we will mine the entrance."

Devlin had little idea what he was talking about but she could see in Carl's face that he did.

Something in his tone annoyed her. "I don't think you are in a position to be making more threats," she said.

"Nonetheless," he said, and gave her a casual salute. "Give my regards to your daughter," he said, and reached forward to cut the call.

Alicia Rodriguez and Bunny O'Hare watched on Bunny's laptop as the icon from Bondarev's quadrotor headed south, escorted by four Su-57s. To the east, their last remaining Fantom was starting its final approach to the airfield at Juneau. Bunny shut her laptop down.

They'd watched Bondarev exit the chute on the rope he swung in on, and had lain in wait with rifles trained on the small square of sky at the end of the chute in case it was all just a ploy to allow a larger Spetsnaz force to take them on. But they'd eventually had to allow that perhaps the Russian officer had kept his word.

This time, after they contacted Coronado and briefed them on developments, and with Russian aircraft clearly pulling out of the Operations Area, Navy agreed to send a chopper from Port Clarence to lift them off.

"Not that I don't like it down here, ma'am," Bunny said. "But perhaps we could wait topside?"

"They could still be up there," Rodriguez said. "A few hours ago he led a Spetsnaz team in here to kill us."

"I know, Boss," Bunny sighed. "But I'll take the chance that the killing is over for now. The trust has to start again somewhere."

It wouldn't be easy, that much she knew. Too many people had died. As they had walked him across the bridge toward the chute, Bunny trailing watchfully with her rifle ready in the crook of her arm, Rodriguez had stopped him.

"Tell me something?" she'd asked. "I couldn't follow your conversation earlier. A lot of good people died. Can you tell me why?"

He'd looked away. "Why did we go to war? For all the usual reasons, I suppose. Power. Greed. Survival." He'd looked back at her and tapped the star on her flight suit. "Ours is not to reason why, Lieutenant Commander."

Bunny had shaken her head and prodded him up the ramp with the barrel of her gun. "Yeah, right. See that's the difference between us, right there," she'd told him. "Decades ago, you stopped asking your leaders why. We never will."

Dave was asking himself why. Why he'd left. Why he hadn't got back faster. Why he hadn't taken the shot when he had it. Why he'd let the Russian get inside the water tank and shoot his friend.

But he'd nailed the guy. As Dave climbed down inside the water tank again, the Russian was slumped against the wall behind Perri, gasping, a new bloodstain spreading across the front of his chest. He wasn't dead, but he couldn't be far away from it this time. Dave ran a couple of steps and picked up his pistol, just to be sure, then knelt down beside Perri.

He was *cold*.

So he'd been dead a while. Was probably already dead when the Russian shot him a few minutes ago. In a way, Dave was relieved; relieved it hadn't been his gutlessness that had killed his friend. Then he felt bad about feeling relieved. And that led to anger.

He looked up at the Russian, still taking heaving, shuddering breaths with his eyes fixed on Dave.

Dave didn't want to listen to him anymore. He lifted his rifle, chambered a round.

The Russian held up a hand, feebly, as if to stop him.

Dave hesitated, lowered his rifle. No, the guy was offering him something.

Dave frowned and looked at it.

Oh, it was a grenade. The Russian was offering him a grenade.

POSTSCRIPT

In the sub-Arctic autumn of Saint Lawrence Island in the Bering Sea, a cadaver can keep for months without spoiling. Whether a whale on a black volcanic beach, a walrus caught in the rocks along the coast, or the body of a man.

So there was no tell-tale stink when Sergeant Dan Kushniruk of the Canadian Mounted Police approached the water tank in the last brief light of day and noticed it was full of bullet holes.

There were shrapnel holes too, and one of the four legs of the tower the water tank was standing on was broken and splintered, but there was no mistaking the perfectly circular pattern of holes stitched across one side of the water tank. He looked at the ground by his feet and saw shell casings.

He knelt and picked one up. Russian, 9mm. Favored short round of the Spetsnaz special forces.

He looked around him. This must be the place.

With a sigh, he tightened the straps on his backpack, hitched a rope over his shoulder and walked over to the ladder that led from the ground, up to the platform on which the tank was resting, and then up the side of the tank to an open manhole cover at the top.

The metal was cold, even through his gloves. Kushniruk was used to the cold. He was a cop from Whitehorse in the Canadian Yukon Territory, and the only difference between the Yukon and this place, as far he was concerned, was a distinct lack of trees, leaving nothing to protect you from the biting wind except the rise and fall of the ground – and the blackened ruins of the US base in which the water tank stood.

As he reached the top of the ladder, he hesitated. He had a pretty good idea what he'd find inside.

Or thought he did.

He'd come to look for a local Yup'ik man. Man? Just a kid, really. A lone, brave, hard as nails kid who had single-handedly turned the tide of a war, not that anyone except Kushniruk would ever know it. Kushniruk had come to Saint Lawrence to find him; he'd been out to the overflowing Savoonga medical clinic but there was no record of him there. Instead he had found the kid's name on a list in the town hall in Savoonga, along with hundreds of others, 'missing, presumed dead'.

His heart had fallen, even though he'd prepared himself. There was a woman there, a round-faced weary woman wearing three sweaters inside the hall because the power and heating weren't reliable yet, and Kushniruk had asked her how he could find the cantonment, or what was left of it.

"Why?" she'd asked. "Nothing out there. We exhumed all the bodies from the graves, gave them a proper burial here in town."

"I'm looking for a water tower?" he'd said. "Might be the only thing left standing. You know it?"

"You a photographer?" the woman had asked. "You need a permit to take photographs out there. Folks around here are pretty sensitive about it."

Kushniruk had shown her his Canadian Mounted Police ID. "No, I'm just following something up. Sorry, I can't really discuss it."

The woman had shrugged, and drawn him a map. Told him he'd have to hustle if he wanted to get out there today, because it would be dusk in two hours.

"You have to declare anything you find to Savoonga police," she'd said. "We don't hold with souvenir hunters."

"I will," he'd told her, and hoped he wouldn't have to. After all, it was still possible the kid had made it. He wasn't from Savoonga, he was from Gambell, a town about fifty miles west. He could have headed back there without registering. Kushniruk hadn't been able to reach his family, because communications with Gambell were still down. The kid could be back home, ripping through the snow on his ATV, or out fishing for halibut with his father and brothers.

Kushniruk paused on his way up the ladder, looking across the blasted wasteland that had until recently been the new US

516

Savoonga radar facility. He could see why the boy had climbed up here. It had a perfect view of the single long runway of the Savoonga airfield – vehicles and aircraft parked alongside it – and he watched as a small two-engined air ambulance began its landing. He grabbed the lip of the manhole and hauled himself up. It was dark inside, the gray light filtering through the shrapnel and bullet holes not enough to light the interior of the tank, so he pulled a flashlight from his belt and held it up.

He panned the light around.

The first thing he saw was that he would have to come back tomorrow.

He'd only brought one body bag.

"He's been dying for you to arrive," Williams told Ambassador McCarthy with a wry smile. He pulled out his only other chair and turned on his electric kettle, putting out two paper coffee cups and spooning instant coffee into them. "How are things above ground?"

She settled wearily on the chair and leaned her head back against the wall. "Getting back to normal." She sighed. "It's amazing how quickly a near nuclear holocaust becomes yesterday's news. State is obsessing over what Navalny is going to do with the coup plotters while CIA is doing its damndest to recruit them before they get arrested and shot."

"May I deliver my briefing, ma'am?" HOLMES' plummy English voice interrupted. "I enjoy delivering briefings," HOLMES said.

"You enjoy showing off is more like it," Williams said. "I know you do, because I taught you to."

"You have something big?" Devlin asked. HOLMES had been forwarding her a daily summary of all critical intelligence on the fast-moving situation within the Russian regime as President Navalny acted to neutralize the coup plotters and re-establish control of his government and armed forces. He was pulling down intel from the CIA, DIA, NSA, FBI, State Department, Cybercommand and sources inside the five-eyes nations of Britain, Canada, Australia and New Zealand too. It meant she had a more complete overview of the situation inside the Kremlin than even the CIA head of station for Moscow, and that was something she *greatly* enjoyed. But HOLMES had asked today to deliver his report 'in person'. "Whatever it is, can you start with a sitrep please? Highlights on predefined interests only."

Carl smiled at how quickly the Ambassador had adjusted to the protocol for talking to his AI system, and now just took it in her stride.

"Yes, ma'am," HOLMES began. "Topic: Coup leaders: all members of the so-called 'Committee for the Special Regime' including former Defense Minister Burkhin and Air Army General Potemkin have now surrendered to Russian authorities and are being held at Lefortovo Prison for interrogation. None have yet been charged. Topic: Civil unrest: Riots between members of the Russian ultra-right wing 'Wolves' movement and the 'Citizens for Protection of the Constitution' continued for a third day with deaths reported in Ekaterinburg, Vladivostok and Moscow. Topic: US cyber-attacks on Russian infrastructure: Russian banking systems were restored yesterday and Moscow stock exchange reopened. Power supplies in major cities are approaching pre-conflict norms except for St. Petersburg. Cell phone and television broadcast networks have been restored in 70% of the country. Topic: Military dispositions: All air, ground and sea units except for interior ministry forces in areas of urban unrest have returned to their pre-conflict bases and readiness levels; however, a continued heightened level of signals traffic across the country persists. Topic: Political: President Navalny has declared that the current nationwide State of Emergency will remain in force until civil unrest subsides. Decrees issued since yesterday include: a decree to disband leftist and nationalist political parties, a decree to ban the New Pravda media group, a decree to postpone elections planned for October indefinitely, a decree to establish a new committee to investigate the coup attempt and propose criminal charges and constitutional amendments. Do you have any specific questions, ma'am?"

"Threats to Embassy property and personnel?" Devlin asked.

"A CIA source in the Moscow chapter of the 'Wolves' reported yesterday that the group is preparing Molotov cocktails and smoke bombs for use in a protest at the Embassy next Monday. The source is rated as 'usually reliable', the report as 'probably true'. No other reports of note."

"Still, thanks for telling me," Devlin said, looking annoyed. "That seemed to have slipped the CIA head of station's attention."

"Ma'am, what he really wants to tell you..." Williams started.

"May I please continue the briefing, Carl?" HOLMES broke in over the top of the analyst again. It was the first time Devlin had heard the AI interrupt its programmer, and even Williams looked surprised.

"Uh, sure. Go for it." He poured water into the paper cups and handed one to Devlin.

"Thank you, Carl. Ma'am, I have identified with an assessed probability of 96% why Russia initiated this conflict."

Devlin sat in the chair opposite the desk. "I'm listening," she said.

"I have prepared a small presentation," HOLMES said, and the screen on the laptop blinked to life, showing a map of what Devlin quickly realized was the Russian Federation, from west to east. The map was divided into the 46 states or oblasts that comprised the Federation, colored various shades of green. HOLMES continued. "This is a map showing the total freshwater supply available for drinking, irrigation or industry in each of the states of the Russian Federation. Green indicates that supply exceeds demand. This map and the timeline I am about to show starts in 1991 with the dissolution of the former Soviet Union. I will now advance the timeline at one year every two seconds." Devlin saw the map begin to change as time moved forward and several provinces went from deep green to light green. Around 2001 one of the oblasts went yellow. "Yellow indicates occasional supply shortages, red will indicate critical supply shortages."

Devlin saw several states turn yellow around 2010, but then a number of them, mostly around the big cities, turned light green again. The timeline paused. "In 2015 a large-scale desalinization program which was started in 2010 began delivering new freshwater supplies into the hardest-hit catchments," HOLMES said. "Following this success, any talk of a crisis in freshwater supplies in the Russian Duma was put aside and the desalinization program was intensified. The availability of large amounts of freshwater for industry and agriculture supported the resurgence of the Russian economy between 2020 and 2030."

Now the screen shifted to show a simple line graph, with dates from 2000 to 2025 on the bottom axis and a line that rose dramatically and then fell just as dramatically toward the outer years. "This graph shows water delivered into Russian groundwater reserves by melting Siberian permafrost. At the same time as Russian desalinization plants were coming online, massive amounts of meltwater were being delivered to the Central Asian aquifers and beyond by underground ice melting due to global warming. This meltwater artificially elevated the levels of available freshwater, but this was not sustainable. I believe I may be the first one outside Russia, either human or AI, to have identified this critical piece of the puzzle," HOLMES said, in a matter of fact way.

The timeline resumed and Devlin saw that around 2025 all the states in yellow had reverted to green. Whatever Russia had done to solve its freshwater problem, it appeared to have worked.

"With increased agricultural and industrial production, climate change-induced droughts, plus uncontrolled urbanization, freshwater demand has begun outpacing supply again, even with the commissioning of hundreds of desalinization plants, and even with the inflow of Siberian meltwater," HOLMES continued. Now the map was showing half green, nearly half yellow, and a deal red. More states turned red, until about a third of the map was red, and a third yellow, with only one or two states still in green. "This is the present day," he said. "I have projected this analysis into the future by ten years and done a sensitivity analysis to arrive at a base case scenario. May I skip directly to my ten-year prognosis, ma'am?"

"Please," Devlin said. She had a fair idea where it was going to land.

With a flicker, the map on the screen turned blood red, from west to east.

Devlin looked at it thoughtfully. What HOLMES had shown her was not news to Williams, so he sat patiently while McCarthy processed it. So did HOLMES.

"I have some questions," Devlin said at last.

"Yes, ma'am," Williams and HOLMES replied together.

Devlin smiled. "HOLMES, your analysis tells me Russia is facing a critical shortage of fresh water in the next ten years. I assume you have allowed for a continued increase in the rate of commissioning desalinization plants, or purification of polluted water sources?"

"Yes, ma'am, the base case scenario I am showing allows for the current rate of growth in desalinization plant and purified water delivered inflow to double, which is against current trends. I have also modeled a modest decline in economic growth, also against current trends. Neither of these adjustments enable Russia to avert the critical water shortages."

"Have you considered the impact of climate change mitigation strategies on current rainfall?"

She felt she was asking dumb questions, but they had to be asked, because someone would very soon be asking her.

"Yes, ma'am, I have incorporated the best-case projections of the Intergovernmental Panel on Climate Change into the base case. Climate change mitigation strategies cannot work quickly enough to change these projections."

She looked at Williams. "Russia is dying of thirst."

"Not yet, but it will be," Williams agreed. "Very soon. And it seems that HOLMES, me, and now you are the only ones outside Russia who know it."

"You haven't copied this analysis to NSA?" She was surprised.

Williams looked sheepish. "He wanted to tell you first, before he uplinked it."

"Are you serious?" she asked. "HOLMES, is that correct?"

The voice that came back had the quality of an English schoolboy, trying to please his teacher. "You were the one who provoked me to revisit my scenarios, ma'am. Your intel regarding the personal reaction of the Russian Foreign Minister when you accused him of making a land grab for Saint Lawrence was pivotal to redirecting my analytical energies. I may not have made the connection to dwindling Siberian meltwater levels without your input."

Williams looked annoyed. "I'm sorry, ma'am. I'm using regularization algorithms like least absolute shrinkage and selection to simplify his alternative 'out of the box' scenario development."

"English?"

"Uh, right. He was creating scenarios that are too intricate and complex to be likely, so I taught him to learn to like simplicity in his scenario building and seek out inputs that force him to simplify," he shrugged. "That's you."

"I'm an input that forces him to simplify?"

"People in my work see the world in shades of gray. You, however, see the world in black and white, ma'am," Williams said gently. "Good guys, bad guys kind of thing. I'm training him to seek out simpler perspectives."

"I like your perspectives, Ambassador," HOLMES said. "They are elegant and appealing."

Williams shrugged. "That's why I apologized. I think he has a brain crush on you."

"Yes. I like the Ambassador," HOLMES said.

Devlin found herself smiling again. "I sincerely appreciate the gesture, but you should share your intel on this quickly, not wait for me next time."

Williams coughed. "If I can interrupt this mutual admiration club, ma'am, we haven't got to the meat of the briefing yet. HOLMES is describing 'cause' to you, he hasn't gotten to 'effect'."

"It was my next question," Devlin admitted. "What are the implications of Russia running out of water? They must be significant to have provoked them to risk global nuclear war."

"Total economic dysfunction," HOLMES said. "Social upheaval. Political destabilization, regime collapse and civil war."

"To name a few things," Williams said.

"Well, that sounds exciting," Devlin said with deliberate irony. "Perhaps too exciting. I suspect as soon as this report hits Washington, I'm going to be asked to start negotiating a treaty with Russia for a water pipeline under the Bering Strait." She swallowed the last of her coffee with a grimace. "Thanks for the coffee. I think."

"You're welcome," Williams nodded. "I think."

She stood, but hesitated by the door. "And thank you for the briefing, HOLMES. Carl, I'd offer to get you a decent coffee machine down here but I hear you're already leaving us."

He looked a little sheepish. "Uh, yeah. It seems I came into a little money. I brought my retirement plan forward."

Devlin tipped him a wink. "At least *something* good came of all this, then." She tapped a hand on the doorframe, not quite ready to go. "When you get that place on the Pacific Coast, send me a note. I'd like to come and see it some time."

"Anytime, ma'am." Carl smiled.

It was the first time Bondarev had seen his old friend in weeks. During his return to Savoonga, he'd ordered Arsharvin to fly to the headquarters of the 3rd Air Army at Khabarovsk and mobilize GRU troops to arrest General Potemkin and his staff. That done, Bondarev had assumed command of the 3rd Air Army and flown to Moscow to meet with the newly liberated and recently appointed Defense Minister, Kelnikov, while Arsharvin had stayed in Khabarovsk to consolidate. In the meantime, Kelnikov had insisted Bondarev stay in Moscow to help with the work of cleaning out the traitor Burkhin's sympathizers inside the Air Army.

Moscow was approaching normality again but pockets of the country were still riven with civil unrest, riots and looting. Syrian forces were being pushed back out of Lebanon and the Syrian regime was screaming for Russian air support, which Kelnikov was not minded to provide, but he had asked Bondarev for options so Bondarev had called a meeting of his operations staff at his temporary office in Moscow.

Arsharvin arrived the evening before they were due to meet and came into Bondarev's office holding a bottle wrapped in brown paper. "I found this when I was packing," he said, and pulled the paper off to reveal a half-full bottle of Macallan whiskey. "You know I don't like leaving a job unfinished."

Bondarev had regarded him from behind a pile of folders, then reached into a drawer for a pair of shot glasses. "Your new uniform suits you, Comrade Colonel."

Arsharvin grinned. "As does yours, Comrade *Lieutenant General.*" He sat down, poured the drinks and held up his glass. "I'm told the best way to drink such a fine whiskey is to use a pipette to place just a single drop of water on the surface, to break the meniscus and let the aromas enfold you." With that, he threw it down in a single gulp and poured himself another.

Bondarev put his glass down on the table without drinking it.

"That's bad luck," Arsharvin warned him.

"I've used up all my luck, Tomas," Bondarev told him. "Bad, and good. All I have left is my wits. So I need to keep them straight."

"Agh, why the sad song?" Arsharvin said, leaning back. "You know, if we hadn't been white-anted by the coup plotters, I think LOSOS could have succeeded."

Bondarev laughed. "It could have succeeded in starting a nuclear war. That is all."

"You still think the US held itself back from an all-out counter-attack because it went straight for the nuclear option," Arsharvin said, running his glass under his nose a little more thoughtfully this time. "Whereas I think they were shocked by our boldness, cowed by our military might and panicked into a weak response that was targeted at the world media, not at our military. If not for the coup, we would have taken Nome and you and I would be sitting in Alaska right now, policing our new demilitarized zone and mixing fresh, clean Yukon glacier water into our whiskey!"

"Our fatherland needs dreamers, friend, now more than ever. I toast you and your dreams." Bondarev took a sip of his whiskey at last, and rolled it around his mouth. He put the glass down again. "But the Americans have moved a flotilla of guided missile destroyers and a squadron of Fantoms into Nome, less than ten minutes' flight time from Lavrentiya. They have announced plans to base HELLADS and anti-air missile batteries along the Alaska coast from Nome to Port Clarence, and rebuild their base in Savoonga. There is a US carrier task force transiting the Strait as we speak. Our so-called allies in Lebanon are having their asses whipped by the Israelis and rightly claiming it is our fault they are even engaged. And the commander of the 126th Center for Special and Physical Training in Kalinka is still refusing to recognize my command authority and insisting he will answer only to the traitor Potemkin." He raised his eyebrows at Arsharvin, as this last problem was one he had tasked the GRU Colonel to assist with.

"If he doesn't hand over command by tomorrow, I will take his base by force," Arsharvin said. "Unless he has the brains to shoot himself first and save us all some trouble."

Bondarev drained his glass and turned it upside down. "And the US base at Little Diomede?"

"No activity since the last personnel were taken off, just after you left. The Americans may attempt to re-establish the radar facility, but as a covert drone base, it is finished," he scoffed.

Bondarev frowned. "And how many others do they have, Tomas? Sitting on our shores, hiding under the ice, under the sea, ready to strike next time?"

Arsharvin sighed. "You are asking me to investigate whether …"

"I am, Colonel Arsharvin, I most definitely am. And I have one more favor to ask, a personal one."

"Name it, Yevgeny," Arsharvin said.

"I would like you to task your intelligence agents to trace the Australian drone aviator I met under that godforsaken rock. I gave you her name. Find her."

"And kill her?"

"What? No. Recruit her! Find her, compromise her and turn her. We are twenty years behind the Americans in the strategic application of drone technology and that woman could be the key to leapfrogging us ahead of the Americans."

To find Bunny right at that moment, all the GRU would have had to do was walk through the door of a small brown weatherboard house in Little Italy, San Diego.

Inside, on pale yellow walls, they would have seen framed sketches in red, blue, green and black. A gallery, of sorts. Except for the strange sound coming from the salons off the reception area. A buzzing, like electric barber clippers.

In one of the salons, sitting in a black leather chair, the GRU would have found Karen O'Hare. And reclining on the chair beside her, Alicia Rodriguez.

"Here you go," the artist said, walking back into the room with a sketch pad. "I don't often get a really original commission like this. Spent way too much time on it, so I hope you like."

He lay the pad down on the table between them and turned it to face them.

A huge smile spread across Bunny's face. It looked like a biker's gang patch. In the middle, white on dark red, was a mushroom cloud, and in a half circle above and below it in gothic script the words: To The Brink / of Hell.

"Uh, I'm not sure…" Rodriguez said, uncertainly.

"It's perfect!" Bunny said, pulling off her shirt, unclipping her bra and rolling onto her stomach.

"Do you want to see some other options?" the tattooist asked Rodriguez. Bunny was glaring at her.

"No, it's good. It's great," she said, and pulled the sleeve of her t-shirt up to her shoulder.

"OK, cool. I'll do the big one," he said, beginning the process of pasting stencil paper on Bunny's back, between her shoulders. "Sienna will do yours, she's just finishing with another client."

Rodriguez took a sip of the energy drink she'd brought in with her as she watched the tattooist work. "I can't believe I'm doing this. I'm not even drunk."

"And I can't believe you've been in the Navy half your life and this is your first tattoo," O'Hare said. Rodriguez leaned forward as the tattooist slowly peeled the stencil away. As the paper came off, Rodriguez saw the Australian had another tattoo, just above her panty line. Some words, in a flowing script.

"*Is ait an mac an saol?*" Rodriguez said, reading them out loud, no doubt pronouncing them wrongly. "What language is that?"

"Gaelic," O'Hare said.

"What does it mean?"

"That, Lieutenant Commander Rodriguez, is for me to know and you to never find out," Bunny grinned.

Sarge hiked back to Savoonga with a heavy heart. There had been three bodies inside the water tank, as far as he could tell.

He had wrapped a scarf around his face and gone down into the tank. He wanted to be sure it was Perri Tungyan and Dave Iworrigan in there. He had found two rifles, a Makarov pistol. And a Russian soldier in a private's uniform. The bodies were pretty torn up, but the freezing weather had stopped them from decomposing. He had seen enough photos of Perri and Dave to recognize them easily.

He knew why Perri and Dave were inside the water tower; he'd probably been the last one to speak to them. But what the Russian was doing there he had no idea. He was a policeman, not a war vet, but he'd be willing to bet the carnage he had seen inside that tank had been caused by a bomb or grenade.

It looked like some bizarre three-way suicide pact but that was ridiculous. Had someone thrown a grenade in from outside, killing them all or leaving them to die? Had they died in a bombing or mortar strike? He shook his head. The island was crawling with war crimes investigators – a special team from The Hague appointed by the UN Security Council. Russia had accused the US of bombing its own citizens at Savoonga, the US had accused Russia of using them as human shields. The US had accused Russian troops of the massacre of the sick and elderly residents of Gambell, while Russia accused US troops of killing its wounded soldiers there and hiding their bodies in a mass grave.

Perri, Dave and the Russian private would probably just be added to the long list of tragic mysteries that Saint Lawrence now held.

The pockets on his cargo trousers were heavy with the wallets he'd taken off the bodies of the boys inside the water tank. The Russian had an ID card on him, too bloodied for him to read, but he took it with him as well to give to the investigators. He had to work out how he was going to get the boys' bodies back to Gambell, and what he was going to tell their families – but that was a problem for tomorrow.

Sarge knew only one thing for sure. If it hadn't been for the boys inside that water tank getting the warning out, the air battle over Little Diomede could have turned out very

528

differently, and with it, the entire conflict. Maybe even the whole of history.

But then, history belonged to small people doing great things, didn't it?

He was pretty sure Dostoyevsky had said that.

/END

(A preview of the next volume in the Future War series follows after the Author notes...)

AUTHOR'S NOTES

Copenhagen, June 2019: Growing up I read a book by British adventure writer Brian Callison called *The Dawn Attack*. It was an hour-by-hour account of a fictional British commando raid on a Norwegian port in World War Two, but what sets it apart is the use of multiple perspectives – both land, sea and air and from either side of the conflict – which served to highlight that wars are started by politicians and generals but fought by ordinary people doing extraordinary things. It does not glorify war; the author successfully paints the picture of an ultimately meaningless action in a brutal conflict, and of painful, lonely and pointless battlefield deaths, but it is an exhilarating read. I'd guess I have read it at least twenty times over the years.

I always told myself one day I'd try to write a book in the style of *Dawn Attack*. This pale attempt is that. So if you enjoyed this one, I strongly recommend you read the book that was the inspiration.

The way this book came to be written was a little unusual, so it bears mentioning. In February 2019 I found myself with time on my hands, a gap in my writing calendar, and an idea for a technothriller. I'd never written a technothriller before. I'm not ex-Army/Navy/Air Force, so I realized I would need experts to help with both the tech and keeping the action grounded in reality. I went online to chat forums and found a fantastic group of volunteer experts, happy to help out with this charity project. They had backgrounds in the armed forces, in special weapons and tactics instruction, in aviation and weapons systems – everything I could ask for.

The way we worked was that I would write a chapter, send it to them, and they would pull it apart, initially focused just on the tech and tactical discussions, but later giving great advice on plot points too! They had very definite opinions on who should live and who should die in the novel, so you can either thank or blame this group (acknowledged in the front of the book) for any emotional trauma suffered through the death of your favorite character(s).

Having a team behind me pushing for the next chapter each time they were finished with the last really moved the project along. *BERING STRAIT* is the length of two traditional 80,000-word novels, but the first draft was written in just six months! The backing team also did a good job of getting the word out about the book before the launch, so that within a month of launch in December 2019, it had hit #1 technothriller in Australia and Canada, and was in the top 50 in the USA and UK, where it has stayed since.

Thanks for reading! You can always contact me on Facebook at https://www.facebook.com/hardcorethrillers if you'd like to chat, ask questions, or just follow the page to find out about giveaways or teasers for upcoming novels. (A preview of Book 2 in the series, *OKINAWA*, follows!)

Cheers,

FX Holden

Other books in the Future War series

All novels in the Future War series are self contained stories and can be read in any order. If you want to read them in the order the conflicts take place then this is a suggested order:

Kobani (2030)
Golan (2030)
Bering Strait (2032)
Okinawa (2033)
Orbital (2034)

Coming December 2021: The Bay (2035)

Read on for a preview of OKINAWA

Preview

OKINAWA
Future War Book 2

"China is leveraging military modernization, influence operations and predatory economics to coerce neighboring countries to reorder the Indo-Pacific region to their advantage. As China continues its economic and military ascendance, asserting power through an all-of-nation long-term strategy, it will continue to pursue a military modernization program that seeks Indo-Pacific regional hegemony in the near-term and displacement of the United States to achieve global pre-eminence in the future."
US Department of Defense.
Summary of the National Defense Strategy of the USA, 2018.

"From competition to co-existence, Japan and China bilateral relations have entered a new phase... With President Xi Jinping, I would like to carve out a new era for China and Japan."
Japanese Prime Minister, Shinzo Abe, speaking in Beijing.
October 2018

April 2033, East China Sea

Lieutenant Takuya Kato believed in omens. On the day he'd turned 30, he'd been promoted to a flight leader on the Japanese aircraft carrier, the *JS Izumo* and then advised his planned shore leave had been canceled because he was needed for exercise RED DOVE, the first-ever joint military exercise between Japan and the People's Republic of China. A birthday and a promotion, that would have been portentous enough. But a birthday, a promotion and an unexpected recall to duty? The Gods, his Kami, were telling him something. Only time would reveal what it was and luckily, Kato-san was a patient man.

But not unnecessarily so. "Close up, Momiji three," he barked, looking down at the panoramic Pilot Vehicle Interface of his F-35E. The tactical situational display was showing his new wingman lagging, as his four-man formation made its last east-west sweep of the skies ahead of the *Izumo*. They were on picket duty, tasked with responding to any threats detected by the Okinawa based *Hawkeye* early warning aircraft circling over the *Izumo*. It could in theory detect enemy aircraft out to a range of 200 kilometers, but the shameful events of two days ago had proven its limitations, when a squadron of Chinese stealth fighters had managed to close within standoff missile range of the *Izumo* before being detected and intercepted. The simulated missiles launched had been few and were judged to have been successfully intercepted by the RED DOVE AI 'referee', but the Chinese fighters should not have been able to penetrate the Japanese fighter screen with such impunity. Japan had come very close to having to accept a strike on the *Izumo*! It was not his flight which was on picket that day and he was determined his flight would not repeat the mistake of relying on the Hawkeye to detect the foe.

His mission was to patrol a grid 200km northeast of the carrier, but after conferring with his superior officer, he had taken his flight 220km out. It meant burning into his fuel safety reserve, but it also meant he might have a slight element of surprise over the 'attacking' Chinese force. There was no guarantee of course that they would attack from his sector, but...

"Momiji one, I have a return. Fast mover, 030 degrees, low," his wingman called, voice supernaturally calm. "Patching data through to Hawkeye." The man had picked up the electronic signature of a Chinese fighter aircraft. *Possibly*.

"Momiji flight, turn to 030, weapons safe, passive arrays only," Kato said, flicking his fighter onto its wingtip and beginning a sweeping starboard turn. "Waiting *Hawkeye* confirmation." He needed the commander aboard the airborne warning aircraft to decide how to react to the possible threat. It could be a false return. Or it could be a feint, designed to draw the Japanese fighter cover away from the real threat. Right now, aboard the *Hawkeye*, they would be trying to triangulate the electronic signature picked up by his flight with their own data, with infrared satellite detection, with data from other fighters. It was the third time today they had seen a Chinese *yurei*, or ghost. Like ghosts, the other two had evaporated. Without thinking, he reached up and touched the silver pendant of his Kami, hanging at his throat. It had the stylized form of a large, breaking wave.

His personal Kami was the *Tsunami*, or Tidal Wave. It had been passed on to him by his grandfather with great solemnity in a personal family ceremony that he had learned had less to do with the Shinto religion, than it did with his family's deeply ingrained nationalism. He had been seventeen years old when his father had ushered him into his grandfather's living room on a hot, grey autumn day. It had been raining all morning and he remembered still the smell of warm steaming bitumen as he blinked his way into the room, eyes struggling to adjust to the darkness. His grandfather sat in his big armchair and beckoned him over.

On the table before him was a blue, velvet-covered box.

"Sit boy, sit," his grandfather had said. He was sitting in a corner in a pool of lamplight. "How old are you today?"

Kato had sat and then looked up at his grandfather in confusion. Had the man not just been to his birthday party? He knew very well how old Kato was.

"Uh, seventeen grandfather."

"Yes. Seventeen. And it is time for you to receive your *Kami*."

"Yes grandfather." Like most of his generation, Kato had been a self-absorbed, ignorant child. More interested in the latest fashion craze from Shimokita, or the newest virtual reality game, than the history of his ancestors. And though he would soon be leaving to join the air defense force academy, he had walked into the dark room thinking about nothing deeper than the pair of Energy Pump Nikes he had just unwrapped and what his girlfriend Ushi might say when she saw him casually charging his phone from his heel.

His grandfather knew enough about his grandson to know he needed to be brought into the now, with a small, sharp shock.

"Your great grandfather Tadao Kato chose this Kami, in April, 1945, the day before he dived his rocket plane into an American destroyer, killing himself..."

"Grandfather..." Kato-san had interrupted. "Was my great grandfather a Kamikaze?"

"Yes. Be quiet," the old man said. "I will read you his *Jisei*. The Jisei was a poem our pilots took with them into combat. He made two copies, one of which he always took with him and one which he sent to my mother." The old man unfolded a piece of ancient rice paper and read aloud.

For the Emperor,
I will fall as a wave
With joy
In my heart
Your jade will shatter.

Kato stayed silent this time. The old man was breathing softly. After a minute, he spoke, "He had with him, on that final flight, a jade ring my mother gave him." He folded the rice paper and placed it in his shirt pocket. "The report of his death stated that officer Tadao Kato set an example for all of his men and for his empire when he sacrificed his life to destroy an American ship off Okinawa." He reached forward out of the lamplight and lifted something from the table. "All pilots were required to choose their Kami on the day before their final mission. Your great grandfather chose the Tsunami. It was recorded that this surprised his superior officer, who asked him why he had chosen this and not an animal spirit like most other pilots ... a tiger, a wolf, or a shark. Your grandfather said that he chose the Tsunami because a tiger can be shot, a shark can be speared, but the Tsunami is unstoppable." The old man's hand lifted a pendant on a silver chain from the table. "In honor of his sacrifice, my father commissioned this necklace from a jeweler in his village," he said and held it out to Kato. "My mother said I should wear it. But I was a poor student, who became a simple accountant and I did not feel myself worthy. I offered it to your father, but he also declined." His hand was shaking, the silver wave at the end of the chain quivering. "You are the first in our family to serve in the military since your great grandfather. I want you to take it."

"Grandfather," Kato had said, "I can't. I haven't earned it."

"Perhaps, but take it now and do your utmost to earn it," the old man had said, pressing it into Kato's palm.

Over the East China sea, his radio pulled him away from his thoughts. "Momiji leader this is Arakashi Control. Target confirmed, you are cleared to intercept. Vectoring support to your sector, you are lead."

His heart caught in his throat but he took a deep breath and forced it down. The target was real! His eyes flicked across his display panels as his fingers tapped commands into a panel beside his throttle, "Roger Control. Momiji flight, targets on your tac monitors, roll out to formation four and follow me in. Select AAM-6s." The Japanese AAM-6 was an adaptation of the British *Meteor* ramjet-powered air to air missile that flew at Mach-4 and had a 'no escape zone' three times that of its Chinese counterpart. If they engaged, they would be firing in simulation mode, but the lethality of the Japanese missiles would weigh in their favor when the AI referees tallied up kills and losses after the merge.

A tone sounded in Kato's ears and six green dots appeared in his heads-up display, bracketed with glowing red circles. His targeting system had analyzed their electronic signatures and was calling them Chinese *Chengdu* stealth fighters. They were heading in at wavetop height, apparently oblivious to the Japanese fighters about to drop on them from above.

His eyes flicked from his instruments, to his visor, to the skies around him as he gripped his stick tight and pushed his throttles forward, "Momiji flight, targets low on our 11 o'clock, *engage engage engage*," he called. With a grunt, he rolled his fighter on its axis, stopped it with the canopy pointing at the ground and pulled it into a screaming dive just as the Chinese aircraft flashed under his nose 30,000 feet below.

And the second he did so, he recognized the nagging uncertainty that had suddenly grabbed him. The *Chengdu* was a *land-based* aircraft. To get to the exercise area north of Okinawa, it would have had to fly from Wenzhou or Shanghai on the Chinese mainland and possibly refuel in flight. There were not supposed to be any land-based aircraft in the Chinese order of battle for exercise RED DOVE! As he closed on the Chinese fighter formation and the missile targeting tone in his helmet began to beep faster indicating his AAM-6s would soon be in range, he knew he had flown his men right into an enemy trap. Even as the thought registered, a missile warning tone screamed in his ears and his combat AI wrenched control of his fighter from his grip and pulled it into a screaming starboard banking turn that snapped his head back and pushed him into his seat as though a giant had just laid a hand on his chest.

Fighting for air, he tried to make sense of the icons in his visor and managed to key his comms, "Momiji flight, J-31 *Snow Falcons*, high on our six! Evade and…"

A new tone sounded. *Miss!* The enemy missile had failed to get a lock.

"…evade and engage with short-range missiles!" he completed, taking control of his aircraft back and flinging his machine into a climbing reverse turn to try to get his nose pointed at the source of his attack. An icon flashed on the visor of his helmet and he screwed his head around – there! High on his four o'clock, a small silver speck. He rolled his F-35E as he and his enemy closed at a combined velocity of twice the speed of sound.

The *Snow Falcon* was the newest and deadliest fighter in the Chinese arsenal; with flight and weapons systems controlled by an advanced combat AI, the human pilot was a more a part of the aircraft, than master of it. The enemy fighter immediately grew from a dot, to a small silver arrow and his offensive system automatically selected the short-range Mitsubishi AAM5-B air to air missile and locked up the enemy plane. *Tone!* He hesitated. For a millisecond. The AAM5 had a poor record for accuracy in a high-speed head-on merge. He canceled the missile and switched to guns, his gun pipper appearing now in his helmet visor and bobbing around, trying to lock onto the enemy aircraft screaming down at him.

Before he could get a lock, a new missile warning alarm screamed in his ears. The enemy had fired! His joystick was pulled from his hand and his machine rolled into a hard inverted turn. His vision began to blur and he just had time to register the G-force warning on his visor before the enemy missile tone became a long, flat, drawn-out screech and his aircraft righted itself as it resumed straight and level flight.

It was a screech designed to bore into a pilot's soul. It was the scream of digital death. Sure enough, the computerized voice of a RED DOVE referee broke in on his comms channel, "Momiji 1 this is RED DOVE control. Please maintain your current altitude and heading and respect radio silence until you exit the exercise area. You are Killed In Action."

He slumped forward against his harness, breathing hard. He should have taken the shot when he had it, could have followed through with guns. Why did he hesitate?!

His fist hammered into the glass over his head. One by one, the icons of the doomed aircraft in his flight flashed and showed red crosses, indicating they too were KIA. They had only claimed one Chinese fighter. Diving on the Chinese decoy flight below, he had exposed himself to their unseen escort above and they had swatted his machines from the sky. The short-ranged Chinese *Chengdu* decoys had done their job and as he watched, they broke off, headed back to the mainland. Switching a display screen to show a feed from the RED DOVE strategic overview – a view only available to ground controllers and 'dead' units – Kato now saw no fewer than 24 attack aircraft from the Chinese carrier, *Liaoning*, speeding into the sector he had just been forced to abandon. And headed straight for his carrier, the *JS Izumo*.

It may only be a 'friendly' exercise, but the Chinese had just blown a hole in the Japanese defenses and they were about to pour pain and humiliation through it.

Red Dove, Red Dragon.

His hacker handle was *Dragon Bird* and he was about to fire the first shot in a new global war.

He stood at a traffic light across from the 24-hour electronics market on Beijing East Road, near the harborside clamor of Shanghai's Bund and at the bottom of one its many skyscrapers. Even at this early time of the morning, the shopping center teemed with customers buying everything from solder, to integrated circuits, chips and power supplies. The store owners were gruff and unfriendly to casual shoppers like Dragon Bird, as they mostly serviced tradesmen, technicians and electronics repair firms. So he rarely shopped there.

Dragon Bird made his way down the steps and through the basement, past the small shop fronts, with weary resentment. He especially disliked the sharp, nostril stinging stink of burning solder and ozone that seemed to pool in the basement and the slap slap slap of his Huili Warrior sneakers across the fake white marble floor. Every day, slap slap slap on his way in, slap slap slap on his way out. Yeah, sure, he could do up his laces and cut down on the slapping, but casual civilian dress was one of the few personal privileges he was allowed and he was milking it.

At the back of the basement he turned a corner to a service elevator marked 'technical staff only'. It had no button, just a card reader. He fished in his bag for his card, shoving aside the thermos of pot noodles, his keys and phone, to pull it out by its lanyard, hang it around his neck and swipe it through the reader. When the reader lit green he stuck his thumb on a thumb pad to confirm his ID. As he waited for the elevator, he reflected he may as well have slept under his desk overnight, since it was only six hours since he had slapped his way out across the tiles in the early morning hours of last night.

But at least today would be a break from the usual routine. Today his system was going *offensive*. The system he and his team had worked to perfect for nearly five years, that no one had believed was possible and that sprung from an idea his former boss, the Golden Idiot, had even mocked in front of his fellow programmers. Not that he would get much credit for it, he was still only a lowly Shàowèi or Captain and his small team of five coders, the ones who had been toiling away all these years to bring them here, would never be recognized. His officers would take all the credit if his system worked and be the first to grab him by the collar and throw him in front of a disciplinary tribunal if it didn't.

The elevator pinged open and he waited as two young privates slouched out, looking more tired and washed out than him, if that was possible. They were not permitted to salute him, so they just nodded and started fishing cigarette packets out of their pockets as they exited the elevator. He stepped into a fug of spicy aftershave and sour sweat. As the elevator clunked into motion, he checked his *WeChat Moments* account one last time before he had to hand the phone over to the security staff. As usual, the only message was one from his mother. His other friends from college had landed themselves jobs at Baidu and Huawei and lived glamorous, glittering lives with high salaries, street clothes and girlfriends with narrow hips and luscious lips, while he had let himself be lured into a job with Unit 61938. He

541

was promised the chance to work on technologies his friends could only dream of, but he hadn't been told he would be doing it in numbing social isolation.

The elevator opened onto what looked like a small airport security gate. He stepped out and walked up to a desk and handed over his shoulder bag, with everything inside it except his lunch thermos. The private behind the desk handed him a bag tag and stuck his bag in a pigeon hole. There were people from another elevator stacking behind him and she waved him out of the way. He put the thermos onto an x-ray belt, then moved over to a body scanner, stepped inside when he was called forward, held his hands in the air and made a circle. The machine beeped. It nearly always did. He stepped out and waited as a soldier ran a detector wand up and down his arms, legs and around his waist. The soldier checked a screen and then waved him into the locker room. From his locker, he took his light green uniform shirt with its green and gold shoulder boards and dark green baseball-style hat. Then he stowed his lunch thermos where his shirt had been, checked himself in a mirror and got ready to go through to his team's work area.

It was the same routine as every other damn day. But today was not every other day. Today, he and his unit were going to *war*.

China's first modern aircraft carrier had started its life as a cold war wreck. Its keel was laid down in 1985 as a Soviet aircraft cruiser, the *Varyag*, but the regime collapsed before it was completed and its hull lay rusting in the Ukraine until China bought it in 1998 and towed it to its Dalian shipyard in Liaoning province.

The rebuilding of the carrier was a herculean task that took nearly twenty years – it wasn't until 2016 that the ship named after the province that had birthed it, the *Liaoning* (pronounced lee-ow-ning), was declared combat-ready.

The announcement sent geopolitical tremors around the world, particularly among the nations that border the disputed

South China sea; the Philippines, Vietnam and Japan. It was more than a military signal, it was a political signal to the region that a resurgent China was going to take a more assertive role at sea. Landlocked for centuries without a true blue-water navy, it nevertheless had a proud naval history dating as far back as 210 BC when the royal sorcerer Xu Fu led a fleet of 60 ships and 5,000 sailors on a search for the elixir of life across the seas to the east of China. He was believed to have made landfall on the western coast of Japan and declared himself emperor. Neither he, nor his ships and crew ever returned.

As a metaphor for China's naval ambitions, the *Liaoning* was apt. Concerned with civil wars and invasions from the west and later from Japan, the rising empire of China had built up a strong 'green water' or coastal navy, but did not pose a naval threat to other Pacific powers in the 20th Century. With the launch of the *Liaoning* in the 21st Century, that all changed. Ship by ship, port by port, China built up its navy, so that by 2030 it had matched the US Navy in blue-water capability. The numbers were telling. In attack submarines, it could field 87 to the US's 42. In ballistic missile submarines it matched the US, 12 to 11. In large surface ships and carriers, it lagged, matching only a third of the US firepower in missile cruisers, but this was due to a focus on smaller surface ships suited to battle in the waters of Korea, Japan and the South China Sea, where it outnumbered the US 123 to 40. In the final stage of its expansion, it launched five amphibious landing ships, each capable of fielding a full marine expeditionary force.

The threat provoked Japan in 2020 to embark on a ten-year race to build up its armed forces to counterbalance the growing Chinese presence in the south China sea and increased assertiveness over Taiwan. But it had started thirty years too late; through that entire period China had been outspending it six to one. Against China's hundreds of heavy ships, submarines and soon-to-be three aircraft carriers, Japan could only muster a half dozen missile frigates or destroyers, two smaller helicopter carriers and a fleet of 20 submarines, a third the size of China's sub fleet. Japan had relied too long on its alliance with a USA that now had bigger troubles with its old enemy Russia and was much less interested in involving itself in the problems of far off nations like Japan.

That its attention and priorities were elsewhere became apparent in 2019 when the US announced it would be suspending its annual wargames with South Korea, as a goodwill gesture toward the North. The suspension became permanent as reunification talks began in 2023 and the US began drawing down its permanent presence in South Korea. In 2025 when a ten-year timetable for the reunification of the two Koreas was announced by the leaders of both of those countries, China and South Korea made clear in the UN Security Council they saw no ongoing role for US forces in the new Korea and the US agreed. But it wasn't going to wait ten years - it started in 2030 to withdraw all combat personnel. A few of the larger US bases were still there, but they were mostly filled with accountants and lawyers, haggling over the details of what should be turned over to the new United Korean Republic government and who would pay what to who.

When South China sea tensions inevitably escalated to an armed confrontation between Chinese and Philippine naval units, resulting in the loss of the Philippine Navy frigate, the *Gregorio del Pilar*, the US response offered no material support and made nothing but the softest of protests at the United Nations. Japanese politicians watched the US turn its back on its former ally with alarm. When Chinese forces landed on the Taiwanese Pescadores Islands and reclaimed them for China, provoking a political crisis on Taiwan and censure in the UN Security Council, the UK proposed a motion calling on China to withdraw its troops. France voted for the motion, China and Russia against. The US abstained. In Tokyo, the newly formed right-wing government of the Party of Hope convened an emergency session of Parliament, voted to increase military spending and to withdraw Japan from the nearly 80-year-old US-Japan Mutual Security Treaty.

Despite centuries of enmity, it was perhaps not surprising that in 2025 Japan intensified diplomatic overtures to China that had first begun in 2018. It softened its stance on key maritime disputes in the South China Sea and closed its representative office on Taiwan. The hotly disputed Senkaku Islands were declared *terra nullius* and a joint China-Japan 'maritime safety' station began operating on Uotsuri-shima island in 2028. The US responded by canceling arms shipments to Japan, but Japan was not concerned. It had stockpiled spare parts and ammunition for its US-made fighter aircraft and immediately announced a joint-venture agreement between Mitsubishi Heavy Industries and the Shenyang Aircraft Corporation for a Japanese version of the Chinese *Chengdu* 'Mighty Dragon' stealth fighter.

The US reacted angrily but pragmatically, just as it had in Korea, announcing an aggressive timetable for closing the three US Air Force bases on the Japanese mainland and Okinawa, plus the US Army Camp Zama base at Kanagawa, leaving only the 10,000 Marines at Camp Smedley on Okinawa; which had already shrunk from a peak of 7 facilities, down to just four – the Marine Corp base at Camp Schwab, the Marine Air Corps at Futenma, the joint Marine and NSA intelligence facility at Camp Hansen and the Navy-run port at White Beach. The move was more than pure posturing however. The troops and equipment stationed in Japan were sorely needed in other theatres and in fact were redeployed well ahead of the deadline; to Guam, Darwin and the bulk of them, to bases bordering a now belligerent and chaotic post-Putin Russia.

As the US drew down its forces and closed its mainland bases, the Japanese Government hit the US with a massive bill for the cleanup of its former installations, which the US refused to acknowledge. And on Okinawa, simmering civilian resentment against the remaining US presence there led to violent protests and then 'citizen occupations' of the largely deserted US facilities. Acts of violence against US service members became commonplace and Japanese police investigation of these was lax.

In 2033, Japan and China announced a new China-Japan Mutual Self Defense Treaty. The two most powerful militaries in the Far East were allied for the first time in their histories. China began to support Japanese calls for the accelerated withdrawal of the remaining US military forces in Japan and in particular, for the US to hand over to Japanese Self Defense Forces full control of the last US Navy run port facility on Okinawa, at White Beach. This, the US refused. It continued to forward base a naval taskforce at White Beach, currently comprising an amphibious assault ship, the USS *Makin Island*, the recently upgraded Ticonderoga Aegis cruiser the *USS Port Royal*, two *Zumwalt* class multirole destroyers and a fleet oiler.

To mark the occasion of the official signing of the new China-Japan defense pact, the two countries announced the **first**-ever joint naval exercises between the Japan Naval Self Defense Force and the Peoples Liberation Army Navy. China allocated no less than a full carrier task force, based around the *Liaoning*, to exercise RED DOVE.

The *Liaoning* may have been the first and oldest of China's carriers, but it was designated officially as a 'training ship' and was the country's testbed for the newest technologies - a mantle it carried proudly. While its sister carriers fielded older navalized *Chengdu* fighters based on stolen US 4th gen stealth technology, the *Liaoning* was nearing the end of very successful trials for the newer *Snow Falcon Snow Falcons* and had been upgraded to be able to field 36 of the new 'very short takeoff and landing' stealth fighters. After an on-again, off-again development program, *Red Dove* was going to be the final exercise before the new *Snow Falcon* aircraft were declared combat-ready. The *Liaoning's* pilots had been looking forward very much indeed to the chance to test themselves against the 28 US made F-35Es of the Japanese Maritime Self Defense Force, flying off the decks of its own carrier, the newly modified former Helicopter Destroyer, the *JS Izumo*.

At the exact moment Dragon Bird was checking his pot noodles through the security scanner, the pilots of the *Liaoning* were engaged with the pilots of the Japanese carriers over the sea off Okinawa. Accompanying the *Liaoning* in this show of Chinese naval power were six air defense destroyers, four anti-submarine frigates, two *Shang* class nuclear submarines and one supply ship. Japan had also brought a formidable naval force to the party, with its newly refitted carrier accompanied by four *Konga* class missile destroyers, a *Towada* class fleet replenishment tanker and two *Soryu-E* class extended-range submarines, supported by maritime surveillance aircraft flying from Okinawa.

Exercise *Red Dove* had four more days to run. After which, in a gesture of international maritime fraternity, the combined Japanese and Chinese fleets were going to proceed to Shanghai for a formal signing ceremony to celebrate the successful conduct of their first-ever joint fleet exercises.

Before the exercise, the Japanese government had issued a warning to Japan-based US warships to avoid military operations in the East China Sea until the passage of the Sino-Japanese carrier strike group was concluded, to prevent any 'maritime misunderstandings' occurring due to heavier than usual naval traffic in Chinese and Japanese waters. A US Navy spokesman responded by stating that its forward-deployed Okinawa expeditionary strike group, Taskforce 44, would stage from White Beach 'as and when the Commander of US Forces in the Pacific so deems.' Off the record, he told journalists that it would be a cold day in Hades when a Japanese admiral told a US admiral where and when he could sail his ships.

Unwelcome Guests

Noriko Fukada had worked at the Kouwa Gardens Nursery near White Beach US Navy Base for a long time. A very long time. These days, she didn't get through as much as she used to in her prime, nor was she getting paid for it either. But she was always at the Nursery at seven in the morning, rain or shine, six days a week. Her specialty was succulents, because Okinawa was full of people who did nothing but work and drink and work and did not have time for high maintenance house plants. A cactus however – a nice *Buiningii* or *Akagurohibotan-Nishiki* – if potted correctly and watered sparingly, any idiot could keep alive. Her favorite customers however were not the collectors, the cacti fanatics who she tolerated but did not encourage. They came only to show her how much they thought they knew, to try to teach her, not to listen, not to learn. Noriko loved the students, the twenty-something boys and girls, who came to Kouwa Gardens looking for nothing more complicated than a plant for their windowsill, or their desk.

"Something that doesn't need much light," they would say. "Something that doesn't need much care."

"Tell me about yourself," she would reply. "And I will find the perfect plant for you." Their stories kept her young.

Most days she would arrive early and stay at the nursery until lunchtime, unless she was sick, or having a bad day. She would eat with the other workers and listen to their prattle, shake her head at their obsession with gadgets and devices, VR game stars she had never seen. After lunch she would walk the two blocks back to her apartment, take a lift to the second floor and gather the things she needed for her afternoon program. In the afternoons she visited the 'old people'. The lonely and the sick and those whose minds had packed up before their body did. She made small cakes for them and took a thermos of tea with her so that they wouldn't need to fuss, though often – if they were brought up correctly - they made a big deal out of serving for her and she let them.

Because in the country which still held the world record for the greatest number of people over the age of 100, Noriko Fukada was a bit of a legend. World-famous on Okinawa, she said with a gap-toothed smile.

Noriko Fukada had been born on January 7, 1931. She was nearly twelve when Japan attacked Pearl Harbor and opened a new front in the Second World War. She had just turned 15 when the Americans stormed ashore on Okinawa in the biggest amphibious assault of the Pacific war. Her father hid her in the cellar of their apartment when the first shells from the big American battleships started roaring in from the sea. She was only allowed up to the apartment to eat lunch, when her father would update them all on what was happening. He was a fireman and worked with everyone from sailors to soldiers and policemen, so he knew everything. "A violent wind of steel is coming Noriko," he told her. "You must be brave and help your mother." She didn't want to stay home and help her mother. Her brother, only fourteen years old, had been drafted into the *Tekketsu Kinnōtai*, the Iron and Blood Corps. She had wanted to go with him, but had been told to go home again. She stood crying beside the line of boys, bereft with shame. An old marine had come up to her and led her to a corner and sat her down. "I have an important mission for you," he said. "You must survive. Above all else, you must live. If you die there will be no one left who knows the truth about the battle of Okinawa. Bear this temporary shame but endure it. I give you this order and expect you to carry it out."

She lived. Her father and brother did not. She was pressed into service at a Japanese field hospital, where people from surrounding Maehara and Suzaki were often rounded up and herded onto the roof to wave flags, so that the American bombers would not bomb them. She and her mother nearly starved, troops from both sides raiding their house for food, leaving them nothing.

She lived. She spent the next ten years hungry, a meal a day if she was lucky, many days without. US forces took their farmland to build their bases, paid the local workers poorly if at all. Only in the late 1950s did things start to improve, as the US needed Okinawa as a staging post for its new war in Korea and Okinawa became a US territory. She worked as a nurse at a US military hospital, for US dollars, until it was closed down when the island was transferred to Japanese government control in 1972.

That was when she had gotten the job at Kouwa Gardens, working in the nursery shop. She showed an aptitude for cultivation, requested a job in the greenhouse and started in the succulents department, where she had stayed since, except for a very brief and unhappy time in the herb gardens, which she found overwhelming. So many scents.

She had carried out the order given to her by that old sergeant in 1945 most faithfully. She was one hundred and three years old and she had lived. Lived through world war 2, the dawn of atomic weapons, Korean wars one and two, the electrification, industrialization and roboticization of Japan. Lived through a husband, but never had children herself. She had outlived the sorrow of that. She had seen the arrival of wireless communications, television, games consoles, internet, nuclear, solar, wind and hydro power and VR. She had seen Russians send a man into space, Americans walk on the moon and a Chinese astronaut orbit Mars.

But she had never seen anything, or anyone, quite like the woman who walked into the Kouwa Gardens Nursery a year ago. Her hair was dyed platinum blonde, cropped so short it reminded Noriko of one of her favorite cactuses, the Extra Hairy Mammillaria Plumosa. She was wearing jeans, a poorly fitting t-shirt verging on immodest and US Navy baseball cap. She had metal through her ears, her nose and a stud in one lip. Tattoos on both arms. She whistled a tune as she entered the nursery, loudly and badly.

The woman had walked up to Noriko, quite boldly and started talking to her in English. Noriko made a pretense of not understanding, hoping she would go away, but she had taken an interest in the arrangement Noriko was making – a simple miniature-garden in a rectangular pot, with four varieties in it, suitable for a wide window with an easterly aspect – and started asking questions about it. Noriko soon realized that the only way to free herself of this very embarrassing situation was to sell the woman something and exchanged a few words with her, eventually selling her a large Biznaga Plumosa, which was much like the Mammillaria, but more vulgar and thus perfectly suited. The woman had departed, whistling and Noriko had taken the rest of the day off.

That was the first time she met Karen 'Bunny' O'Hare.

Bunny O'Hare was staring at the stubbornly unflowering cactus sitting on top of her microwave oven and feeling like she was headed for a cold Saturday in hell. Some Saturdays, she woke up in the humidity of an Okinawa morning, got that first cup of coffee inside her and then sat back with her hands locked behind her head, the whole weekend stretching out in front of her like a runway in front of superjumbo jet. Nothing to do, nowhere to go, just a slow takeoff toward total freedom.

This was not going to be a superjumbo day.

She'd had her morning coffee Vietnamese style (with condensed milk because she still didn't have a fridge) and checked her email inbox. There were the usual thousand unread messages, but nothing screaming READ ME at her. At that point, she had been thinking maybe it was going to be A Good Day. Which didn't happen too often when you were stationed on the last remaining operational US base in Japan.

Then Master at Arms James Jensen, of the 3rd Marines, 1st Battalion, White Beach Naval Base Okinawa, knocked on her door.

"Hey O'Hare, wassup?" he said, giving her his usual lopsided health-nut quarterback six-pack wonderboy grin.

Wassup number one was that Chief Petty Officer Jensen had rarely called at her off-base apartment across the road from Koza Music Town and never on a Saturday morning. Wassup number two was that Agent Smith from the classic *Matrix* movies was standing there beside him. It was O'Hare's incontrovertible experience that when a man in his mid-30s dressed in a dark suit, white shirt, dark tie and sunglasses turned up unannounced at your front door and just stood there without mentioning Jehovah, then you were about to have a very non-superjumbo kind of day.

She shot a curious frown at Jensen but he just shrugged, "This is Chuck, can we come in?" 'Chuck' smiled but didn't hold out his hand. He reeked of Spook.

Bunny stepped aside and waved them into the living room of her apartment. A two-room apartment above the Galaxy Bar, which she could barely afford on her DARPA housing allowance.

Chuck didn't know where to sit. Jensen solved the problem for him by pushing O'Hare's newspapers and magazines off her sofa and onto the floor and pointing to where Chuck could park his butt.

"I was reading those," Bunny told Jensen, pulling over one of her dining chairs.

He looked down at them, "Same magazines and papers that were on the sofa three weeks ago when I visited."

"There's some good articles. Long-read features kind of thing," Bunny said defensively.

"Open at the same pages," he said.

Chuck was holding out a badge for her to see and waving it to get her attention, "Ms. O'Hare, I'm from the NSA."

"It's Bunny," Jensen said. "Get it? O'Hare – Bunny? It's a pilot thing."

"To friends," she said, looking at Agent Smith. "And we're not there yet." She glowered at Jensen. What was he doing in her flat with the NSA in tow? The NSA was the National Security Agency of the USA, the world's biggest ugliest Cyber Spooks.

Bunny stared at him curiously. OK, so Chief Jensen was Navy Security Force and Chuckie was a cyberspook. What did they want with a lowly DARPA contractor, like her?

Over the next few minutes, Bunny O'Hare got the unwelcome feeling she was under investigation. The thing that had her curiosity, as she bustled around in her kitchen making tea for Jensen (black) and coffee for Chuck (black) and a double shot Vietnamese for herself was what she might have done that warranted an unannounced visit from both the NSA and a Navy Security Force master at arms. Bunny got on first names terms with Chief Jensen thanks to a small situation involving a bunch of marines who'd gotten into trouble using karaoke microphones to beat the crap out of a local Yakuza mobster downstairs in the Galaxy Bar, which took up the whole first and second floors of her apartment complex. She'd been walking up the stairs to her apartment and heard a lot of shouting in English and Japanese. Stopping at the karaoke bar level she stuck her head in and saw half the staff of the Galaxy had surrounded some young marines, who were swinging microphones on their leads around their heads, to hold the staff at bay. A Yakuza mobster was propped against a wall, holding his bleeding forehead and cursing, too drunk to stand.

Bunny knew the staff at the Galaxy pretty well, seeing they'd been neighbors for a year. And she did most of her drinking there, when she wasn't at the Mohito Bar down the road, which they also owned. She calmed things down, took the three marines upstairs to her place and telephoned base security. Jensen had come personally with a couple of his men to collect them.

"I looked you up when you called," he said, after thanking Bunny for stepping in and sending his men downstairs to a waiting van. "You're DARPA."

"Yep," she confirmed.

"That why you live off-base?" It was a fair question, since the local population was quite ambivalent about seeing the US military on their streets these days and most personnel chose to live and socialize on-base.

"No, I took this place for the view," she told him, nodding at the view out her loungeroom window, across Kozagate street to the rusting neon sign over Music Town.

He looked out the window, looked around the tiny apartment and looked O'Hare up and down, from face piercings to tattoos to army combat boots.

"I think this is going to be the start of a beautiful friendship, Lieutenant," he said.

"That's my *former* air force rank," she said.

"Well I'm not going to call you Ms. DARPA Project Lead," he smiled. "What else do you go by?"

"Bunny. And O'Hare."

"I'll go with O'Hare." He'd tipped her a salute. "Thanks again for the help, O'Hare."

When she'd signed up for a hiking tour at White Beach, she'd found herself on a full day trek through the Gangala Valley with a bunch of base nurses and ... Jensen. They'd clicked. Turned out she wasn't the only one on the island with a warped view of the world.

She tipped a half packet of old Oreos onto a plate. She'd messed up plenty in her life, but whatever this was, she decided she must be in big trouble, looking at Chuck sitting there impatiently while Jensen stirred sugar into his coffee and reached for a cookie. He took two.

She pulled the plate away from him and handed it to Chuck, but he just looked at it like he'd never seen a cookie before in his life and then looked at her, "Ms. O'Hare, we need your help."

She gave Jensen a 'what the hell' look, but he just shrugged.

"I am a Remotely Piloted Submersible Pilot and Sensor Operator," she told Chuck, emphasizing the capital letters. "And DARPA project lead for the Stingray program here at White Beach. I am still getting stopped at the gates every time there is a new guy, having to explain that I really work there and reminding him he should be saluting me." He looked as though this did not surprise him. "There is no capacity in which I can possibly be of help to the US National Security Agency, unless you want advice on pubs and clubs in downtown Koza."

He smiled his non-smile again. In a movie, at this point he'd have been pulling out a big fat manila folder from his briefcase and it would have had 'O'Hare, K' written on the front and he would have unclipped it slowly and taken out some surveillance photos of her and started telling her about her life story, just to intimidate her. But he didn't have a briefcase. So he didn't have a manila folder. He didn't even take out his smartphone and look up some notes. He'd memorized it.

"Well, actually there is. Your latest security vetting was less than two years ago..."

"Yep. I think it was right before your Secretary of Navy pinned a Navy Cross on me. Or maybe it was after?"

"After," he said, without a pause. "But you do not have sufficient clearances for what we are about to discuss."

554

She pointed at Jensen. "But *he* does?"

Chuck didn't look happy. "I've had to indoctrinate Chief Petty Officer Jensen, for the purposes of our discussion today."

"Oooh, you've been *indoctrinated*," she said to Jensen. "Did it hurt?"

"Walking like a cowboy," he said. "Seriously though O'Hare, just hear him out so we can go and get a proper breakfast, OK?"

That was his nice way of saying STFU O'Hare, so she did.

"Can I just confirm a few details?" Chuck asked. He took off his sunglasses, showing ice blue eyes.

"Sure."

"Thank you ma'am. You served six years with the Royal Australian Air Force and were recruited by DARPA Aerospace during the Turkey-Syria conflict, where you were based in Incirlik..." He still wasn't looking at notes. It was quite unnerving.

"Classified," she told him.

"Yes, flying F-35s."

"No comment."

"But you were removed from active duty due to multiple disciplinary breaches and then recruited to the DARPA Unmanned Combat Air Vehicle program."

"Again, no comment."

"Then transferred to the F-47 *Fantom* amphibious conversion program..."

"Also, classified." He was good. He was all over her CV, she had to give him that.

"From there you were posted to a covert second-strike facility on Little Diomede Island in the Bering Strait, during the Russia-USA maritime dispute..."

"War, not dispute. And still classified. And now I'll have to ask Chief Jensen to kill you."

"...In which service you became the first Australian since Admiral Harold Farncomb in WW2 to be awarded the US Navy Cross for valor under fire and a purple heart."

Jensen arched his eyebrows in surprise. This was apparently something he hadn't picked up on, even though it was in the public domain. "They hand them out like crackerjack prizes these days," she said.

"After which you were placed on long term medical impairment leave..." he said like he was reading off a mental shopping list.

"Shortish," she told him. "Shortish-term medical leave."

"Fine," he said, all polite about it. "And now, as you explained, you are attached to DARPA again, leading the final pre-deployment trials of the advanced undersea payload delivery system for Extra-Large Unmanned Underwater Vehicles before DARPA hands the project over to the Office of Naval Research."

"XLUUVs, we call them," she told him. "The Orca was the first. This new generation are called Stingrays. Sounds edgier."

"Do we have to go through O'Hare's whole life story?" Jensen asked. "Because there is some really ugly stuff in there if you get to her taste in music..."

"He's just trying to protect me, bless him. He actually loves bro-country," she quipped.

Chuck ignored them, "While on medical leave, you were prescribed anti-depressants."

O'Hare glared at him, "Seriously, you want to go *there*?" She didn't care what he said in front of Jensen – the guy had used her bathroom so he'd probably sneaked a peek in her medicine cabinet. But it unsettled her that the NSA would have dug into her personal life so deeply. "Have you ever been in combat Chuck?"

"No. But this is about you, not me. You have not filled a prescription for nearly a year," he said, conversationally. "So your mental state is, what ... stable would you say?" He waited for her reply with an inscrutably blank expression.

"I haven't woken up screaming for months, if that's your question."

"Seriously, can we speed this up?" Jensen said, crossing and uncrossing his legs. "I'll be turning forty in a few years."

556

Chuck gave Jensen a polite death-look. Wiped his face clean from the inside, reached into his inside jacket pocket and pulled out a couple of pieces of paper and a pen. "This is a Secrecy Agreement, please sign at the bottom."

She looked at Jensen. "*I* already signed mine," he said. "I'm good."

The paper had the usual guff across the top: TOP SECRET UMBRA ORCON dot dot dot. Then the standard threats of death and dismemberment if the signatory (Karen O'Hare) disclosed anything about said project to anyone not authorized to receive information about said project. And then the project name...

"Project LOKI?" she asked as she signed.

"Yup. Thank you," Chuck said, taking back his paper and pen and putting them both in his pocket. As he reached across her, O'Hare picked up a whiff of...what? She was usually pretty good at aftershaves and perfumes, but couldn't nail his. Probably because he also smelled like he just got off a plane after a three-hour flight. He sat back, looking at her as though waiting for her to ask a question. When she didn't, he spoke up, "Loki. Norse god of mischief," he said. "Usually we use random name generators for our operations, but I came up with that one myself."

"Cute," she said. "Care to tell me what Project LOKI is about?"

"Of course." He looked at Jensen, who was already in on the secret and looking at O'Hare with an annoyingly knowing smile, then turned his gaze back on her. "NSA has for some time been concerned at the increasing automation of our most advanced weapons systems. Aircraft, ships, tanks and subs are going from being manned, to semi-autonomous, or in the case of your Stingray, almost entirely autonomous."

"Autonomous AI is a force multiplier. It frees human resources to be used across multiple weapons systems instead of having dedicated crews which need training, fielding, rest and recreation. The Stingray has the offensive capabilities of a Los Angeles class submarine, but can be piloted remotely by just myself and a systems officer, whereas an LA class boat requires a crew of one hundred and twenty-nine. Why is NSA concerned?" O'Hare asked.

"NSA is concerned that weapons systems like your Stingray are in essence just highly armed and mobile computer systems." He brushed an invisible crumb from his trousers, "And like any computer, they are vulnerable to cyber-attack."

A light finally clicked on in Bunny O'Hare's still half-asleep mind. The NSA and its Cyber Command were America's cyber-attack dogs. Jensen was the base security officer. Chuck was interested in her Stingray. She pointed a finger at him, "NSA is going to try to hack my Stingray, right?"

"That will depend." he shrugged, "On what I find when I start looking under the hood."

A Ribbon Around A Bomb

"I want to see some action, people!" *Dragon Bird* said, looking around him. He'd walked into his team's cube to find *Frangipani* with her headphones on, buried in code as usual, but *Po* was sitting with his feet up on his desk flicking through anime images on a tablet and *Tanken* looked like he was browsing the banned BBC news website. Banned for citizens, not for members of Unit APT (Advanced Persistent Threat) 23 of course. Nothing on the web was off-limits to his people; still it irked him to see them waiting around for him to arrive, rather than already hard at work.

Today was their day!

"I am already in action, Sir," Tanken said. His handle meant 'blade' and he had the movie star good looks of Huang Jiaoming. Frangi flicked her eyes to glance at him briefly as he spoke. DB knew she was secretly in love with him, but she had sworn him to silence about it and it had made him very uncomfortable that she had even confided the secret to him. "I can confirm that there are no reports on western media today regarding our successful penetration." Tanken continued.

"We have a media monitoring service that will do that," DB said. "I doubt that you will add greatly to their analysis from your reading of the BBC Sport pages."

Po swung his feet down, "I forgot to eat breakfast, Sir." He rubbed his eyes. "It's only five hours since I went home. I went home, brushed my teeth, went to bed, woke up, brushed my teeth and came here," he said. "And when I got here, I realized I had forgotten to have breakfast."

"You had toothpaste," Frangi said without looking at him, or even smiling. "And you are overweight. You need to eat less anyway." Po was indeed struggling with his weight. He hadn't chosen his own handle, it had been given him in a different unit, where he was named after a cartoon panda who loved noodles.

DB looked at his motley band of recruits with pride. It was true, he had been working them around the clock on this assignment. But they had achieved miracles. His immediate superior, Major Shaofeng, had said as much yesterday after DB sent his daily status report to him. The Major had called him into his office within minutes of receiving it.

Shaofeng had printed the email and it was on his desk in front of him. DB stood at attention, nervous but not afraid. He had done nothing wrong. Had he?

"Is this report accurate?" Shaofeng had asked.

"Yes sir."

"You have not exaggerated?"

"No sir," DB had replied. "We have completed our preparations and are ready to take covert control of the target system. We are just waiting for the Ministry of State Security's human agent to get in position to give us real-time intelligence."

Shaofeng tapped a finger on the email, "The alternatives you propose have already been discussed. We can continue to use the KAHLO system to gather intelligence, or we can use it as we have been tasked to use it. Why should we reconsider, now that your unit has successfully done as ordered?"

"I was merely reminding the Major of his options," DB said carefully. "In case the strategic situation had changed in any way I was unaware of."

559

Shaofeng flicked the email across his desk to the floor in front of DB, "The strategic situation has not changed. Our main enemy is still our main enemy. And as long as that enemy has military bases on our borders, our mission is clear and your orders are unchanged."

"Yes sir."

"Is anything about this confusing to you?"

"No sir."

"Then at 1220 hours tomorrow, you will initiate the operation, as ordered."

"Yes sir!" DB had said. "We will not fail."

Shaofeng's voice softened. He was a portly, fatherly figure who dressed like an office worker, in a white shirt and black suit and when he smiled his rather large ears lifted a little in a comical way. "I know you will not, Captain. APT 23 is setting new standards in stealth infiltration. You should be proud."

"I am proud sir!" DB had replied. "But this attack *will* be discovered. By its very nature, it must reveal itself in order to be effective and then our new capabilities will also be revealed. If we had more time, we could leverage the existing infiltration to..."

Shaofeng had held up his hand and stood up from his chair. On the wall beside his desk, he had a huge antique map of Asia, a copy of a map drawn up by the Chinese navy in the Tang dynasty, in about 900 AD. It showed Southeast China, the Korean Peninsula, Japan and its southerly chain of islands, including Okinawa. He stood next to it and pointed to a spot in the East China sea. "The *Liaoning* task force is here, 200 km south of Jeju, executing the final maneuvers of Exercise *Red Dove* together with our new Japanese allies." He moved his finger south. "At 1200 hours it will recover the last of its fighter aircraft and together with the Japanese fleet, begin sailing south, for a celebration of international fraternity and a ceremony to mark the official signing of the new China-Japan Defense Treaty." Shaofeng moved his finger again, "And the last significant US military presence in the Sino-Japanese co-prosperity sphere is here. US Navy Base White Beach, Okinawa, Japan."

"Yes sir."

"You know what you need to do, *Dragon Bird*."

DB had squared his shoulders at the Captain's use of his hacker handle instead of his military rank. It had been a mark of the deepest respect.

Listening to his crew give each other a ribbing, DB decided not to come down hard on them. "Frangi, are you in?"

"Yes Comrade Team Leader," she said. Although his rank was captain, the special informality in Unit 61938 went beyond not wearing uniforms. They also referred to their units as teams and their officers as team leaders. "Traffic appears normal. Intercepting and re-routing. KAHLO is successfully capturing 97 percent of communications in and out of the target system."

She was the chief systems officer for their KAHLO system and the cyber equivalent of the pilot in a jet fighter. DB's team had gone from twenty-plus coders at its peak, to these three now, supported by a backroom team of system techs. His small project leadership group was not a sign of decreased importance, it was a sign they had been so successful that the mission objectives could now be met by just this small team – minimizing security risks and maximizing their efficiency.

"Po, anything on your radar?" he asked. Po stopped his moaning and turned to his desk where an array of three screens flickered with numbers and readouts. He was DB's systems vulnerability engineer and his job right now was to monitor for and intercept any counter-attack.

"All quiet Comrade Captain," Po said. He pointed to a red police siren and light mounted on a stand above his screens. "You'll know if they send anything against us. I rigged that just up just in case I fall asleep." He glared at Frangi, "From starvation."

DB turned to Tanken, "Is your agent in motion?"

Tanken sighed. He was the only one who was not Unit 61938. He had been seconded to DB's team from the People's Liberation Army Strategic Support Force or SSF. He had no role in the immediate cyber-attack. His mission would only be initiated if they were successful. He tossed a sardonic salute at DB, "Yes sir, Captain." His work station contained one laptop, a couple of screens and a joystick rig that looked like something a computer gamer would use. "He reported in two hours ago, right on schedule."

DB's KAHLO operators, Frangi and Po, both looked up from their desks briefly and glanced at each other, then went back to work. They were unaware of the full scope of the operation and knew nothing about the actual identity of the Chinese human source on which so much of their mission depended. No one in Unit APT 23, including DB, knew more than they needed to know right now.

He looked at his crew fondly. KAHLO was DB's foster-child and China's newest and most potent cyber-attack system. One of DB's early crew members, Jin Tan, got the idea for KAHLO several years ago, when she was watching a nature documentary about the katydid insect, a predator which preys specifically on male cicadas. Except it doesn't have to hunt them, its prey runs eagerly to its death. The katydid parks itself on a nice prominent leaf or branch near a colony of cicadas and mimics the wing clicks of a horny female cicada. A nearby male, thinking it's got lucky, comes galloping at the katydid hoping to mate and the next thing it knows, it's dinner.

It took her a while to operationalize the thought buzzing around her head, but when she finally did, she shared her thinking with DB and he found Frangipani in another unit with exactly the skills he had needed to bring KAHLO to life. With Jin and Frangi working together, side by side, after nearly two years, KAHLO was born. When Unit 61938 realized what it had, Jin Tan was moved out of DB's unit due to 'questionable political alliances' – her family had been members of the Falun Gong movement. DB had taken over the project, kept Frangi with him and brought it to where it was today. He had no idea what had happened to Jin Tan, but often thought of her. He hoped she had received the credit she was due for gifting such a powerful weapon to China.

KAHLO was a neural network learning system that piggybacked on standard hacker exploits to penetrate enemy systems in a way that DB had termed 'cyber mimicry'. Once inside, it just laid low and studied the enemy system, captured its comms and learned how to regurgitate its encrypted code - but it didn't try to break it down and exploit it immediately. It was a katydid, learning how to make cicada wing clicks to fool the host system into thinking it was just a completely normal part of the host. If successful, it would be invisible to any host audit, because all that audit would show was what it expected to see – just another part of itself. Meanwhile KAHLO kept studying and learning, until it had learned enough to be able to take over critical parts of the host system, without the host realizing. It didn't just attack a target system, it *possessed* it.

DB was an art lover and to him, in all modesty, KAHLO was a work of cyber art. So he'd named it after his favorite artist, the Mexican Frida Kahlo de Rivera, whose work had been so seductively subversive. He'd heard that Picasso had once described her art as being like 'a ribbon around a bomb'. The thought described KAHLO beautifully.

"OK team," DB said, trying to keep his voice steady and not show the excitement he was feeling. "It is 1220 a.m." He swallowed and turned to Tanken. "You may advise your SSF superiors. We are ready to initiate phase 1."

'OKINAWA', the new future war thriller from FX Holden, is out NOW.

Made in the USA
Columbia, SC
10 January 2022

54065378R00336